Tales from the Arabian Nights

TALES FROM THE ARABIAN NIGHTS

TRANSLATED BY

SIR RICHARD FRANCIS BURTON

FALL RIVER PRESS

New York

FALL RIVER PRESS

New York

An Imprint of Sterling Publishing Co., Inc.
1166 Avenue of the Americas
New York, NY 10036

ISBN 978-1-4351-6656-1

Distributed in Canada by Sterling Publishing Co., Inc.
c/o Canadian Manda Group, 664 Annette Street
Toronto, Ontario, Canada M6S 2C8
Distributed in the United Kingdom by GMC Distribution Services
Castle Place, 166 High Street, Lewes, East Sussex, England BN7 1XU
Distributed in Australia by NewSouth Books
45 Beach Street, Coogee, NSW 2034, Australia

For information about custom editions, special sales, and premium and corporate purchases, please contact Sterling Special Sales at 800-805-5489 or specialsales@sterlingpublishing.com.

Manufactured in the United States of America

2 4 6 8 10 9 7 5 3 1

sterlingpublishing.com

Jacket typeface Fortunaschwein by anke-art

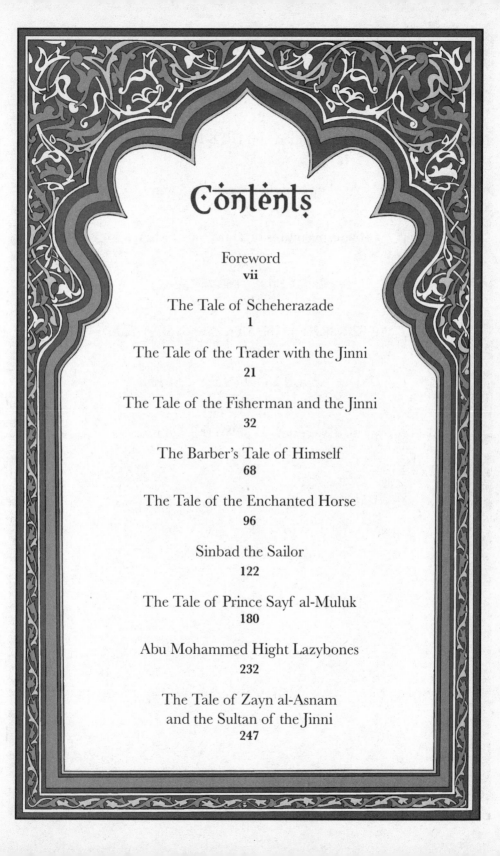

Contents

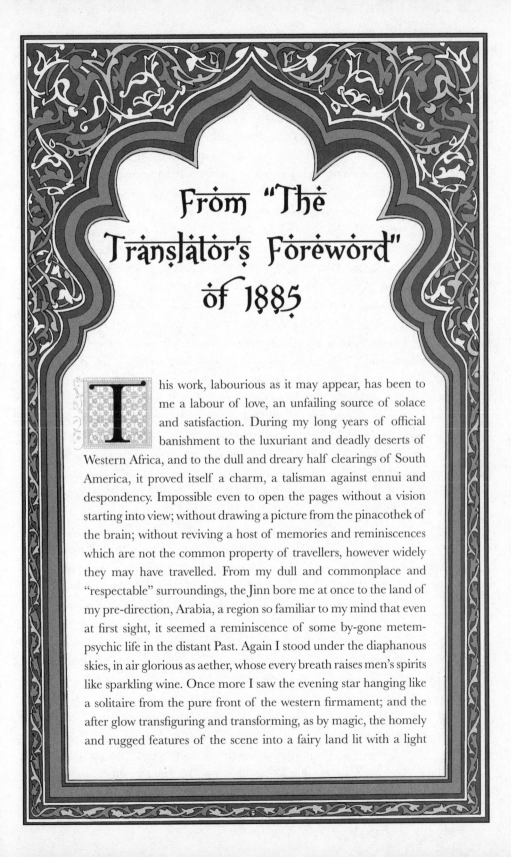

From "The Translator's Foreword" of 1885

This work, labourious as it may appear, has been to me a labour of love, an unfailing source of solace and satisfaction. During my long years of official banishment to the luxuriant and deadly deserts of Western Africa, and to the dull and dreary half clearings of South America, it proved itself a charm, a talisman against ennui and despondency. Impossible even to open the pages without a vision starting into view; without drawing a picture from the pinacothek of the brain; without reviving a host of memories and reminiscences which are not the common property of travellers, however widely they may have travelled. From my dull and commonplace and "respectable" surroundings, the Jinn bore me at once to the land of my pre-direction, Arabia, a region so familiar to my mind that even at first sight, it seemed a reminiscence of some by-gone metempsychic life in the distant Past. Again I stood under the diaphanous skies, in air glorious as aether, whose every breath raises men's spirits like sparkling wine. Once more I saw the evening star hanging like a solitaire from the pure front of the western firmament; and the after glow transfiguring and transforming, as by magic, the homely and rugged features of the scene into a fairy land lit with a light which never shines on other soils or seas. Then would appear the woollen tents, low and black, of the true Badawin, mere dots in the boundless waste of lion tawny clays and gazelle brown gravels, and the camp fire dotting like a glow worm the village centre. Presently, sweetened by distance, would be heard the wild weird song of lads and lasses, driving or rather pelting, through the gloaming their sheep and goats; and the measured chant of the spearsmen gravely stalking behind their charge, the camels; mingled with bleating of the flocks and the bellowing of the humpy herds; while the reremouse flitted overhead with his tiny shriek, and the rave of the jackal resounded through deepening glooms, and—most musical of music—the palm trees answered the whispers of the night breeze with the softest tones of falling water.

And then a shift of scene. The Shaykhs and "white beards" of the tribe gravely take their places, sitting with outspread skirts like hillocks on the plain, as the Arabs say, around the camp fire, whilst I reward their hospitality and secure its continuance by reading or reciting a few pages of their favourite tales. The women and children stand motionless as silhouettes outside the ring; and all are breathless with attention; they seem to drink in the words with eyes and mouths as well as with ears. The most fantastic flights of fancy, the wildest improbabilities, the most impossible of impossibilities, appear to them utterly natural, mere matters of every day occurrence. They enter thoroughly into each phase of feeling touched upon by the author: they take a personal pride in the chivalrous nature and knightly prowess of Taj al-Muluk; they are touched with tenderness by the self sacrificing love of Azizah; their mouths water as they hear of heaps of untold gold given away in largesse like clay; they chuckle with delight every time a Kazi or a Fakir—a judge or a reverend—is scurvily entreated by some Pantagruelist of the Wilderness; and, despite their normal solemnity and impassibility, all roar with laughter, sometimes rolling upon the ground till the reader's gravity is sorely tried, at the tales of the garrulous Barber and of Ali and the Kurdish Sharper. To this magnetising mood the sole exception is when a Badawi of superior accomplishments, who sometimes says his prayers, ejaculates a startling "Astagh-faru'llah"—I pray Allah's pardon!—for listening, not to Carlyle's "downright lies," but to light mention of the sex whose name is never heard amongst the nobility of the Desert.

Nor was it only in Arabia that the immortal Nights did me such notable service: I found the wildlings of Somali land equally amenable to its discipline; no one was deaf to the charm and the two women cooks of my caravan, on its way to Harar, were incontinently dubbed by my men "Shahrazad" and "Dinazad."

It may be permitted me also to note that this translation is a natural outcome of my Pilgrimage to Al-Medinah and Meccah. Arriving at Aden in the (so called) winter of 1852, I put up with my old and dear friend, Steinhaeuser, to whose memory this volume is inscribed; and, when talking over Arabia and the Arabs, we at once came to the same conclusion that, while the name of this wondrous treasury of Moslem folk lore is familiar to almost every English child, no general reader is aware of the valuables it contains, nor indeed will the door open to any but Arabists. Before parting we agreed to "collaborate" and produce a full, complete, unvarnished, uncastrated copy of the great original, my friend taking the prose and I the metrical part; and we corresponded upon the subject for years. But whilst I was in the Brazil, Steinhaeuser died suddenly of apoplexy at Berne in Switzerland and, after the fashion of Anglo India, his valuable MSS. left at Aden were dispersed, and very little of his labours came into my hands.

Thus I was left alone to my work, which progressed fitfully amid a host of obstructions. At length, in the spring of 1879, the tedious process of copying began and the book commenced to take finished form. But, during the winter of 1881–82, I saw in the literary journals a notice of a new version by Mr. John Payne, well known to scholars for his prowess in English verse, especially for his translation of "The Poems of Master Francis Villon, of Paris." Being then engaged on an expedition to the Gold Coast (for gold), which seemed likely to cover some months, I wrote to the *Athenaeum* (Nov. 13, 1881) and to Mr. Payne, who was wholly unconscious that we were engaged on the same work, and freely offered him precedence and possession of the field till no longer wanted. He accepted my offer as frankly, and his priority entailed another delay lasting till the spring of 1885. These details will partly account for the lateness of my appearing, but there is yet another cause. Professional ambition suggested that literary labours, unpopular with the vulgar and the half educated, are not likely to help a man up the ladder of promotion. But common sense presently suggested to me that, professionally speaking, I was not a success, and, at the same time, that I had no cause to be ashamed of my failure. In our day, when we live under a despotism of the lower "middle class" Philister who can pardon anything but superiority, the prizes of competitive services are monopolized by certain "pets" of the Mediocratie, and prime favourites of that jealous and potent majority—the Mediocrities who know "no nonsense about merit." It is hard for an outsider to realise how perfect is

the monopoly of common place, and to comprehend how fatal a stumbling stone that man sets in the way of his own advancement who dares to think for himself, or who knows more or who does more than the mob of gentlemen employee who know very little and who do even less.

Yet, however behindhand I may be, there is still ample room and verge for an English version of the *Arabian Nights' Entertainments*.

Sir Richard Francis Burton

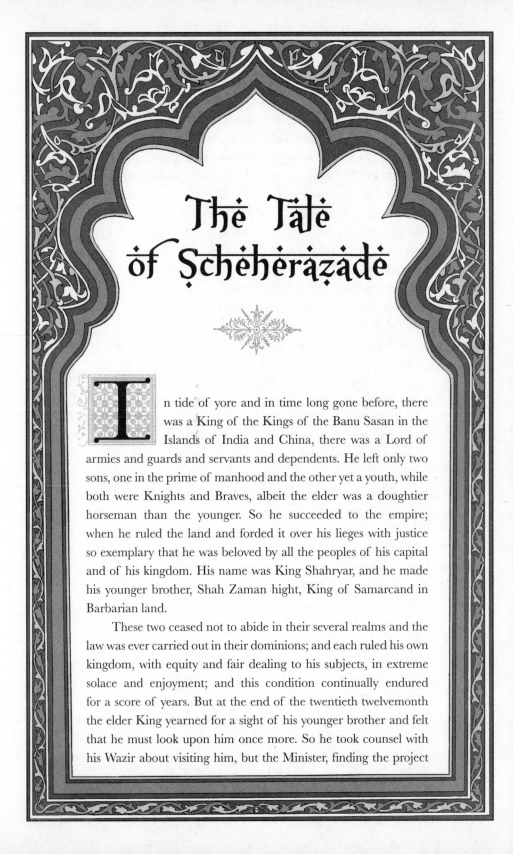

The Tale of Scheherazade

In tide of yore and in time long gone before, there was a King of the Kings of the Banu Sasan in the Islands of India and China, there was a Lord of armies and guards and servants and dependents. He left only two sons, one in the prime of manhood and the other yet a youth, while both were Knights and Braves, albeit the elder was a doughtier horseman than the younger. So he succeeded to the empire; when he ruled the land and forded it over his lieges with justice so exemplary that he was beloved by all the peoples of his capital and of his kingdom. His name was King Shahryar, and he made his younger brother, Shah Zaman hight, King of Samarcand in Barbarian land.

These two ceased not to abide in their several realms and the law was ever carried out in their dominions; and each ruled his own kingdom, with equity and fair dealing to his subjects, in extreme solace and enjoyment; and this condition continually endured for a score of years. But at the end of the twentieth twelvemonth the elder King yearned for a sight of his younger brother and felt that he must look upon him once more. So he took counsel with his Wazir about visiting him, but the Minister, finding the project unadvisable, recommended that a letter be written and a present be sent under his charge to the younger brother with an invitation to visit the elder. Having accepted this advice the King forthwith bade prepare handsome gifts, such as horses with saddles of gem encrusted gold; Mamelukes, or white slaves; beautiful handmaids; high-breasted virgins; and splendid stuffs and costly. He then wrote a letter to Shah Zaman expressing his warm love and great wish to see him, ending with these words, "We therefore hope of the favour and affection of the beloved brother that he will condescend to bestir himself and turn his face us-wards. Furthermore we have sent our Wazir to make all ordinance for the march, and our one and only desire is to see thee ere we die; but if thou delay or disappoint us we shall not survive the blow. Wherewith peace be upon thee!"

Then King Shahryar, having sealed the missive and given it to the Wazir with the offerings aforementioned, commanded him to shorten his skirts and strain his strength and make all expedition in going and returning.

"Harkening and obedience!" quoth the Minister, who fell to making ready without stay and packed up his loads and prepared all his requisites without delay. This occupied him three days, and on the dawn of the fourth he took leave of his King and marched right away, over desert and hill-way, stony waste and pleasant lea without halting by night or by day. But whenever he entered a realm whose ruler was subject to his Suzerain, where he was greeted with magnificent gifts of gold and silver and all manner of presents fair and rare, he would tarry there three days, the term of the guest rite; and, when he left on the fourth, he would be honourably escorted for a whole day's march. As soon as the Wazir drew near Shah Zaman's court in Samarcand he despatched to report his arrival one of his high officials, who presented himself before the King; and, kissing ground between his hands, delivered his message. Hereupon the King commanded sundry of his Grandees and Lords of his realm to fare forth and meet his brother's Wazir at the distance of a full day's journey; which they did, greeting him respectfully and wishing him all prosperity and forming an escort and a procession.

When he entered the city he proceeded straightway to the palace, where he presented himself in the royal presence; and, after kissing ground and praying for the King's health and happiness and for victory over all his enemies, he informed him that his brother was yearning to see him, and prayed for the pleasure of a visit. He then delivered the letter which Shah Zaman took from his hand and read: it contained sundry hints and allusions which required thought; but, when the King had fully comprehended its import, he said, "I hear and I obey the commands of the beloved brother!" adding to the Wazir, "But we will not march till after the third day's hospitality." He appointed for the Minister fitting quarters of the palace; and, pitching tents for the troops, rationed them with whatever they might require of meat and drink and other necessaries.

On the fourth day he made ready for wayfare and got together sumptuous presents befitting his elder brother's majesty, and 'stablished his chief Wazir viceroy of the land during his absence. Then he caused his tents and camels and mules to be brought forth and encamped, with their bales and loads, attendants and guards, within sight of the city, in readiness to set out next morning for his brother's capital. But when the night was half spent he bethought him that he had forgotten in his palace somewhat which he should have brought with him, so he returned privily and entered his apartments, where he found the Queen, his wife, asleep on his own carpet bed, embracing with both arms a black cook of loathsome aspect and foul with kitchen grease and grime. When he saw this the world waxed black before his sight and he said, "If such case happen while I am yet within sight of the city what will be the doings of this damned whore during my long absence at my brother's court?"

So he drew his scymitar and, cutting the two in four pieces with a single blow, left them on the carpet and returned presently to his camp without letting anyone know of what had happened. Then he gave orders for immediate departure and set out at once and began his travel; but he could not help thinking over his wife's treason and he kept ever saying to himself, "How could she do this deed by me? How could she work her own death?" till excessive grief seized him, his colour changed to yellow, his body waxed weak and he was threatened with a dangerous malady, such an one as bringeth men to die. So the Wazir shortened his stages and tarried long at the watering stations and did his best to solace the King.

Now when Shah Zaman drew near the capital of his brother he despatched vaunt couriers and messengers of glad tidings to announce his arrival, and Shahryar came forth to meet him with his Wazirs and Emirs and Lords and Grandees of his realm; and saluted him and joyed with exceeding joy and caused the city to be decorated in his honour. When, however, the brothers met, the elder could not but see the change of complexion in the younger and questioned him of his case whereto he replied, "'Tis caused by the travails of wayfare and my case needs care, for I have suffered from the change of water and air! but Allah be praised for

reuniting me with a brother so dear and so rare!" On this wise he dissembled and kept his secret, adding, "O King of the time and Caliph of the tide, only toil and moil have tinged my face yellow with bile and hath made my eyes sink deep in my head."

Then the two entered the capital in all honour; and the elder brother lodged the younger in a palace overhanging the pleasure garden; and, after a time, seeing his condition still unchanged, he attributed it to his separation from his country and kingdom. So he let him wend his own ways and asked no questions of him till one day when he again said, "O my brother, I see thou art grown weaker of body and yellower of colour."

"O my brother," replied Shah Zaman "I have an internal wound": still he would not tell him what he had witnessed in his wife. Thereupon Shahryar summoned doctors and surgeons and bade them treat his brother according to the rules of art, which they did for a whole month; but their sherbets and potions naught availed, for he would dwell upon the deed of his wife, and despondency, instead of diminishing, prevailed, and leach craft treatment utterly failed.

One day his elder brother said to him, "I am going forth to hunt and course and to take my pleasure and pastime; maybe this would lighten thy heart." Shah Zaman, however, refused, saying, "O my brother, my soul yearneth for naught of this sort and I entreat thy favour to suffer me tarry quietly in this place, being wholly taken up with my malady."

So King Shah Zaman passed his night in the palace and, next morning, when his brother had fared forth, he removed from his room and sat him down at one of the lattice windows overlooking the pleasure grounds; and there he abode thinking with saddest thought over his wife's betrayal and burning sighs issued from his tortured breast. And as he continued in this case lo! a pastern of the palace, which was carefully kept private, swung open and out of it came twenty slave girls surrounding his bother's wife who was wondrous fair, a model of beauty and comeliness and symmetry and perfect loveliness and who paced with the grace of a gazelle which panteth for the cooling stream. Thereupon Shah Zaman drew back from the window, but he kept the bevy in sight espying them from a place whence he could not be espied. They walked under the very lattice and advanced a little way into the garden till they came to a jetting fountain amiddlemost a great basin of water; then they stripped off their clothes and behold, ten of them were women, concubines of the King, and the other ten were white slaves. Then they all paired off, each with each: but the Queen, who was left alone, presently cried out in a loud voice, "Here to me, O my lord Saeed!"

and then sprang with a drop leap from one of the trees a big slobbering blackamoor with rolling eyes which showed the whites, a truly hideous sight. He walked boldly up to her and threw his arms round her neck while she embraced him as warmly; then he bussed her and winding his legs round hers, as a button loop clasps a button, he threw her and enjoyed her. On like wise did the other slaves with the girls till all had satisfied their passions, and they ceased not from kissing and clipping, coupling and carousing till day began to wane; when the Mamelukes rose from the damsels' bosoms and the blackamoor slave dismounted from the Queen's breast; the men resumed their disguises and all, except the negro who swarmed up the tree, entered the palace and closed the postern door as before.

Now, when Shah Zaman saw this conduct of his sister-in-law he said in himself, "By Allah, my calamity is lighter than this! My brother is a greater King among the kings than I am, yet this infamy goeth on in his very palace, and his wife is in love with that filthiest of filthy slaves. But this only showeth that they all do it and that there is no woman but who cuckoldeth her husband, then the curse of Allah upon one and all and upon the fools who lean against them for support or who place the reins of conduct in their hands." So he put away his melancholy and despondency, regret and repine, and allayed his sorrow by constantly repeating those words, adding, "'Tis my conviction that no man in this world is safe from their malice!"

When supper time came they brought him the trays and he ate with voracious appetite, for he had long refrained from meat, feeling unable to touch any dish however dainty. Then he returned grateful thanks to Almighty Allah, praising Him and blessing Him, and he spent a most restful night, it having been long since he had savoured the sweet food of sleep.

Next day he broke his fast heartily and began to recover health and strength, and presently regained excellent condition. His brother came back from the chase ten days after, when he rode out to meet him and they saluted each other; and when King Shahryar looked at King Shah Zaman he saw how the hue of health had returned to him, how his face had waxed ruddy and how he ate with an appetite after his late scanty diet. He wondered much and said, "O my brother, I was so anxious that thou wouldst join me in hunting and chasing, and wouldst take thy pleasure and pastime in my dominion!" He thanked him and excused himself; then the two took horse and rode into the city and, when they were seated at their ease in the palace, the food trays were set before them and they ate their sufficiency.

After the meats were removed and they had washed their hands, King Shahryar turned to his brother and said, "My mind is overcome with

wonderment at thy condition. I was desirous to carry thee with me to the chase but I saw thee changed in hue, pale and wan to view, and in sore trouble of mind too. But now Alhamdolillah—glory be to God!—I see thy natural colour hath returned to thy face and that thou art again in the best of case. It was my belief that thy sickness came of severance from thy family and friends, and absence from capital and country, so I refrained from troubling thee with further questions. But now I beseech thee to expound to me the cause of thy complaint and thy change of colour, and to explain the reason of thy recovery and the return to the ruddy hue of health which I am wont to view. So speak out and hide naught!"

When Shah Zaman heard this he bowed groundwards awhile his head, then raised it and said, "I will tell thee what caused my complaint and my loss of colour; but excuse my acquainting thee with the cause of its return to me and the reason of my complete recovery: indeed I pray thee not to press me for a reply."

Said Shahryar, who was much surprised by these words, "Let me hear first what produced thy pallor and thy poor condition."

"Know, then, O my brother," rejoined Shah Zaman, "that when thou sentest thy Wazir with the invitation to place myself between thy hands, I made ready and marched out of my city; but presently I minded me having left behind me in the palace a string of jewels intended as a gift to thee. I returned for it alone and found my wife on my carpet bed and in the arms of a hideous black cook. So I slew the twain and came to thee, yet my thoughts brooded over this business and I lost my bloom and became weak. But excuse me if I still refuse to tell thee what was the reason of my complexion returning."

Shahryar shook his head, marvelling with extreme marvel, and with the fire of wrath flaming up from his heart, he cried, "Indeed, the malice of woman is mighty!" Then he took refuge from them with Allah and said, "In very sooth, O my brother, thou hast escaped many an evil by putting thy wife to death, and right excusable were thy wrath and grief for such mishap which never yet befel crowned King like thee. By Allah, had the case been mine, I would not have been satisfied without slaying a thousand women and that way madness lies! But now praise be to Allah who hath tempered to thee thy tribulation, and needs must thou acquaint me with that which so suddenly restored to thee complexion and health, and explain to me what causeth this concealment."

"O King of the Age, again I pray thee excuse my so doing!"

"Nay, but thou must."

"I fear, O my brother, lest the recital cause thee more anger and sorrow than afflicted me."

"That were but a better reason," quoth Shahryar, "for telling me the whole history, and I conjure thee by Allah not to keep back aught from me."

Thereupon Shah Zaman told him all he had seen, from commencement to conclusion, ending with these words, "When I beheld thy calamity and the treason of thy wife, O my brother, and I respected that thou art in years my senior and in sovereignty my superior, mine own sorrow was belittled by the comparison, and my mind recovered tone and temper: so throwing off melancholy and despondency, I was able to eat and drink and sleep, and thus I speedily regained health and strength. Such is the truth and the whole truth."

When King Shahryar heard this he waxed wroth with exceeding wrath, and rage was like to strangle him; but presently he recovered himself and said, "O my brother, I would not give thee the lie in this matter, but I cannot credit it till I see it with mine own eyes."

"An thou wouldst look upon thy calamity," quoth Shah Zaman, "rise at once and make ready again for hunting and coursing, and then hide thyself with me, so shalt thou witness it and thine eyes shall verify it."

"True," quoth the King; whereupon he let make proclamation of his intent to travel, and the troops and tents fared forth without the city, camping within sight, and Shahryar sallied out with them and took seat amidmost his host, bidding the slaves admit no man to him.

When night came on he summoned his Wazir and said to him, "Sit thou in my stead and let none wot of my absence till the term of three days." Then the brothers disguised themselves and returned by night with all secrecy to the palace, where they passed the dark hours: and at dawn they seated themselves at the lattice overlooking the pleasure grounds, when presently the Queen and her handmaids came out as before, and passing under the windows made for the fountain. Here they stripped, ten of them being men to ten women, and the King's wife cried out, "Where art thou, O Saeed?" The hideous blackamoor dropped from the tree straightway; and, rushing into her arms without stay or delay, cried out, "I am Sa'ad al Din Saood!" The lady laughed heartily, and all fell to satisfying their lusts, and remained so occupied for a couple of hours, when the white slaves rose up from the handmaidens' breasts and the blackamoor dismounted from the Queen's bosom: then they went into the basin and, after performing the Ghusl, or complete ablution, donned their dresses and retired as they had done before.

When King Shahryar saw this infamy of his wife and concubines he became as one distraught and he cried out, "Only in utter solitude can man be safe from the doings of this vile world! By Allah, life is naught but one great wrong." Presently he added, "Do not thwart me, O my brother, in what I propose;" and the other answered, "I will not."

So he said, "Let us up as we are and depart forthright hence, for we have no concern with Kingship, and let us overwander Allah's earth, worshipping the Almighty till we find some one to whom the like calamity hath happened; and if we find none then will death be more welcome to us than life."

So the two brothers issued from a second private postern of the palace; and they never stinted wayfaring by day and by night, until they reached a tree a-middle of a meadow hard by a spring of sweet water on the shore of the salt sea. Both drank of it and sat down to take their rest; and when an hour of the day had gone by: lo! they heard a mighty roar and uproar in the middle of the main as though the heavens were falling upon the earth; and the sea brake with waves before them, and from it towered a black pillar, which grew and grew till it rose skywards and began making for that meadow. Seeing it, they waxed fearful exceedingly and climbed to the top of the tree, which was a lofty; whence they gazed to see what might be the matter. And behold, it was a Jinni, huge of height and burly of breast and bulk, broad of brow and black of blee, bearing on his head a coffer of crystal. He strode to land, wading through the deep, and coming to the tree whereupon were the two Kings, seated himself beneath it. He then set down the coffer on its bottom and out it drew a casket, with seven padlocks of steel, which he unlocked with seven keys of steel he took from beside his thigh, and out of it a young lady to come was seen, white-skinned and of winsomest mien, of stature fine and thin, and bright as though a moon of the fourteenth night she had been, or the sun raining lively sheen. Even so the poet Utayyah hath excellently said:

> She rose like the morn as she shone through the night
> And she gilded the grove with her gracious sight:
> From her radiance the sun taketh increase when
> She unveileth and shameth the moonshine bright.
> Bow down all beings between her hands
> As she showeth charms with her veil undight.
> And she foodeth cities with torrent tears
> When she flasheth her look of leven-light.

The Jinni seated her under the tree by his side and looking at her said, "O choicest love of this heart of mine! O dame of noblest line, whom I snatched away on thy bride night that none might prevent me taking thy maidenhead or tumble thee before I did, and whom none save myself hath loved or hath enjoyed: O my sweetheart! I would fief sleep a little while." He then laid his head upon the lady's thighs; and, stretching out his legs which extended down to the sea, slept and snored and sparked like the roll of thunder.

Presently she raised her head towards the tree top and saw the two Kings perched near the summit; then she softly lifted off her lap the Jinni's pate which she was tired of supporting and placed it upon the ground; then standing upright under the tree signed to the Kings, "Come ye down, ye two, and fear naught from this Ifrit."

They were in a terrible fright when they found that she had seen them and answered her in the same manner, "Allah upon thee and by thy modesty, O lady, excuse us from coming down!"

But she rejoined by saying, "Allah upon you both, that ye come down forthright, and if ye come not, I will rouse upon you my husband, this Ifrit, and he shall do you to die by the illest of deaths"; and she continued making signals to them.

So, being afraid, they came down to her and she rose before them and said, "Stroke me a strong stroke, without stay or delay, otherwise will I arouse and set upon you this Ifrit who shall slay you straightway."

They said to her, "O our lady, we conjure thee by Allah, let us off this work, for we are fugitives from such and in extreme dread and terror of this thy husband. How then can we do it in such a way as thou desires?"

"Leave this talk: it needs must be so"; quoth she, and she swore them by Him who raised the skies on high, without prop or pillar, that, if they worked not her will, she would cause them to be slain and cast into the sea. Whereupon out of fear King Shahryar said to King Shah Zaman, "O my brother, do thou what she biddeth thee do"; but he replied, "I will not do it till thou do it before I do."

And they began disputing about futtering her. Then quoth she to the twain, "How is it I see you disputing and demurring; if ye do not come forward like men and do the deed of kind ye two, I will arouse upon you the Ifrit."

At this, by reason of their sore dread of the Jinni, both did by her what she bade them do; and, when they had dismounted from her, she said, "Well done!" She then took from her pocket a purse and drew out a knotted string, whereon were strung five hundred and seventy seal rings, and asked, "Know ye what be these?"

They answered her saying, "We know not!"

Then quoth she: "These be the signets of five hundred and seventy men who have all futtered me upon the horns of this foul, this foolish, this filthy Ifrit; so give me also your two seal rings, ye pair of brothers." When they had drawn their two rings from their hands and given them to her, she said to them, "Of a truth this Ifrit bore me off on my bride night, and put me into a casket and set the casket in a coffer and to the coffer he affixed seven strong padlocks of steel and deposited me on the deep bottom of the sea that raves, dashing and clashing with waves; and guarded me so that I might remain chaste and honest, quotha! that none save himself might have connexion with me. But I have lain under as many of my kind as I please, and this wretched Jinni wotteth not that Destiny may not be averted nor hindered by aught, and that whatso woman willeth the same she fulfilleth however man nilleth. Even so saith one of them:

> "Rely not on women;
>   Trust not to their hearts,
> Whose joys and whose sorrows
> Are hung to their parts!
> Lying love they will swear thee
> Whence guile ne'er departs:
> Take Yusuf for sample
> 'Ware sleights and 'ware smarts!
> Iblis ousted Adam
> (See ye not?) thro' their arts.

"And another saith:

> "Stint thy blame, man!
>   'Twill drive to a passion without bound;
> My fault is not so heavy as fault in it hast found.
> If true lover I become, then to me there cometh not
> Save what happened unto many in the bygone 'stound.
> For wonderful is he and right worthy of our praise
> Who from wiles of female wits kept him safe and kept
>   him sound."

Hearing these words they marvelled with exceeding marvel, and she went from them to the Ifrit and, taking up his head on her thigh as before, said to them softly, "Now wend your ways and bear yourselves beyond the bounds of his malice."

So they fared forth saying either to other, "Allah! Allah!" and, "There be no Majesty and there be no Might save in Allah, the Glorious, the Great; and with Him we seek refuge from women's malice and sleight, for of a truth it hath no mate in might. Consider, O my brother, the ways of this marvellous lady with an Ifrit who is so much more powerful than we are. Now since there hath happened to him a greater mishap than that which befel us and which should bear us abundant consolation, so return we to our countries and capitals, and let us decide never to intermarry with womankind and presently we will show them what will be our action."

Thereupon they rode back to the tents of King Shahryar, which they reached on the morning of the third day; and, having mustered the Wazirs and Emirs, the Chamberlains and high officials, he gave a robe of honour to his Viceroy and issued orders for an immediate return to the city. There he sat him upon his throne and sending for the Chief Minister, the father of the two damsels who (Inshallah!) will presently be mentioned, he said, "I command thee to take my wife and smite her to death; for she hath broken her plight and her faith." So he carried her to the place of execution and did her die.

Then King Shahryar took brand in hand and repairing to the Serraglio slew all the concubines and their Mamelukes. He also sware himself by a binding oath that whatever wife he married he would abate her maidenhead at night and slay her next morning to make sure of his honour; "For," said he, "there never was nor is there one chaste woman upon face of earth."

Then Shah Zaman prayed for permission to fare homewards; and he went forth equipped and escorted and travelled till he reached his own country. Meanwhile Shahryar commanded his Wazir to bring him the bride of the night that he might go in to her; so he produced a most beautiful girl, the daughter of one of the Emirs and the King went in unto her at eventide and when morning dawned he bade his Minister strike off her head; and the Wazir did accordingly for fear of the Sultan.

On this wise he continued for the space of three years; marrying a maiden every night and killing her the next morning, till folk raised an outcry against him and cursed him, praying Allah utterly to destroy him and his rule; and women made an uproar and mothers wept and parents fled with their daughters till there remained not in the city a young person fit for carnal copulation.

Presently the King ordered his Chief Wazir, the same who was charged with the executions, to bring him a virgin as was his wont; and the Minister went forth and searched and found none; so he returned home in sorrow and anxiety fearing for his life from the King.

Now he had two daughters, Scheherazade and Dunyazad hight, of whom the elder had perused the books, annals and legends of preceding Kings, and the stories, examples and instances of bygone men and things; indeed it was said that she had collected a thousand books of histories relating to antique races and departed rulers. She had perused the works of the poets and knew them by heart; she had studied philosophy and the sciences, arts and accomplishments; and she was pleasant and polite, wise and witty, well read and well bred. Now on that day she said to her father, "Why do I see thee thus changed and laden with cark and care? Concerning this matter quoth one of the poets:

> "Tell whoso hath sorrow
> Grief never shall last:
> E'en as joy hath no morrow
> So woe shall go past."

When the Wazir heard from his daughter these words he related to her, from first to last, all that had happened between him and the King. Thereupon said she, "By Allah, O my father, how long shall this slaughter of women endure? Shall I tell thee what is in my mind in order to save both sides from destruction?"

"Say on, O my daughter," quoth he, and quoth she, "I wish thou wouldst give me in marriage to this King Shahryar; either I shall live or I shall be a ransom for the virgin daughters of Moslems and the cause of their deliverance from his hands and thine."

"Allah upon thee!" cried he in wrath exceeding that lacked no feeding, "O scanty of wit, expose not thy life to such peril! How durst thou address me in words so wide from wisdom and un-far from foolishness? Know that one who lacketh experience in worldly matters readily falleth into misfortune; and whoso considereth not the end keepeth not the world to friend, and the vulgar say, 'I was lying at mine ease: nought but my officiousness brought me unease.'"

"Needs must thou," she broke in, "make me a doer of this good deed, and let him kill me an he will: I shall only die a ransom for others."

"O my daughter," asked he, "and how shall that profit thee when thou shalt have thrown away thy life?" and she answered, "O my father it must be, come of it what will!"

The Wazir was again moved to fury and blamed and reproached her, ending with, "In very deed—I fear lest the same befal thee which befel the Bull and the Ass with the Husbandman." "And what," asked she, "befel them, O my father?" Whereupon the Wazir began "The Tale of the Bull and the Ass."

Know, O my daughter, that there was once a merchant who owned much money and many men, and who was rich in cattle and camels; he had also a wife and family and he dwelt in the country, being experienced in husbandry and devoted to agriculture. Now Allah Most High had endowed him with understanding the tongues of beasts and birds of every kind, but under pain of death if he divulged the gift to any. So he kept it secret for very fear. He had in his cowhouse a Bull and an Ass each tethered in his own stall one hard by the other.

As the merchant was sitting near hand one day with his servants and his children were playing about him, he heard the Bull say to the Ass, "Hail and health to thee O Father of Waking! for that thou enjoyest rest and good ministering; all under thee is clean-swept and fresh-sprinkled; men wait upon thee and feed thee, and thy provaunt is sifted barley and thy drink pure spring water, while I (unhappy creature!) am led forth in the middle of the night, when they set on my neck the plough and a something called Yoke; and I tire at cleaving the earth from dawn of day till set of sun. I am forced to do more than I can and to bear all manner of ill treatment from night to night; after which they take me back with my sides torn, my neck flayed, my legs aching and mine eyelids sored with tears. Then they shut me up in the byre and throw me beans and crushed straw, mixed with dirt and chaff; and I lie in dung and filth and foul stinks through the livelong night. But thou art ever in a place swept and sprinkled and cleansed, and thou art always lying at ease, save when it happens (and seldom enough!) that the master hath some business, when he mounts thee and rides thee to town and returns with thee forthright. So it happens that I am toiling and distress while thou takest thine ease and thy rest; thou sleepest while I am sleepless; I hunger still while thou eatest thy fill, and I win contempt while thou winnest good will."

When the Bull ceased speaking, the Ass turned towards him and said, "O Broad o' Brow, O thou lost one! he lied not who dubbed thee Bull-head, for thou, O father of a Bull, hast neither forethought nor contrivance; thou art the simplest of simpletons, and thou knowest naught of good advisers. Hast thou not heard the saying of the wise:

> "For others these hardships and labours I bear
> And theirs is the pleasure and mine is the care;
> As the bleacher who blacketh his brow in the sun
> To whiten the raiment which other men wear.

"But thou, O fool, art full of zeal and thou toilest and moilest before the master; and thou tearest and wearest and slayest thyself for the comfort of another. Hast thou never heard the saw that saith, None to guide and from the way go wide? Thou wendest forth at the call to dawn prayer and thou returnest not till sundown; and through the livelong day thou endurest all manner hardships; to wit, beating and belabouring and bad language. Now hearken to me, Sir Bull! when they tie thee to thy stinking manger, thou pawest the ground with thy forehand and lashest out with thy hind hoofs and pushest with thy horns and bellowest aloud, so they deem thee contented. And when they throw thee thy fodder thou fallest on it with greed and hastenest to line thy fair fat paunch. But if thou accept my advice it will be better for thee and thou wilt lead an easier life even than mine. When thou goest afield and they lay the thing called Yoke on thy neck, lie down and rise not again though haply they swinge thee; and, if thou rise, lie down a second time; and when they bring thee home and offer thee thy beans, fall backwards and only sniff at thy meat and withdraw thee and taste it not, and be satisfied with thy crushed straw and chaff; and on this wise feign thou art sick, and cease not doing thus for a day or two days or even three days, so shalt thou have rest from toil and moil."

When the Bull heard these words he knew the Ass to be his friend and thanked him, saying, "Right is thy rede"; and prayed that all blessings might requite him, and cried, "O Father Wakener! thou hast made up for my failings."

Now the merchant, O my daughter, understood all that passed between them. Next day the driver took the Bull, and settling the plough on his neck, made him work as wont; but the Bull began to shirk his ploughing, according to the advice of the Ass, and the ploughman drubbed him till he broke the yoke and made off; but the man caught him up and leathered him till he despaired of his life. Not the less, however, would he do nothing but stand still and drop down till the evening. Then the herd led him home and stabled him in his stall: but he drew back from his manger and neither stamped nor ramped nor butted nor bellowed as he was wont to do; whereat the man wondered. He brought him the beans and husks, but he sniffed at them and left them and lay down as far from them as he could and passed the whole night fasting.

The peasant came next morning; and, seeing the manger full of beans, the crushed straw untasted and the ox lying on his back in sorriest plight, with legs outstretched and swollen belly, he was concerned for him, and said to himself, "By Allah, he hath assuredly sickened and this is the cause why he would not plough yesterday." Then he went to the merchant and reported, "O my master, the Bull is ailing; he refused his fodder last night; nay more, he hath not tasted a scrap of it this morning."

Now the merchant farmer understood what all this meant, because he had overheard the talk between the Bull and the Ass, so quoth he, "Take that rascal donkey, and set the yoke on his neck, and bind him to the plough and make him do Bull's work."

Thereupon the ploughman took the Ass, and worked him through the livelong day at the Bull's task; and, when he failed for weakness, he made him eat stick till his ribs were sore and his sides were sunken and his neck was flayed by the yoke; and when he came home in the evening he could hardly drag his limbs along, either fore-hand or hind-legs. But as for the Bull, he had passed the day lying at full length and had eaten his fodder with an excellent appetite, and he ceased not calling down blessings on the Ass for his good advice, unknowing what had come to him on his account.

So when night set in and the Ass returned to the byre the Bull rose up before him in honour, and said, "May good tidings gladden thy heart, O Father Wakener! through thee I have rested all this day and I have eaten my meat in peace and quiet."

But the Ass returned no reply, for wrath and heart-burning and fatigue and the beating he had gotten; and he repented with the most grievous of repentance; and quoth he to himself: "This cometh of my folly in giving good counsel; as the saw saith, I was in joy and gladness, nought save my officiousness brought me this sadness. But I will bear in mind my innate worth and the nobility of my nature; for what saith the poet?

"Shall the beautiful hue of the Basil fail
Tho' the beetle's foot o'er the Basil crawl?
And though spider and fly be its denizens
Shall disgrace attach to the royal hall?
The cowrie, I ken, shall have currency
But the pearl's clear drop, shall its value fall?

"And now I must take thought and put a trick upon him and return him to his place, else I die."

Then he went aweary to his manger, while the Bull thanked him and blessed him. "And even so, O my daughter," said the Wazir, "thou wilt die for lack of wits; therefore sit thee still and say naught and expose not thy life to such stress; for, by Allah, I offer thee the best advice, which cometh of my affection and kindly solicitude for thee."

"O my father," she answered, "needs must I go up to this King and be married to him."

Quoth he, "Do not this deed;" and quoth she, "Of a truth I will:" whereat he rejoined, "If thou be not silent and bide still, I will do with thee even what the merchant did with his wife."

"And what did he?" asked she.

Know then, answered the Wazir, that after the return of the Ass the merchant came out on the terrace roof with his wife and family, for it was a moonlit night and the moon at its full. Now the terrace overlooked the cowhouse and presently, as he sat there with his children playing about him, the trader heard the Ass say to the Bull, "Tell me, O Father Broad o' Brow, what thou purposest to do to-morrow?"

The Bull answered, "What but continue to follow thy counsel, O Aliboron? Indeed it was as good as good could be and it hath given me rest and repose; nor will I now depart from it one little: so, when they bring me my meat, I will refuse it and blow out my belly and counterfeit crank."

The Ass shook his head and said, "Beware of so doing, O Father of a Bull!" The Bull asked, "Why," and the Ass answered, "Know that I am about to give thee the best of counsel, for verily I heard our owner say to the herd, If the Bull rise not from his place to do his work this morning and if he retire from his fodder this day, make him over to the butcher that he may slaughter him and give his flesh to the poor, and fashion a bit of leather from his hide. Now I fear for thee on account of this. So take my advice ere a calamity befal thee; and when they bring thee thy fodder eat it and rise up and bellow and paw the ground, or our master will assuredly slay thee: and peace be with thee!"

Thereupon the Bull arose and lowed aloud and thanked the Ass, and said, "To-morrow I will readily go forth with them"; and he at once ate up all his meat and even licked the manger. (All this took place and the owner was listening to their talk.)

Next morning the trader and his wife went to the Bull's crib and sat down, and the driver came and led forth the Bull who, seeing his owner, whisked his tail and brake wind, and frisked about so lustily that the merchant laughed a loud laugh and kept laughing till he fell on his back. His wife asked him, "Whereat laughest thou with such loud laughter as this?"; and he answered her, "I laughed at a secret something which I have heard and seen but cannot say lest I die my death."

She returned, "Perforce thou must discover it to me, and disclose the cause of thy laughing even if thou come by thy death!"

But he rejoined, "I cannot reveal what beasts and birds say in their lingo for fear I die."

Then quoth she, "By Allah, thou liest! this is a mere pretext: thou laughest at none save me, and now thou wouldest hide somewhat from me. But by the Lord of the Heavens! and thou disclose not the cause I will no longer cohabit with thee: I will leave thee at once." And she sat down and cried.

Whereupon quoth the merchant, "Woe betide thee! what means thy weeping? Fear Allah and leave these words and query me no more questions."

"Needs must thou tell me the cause of that laugh," said she, and he replied, "Thou wottest that when I prayed Allah to vouchsafe me understanding of the tongues of beasts and birds, I made a vow never to disclose the secret to any under pain of dying on the spot."

"No matter," cried she, "tell me what secret passed between the Bull and the Ass and die this very hour an thou be so minded"; and she ceased not to importune him till he was worn out and clean distraught.

So at last he said, "Summon thy father and thy mother and our kith and kin and sundry of our neighbours," which she did; and he sent for the Kazi and his assessors, intending to make his will and reveal to her his secret and die the death; for he loved her with love exceeding because she was his cousin, the daughter of his father's brother, and the mother of his children, and he had lived with her a life of an hundred and twenty years. Then, having assembled all the family and the folk of his neighbourhood, he said to them, "By me there hangeth a strange story, and 'tis such that if I discover the secret to any, I am a dead man."

Therefore quoth every one of those present to the woman, "Allah upon thee, leave this sinful obstinacy and recognise the right of this matter, lest haply thy husband and the father of thy children die."

But she rejoined, "I will not turn from it till he tell me, even though he come by his death." So they ceased to urge her; and the trader rose from amongst them and repaired to an outhouse to perform Wuzu-ablution, and he purposed thereafter to return and to tell them his secret and to die.

Now, daughter Scheherazade, that merchant had in his outhouses some fifty hens under one cock, and whilst making ready to farewell his folk he heard one of his many farm dogs thus address in his own tongue the Cock, who was flapping his wings and crowing lustily and jumping from one hen's back to another and treading all in turn, saying "O Chanticlear! how mean is thy wit and how shameless is thy conduct! Be he disappointed who brought thee up! Art thou not ashamed of thy doings on such a day as this!"

"And what," asked the Rooster, "hath occurred this day?" when the Dog answered, "Dost thou not know that our master is this day making ready for his death? His wife is resolved that he shall disclose the secret taught to him by Allah, and the moment he so doeth he shall surely die. We dogs are all a-mourning; but thou clappest thy wings and clarionest thy loudest and treadest hen after hen. Is this an hour for pastime and pleasuring? Art thou not ashamed of thyself?"

"Then by Allah," quoth the Cock, "is our master a lack-wit and a man scanty of sense: if he cannot manage matters with a single wife, his life is not worth prolonging. Now I have some fifty Dame Partlets; and I please this and provoke that and starve one and stuff another; and through my good governance they are all well under my control. This our master pretendeth to wit and wisdom, and he hath but one wife, and yet knoweth not how to manage her."

Asked the Dog, "What then, O Cock, should the master do to win clear of his strait?"

"He should arise forthright," answered the Cock, "and take some twigs from yon mulberry tree and give her a regular back basting and rib roasting till she cry: I repent, O my lord! I will never ask thee a question as long as I live! Then let him beat her once more and soundly, and when he shall have done this he shall sleep free from care and enjoy life. But this master of ours owns neither sense nor judgment."

"Now, daughter Scheherazade," continued the Wazir, "I will do to thee as did that husband to that wife."

Said Scheherazade, "And what did he do?"

He replied, "When the merchant heard the wise words spoken by his Cock to his Dog, he arose in haste and sought his wife's chamber, after cutting for her some mulberry twigs and hiding them there; and then he called to her, 'Come into the closet that I may tell thee the secret while no one seeth me and then die.' She entered with him and he locked the door and came down upon her with so sound a beating of back and shoulders, ribs, arms and legs, saying the while, 'Wilt thou ever be asking questions about what concerneth thee not?' that she was well nigh senseless. Presently she cried out, 'I am of the repentant! By Allah, I will ask thee no more questions, and indeed I repent sincerely and wholesomely.' Then she kissed his hand and feet and he led her out of the room submissive as a wife should be. Her parents and all the company rejoiced and sadness and mourning were changed into joy and gladness. Thus the merchant learnt family discipline from his Cock and he and his wife lived together the happiest of lives until death.

"And thou also, O my daughter!" continued the Wazir, "Unless thou turn from this matter I will do by thee what that trader did to his wife." But she answered him with much decision, "I will never desist, O my father, nor shall this tale change my purpose. Leave such talk and tattle. I will not listen to thy words and, if thou deny me, I will marry myself to him despite the nose of thee. And first I will go up to the King myself and alone and I will say to him: I prayed my father to wive me with thee, but he refused, being resolved to disappoint his lord, grudging the like of me to the like of thee."

Her father asked, "Must this needs be?" and she answered, "Even so."

Hereupon the Wazir being weary of lamenting and contending, persuading and dissuading her, all to no purpose, went up to King Shahryar and, after blessing him and kissing the ground before him, told him all about his dispute with his daughter from first to last and how he designed to bring her to him that night. The King wondered with exceeding wonder; for he had made an especial exception of the Wazir's daughter, and said to him, "O most faithful of Counsellors, how is this? Thou wottest that I have sworn by the Raiser of the Heavens that after I have gone in to her this night I shall say to thee on the morrow's morning: Take her and slay her! and, if thou slay her not, I will slay thee in her stead without fail."

"Allah guide thee to glory and lengthen thy life, O King of the age," answered the Wazir, "it is she that hath so determined: all this have I told her and more; but she will not hearken to me and she persisteth in passing this coming night with the King's Majesty."

So Shahryar rejoiced greatly and said, "'Tis well; go get her ready and this night bring her to me."

The Wazir returned to his daughter and reported to her the command saying, "Allah make not thy father desolate by thy loss!"

But Scheherazade rejoiced with exceeding joy and got ready all she required and said to her younger sister, Dunyazad, "Note well what directions I entrust to thee! When I have gone in to the King I will send for thee and when thou comest to me and seest that he hath had his carnal will of me, do thou say to me: O my sister, an thou be not sleepy, relate to me some new story, delectable and delightsome, the better to speed our waking hours;" and I will tell thee a tale which shall be our deliverance, if so Allah please, and which shall turn the King from his blood-thirsty custom."

Dunyazad answered "With love and gladness."

So when it was night their father the Wazir carried Scheherazade to the King who was gladdened at the sight and asked, "Hast thou brought me my need?" and he answered, "I have." But when the King took her to his bed and fell to toying with her and wished to go in to her she wept; which made him ask, "What aileth thee?"

She replied, "O King of the age, I have a younger sister and lief would I take leave of her this night before I see the dawn."

So he sent at once for Dunyazad and she came and kissed the ground between his hands, when he permitted her to take her seat near the foot of the couch. Then the King arose and did away with his bride's maidenhead and the three fell asleep. But when it was midnight Scheherazade awoke and signalled to her sister Dunyazad who sat up and said, "Allah upon thee, O my sister, recite to us some new story, delightsome and delectable, wherewith to while away the waking hours of our latter night."

"With joy and goodly gree," answered Scheherazade, "if this pious and auspicious King permit me."

"Tell on," quoth the King who chanced to be sleepless and restless and therefore was pleased with the prospect of hearing her story. So Scheherazade rejoiced; and thus, on the first night of the storytelling she began with "The Tale of the Trader with the Jinni."

The Tale of the Trader with the Jinni

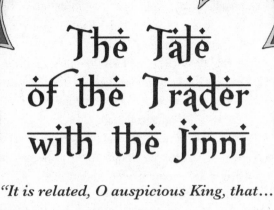

"It is related, O auspicious King, that…

There was a merchant of the merchants who had much wealth, and business in various cities. Now on a day he mounted horse and went forth to recover monies in certain towns, and the heat sore oppressed him; so he sat beneath a tree and, putting his hand into his saddle bags, took thence some broken bread and dry dates and began to break his fast. When he had ended eating the dates he threw away the stones with force and lo! an Ifrit appeared, huge of stature and brandishing a drawn sword, wherewith he approached the merchant and said, "Stand up that I may slay thee, even as thou slewest my son!"

Asked the merchant, "How have I slain thy son?" and he answered, "When thou atest dates and threwest away the stones they struck my son full in the breast as he was walking by, so that he died forthwith."

Quoth the merchant, "Verily from Allah we proceeded and unto Allah are we returning. There is no Majesty, and there is no Might save in Allah, the Glorious, the Great! If I slew thy son, I slew him by chance medley. I pray thee now pardon me."

Rejoined the Jinni, "There is no help but I must slay thee."

Then he seized him and dragged him along and, casting him to the earth, raised the sword to strike him; whereupon the merchant wept, and said, "I commit my case to Allah," and began repeating these couplets:

> "Containeth Time a twain of days, this of blessing that of bane
> And holdeth Life a twain of halves, this of pleasure that of pain.
> See'st not when blows the hurricane, sweeping stark and
>   striking strong
> None save the forest giant feels the suffering of the strain?
> How many trees earth nourisheth of the dry and of the green
> Yet none but those which bear the fruits for cast of
>   stone complain.
> See'st not how corpses rise and float on the surface of the tide
> While pearls o'price lie hidden in the deepest of the main!
> In Heaven are unnumbered the many of the stars
> Yet ne'er a star but Sun and Moon by eclipse is overta'en.
> Well judgedst thou the days that saw thy faring sound and well
> And countedst not the pangs and pain whereof Fate is ever fain.
> The nights have kept thee safe and the safety brought
>   thee pride
> But bliss and blessings of the night are 'genderers of bane!"

When the merchant ceased repeating his verses the Jinni said to him, "Cut thy words short, by Allah! needs must I slay thee."

But the merchant spake him thus, "Know, O thou Ifrit, that I have debts due to me and much wealth and children and a wife and many pledges in hand; so permit me to go home and discharge to every claimant his claim; and I will come back to thee at the head of the new year. Allah be my testimony and surety that I will return to thee; and then thou mayest do with me as thou wilt and Allah is witness to what I say."

The Jinni took sure promise of him and let him go; so he returned to his own city and transacted his business and rendered to all men their dues and after informing his wife and children of what had betided him, he appointed a guardian and dwelt with them for a full year. Then he arose, and made the Wuzu ablution to purify himself before death and took his shroud under his arm and bade farewell to his people, his neighbours and all his kith and kin, and went forth despite his own nose. They then began weeping and wailing and beating their breasts over him; but he travelled until he arrived at the same garden, and the day of his arrival was the head of the New Year.

As he sat weeping over what had befallen him, behold, a Shaykh, a very ancient man, drew near leading a chained gazelle; and he saluted that merchant and wishing him long life said, "What is the cause of thy sitting in this place and thou alone and this be a resort of evil spirits?" The merchant related to him what had come to pass with the Ifrit, and the old man, the owner of the gazelle, wondered and said, "By Allah, O brother, thy faith is none other than exceeding faith and thy story right strange; were it graven with gravers on the eye corners, it were a warner to whoso would be warned." Then seating himself near the merchant he said, "By Allah, O my brother, I will not leave thee until I see what may come to pass with thee and this Ifrit."

And presently as he sat and the two were at talk the merchant began to feel fear and terror and exceeding grief and sorrow beyond relief and ever growing care and extreme despair. And the owner of the gazelle was hard by his side; when behold, a second Shaykh approached them, and with him were two dogs both of greyhound breed and both black. The second old man after saluting them with the salam, also asked them of their tidings and said "What causeth you to sit in this place, a dwelling of the Jann?" So they told him the tale from beginning to end, and their stay there had not lasted long before there came up a third Shaykh, and with him a she mule of bright bay coat; and he saluted them and asked them why they were seated in that place. So they told him the story from first to last: and of no avail, O my master, is a twice told tale! There he sat down with them, and lo! a dust cloud advanced and a mighty send devil appeared amidmost of the waste. Presently the cloud opened and behold, within it was that Jinni hending in hand a drawn sword, while his eyes were shooting fire sparks of rage. He came up to them and, haling away the merchant from among them, cried to him, "Arise that I may slay thee, as thou slewest my son, the life stuff of my liver." The merchant wailed and wept, and the three old men began sighing and crying and weeping and wailing with their companion.

Presently the first old man (the owner of the gazelle) came out from among them and kissed the hand of the Ifrit and said, "O Jinni, thou Crown of the Kings of the Jann! were I to tell thee the story of me and this gazelle and thou shouldst consider it wondrous wouldst thou give me a third part of this merchant's blood?"

Then quoth the Jinni "Even so, O Shaykh ! if thou tell me this tale, and I hold it a marvellous, then will I give thee a third of his blood." Thereupon the old man began to tell the First Shaykh's Story.

The First Shaykh's Story

Know O Jinni! that this gazelle is the daughter of my paternal uncle, my own flesh and blood, and I married her when she was a young maid, and I lived with her well nigh thirty years, yet was I not blessed with issue by her. So I took me a concubine who brought to me the boon of a male child fair as the full moon, with eyes of lovely shine and eyebrows which formed one line, and limbs of perfect design. Little by little he grew in stature and waxed tall; and when he was a lad fifteen years old, it became needful I should journey to certain cities and I travelled with great store of goods. But the daughter of my uncle (this gazelle) had learned gramarye and egromancy and clerkly craft from her childhood; so she bewitched that son of mine to a calf, and my handmaid (his mother) to a heifer, and made them over to the herdsman's care.

Now when I returned after a long time from my journey and asked for my son and his mother, she answered me, saying "Thy slave girl is dead, and thy son hath fled and I know not whither he is sped."

So I remained for a whole year with grieving heart, and streaming eyes until the time came for the Great Festival of Allah. Then sent I to my herdsman bidding him choose for me a fat heifer; and he brought me one which was the damsel, my handmaid, whom this gazelle had ensorcelled. I tucked up my sleeves and skirt and, taking a knife, proceeded to cut her throat, but she lowed aloud and wept bitter tears. Thereat I marvelled and pity seized me and I held my hand, saying to the herd, "Bring me other than this."

Then cried my cousin, "Slay her, for I have not a fatter nor a fairer!"

Once more I went forward to sacrifice her, but she again lowed aloud upon which in ruth I refrained and commanded the herdsman to slay her and flay her. He killed her and skinned her but found in her neither fat nor flesh, only hide and bone; and I repented when penitence availed me naught.

I gave her to the herdsman and said to him, "Fetch me a fat calf"; so he brought my son ensorcelled. When the calf saw me, he brake his tether and ran to me, and fawned upon me and wailed and shed tears; so that I took pity on him and said to the herdsman, "Bring me a heifer and let this calf go!"

Thereupon my cousin (this gazelle) called aloud at me, saying, "Needs must thou kill this calf; this is a holy day and a blessed, whereon naught is slain save what be perfect pure; and we have not amongst our calves any fatter or fairer than this!"

Quoth I, "Look thou upon the condition of the heifer which I slaughtered at thy bidding and how we turn from her in disappointment and she profited us on no wise; and I repent with an exceeding repentance of having killed her: so this time I will not obey thy bidding for the sacrifice of this calf."

Quoth she, "By Allah the Most Great, the Compassionating, the Compassionate! there is no help for it; thou must kill him on this holy day, and if thou kill him not to me thou art no man and I to thee am no wife."

When the merchant purposed the sacrifice of the calf but saw it weeping, his heart relented and he said to the herdsman, "Keep the calf among my cattle."

All this the old Shaykh told the Jinni who marvelled much at these strange words. Then the owner of the gazelle continued:

O Lord of the Kings of the Jann, this much took place and my uncle's daughter, this gazelle, looked on and saw it, and said, "Butcher me this calf, for surely it is a fat one"; but I bade the herdsman take it away and he took it and turned his face homewards. On the next day as I was sitting in my own house, lo! the herdsman came and, standing before me said, "O my master, I will tell thee a thing which shall gladden thy soul, and shall gain me the gift of good tidings."

I answered, "Even so."

Then said he, "O merchant, I have a daughter, and she learned magic in her childhood from an old woman who lived with us. Yesterday when thou gavest me the calf, I went into the house to her, and she looked upon it and veiled her face; then she wept and laughed alternately and at last she said:

"O my father, hath mine honour become so cheap to thee that thou bringest in to me strange men?"

I asked her: "Where be these strange men and why wast thou laughing, and crying?" and she answered, "Of a truth this calf which is with thee is the son of our master, the merchant; but he is ensorcelled by his stepdame who bewitched both him and his mother: such is the cause of my laughing; now the reason of his weeping is his mother, for that his father slew her unawares." Then I marvelled at this with exceeding marvel and hardly made sure that day had dawned before I came to tell thee.

When I heard, O Jinni, my herdsman's words, I went out with him, and I was drunken without wine, from the excess of joy and gladness which came upon me, until I reached his house. There his daughter welcomed me and kissed my hand, and forthwith the calf came and fawned upon me as before.

Quoth I to the herdsman's daughter, "Is this true that thou sayest of this calf?"

Quoth she, "Yea, O my master, he is thy son, the very core of thy heart."

I rejoiced and said to her, "O maiden, if thou wilt release him thine shall be whatever cattle and property of mine are under thy father's hand."

She smiled and answered, "O my master, I have no greed for the goods nor will I take them save on two conditions; the first that thou marry me to thy son and the second that I may bewitch her who bewitched him and imprison her, otherwise I cannot be safe from her malice and malpractices."

Now when I heard, O Jinni, these, the words of the herdsman's daughter, I replied, "Beside what thou askest all the cattle and the house hold stuff in thy father's charge are thine and, as for the daughter of my uncle, her blood is lawful to thee."

When I had spoken, she took a cup and filled it with water: then she recited a spell over it and sprinkled it upon the calf, saying, "If Almighty Allah created thee a calf, remain so shaped, and change not; but if thou be enchanted, return to thy whilom form, by command of Allah Most Highest!" and lo! he trembled and became a man.

Then I fell on his neck and said, "Allah upon thee, tell me all that the daughter of my uncle did by thee and by thy mother." And when he told me what had come to pass between them I said, " O my son, Allah favoured thee with one to restore thee, and thy right hath returned to thee." Then, O Jinni, I married the herdsman's daughter to him, and she transformed my wife into this gazelle, saying: "Her shape is a comely and by no means loathsome."

After this she abode with us night and day, day and night, till the Almighty took her to Himself. When she deceased, my son fared forth to the cities of Hind, even to the city of this man who hath done to thee what hath been done; and I also took this gazelle (my cousin) and wandered with her from town to town seeking tidings of my son, till Destiny drove me to this place where I saw the merchant sitting in tears. Such is my tale!

Quoth the Jinni, "This story is indeed strange, and therefore I grant thee the third part of his blood."

There upon the second old man, who owned the two greyhounds, came up and said, " O Jinni, if I recount to thee what befel me from my brothers, these two hounds, and thou see that it is a tale even more wondrous and marvellous than what thou hast heard, wilt thou grant to me also the third of this man's blood?"

Replied the Jinni, "Thou hast my word for it, if thine adventures be more marvellous and wondrous." Thereupon he thus began the Second Shaykh's Story.

THE SECOND SHAYKH'S STORY

Know, O lord of the Kings of the Jann! that these two dogs are my brothers and I am the third. Now when our father died and left us a capital of three thousand gold pieces, I opened a shop with my share, and bought and sold therein, and in like guise did my two brothers, each setting up a shop. But I had been in business no long while before the elder sold his stock for a thousand dinars, and after buying outfit and merchandise, went his ways to foreign parts. He was absent one whole year with the caravan; but one day as I sat in my shop, behold, a beggar stood before me asking alms, and I said to him, "Allah open thee another door!" Whereupon he answered, weeping the while, "Am I so changed that thou knowest me not?" Then I looked at him narrowly, and lo! it was my brother, so I rose to him and welcomed him; then I seated him in my shop and put questions concerning his case.

"Ask me not," answered he; "my wealth is awaste and my state hath waxed unstated!" So I took him to the Hammam bath and clad him in a suit of my own and gave him lodging in my house. Moreover, after looking over the accounts of my stock in trade and the profits of my business, I found that industry had gained me one thousand dinars, while my principal, the head of my wealth, amounted to two thousand. So I shared the whole with him saying, "Assume that thou hast made no journey abroad but hast remained at home; and be not cast down by thine ill luck."

He took the share in great glee and opened for himself a shop; and matters went on quietly for a few nights and days. But presently my second brother (yon other dog), also setting his heart upon travel, sold off what goods and stock in trade he had, and albeit we tried to stay him he would not be stayed: he laid in an outfit for the journey and fared forth with certain wayfarers. After an absence of a whole year he came back to me, even as my elder brother had come back; and when I said to him, "O my brother, did I not dissuade thee from travel?" he shed tears and cried, "O my brother, this be destiny's decree: here I am a mere beggar, penniless and without a shirt to my back."

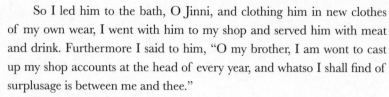

28

So I led him to the bath, O Jinni, and clothing him in new clothes of my own wear, I went with him to my shop and served him with meat and drink. Furthermore I said to him, "O my brother, I am wont to cast up my shop accounts at the head of every year, and whatso I shall find of surplusage is between me and thee."

So I proceeded, O Ifrit, to strike a balance and, finding two thousand dinars of profit, I returned praises to the Creator (be He extolled and exalted!) and made over one half to my brother, keeping the other to my self. Thereupon he busied himself with opening a shop and on this wise we abode many days. After a time my brothers began pressing me to travel with them; but I refused saying, "What gained ye by travel voyage that I should gain thereby?" As I would not give ear to them we went back each to his own shop where we bought and sold as before. They kept urging me to travel for a whole twelvemonth, but I refused to do so till full six years were past and gone when I consented with these words, "O my brothers, here am I, your companion of travel: now let me see what monies you have by you." I found, however, that they had not a doit, having squandered their substance in high diet and drinking and carnal delights. Yet I spoke not a word of reproach; so far from it I looked over my shop accounts once more, and sold what goods and stock in trade were mine; and, finding myself the owner of six thousand ducats, I gladly proceeded to divide that sum in halves, saying to my brothers, "These three thousand gold pieces are for me and for you to trade withal," adding, "Let us bury the other moiety underground that it may be of service in case any harm befal us, in which case each shall take a thousand wherewith to open shops."

Both replied, "Right is thy recking"; and I gave to each one his thousand gold pieces, keeping the same sum for myself, to wit, a thousand dinars. We then got ready suitable goods and hired a ship and, having embarked our merchandise, proceeded on our voyage, day following day, a full month, after which we arrived at a city, where we sold our venture; and for every piece of gold we gained ten.

And as we turned again to our voyage we found on the shore of the sea a maiden clad in worn and ragged gear, and she kissed my hand and said, "O master, is there kindness in thee and charity? I can make thee a fitting return for them."

I answered, "Even so; truly in me are benevolence and good works, even though thou render me no return."

Then she said, "Take me to wife, O my master, and carry me to thy city, for I have given myself to thee; so do me a kindness and I am of those who be meet for good works and charity: I will make thee a fitting return for these and be thou not shamed by my condition." When I heard her words, my heart yearned towards her, in such sort as willed it Allah (be He extolled and exalted!); and took her and clothed her and made ready for her a fair resting place in the vessel, and honourably entreated her.

So we voyaged on, and my heart became attached to her with exceeding attachment, and I was separated from her neither night nor day, and I paid more regard to her than to my brothers. Then they were estranged from me, and waxed jealous of my wealth and the quantity of merchandise I had, and their eyes were opened covetously upon all my property. So they took counsel to murder me and seize my wealth, saying, "Let us slay our brother and all his monies will be ours"; and Satan made this deed seem fair in their sight; so when they found me in privacy (and I sleeping by my wife's side) they took us both up and cast us into the sea. My wife awoke startled from her sleep and, forthright becoming an Ifritah, she bore me up and carried me to an island and disappeared for a short time; but she returned in the morning and said, "Here am I, thy faithful slave, who hath made thee due recompense; for I bore thee up in the waters and saved thee from death by command of the Almighty. Know—that I am a Jinniyah, and as I saw thee my heart loved thee by will of the Lord, for I am a believer in Allah and in His Apostle (whom Heaven bless and preserve!). Thereupon I came to thee conditioned as thou sawest me and thou didst marry me, and see now I have saved thee from sinking. But I am angered against thy brothers and assuredly I must slay them."

When I heard her story I was surprised and, thanking her for all she had done, I said, "But as to slaying my brothers this must not be."

Then I told her the tale of what had come to pass with them from the beginning of our lives to the end, and on hearing it quoth she, "This night will I fly as a bird over them and will sink their ship and slay them."

Quoth I, "Allah upon thee, do not thus, for the proverb saith, O thou who doest good to him that doth evil, leave the evil doer to his evil deeds. Moreover they are still my brothers."

But she rejoined, "By Allah, there is no help for it but I slay them."

I humbled myself before her for their pardon, whereupon she bore me up and flew away with me till at last she set me down on the terrace roof of my own house. I opened the doors and took up what I had hidden in the ground; and after I had saluted the folk I opened my shop and bought me merchandise. Now when night came on I went home, and there I saw these two hounds tied up; and, when they sighted me, they arose and whined and fawned upon me; but ere I knew what happened my wife said, "These two dogs be thy brothers!"

I answered, "And who hath done this thing by them?" and she rejoined, "I sent a message to my sister and she entreated them on this wise, nor shall these two be released from their present shape till ten years shall have passed."

And now I have arrived at this place on my way to my wife's sister that she may deliver them from this condition, after their having endured it for half a score of years. As I was wending onwards I saw this young man, who acquainted me with what had befallen him, and I determined not to fare hence until I should see what might occur between thee and him. Such is my tale!

Then said the Jinni, "Surely this is a strange story and therefore I give thee the third portion of his blood and his crime."

Thereupon quoth the third Shaykh, the master of the mare mule, to the Jinni, "I can tell thee a tale more wondrous than these two, so thou grant me the remainder of his blood and of his offense," and the Jinni answered, "So be it!" Then the old man began the Third Shaykh's Story.

The Third Shaykh's Story

Know, O Sultan and head of the Jann, that this mule was my wife. Now it so happened that I went forth and was absent one whole year; and when I returned from my journey I came to her by night, and saw a black slave lying with her on the carpet bed and they were talking, and dallying, and laughing, and kissing and playing the close buttock game. When she saw me, she rose and came hurriedly at me with a gugglet of water; and, muttering spells over it, she besprinkled me and said, "Come forth from this thy shape into the shape of a dog"; and I became on the instant a dog. She drove me out of the house, and I ran through the doorway nor ceased running until I came to a butcher's stall, where I stopped and began to eat what bones were there.

When the stall owner saw me, he took me and led me into his house, but as soon as his daughter had sight of me she veiled her face from me, crying out, "Dost thou bring men to me and dost thou come in with them to me?"

Her father asked, "Where is the man?"; and she answered, "This dog is a man whom his wife hath ensorcelled and I am able to release him." When her father heard her words, he said, "Allah upon thee, O my daughter, release him." So she took a gugglet of water and, after uttering words over it, sprinkled upon me a few drops, saying, "Come forth from that form into thy former form." And I returned to my natural shape.

Then I kissed her hand and said, "I wish thou wouldest transform my wife even as she bans formed me."

Thereupon she gave me some water, saying, "As soon as thou see her asleep, sprinkle this liquid upon her and speak what words thou heardest me utter, so shall she become whatsoever thou desirest."

I went to my wife and found her fast asleep; and, while sprinkling the water upon her, I said, "Come forth from that form into the form of a mare mule." So she became on the instant a she mule, and she it is whom thou seest with thine eyes, O Sultan and head of the Kings of the Jann!

Then the Jinni turned towards her and said, "Is this sooth?" And she nodded her head and replied by signs, "Indeed, 'tis the truth: for such is my tale and this is what hath befallen me."

When the third old man told a tale to the Jinni more wondrous than the two preceding, the Jinni marvelled with exceeding marvel, and, shaking with delight, cried, "Lo! I have given thee the remainder of the merchant's punishment and for thy sake have I released him." Thereupon the merchant embraced the old men and thanked them, and these Shaykhs wished him joy on being saved and fared forth each one for his own city.

"Yet this tale is not more wondrous than the fisherman's story," quoth Scheherazade.

Asked the King, "What is the fisherman's story?"

And she answered by relating "The Tale of the Fisherman and the Jinni."

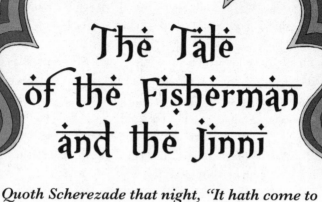

The Tale of the Fisherman and the Jinni

Quoth Scherezade that night, "It hath come to me, O auspicious King, that…

There was a Fisherman well stricken in years who had a wife and three children, and withal was of poor condition. Now it was his custom to cast his net every day four times, and no more. On a day he went forth about noontide to the sea shore, where he laid down his basket; and, tucking up his shirt and plunging into the water, made a cast with his net and waited till it settled to the bottom. Then he gathered the cords together and haled away at it, but found it weighty; and however much he drew it landwards, he could not pull it up; so he carried the ends ashore and drove a stake into the ground and made the net fast to it. Then he stripped and dived into the water all about the net, and left not off working hard until he had brought it up. He rejoiced thereat and, donning his clothes, went to the net, when he found in it a dead jackass which had torn the meshes. Now when he saw it, he exclaimed in his grief, "There is no Majesty, and there is no Might save in Allah the Glorious, the Great!" Then quoth he, "This is a strange manner of daily bread"; and he began reciting in extempore verse:

"O toiler through the glooms of night in peril and in pain
Thy toiling stint for daily bread comes not by might and main!
Seest thou not the fisher seek afloat upon the sea
His bread, while glimmer stars of night as set in tangled skein.
Anon he plungeth in despite the buffet of the waves
The while to sight the bellying net his eager glances strain;
Till joying at the night's success, a fish he bringeth home
Whose gullet by the hook of Fate was caught and cut in twain.
When buys that fish of him a man who spent the hours of night
Reckless of cold and wet and gloom in ease and comfort fain,
Laud to the Lord who gives to this, to that denies his wishes
And dooms one toil and catch the prey and other eat the fishes."

Then quoth he, "Up and to it; I am sure of His beneficence, Inshallah!"
So he continued:

"When thou art seized of Evil Fate, assume
The noble soul's long suffering: 'tis thy best
Complain not to the creature; this be 'plaint
From one most ruthful to the ruthlessest."

The Fisherman, when he had looked at the dead ass, got it free of the
toils and wrung out and spread his net; then he plunged into the sea, saying,
"In Allah's name!" and made a cast and pulled at it, but it grew heavy and
settled down more firmly than the first time. Now he thought that there
were fish in it, and he made it fast, and doffing his clothes went into the
water, and dived and haled until he drew it up upon dry land. Then found
he in it a large earthen pitcher which was full of sand and mud; and seeing
this he was greatly troubled and began repeating these verses:

"Forbear, O troubles of the world,
And pardon an ye nill forbear:
I went to seek my daily bread
I find that breadless I must fare:
For neither handcraft brings me aught
Nor Fate allots to me a share:
How many fools the Pleiads reach
While darkness whelms the wise and ware."

So he prayed pardon of Allah and, throwing away the jar, wrung his net and cleansed it and returned to the sea the third time to cast his net and waited till it had sunk. Then he pulled at it and found therein potsherds and broken glass; whereupon he began to speak these verses:

> "He is to thee that daily bread thou canst nor loose nor bind
> Nor pen nor writ avail thee aught thy daily bread to find:
> For joy and daily bread are what Fate deigneth to allow;
> This soil is sad and sterile ground, while that makes glad
> the hind.
> The shafts of Time and Life bear down full many a man
> of worth
> While bearing up to high degree wights of ignoble mind.
> So come thou, Death! for verily life is not worth a straw
> When low the falcon falls withal the mallard wings the wind:
> No wonder 'tis thou seest how the great of soul and mind
> Are poor, and many a loser carle to height of luck designed.
> This bird shall overfly the world from east to furthest west
> And that shall win her every wish though ne'er she leave the nest."

Then raising his eyes heavenwards he said, "O my God! verily Thou wottest that I cast not my net each day save four times; the third is done and as yet Thou hast vouchsafed me nothing. So this time, O my God, deign give me my daily bread." Then, having called on Allah's name, he again threw his net and waited its sinking and settling; whereupon he haled at it but could not draw it in for that it was entangled at the bottom. He cried out in his vexation "There is no Majesty and there is no Might save in Allah!" and he began reciting:

> "Fie on this wretched world, an so it be
> I must be whelmed by grief and misery:
> Tho' gladsome be man's lot when dawns the morn
> He drains the cup of woe ere eve he see:
> Yet was I one of whom the world when asked
> 'Whose lot is happiest?' oft would say ''Tis he!'"

Thereupon he stripped and, diving down to the net, busied himself with it till it came to land. Then he opened the meshes and found therein a cucumber-shaped jar of yellow copper, evidently full of something, whose mouth was made fast with a leaden cap, stamped with the seal ring of our Lord Sulayman son of David (Allah accept the twain!). Seeing this the Fisherman rejoiced and said, "If I sell it in the brass bazar 'tis worth ten golden dinars." He shook it and finding it heavy continued, "Would to Heaven I knew what is herein. But I must and will open it and look to its contents and store it in my bag and sell it in the brass market." And taking out a knife he worked at the lead till he had loosened it from the jar; then he laid the cup on the ground and shook the vase to pour out whatever might be inside. He found nothing in it; whereat he marvelled with an exceeding marvel. But presently there came forth from the jar a smoke which spired heavenwards into aether (whereat he again marvelled with mighty marvel), and which trailed along earth's surface till presently, having reached its full height, the thick vapour condensed, and became an Ifrit, huge of bulk, whose crest touched the clouds while his feet were on the ground. His head was as a dome, his hands like pitchforks, his legs long as masts and his mouth big as a cave; his teeth were like large stones, his nostrils ewers, his eyes two lamps and his look was fierce and lowering.

Now when the Fisherman saw the Ifrit his side muscles quivered, his teeth chattered, his spittle dried up and he became blind about what to do. Upon this the Ifrit looked at him and cried, "There is no god but *the* God, and Sulayman is the prophet of God"; presently adding, "O Apostle of Allah, slay me not; never again will I gainsay thee in word nor sin against thee in deed."

Quoth the Fisherman, "O Marid, diddest thou say, Sulayman the Apostle of Allah; and Sulayman is dead some thousand and eight hundred years ago, and we are now in the last days of the world! What is thy story, and what is thy account of thyself, and what is the cause of thy entering into this cucurbit?"

Now when the Evil Spirit heard the words of the Fisherman, quoth he, "There is no god but *the* God: be of good cheer, O Fisherman!"

Quoth the Fisherman, "Why biddest thou me to be of good cheer?" and he replied, "Because of thy having to die an ill death in this very hour."

Said the Fisherman, "Thou deservest for thy good tidings the withdrawal of Heaven's protection, O thou distant one! Wherefore shouldest thou kill me and what thing have I done to deserve death, I who freed thee from the jar, and saved thee from the depths of the sea, and brought thee up on the dry land?"

Replied the Ifrit, "Ask of me only what mode of death thou wilt die, and by what manner of slaughter shall I slay thee."

Rejoined the Fisherman, "What is my crime and wherefore such retribution?" Quoth the Ifrit, "Hear my story, O Fisherman!" and he answered, "Say on, and be brief in thy saying, for of very sooth my life breath is in my nostrils."

Thereupon quoth the Jinni, "Know, that I am one among the heretical Jann and I sinned against Sulayman, David's son (on the twain be peace!), I together with the famous Sakhr al Jinni; whereupon the Prophet sent his minister, Asaf son of Barkhiya, to seize me; and this Wazir brought me against my will and led me in bonds to him (I being downcast despite my nose) and he placed me standing before him like a suppliant. When Sulayman saw me, he took refuge with Allah and bade me embrace the True Faith and obey his behests; but I refused, so sending for this cucurbit he shut me up therein, and stopped it over with lead whereon he impressed the Most High Name, and gave his orders to the Jann who carried me off, and cast me into the midmost of the ocean. There I abode an hundred years, during which I said in my heart, 'Whoso shall release me, him will I enrich for ever and ever.' But the full century went by and, when no one set me free, I entered upon the second five score saying, 'Whoso shall release me, for him I will open the hoards of the earth.' Still no one set me free and thus four hundred years passed away. Then quoth I, 'Whoso shall release me, for him will I fulfil three wishes.' Yet no one set me free. Thereupon I waxed wroth with exceeding wrath and said to myself, 'Whoso shall release me from this time forth, him will I slay and I will give him choice of what death he will die; and now, as thou hast released me, I give thee full choice of deaths.'"

The Fisherman, hearing the words of the Ifrit, said, "O Allah! the wonder of it that I have not come to free thee save in these days!" adding, "Spare my life, so Allah spare thine; and slay me not, lest Allah set one to slay thee."

Replied the Contumacious One, "There is no help for it; die thou must; so ask me by way of boon what manner of death thou wilt die."

Albeit thus certified the Fisherman again addressed the Ifrit saying, "Forgive me this my death as a generous reward for having freed thee"; and the Ifrit, "Surely I would not slay thee save on account of that same release."

"O Chief of the Ifrits," said the Fisherman, "I do thee good and thou requitest me with evil! in very sooth the old saw lieth not when it saith:

"We wrought them weal, they met our weal with ill;
   Such, by my life! is every bad man's labour:
   To him who benefits unworthy wights
   Shall hap what hapt to Ummi Amir's neighbor."

Now when the Ifrit heard these words he answered, "No more of this talk, needs must I kill thee."

Upon this the Fisherman said to himself, "This is a Jinni; and I am a man to whom Allah hath given a passably cunning wit, so I will now cast about to compass his destruction by my contrivance and by mine intelligence; even as he took counsel only of his malice and his frowardness." He began by asking the Ifrit, "Hast thou indeed resolved to kill me?" and, receiving for all answer, "Even so," he cried, "now in the Most Great Name, graven on the seal ring of Sulayman the Son of David (peace be with the holy twain!), and I question thee on a certain matter wilt thou give me a true answer?"

The Ifrit replied "Yea"; but, hearing mention of the Most Great Name, his wits were troubled and he said with trembling, "Ask and be brief."

Quoth the Fisherman, "How didst thou fit into this bottle which would not hold thy hand; no, nor even thy foot, and how came it to be large enough to contain the whole of thee?"

Replied the Ifrit, "What! dost not believe that I was all there?" and the Fisherman rejoined, "Nay! I will never believe it until I see thee inside with my own eyes."

The Evil Spirit on the instant shook and became a vapour, which condensed, and entered the jar little and little, till all was well inside when lo! the Fisherman in hot haste took the leaden cap with the seal and stoppered therewith the mouth of the jar and called out to the Ifrit, saying, "Ask me by way of boon what death thou wilt die! By Allah, I will throw thee into the sea before us and here will I build me a lodge; and whoso cometh hither I will warn him against fishing and will say: 'In these waters abideth an Ifrit who giveth as a last favour a choice of deaths and fashion of slaughter to the man who saveth him!'"

Now when the Ifrit heard this from the Fisherman and saw himself in limbo, he was minded to escape, but this was prevented by Solomon's seal; so he knew that the Fisherman had cozened and outwitted him, and he waxed lowly and submissive and began humbly to say, "I did but jest with thee."

But the other answered, "Thou liest, O vilest of the Ifrits, and meanest and filthiest!" and he set off with the bottle for the sea side; the Ifrit calling out "Nay! Nay!" and he calling out "Aye! Aye!"

Thereupon the Evil Spirit softened his voice and smoothed his speech and abased himself, saying, "What wouldest thou do with me, O Fisherman?"

"I will throw thee back into the sea," he answered; "where thou hast been housed and homed for a thousand and eight hundred years; and now I will leave thee therein till Judgment day; did I not say to thee: 'Spare me and Allah shall spare thee; and slay me not lest Allah slay thee? yet thou spurnedst my supplication and hadst no intention save to deal ungraciously by me, and Allah hath now thrown thee into my hands and I am cunninger than thou.'"

Quoth the Ifrit, "Open for me and I may bring thee weal." Quoth the Fisherman, "Thou liest, thou accursed! my case with thee is that of the Wazir of King Yunan with the sage Duban."

"And who was the Wazir of King Yunan and who was the sage Duban; and what was the story about them?" quoth the Ifrit, whereupon the Fisherman began to tell

The Tale of the Wazir and the Sage Duban

Know, O thou Ifrit, that in days of yore and in ages long gone before, a King called Yunan reigned over the city of Fars of the land of the Roum. He was a powerful ruler and a wealthy, who had armies and guards and allies of all nations of men; but his body was afflicted with a leprosy which leaches and men of science failed to heal. He drank potions and he swallowed powders and he used unguents, but naught did him good and none among the host of physicians availed to procure him a cure. At last there came to his city a mighty healer of men and one well stricken in years, the sage Duban highs. This man was a reader of books, Greek, Persian, Roman, Arabian, and Syrian; and he was skilled in astronomy and in leechcraft, the theorick as well as the practick; he was experienced in all that healeth and that hurteth the body; conversant with the virtues of every plant, grass and herb, and their benefit and bane; and he understood philosophy and had compassed the whole range of medical science and other branches of the knowledge tree.

Now this physician passed but few days in the city, ere he heard of the King's malady and all his bodily sufferings through the leprosy with which Allah had smitten him; and how all the doctors and wise men had failed to heal him. Upon this he sat up through the night in deep thought and, when broke the dawn and appeared the morn and light was again born, and the Sun greeted the Good whose beauties the world adorn, he donned his handsomest dress and going in to King Yunan, he kissed the ground before him: then he prayed for the endurance of his honour and prosperity in fairest language and made himself known saying, 'O King, tidings have reached I me of what befel thee through that which is in thy person; and how the host of physicians have proved themselves unavailing to abate it; and lo! I can cure thee, O King; and yet will I not make thee drink of draught or anoint thee with ointment.'

Now when King Yunan heard his words he said in huge surprise, "How wilt thou do this? By Allah, if thou make me whole I will enrich thee even to thy son's son and I will give thee sumptuous gifts; and whatso thou wishest shall be thine and thou shalt be to me a cup companion and a friend."

The King then robed him with a dress of honour and entreated him graciously and asked him, "Canst thou indeed cure me of this complaint without drug and unguent?" and he answered, "Yes! I will heal I thee without the pains and penalties of medicine."

The King marvelled with exceeding marvel and said, "O physician, when shall be this whereof thou speakest, and in how many days shall it take place? Haste thee, O my son!" He replied, "I hear and I obey; the cure shall begin to-morrow."

So saying he went forth from the presence, and hired himself a house in the city for the better storage of his books and scrolls, his medicines and his aromatic roots. Then he set to work at choosing the fittest drugs and simples and he fashioned a bat hollow within, and furnished with a handle without, for which he made a ball; the two being prepared with consummate art.

On the next day when both were ready for use and wanted nothing more, he went up to the King; and, kissing the ground between his hands bade him ride forth on the parade ground there to play at pall and mall. He was accompanied by his suite, Emirs and Chamberlains, Wazirs and Lords of the realm and, ere he was seated, the sage Duban came up to him, and handing him the bat said, "Take this mall and grip it as I do; so! and now push for the plain and leaning well over thy horse drive the ball with all thy might until thy palm be moist and thy body perspire: then the medicine will penetrate through thy palm and will permeate thy person. When thou hast done with playing and thou feelest the effects of the medicine, return to thy palace, and make the Ghusl ablation in the Hammam bath, and lay thee down to sleep; so shalt thou become whole; and now peace be with thee!"

Thereupon King Yunan took the bat from the Sage and grasped it firmly; then, mounting steed, he drove the ball before him and gallopped after it till he reached it, when he struck it with all his might, his palm gripping the bat handle the while; and he ceased not malling the ball till his hand waxed moist and his skin, perspiring, imbibed the medicine from the wood. Then the sage Duban knew that the drugs had penetrated his person and bade him return to the palace and enter the Hammam without stay or delay; so King Yunan forthright returned and ordered them to clear for him the bath. They did so, the carpet spreaders making all haste, and the slaves all hurry and got ready a change of raiment for the King. He entered the bath and made the total ablution long and thoroughly; then donned his clothes within the Hammam and rode therefrom to his palace where he lay him down and slept. Such was the case with King Yunan, but as regards the sage Duban, he returned home and slept as usual and when morning dawned he repaired to the palace and craved audience. The King ordered him to be admitted; then, having kissed the ground between his hands, in allusion to the King he recited these couplets with solemn intonation:

> "Happy is Eloquence when thou art named her sire
> But mourns she whenas other man the title claimed.
> O Lord of fairest presence, whose illuming rays
> Clear off the fogs of doubt aye veiling deeds high famed,
> Ne'er cease thy face to shine like Dawn and rise of Morn
> And never show Time's face with heat of ire inflamed!
> Thy grace hath favoured us with gifts that worked such wise
> As rain clouds raining on the hills by words enframed:
> Freely thou lavishedst thy wealth to rise on high
> Till won from Time the heights whereat thy grandeur aimed."

Now when the Sage ceased reciting, the King rose quickly to his feet and fell on his neck; then, seating him by his side he bade dress him in a sumptuous dress; for it had so happened that when the King left the Hammam he looked on his body and saw no trace of leprosy: the skin was all clean as virgin silver. He joyed thereat with exceeding joy, his breast broadened with delight and he felt thoroughly happy. Presently, when it was full day he entered his audience hall and sat upon the throne of his kingship whereupon his Chamberlains and Grandees flocked to the presence and with them the Sage Duban. Seeing the leach the King rose to him in honour and seated him by his side; then the food trays furnished with the daintiest viands were brought and the physician ate with the King, nor did he cease companying him all that day. Moreover, at nightfall he gave the physician Duban two thousand gold pieces, besides the usual dress of honour and other gifts galore, and sent him home on his own steed.

After the Sage had fared forth King Yunan again expressed his amazement at the leach's art, saying, "This man medicined my body from without nor anointed me with aught of ointments: by Allah, surely this is none other than consummate skill! I am bound to honour such a man with rewards and distinction, and take him to my companion and my friend during the remainder of my days." So King Yunan passed the night in joy and gladness for that his body had been made whole and had thrown off so pernicious a malady.

On the morrow the King went forth from his Serraglio and sat upon his throne, and the Lords of Estate stood about him, and the Emirs and Wazirs sat as was their wont on his right hand and on his left. Then he asked for the Sage Duban, who came in and kissed the ground before him, when the King rose to greet him and, seating him by his side, ate with him and wished him long life. Moreover he robed him and gave him gifts, and ceased not conversing with him until night approached. Then the King ordered him, by way of salary, five dresses of honour and a thousand dinars. The physician returned to his own house full of gratitude to the King.

Now when next morning dawned the King repaired to his audience hall, and his Lords and Nobles surrounded him and his Chamberlains and his Ministers, as the white encloseth the black of the eye. Now the King had a Wazir among his Wazirs, unsightly to look upon, an ill omened spectacle; sordid, ungenerous, full of envy and evil will. When this Minister saw the King place the physician near him and give him all these gifts, he jaloused him and planned to do him a harm, as in the saying on such subject, "Envy lurks in every body"; and the saying, "Oppression hideth in every heart: power revealeth it and weakness concealeth it." Then the Minister came before the King and, kissing the ground between his hands, said, "O King of the age and of all time, thou in whose benefits I have grown to manhood, I have weighty advice to offer thee, and if I withhold it I were a son of adultery and no true born man; wherefore an thou order me to disclose it I will so do forthwith."

Quoth the King (and he was troubled at the words of the Minister), "And what is this counsel of thine?"

Quoth he, "O glorious monarch, the wise of old have said: 'Whoso regardeth not the end, hath not Fortune to friend'; and indeed I have lately seen the King on far other than the right way; for he lavisheth largesse on his enemy, on one whose object is the decline and fall of his kingship: to this man he hath shown favour, honouring him with over honour and making of him an intimate. Wherefore I fear for the King's life."

The King, who was much troubled and changed colour, asked, "Whom dost thou suspect and anent whom doest thou hint?" and the Minister answered, "O King, an thou be asleep, wake up! I point to the physician Duban."

Rejoined the King, "Fie upon thee! This is a true friend who is favoured by me above all men, because he cured me with some thing which I held in my hand, and he healed my leprosy which had baffled all physicians; indeed he is one whose like may not be found in these days—no, not in the whole world from furthest east to utmost west! And it is of such a man thou sayest such hard sayings. Now from this day forward I allot him a settled solde and allowances, every month a thousand gold pieces; and, were I to share with him my realm 'twere but a little matter. Perforce I must suspect that thou speakest on this wise from mere envy and jealousy as they relate of the King Sindibad."

King Yunan said to his Minister, "O Wazir, thou art one whom the evil spirit of envy hath possessed because of this physician, and thou plottest for my putting him to death, after which I should repent me full sorely, even as repented King Sindibad for killing his falcon."

"Quoth the Wazir, "Pardon me, O King of the age, how was that?" So the King began the story of

KING SINDIBAD AND HIS FALCON

It is said (but Allah is All knowing!) that there was a King of the Kings of Fars, who was fond of pleasuring and diversion, especially coursing end hunting. He had reared a falcon which he carried all night on his fist, and whenever he went a chasing he took with him this bird; and he bade make for her a golden cuplet hung around her neck to give her drink therefrom. One day as the King was sitting quietly in his palace, behold, the high falcaner of the household suddenly addressed him, "O King of the age, this is indeed a day fit for birding."

The King gave orders accordingly and set out taking the hawk on fist; and they fared merrily forwards till they made a Wady where they planted a circle of nets for the chase; when lo! a gazelle came within the toils and the King cried, "Whoso alloweth yon gazelle to spring over his head and loseth her, that man will I surely slay." They narrowed the nets about the gazelle when she drew near the King's station; and, planting herself on her hind quarter, crossed her forehand over her breast, as if about to kiss the earth before the King. He bowed his brow low in acknowledgment to the beast; when she bounded high over his head and took the way of the waste. Thereupon the King turned towards his troops and seeing them winking and pointing at him, he asked, "O Wazir, what are my men saying?" and the Minister answered, "They say thou didst proclaim that whoso alloweth the gazelle to spring over his head, that man shall be put to death."

Quoth the King, "Now, by the life of my head! I will follow her up till I bring her back." So he set off gallopping on the gazelle's trail and gave not over tracking till he reached the foot hills of a mountain chain where the quarry made for a cave. Then the King cast off at it the falcon which presently caught it up and, swooping down, drove her talons into its eyes, bewildering and blinding it; and the King drew his mace and struck a blow which rolled the game over. He then dismounted; and, after cutting the antelope's throat and flaying the body, hung it to the pommel of his saddle.

Now the time was that of the siesta and the wold was parched and dry, nor was any water to be found anywhere; and the King thirsted and his horse also; so he went about searching till he saw a tree dropping water, as it were melted butter, from its boughs. Thereupon the King who wore gauntlets of skin to guard him against poisons took the cup from the hawk's neck, and filling it with the water set it before the bird, and lo! the falcon struck it with her pounces and upset the liquid. The King filled it a second time with the dripping drops, thinking his hawk was thirsty; but the bird again struck at the cup with her talons and overturned it. Then the King waxed wroth with the hawk and filling the cup a third time offered it to his horse: but the hawk upset it with a flirt of wings. Quoth the King, "Allah confound thee, thou unluckiest of flying things! thou keepest me from drinking, and thou deprivest thyself also, and the horse."

So he struck the falcon with his sword and cut off her wing; but the bird raised her head and said by signs, "Look at that which hangeth on the tree!" The King lifted up his eyes accordingly and caught sight of a brood of vipers, whose poison drops he mistook for water; thereupon he repented him of having struck off his falcon's wing, and mounting horse, fared on with the dead gazelle, till he arrived at the camp, his starting place. He threw the quarry to the cook saying, "Take and broil it," and sat down on his chair, the falcon being still on his fist when suddenly the bird gasped and died; whereupon the King cried out in sorrow and remorse for having slain that falcon which had saved his life. Now this is what occurred in the case of King Sindibad; and I am assured that were I to do as thou desirest I should repent even as the man who killed his parrot.

Quoth the Wazir, "And how was that?" And the King began to tell

The Tale of the Husband and the Parrot

A certain man and a merchant to boot had married a fair wife, a woman of perfect beauty and grace, symmetry and loveliness, of whom he was mad-jealous, and who contrived successfully to keep him from travel. At last an occasion compelling him to leave her, he went to the bird market and bought him for one hundred gold pieces a she parrot which he set in his house to act as duenna, expecting her to acquaint him on his return with what had passed during the whole time of his absence; for the bird was kenning and cunning and never forgot what she had seen and heard. Now his fair wife had fallen in love with a young Turk, who used to visit her, and she feasted him by day and lay with him by night. When the man had made his journey and won his wish he came home; and, at once causing the Parrot be brought to him, questioned her concerning the conduct of his consort whilst he was in foreign parts.

Quoth she, "Thy wife hath a man friend who passed every night with her during thine absence."

Thereupon the husband went to his wife in a violent rage and bashed her with a bashing severe enough to satisfy any body. The woman, suspecting that one of the slave girls had been tattling to the master, called them together and questioned them upon their oaths, when all swore that they had kept the secret, but that the Parrot had not, adding, "And we heard her with our own ears."

Upon this the woman bade one of the girls to set a hand mill under the cage and grind therewith and a second to sprinkle water through the cage roof and a third to run about, right and left, dashing a mirror of bright steel through the livelong night. Next morning when the husband returned home after being entertained by one of his friends, he bade bring the Parrot before him and asked what had taken place whilst he was away.

"Pardon me, O my master," quoth the bird, "I could neither hear nor see aught by reason of the exceeding murk and the thunder and lightning which lasted throughout the night."

As it happened to be the summer tide the master was astounded and cried, "But we are now in mid Tammuz, and this is not the time for rains and storms."

"Ay, by Allah," rejoined the bird, "I saw with these eyes what my tongue hath told thee."

Upon this the man, not knowing the case nor smoking the plot, waxed exceeding wroth; and, holding that his wife had been wrongously accused, put forth his hand and pulling the Parrot from her cage dashed her upon the ground with such force that he killed her on the spot. Some days after wards one of his slave girls confessed to him the whole truth, yet would he not believe it till he saw the young Turk, his wife's lover, coming out of her chamber, when he bared his blade and slew him by a blow on the back of the neck; and he did the same by the adulteress; and thus the twain, laden with mortal sin, went straightways to Eternal Fire. Then the merchant knew that the Parrot had told him the truth anent all she had seen and he mourned grievously for her loss, when mourning availed him not.

The Minister, hearing the words of King Yunan, rejoined, "O Monarch, high in dignity, and what harm have I done him, or what evil have I seen from him that I should compass his death? I would not do this thing, save to serve thee, and soon shalt thou sight that it is right; and if thou accept my advice thou shalt be saved, otherwise thou shalt be destroyed even as a certain Wazir who acted treacherously by the young Prince."

Asked the King, "How was that?" and the Minister thus began

THE TALE OF THE PRINCE AND THE OGRESS

A certain King, who had a son over much given to hunting and coursing, ordered one of his Wazirs to be in attendance upon him whithersoever he might wend. One day the youth set out for the chase accompanied by his father's Minister; and, as they jogged on together, a big wild beast came in sight.

Cried the Wazir to the King's son, "Up and at yon noble quarry!"

So the Prince followed it until he was lost to every eye and the chase got away from him in the waste; whereby he was confused and he knew not which way to turn, when lo! a damsel appeared ahead and she was in tears. The King's son asked, "Who art thou?" and she answered, "I am daughter to a King among the Kings of Hind, and I was travelling with a caravan in the desert when drowsiness overcame me, and I fell from my beast unwittingly whereby I am cut off from my people and sore bewildered."

46

The Prince, hearing these words, pitied her case and, mounting her on his horse's crupper, travelled until he passed by an old ruin, when the damsel said to him, "O my master, I wish to obey a call of nature": he therefore set her down at the ruin where she delayed so long that the King's son thought that she was only wasting time; so he followed her without her knowledge and behold, she was a Ghulah, a wicked Ogress, who was saying to her brood, "O my children, this day I bring you a fine fat youth, for dinner;" whereto they answered, "Bring him quick to us, O our mother, that we may browse upon him our bellies full."

The Prince hearing their talk, made sure of death and his side muscles quivered in fear for his life, so he turned away and was about to fly. The Ghulah came out and seeing him in sore affright (for he was trembling in every limb) cried, "Wherefore art thou afraid?" and he replied, "I have hit upon an enemy whom I greatly fear."

Asked the Ghulah, "Diddest thou not say: 'I am a King's son?'" and he answered, "Even so."

Then quoth she, "Why dost not give thine enemy something of money and so satisfy him?"

Quoth he, "He will not be satisfied with my purse but only with my life, and I mortally fear him and am a man under oppression."

She replied, "If thou be so distressed, as thou deemest, ask aid against him from Allah, who will surely protect thee from his ill doing and from the evil whereof thou art afraid."

Then the Prince raised his eyes heavenwards and cried, "O Thou who answerest the necessitous when he calleth upon Thee and dispellest his distress; O my God ! grant me victory over my foe and turn him from me, for Thou over all things art Almighty."

The Ghulah, hearing his prayer, turned away from him, and the Prince returned to his father, and told him the tale of the Wazir; whereupon the King summoned the Minister to his presence and then and there slew him. Thou likewise, O King, if thou continue to trust this leach, shalt be made to die the worst of deaths. He verily thou madest much of and whom thou entreatedest as an intimate, will work thy destruction. Seest thou not how he healed the disease from outside thy body by something grasped in thy hand? Be not assured that he will not destroy thee by something held in like manner!

Replied King Yunan, "Thou hast spoken sooth, O Wazir, it may well be as thou hintest O my well advising Minister; and belike this Sage hath come as a spy searching to put me to death; for assuredly if he cured me by a something held in my hand, he can kill me by a something given me to smell." Then asked King Yunan, "O Minister, what must be done with him?" and the Wazir answered, "Send after him this very instant and summon him to thy presence; and when he shall come strike him across the neck; and thus shalt thou rid thyself of him and his wickedness, and deceive him ere he can deceive thee."

"Thou hast again spoken sooth, O Wazir," said the King and sent one to call the Sage who came in joyful mood for he knew not what had appointed for him the Compassionate; as a certain poet saith by way of illustration:

> "O Thou who fearest Fate, confiding fare
> Trust all to Him who built the world and wait:
> What Fate saith 'Be' perforce must be, my lord!
> And safe art thou from the undecreed of Fate."

As Duban the physician entered he addressed the King in these lines:

> "An fail I of my thanks to thee nor thank thee day by day
> For whom composed I prose and verse, for whom my say
> and lay?
> Thou lavishedst thy generous gifts ere they were craved by me
> Thou lavishedst thy boons unsought sans pretext or delay:
> How shall I stint my praise of thee, how shall I cease to laud
> The grace of thee in secresy and patentest display?
> Nay; I will thank thy benefits, for aye thy favours lie
> Light on my thought and tongue, though heavy on my
> back they weigh."

And he said further on the same theme:

> "Turn thee from grief nor care a jot!
> Commit thy needs to Fate and Lot!
> Enjoy the Present passing well
> And let the Past be clean forgot
> For whatso haply seemeth worse
> Shall work thy weal as Allah wot
> Allah shall do whate'er He wills
> And in His will oppose Him not."

And further still:

> "To th' All wise Subtle One trust worldly things
> Rest thee from all whereto the worldling clings:
> Learn wisely well naught cometh by thy will
> But e'en as willeth Allah, King of Kings."

And lastly:

> "Gladsome and gay forget thine every grief
> Full often grief the wisest hearts outwore:
> Thought is but folly in the feeble slave
> Shun it and so be saved evermore."

Said the King for sole return, "Knowest thou why I have summoned thee?" and the Sage replied, "Allah Most Highest alone kenneth hidden things!"

But the King rejoined, "I summoned thee only to take thy life and utterly to destroy thee."

Duban the Wise wondered at this strange address with exceeding wonder and asked, "O King, and wherefore wouldest thou slay me, and what ill have I done thee?" and the King answered, "Men tell me thou art a spy sent hither with intent to slay me; and lo! I will kill thee ere I be killed by thee"; then he called to his Sworder, and said, "Strike me off the head of this traitor and deliver us from his evil practices."

Quoth the Sage, "Spare me and Allah will spare thee; slay me not or Allah shall slay thee."

And he repeated to him these very words, even as I to thee, O Ifrit, and yet thou wouldst not let me go, being bent upon my death. King Yunan only rejoined, "I shall not be safe without slaying thee; for, as thou healedst me by something held in hand, so am I not secure against thy killing me by something given me to smell or otherwise."

Said the physician, "This then, O King, is thy requital and reward; thou returnest only evil for good."

The King replied, "There is no help for it; die thou must and without delay."

Now when the physician was certified that the King would slay him without waiting, he wept and regretted the good he had done to other than the good. As one hath said on this subject:

"Of wit and wisdom is Maymunah bare
Whose sire in wisdom all the wits outstrippeth:
Man may not tread on mud or dust or clay
Save by good sense, else trippeth he and slippeth."

Hereupon the Sworder stepped forward and bound the Sage Duban's eyes and bared his blade, saying to the King, "By thy leave;" while the physician wept and cried, "Spare me and Allah will spare thee, and slay me not or Allah shall slay thee," and began repeating:

"I was kind and 'scaped not, they were cruel and escaped;
And my kindness only led me to Ruination Hall,
If I live I'll ne'er be kind; if I die, then all be damned
Who follow me, and curses their kindliness befal."

"Is this," continued Duban, "the return I meet from thee? Thou givest me, meseems, but crocodile boon."

Quoth the King, "What is the tale of the crocodile?" and quoth the physician, "Impossible for me to tell it in this my state; Allah upon thee, spare me, as thou hopest Allah shall spare thee."

And he wept with exceeding weeping. Then one of the King's favourites stood up and said, "O King! grant me the blood of this physician; we have never seen him sin against thee, or doing aught save healing thee from a disease which baffled every leach and man of science."

Said the King, "Ye wot not the cause of my putting to death this physician, and this it is. If I spare him, I doom myself to certain death; for one who healed me of such a malady by something held in my hand, surely can slay me by something held to my nose; and I fear lest he kill me for a price, since haply he is some spy whose sole purpose in coming hither was to compass my destruction. So there is no help for it; die he must, and then only shall I be sure of my own life."

Again cried Duban, "Spare me and Allah shall spare thee; and slay me not or Allah shall slay thee." But it was in vain.

When the physician knew for certain that the King would kill him, he said, "O King, if there be no help but I must die, grant me some little delay that I may go down to my house and release myself from mine obligations and direct my folk and my neighbours where to bury me and distribute my books of medicine. Amongst these I have one, the rarest of rarities, which I would present to thee as an offering: keep it as a treasure in thy treasury."

"And what is in the book?" asked the King and the Sage answered, "Things beyond compt; and the least of secrets is that if, directly after thou hast cut off my head, thou open three leaves and read three lines of the page to thy left hand, my head shall speak and answer every question thou deignest ask of it."

The King wondered with exceeding wonder and shaking with delight at the novelty, said, "O physician, cost thou really tell me that when I cut off thy head it will speak to me?"

He replied, "Yes, O King!"

Quoth the King, "This is indeed a strange matter!" and forthwith sent him closely guarded to his house, and Duban then and there settled all his obligations.

Next day he went up to the King's audience hall, where Emirs and Wazirs, Chamberlains and Nabobs, Grandees and Lords of Estate were gathered together, making the presence chamber gay as a garden of flower beds. And lo! the physician came up and stood before the King, bearing a worn old volume and a little etui of metal full of powder, like that used for the eyes. Then he sat down and said, "Give me a tray." So they brought him one and he poured the powder upon it and levelled it and lastly spake as follows: "O King, take this book but do not open it till my head falls; then set it upon this tray, and bid press it down upon the powder, when forthright the blood will cease flowing. That is the time to open the book."

The King thereupon took the book and made a sign to the Sworder, who arose and struck off the physician's head, and placing it on the middle of the tray, pressed it down upon the powder. The blood stopped flowing, and the Sage Duban unclosed his eyes and said, "Now open the book, O King!" The King opened the book, and found the leaves stuck together; so he put his finger to his mouth and, by moistening it, he easily turned over the first leaf, and in like way the second, and the third, each leaf opening with much trouble; and when he had unstuck six leaves he looked over them and, finding nothing written thereon, said, "O physician, there is no writing here!"

Duban replied, "Turn over yet more;" and he turned over three others in the same way. Now the book was poisoned; and before long the venom penetrated his system, and he fell into strong convulsions and he cried out, "The poison hath done its work!" Whereupon the Sage Duban's head began to improvise:

"There be rulers who have ruled with a foul tyrannic sway
    But they soon became as though they had never, never been:

Just, they had won justice: they oppressed and were oppress
By Fortune, who requited them with ban and bane and teen:
So they faded like the morn, and the tongue of things repeats
'Take this far that, nor vent upon Fortune's ways thy spleen.'"

No sooner had the head ceased speaking than the King rolled over dead.

"Now I would have thee know, O Ifrit, that if King Yunan had spared the Sage Duban, Allah would have spared him, but he refused so to do and decreed to do him dead, wherefore Allah slew him; and thou too, O Ifrit, if thou hadst spared me, Allah would have spared thee.

When the Fisherman said to the Ifrit, "If thou hadst spared me I would have spared thee, but nothing would satisfy thee save my death; so now I will do thee die by jailing thee in this jar and I will hurl thee into this sea."

Then the Marid roared aloud and cried, "Allah upon thee, O Fisherman, don't! Spare me, and pardon my past doings; and, as I have been tyrannous, so be thou generous, for it is said among sayings that go current: O thou who doest good to him who hath done thee evil, suffice for the ill doer his ill deeds, and do not deal with me as did Umamah to 'Atikah."

Asked the Fisherman, "And what was their case?" and the Ifrit answered, "This is not the time for story telling and I in this prison; but set me free and I will tell thee the tale."

Quoth the Fisherman, "Leave this language: there is no help but that thou be thrown back into the sea nor is there any way for thy getting out of it for ever and ever. Vainly I placed myself under thy protection, and I humbled myself to thee with weeping, while thou soughtest only to slay me, who had done thee no injury deserving this at thy hands; nay, so far from injuring thee by any evil act, I worked thee nought but weal in releasing thee from that jail of thine. Now I knew thee to be an evil doer when thou diddest to me what thou didst, and know, that when I have cast thee back into the sea, I will warn whomsoever may fish thee up of what hath befallen me with thee, and I will advise him to toss thee back again; so shalt thou abide here under these waters till the End of Time shall make an end of thee."

But the Ifrit cried aloud, "Set me free; this is a noble occasion for generosity and I make covenant with thee and vow never to do thee hurt and harm; nay, I will help thee to what shall put thee out of want."

The Fisherman accepted his promises on both conditions, not to trouble him as before, but on the contrary to do him service; and, after making firm the plight and swearing him a solemn oath by Allah Most Highest he opened the cucurbit. Thereupon the pillar of smoke rose up till all of it was fully out; then it thickened and once more became an Ifrit of hideous presence, who forthright administered a kick to the bottle and sent it flying into the sea. The Fisherman, seeing how the cucurbit was treated and making sure of his own death, piddled in his clothes and said to himself, "This promiseth badly"; but he fortified his heart, and cried, "O Ifrit, Allah hath said: 'Perform your covenant; for the performance of your covenant shall be inquired into hereafter.' Thou hast made a vow to me and hast sworn an oath not to play me false lest Allah play thee false, for verily he is a jealous God who respiteth the sinner, but letteth him not escape. I say to thee as said the Sage Duban to King Yunan, 'Spare me so Allah may spare thee!'"

The Ifrit burst into laughter and stalked away, saying to the Fisherman, "Follow me"; and the man paced after him at a safe distance (for he was not assured of escape) till they had passed round the suburbs of the city. Thence they struck into the uncultivated grounds, and crossing them descended into a broad wilderness, and lo! in the midst of it stood a mountain tarn. The Ifrit waded in to the middle and again cried, "Follow me"; and when this was done he took his stand in the centre and bade the man cast his net and catch his fish.

The Fisherman looked into the water and was much astonished to see therein vari-coloured fishes, white and red, blue and yellow; however he cast his net and, hauling it in, saw that he had netted four fishes, one of each colour. Thereat he rejoiced greatly and more when the Ifrit said to him, "Carry these to the Sultan and set them in his presence; then he will give thee what shall make thee a wealthy man; and now accept my excuse, for by Allah at this time I wot none other way of benefiting thee, inasmuch I have lain in this sea eighteen hundred years and have not seen the face of the world save within this hour. But I would not have thee fish here save once a day."

The Ifrit then gave him God speed, saying, "Allah grant we meet again"; and struck the earth with one foot, whereupon the ground clove asunder and swallowed him up. The Fisherman, much marvelling at what had happened to him with the Ifrit, took the fish and made for the city; and as soon as he reached home he filled an earthen bowl with water and there-in threw the fish which began to struggle and wriggle about. Then he bore off the bowl upon his head and repairing to the King's palace (even as the Ifrit had bidden him) laid the fish before the presence; and the King wondered with exceeding wonder at the sight, for never in his lifetime had he seen fishes like these in quality or in conformation. So he said, "Give those fish to the stranger slave girl who now cooketh for us," meaning the bond maiden whom the King of Roum had sent to him only three days before, so that he had not yet made trial of her talents in the dressing of meat.

Thereupon the Wazir carried the fish to the cook and bade her fry them saying, "O damsel, the King sendeth this say to thee: 'I have not treasured thee, O tear o' me! save for stress time of me; approve, then, to us this day thy delicate handiwork and thy savoury cooking; for this dish of fish is a present sent to the Sultan and evidently a rarity.'"

The Wazir, after he had carefully charged her, returned to the King, who commanded him to give the Fisherman four hundred dinars: he gave them accordingly, and the man took them to his bosom and ran off home stumbling and falling and rising again and deeming the whole thing to be a dream. However, he bought for his family all they wanted and lastly he went to his wife in huge joy and gladness.

So far concerning him; but as regards the cookmaid, she took the fish and cleansed them and set them in the frying pan, basting them with oil till one side was dressed. Then she turned them over and, behold, the kitchen wall crave asunder, and therefrom came a young lady, fair of form, oval of face, perfect in grace, with eyelids which Kohl lines enchase. Her dress was a silken head kerchief fringed and tasseled with blue: a large ring hung from either ear; a pair of bracelets adorned her wrists; rings with bezels of priceless gems were on her fingers; and she hent in hand a long rod of rattan cane which she thrust into the frying pan, saying, "O fish! O fish! be ye constant to your covenant?"

When the cookmaiden saw this apparition she swooned away. The young lady repeated her words a second time and a third time, and at last the fishes raised their heads from the pan, and saying in articulate speech "Yes! Yes!" began with one voice to recite:

"Come back and so will I! Keep faith and so will I!
And if ye fain forsake, I'll requite till quits we cry!"

After this the young lady upset the frying pan and went forth by the way she came in and the kitchen wall closed upon her. When the cook maiden recovered from her fainting fit, she saw the four fishes charred black as charcoal, and crying out, "His staff brake in his first bout," she again fell swooning to the ground. Whilst she was in this case the Wazir came for the

fish and looking upon her as insensible she lay, not knowing Sunday from Thursday, shoved her with his foot and said, "Bring the fish for the Sultan!" Thereupon recovering from her fainting fit she wept and informed him of her case and all that had befallen her.

The Wazir marvelled greatly and exclaiming, "This is none other than a right strange matter!" he sent after the Fisherman and said to him, "Thou, O Fisherman, must needs fetch us four fishes like those thou broughtest before." Thereupon the man repaired to the tarn and cast his net; and when he landed it, lo! four fishes were therein exactly like the first. These he at once carried to the Wazir, who went in with them to the cook maiden and said, "Up with thee and fry these in my presence, that I may see this business."

The damsel arose and cleansed the fish, and set them in the frying pan over the fire; however they remained there but a little while ere the wall crave asunder and the young lady appeared, clad as before and holding in hand the wand which she again thrust into the frying pan, saying, "O fish! O fish! be ye constant to your olden covenant?"

And behold, the fish lifted their heads, and repeated "Yes! Yes!" and recited this couplet:

> "Come back and so will I! Keep faith and so will I!
> But if ye fain forsake, I'll requite till quits we cry!"

When the fishes spoke, and the young lady upset the frying pan with her rod, and went forth by the way she came and the wall closed up, the Wazir cried out, "This is a thing not to be hidden from the King."

So he went and told him what had happened, where upon quoth the King, "There is no help for it but that I see this with mine own eyes." Then he sent for the Fisherman and commended him to bring four other fish like the first and to take with him three men as witnesses. The Fisherman at once brought the fish: and the King, after ordering them to give him four hundred gold pieces, turned to the Wazir and said, "Up and fry me the fishes here before me!"

The Minister, replying, "To hear is to obey," bade bring the frying pan, threw therein the cleansed fish and set it over the fire; when lo! the wall crave asunder, and out burst a black slave like a huge rock or a remnant of the tribe Ad bearing in hand a branch of a green tree; and he cried in loud and terrible tones, "O fish! O fish! be ye all constant to your antique covenant?" whereupon the fishes lifted their heads from the frying pan and said, "Yes! Yes! we be true to our vow"; and they again recited the couplet:

> "Come back and so will I! Keep faith and so will I!
> But if ye fain forsake, I'll requite till quits we cry!"

Then the huge blackamoor approached the frying pan and upset it with the branch and went forth by the way he came in. When he vanished from their sight the King inspected the fish; and finding them all charred black as charcoal, was utterly bewildered and said to the Wazir, "Verily this is a matter whereanent silence cannot be kept, and as for the fishes, assuredly some marvellous adventure connects with them."

So he bade bring the Fisherman and asked him, saying "Fie on thee, fellow! whence came these fishes?" and he answered, "From a tarn between four heights lying behind this mountain which is in sight of thy city."

Quoth the King, "How many days' march?"

Quoth he, "O our lord the Sultan, a walk of half hour."

The King wondered and, straight way ordering his men to march and horsemen to mount, led off the Fisherman who went before as guide, privily damning the Ifrit. They fared on till they had climbed the mountain and descended unto a great desert which they had never seen during all their lives; and the Sultan and his merry men marvelled much at the wold set in the midst of four mountains, and the tarn and its fishes of four colours, red and white, yellow and blue. The King stood fixed to the spot in wonderment and asked his troops and all present, "Hath any one among you ever seen this piece of water before now?" and all made answer, "O King of the age never did we set eyes upon it during all our days."

They also questioned the oldest inhabitants they met, men well stricken in years, but they replied, each and every, "A lakelet this we never saw in this place." Thereupon quoth the King, "By Allah I will neither return to my capital nor sit upon the throne of my forbears till I learn the truth about this tarn and the fish therein."

He then ordered his men to dismount and bivouac all around the mountain; which they did; and summoning his Wazir, a Minister of much experience, sagacious, of penetrating wit and well versed in affairs, said to him, "'Tis in my mind to do a certain thing whereof I will inform thee; my heart telleth me to fare forth alone this night and root out the mystery of this tarn and its fishes. Do thou take thy seat at my tent door, and say to the Emirs and Wazirs, the Nabobs and the Chamberlains, in fine to all who ask thee: 'The Sultan is ill at ease, and he hath ordered me to refuse all admittance'; and be careful thou let none know my design." And the Wazir could not oppose him.

Then the King changed his dress and ornaments and, slinging his sword over his shoulder, took a path which led up one of the mountains and marched for the rest of the night till morning dawned; nor did he cease wayfaring till the heat was too much for him. After his long walk he rested for a while, and then resumed his march and fared on through the second night till dawn, when suddenly there appeared a black point in the far distance. Hereat he rejoiced and said to himself, "Haply someone here shall acquaint me with the mystery of the tarn and its fishes."

Presently drawing near the dark object he found it a palace built of swart stone plated with iron; and, while one leaf of the gate stood wide open, the other was shut. The King's spirits rose high as he stood before the gate and rapped a light rap; but hearing no answer he knocked a second knock and a third; yet there came no sign. Then he knocked his loudest but still no answer, so he said, "Doubtless 'tis empty." Thereupon he mustered up resolution and boldly walked through the main gate into the great hall and there cried out aloud, "Holla, ye people of the palace! I am a stranger and a wayfarer; have you aught here of victual?" He repeated his cry a second time and a third but still there came no reply; so strengthening his heart and making up his mind he stalked through the vestibule into the very middle of the palace and found no man in it. Yet it was furnished with silken stuffs gold starred; and the hangings were let down over the doorways. In the midst was a spacious court off which set four open saloons each with its raised dais, saloon facing saloon; a canope shaded the court and in the centre was a jetting fount with four figures of lions made of red gold, spouting from their mouths water clear as pearls and diaphanous gems. Round about the palace birds were let loose and over it stretched a net of golden wire, hindering them from flying off; in brief there was everything but human beings. The King marvelled mightily thereat, yet felt he sad at heart for that he saw no one to give him account of the waste and its tarn, the fishes, the mountains and the palace itself. Presently as he sat between the doors in deep thought behold, there came a voice of lament, as from a heart grief spent and he heard the voice chanting these verses:

"I hid what I endured of him and yet it came to light,
And nightly sleep mine eyelids fled and changed to
sleepless night:

Oh world! Oh Fate! withhold thy hand and cease thy hurt
    and harm
Look and behold my hapless sprite in colour and affright:
Wilt ne'er show ruth to highborn youth who lost him on the way
Of Love, and fell from wealth and fame to lowest basest wight.
Jealous of Zephyr's breath was I as on your form he breathed
But whenas Destiny descends she blindeth human sight
What shall the hapless archer do who when he fronts his foe
And bends his bow to shoot the shaft shall find his string undight?
When cark and care so heavy bear on youth of generous soul
How shall he 'scape his lot and where from Fate his
    place of flight?"

Now when the Sultan heard the mournful voice he sprang to his feet;
and, following the sound, found a curtain let down over a chamber door.
He raised it and saw behind it a young man sitting upon a couch about a
cubit above the ground; and he fair to the sight, a well shaped wight, with
eloquence dight; his forehead was flower white, his cheek rosy bright, and
a mole on his cheek breadth like an ambergris mite; even as the poet cloth
indite:

A youth slim waisted from whose locks and brow
The world in blackness and in light is set.
Throughout Creation's round no fairer show
No rarer sight thine eye hath ever met:
A nut brown mole sits throned upon a cheek
Of rosiest red beneath an eye of jet.

The King rejoiced and saluted him, but he remained sitting in his
caftan of silken stuff pureed with Egyptian gold and his crown studded with
gems of sorts; but his face was sad with the traces of sorrow. He returned
the royal salute in most courteous wise adding, "O my lord, thy dignity
demandeth my rising to thee; and my sole excuse is to crave thy pardon."

Quoth the King, "Thou art excused, O youth; so look upon me as thy
guest come hither on an especial object. I would thou acquaint me with
the secrets of this tarn and its fishes and of this palace and thy loneliness
therein and the cause of thy groaning and wailing."

When the young man heard these words he wept with sore weeping;
till his bosom was drenched with tears and began reciting:

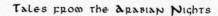

"Say him who careless sleeps what while the shaft of Fortune flies
How many cloth this shifting world lay low and raise to rise?
Although thine eye be sealed in sleep, sleep not th'
    Almighty's eyes
And who hath found Time ever fair, or Fate in constant guise?"

Then he sighed a long fetched sigh and recited:

"Confide thy case to Him, the Lord who made mankind;
Quit cark and care and cultivate content of mind;
Ask not the Past or how or why it came to pass:
All human things by Fate and Destiny were designed!"

The King marvelled and asked him, "What maketh thee weep, O young man?" and he answered, "How should I not weep, when this is my case!" Thereupon he put out his hand and raised the skirt of his garment, when lo! the lower half of him appeared stone down to his feet while from his navel to the hair of his head he was man.

The King, seeing this his plight, grieved with sore grief and of his compassion cried, "Alack and well away! in very sooth, O youth, thou heapest sorrow upon my sorrow. I was minded to ask thee the mystery of the fishes only: whereas now I am concerned to learn thy story as well as theirs. But there is no Majesty and there is no Might save in Allah, the Glorious, the Great! Lose no time, O youth, but tell me forthright thy whole tale."

Quoth he, "Lend me thine ears, thy sight and thine insight"; and quoth the King, "All are at thy service!"

Thereupon the youth began, "Right wondrous and marvellous is my case and that of these fishes; and were it graven with gravers upon the eye corners it were a warner to whoso would be warned."

"How is that?" asked the King, and the young man began to tell

THE TALE OF THE ENSORCELLED PRINCE

Know then, O my lord, that whilome my sire was King of this city, and his name was Mahmud, entitled Lord of the Black Islands, and owner of what are now these four mountains. He ruled three score and ten years, after which he went to the mercy of the Lord and I reigned as Sultan in his stead. I took to wife my cousin, the daughter of my paternal uncle, and she loved me with such abounding love that whenever I was absent she

ate not and she drank not until she saw me again. She cohabited with me for five years till a certain day when she went forth to the Hammam bath; and I bade the cook hasten to get ready all requisites for our supper. And I entered this palace and lay down on the bed where I was wont to sleep and bade two damsels to fan my face, one sitting by my head and the other at my feet. But I was troubled and made restless by my wife's absence and could not sleep; for although my eyes were closed my mind and thoughts were wide awake.

Presently I heard the slave girl at my head say to her at my feet, "O Mas'udah, how miserable is our master and how wasted in his youth and oh! the pity of his being so betrayed by our mistress, the accursed whore!"

The other replied, "Yes indeed: Allah curse all faithless women and adulterous; but the like of our master, with his fair gifts, deserveth something better than this harlot who lieth abroad every night."

Then quoth she who sat by my head, "Is our lord dumb or fit only for bubbling that he questioneth her not!" and quoth the other, "Fie on thee! doth our lord know her ways or doth she allow him his choice? Nay, more, doth she not drug every night the cup she giveth him to drink before sleep time, and put Bhang into it? So he sleepeth and wotteth not whither she goeth, nor what she doeth; but we know that after giving him the drugged wine, she donneth her richest raiment and perfumeth herself and then she fareth out from him to be away till break of day; then she cometh to him, and burneth a pastile under his nose and he awaketh from his deathlike sleep."

When I heard the slave girl's words, the light became black before my sight and I thought night would never fall. Presently the daughter of my uncle came from the baths; and they set the table for us and we ate and sat together a fair half hour quaffing our wine as was ever our wont. Then she called for the particular wine I used to drink before sleeping and reached me the cup; but, seeming to drink it according to my wont, I poured the contents into my bosom; and, lying down, let her hear that I was asleep.

Then, behold, she cried, "Sleep out the night, and never wake again: by Allah, I loathe thee and I loathe thy whole body, and my soul turneth in disgust from cohabiting with thee; and I see not the moment when Allah shall snatch away thy life!" Then she rose and donned her fairest dress and perfumed her person and slung my sword over her shoulder; and, opening the gates of the palace, went her ill way.

I rose and followed her as she left the palace and she threaded the streets until she came to the city gate, where she spoke words I understood

not, and the padlocks dropped of themselves as if broken and the gate leaves opened. She went forth (and I after her without her noticing aught) till she came at last to the outlying mounds and a reed fence built about a round roofed hut of mud bricks. As she entered the door, I climbed upon the roof which commanded a view of the interior, and lo! my fair cousin had gone in to a hideous negro slave with his upper lip like the cover of a pot, and his lower like an open pot; lips which might sweep up sand from the gravel-floor of the cot. He was to boot a leper and a paralytic, lying upon a strew of sugar cane trash and wrapped in an old blanket and the foulest rags and tatters. She kissed the earth before him, and he raised his head so as to see her and said, "Woe to thee! what call hadst thou to stay away all this time? Here have been with me sundry of the black brethren, who drank their wine and each had his young lady, and I was not content to drink because of thine absence."

Then she, "O my lord, my heart's love and coolth of my eyes, knowest thou not that I am married to my cousin whose very look I loathe, and hate myself when in his company? And did not I fear for thy sake, I would not let a single sun arise before making his city a ruined heap wherein raven should croak and howlet hoot, and jackal and wolf harbour and loot; nay I had removed its very stones to the back side of Mount Kaf."

Rejoined the slave, "Thou liest, damn thee! Now I swear an oath by the valour and honour of blackamoor men (and deem not our manliness to be the poor manliness of white men), from to-day forth if thou stay away till this hour, I will not keep company with thee nor will I glue my body with thy body and strum and belly bump. Dost play fast and loose with us, thou cracked pot, that we may satisfy thy dirty lusts? stinkard! bitch! vilest of the vile whites!"

When I heard his words, and saw with my own eyes what passed between these two wretches, the world waxed dark before my face and my soul knew not in what place it was. But, my wife humbly stood up weeping before and wheedling the slave, and saying, "O my beloved, and very fruit of my heart, there is none left to cheer me but thy dear self; and, if thou cast me off who shall take me in, O my beloved, O light of my eyes?" And she ceased not weeping and abasing herself to him until he deigned be reconciled with her.

Then was she right glad and stood up and doffed her clothes, even to her petticoat trousers, and said, "O my master what hast thou here for thy handmaiden to eat?"

"Uncover the basin," he grumbled, "and thou shalt find at the bottom the broiled bones of some rats we dined on, pick at them, and then go to that slop pot where thou shalt find some leavings of beer which thou mayest drink."

So she ate and drank and washed her hands, and went and lay down by the side of the slave, upon the cane trash and, stripping herself stark naked, she crept in with him under his foul coverlet and his rags and tatters.

When I saw my wife, my cousin, the daughter of my uncle, do this deed I clean lost my wits, and climbing down from the roof, I entered and took the sword which she had with her and drew it, determined to cut down the twain. I first struck at the slave's neck and thought that the death decree had fallen on him.

When I smote the slave with intent to strike off his head, I thought that I had slain him; for he groaned a loud hissing groan, but I had cut only the skin and flesh of the gullet and the two arteries! It awoke the daughter of my uncle, so I sheathed the sword and fared forth for the city; and, entering the palace, lay upon my bed and slept till morning when my wife aroused me and I saw that she had cut off her hair and had donned mourning garments.

Quoth she: 'O son of my uncle, blame me not for what I do; it hath just reached me that my mother is dead, and my father hath been killed in holy war, and of my brothers one hath lost his life by a snake sting and the other by falling down some precipice; and I can and should do naught save weep and lament.'

When I heard her words I refrained from all reproach and said only: "Do as thou list; I certainly will not thwart thee."

She continued sorrowing, weeping and wailing one whole year from the beginning of its circle to the end, and when it was finished she said to me: "I wish to build me in thy palace a tomb with a cupola, which I will set apart for my mourning and will name the House of Lamentations."

Quoth I again: "Do as thou list!"

Then she builded for herself a cenotaph wherein to mourn, and set on its centre a dome under which showed a tomb like a Santon's sepulchre. Thither she carried the slave and lodged him; but he was exceeding weak by reason of his wound, and unable to do her love service; he could only drink wine and from the day of his hurt he spake not a word, yet he lived on because his appointed hour was not come. Every day, morning and evening, my wife went to him and wept and wailed over him and gave him wine and strong soups, and left not off doing after this manner a second year; and I bore with her patiently and paid no heed to her.

62

One day, however, I went in to her unawares; and I found her weeping and beating her face and crying: "Why art thou absent from my sight, O my heart's delight? Speak to me, O my life; talk with me, O my love?"

Then she recited these verses:

> "For your love my patience fails and albeit you forget
> I may not, nor to other love my heart can make reply:
> Bear my body, bear my soul wheresoever you may fare
> And where you pitch the camp let my body buried lie:
> Cry my name above my grave, and an answer shall return
> The moaning of my bones responsive to your cry."

Then she recited, weeping bitterly the while:

> "The day of my delight is the day when draw you near
> And the day of mine affright is the day you turn away:
> Though I tremble through the night in my bitter dread
> of death
> When I hold you in my arms I am free from all affray"

Once more she began reciting:

> "Though a morn I may awake with all happiness in hand
> Though the world all be mine and like Kisra-kings I reign;
> To me they had the worth of the winglet of the gnat
> When I fail to see thy form, when I look for thee in vain"

When she had ended for a time her words and her weeping I said to her: "O my cousin, let this thy mourning suffice, for in pouring forth tears there is little profit!"

"Thwart me not," answered she, "in aught I do, or I will lay violent hands on myself!"

So I held my peace and left her to go her own way; and she ceased not to cry and keen and indulge her affliction for yet another year. At the end of the third year I waxed aweary of this longsome mourning, and one day I happened to enter the cenotaph when vexed and angry with some matter which had thwarted me, and suddenly I heard her say: "O my lord, I never hear thee vouch safe a single word to me! Why cost thou not answer me, O my master?" And she began reciting:

"O thou tomb! O, thou tomb! be his beauty set in shade?
    Hast thou darkened that countenance all sheeny as the noon?
    O thou tomb! neither earth nor yet heaven art to me
    Then how cometh it in thee are conjoined my sun and moon?"

"When I heard such verses as these rage was heaped upon my rage; I cried out: 'Well away! how long is this sorrow to last?' and I began repeating:

"O thou tomb! O thou tomb! be his horrors set in blight?
    Hast thou darkened his countenance that sickeneth the soul?
    O thou tomb! neither cesspool nor pipkin art to me
    Then how cometh it in thee are conjoined soil and coal?"

When she heard my words she sprang to her feet crying: "Fie upon thee, thou cur! all this is of thy doings; thou hast wounded my heart's darling and thereby worked me sore woe and thou hast wasted his youth so that these three years he hath lain abed more dead than alive!"

In my wrath I cried: "O thou foulest of harlots and filthiest of whores ever futtered by negro slaves who are hired to have at thee! Yes indeed it was I who did this good deed"; and snatching up my sword I drew it and made at her to cut her down.

But she laughed my words and mine intent to scorn crying: "To heel, hound that thou art! Alas for the past which shall no more come to pass nor shall any one avail the dead to raise. Allah hath indeed now given into my hand him who did to me this thing, a deed that hath burned my heart with a fire which died not and a flame which might not be quenched!" Then she stood up; and, pronouncing some words to me unintelligible, she said: "By virtue of my egromancy become thou half stone and half man"; whereupon I became what thou seest, unable to rise or to sit, and neither dead nor alive. Moreover she ensorcelled the city with all its streets and garths, and she turned by her gramarye the four islands into four mountains around the tarn whereof thou questionest me; and the citizens, who were of four different faiths, Moslem, Nazarene, Jew and Magian, she transformed by her enchantments into fishes; the Moslems are the white, the Magians red, the Christians blue and the Jews yellow. And every day she tortureth me and scourgeth me with an hundred stripes, each of which draweth floods of blood and cutteth the skin of my shoulders to strips; and lastly she clotheth my upper half with a hair cloth and then throweth over them these robes.

64

Hereupon the young man again shed tears and began reciting:

"In patience, O my God, I endure my lot and fate;
I will bear at will of Thee whatsoever be my state:
They oppress me; they torture me; they make my life a woe
Yet haply Heaven's happiness shall compensate my strait:
Yea, straitened is my life by the bane and hate o' foes
But Mustafa and Murtaza shall ope me Heaven's gate."

After this the Sultan turned towards the young Prince and said, "O youth, thou hast removed one grief only to add another grief; but now, O my friend, where is she; and where is the mausoleum wherein lieth the wounded slave?"

"The slave lieth under yon dome," quoth the young man, "and she sitteth in the chamber fronting yonder door. And every day at sunrise she cometh forth, and first strippeth me, and whippeth me with an hundred strokes of the leathern scourge, and I weep and shriek; but there is no power of motion in my lower limbs to keep her off me. After ending her tormenting me she visiteth the slave, bringing him wine and boiled meats. And to morrow at an early hour she will be here."

Quoth the King, "By Allah, O youth, I will assuredly do thee a good deed which the world shall not willingly let die, and an act of derring do which shall be chronicled long after I am dead and gone by."

Then the King sat him by the side of the young Prince and talked till nightfall, when he lay down and slept; but, as soon as the false dawn showed, he arose and doffing his outer garments bared his blade and hastened to the place wherein lay the slave. Then was he ware of lighted candles and lamps, and the perfume of incenses and unguents, and directed by these, he made for the slave and struck him one stroke killing him on the spot: after which he lifted him on his back and threw him into a well that was in the palace. Presently he returned and, donning the slave's gear, lay down at length within the mausoleum with the drawn sword laid close to and along his side.

After an hour or so the accursed witch came; and, first going to her husband, she stripped off his clothes and, taking a whip, flogged him cruelly while he cried out, "Ah! enough for me the case I am in! take pity on me, O my cousin!"

But she replied, "Didst thou take pity on me and spare the life of my true love on whom I doated?" Then she drew the cilice over his raw and bleeding skin and threw the robe upon all and went down to the slave with a goblet of wine and a bowl of meat broth in her hands. She entered under the dome weeping and wailing, "Well-away!" and crying, "O my lord! speak a word to me! O my master! talk awhile with me!" and began to recite these couplets:

> "How long this harshness, this unlove, shall bide?
> Suffice thee not tear floods thou hast espied?
> Thou dost prolong our parting purposely
> And if wouldst please my foe, thou'rt satisfied!"

Then she wept again and said, "O my lord! speak to me, talk with me!"

The King lowered his voice and, twisting his tongue, spoke after the fashion of the blackamoors and said "'lack! 'lack! there be no Ma'esty and there be no Might save in Allauh, the Gloriose, the Great!"

Now when she heard these words she shouted for joy, and fell to the ground fainting; and when her senses returned she asked, "O my lord, can it be true that thou hast power of speech?" and the King making his voice small and faint answered, "O my cuss! dost thou deserve that I talk to thee and speak with thee?"

"Why and wherefore?" rejoined she; and he replied "The why is that all the livelong day thou tormentest thy hubby; and he keeps calling on 'eaven for aid until sleep is strange to me even from evenin' till mawnin', and he prays and damns, cussing us two, me and thee, causing me disquiet and much bother: were this not so, I should long ago have got my health; and it is this which prevents my answering thee."

Quoth she, "With thy leave I will release him from what spell is on him;" and quoth the King, "Release him and let's have some rest!"

She cried, "To hear is to obey;" and, going from the cenotaph to the palace, she took a metal bowl and filled it with water and spake over it certain words which made the contents bubble and boil as a cauldron seetheth over the fire. With this she sprinkled her husband saying, "By virtue of the dread words I have spoken, if thou becamest thus by my spells, come forth out of that form into thine own former form."

And lo and behold! the young man shook and trembled; then he rose to his feet and, rejoicing at his deliverance, cried aloud, "I testify that there is no god but *the* God, and in very truth Mohammed is His Apostle, whom Allah bless and keep!"

Then she said to him, "Go forth and return not hither, for if thou do I will surely slay thee;" screaming these words in his face. So he went from

between her hands; and she returned to the dome and, going down to the sepulchre, she said, "O my lord, come forth to me that I may look upon thee and thy goodliness!"

The King replied in faint low words, "What thing hast thou done? Thou hast rid me of the branch but not of the root."

She asked, "O my darling! O my negro ring! what is the root?"

And he answered, "Fie on thee, O my cuss! The people of this city and of the four islands every night when it's half passed lift their heads from the tank in which thou hast turned them to fishes and cry to Heaven and call down its anger on me and thee; and this is the reason why my body's baulked from health. Go at once and set them free, then come to me and take my hand, and raise me up, for a little strength is already back in me."

When she heard the King's words (and she still supposed him to be the slave) she cried joyously, "O my master, on my head and on my eyes be thy command, Bismillah!"

So she sprang to her feet and, full of joy and gladness, ran down to the tarn and took a little of its water in the palm of her hand and spake over it words not to be understood, the fishes lifted their heads and stood up on the instant like men, the spell on the people of the city having been removed. What was the lake again became a crowded capital; the bazars were thronged with folk who bought and sold; each citizen was occupied with his own calling and the four hills became islands as they were whilome.

Then the young woman, that wicked sorceress, returned to the King and (still thinking he was the negro) said to him, "O my love! stretch forth thy honoured hand that I may assist thee to rise."

"Nearer to me," quoth the King in a faint and feigned tone. She came close as to embrace him when he took up the sword lying hid by his side and smote her across the breast, so that the point showed gleaming behind her back. Then he smote her a second time and cut her in twain and cast her to the ground in two halves. After which he fared forth and found the young man, now freed from the spell, awaiting him and gave him joy of his happy release while the Prince kissed his hand with abundant thanks. Quoth the King, "Wilt thou abide in this city or go with me to my capital?"

Quoth the youth, "O King of the age, wottest thou not what journey is between thee and thy city?"

"Two days and a half," answered he, whereupon said the other, "An thou be sleeping, O King, awake! Between thee and thy city is a year's march for a well girt walker, and thou haddest not come hither in two days and a half save that the city was under enchantment. And I, O King, will never part from thee; no, not even for the twinkling of an eye."

The King rejoiced at his words and said, "Thanks be to Allah who hath bestowed thee upon me! From this hour thou art my son and my only son, for that in all my life I have never been blessed with issue."

67

Thereupon they embraced and joyed with exceeding great joy; and, reaching the palace, the Prince who had been spell-bound informed his lords and his grandees that he was about to visit the Holy Places as a pilgrim, and bade them get ready all things necessary for the occasion. The preparations lasted ten days, after which he set out with the Sultan, whose heart burned in yearning for his city whence he had been absent a whole twelvemonth. They journeyed with an escort of Mamelukes carrying all manners of precious gifts and rarities, nor stinted they wayfaring day and night for a full year until they approached the Sultan's capital, and sent on messengers to announce their coming. Then the Wazir and the whole army came out to meet him in joy and gladness, for they had given up all hope of ever seeing their King; and the troops kissed the ground before him and wished him joy of his safety. He entered and took seat upon his throne and the Minister came before him and, when acquainted with all that had befallen the young Prince, he congratulated him on his narrow escape. When order was restored throughout the land the King gave largesse to many of his people, and said to the Wazir, "Hither the Fisherman who brought us the fishes!"

So he sent for the man who had been the first cause of the city and the citizens being delivered from enchantment and, when he came in to the presence, the Sultan bestowed upon him a dress of honour, and questioned him of his condition and whether he had children. The Fisherman gave him to know that he had two daughters and a son, so the King sent for them and, taking one daughter to wife, gave the other to the young Prince and made the son his head treasurer. Furthermore he invested his Wazir with the Sultanate of the City in the Black Islands whilome belonging to the young Prince, and dispatched with him the escort of fifty armed slaves together with dresses of honour for all the Emirs and Grandees. The Wazir kissed hands and fared forth on his way; while the Sultan and the Prince abode at home in all the solace and the delight of life; and the Fisherman became the richest man of his age, and his daughters wived with Kings, until death came to them.

"And yet, O King!" quoth Scheherezade, "this tale is not more wondrous than 'The Barber's Tale of Himself.'"

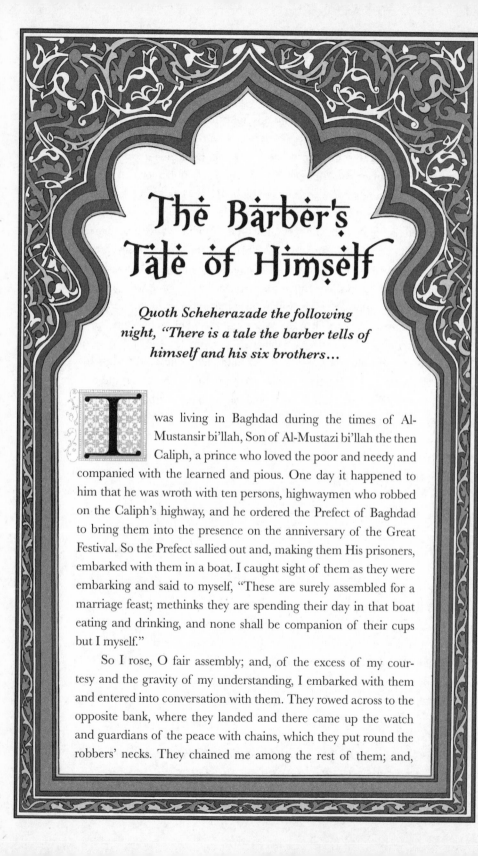

The Barber's Tale of Himself

Quoth Scheherazade the following night, "There is a tale the barber tells of himself and his six brothers…

I was living in Baghdad during the times of Al-Mustansir bi'llah, Son of Al-Mustazi bi'llah the then Caliph, a prince who loved the poor and needy and companied with the learned and pious. One day it happened to him that he was wroth with ten persons, highwaymen who robbed on the Caliph's highway, and he ordered the Prefect of Baghdad to bring them into the presence on the anniversary of the Great Festival. So the Prefect sallied out and, making them His prisoners, embarked with them in a boat. I caught sight of them as they were embarking and said to myself, "These are surely assembled for a marriage feast; methinks they are spending their day in that boat eating and drinking, and none shall be companion of their cups but I myself."

So I rose, O fair assembly; and, of the excess of my courtesy and the gravity of my understanding, I embarked with them and entered into conversation with them. They rowed across to the opposite bank, where they landed and there came up the watch and guardians of the peace with chains, which they put round the robbers' necks. They chained me among the rest of them; and,

O people, is it not a proof of my courtesy and spareness of speech, that I held my peace and did not please to speak? Then they took us away in bilbos and next morning carried us all before Al-Mustansir bi'llah, Commander of the Faithful, who bade smite the necks of the ten robbers. So the Sworder came forward after they were seated on the leather of blood; then drawing his blade, struck off one head after another until he had smitten the neck of the tenth; and I alone remained.

The Caliph looked at me and asked the Headsman, saying, "What ails thee that thou hast struck off only nine heads?"; and he answered, "Allah forbid that I should behead only nine, when thou biddest me behead ten!"

Quoth the Caliph, "Meseems thou hast smitten the necks of only nine, and this man before thee is the tenth."

"By thy beneficence!" replied the Headsman, "I have beheaded ten."

"Count them!" cried the Caliph and whenas they counted heads, lo! there were ten. The Caliph looked at me and said, "What made thee keep silence at a time like this and how camest thou to company with these men of blood? Tell me the cause of all this, for albeit thou art a very old man, assuredly thy wits are weak."

Now when I heard these words from the Caliph I sprang to my feet and replied, "Know, O Prince of the Faithful, that I am the Silent Shaykh and am thus called to distinguish me from my six brothers. I am a man of immense learning whilst, as for the gravity of my understanding, the wiliness of my wits and the spareness of my speech, there is no end of them; and my calling is that of a barber. I went out early on yesterday morning and saw these men making for a skiff; and, fancying they were bound for a marriage feast, I joined them and mixed with them. After a while up came the watch and guardians of the peace, who put chains round their necks and round mine with the rest; but, in the excess of my courtesy, I held my peace and spake not a word; nor was this other but generosity on my part. They brought us into thy presence, and thou gavest an order to smite the necks of the ten; yet did I not make myself known to thee and remained silent before the Sworder, purely of my great generosity and courtesy which led me to share with them in their death. But all my life long have I dealt thus nobly with mankind, and they requite me the foulest and evillest requital!"

When the Caliph heard my words and knew that I was a man of exceeding generosity and of very few words, one in whom is no forwardness (as this youth would have it whom I rescued from mortal risk and who hath so scurvily repaid me), he laughed with excessive laughter till he fell upon his back. Then said he to me, "O Silent Man, do thy six brothers favour thee in wisdom and knowledge and spareness of speech?"

I replied, "Never were they like me! Thou puttest reproach upon me, O Commander of the Faithful, and it becomes thee not to even my brothers with me; for, of the abundance of their speech and their deficiency of courtesy and gravity, each one of them hath gotten some maim or other. One is a monocular, another palsied, a third stone blind, a fourth cropped of ears and nose and a fifth shorn of both lips, while the sixth is a hunchback and a cripple. And conceive not, O Commander of the Faithful, that I am prodigal of speech; but I must perforce explain to thee that I am a man of greater worth and fewer words than any of them. From each one of my brothers hangs a tale of how he came by his bodily defect and these I will relate to thee."

So the Caliph gave ear to

THE BARBER'S TALE OF HIS FIRST BROTHER

Know then, O Commander of the Faithful, that my first brother, Al Bakbuk, the Prattler, is a Hunchback who took to tailoring in Baghdad, and he used to sew in a shop hired from a man of much wealth, who dwelt over the shop, and there was also a flour-mill in the basement. One day as my brother, the Hunchback, was sitting in his shop a tailoring, he chanced to raise his head and saw a lady like the rising full moon at a balconied window of his landlord's house, engaged in looking out at the passers by. When my brother beheld her, his heart was taken with love of her and he passed his whole day gazing at her and neglected his tailoring till eventide.

Next morning he opened his shop and sat him down to sew; but, as often as he stitched a stitch, he looked to the window and saw her as before; and his passion and infatuation for her increased. On the third day as he was sitting in his usual place gazing on her, she caught sight of him and, perceiving that he had been captivated with love of her, laughed in his face and he smiled back at her. Then she disappeared and presently sent her slave girl to him with a bundle containing a piece of red cowered silk. The handmaid accosted him and said, "My lady salameth to thee and desireth thee, of thy skill and good will, to fashion for her a shift of this piece and to sew it handsomely with thy best sewing.

He replied, "Hearkening and obedience"; and shaped for her a chemise and finished sewing it the same day.

When the morning morrowed the girl came back and said to him,

"My lady salameth to thee and asks how thou hast passed yesternight; for she hath not tasted sleep by reason of her heart being taken up with thee." Then she laid before him a piece of yellow satin and said, "My lady biddeth thee cut her two pair of petticoat trousers out of this piece and sew them this very day."

"Hearkening and obedience!" replied he, "greet her for me with many greetings and say to her, Thy slave is obedient to thine order; so command him as thou wilt." Then he applied himself to cutting out and worked hard at sewing the trousers; and after an hour the lady appeared at the lattice and saluted him by signs, now casting down her eyes, then smiling in his face, and he began to assure himself that he would soon make a conquest. She did not let him stir till he had finished the two pair of trousers, when she withdrew and sent the handmaid to whom he delivered them; and she took them and went her ways.

When it was night, he threw himself on his carpet bed, and lay tossing about from side to side till morning, when he rose and sat down in his place. Presently the damsel came to him and said, "My master calleth for thee."

Hearing these words he feared with exceeding fear; but the slave girl, seeing his affright, said to him, "No evil is meant to thee: naught but good awaiteth thee. My lady would have thee make acquaintance with my lord."

So my brother the tailor, rejoicing with great joy, went with her; and when he came into the presence of his landlord, the lady's husband, he kissed the ground before him, and the master of the house returned his greeting and gave him a great piece of linen saying, "Shape me shirts out of this stuff and sew them well"; and my brother answered, "To hear is to obey." Thereupon he fell to work at once, snipping, shaping and sewing till he had finished twenty shirts by supper time, without stopping to taste food.

The house master asked him, "How much the wage for this?"; and he answered, "Twenty dirhams."

So the gentleman cried out to the slave girl, "Bring me twenty dirhams," and my brother spake not a word; but the lady signed, "Take nothing from him"; whereupon my brother said, "By Allah I will take naught from thy hand." And he carried off his tailor's gear and returned to his shop, although he was destitute even to a red cent. Then he applied himself to do their work; eating, in his zeal and diligence, but a bit of bread and drinking only a little water for three days.

At the end of this time came the handmaid and said to him, "What hast thou done?"

Quoth he, "They are finished," and carried the shirts to the lady's husband, who would have paid him his hire: but he said, "I will take nothing," for fear of her and, returning to his shop, passed the night without sleep because of his hunger.

72

Now the dame had informed her husband how the case stood (my brother knowing naught of this); and the two had agreed to make him tailor for nothing, the better to mock and laugh at him. Next morning he went to his shop, and, as he sat there, the handmaid came to him and said, "Speak with my master."

So he accompanied her to the husband who said to him, "I wish thee to cut out for me five long sleeved robes."

So he cut them out and took the stuff and went away. Then he sewed them and carried them to the gentleman, who praised his sewing and offered him a purse of silver. He put out his hand to take it, but the lady signed to him from behind her husband not to do so, and he replied, "O my lord, there is no hurry, we have time enough for this."

Then he went forth from the house meaner and meeker than a donkey, for verily five things were gathered together in him viz.: love, beggary, hunger, nakedness, and hard labour. Nevertheless he heartened himself with the hope of gaining the lady's favours. When he had made an end of all their jobs, they played him another trick and married him to their slave girl; but, on the night when he thought to go in to her, they said to him, "Lie this night in the mill; and to morrow all will go well."

My brother concluded that there was some good cause for this and nighted alone in the mill. Now the husband had set on the miller to make the tailor turn the mill: so when night was half spent the man came in to him and began to say, "This bull of ours hath become useless and standeth still instead of going round: he will not turn the mill this night, and yet we have great store of corn to be ground. However, I'll yoke him perforce and make him finish grinding it before morning, as the folk are impatient for their flour." So he filled the hoppers with grain and, going up to my brother with a rope in his hand, tied it round his neck and said to him, "Gee up! Round with the mill! thou, O bull, wouldst do nothing but grub and stale and dung!" Then he took a whip and laid it on the shoulders and calves of my brother, who began to howl and bellow; but none came to help him; and he was forced to grind the wheat till hard upon dawn, when the house master came in and, seeing my brother still tethered to the yoke and the man flogging him, went away.

At day break the miller returned home and left him still yoked and

half dead; and soon after in came the slave girl who unbound him, and said
to him, "I and my lady are right sorry for what hath happened and we have
borne thy grief with thee." But he had no tongue wherewith to answer her
from excess of beating and mill turning.

Then he retired to his lodging and behold, the clerk who had drawn
up the marriage deed came to him and saluted him, saying, "Allah give thee
long life! May thy espousal be blessed! This face telleth of pleasant doings
and dalliance and kissing and clipping from dusk to dawn."

"Allah grant the liar no peace, O thou thousandfold cuckold!" my
brother replied, "by Allah, I did nothing but turn the mill in the place of
the bull all night till morning!"

"Tell me thy tale," quoth he; and my brother recounted what had
befallen him and he said, "Thy star agrees not with her star; but an thou
wilt I can alter the contract for thee," adding, "'Ware lest another cheat be
not in store for thee."

And my brother answered him, "See if thou have not another
contrivance."

Then the clerk left him and he sat in his shop, looking for some one
to bring him a job whereby he might earn his day's bread. Presently the
handmaid came to him and said, "Speak with my lady."

"Begone, O my good girl," replied he, "there shall be no more dealings
between me and thy lady."

The handmaid returned to her mistress and told her what my brother
had said and presently she put her head out of the window, weeping and
saying, "Why, O my beloved, are there to be no more dealings 'twixt me
and thee?" But he made her no answer. Then she wept and conjured him,
swearing that all which had befallen him in the mill was not sanctioned
by her and that she was innocent of the whole matter. When he looked
upon her beauty and loveliness and heard the sweetness of her speech, the
sorrow which had possessed him passed from his heart; he accepted her
excuse and he rejoiced in her sight. So he saluted her and talked with her
and sat tailoring awhile, after which the handmaid came to him and said,
"My mistress greeteth thee and informeth thee that her husband purposeth
to lie abroad this night in the house of some intimate friends of his; so,
when he is gone, do thou come to us and spend the night with my lady in
delightsomest joyance till the morning."

Now her husband had asked her, "How shall we manage to turn him
away from thee?"; and she answered, "Leave me to play him another trick
and make him a laughing stock for all the town." But my brother knew

naught of the malice of women.

As soon as it was dusk, the slave girl came to him and carried him to the house, and when the lady saw him she said to him, "By Allah, O my lord, I have been longing exceedingly for thee."

"By Allah," cried he, "kiss me quick before thou give me aught else."

Hardly had he spoken, when the lady's husband came in from the next room and seized him, saying, "By Allah, I will not let thee go, till I deliver thee to the chief of the town watch."

My brother humbled himself to him; but he would not listen to him and carried him before the Prefect who gave him an hundred lashes with a whip and, mounting him on a camel, promenaded him round about the city, whilst the guards proclaimed aloud, "This is his reward who violateth the Harims of honourable men!" Moreover, he fell off the camel and broke his leg and so became lame. Then the Prefect banished him from the city; and he went forth unknowing whither he should wend; but I heard of him and fearing for him went out after him and brought him back secretly to the city and restored him to health and took him into my house where he still liveth.

The Caliph laughed at my story and said, "Thou hast done well, O Samit, O Silent Man, O spare of speech!"; and he bade me take a present and go away.

But I said, "I will accept naught of thee except I tell thee what befell all my other brothers; and do not think me a man of many words." So the Caliph gave ear to

THE BARBER'S TALE OF HIS SECOND BROTHER

Know, O Commander of the Faithful, that my second brother's name was Al-Haddar, that is the Babbler, and he was the paralytic. Now it happened to him one day, as he was going about his business, that an old woman accosted him and said, "Stop a little, my good man, that I may tell thee of somewhat which, if it be to thy liking, thou shalt do for me and I will pray Allah to give thee good of it!" My brother stopped and she went on, "I will put thee in the way of a certain thing, so thou not be prodigal of speech."

"On with thy talk," quoth he; and she, "What sayest thou to handsome quarters and a fair garden with flowing waters, flowers blooming, and fruit growing, and old wine going and a pretty young face whose owner thou mayest embrace from dark till dawn? If thou do whatso I bid thee thou shalt see something greatly to thy advantage."

"And is all this in the world?" asked my brother; and she answered, "Yes, and it shall be thine, so thou be reasonable and leave idle curiosity and many words, and do my bidding."

"I will indeed, O my lady," said he, "how is it thou hast preferred me in this matter before all men and what is it that so much pleaseth thee in me?"

Quoth she, "Did I not bid thee be spare of speech? Hold thy peace and follow me. Know, that the young lady, to whom I shall carry thee, loveth to have her own way and hateth being thwarted and all who gainsay; so, if thou humour her, thou shalt come to thy desire of her."

And my brother said, "I will not cross her in anything."

Then she went on and my brother followed her, an hungering after what she described to him till they entered a fine large house, handsome and choicely furnished, full of eunuchs and servants and showing signs of prosperity from top to bottom. And she was carrying him to the upper story when the people of the house said to him, "What dost thou here?"

But the old woman answered them, "Hold your peace and trouble him not: he is a workman and we have occasion for him."

Then she brought him into a fine great pavilion, with a garden in its midst, never eyes saw a fairer; and made him sit upon a handsome couch. He had not sat long, before he heard a loud noise and in came a troop of slave girls surrounding a lady like the moon on the night of its fullest. When he saw her, he rose up and made an obeisance to her, whereupon she welcomed him and bade him be seated.

So he sat down and she said to him, "Allah advance thee to honour! Is all well with thee?"

"O my lady," he answered, "all with me is right well." Then she bade bring in food, and they set before her delicate viands; so she sat down to eat, making a show of affection to my brother and jesting with him, though all the while she could not refrain from laughing; but as often as he looked at her, she signed towards her handmaidens as though she were laughing at them. My brother (the ass!) understood nothing; but, in the excess of his ridiculous passion, he fancied that the lady was in love with him and that she would soon grant him his desire. When they had done eating, they set on the wine and there came in ten maidens like moons, with lutes ready strung in their hands, and fell to singing with full voices, sweet and sad, whereupon delight gat hold upon him and he took the cup from the lady's hands and drank it standing.

Then she drank a cup of wine and my brother (still standing) said to her "Health," and bowed to her. She handed him another cup and he drank it off, when she slapped him hard on the nape of his neck. Upon this my brother would have gone out of the house in anger; but the old woman followed him and winked to him to return. So he came back and the lady bade him sit and he sat down without a word. Then she again slapped him on the nape of his neck; and the second slapping did not suffice her, she must needs make all her handmaidens also slap and cuff him, while he kept saying to the old woman, "I never saw aught nicer than this."

She on her side ceased not exclaiming, "Enough, enough, I conjure thee, O my mistress!"; but the women slapped him till he well nigh swooned away.

Presently my brother rose and went out to obey a call of nature, but the old woman overtook him, and said, "Be patient a little and thou shalt win to thy wish."

"How much longer have I to wait," my brother replied, "this slapping hath made me feel faint." "As soon as she is warm with wine," answered she, "thou shalt have thy desire."

So he returned to his place and sat down, where upon all the handmaidens stood up and the lady bade them perfume him with pastiles and besprinkle his face with rose-water. Then said she to him, "Allah advance thee to honour! Thou hast entered my house and hast borne with my conditions, for whoso thwarteth me I turn him away, and whoso is patient hath his desire."

"O mistress mine," said he, "I am thy slave and in the hollow of thine hand!"

"Know, then," continued she, "that Allah hath made me passionately fond of frolic; and whoso falleth in with my humour cometh by whatso he wisheth."

Then she ordered her maidens to sing with loud voices till the whole company was delighted; after which she said to one of them, "Take thy lord, and do what is needful for him and bring him back to me forthright."

So the damsel took my brother (and he not knowing what she would do with him); but the old woman overtook him and said, "Be patient; there remaineth but little to do."

At this his face brightened and he stood up before the lady while the old woman kept saying, "Be patient; thou wilt now at once win to thy wish!"; till he said, "Tell me what she would have the maiden do with me?"

"Nothing but good," replied she, "as I am thy sacrifice! She wisheth only to dye thy eyebrows and pluck out thy mustachios."

Quoth he, "As for the dyeing of my eyebrows, that will come off with washing, but for the plucking out of my mustachios, that indeed is a somewhat painful process."

"Be cautious how thou cross her," cried the old woman; "for she hath set her heart on thee." So my brother patiently suffered her to dye his eyebrows and pluck out his mustachios, after which the maiden returned to her mistress and told her.

Quoth she "Remaineth now only one other thing to be done; thou must shave his beard and make him a smooth o' face."

So the maiden went back and told him what her mistress had bidden her do; and my brother (the blockhead!) said to her, "How shall I do what will disgrace me before the folk?"

But the old woman said, "She would do on this wise only that thou mayst be as a beardless youth and that no hair be left on thy face to scratch and prick her delicate cheeks; for indeed she is passionately in love with thee. So be patient and thou shalt attain thine object."

My brother was patient and did her bidding and let shave off his beard and, when he was brought back to the lady, lo! he appeared dyed red as to his eyebrows, plucked of both mustachios, shorn of his beard, rouged on both cheeks. At first she was affrighted at him; then she made mockery of him and, laughing till she fell upon her back, said, "O my lord, thou hast indeed won my heart by thy good nature!" Then she conjured him, by her life, to stand up and dance, and he arose, and capered about, and there was not a cushion in the house but she threw it at his head, and in like manner did all her women who also kept pelting him with oranges and lemons and citrons till he fell down senseless from the cuffing on the nape of the neck, the pillowing and the fruit pelting.

"Now thou hast attained thy wish," said the old woman when he came round; "there are no more blows in store for thee and there remaineth but one little thing to do. It is her wont, when she is in her cups, to let no one have her until she put off her dress and trousers and remain stark naked. Then she will bid thee doff thy clothes and run; and she will run before thee as if she were flying from thee; and do thou follow her from place to place till thy prickle stands at fullest point, when she will yield to thee"; adding, "Strip off thy clothes at once."

So he rose, well nigh lost in ecstasy and, doffing his raiment, showed himself mother naked. Whereupon the lady stripped also and said to my brother, "If thou want anything run after me till thou catch me."

Then she set out at a run and he ran after her while she rushed into room after room and rushed out of room after room, my brother scampering after her in a rage of desire like a veritable madman, with yard standing terribly tall. After much of this kind she dashed into a darkened place, and he dashed after her; but suddenly he trod upon a yielding spot, which gave way under his weight; and, before he was aware where he was, he found himself in the midst of a crowded market, part of the bazaar of the leather sellers who were crying the prices of skins and hides and buying and selling. When they saw him in his plight, naked, with standing yard, shorn of beard and mustachios, with eyebrows dyed red, and cheeks ruddied with rouge, they shouted and clapped their hands at him, and set to flogging him with skins upon his bare body till a swoon came over him. Then they threw him on the back of an ass and carried him to the Chief of Police.

Quoth the Chief, "What is this?"

Quoth they, "This fellow fell suddenly upon us out of the Wazir's house in this state."

So the Prefect gave him an hundred lashes and then banished him from Baghdad. However, I went out after him and brought him back secretly into the city and made him a daily allowance for his living: although, were it not for my generous humour, I could not have put up with the like of him. Then the Caliph gave ear to

The Barber's Tale of His Third Brother

My third brother's name was Al-Fakik, the Gabbler, who was blind. One day Fate and Fortune drove him to a fine large house, and he knocked at the door, desiring speech of its owner that he might beg somewhat of him.

Quoth the master of the house, "Who is at the door?" But my brother spake not a word and presently he heard him repeat with a loud voice, "Who is this?" Still he made no answer and immediately heard the master walk to the door and open it and say, "What dost thou want?"

My brother answered "Something for Allah Almighty's sake."

"Art thou blind?" asked the man, and my brother answered "Yes."

Quoth the other, "Stretch me out thy hand." So my brother put out his hand thinking that he would give him something; but he took it and, drawing him into the house, carried him up from stair to stair till they reached the terrace on the house top, my brother thinking the while that he would surely give him something of food or money.

Then he asked my brother, "What dost thou want, O blind man?" and he answered, "Something for the Almighty's sake."

"Allah open for thee some other door!"

"O thou! why not say so when I was below stairs?"

"O cadger, why not answer me when I first called to thee?"

"And what meanest thou to do for me now?"

"There is nothing in the house to give thee."

"Then take me down the stair."

"The path is before thee."

So my brother rose and made his way downstairs, till he came within twenty steps of the door, when his foot slipped and he rolled to the bottom and broke his head. Then he went out, unknowing whither to turn, and presently fell in with two other blind men, companions of his, who said to him, "What didst thou gain to day?"

He told them what had befallen him and added, "O my brothers, I wish to take some of the money in my hands and provide myself with it."

Now the master of the house had followed him and was listening to what they said; but neither my brother nor his comrades knew of this. So my brother went to his lodging and sat down to await his companions, and the house owner entered after him without being perceived. When the other blind men arrived, my brother said to them, "Bolt the door and search the house lest any stranger have followed us."

The man, hearing this, caught hold of a cord that hung from the ceiling and clung to it, whilst they went round about the house and searched but found no one. So they came back, and, sitting beside my brother, brought out their money which they counted and lo! it was twelve thousand dirhams. Each took what he wanted and they buried the rest in a corner of the room. Then they set on food and sat down, to eat.

Presently my brother, hearing a strange pair of jaws munching by his side, said to his friends, "There is a stranger amongst us"; and, putting forth his hand, caught hold of that of the house master. Thereupon all fell on him and beat him; and when tired of belabouring him they shouted, "O ye Moslems! a thief is come in to us, seeking to take our money!"

A crowd gathered around them, whereupon the intruder hung on to them; and complained with them as they complained, and, shutting his eyes like them, so that none might doubt his blindness, cried out, "O Moslems, I take refuge with Allah and the Governor, for I have a matter to make known to him!"

Suddenly up came the watch and, laying hands on the whole lot (my brother being amongst them), drove them to the Governor's who set them

before him and asked, "What news with you?"

Quoth the intruder, "Look and find out for thyself, not a word shall be wrung from us save by torture, so begin by beating me and after me beat this man our leader." And he pointed to my brother.

So they threw the man at full length and gave him four hundred sticks on his backside. The beating pained him, whereupon he opened one eye and, as they redoubled their blows, he opened the other eye.

When the Governor saw this he said to him, "What have we here, O accursed?"; whereto he replied, "Give me the seal-ring of pardon! We four have shammed blind, and we impose upon people that we may enter houses and look upon the unveiled faces of the women and contrive for their corruption. In this way we have gotten great gain and our store amounts to twelve thousand dirhams. Said I to my company, 'Give me my share, three thousand'; but they rose and beat me and took away my money, and I seek refuge with Allah and with thee; better thou have my share than they. So, if thou wouldst know the truth of my words, beat one and every of the others more than thou hast beaten me, and he will surely open his eyes."

The Governor gave orders for the question to begin with my brother, and they bound him to the whipping post, and the Governor said, "O scum of the earth, do ye abuse the gracious gifts of Allah and make as if ye were blind!"

"Allah! Allah!" cried my brother, "by Allah, there is none among us who can see."

Then they beat him till he swooned away and the Governor cried, "Leave him till he come to and then beat him again."

After this he caused each of the companions to receive more than three hundred sticks, whilst the sham Abraham kept saying to them "Open your eyes or you will be beaten afresh."

At last the man said to the Governor, "Dispatch someone with me to bring thee the money; for these fellows will not open their eyes, lest they incur disgrace before the folk."

So the Governor sent to fetch the money and gave the man his pretended share, three thousand dirhams; and, keeping the rest for himself, banished the three blind men from the city. But I, O Commander of the Faithful, went out and overtaking my brother questioned him of his case; whereupon he told me of what I have told thee; so I brought him secretly into the city, and appointed him (in the strictest privacy) an allowance for meat and drink!

The Caliph laughed at my story and said, "Give him a gift and let him go;" but I said, "By Allah! I will take naught till I have made known to the Commander of the Faithful what came to pass with the rest of my brothers; for truly I am a man of few words and spare of speech."

Then the Caliph gave ear to

THE BARBER'S TALE OF HIS FOURTH BROTHER

Now as for my fourth brother, O Commander of the Faithful, Al-Kuz al-aswani, or the long necked Gugglet hight, from his brimming over with words, the same who was blind of one eye, he became a butcher in Baghdad and he sold flesh and fattened rams; and great men and rich bought their meat of him, so that he amassed much wealth and got him cattle and houses. He fared thus a long while, till one day, as he was sitting in his shop, there came up an old man and long o' the beard, who laid down some silver and said, "Give me meat for this." He gave him his money's worth of flesh and the oldster went his ways.

My brother examined the Shaykh's silver, and, seeing that the dirhams were white and bright, he set them in a place apart. The greybeard continued to return to the shop regularly for five months, and my brother ceased not to lay up all the coin he received from him in its own box. At last he thought to take out the money to buy sheep; so he opened the box and found in it nothing, save bits of white paper cut round to look like coin; so he buffeted his face and cried aloud till the folk gathered about him, whereupon he told them his tale which made them marvel exceedingly. Then he rose as was his wont, and slaughtering a ram hung it up inside his shop; after which he cut off some of the flesh, and hanging it outside kept saying to himself, "O Allah, would the ill omened old fellow but come!"

And an hour had not passed before the Shaykh came with his silver in hand; where upon my brother rose and caught hold of him calling out, "Come aid me, O Moslems, and learn my story with this villain!"

When the old man heard this, he quietly said to him, "Which will be the better for thee, to let go of me or to be disgraced by me amidst the folk?"

"In what wilt thou disgrace me?"

"In that thou sellest man's flesh for mutton!"

"Thou liest, thou accursed!"

"Nay, he is the accursed who hath a man hanging up by way of meat in his shop. If the matter be as thou sayest, I give thee lawful leave to take my money and my life."

Then the old man cried out aloud, "Ho, ye people! if you would prove the truth of my words, enter this man's shop."

The folk rushed in and found that the ram was become a dead man hung up for sale. So they set upon my brother crying out, "O Infidel! O villain!"; and his best friends fell to cuffing and kicking him and kept saying, "Dost thou make us eat flesh of the sons of Adam?" Furthermore, the old man struck him on the eye and put it out.

Then they carried the carcass, with the throat cut, before the Chief of the city watch, to whom the old man said, "O Emir, this fellow butchers men and sells their flesh for mutton and we have brought him to thee; so arise and execute the judgments of Allah (to whom be honour and glory!)."

My brother would have defended himself, but the Chief refused to hear him and sentenced him to receive five hundred sticks and to forfeit the whole of his property. And, indeed, had it not been for that same property which he expended in bribes, they would have surely slain him. Then the Chief banished him from Baghdad; and my brother fared forth at a venture, till he came to a great town, where he thought it best to set up as a cobbler; so he opened a shop and sat there doing what he could for his livelihood.

One day, as he went forth on his business, he heard the distant tramp of horses and, asking the cause, was told that the King was going out to hunt and course; so my brother stopped to look at the fine suite. It so fortuned that the King's eye met my brother's; whereupon the King hung down his head and said, "I seek refuge with Allah from the evil of this day!"; and turned the reins of his steed and returned home with all his retinue. Then he gave orders to his guards, who seized my brother and beat him with a beating so painful that he was well nigh dead; and my brother knew not what could be the cause of his maltreatment, after which he returned to his place in sorriest plight.

Soon afterwards he went to one of the King's household and related what had happened to him; and the man laughed till he fell upon his back and cried, "O brother mine, know that the King cannot bear to look at a monocular, especially if he be blind of the right eye, in which case he doth not let him go without killing him."

When my brother heard this, he resolved to fly from that city; so he went forth from it to another wherein none knew him and there he abode a long while. One day, being full of sorrowful thought for what had befallen him, he sallied out to solace himself; and, as he was walking along, he heard the distant tramp of horses behind him and said, "The judgement of Allah is upon me!" and looked about for a hiding place but found none.

At last he saw a closed door which he pushed hard: it yielded. and he entered a long gallery in which he took refuge, but hardly had he done so, when two men set upon him crying out, "Allah be thanked for having delivered thee into our hands, O enemy of God! These three nights thou hast robbed us of our rest and sleep, and verily thou hast made us taste of the death cup."

My brother asked, "O folk, what ails you?"; and they answered, "Thou givest us the change and goest about to disgrace us and plannest some plot to cut the throat of the house master! Is it not enough that thou hast brought him to beggary, thou and thy fellows? But now give us up the knife wherewith thou threatenest us every night."

Then they searched him and found in his waist belt the knife used for his shoe leather; and he said, "O people, have the fear of Allah before your eyes and maltreat me not, for know that my story is a right strange!"

"And what is thy story?" said they: so he told them what had befallen him, hoping they would let him go; however they paid no heed to what he said and, instead of showing some regard, beat him grievously and tore off his clothes: then, finding on his sides the scars of beating with rods, they said, "O accursed! these marks are the manifest signs of thy guilt!"

They carried him before the Governor, whilst he said to himself, "I am now punished for my sins and none can deliver me save Allah Almighty!"

The Governor addressing my brother asked him, "O villain, what led thee to enter their house with intention to murther?"; and my brother answered, "I conjure thee by Allah, O Emir, hear my words and be not hasty in condemning me!"

But the Governor cried, "Shall we listen to the words of a robber who hath beggared these people, and who beareth on his back the scar of his stripes?" adding, "They surely had not done this to thee, save for some great crime." So he sentenced him to receive an hundred cuts with the scourge, after which they set him on a camel and paraded him about the city, proclaiming, "This is the requital and only too little to requite him who breaketh into people's houses."

Then they thrust him out of the city, and my brother wandered at random, till I heard what had befallen him; and, going in search of him, questioned him of his case; so he acquainted me with his story and all his mischances, and I carried him secretly to the city where I made him an allowance for his meat and drink.

Then the Caliph gave ear to

THE BARBER'S TALE OF HIS FIFTH BROTHER

My fifth brother, Al-Nashshar, the Babbler, the same who was cropped of both ears, O Commander of the Faithful, was an asker wont to beg of folk by night and live on their alms by day. Now when our father, who was an old man well stricken in years sickened and died, he left us seven hundred dirhams whereof each son took his hundred; but, as my fifth brother received his portion, he was perplexed and knew not what to do with it. While in this uncertainty he bethought him to lay it out on glass ware of all sorts and turn an honest penny on its price. So he bought an hundred dirhams worth of verroterie and, putting it into a big tray, sat down to sell it on a bench at the foot of a wall against which he leant back. As he sat with the tray before him he fell to musing and said to himself, "Know, O my good Self, that the head of my wealth, my principal invested in this glass ware, is an hundred dirhams. I will assuredly sell it for two hundred with which I will forthright buy other glass and make by it four hundred; nor will I cease to sell and buy on this wise, till I have gotten four thousand and soon find myself the master of much money. With these coins I will buy merchandise and jewels and ottars and gain great profit on them; till, Allah willing, I will make my capital an hundred thousand dirhams. Then I will purchase a fine house with white slaves and eunuchs and horses; and I will eat and drink and disport myself; nor will I leave a singing man or a singing woman in the city, but I will summon them to my palace and make them perform before me."

All this he counted over in his mind, while the tray of glass ware, worth an hundred dirhams, stood on the bench before him, and, after looking at it, he continued, "And when, Inshallah! my capital shall have become one hundred thousand dinars, I will send out marriage brokeresses to require for me in wedlock the daughters of Kings and Wazirs; and I will demand to wife the eldest daughter of the Prime Minister; for it hath reached me that she is perfect in beauty and prime in loveliness and rare in accomplishments. I will give a marriage settlement of one thousand dinars; and, if her father consent, well: but if not I will take her by force from under his very nose. When she is safely homed in my house, I will buy ten little eunuchs and for myself a robe of the robes of Kings and Sultans; and get me a saddle of gold and a bridle set thick with gems of price. Then I will mount with the Mamelukes preceding me and surrounding me, and I will make the round of the city whilst the folk salute me and bless me; after which I will repair to the Wazir (he that is father of the girl) with armed white slaves

before and behind me and on my right and on my left. When he sees me, the Wazir stands up, and seating me in his own place sits down much below me; for that I am to be his son in law.

"Now I have with me two eunuchs carrying purses, each containing a thousand dinars; and of these I deliver to him the thousand, his daughter's marriage settlement, and make him a free gift of the other thousand, that he may have reason to know my generosity and liberality and my greatness of spirit and the littleness of the world in my eyes. And for ten words he addresses to me I answer him two. Then back I go to my house, and if one come to me on the bride's part, I make him a present of money and throw on him a dress of honour; but if he bring me a gift, I give it back to him and refuse to accept it, that they may learn what a proud spirit is mine which never condescends to derogate. Thus I establish my rank and status. When this is done I appoint her wedding night and adorn my house showily! gloriously! And as the time for parading the bride is come, I don my finest attire and sit down on a mattress of gold brocade, propping up my elbow with a pillow, and turning neither to the right nor to the left; but looking only straight in front for the haughtiness of my mind and the gravity of my understanding. And there before me stands my wife in her raiment and ornaments, lovely as the full moon; and I, in my loftiness and dread lordliness, will not glance at her till those present say to me, 'O our lord and our master, thy wife, thy handmaid, standeth before thee; vouchsafe her one look, for standing wearieth her.' Then they kiss the ground before me many times; whereupon I raise my eyes and cast at her one single glance and turn my face earthwards again. Then they bear her off to the bride chamber, and I arise and change my clothes for a far finer suit; and, when they bring in the bride a second time, I deign not to throw her a look till they have begged me many times; after which I glance at her out of the corner of one eye, and then bend down my head. I continue acting after this fashion till the parading and displaying are completed.

"Then I bend down my head and continue acting after this fashion till her parading and displaying are completed. Thereupon I order one of my eunuchs to bring me a bag of five hundred dinars which I give as largesse to the tire women present and bid them one and all lead me to the bride chamber. When they leave me alone with her I neither look at her nor speak to her, but lie by her side with my face to the wall showing my contempt, that each and every may again remark how high and haughty I am. Presently her mother comes in to me, and kissing my head and hand, says to me, 'O my lord, look upon thine handmaid who longs for thy favour; so heal her broken spirit!'

"I give her no answer; and when she sees this she rises and busses my feet many times and says, 'O my lord, in very sooth my daughter is a beautiful maid, who hath never known man; and if thou show her this backwardness and aversion, her heart will break; so do thou incline to her and speak to her and soothe her mind and spirit.' Then she rises and fetches a cup of wine; and says to her daughter, 'Take it and hand it to thy lord.' But as she approaches me I leave her standing between my hands and sit, propping my elbow on a round cushion purfled with gold thread, leaning lazily back, and without looking at her in the majesty of my spirit, so that she may deem me indeed a Sultan and a mighty man.

"Then she says to me, 'O my lord, Allah upon thee, do not refuse to take the cup from the hand of thine handmaid, for verily I am thy bondswoman.' But I do not speak to her and she presses me, saying, 'There is no help but that thou drink it'; and she puts it to my lips. Then I shake my fist in her face and kick her with my foot thus."

So he let out with his toe an knocked over the tray of glass ware which fell to the ground and, falling from the bench, all that was on it was broken to bits. "O foulest of pimps, this comes from the pride of my spirit" cried my brother; and then, O Commander of the Faithful, he buffeted his face and rent his garments and kept on weeping and beating himself.

The folk who were flocking to their Friday prayers saw him; and some of them looked at him and pitied him, whilst others paid no heed to him, and in this way my brother lost both capital and profit. He remained weeping a long while, and at last up came a beautiful lady, the scent of musk exhaling from her, who was going to Friday prayers riding a mule with a gold saddle and followed by several eunuchs. When she saw the broken glass and my brother weeping, her kind heart was moved to pity for him, and she asked what ailed him and was told that he had a tray full of glass ware by the sale of which he hoped to gain his living, but it was broken, and (said they), "There befell him what thou seest."

Thereupon she called up one of her eunuchs and said to him, "Give what thou hast with thee to this poor fellow!" And he gave my brother a purse in which he found five hundred dinars; and when it touched his hand he was well nigh dying for excess of joy and he offered up blessings for her. Then he returned to his abode a substantial man; and, as he sat considering, someone rapped at the door. So he rose and opened and saw an old woman whom he had never seen.

"O my son," said she, "know that prayer tide is near and I have not yet made my Wuzu-ablution; so kindly allow me the use of thy lodging for the purpose."

My brother answered, "To hear is to comply"; and going in bade her follow him. So she entered and he brought her an ewer wherewith to wash, and sat down like to fly with joy because of the dinars which he had tied up in his belt for a purse.

When the old woman had made an end of her ablution, she came up to where he sat, and prayed a two bow prayer; after which she blessed my brother with a godly benediction, and he while thanking her put his hand to the dinars and gave her two, saying to himself "These are my voluntaries."

When she saw the gold she cried, "Praise be to Allah! why dost thou look on one who loveth thee as if she were a beggar? Take back thy money: I have no need of it; or, if thou want it not, return it to her who gave it thee when thy glass ware was broken. Moreover, if thou wish to be united with her, I can manage the matter, for she is my mistress."

"O my mother," asked my brother, "by what manner of means can I get at her?"; and she answered, "O my son! she hath an inclination for thee, but she is the wife of a wealthy man; so take the whole of thy money with thee and follow me, that I may guide thee to thy desire: and when thou art in her company spare neither persuasion nor fair words , but bring them all to bear upon her; so shalt thou enjoy her beauty and wealth to thy heart's content."

My brother took all his gold and rose and followed the old woman, hardly believing in his luck. She ceased not faring on, and my brother following her, till they came to a tall gate at which she knocked and a Roumi slave-girl came out and opened to them. Then the old woman led my brother into a great sitting room spread with wondrous fine carpets and hung with curtains, where he sat down with his gold before him, and his turband on his knee. He had scarcely taken seat before there came to him a young lady (never eye saw fairer) clad in garments of the most sumptuous; whereupon my brother rose to his feet, and she smiled in his face and welcomed him, signing to him to be seated. Then she bade shut the door and, when it was shut, she turned to my brother, and taking his hand conducted him to a private chamber furnished with various kinds of brocades and gold cloths. Here he sat down and she sat by his side and toyed with him awhile; after which she rose and saying, "Stir not from thy seat till I come back to thee," disappeared.

Meanwhile as he was on this wise, lo! there came in to him a black slave big of body and bulk and holding a drawn sword in hand, who said to him, "Woe to thee! Who brought thee hither and what dost thou want here?"

My brother could not return him a reply, being tongue tied for terror; so the blackamoor seized him and stripped him of his clothes and bashed him with the flat of his sword blade till he fell to the ground, swooning from excess of belabouring. The ill-omened negro fancied that there was an end of him and my brother heard him cry, "Where is the salt wench?" Whereupon in came a handmaid holding in hand a large tray of salt, and the slave kept rubbing it into my brother's wounds; but he did not stir fearing lest the slave might find out that he was not dead and kill him outright.

Then the salt girl went away, and the slave cried "Where is the souterrain guardianess?" Whereupon in came the old woman and dragged my brother by his feet to a souterrain and threw him down upon a heap of dead bodies. In this place he lay two full days, but Allah made the salt the means of preserving his life by staunching the blood and staying its flow.

Presently, feeling himself able to move, Al-Nashshar rose and opened the trap door in fear and trembling and crept out into the open; and Allah protected him, so that he went on in the darkness and hid himself in the vestibule till dawn, when he saw the accursed beldam sally forth in quest of other quarry. He followed in her wake without her knowing it, and made for his own lodging where he dressed his wounds and medicined himself till he was whole.

Meanwhile he used to watch the old woman, tracking her at all times and seasons, and saw her accost one man after another and carry them to the house. However he uttered not a word; but, as soon as he waxed hale and hearty, he took a piece of stuff and made it into a bag which he filled with broken glass and bound about his middle. He also disguised himself as a Persian that none might know him, and hid a sword under his clothes of foreign cut. Then he went out and presently, falling in with the old woman, said to her, speaking Arabic with a Persian accent, "Venerable lady, I am a stranger arrived but this day here where I know no one. Hast thou a pair of scales wherein I may weigh eleven hundred dinars? I will give thee somewhat of them for thy pains."

"I have a son, a money changer, who keepeth all kinds of scales," she answered, "so come with me to him before he goeth out and he will weigh thy gold."

My brother answered "Lead the way!" She led him to the house and the young lady herself came out and opened it, whereupon the old woman smiled in her face and said, "I bring thee fat meat to-day."

Then the damsel took my brother by the hand, and led him to the same chamber as before; where she sat with him awhile then rose and went forth saying, "Stir not from thy seat till I come back to thee."

Presently in came the accursed slave with the drawn sword and cried to my brother, "Up and be damned to thee."

So he rose, and as the slave walked on before him he drew the sword from under his clothes and smote him with it, making head fly from body. Then he dragged the corpse by the feet to the souterrain and called out, "Where is the salt wench?"

Up came the girl carrying the tray of salt and, seeing my brother sword in hand, turned to fly; but he followed her and struck off her head. Then he called out, "Where is the souterrain guardianess?" and in came the old woman to whom he said, "Dost know me again, ill omened hag?"

"No my lord," she replied, and he said, "I am the owner of the five hundred gold pieces, whose house thou enteredst to make the ablution and to pray, and whom thou didst snare hither and betray."

"Fear Allah and spare me," cried she; but he regarded her not and struck her with the sword till he had cut her in four. Then he went to look for the young lady; and when she saw him her reason fled and she cried out piteously "Aman! Mercy!"

So he spared her and asked, "What made thee consort with this blackamoor?" and she answered, "I was slave to a certain merchant, and the old woman used to visit me till I took a liking to her. One day she said to me, 'We have a marriage festival at our house the like of which was never seen and I wish thee to enjoy the sight.'

"'To hear is to obey,' answered I, and rising arrayed myself in my finest raiment and ornaments, and took with me a purse containing an hundred gold pieces. Then she brought me hither and hardly had I entered the house when the black seized on me, and I have remained in this case three whole years through the perfidy of the accursed beldam."

Then my brother asked her, "Is there anything of his in the house?" whereto she answered, "Great store of wealth, and if thou art able to carry it away, do so and Allah give thee good of it."

My brother went with her and she opened to him sundry chests wherein were money bags, at which he was astounded; then she said to him, "Go now and leave me here, and fetch men to remove the money."

He went out and hired ten men, but when he returned he found the door wide open, the damsel gone and nothing left but some small matter of coin and the household stuffs. By this he knew that the girl had overreached him; so he opened the store rooms and seized what was in them, together with the rest of the money, leaving nothing in the house. He passed the night rejoicing, but when morning dawned he found at the door some twenty troopers who laid hands on him saying, "The Governor wants thee!"

My brother implored them hard to let him return to his house; and even offered them a large sum of money; but they refused and, binding him fast with cords, carried him off. On the way they met a friend of my brother who clung to his skirt and implored his protection, begging him to stand by him and help to deliver him out of their hands. The man stopped, and asked them what was the matter, and they answered, "The Governor hath ordered us to bring this fellow before him and, look ye, we are doing so."

My brother's friend urged them to release him, and offered them five hundred dinars to let him go, saying, "When ye return to the Governor tell him that you were unable to find him."

But they would not listen to his words and took my brother, dragging him along on his face, and set him before the Governor who asked him, "Whence gottest thou these stuffs and monies?" and he answered, "I pray for mercy!" So the Governor gave him the kerchief of mercy; and he told him all that had befallen him from first to last with the old woman and the flight of the damsel; ending with, "Whatso I have taken, take of it what thou wilt, so thou leave me sufficient to support life."

But the Governor took the whole of the stuffs and all the money for himself; and, fearing lest the affair come to the Sultan's ears, he summoned my brother and said, "Depart from this city, else I will hang thee."

"Hearing and obedience" quoth my brother and set out for another town. On the way thieves fell foul of him and stripped and beat him and docked his ears; but I heard tidings of his misfortunes and went out after him taking him clothes; and brought him secretly into the city where I assigned to him an allowance for meat and drink.

And presently the Caliph gave ear to

THE BARBER'S TALE OF HIS SIXTH BROTHER

My sixth brother, O Commander of the Faithful, Shakashik, or Many Clamours, the shorn of both lips, was once rich and became poor, so one day he went out to beg somewhat to keep life in him. As he was on the road he suddenly caught sight of a large and handsome mansion, with a detached building wide and lofty at the entrance, where sat sundry eunuchs bidding and forbidding. My brother enquired of one of those idling there and he replied "The palace belongs to a scion of the Barmaki house"; so he stepped up to the door keepers and asked an alms of them. "Enter," said they, "by the great gate and thou shalt get what thou seekest from the Wazir our master."

Accordingly he went in and, passing through the outer entrance, walked on a while and presently came to a mansion of the utmost beauty and elegance, paved with marble, hung with curtains and having in the midst of it a flower garden whose like he had never seen. My brother stood awhile as one bewildered not knowing whither to turn his steps; then, seeing the farther end of the sitting chamber tenanted, he walked up to it and there found a man of handsome presence and comely beard. When this personage saw my brother he stood up to him and welcomed him and asked him of his case; whereto he replied that he was in want and needed charity. Hearing these words the grandee showed great concern and, putting his hand to his fine robe, rent it exclaiming, "What! am I in a City, and thou here an hungered? I have not patience to bear such disgrace!"

Then he promised him all manner of good cheer and said, "There is no help but that thou stay with me and eat of my salt."

"O my lord," answered my brother, "I can wait no longer; for I am indeed dying of hunger."

So he cried, "Ho boy! bring basin and ewer"; and, turning to my brother, said, "O my guest come forward and wash thy hands."

My brother rose to do so but he saw neither ewer nor basin; yet his host kept washing his hands with invisible soap in imperceptible water and cried, "Bring the table!" But my brother again saw nothing.

Then said the host, "Honour me by eating of this meat and be not ashamed." And he kept moving his hand to and fro as if he ate and saying to my brother, "I wonder to see thee eating thus sparely: do not stint thyself for I am sure thou art famished."

So my brother began to make as though he were eating whilst his host kept saying to him, "Fall to, and note especially the excellence of this bread and its whiteness!" But still my brother saw nothing.

Then said he to himself, "This man is fond of poking fun at people"; and replied, "O my lord, in all my days I never knew aught more winsome than its whiteness or sweeter than its savour."

The Barmecide said, "This bread was baked by a hand maid of mine whom I bought for five hundred dinars." Then he called out, "Ho boy,

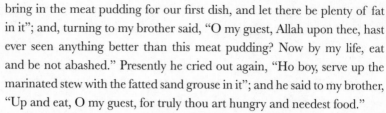

92

bring in the meat pudding for our first dish, and let there be plenty of fat in it"; and, turning to my brother said, "O my guest, Allah upon thee, hast ever seen anything better than this meat pudding? Now by my life, eat and be not abashed." Presently he cried out again, "Ho boy, serve up the marinated stew with the fatted sand grouse in it"; and he said to my brother, "Up and eat, O my guest, for truly thou art hungry and needest food."

So my brother began wagging his jaws and made as if champing and chewing, whilst the host continued calling for one dish after another and yet produced nothing save orders to eat. Presently he cried out, "Ho boy, bring us the chickens stuffed with pistachio nuts"; and said to my brother, "By thy life, O my guest, I have fattened these chickens upon pistachios; eat, for thou hast never eaten their like."

"O my lord," replied my brother, "they are indeed first rate." Then the host began motioning with his hand as though he were giving my brother a mouthful; and ceased not to enumerate and expatiate upon the various dishes to the hungry man whose hunger waxt still more violent, so that his soul lusted after a bit of bread, even a barley scone.

Quoth the Barmecide, "Didst thou ever taste anything more delicious than the seasoning of these dishes?"; and quoth my brother, "Never, O my lord!"

"Eat heartily and be not ashamed," said the host, and the guest, "I have eaten my fill of meat."

So the entertainer cried, "Take away and bring in the sweets;" and turning to my brother said, "Eat of this almond conserve for it is prime and of these honey fritters; take this one, by my life, the syrup runs out of it."

"May I never be bereaved of thee, O my lord," replied the hungry one and began to ask him about the abundance of musk in the fritters.

"Such is my custom," he answered, "they put me a dinar weight of musk in every honey fritter and half that quantity of ambergris."

All this time my brother kept wagging head and jaws till the master cried, "Enough of this. Bring us the dessert!" Then said he to him, "Eat of these almonds and walnuts and raisins; and of this and that (naming diverse kinds of dried fruits), and be not abashed."

But my brother replied, "O my lord, indeed I am full: I can eat no more."

"O my guest," repeated the host, "if thou have a mind to these good things eat: Allah! Allah! do not remain hungry"; but my brother rejoined, "O my lord, he who hath eaten of all these dishes how can he be hungry?"

Then he considered and said to himself, "I will do that shall make him repent of these pranks."

Presently the entertainer called out "Bring me the wine"; and, moving his hands in the air, as though they had set it before them, he gave my brother a cup and said, "Take this cup and, if it please thee, let me know."

"O my lord," he replied, "it is notable good as to nose but I am wont to drink wine some twenty years old."

"Knock then at this door," quoth the host "for thou canst not drink of aught better."

"By thy kindness," said my brother, motioning with his hand as though he were drinking.

"Health and joy to thee," exclaimed the house master and feigned to fill a cup and drink it off; then he handed another to my brother who quaffed it and made as if he were drunken.

Presently he took the host unawares; and, raising his arm till the white of his armpit appeared, dealt him such a cuff on the nape of his neck that the palace echoed to it. Then he came down upon him with a second cuff and the entertainer cried aloud "What is this, O thou scum of the earth?"

"O my lord," replied my brother, "thou hast shown much kindness to thy slave, and admitted him into thine abode and given him to eat of thy victual; then thou madest him drink of thine old wine till he became drunken and boisterous; but thou art too noble not to bear with his ignorance and pardon his offence."

When the Barmaki heard my brother's words he laughed his loudest and said, "Long have I been wont to make mock of men and play the madcap among my intimates, but never yet have I come across a single one who had the patience and the wit to enter into all my humours save thyself: so I forgive thee, and thou shalt be my boon companion in very sooth and never leave me." Then he ordered the servants to lay the table in earnest and they set on all the dishes of which he had spoken in sport; and he and my brother ate till they were satisfied; after which they removed to the drinking chamber, where they found damsels like moons who sang all manner songs and played on all manner instruments. There they remained drinking till their wine got the better of them and the host treated my brother like a familiar friend, so that he became as it were his brother, and bestowed on him a robe of honour and loved him with exceeding love.

Next morning the two fell again to feasting and carousing, and ceased not to lead this life for a term of twenty years; at the end of which the Barmecide died and the Sultan took possession of all his wealth and squeezed my brother of his savings, till he was left a pauper without a penny

to handle. So he quitted the city and fled forth following his face; but, when he was half way between two towns, the wild Arabs fell on him and bound him and carried him to their camp, where his captor proceeded to torture him, saying, "Buy thy life of me with thy money, else I will slay thee!"

My brother began to weep and replied, "By Allah, I have nothing, neither gold nor silver; but I am thy prisoner; so do with me what thou wilt."

Then the Badawi drew a knife, broad bladed and so sharp grinded that if plunged into a camel's throat it would sever it clean across from one jugular to the other, and cut off my brother's lips and waxed more instant in requiring money.

Now this Badawi had a fair wife who in her husband's absence used to make advances to my brother and offer him her favours, but he held off from her. One day she began to tempt him as usual and he played with her and made her sit on his lap, when behold, in came the Badawi who, seeing this, cried out, "Woe to thee, O accursed villain, wouldest thou debauch my wife for me?"

Then he took out a knife and cut off my brother's yard, after which he bound him on the back of a camel and, carrying him to a mountain, left him there. He was at last found by some who recognised him and gave him meat and drink and acquainted me with his condition; whereupon I went forth to him and brought him back to Baghdad where I made him an allowance sufficient to live on.

This, then, O Commander of the Faithful, is the history of my six brothers, and I feared to go away without relating it all to thee and leave thee in the error of judging me to be like them. And now thou knowest that I have six brothers upon my hands and, being more upright than they, I support the whole family.

When the Caliph heard my story and all I told him concerning my brothers, he laughed and said, "Thou sayest sooth, O Silent Man! thou art indeed spare of speech nor is there aught of forwardness in thee; but now go forth out of this city and settle in some other." And he banished me under edict.

I left Baghdad and travelled in foreign parts till I heard of his death and the accession of another to the Caliphate. Then I returned to Baghdad where I found all my brothers dead and chanced upon this young man, to whom I rendered the kindliest service, for without me he had surely been killed. Indeed he slanders me and accuses me of a fault which is not in my nature; and what he reports concerning impudence and meddling and forwardness is idle and false; for verily on his account I left Baghdad and travelled about full many a country till I came to this city and met him here in your company. And was not this, O worthy assemblage, of the generosity of my nature?

And Scheherazade perceived the dawn of day and ceased saying her permitted say. Then quoth Dunyazad, "O my sister, how pleasant is thy tale, and how tasteful; how sweet, and how grateful!" And Scheherazade replied, "And where is this compared with 'The Tale of the Enchanted Horse' that I could tell thee this coming night, if I live and the King spare me?"

Said the King in himself, "By Allah, I will not slay her until I hear her story, for her tale telling truly is wondrous."

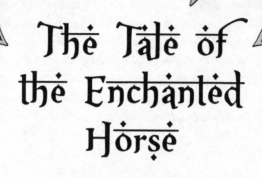

The Tale of the Enchanted Horse

The next night Scheherazade continued:
"It hath reached me, O auspicious King, that…

There was once in times of yore and ages long gone before, a great and puissant King, of the Kings of the Persians, Sabur by name, who was the richest of all the Kings in store of wealth and dominion and surpassed each and every in wit and wisdom. He was generous, open handed and beneficent, and he gave to those who sought him and repelled not those who resorted to him; and he comforted the broken-hearted and honourably entreated those who fled to him for refuge. Moreover, he loved the poor and was hospitable to strangers and did the oppressed justice upon the oppressor. He had three daughters, like full moons of shining light or flower-gardens blooming bright; and a son as he were the moon; and it was his wont to keep two festivals in the twelvemonth, those of the Nau-Roz, or New Year, and Mihrgan the Autumnal Equinox, on which occasions he threw open his palaces and gave largesse and made proclamation of safety and security and promoted his chamberlains and viceroys; and the people of his realm came in to him and saluted him and gave him joy of the holy day, bringing him gifts and servants and eunuchs.

Now he loved science and geometry, and one festival-day as he sat on his kingly throne there came in to him three wise men, cunning artificers and past masters in all manner of craft and inventions, skilled in making things curious and rare, such as confound the wit; and versed in the knowledge of occult truths and perfect in mysteries and subtleties. And they were of three different tongues and countries, the first a Hindi or Indian, the second a Roumi or Greek and the third a Farsi or Persian.

The Indian came forwards and, prostrating himself before the King, wished him joy of the festival and laid before him a present befitting his dignity; that is to say, a man of gold, set with precious gems and jewels of price and hending in hand a golden trumpet. When Sabur saw this, he asked, "O sage, what is the virtue of this figure?" and the Indian answered, "O my lord, if this figure be set at the gate of thy city, it will be a guardian over it; for, if an enemy enter the place, it will blow this clarion against him and he will be seized with a palsy and drop down dead." Much the King marvelled at this and cried, "By Allah, O sage, and this thy word be true, I will grant thee thy wish and thy desire."

Then came forward the Greek and, prostrating himself before the King, presented him with a basin of silver, in whose midst was a peacock of gold, surrounded by four-and-twenty chicks of the same metal. Sabur looked at them and turning to the Greek, said to him, "O sage, what is the virtue of this peacock?" "O my lord," answered he, "as often as an hour of the day or night passeth, it pecketh one of its young and crieth out and flappeth its wings, till the four-and-twenty hours are accomplished; and when the month cometh to an end, it will open its mouth and thou shalt see the crescent therein." And the King said, "An thou speak sooth, I will bring thee to thy wish and thy desire."

Then came forward the Persian sage and, prostrating himself before the King, presented him with a horse of the blackest ebony-wood inlaid with gold and jewels, and ready harnessed with saddle, bridle and stirrups such as befit Kings; which when Sabur saw, he marvelled with exceeding marvel and was confounded at the beauty of its form and the ingenuity of its fashion. So he asked, "What is the use of this horse of wood, and what is its virtue and what the secret of its movement?" and the Persian answered, "O my lord, the virtue of this horse is that, if one mount him, it will carry him whither he will and fare with its rider through the air and cover the space of a year in a single day." The King marvelled and was amazed at these three wonders, following thus hard upon one another on the same day, and turning to the sage, said to him, "By Allah the Omnipotent, and

our Lord the Beneficent, who created all creatures and feedeth them with meat and drink, an thy speech be veritable and the virtue of thy contrivance appear, I will assuredly give thee whatsoever thou lustest for and will bring thee to thy desire and thy wish!"

Then he entertained the sages three days, that he might make trial of their gifts; after which they brought the figures before him and each took the creature he had wroughten and showed him the mystery of its movement. The trumpeter blew the trump; the peacock pecked its chicks and the Persian sage mounted the ebony house, whereupon it soared with him high in air and descended again. When King Sabur saw all this, he was amazed and perplexed and felt like to fly for joy and said to the three sages, "Now I am certified of the truth of your words and it behoveth me to quit me of my promise. Ask ye, therefore, what ye will, and I will give you that same." Now the report of the King's daughters had reached the sages, so they answered, "If the King be content with us and accept of our gifts and allow us to prefer a request to him, we crave of him that he give us his three daughters in marriage, that we may be his sons-in-law; for that the stability of Kings may not be gainsaid."

Quoth the King, "I grant you that which you wish and you desire," and bade summon the Kazi forthright, that he might marry each of the sages to one of his daughters.

Now it fortuned that the Princesses were behind a curtain, looking on; and when they heard this, the youngest considered her husband to be and behold, he was an old man, an hundred years of age, with hair frosted, forehead drooping, eyebrows mangy, ears slitten, beard and mustachios stained and dyed; eyes red and goggle; cheeks bleached and hollow; flabby nose like a brinjall, or eggplant; face like a cobbler's apron, teeth overlapping and lips like camel's kidneys, loose and pendulous; in brief a terror, a horror, a monster, for he was of the folk of his time the unsightliest and of his age the frightfullest; sundry of his grinders had been knocked out and his eye-teeth were like the tusks of the Jinni who frighteneth poultry in hen-houses. Now the girl was the fairest and most graceful of her time, more elegant than the gazelle however tender, than the gentlest zephyr blander and brighter than the moon at her full; for amorous fray right suitable; confounding in graceful sway the waving bough and outdoing in swimming gait the pacing roe; in fine she was fairer and sweeter by far than all her sisters. So, when she saw her suitor, she went to her chamber and strewed dust on her head and tore her clothes and fell to buffeting her face and weeping and wailing.

Now the Prince, her brother, Kamar al-Akmar, or the Moon of Moons hight, was then newly returned from a journey and, hearing her weeping and crying came in to her (for he loved her with fond affection, more than his other sisters) and asked her, "What aileth thee? What hath befallen thee? Tell me and conceal naught from me."

So she smote her breast and answered, "O my brother and my dear one, I have nothing to hide. If the palace be straitened upon thy father, I will go out; and if he be resolved upon a foul thing, I will separate myself from him, though he consent not to make provision for me; and my Lord will provide."

Quoth he, "Tell me what meaneth this talk and what hath straitened thy breast and troubled thy temper."

"O my brother and my dear one," answered the Princess, "Know that my father hath promised me in marriage to a wicked magician who brought him, as a gift, a horse of black wood, and hath bewitched him with his craft and his egromancy; but, as for me, I will none of him, and would, because of him, I had never come into this world!"

Her brother soothed her and solaced her, then fared to his sire and said, "What be this wizard to whom thou hast given my youngest sister in marriage, and what is this present which he hath brought thee, so that thou hast killed my sister with chagrin? It is not right that this should be."

Now the Persian was standing by and, when he heard the Prince's words, he was mortified and filled with fury and the King said, "O my son, an thou sawest this horse, thy wit would be confounded and thou wouldst be amated with amazement." Then he bade the slaves bring the horse before him and they did so; and, when the Prince saw it, it pleased him. So (being an accomplished cavalier) he mounted it forthright and struck its sides with the shovel-shaped stirrup-irons; but it stirred not and the King said to the Sage, "Go show him its movement, that he also may help thee to win thy wish."

Now the Persian bore the Prince a grudge because he willed not he should have his sister; so he showed him the pin of ascent on the right side of the horse and saying to him, "Trill this," left him. Thereupon the Prince trilled the pin and lo! the horse forthwith soared with him high in ether, as it were a bird, and gave not overflying till it disappeared from men's espying, whereat the King was troubled and perplexed about his case and said to the Persian, "O sage, look how thou mayest make him descend."

But he replied, "O my lord, I can do nothing, and thou wilt never see him again till Resurrection-day, for he, of his ignorance and pride, asked me not of the pin of descent and I forgot to acquaint him therewith."

When the King heard this, he was enraged with sore rage; and bade bastinado the sorcerer and clap him in jail, whilst he himself cast the crown from his head and beat his face and smote his breast. Moreover, he shut the doors of his palaces and gave himself up to weeping and keening, he and his wife and daughters and all the folk of the city; and thus their joy was turned to annoy and their gladness changed into sore affliction and sadness.

Thus far concerning them; but as regards the Prince, the horse gave not over soaring with him till he drew near the sun, whereat he gave himself up for lost and saw death in the skies, and was confounded at his case, repenting him of having mounted the horse and saying to himself, "Verily, this was a device of the Sage to destroy me on account of my youngest sister; but there is no Majesty and there is no Might save in Allah, the Glorious, the Great! I am lost without recourse; but I wonder, did not he who made the ascent-pin make also a descent-pin?"

Now he was a man of wit and knowledge and intelligence; so he fell to feeling all the parts of the horse, but saw nothing save a screw, like a cock's head, on its right shoulder and the like on the left, when quoth he to himself, "I see no sign save these things like buttons." Presently he turned the right-hand pin, whereupon the horse flew heavenwards with increased speed. So he left it and looking at the sinister shoulder and finding another pin, he wound it up and immediately the steed's upwards motion slowed and ceased and it began to descend, little by little, towards the face of the earth, while the rider became yet more cautious and careful of his life. And when he saw this and knew the uses of the horse, his heart was filled with joy and gladness and he thanked Almighty Allah for that He had deigned deliver him from destruction.

Then he began to turn the horse's head whithersoever he would, making it rise and fall at pleasure, till he had gotten complete mastery over its every movement. He ceased not to descend the whole of that day, for that the steed's ascending flight had borne him afar from the earth; and, as he descended, he diverted himself with viewing the various cities and countries over which he passed and which he knew not, never having seen them in his life. Amongst the rest, he descried a city ordered after the fairest fashion in the midst of a verdant and riant land, rich in trees and streams, with gazelles pacing daintily over the plains; whereat he fell a-musing and said to himself, "Would I knew the name of yon town and in what land it is!" And he took to circling about it and observing it right and left.

By this time, the day began to decline and the sun drew near to its

downing; and he said in his mind, "Verily I find no goodlier place to night in than this city; so I will lodge here and early on the morrow I will return to my kith and kin and my kingdom; and tell my father and family what hath passed and acquaint him with what mine eyes have seen." Then he addressed himself to seeking a place wherein he might safely bestow himself and his horse and where none should descry him, and presently behold, he espied a-middlemost of the city a palace rising high in upper air surrounded by a great wall with lofty crenelles and battlements, guarded by forty black slaves, clad in complete mail and armed with spears and swords, bows and arrows. Quoth he, "This is a goodly place," and turned the descent-pin, whereupon the horse sank down with him like a weary bird, and alighted gently on the terrace-roof of the palace. So the Prince dismounted and ejaculating "Alhamdolillah"—praise be to Allah—he began to go round about the horse and examine it, saying, "By Allah, he who fashioned thee with these perfections was a cunning craftsman, and if the Almighty extend the term of my life and restore me to my country and kinsfolk in safety and reunite me with my father, I will assuredly bestow upon him all manner bounties and benefit him with the utmost beneficence."

By this time night had overtaken him and he sat on the roof till he was assured that all in the palace slept; and indeed hunger and thirst were sore upon him, for that he had not tasted food nor drunk water since he parted from his sire. So he said within himself, "Surely the like of this palace will not lack of victual"; and, leaving the horse above, went down in search of somewhat to eat. Presently, he came to a staircase and descending it to the bottom, found himself in a court paved with white marble and alabaster, which shone in the light of the moon. He marvelled at the place and the goodliness of its fashion, but sensed no sound of speaker and saw no living soul and stood in perplexed surprise, looking right and left and knowing not whither he should wend. Then said he to himself, "I may not do better than return to where I left my horse and pass the night by it; and as soon as day shall dawn I will mount and ride away."

However, as he tarried talking to himself, he espied a light within the palace, and making towards it, found that it came from a candle that stood before a door of the Harim, at the head of a sleeping eunuch, as he were one of the Ifrits of Solomon or a tribesman of the Jinn, longer than lumber and broader than a bench. He lay before the door, with the pommel of his sword gleaming in the flame of the candle, and at his head was a bag of leather hanging from a column of granite. When the Prince saw this, he was affrighted and said, "I crave help from Allah the Supreme! O mine

Holy One, even as Thou hast already delivered me from destruction, so vouchsafe me strength to quit myself of the adventure of this palace!"

So saying, he put out his hand to the budget and taking it, carried it aside and opened it and found in it food of the best. He ate his fill and refreshed himself and drank water, after which he hung up the provision-bag in its place and drawing the eunuch's sword from its sheath, took it, whilst the slave slept on, knowing not whence destiny should come to him. Then the Prince fared forwards into the palace and ceased not till he came to a second door, with a curtain drawn before it; so he raised the curtain and behold, on entering he saw a couch of the whitest ivory, inlaid with pearls and jacinths and jewels, and four slave-girls sleeping about it. He went up to the couch, to see what was thereon, and found a young lady lying asleep, chemised with her hair as she were the full moon rising over the Eastern horizon, with flower-white brow and shining hair-paring and cheeks like blood-red anemones and dainty moles thereon. He was amazed at her as she lay in her beauty and loveliness, her symmetry and grace, and he recked no more of death.

So he went up to her, trembling in every nerve and, shuddering with pleasure, kissed her on the right cheek; whereupon she awoke forthright and opened her eyes, and seeing the Prince standing at her head, said to him, "Who art thou and whence comest thou?"

Quoth he, "I am thy slave and thy lover." Asked she, "And who brought thee hither?" and he answered, "My Lord and my fortune."

Then said Shams al-Nahar (for such was her name), "Haply thou art he who demanded me yesterday of my father in marriage and he rejected thee, pretending that thou wast foul of favour. By Allah, my sire lied in his throat when he spoke this thing, for thou art not other than beautiful."

Now the son of the King of Hind had sought her in marriage, but her father had rejected him, for that he was ugly and uncouth, and she thought the Prince was he. So, when she saw his beauty and grace (for indeed he was like the radiant moon) the syntheism of love gat hold of her heart as it were a flaming fire, and they fell to talk and converse. Suddenly, her waiting-women awoke and, seeing the Prince with their mistress, said to her, "Oh my lady, who is this with thee?"

Quoth she, "I know not; I found him sitting by me, when I woke up: haply 'tis he who seeketh me in marriage of my sire."

Quoth they, "O my lady, by Allah the All-Father, this is not he who seeketh thee in marriage, for he is hideous and this man is handsome and of high degree. Indeed, the other is not fit to be his servant."

Then the handmaidens went out to the eunuch, and finding him slumbering awoke him, and he started up in alarm. Said they, "How happeth it that thou art on guard at the palace and yet men come in to us, whilst we are asleep?" When the black heard this, he sprang in haste to his sword, but found it not; and fear took him and trembling. Then he went in, confounded, to his mistress and seeing the Prince sitting at talk with her, said to him, "O my lord, art thou man or Jinni?"

Replied the Prince, "Woe to thee, O unluckiest of slaves: how darest thou even the sons of the royal Chosroes with one of the unbelieving Satans?" And he was as a raging lion.

Then he took the sword in his hand and said to the slave, "I am the King's son-in-law, and he hath married me to his daughter and bidden me go in to her."

And when the eunuch heard these words he replied, "O my lord, if thou be indeed of kind a man as thou avouchest, she is fit for none but for thee, and thou art worthier of her than any other."

Thereupon the eunuch ran to the King, shrieking loud and rending his raiment and heaving dust upon his head; and when the King heard his outcry, he said to him, "What hath befallen thee? Speak quickly and be brief; for thou hast fluttered my heart."

Answered the eunuch, "O King, come to thy daughter's succour; for a devil of the Jinn, in the likeness of a King's son, hath got possession of her; so up and at him!"

When the King heard this, he thought to kill him and said, "How camest thou to be careless of my daughter and let this demon come at her?" Then he betook himself to the Princess's palace, where he found her slave-women standing to await him and asked them, "What is come to my daughter?"

"O King," answered they, "slumber overcame us and, when we awoke, we found a young man sitting upon her couch in talk with her, as he were the full moon; never saw we aught fairer of favour than he. So we questioned him of his case and he declared that thou hadst given him thy daughter in marriage. More than this we know not, nor do we know if he be a man or a Jinni; but he is modest and well bred, and doth nothing unseemly or which leadeth to disgrace."

Now when the King heard these words, his wrath cooled and he raised the curtain little by little and looking in, saw sitting at talk with his daughter a Prince of the goodliest with a face like the full moon for sheen. At this sight he could not contain himself, of his jealousy for his daughter's honour;

and, putting aside the curtain, rushed in upon them drawn sword in hand like a furious Ghul. Now when the Prince saw him he asked the Princess, "Is this thy sire?" and she answered, "Yes." Whereupon he sprang to his feet and, seizing his sword, cried out at the King with so terrible a cry that he was confounded.

Then the youth would have fallen on him with the sword; but the King seeing that the Prince was doughtier than he, sheathed his scymitar and stood till the young man came up to him, when he accosted him courteously and said to him, "O youth, art thou a man or a Jinni?"

Quoth the Prince, "Did I not respect thy right as mine host and thy daughter's honour, I would spill thy blood! How darest thou fellow me with devils, me that am a Prince of the sons of the royal Chosroes who, had they wished to take thy kingdom, could shake thee like an earthquake from thy glory and thy dominions and spoil thee of all thy possessions?"

Now when the King heard his words, he was confounded with awe and bodily fear of him and rejoined, "If thou indeed be of the sons of the Kings, as thou pretendest, how cometh it that thou enterest my palace without my permission, and smirchest mine honour, making thy way to my daughter and feigning that thou art her husband and claiming that I have given her to thee to wife, I that have slain Kings and Kings' sons, who sought her of me in marriage? And now who shall save thee from my might and majesty when, if I cried out to my slaves and servants and bade them put thee to the vilest of deaths they would slay thee forthright? Who shall deliver thee out of my hand?"

When the Prince heard this speech of the King he answered, "Verily, I wonder at thee and at the shortness and denseness of thy wit! Say me, canst covet for thy daughter a mate comelier than myself, and hast ever seen a stouter hearted man or one better fitted for a Sultan or a more glorious in rank and dominion than I?"

Rejoined the King, "Nay, by Allah! but I would have had thee, O youth, act after the custom of Kings and demand her from me to wife before witnesses, that I might have married her to thee publicly; and now, even were I to marry her to thee privily, yet hast thou dishonoured me in her person."

Rejoined the Prince, "Thou sayest sooth, O King, but if thou summon thy slaves and thy soldiers and they fall upon me and slay me, as thou pretendest, thou wouldst but publish thine own disgrace, and the folk would be divided between belief in thee and disbelief in thee. Wherefore,

O King, thou wilt do well, meseemeth, to turn from this thought to that which I shall counsel thee."

Quoth the King, "Let me hear what thou hast to advise"; and quoth the Prince, "What I have to propose to thee is this: either do thou meet me in combat singular, I and thou; and he who slayeth his adversary shall be held the worthier and having a better title to the kingdom; or else, let me be this night and, whenas dawns the morn, draw out against me thy horsemen and footmen and servants; but first tell me their number."

Said the King, "They are forty thousand horse, beside my own slaves and their followers, who are the like of them in number."

Thereupon said the Prince, "When the day shall break, do thou array them against me and say to them: 'This man is a suitor to me for my daughter's hand, on condition that he shall do battle single-handed against you all; for he pretendeth that he will overcome you and put you to the rout, and indeed that ye cannot prevail against him.' After which, leave me to do battle with them: if they slay me, then is thy secret surer guarded and thine honour the better warded; and if I overcome them and see their backs, then is it the like of me a King should covet to his son-in-law."

So the King approved of his opinion and accepted his proposition, despite his awe at the boldness of his speech and amaze at the pretensions of the Prince to meet in fight his whole host, such as he had described to him, being at heart assured that he would perish in the fray and so he should be quit of him and freed from the fear of dishonour. Thereupon he called the eunuch and bade him go to his Wazir without stay and delay and command him to assemble the whole of the army and cause them don their arms and armour and mount their steeds.

So the eunuch carried the King's order to the Minister, who straightaway summoned the Captains of the host and the Lords of the realm and bade them don their harness of derring-do and mount horse and sally forth in battle array. Such was their case; but as regards the King, he sat a long while conversing with the young Prince, being pleased with his wise speech and good sense and fine breeding. And when it was day-break he returned to his palace and, seating himself on his throne, commanded his merry men to mount and bade them saddle one of the best of the royal steeds with handsome selle and housings and trappings and bring it to the Prince. But the youth said, "O King, I will not mount horse, till I come in view of the troops and review them."

"Be it as thou wilt," replied the King. Then the two repaired to the parade-ground, where the troops were drawn up, and the young Prince

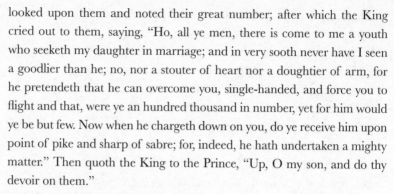

looked upon them and noted their great number; after which the King cried out to them, saying, "Ho, all ye men, there is come to me a youth who seeketh my daughter in marriage; and in very sooth never have I seen a goodlier than he; no, nor a stouter of heart nor a doughtier of arm, for he pretendeth that he can overcome you, single-handed, and force you to flight and that, were ye an hundred thousand in number, yet for him would ye be but few. Now when he chargeth down on you, do ye receive him upon point of pike and sharp of sabre; for, indeed, he hath undertaken a mighty matter." Then quoth the King to the Prince, "Up, O my son, and do thy devoir on them."

Answered he, "O King, thou dealest not justly and fairly by me: how shall I go forth against them, seeing that I am afoot and the men be mounted?"

The King retorted, "I bade thee mount, and thou refusedst; but choose thou which of my horses thou wilt."

Then he said, "Not one of thy horses pleaseth me, and I will ride none but that on which I came."

Asked the King, "And where is thy horse?"

"Atop of thy palace."

"In what part of my palace?"

"On the roof." Now when the King heard these words, he cried, "Out on thee! this is the first sign thou hast given of madness. How can the horse be on the roof? But we shall at once see if thou speak the truth or lies." Then he turned to one of his chief officers and said to him, "Go to my palace and bring me what thou findest on the roof."

So all the people marvelled at the young Prince's words, saying one to other, "How can a horse come down the steps from the roof? Verily this is a thing whose like we never heard."

In the meantime the King's messenger repaired to the palace and mounting to the roof, found the horse standing there and never had he looked on a handsomer; but when he drew near and examined it, he saw that it was made of ebony and ivory. Now the officer was accompanied by other high officers, who also looked on and they laughed to one another, saying, "Was it of the like of this horse that the youth spake? We cannot deem him other than mad; however, we shall soon see the truth of his case. Peradventure herein is some mighty matter, and he is a man of high degree."

Then they lifted up the horse bodily and, carrying it to the King, set it down before him, and all the lieges flocked round to look at it, marvelling at the beauty of its proportions and the richness of its saddle and bridle.

The King also admired it and wondered at it with extreme wonder; and he asked the Prince, "O youth, is this thy horse?"

He answered, "Yes, O King, this is my horse, and thou shalt soon see the marvel it showeth." Rejoined the King, "Then take and mount it," and the Prince retorted, "I will not mount till the troops withdraw afar from it."

So the King bade them retire a bowshot from the horse; whereupon quoth its owner, "O King, see thou; I am about to mount my horse and charge upon thy host and scatter them right and left and split their hearts asunder."

Said the King, "Do as thou wilt; and spare not their lives, for they will not spare thine."

Then the Prince mounted, whilst the troops ranged themselves in ranks before him, and one said to another, "When the youth cometh between the ranks, we will take him on the points of our pikes and the sharps of our sabres."

Quoth another, "By Allah, this a mere misfortune: how shall we slay a youth so comely of face and shapely of form?"

And a third continued, "Ye will have hard work to get the better of him; for the youth had not done this, but for what he knew of his own prowess and pre-eminence of valour."

Meanwhile, having settled himself in his saddle, the Prince turned the pin of ascent; whilst all eyes were strained to see what he would do, whereupon the horse began to heave and rock and sway to and fro and make the strangest of movements steed ever made, till its belly was filled with air and it took flight with its rider and soared high into the sky. When the King saw this, he cried out to his men, saying, "Woe to you! catch him, catch him, ere he 'scape you!"

But his Wazirs and Viceroys said to him, "O King, can a man overtake the flying bird? This is surely none but some mighty magician or Marid of the Jinn or devil, and Allah save thee from him. So praise thou the Almighty for deliverance of thee and of all thy host from his hand."

Then the King returned to his palace after seeing the feat of the Prince and, going in to his daughter, acquainted her with what had befallen them both on the parade-ground. He found her grievously afflicted for the Prince and bewailing her separation from him; wherefore she fell sick with violent sickness and took to her pillow.

Now when her father saw her on this wise, he pressed her to his breast and kissing her between the eyes, said to her, "O my daughter, praise Allah Almighty and thank Him for that He hath delivered us from this crafty enchanter, this villain, this low fellow, this thief who thought only of seducing thee!" And he repeated to her the story of the Prince and how he had disappeared in the firmament; and he abused him and cursed him knowing not how dearly his daughter loved him. But she paid no heed to his words and did but redouble in her tears and wails, saying to herself, "By Allah, I will neither eat meat nor drain drink, till Allah reunite me with him!" Her father was greatly concerned for her case and mourned much over her plight; but, for all he could do to soother her, love-longing only increased on her.

Thus far concerning the King and Princess Shams al-Nahar; but as regards Prince Kamar al-Akmar, when he had risen high in air, he turned his horse's head towards his native land, and being alone mused upon the beauty of the Princess and her loveliness. Now he had enquired of the King's people the name of the city and of its King and his daughter; and men had told him that it was the city of Sana'a. So he journeyed with all speed, till he drew near his father's capital and, making an airy circuit about the city, alighted on the roof of the King's palace, where he left his horse, whilst he descended into the palace and seeing its threshold strewn with ashes, thought that one of his family was dead. Then he entered, as of wont, and found his father and mother and sisters clad in mourning raiment of black, all pale of faces and lean of frames. When his sire descried him and was assured that it was indeed his son, he cried out with a great cry and fell down in a fit, but after a time coming to himself, threw himself upon him and embraced him, clipping him to his bosom and rejoicing in him with exceeding joy and extreme gladness. His mother and sisters heard this; so they came in and seeing the Prince, fell upon him, kissing him and weeping, and joying with exceeding joyance. Then they questioned him of his case; so he told them all that had passed from first to last, and his father said to him, "Praised be Allah for thy safety, O coolth of my eyes and core of my heart!" Then the King bade hold high festival, and the glad tidings flew through the city.

So they beat drums and cymbals and, doffing the weed of mourning, they donned the gay garb of gladness and decorated the streets and markets; whilst the folk vied with one another who should be the first to give the King joy, and the King proclaimed a general pardon and opening the prisons, released those who were therein prisoned. Moreover, he made banquets for the people, with great abundance of eating and drinking, for seven days and nights and all creatures were gladsomest; and he took horse with his son and rode out with him, that the folk might see him and rejoice.

After awhile the Prince asked about the maker of the horse, saying, "O my father, what hath fortune done with him?" and the King answered, "Allah never bless him nor the hour wherein I set eyes on him! For he was the cause of thy separation from us, O my son, and he hath lain in gaol since the day of thy disappearance."

Then the King bade release him from prison and, sending for him, invested him in a dress of satisfaction and entreated him with the utmost favour and munificence, save that he would not give him his daughter to wife; whereat the Sage raged with sore rage and repented of that which he had done, knowing that the Prince had secured the secret of the steed and the manner of its motion. Moreover, the King said to his son, "I reck thou wilt do will not to go near the horse henceforth and more especially not to mount it after this day; for thou knowest not its properties, and belike thou art in error about it."

Not the Prince had told his father of his adventure with the King of Sana'a and his daughter and he said, "Had the King intended to kill thee, he had done so; but thine hour was not yet come."

When the rejoicings were at an end, the people returned to their places and the King and his son to the palace, where they sat down and fell to eating and drinking and making merry. Now the King had a handsome handmaiden who was skilled in playing the lute; so she took it and began to sweep the strings and sing thereto before the King and his son of separation of lovers, and she chanted the following verses:

> "Deem not that absence breeds in me aught of forgetfulness;
> What should remember I did you fro' my remembrance wane?
> Time dies but never dies the fondest love for you we bear;
> And in your love I'll die and in your love I'll arise again."

When the Prince heard these verses, the fires of longing flamed up in his heart and pine and passion redoubled upon him. Grief and regret were sore upon him and his bowels yearned in him for love of the King's daughter of Sana'a; so he rose forthright and, escaping his father's notice, went forth the palace to the horse and mounting it, turned the pin of ascent, whereupon bird-like it flew with him high in air and soared towards the upper regions of the sky. In early morning his father missed him and, going up to the pinnacle of the palace, in great concern, saw his son rising into the firmament; whereat he was sore afflicted and repented in all penitence that he had not taken the horse and hidden it; and he said to himself, "By Allah,

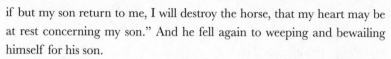

if but my son return to me, I will destroy the horse, that my heart may be at rest concerning my son." And he fell again to weeping and bewailing himself for his son.

Such was his case; but as regards the Prince, he ceased not flying on through air till he came to the city of Sana'a and alighted on the roof as before. Then he crept down stealthily and, finding the eunuch asleep, as of wont, raised the curtain and went on little by little, till he came to the door of the Princess's alcove-chamber and stopped to listen; when lo! he heard her shedding plenteous tears and reciting verses, whilst her women slept round her. Presently, overhearing her weeping and wailing quoth they, "O our mistress, why wilt thou mourn for one who mourneth not for thee?"

Quoth she, "O ye little of wit, is he for whom I mourn of those who forget or who are forgotten?" And she fell again to wailing and weeping, till sleep overcame her. Hereat the Prince's heart melted for her and his gall-bladder was like to burst, so he entered and, seeing her lying asleep without covering, touched her with his hand; whereupon she opened her eyes and espied him standing by her. Said he, "Why all this crying and mourning?"

And when she knew him, she threw herself upon him, and took him around the neck and kissed him and answered, "For thy sake and because of my separation from thee."

Said he, "O my lady, I have been made desolate by thee all this long time!"

But she replied, "'Tis thou who hast desolated me; and hadst thou tarried longer, I had surely died!"

Rejoined he, "O my lady, what thinkest thou of my case with thy father and how he dealt with me? Were it not for my love of thee, O temptation and seduction of the Three Worlds, I had certainly slain him and made him a warning to all beholders; but, even as I love thee, so I love him for thy sake."

Quoth she, "How couldst thou leave me: can my life be sweet to me after thee?"

Quoth he, "Let what hath happened suffice: I am now hungry, and thirsty."

So she bade her maidens make ready meat and drink, and they sat eating and drinking and conversing till night was well nigh ended; and when day broke he rose to take leave of her and depart, ere the eunuch should awake. Shams al-Nahar asked him, "Whither goest thou?" and he answered, "To my father's house, and I plight thee my troth that I will come to thee once in every week."

But she wept and said, "I conjure thee, by Allah the Almighty, take me with thee whereso thou wendest and make me not taste anew the bitter gourd of separation from thee."

Quoth he, "Wilt thou indeed go with me?" and quoth she, "Yes."

"Then," said he, "arise that we depart."

So she rose forthright and going to a chest, arrayed herself in what was richest and dearest to her of her trinkets of gold and jewels of price, and she fared forth, her handmaids recking naught. So he carried her up to the roof of the palace and, mounting the ebony horse, took her up behind him and made her fast to himself, binding her with strong bonds; after which he turned the shoulder-pin of ascent, and the horse rose with him high in air. When her slave-women saw this, they shrieked aloud and told her father and mother, who in hot haste ran to the palace-roof and looking up, saw the magical horse flying away with the Prince and Princess. At this the King was troubled with ever-increasing trouble and cried out, saying, "O King's son, I conjure thee, by Allah, have ruth on me and my wife and bereave us not of our daughter!"

The Prince made him no reply; but, thinking in himself that the maiden repented of leaving father and mother, asked her, "O ravishment of the age, say me, wilt thou that I restore thee to thy mother and father?" whereupon she answered, "By Allah, O my lord, that is not my desire: my only wish is to be with thee, wherever thou art; for I am distracted by the love of thee from all else, even from my father and mother."

Hearing these words the Prince joyed with great joy, and made the horse fly and fare softly with them, so as not to disquiet her; nor did they stay their flight till they came in sight of a green meadow, wherein was a spring of running water. Here they alighted and ate and drank; after which the Prince took horse again and set her behind him, binding her in his fear for her safety; after which they fared on till they came in sight of his father's capital. At this, the Prince was filled with joy and bethought himself to show his beloved the seat of his dominion and his father's power and dignity and give her to know that it was greater than that of her sire. So he set her down in one of his father's gardens without the city where his parent was wont to take his pleasure; and, carrying her into a domed summer-house prepared there for the King, left the ebony horse at the door and charged the damsel keep watch over it, saying, "Sit here, till my messenger come to thee; for I go now to my father, to make ready a palace for thee and show thee my royal estate."

She was delighted when she heard these words and said to him, "Do as thou wilt"; for she thereby understood that she should not enter the city but with due honour and worship, as became her rank.

Then the Prince left her and betook himself to the palace of the King his father, who rejoiced in his return and met him and welcomed him; and the Prince said to him, "Know that I have brought with me the King's daughter of whom I told thee; and have left her without the city in such a garden and come to tell thee, that thou mayst make ready the procession of estate and go forth to meet her and show her thy royal dignity and troops and guards."

Answered the King, "With joy and gladness"; and straightaway bade decorate the town with the goodliest adornment.

Then he took horse and rode out in all magnificence and majesty, he and his host, high officers and household, with drums and kettle-drums, fifes and clarions and all manner instruments; whilst the Prince drew forth of his treasuries jewellery and apparel and what else of the things which Kings hoards and made a rare display of wealth and splendour: moreover he got ready for the Princess a canopied litter of brocades, green, red and yellow, wherein he set Indian and Greek and Abyssinian slave-girls. Then he left the litter and those who were therein and preceded them to the pavilion where he had set her down; and searched but found naught, neither Princess nor horse. When he saw this, he beat his face, and rent his raiment and began to wander round about the garden, as he had lost his wits; after which he came to his senses and said to himself, "How could she have come at the secret of this horse, seeing I told her nothing of it? Maybe the Persian sage who made the horse hath chanced upon her and stolen her away, in revenge for my father's treatment of him."

Then he sought the guardians of the garden and asked them if they had seen any pass the precincts; and said, "Hath any one come in here? Tell me the truth and the whole truth or I will at once strike off your heads."

They were terrified by his threats; but they answered with one voice, "We have seen no man enter save the Persian sage, who came to gather healing herbs." So the Prince was certified that it was indeed he that had taken away the maiden, and abode confounded and perplexed concerning his case. And he was abashed before the folk and, turning to his sire, told him what had happened and said to him, "Take the troops and march them back to the city. As for me, I will never return till I have cleared up this affair."

When the King heard this, he wept and beat his breast and said to him, "O my son, calm thy choler and master thy chagrin and come home with us and look what King's daughter thou wouldst fain have, that I may marry thee to her." But the Prince paid no heed to his words and farewelling him departed, whilst the King returned to the city and their joy was changed into sore annoy.

Now, as Destiny issued her decree, when the Prince left the Princess in the garden-house and betook himself to his father's palace, for the ordering of his affair, the Persian entered the garden to pluck certain simples and, scenting the sweet savour of musk and perfumes that exhaled from the Princess and impregnated the whole place, followed it till he came to the pavilion and saw standing at the door the horse which he had made with his own hands. His heart was filled with joy and gladness, for he had bemourned its loss much since it had gone out of his hand: so he went up to it and, examining its every part, found it whole and sound; whereupon he was about to mount and ride away, when he bethought himself and said, "Needs must I first look what the Prince hath brought and left here with the horse."

So he entered the pavilion and, seeing the Princess sitting there, as she were the sun shining sheen in the sky serene, knew her at the first glance to be some high-born lady and doubted not but the Prince had brought her thither on the horse and left her in the pavilion, whilst he went to the city, to make ready for her entry in state procession with all splendor. Then he went up to her and kissed the earth between her hands, whereupon she raised her eyes to him and, finding him exceedingly foul of face and favour, asked, "Who art thou?" and he answered, "O my lady, I am a messenger sent by the Prince who hath bidden me bring thee to another pleasance nearer the city; for that my lady the Queen cannot walk so far and is unwilling, of her joy in thee, that another should forestall her with thee."

Quoth she, "Where is the Prince?" and quoth the Persian, "He is in the city, with his sire and forthwith he shall come for thee in great state."

Said she, "O thou! say me, could he find none handsomer to send to me?" whereat loud laughed the Sage and said, "Yea verily, he hath not a Mameluke as ugly as I am; but, O my lady, let not the ill-favour of my face and the foulness of my form deceive thee. Hadst thou profited of me as hath the Prince, verily thou wouldst praise my affair. Indeed, he chose me as his messenger to thee, because of my uncomeliness and loathsomeness in his jealous love of thee; else hath he Mamelukes and negro slaves, pages, eunuchs and attendants out of number, each goodlier than other."

Whenas she heard this, it commended itself to her reason and she believed him; so she rose forthright; and, putting her hand in his, said, "O my father, what hast thou brought me to ride?"

He replied, "O my lady, thou shalt ride the horse thou camest on;" and she, "I cannot ride it by myself."

Whereupon he smiled and knew that he was her master and said, "I will ride with thee myself."

So he mounted and, taking her up behind him bound her to himself with firm bonds, while she knew not what he would with her. Then he turned the ascent-pin, whereupon the belly of the horse became full of wind and it swayed to and fro like a wave of the sea, and rose with them high in air nor slackened in its flight, till it was out of sight of the city.

Now when Shams al-Nahir saw this, she asked him, "Ho thou! what is become of that thou toldest me of my Prince, making me believe that he sent thee to me?"

Answered the Persian, "Allah damn the Prince! he is a mean and skinflint knave."

She cried, "Woe to thee! How darest thou disobey thy lord's commandment?"

Whereto the Persian replied, "He is no lord of mine: knowest thou who I am?"

Rejoined the Princess, "I know nothing of thee save what thou toldest me"; and retorted he, "What I told thee was a trick of mine against thee and the King's son: I have long lamented the loss of this horse which is under us; for I constructed it and made myself master of it. But now I have gotten firm hold of it and of thee too, and I will burn his heart even as he hath burnt mine; nor shall he ever have the horse again; no, never! So be of good cheer and keep thine eyes cool and clear; for I can be of more use to thee than he; and I am generous as I am wealthy; my servants and slaves shall obey thee as their mistress; I will robe thee in finest raiment and thine every wish shall be at thy will."

When she heard this, she buffeted her face and cried out, saying, "Ah, well-away! I have not won my beloved and I have lost my father and mother!" And she wept bitter tears over what had befallen her, whilst the Sage fared on with her, without ceasing, till he came to the land of the Greeks and alighted in a verdant mead, abounding in streams and trees.

Now this meadow lay near a city wherein was a King of high puissance, and it chanced that he went forth that day to hunt and divert himself. As he passed by the meadow, he saw the Persian standing there, with the damsel and the horse by his side; and, before the Sage was ware, the King's slaves fell upon him and carried him and the lady and the horse to their master who, noting the foulness of the man's favour and his loathsomeness and the beauty of the girl and her loveliness, said, "O my lady, what kin is this oldster to thee?"

The Persian made haste to reply, saying, "She is my wife and the daughter of my father's brother."

But the lady at once gave him the lie and said, "O King, by Allah, I know him not, nor is he my husband; nay, he is a wicked magician who hath stolen me away by force and fraud." Thereupon the King bade bastinado the Persian and they beat him till he was well-nigh dead; after which the King commanded to carry him to the city and cast him into jail; and, taking from him the damsel and the ebony horse (though he knew not its properties nor the secret of its motion), set the girl in his serraglio and the horse amongst his hoards.

Such was the case with the Sage and the lady; but as regards Prince Kamar al-Akmar, he garbed himself in travelling gear and taking what he needed of money, set out tracking their trail in very sorry plight; and journeyed from country to country and city to city seeking the Princess and enquiring after the ebony horse, whilst all who heard him marvelled at him and deemed his talk extravagant. Thus he continued doing a long while; but, for all his enquiry and quest, he could hit on no new news of her. At last he came to her father's city of Sana'a and there asked for her, but could get no tidings of her and found her father mourning her loss. So he turned back and made for the land of the Greeks, continuing to enquire concerning the twain as he went along, till, as chance would have it, he alighted at a certain Khan and saw a company of merchants sitting at talk. So he sat down near them and heard one say, "O my friends, I lately witnessed a wonder of wonders."

They asked, "What was that?" and he answered, "I was visiting such a district in such a city (naming the city wherein was the Princess), and I heard its people chatting of a strange thing which had lately befallen. It was that their King went out one day hunting and coursing with a company of his courtiers and the lords of his realm; and, issuing from the city, they came to a green meadow where they espied an old man standing, with a woman sitting hard by a horse of ebony. The man was foulest-foul of face and loathly of form, but the woman was a marvel of beauty and loveliness and elegance and perfect grace; and as for the wooden horse, it was a miracle, never saw eyes aught goodlier than it nor more gracious than its make."

Asked the others, "And what did the King with them?" and the merchant answered, "As for the man the King seized him and questioned him of the damsel and he pretended that she was his wife and the daughter

of his paternal uncle; but she gave him the lie forthright and declared that he was a sorcerer and a villain. So the King took her from the old man and bade beat him and cast him into the trunk-house. As for the ebony horse, I know not what became of it."

When the Prince heard these words, he drew near to the merchant and began questioning him discreetly and courteously touching the name of the city and of its King; which when he knew, he passed the night full of joy. And as soon as dawned the day he set out and travelled sans surcease till he reached that city; but, when he would have entered, the gate-keepers laid hands on him, that they might bring him before the King to question him of his condition and the craft in which he was skilled and the cause of his coming thither-such being the usage and custom of their ruler.

Now it was supper-time when he entered the city, and it was then impossible to go in to the King or take counsel with him respecting the stranger. So the guards carried him to the jail, thinking to lay him by the heels there for the night; but, when the warders saw his beauty and loveliness, they could not find it in their hearts to imprison him: they made him sit with them without the walls; and, when food came to them, he ate with them what sufficed him. As soon as they had made an end of eating, they turned to the Prince and said, "What countryman art thou?"

"I come from Fars," answered he, "the land of the Chosroes."

When they heard this they laughed and one of them said, "O Chosroan, I have heard the talk of men and their histories and I have looked into their conditions; but never saw I or heard I a bigger liar than the Chosroan which is with us in the jail."

Quoth another, "And never did I see aught fouler than his favour or more hideous than his visnomy."

Asked the Prince, "What have ye seen of his lying?" and they answered, "He pretendeth that he is one of the wise!"

"Now the King came upon him, as he went a-hunting, and found with him a most beautiful woman and a horse of the blackest ebony, never saw I a handsomer. As for the damsel, she is with the King, who is enamoured of her and would fain marry her; but she is mad, and were this man a leach as he claimeth to be, he would have healed her, for the King doth his utmost to discover a cure for her case and a remedy for her disease, and this whole year past hath he spent treasure upon physicians and astrologers, on her account; but none can avail to cure her. As for the horse, it is in the royal hoard-house, and the ugly man is here with us in prison; and as soon as night falleth, he weepeth and bemoaneth himself and will not let us sleep."

When the warders had recounted the case of the Persian egromancer they held in prison and his weeping and wailing, the Prince at once devised a device whereby he might compass his desire; and presently the guards of the gate, being minded to sleep, led him into the jail and locked the door. So he overheard the Persian weeping and bemoaning himself, in his own tongue, and saying, "Alack, and alas for my sin, that I sinned against myself and against the King's son, in that which I did with the damsel; for I neither left her nor won my will of her! All this cometh of my lack of sense, in that I sought for myself that which I deserved not and which befitted not the like of me; for whoso seeketh what suiteth him not at all, falleth with the like of my fall."

Now when the King's son heard this, he accosted him in Persian, saying, "How long will this weeping and wailing last? Say me, thinkest thou that hath befallen thee that which never befel other than thou?"

Now when the Persian heard this, he made friends with him and began to complain to him of his case and misfortunes. And as soon as the morning morrowed, the warders took the Prince and carried him before their King, informing him that he had entered the city on the previous night, at a time when audience was impossible.

Quoth the King to the Prince, "Whence comest thou and what is thy name and trade and why hast thou travelled hither?"

He replied, "As to my name I am called in Persian Harjah; as to my country I come from the land of Fars; and I am of the men of art and especially of the art of medicine and healing the sick and those whom the Jinns drive mad. For this I go round about all countries and cities, to profit by adding knowledge to my knowledge, and whenever I see a patient I heal him and this is my craft."

Now when the King heard this, he rejoiced with exceeding joy and said, "O excellent Sage, thou hast indeed come to us at a time when we need thee." Then he acquainted him with the case of the Princess, adding, "If thou cure her and recover her from her madness, thou shalt have of me everything thou seekest."

Replied the Prince, "Allah save and favour the King: describe to me all thou hast seen of her insanity and tell me how long it is since the access attacked her; also how thou camest by her and the horse and the Sage."

So the King told him the whole story, from first to last, adding, "The Sage is in gaol."

Quoth the Prince, "O auspicious King, and what hast thou done with the horse?"

Quoth the King, "O youth, it is with me yet, laid up in one of my treasure-chambers," whereupon said the Prince within himself, "The best thing I can do is first to see the horse and assure myself of its condition. If it be whole and sound, all will be well and end well; but, if its motor-works be destroyed, I must find some other way of delivering my beloved."

Thereupon he turned to the King and said to him, "O King, I must see the horse in question: haply I may find in it somewhat that will serve me for the recovery of the damsel."

"With all my heart," replied the King, and taking him by the hand, showed him into the place where the horse was. The Prince went round about it, examining its condition, and found it whole and sound, whereat he rejoiced greatly and said to the King, "Allah save and exalt the King! I would fain go in to the damsel, that I may see how it is with her; for I hope in Allah to heal her by my healing hand through means of the horse."

Then he bade them take care of the horse and the King carried him to the Princess's apartment where her lover found her wringing her hands and writhing and beating herself against the ground, and tearing her garments to tatters as was her wont; but there was no madness of Jinn in her, and she did this but that none might approach her. When the Prince saw her thus, he said to her, "No harm shall betide thee, O ravishment of the three worlds"; and went on to soothe her and speak her fair, till he managed to whisper, "I am Kamar al-Akmar"; whereupon she cried out with a loud cry and fell down fainting for excess of joy; but the King thought this was epilepsy brought on by her fear of him, and by her suddenly being startled.

Then the Prince put his mouth to her ear and said to her, "O Shams al-Nahar, O seduction of the universe, have a care for thy life and mine and be patient and constant; for this our position needeth sufferance and skilful contrivance to make shift for our delivery from the tyrannical King. My first move will be now to go out to him and tell him that thou art possessed of a Jinn and hence thy madness; but that I will engage to heal thee and drive away the evil spirit, if he will at once unbind thy bonds. So when he cometh in to thee, do thou speak him smooth words, that he may think I have cured thee, and all will be done for us as we desire."

Quoth she, "Hearkening and obedience"; and he went out to the King in joy and gladness, and said to him, "O august King, I have, by thy good fortune, discovered her disease and its remedy, and have cured her for thee. So now do thou go in to her and speak her softly and treat her kindly, and promise her what may please her; so shall all thou desirest of her be accomplished to thee."

Thereupon the King went in to her and when she saw him, she rose and kissing the ground before him, bade him welcome and said, "I admire how thou hast come to visit thy handmaid this day"; whereat he was ready to fly for joy and bade the waiting-women and the eunuchs attend her and carry her to the Hammam and make ready for her dresses and adornment.

So they went in to her and saluted her, and she returned their salams with the goodliest language and after the pleasantest fashion; whereupon they clad her in royal apparel and, clasping a collar of jewels about her neck, carried her to the bath and served her there. Then they brought her forth, as she were the full moon; and, when she came into the King's presence, she saluted him and kissed ground before him; whereupon he joyed in her with joy exceeding and said to the Prince, "O Sage, O philosopher, all this is of thy blessing. Allah increase to us the benefit of thy healing breath!"

The Prince replied, "O King, for the completion of her cure it behoveth that thou go forth, thou and all thy troops and guards, to the place where thou foundest her, not forgetting the beast of black wood which was with her; for therein is a devil; and, unless I exorcise him, he will return to her and afflict her at the head of every month."

"With love and gladness," cried the King, "O thou Prince of all philosophers and most learned of all who see the light of day." Then he brought out the ebony horse to the meadow in question and rode thither with all his troops and the Princess, little weeting the purpose of the Prince.

Now when they came to the appointed place, the Prince, still habited as a leach, bade them set the Princess and the steed as far as eye could reach from the King and his troops, and said to him, "With thy leave, and at thy word, I will now proceed to the fumigations and conjurations, and here imprison the adversary of mankind, that he may never more return to her. After this, I shall mount this wooden horse which seemeth to be made of ebony, and take the damsel up behind me; whereupon it will shake and sway to and fro and fare forwards, till it come to thee, when the affair will be at an end; and after this thou mayst do with her as thou wilt."

When the King heard his words, he rejoiced with extreme joy; so the Prince mounted the horse and, taking the damsel up behind him, whilst the King and his troops watched him, bound her fast to him. Then he turned the ascending-pin and the horse took flight and soared with them high in air, till they disappeared from every eye. After this the King abode half the day, expecting their return; but they returned not. So when he despaired of them, repenting him greatly of that which he had done and grieving sore for the loss of the damsel, he went back to the city with his troops. He then sent for the Persian who was in prison and said to him, "O thou traitor, O thou villian, why didst thou hide from me the mystery of the ebony horse? And now a sharper hath come to me and hath carried it off, together with a slave-girl whose ornaments are worth a mint of money, and I shall never see anyone or anything of them again!"

So the Persian related to him all his past, first and last, and the King was seized with a fit of fury which well-nigh ended his life. He shut himself up in his palace for a while, mourning and afflicted; but at last his Wazirs came in to him and applied themselves to comfort him, saying, "Verily, he who took the damsel is an enchanter, and praised be Allah who hath delivered thee from his craft and sorcery!" And they ceased not from him, till he was comforted for her loss.

Thus far concerning the King; but as for the Prince, he continued his career towards his father's capital in joy and cheer, and stayed not till he alighted on his own palace, where he set the lady in safety; after which he went in to his father and mother and saluted them and acquainted them with her coming, whereat they were filled with solace and gladness. Then he spread great banquets for the towns-folk, and they held high festival a whole month, at the end of which time he went in to the Princess and they took their joy of each other with exceeding joy. But his father brake the ebony horse in pieces and destroyed its mechanism for flight; moreover the Prince wrote a letter to the Princess's father, advising him of all that had befallen her and informing him how she was now married to him and in all health and happiness, and sent it by a messenger, together with costly presents and curious rarities. And when the messenger arrived at the city which was Sana'a and delivered the letter and the presents to the King, he read the missive and rejoiced greatly thereat and accepted the presents, honouring and rewarding the bearer handsomely. Moreover, he forwarded rich gifts to his son-in-law by the same messenger, who returned to his master and acquainted him with what had passed; whereat he was much cheered. And after this the Prince wrote a letter every year to his father-in-law and sent him presents till, in course of time, his sire King Sabur deceased and he reigned in his stead, ruling justly over his lieges and conducting himself well and righteously towards them, so that the land submitted to him and his subjects did him loyal service; and Kamar al-Akmar and his wife Shams al-Nahar abode in the enjoyment of all satisfaction and solace of life, till there came to them the Destroyer of delights and Sunderer of societies; the Plunderer of palaces, the Caterer for cemeteries, and the Garnerer of graves.

Quoth Scheherazade, "And now glory be to the Living One who dieth not and in whose hand is the dominion of the worlds visible and invisible! Moreover I have heard tell the tale of Sinbad the Sailor."

121

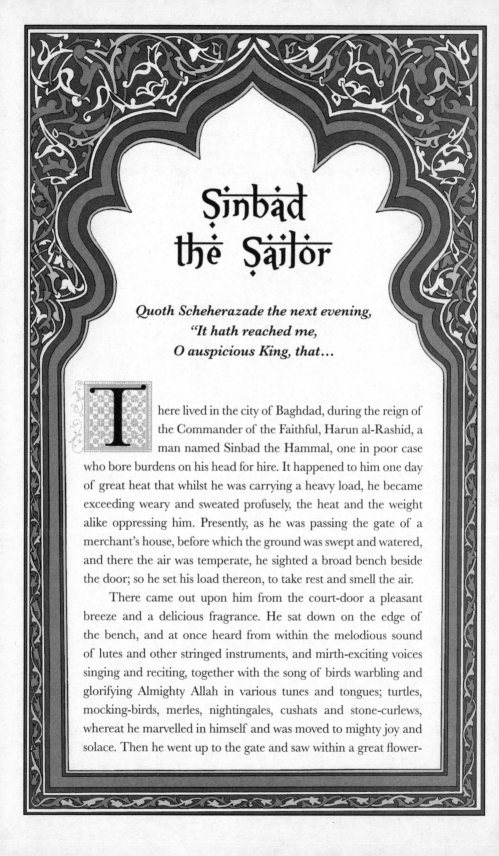

Sinbad
the Sailor

Quoth Scheherazade the next evening,
"It hath reached me,
O auspicious King, that...

There lived in the city of Baghdad, during the reign of the Commander of the Faithful, Harun al-Rashid, a man named Sinbad the Hammal, one in poor case who bore burdens on his head for hire. It happened to him one day of great heat that whilst he was carrying a heavy load, he became exceeding weary and sweated profusely, the heat and the weight alike oppressing him. Presently, as he was passing the gate of a merchant's house, before which the ground was swept and watered, and there the air was temperate, he sighted a broad bench beside the door; so he set his load thereon, to take rest and smell the air.

There came out upon him from the court-door a pleasant breeze and a delicious fragrance. He sat down on the edge of the bench, and at once heard from within the melodious sound of lutes and other stringed instruments, and mirth-exciting voices singing and reciting, together with the song of birds warbling and glorifying Almighty Allah in various tunes and tongues; turtles, mocking-birds, merles, nightingales, cushats and stone-curlews, whereat he marvelled in himself and was moved to mighty joy and solace. Then he went up to the gate and saw within a great flower-garden wherein were pages and black slaves and such a train of servants and attendants and so forth as is found only with Kings and Sultans; and his nostrils were greeted with the savoury odours of all manner meats rich and delicate, and delicious and generous wines. So he raised his eyes heavenwards and said, "Glory to Thee, O Lord, O Creator and Provider, who providest whomso Thou wilt without count or stint! O mine Holy One, I cry Thee pardon for all sins and turn to Thee repenting of all offences! O Lord, there is no gainsaying Thee in Thine ordinance and Thy dominion, neither wilt Thou be questioned of that Thou dost, for Thou indeed over all things art Almighty! Extolled be Thy perfection: whom Thou wilt Thou makest poor and whom Thou wilt Thou makest rich! Whom Thou wilt Thou exaltest and whom Thou wilt Thou abasest and there is no god but Thou! How mighty is Thy majesty and how enduring Thy dominion and how excellent Thy government! Verily, Thou favourest whom Thou wilt of Thy servants, whereby the owner of this place abideth in all joyance of life and delighteth himself with pleasant scents and delicious meats and exquisite wines of all kinds. For indeed Thou appointest unto Thy creatures that which Thou wilt and that which Thou hast foreordained unto them; wherefore are some weary and others are at rest and some enjoy fair fortune and affluence, whilst others suffer the extreme of travail and misery, even as I do." And he fell to reciting:

"How many by my labours, that evermore endure,
   All goods of life enjoy and in cooly shade recline?
Each morn that dawns I wake in travail and in woe,
   And strange is my condition and my burden gars me pine:
Many others are in luck and from miseries are free,
   And Fortune never loads them with loads the like o' mine:
They live their happy days in all solace and delight;
   Eat, drink and dwell in honour 'mid the noble and the digne:
All living things were made of a little drop of sperm,
   Thine origin is mine and my provenance is thine;
Yet the difference and distance 'twixt the twain of us are far
   As the difference of savour 'twixt vinegar and wine:
But at Thee, O God All-wise! I venture not to rail
   Whose ordinance is just and whose justice cannot fail."

When Sinbad the Porter had made an end of reciting his verses, he bore up his burden and was about to fare on, when there came forth to him from the gate a little foot-page, fair of face and shapely of shape and dainty of dress who caught him by the hand saying, "Come in and speak with my lord, for he calleth for thee." The Porter would have excused himself to the page but the lad would take no refusal; so he left his load with the doorkeeper in the vestibule and followed the boy into the house, which he found to be a goodly mansion, radiant and full of majesty, till he brought him to a grand sitting-room wherein he saw a company of nobles and great lords, seated at tables garnished with all manner of flowers and sweet-scented herbs, besides great plenty of dainty viands and fruits dried and fresh and confections and wines of the choicest vintages. There also were instruments of music and mirth and lovely slave-girls playing and singing. All the company was ranged according to rank; and in the highest place sat a man of worshipful and noble aspect whose beard-sides hoariness had stricken; and he was stately of stature and fair of favour, agreeable of aspect and full of gravity and dignity and majesty. So Sinbad the Porter was confounded at that which he beheld and said in himself, "By Allah, this must be either a piece of Paradise or some King's palace!" Then he saluted the company with much respect praying for their prosperity, and kissing the ground before them, stood with his head bowed down in humble attitude.

Sinbad the Porter, after kissing ground between their hands, stood with his head bowed down in humble attitude. The master of the house bade him draw near and be seated and bespoke him kindly, bidding him welcome. Then he set before him various kinds of viands, rich and delicate and delicious, and the Porter, after saying his Bismillah, fell to and ate his fill, after which he exclaimed, "Praised be Allah whatso be our case!" and, washing his hands, returned thanks to the company for his entertainment.

Quoth the host, "Thou art welcome and thy day is a blessed. But what is thy name and calling?"

Quoth the other, "O my lord, my name is Sinbad the Hammal, and I carry folk's goods on my head for hire."

The house-master smiled and rejoined, "Know, O Porter that thy name is even as mine, for I am Sinbad the Sailor; and now, O Porter, I would have thee let me hear the couplets thou recitedst at the gate anon."

The Porter was abashed and replied, "Allah upon thee! Excuse me, for toil and travail and lack of luck when the hand is empty, teach a man ill manners and boorish ways."

Said the host, "Be not ashamed; thou art become my brother; but repeat to me the verses, for they pleased me whenas I heard thee recite them at the gate."

Hereupon the Porter repeated the couplets and they delighted the merchant, who said to him, "Know, O Hammal, that my story is a wonderful one, and thou shalt hear all that befel me and all I underwent ere I rose to this state of prosperity and became the lord of this place wherein thou seest me; for I came not to this high estate save after travail sore and perils galore, and how much toil and trouble have I not suffered in days of yore! I have made seven voyages, by each of which hangeth a marvellous tale, such as confoundeth the reason, and all this came to pass by doom of fortune and fate; for from what destiny doth write there is neither refuge nor flight. Know, then, good my lords (continued he) that I am about to relate

THE FIRST VOYAGE OF SINBAD THE SAILOR

My father was a merchant, one of the notables of my native place, a monied man and ample of means, who died whilst I was yet a child, leaving me much wealth in money and lands and farmhouses. When I grew up, I laid hands on the whole and ate of the best and drank freely and wore rich clothes and lived lavishly, companioning and consorting with youths of my own age, and considering that this course of life would continue for ever and ken no change. Thus did I for a long time, but at last I awoke from my heedlessness and, returning to my senses, I found my wealth had become unwealth and my condition ill-conditioned and all I once hent had left my hand. And recovering my reason I was stricken with dismay and confusion and bethought me of a saying of our lord Solomon, son of David (on whom be peace!), which I had heard aforetime from my father, "Three things are better than other three; the day of death is better than the day of birth, a live dog is better than a dead lion and the grave is better than want." Then I got together my remains of estates and property and sold all, even my clothes, for three thousand dirhams, with which I resolved to travel to foreign parts, remembering the saying of the poet,

> By means of toil man shall scale the height;
> Who to fame aspires mustn't sleep o' night:
> Who seeketh pearl in the deep must dive,
> Winning weal and wealth by his main and might:
> And who seeketh Fame without toil and strife
> Th' impossible seeketh and wasteth life.

So taking heart I bought me goods, merchandise and all needed for a voyage and, impatient to be at sea, I embarked, with a company of merchants, on board a ship bound for Bassorah. There we again embarked and sailed many days and nights, and we passed from isle to isle and sea to sea and shore to shore, buying and selling and bartering everywhere the ship touched, and continued our course till we came to an island as it were a garth of the gardens of Paradise. Here the captain cast anchor and making fast to the shore, put out the landing planks. So all on board landed and made furnaces and lighting fires therein, busied themselves in various ways, some cooking and some washing, whilst other some walked about the island for solace, and the crew fell to eating and drinking and playing and sporting. I was one of the walkers but, as we were thus engaged, behold the master who was standing on the gunwale cried out to us at the top of his voice, saying, "Ho there! passengers, run for your lives and hasten back to the ship and leave your gear and save yourselves from destruction, Allah preserve you! For this island whereon ye stand is no true island, but a great fish stationary a-middlemost of the sea, whereon the sand hath settled and trees have sprung up of old time, so that it is become like unto an island; but, when ye lighted fires on it, it felt the heat and moved; and in a moment it will sink with you into the sea and ye will all be drowned. So leave your gear and seek your safety ere ye die!"

All who heard him left gear and goods, clothes washed and unwashed, fire pots and brass cooking-pots, and fled back to the ship for their lives, and some reached it while others (amongst whom was I) did not, for suddenly the island shook and sank into the abysses of the deep, with all that were thereon, and the dashing sea surged over it with clashing waves. I sank with the others down, down into the deep, but Almighty Allah preserved me from drowning and threw in my way a great wooden tub of those that had served the ship's company for tubbing. I gripped it for the sweetness of life and, bestriding it like one riding, paddled with my feet like oars, whilst the waves tossed me as in sport right and left. Meanwhile the captain made sail and departed with those who had reached the ship, regardless of the drowning and the drowned; and I ceased not following the vessel with my eyes, till she was hid from sight and I made sure of death. Darkness closed in upon me while in this plight and the winds and waves bore me on all that night and the next day, till the tub brought to with me under the lee of a lofty island, with trees overhanging the tide. I caught hold of a branch and by its aid clambered up on to the land, after coming nigh upon death; but when I reached the shore, I found my legs cramped and numbed and my feet bore traces of the nibbling of fish upon their soles; withal I had felt nothing for excess of anguish and fatigue. I threw myself down on the island ground, like a dead man, and drowned in desolation swooned away, nor did I return to my senses till next morning, when the sun rose and revived me. But I found my feet swollen, so made shift to move by shuffling on my breech and crawling on my knees, for in that island were found store of fruits and springs of sweet water. I ate of the fruits which strengthened me; and thus I abode days and nights, till my life seemed to return and my spirits began to revive and I was better able to move about. So, after due consideration, I fell to exploring the island and diverting myself with gazing upon all things that Allah Almighty had created there; and rested under the trees from one of which I cut me a staff to lean upon. One day as I walked along the marge, I caught sight of some object in the distance and thought it a wild beast or one of the monster-creatures of the sea; but, as I drew near it, looking hard the while, I saw that it was a noble mare, tethered on the beach. Presently I went up to her, but she cried out against me with a great cry, so that I trembled for fear and turned to go away, when there came forth a man from under the earth and followed me, crying out and saying, "Who and whence art thou, and what caused thee to come hither?"

"O my lord," answered I, "I am in very sooth, a waif, a stranger, and was left to drown with sundry others by the ship we voyaged in; but Allah graciously sent me a wooden tub; so I saved myself thereon and it floated with me, till the waves cast me up on this island."

When he heard this, he took my hand and saying, "Come with me," carried me into a great Sardab, or underground chamber, which was spacious as a saloon. He made me sit down at its upper end; then he brought me somewhat of food and, being a hungered, I ate till I was satisfied and refreshed; and when he had put me at mine ease he questioned me of myself, and I told him all that had befallen me from first to last; and, as he wondered at my adventure, I said, "By Allah, O my lord, excuse me; I have told thee the truth of my case and the accident which betided me; and now I desire that thou tell me who thou art and why thou abidest here under the earth and why thou hast tethered yonder mare on the brink of the sea."

Answered he, "Know, that I am one of the several who are stationed in different parts of this island, and we are of the grooms of King Mihrjan and under our hand are all his horses. Every month, about new-moon tide we bring hither our best mares which have never been covered, and picket them on the sea-shore and hide ourselves in this place under the ground, so that none may espy us. Presently, the stallions of the sea scent the mares

and come up out of the water and seeing no one, leap the mares and do their will of them. When they have covered them, they try to drag them away with them, but cannot, by reason of the leg-ropes; so they cry out at them and butt at them and kick them, which we hearing, know that the stallions have dismounted; so we run out and shout at them, whereupon they are startled and return in fear to the sea. Then the mares conceive by them and bear colts and fillies worth a mint of money, nor is their like to be found on earth's face. This is the time of the coming forth of the sea-stallions; and Inshallah! I will bear thee to King Mihrjan and show thee our country. And know that hadst thou not happened on us thou hadst perished miserably and none had known of thee: but I will be the means of the saving of thy life and of thy return to thine own land."

I called down blessings on him and thanked him for his kindness and courtesy; and, while we were yet talking, behold, the stallion came up out of the sea; and, giving a great cry, sprang upon the mare and covered her. When he had done his will of her, he dismounted and would have carried her away with him, but could not by reason of the tether. She kicked and cried out at him, whereupon the groom took a sword and target and ran out of the underground saloon, smiting the buckler with the blade and calling to his company, who came up shouting and brandishing spears; and the stallion took fright at them and plunging into the sea, like a buffalo, disappeared under the waves. After this we sat awhile, till the rest of the grooms came up, each leading a mare, and seeing me with their fellow-Syce, questioned me of my case and I repeated my story to them. Thereupon they drew near me and spreading the table, ate and invited me to eat; so I ate with them, after which they took horse and mounting me on one of the mares, set out with me and fared on without ceasing, till we came to the capital city of King Mihrjan, and going in to him acquainted him with my story. Then he sent for me, and when they set me before him and salams had been exchanged, he gave me a cordial welcome and wishing me long life bade me tell him my tale. So I related to him all that I had seen and all that had befallen me from first to last, whereat he marvelled and said to me, "By Allah, O my son, thou hast indeed been miraculously preserved! Were not the term of thy life a long one, thou hadst not escaped from these straits; but praised by Allah for safety!"

Then he spoke cheerily to me and entreated me with kindness and consideration: moreover, he made me his agent for the port and registrar of all ships that entered the harbour. I attended him regularly, to receive his commandments, and he favoured me and did me all manner of kindness and invested me with costly and splendid robes. Indeed, I was high in credit with him, as an intercessor for the folk and an intermediary between them and him, when they wanted aught of him. I abode thus a great while and, as often as I passed through the city to the port, I questioned the merchants and travellers and sailors of the city of Baghdad; so haply I might hear of an occasion to return to my native land, but could find none who knew it or knew any who resorted thither. At this I was chagrined, for I was weary of long strangerhood; and my disappointment endured for a time till one day, going in to King Mihrjan, I found him with a company of Indians. I saluted them and they returned my salam; and politely welcomed me and asked me of my country. When they asked me of my country I questioned them of theirs and they told me that they were of various castes, some being called Shakiriyah who are the noblest of their castes and neither oppress nor offer violence to any, and others Brahmans, a folk who abstain from wine, but live in delight and solace and merriment and own camels and horses and cattle. Moreover, they told me that the people of India are divided into two-and-seventy castes, and I marvelled at this with exceeding marvel. Amongst other things that I saw in King Mihrjan's dominions was an island called Kasil, wherein all night is heard the beating of drums and tabrets; but we were told by the neighbouring islanders and by travellers that the inhabitants are people of diligence and judgment. In this sea I saw also a fish two hundred cubits long and the fishermen fear it; so they strike together pieces of wood and put it to flight. I also saw another fish, with a head like that of an owl, besides many other wonders and rarities, which it would be tedious to recount. I occupied myself thus in visiting the islands till, one day, as I stood in the port, with a staff in my hand, according to my custom, behold, a great ship, wherein were many merchants, came sailing for the harbour.

When it reached the small inner port where ships anchor under the city, the master furled his sails and making fast to the shore, put out the landing-planks, whereupon the crew fell to breaking bulk and landing cargo whilst I stood by, taking written note of them. They were long in bringing the goods ashore so I asked the master, "Is there aught left in thy ship?" and he answered, "O my lord, there are divers bales of merchandise in the hold, whose owner was drowned from amongst us at one of the islands on our course; so his goods remained in our charge by way of trust and we purpose to sell them and note their price, that we may convey it to his people in the city of Baghdad, the Home of Peace."

"What was the merchant's name?" quoth I, and quoth he, "Sinbad the Sailor"; whereupon I straitly considered him and knowing him, cried

129

out to him with a great cry, saying, "O captain, I am that Sinbad the Sailor who travelled with other merchants; and when the fish heaved and thou calledst to us some saved themselves and others sank, I being one of them. But Allah Almighty threw in my way a great tub of wood, of those the crew had used to wash withal, and the winds and waves carried me to this island, where by Allah's grace, I fell in with King Mihrjan's grooms and they brought me hither to the King their master. When I told him my story, he entreated me with favour and made me his harbour-master, and I have prospered in his service and found acceptance with him. These bales, therefore are mine, the goods which God hath given me."

The other exclaimed, "There is no Majesty and there is no Might save in Allah, the Glorious, the Great! Verily, there is neither conscience nor good faith left among men!"

Said I, "O Rais, what mean these words, seeing that I have told thee my case?"

And he answered, "Because thou heardest me say that I had with me goods whose owner was drowned, thou thinkest to take them without right; but this is forbidden by law to thee, for we saw him drown before our eyes, together with many other passengers, nor was one of them saved. So how canst thou pretend that thou art the owner of the goods?"

"O captain," said I, "listen to my story and give heed to my words, and my truth will be manifest to thee; for lying and leasing are the letter-marks of the hypocrites." Then I recounted to him all that had befallen me since I sailed from Baghdad with him to the time when we came to the fish-island where we were nearly drowned; and I reminded him of certain matters which had passed between us; whereupon both he and the merchants were certified at the truth of my story and recognized me and gave me joy of my deliverance, saying, "By Allah, we thought not that thou hadst escaped drowning! But the Lord hath granted thee new life." Then they delivered my bales to me, and I found my name written thereon, nor was aught thereof lacking.

So I opened them and making up a present for King Mihrjan of the finest and costliest of the contents, caused the sailors carry it up to the palace, where I went in to the King and laid my present at his feet, acquainting him with what had happened, especially concerning the ship and my goods; whereat he wondered with exceeding wonder and the truth of all that I had told him was made manifest to him. His affection for me redoubled after that and he showed me exceeding honour and bestowed on me a great present in return for mine. Then I sold my bales and what other matters

I owned making a great profit on them, and bought me other goods and gear of the growth and fashion of the island-city. When the merchants were about to start on their homeward voyage, I embarked on board the ship all that I possessed, and going in to the King, thanked him for all his favours and friendship and craved his leave to return to my own land and friends. He farewelled me and bestowed on me great store of the country-stuffs and produce; and I took leave of him and embarked. Then we set sail and fared on nights and days, by the permission of Allah Almighty; and Fortune served us and Fate favoured us, so that we arrived in safety at Bassorah-city where I landed rejoiced at my safe return to my natal soil. After a short stay, I set out for Baghdad, the House of Peace, with store of goods and commodities of great price. Reaching the city in due time, I went straight to my own quarter and entered my house where all my friends and kinsfolk came to greet me. Then I bought me eunuchs and concubines, servants and negro slaves till I had a large establishment, and I bought me houses, and lands and gardens, till I was richer and in better case than before, and returned to enjoy the society of my friends and familiars more assiduously than ever, forgetting all I had suffered of fatigue and hardship and strangerhood and every peril of travel; and I applied myself to all manner joys and solaces and delights, eating the dantiest viands and drinking the deliciousest wines; and my wealth allowed this state of things to endure.

"This, then, is the story of my first voyage, and to-morrow, Inshallah! I will tell you the tale of the second of my seven voyages" (saith he who telleth the tale). Then Sinbad the Sailor made Sinbad the Landsman sup with him and bade give him an hundred gold pieces, saying, "Thou hast cheered us with thy company this day." The Porter thanked him and, taking the gift, went his way, pondering that which he had heard and marvelling mightily at what things betide mankind. He passed the night in his own place and with early morning repaired to the abode of Sinbad the Sailor, who received him with honour and seated him by his side. As soon as the rest of the company was assembled, he set meat and drink before them and, when they had well eaten and drunken and were merry, he took up his discourse and recounted to them in these words the narrative of

THE SECOND VOYAGE OF SINBAD THE SAILOR

Know, O my brother, that I was living a most comfortable and enjoyable life, in all solace and delight, as I told you yesterday, until my

mind became possessed with the thought of travelling about the world of men and seeing their cities and islands; and a longing seized me to traffic and to make money by trade. Upon this resolve I took a great store of cash and, buying goods and gear fit for travel, bound them up in bales. Then I went down to the river-bank, where I found a noble ship and brand-new about to sail, equipped with sails of fine cloth and well manned and provided; so I took passage in her, with a number of other merchants, and after embarking our goods we weighed anchor the same day. Right fair was our voyage and we sailed from place to place and from isle to isle; and whenever we anchored we met a crowd of merchants and notables and customers, and we took to buying and selling and bartering. At last Destiny brought us to an island, fair and verdant, in trees abundant, with yellow-ripe fruits luxuriant, and flowers fragrant and birds warbling soft descant; and streams crystalline and radiant; but no sign of man showed to the descrier, no, not a blower of the fire. The captain made fast with us to this island, and the merchants and sailors landed and walked about, enjoying the shade of the trees and the song of the birds, that chanted the praises of the One, the Victorious, and marvelling at the works of the Omnipotent King. I landed with the rest; and, sitting down by a spring of sweet water that welled up among the trees, took out some vivers I had with me and ate of that which Allah Almighty had allotted unto me. And so sweet was the zephyr and so fragrant were the flowers, that presently I waxed drowsy and, lying down in that place, was soon drowned in sleep.

When I awoke, I found myself alone, for the ship had sailed and left me behind, nor had one of the merchants or sailors bethought himself of me. I seared the island right and left, but found neither man nor Jinn, whereat I was beyond measure troubled and my gall was like to burst for stress of chagrin and anguish and concern, because I was left quite alone, without aught of wordly gear or meat or drink, weary and heart-broken. So I gave myself up for lost and said, "Not always doth the crock escape the shock. I was saved the first time by finding one who brought me from the desert island to an inhabited place, but now there is no hope for me."

Then I fell to weeping and wailing and gave myself up to an access of rage, blaming myself for having again ventured upon the perils and hardships of voyage, whenas I was at my ease in mine own house in mine own land, taking my pleasure with good meat and good drink and good clothes and lacking nothing, neither money nor goods. And I repented me of having left Baghdad, and this the more after all the travails and dangers I had undergone in my first voyage, wherein I had so narrowly escaped destruction, and exclaimed "Verily we are Allah's and unto Him we are returning!" I was indeed even as one mad and Jinn-struck and presently I rose and walked about the island, right and left and every whither, unable for trouble to sit or tarry in any one place.

Then I climbed a tall tree and looked in all directions, but saw nothing save sky and sea and trees and birds and isles and sands. However, after a while my eager glances fell upon some great white thing, afar off in the interior of the island; so I came down from the tree and made for that which I had seen; and behold, it was a huge white dome rising high in air and of vast compass. I walked all around it, but found no door thereto, nor could I muster strength or nimbleness by reason of its exceeding smoothness and slipperiness. So I marked the spot where I stood and went round about the dome to measure its circumference which I found fifty good paces. And as I stood, casting about how to gain an entrance the day being near its fall and the sun being near the horizon, behold, the sun was suddenly hidden from me and the air became dull and dark. Methought a cloud had come over the sun, but it was the season of summer; so I marvelled at this and lifting my head looked steadfastly at the sky, when I saw that the cloud was none other than an enormous bird, of gigantic girth and inordinately wide of wing which, as it flew through the air, veiled the sun and hid it from the island.

At this sight my wonder redoubled and I remembered a story I had heard aforetime of pilgrims and travellers, how in a certain island dwelleth a huge bird, called the "Rukh" which feedeth its young on elephants; and I was certified that the dome which caught my sight was none other than a Rukh's egg. As I looked and wondered at the marvellous works of the Almighty, the bird alighted on the dome and brooded over it with its wings covering it and its legs stretched out behind it on the ground, and in this posture it fell asleep, glory be to Him who sleepeth not! When I saw this, I arose and, unwinding my turband from my head, doubled it and twisted it into a rope, with which I girt my middle and bound my waist fast to the legs of the Rukh, saying in myself, "Peradventure, this bird may carry me to a land of cities and inhabitants, and that will be better than abiding in this desert island."

I passed the night watching and fearing to sleep, lest the bird should fly away with me unawares; and, as soon as the dawn broke and morn shone, the Rukh rose off its egg and spreading its wings with a great cry flew up into the air dragging me with it; nor ceased it to soar and to tower till I thought it had reached the limit of the firmament; after which it descended, earthwards, little by little, till it lighted on the top of a high hill. As soon as I

133

found myself on the hard ground, I made haste to unbind myself, quaking for fear of the bird, though it took no heed of me nor even felt me; and, loosing my turband from its feet, I made off with my best speed. Presently, I saw it catch up in its huge claws something from the earth and rise with it high in air, and observing it narrowly I saw it to be a serpent big of bulk and gigantic of girth, wherewith it flew away clean out of sight. I marvelled at this and faring forwards found myself on a peak overlooking a valley, exceeding great and wide and deep, and bounded by vast mountains that spired high in air: none could descry their summits, for the excess of their height, nor was any able to climb up thereto. When I saw this, I blamed myself for that which I had done and said, "Would Heaven I had tarried in the island! It was better than this wild desert; for there I had at least fruits to eat and water to drink, and here are neither trees nor fruits nor streams. But there is no Majesty and there is no Might save in Allah, the Glorious, the Great! Verily, as often as I am quit of one peril, I fall into a worse danger and a more grievous." However, I took courage and walking along the Wady found that its soil was of diamond, the stone wherewith they pierce minerals and precious stones and porcelain and the onyx, for that it is a dense stone and a dure, whereon neither iron nor hardhead hath effect, neither can we cut off aught therefrom or break it, save by means of leadstone. Moreover, the valley swarmed with snakes and vipers, each big as a palm tree, that would have made but one gulp of an elephant; and they came out by night, hiding during the day, lest the Rukhs and eagles pounce on them and tear them to pieces, as was their wont, why I wot not. And I repented of what I had done and said, "By Allah, I have made haste to bring destruction upon myself!"

The day began to wane as I went along and I looked about for a place where I might pass the night, being in fear of the serpents; and I took no thought of meat and drink in my concern for my life. Presently, I caught sight of a cave near-hand, with a narrow doorway; so I entered and seeing a great stone close to the mouth, I rolled it up and stopped the entrance, saying to myself, "I am safe here for the night; and as soon as it is day, I will go forth and see what destiny will do." Then I looked within the cave and saw to the upper end a great serpent brooding on her eggs, at which my flesh quaked and my hair stood on end; but I raised my eyes to Heaven and, committing my case to fate and lot, abode all that night without sleep till daybreak, when I rolled back the stone from the mouth of the cave and went forth, staggering like a drunken man and giddy with watching and fear and hunger. As in this sore case I walked along the valley, behold, there fell down before me a slaughtered beast; but I saw no one, whereat I marvelled with great marvel and presently remembered a story I had heard aforetime of traders and pilgrims and travellers; how the mountains where are the diamonds are full of perils and terrors, nor can any fare through them; but the merchants who traffic in diamonds have a device by which they obtain them, that is to say, they take a sheep and slaughter and skin it and cut it in pieces and cast them down from the mountain-tops into the valley-sole, where the meat being fresh and sticky with blood, some of the gems cleave to it. There they leave it till mid-day, when the eagles and vultures swoop down upon it and carry it in their claws to the mountain-summits, whereupon the merchants come and shout at them and scare them away from the meat. Then they come and, taking the diamonds which they find sticking to it, go their ways with them and leave the meat to the birds and beasts; nor can any come at the diamonds but by this device. So, when I saw the slaughtered beast fall (he pursued) and bethought me of the story, I went up to it and filled my pockets and shawl-girdle and turband and the folds of my clothes with the choicest diamonds; and, as I was thus engaged, down fell before me another great piece of meat. Then with my unrolled turband and lying on my back, I set the bit on my breast so that I was hidden by the meat, which was thus raised above the ground. Hardly had I gripped it, when an eagle swooped down upon the flesh and, seizing it with his talons, flew up with it high in air and me clinging thereto, and ceased not its flight till it alighted on the head of one of the mountains where, dropping the carcass he fell to rending it; but, behold, there arose behind him a great noise of shouting and clattering of wood, whereat the bird took fright and flew away. Then I loosed off myself the meat, with clothes daubed with blood therefrom, and stood up by its side; whereupon up came the merchant, who had cried out at the eagle, and seeing me standing there, bespoke me not, but was affrighted at me and shook with fear. However, he went up to the carcass and turning it over, found no diamonds sticking to it, whereat he gave a great cry and exclaimed, "Harrow, my disappointment! There is no Majesty and there is no Might save in Allah with whom we seek refuge from Satan the stoned!" And he bemoaned himself and beat hand upon hand, saying, "Alas, the pity of it! How cometh this?"

Then I went up to him and he said to me, "Who art thou and what causeth thee to come hither?"

And I, "Fear not, I am a man and a good man and a merchant. My story is a wondrous and my adventures marvellous and the manner of my

135

coming hither is prodigious. So be of good cheer, thou shalt receive of me what shall rejoice thee, for I have with me great plenty of diamonds and I will give thee thereof what shall suffice thee; for each is better than aught thou couldst get otherwise. So fear nothing." The man rejoiced thereat and thanked and blessed me; then we talked together till the other merchants, hearing me in discourse with their fellow, came up and saluted me; for each of them had thrown down his piece of meat. And as I went off with them I told them my whole story, how I had suffered hardships at sea and the fashion of my reaching the valley. But I gave the owner of the meat a number of the stones I had by me, so they all wished me joy of my escape, saying, "By Allah a new life hath been decreed to thee, for none ever reached yonder valley and came off thence alive before thee; but praised be Allah for thy safety!"

We passed the night together in a safe and pleasant place, beyond measure rejoiced at my deliverance from the Valley of Serpents and my arrival in an inhabited land; and on the morrow we set out and journeyed over the mighty range of mountains, seeing many serpents in the valley, till we came to a fair great island, wherein was a garden of huge camphor trees under each of which an hundred men might take shelter. When the folk have a mind to get camphor, they bore into the upper part of the bole with a long iron; whereupon the liquid camphor, which is the sap of the tree, floweth out and they catch it in vessels, where it concreteth like gum; but, after this, the tree dieth and becometh firewood. Moreover, there is in this island a kind of wild beast, called "Rhinoceros," that pastureth as do steers and buffalos with us; but it is a huge brute, bigger of body than the camel and like it feedeth upon the leaves and twigs of trees. It is a remarkable animal with a great and thick horn, ten cubits long, amiddleward its head; wherein, when cleft in twain, is the likeness of a man. Voyagers and pilgrims and travellers declare that this beast called "Karkadan" will carry off a great elephant on its horn and graze about the island and the sea-coast therewith and take no heed of it, till the elephant dieth and its fat, melting in the sun, runneth down into the rhinoceros's eyes and blindeth him, so that he lieth down on the shore. Then comes the bird Rukh and carrieth off both the rhinoceros's eyes and blindeth him, so that he lieth down on the shore. Then comes the bird Rukh and carrieth off both the rhinoceros and that which is on its horn to feed its young withal. Moreover, I saw in this island many kinds of oxen and buffalos, whose like are not found in our country. Here I sold some of the diamonds which I had by me for gold dinars and silver dirhams and bartered others for the produce of the country; and, loading them upon beasts of burden, fared on with the merchants from valley to valley and town to town, buying and selling and viewing foreign countries and the works and creatures of Allah, till we came to Bassorah-city, where we abode a few days, after which I continued my journey to Baghdad.

I foregathered with my friends and relations and gave alms and largesse and bestowed curious gifts and made presents to all my friends and companions. Then I betook myself to eating well and drinking well and wearing fine clothes and making merry with my fellows, and forgot all my sufferings in the pleasures of return to the solace and delight of life, with light heart and broadened breast. And every one who heard of my return came and questioned me of my adventures and of foreign countries, and I related to them all that had befallen me, and the much I had suffered, whereat they wondered and gave me joy of my safe return.

"This, then is the end of the story of my second voyage; and to-morrow, Inshallah! I will tell you what befel me in my third voyage." The company marvelled at his story and supped with him; after which he ordered an hundred dinars of gold to be given to the Porter, who took the sum with many thanks and blessings (which he stinted not even when he reached home) and went his way, wondering at what he had heard. Next morning as soon as day came in its sheen and shone, he rose and praying the dawn-prayer, repaired to the house of Sinbad the Sailor, and went in and gave him good-morrow. The merchant welcomed him and made him sit with him, till the rest of the company arrived; and when they had well eaten and drunken and were merry, their host began by saying, "Hearken, O my brothers, to what I am about to tell you; for it is even more wondrous than what you have already heard; but Allah alone kenneth what things His Omniscience concealed from man! And listen to

THE THIRD VOYAGE OF SINBAD THE SAILOR

As I told you yesterday, I returned from my second voyage overjoyed at my safety and with great increase of wealth, Allah having requited me all that I had wasted and lost, and I abode awhile in Baghdad-city savouring the utmost ease and prosperity and comfort and happiness, till the carnal man was once more seized with longing for travel and diversion and adventure, and yearned after traffic and lucre and emolument, for that the human heart is naturally prone to evil. So making up my mind I laid in great plenty of goods suitable for a sea-voyage and repairing to Bassorah, went down to the shore and found there a fine ship ready to sail, with a full crew and a numerous company of merchants, men of worth and substance; faith, piety and consideration. I embarked with them and we set sail on the blessing of Allah Almighty and on His aidance and His favour to bring our voyage to a safe and prosperous issue and already we congratulated one another on our good fortune and boon voyage. We fared on from sea to sea and from island to island and city to city, in all delight and contentment, buying and selling wherever we touched, and taking our solace and our pleasure, till one day when, as we sailed athwart the dashing sea, swollen with clashing billows, behold, the master (who stood on the gunwale examining the ocean in all directions) cried out with a great cry, and buffeted his face and pluckt out his beard and rent his raiment, and bade furl the sail and cast the anchors. So we said to him, "O Rais, what is the matter?"

"Know, O my brethren (Allah preserve you!), that the wind hath gotten the better of us and hath driven us out of our course into mid-ocean, and destiny, for our ill luck, hath brought us to the Mountain of the Zughb, a hairy folk like apes, among whom no man ever fell and came forth alive; and my heart presageth that we all be dead men."

Hardly had the master made an end of his speech when the apes were upon us. They surrounded the ship on all sides swarming like locusts and crowding the shore. They were the most frightful of wild creatures, covered with black hair like felt, foul of favour and small of stature, being but four spans high, yellow-eyed and black-faced; none knoweth their language nor what they are, and they shun the company of men. We feared to slay them or strike them or drive them away, because of their inconceivable multitude; lest, if we hurt one, the rest fall on us and slay us, for numbers prevail over courage; so we let them do their will, albeit we feared they would plunder our goods and gear. They swarmed up the cables and gnawed them asunder, and on like wise they did with all the ropes of the ship, so that it fell off from the wind and stranded upon their mountainous coast. Then they laid hands on all the merchants and crew, and landing us on the island, made off with the ship and its cargo and went their ways, we wot not whither.

We were thus left on the island, eating of its fruits and pot-herbs and drinking of its streams till, one day, we espied in its midst what seemed an inhabited house. So we made for it as fast as our feet could carry us and behold, it was a castle strong and tall, compassed about with a lofty wall, and having a two-leaved gate of ebony-wood both of which leaves open stood. We entered and found within a space wide and bare like a great square, round which stood many high doors open thrown, and at the farther end a long bench of stone and brasiers, with cooking gear hanging thereon and about it great plenty of bones; but we saw no one and marvelled thereat with exceeding wonder. Then we sat down in the courtyard a little while and presently falling asleep, slept from the forenoon till sundown, when lo! the earth trembled under our feet and the air rumbled with a terrible tone. Then there came down upon us, from the top of the castle, a huge creature in the likeness of a man, black of colour, tall and big of bulk, as he were a great date-tree, with eyes like coals of fire and eye-teeth like boar's tusks and a vast big gape like the mouth of a well. Moreover, he had long loose lips like camel's, hanging down upon his breast and ears like two Jarms falling over his shoulder-blades and the nails of his hands were like the claws of a lion. When we saw this frightful giant, we were like to faint and every moment increased our fear and terror; and we became as dead men for excess of horror and affright.

After trampling upon the earth, he sat awhile on the bench; then he arose and coming to us seized me by the arm choosing me out from among my comrades the merchants. He took me up in his hand and turning me over felt me, as a butcher feeleth a sheep he is about to slaughter, and I but a little mouthful in his hands; but finding me lean and fleshless for stress of toil and trouble and weariness, let me go and took up another, whom in like manner he turned over and felt and let go; nor did he cease to feel and turn over the rest of us, one after another, till he came to the master of the ship. Now he was a sturdy, stout, broad-shouldered wight, fat and in full vigour; so he pleased the giant, who seized him, as a butcher seizeth a beast, and throwing him down, set his foot on his neck and brake it; after which he fetched a long spit and thrusting it up his backside, brought it forth of the crown of his head. Then, lighting a fierce fire, he set over it the spit with the Rais thereon, and turned it over the coals, till the flesh was roasted, when he took the spit off the fire and set it like a Kabab-stick before him. Then he tore the body, limb from limb, as one jointeth a chicken and, rending the flesh with his nails, fell to eating of it and gnawing the bones, till there was nothing left but some of these, which he threw on one side of the wall. This done, he sat for a while; then he lay down on the stone-bench and fell asleep, snarking and snoring like the gurgling of a lamb or a cow with its throat cut; nor did he awake till morning, when he rose and fared forth and went his ways.

As soon as we were certified that he was gone, we began to talk with one another, weeping and bemoaning ourselves for the risk we ran, and saying, "Would Heaven we had been drowned in the sea or that the apes had eaten us! That were better than to be roasted over the coals; by Allah, this is a vile, foul death! But whatso the Lord willeth must come to pass and there is no Majesty and there is no Might, save in Him, the Glorious, the Great! We shall assuredly perish miserably and none will know of us; as there is no escape for us from this place."

Then we arose and roamed about the island, hoping that haply we might find a place to hide us in or a means of flight, for indeed death was a light matter to us, provided we were not roasted over the fire and eaten. However, we could find no hiding-place and the evening overtook us; so, of the excess of our terror, we returned to the castle and sat down awhile. Presently, the earth trembled under our feet and the black ogre came up to us and turning us over, felt one after other, till he found a man to his liking, whom he took and served as he had done the captain, killing and roasting and eating him: after which he lay down on the bench and slept all night, snarking and snoring like a beast with its throat cut, till daybreak, when he arose and went out as before.

Then we drew together and conversed and said one to other, "By Allah, we had better throw ourselves into the sea and be drowned than die roasted; for this is an abominable death!"

Quoth one of us, "Hear ye my words! let us cast about to kill him, and be at peace from the grief of him and rid the Moslems of his barbarity and tyranny."

Then said I, "Hear me, O my brothers; if there is nothing for it but to slay him, let us carry some of this firewood and planks down to the sea-shore and make us a boat wherein, if we succeed in slaughtering him, we may either embark and let the waters carry us whither Allah willeth, or else abide here till some ship pass, when we will take passage in it. If we fail to kill him, we will embark in the boat and put out to sea; and if we be drowned, we shall at least escape being roasted over a kitchen fire with sliced weasands; whilst, if we escape, we escape, and if we be drowned, we die martyrs."

"By Allah," said they all, "this rede is a right"; and we agreed upon this, and set about carrying it out.

So we haled down to the beach the pieces of wood which lay about the bench; and, making a boat, moored it to the strand, after which we stowed therein somewhat of victual and returned to the castle. As soon as evening fell the earth trembled under our feet and in came the blackamoor upon us, snarling like a dog about to bite. He came up to us and feeling us and turning us over one by one, took one of us and did with him as he had done before and ate him, after which he lay down on the bench and snored and snorted like thunder. As soon as we were assured that he slept, we arose and taking two iron spits of those standing there, heated them in the fiercest of the fire, till they were red-hot, like burning coals, when we gripped fast hold of them and going up to the giant, as he lay snoring on the bench, thrust them into his eyes and pressed upon them, all of us, with our united might, so that his eyeballs burst and he became stone blind. Thereupon he cried with a great cry, whereat our hearts trembled, and springing up from the bench, he fell a-groping after us, blind-fold. We fled from him right and left and he saw us not, for his sight was altogether blent; but we were in terrible fear of him and made sure we were dead men despairing of escape. Then he found the door, feeling for it with his hands and went out roaring aloud; and behold, the earth shook under us, for the noise of his roaring, and we quaked for fear. As he quitted the castle we followed him and betook ourselves to the place where we had moored our boat, saying to one another, "If this accursed abide absent till the going down of the sun and come not to the castle, we shall know that he is dead; and if he come back, we will embark in the boat and paddle till we escape, committing our affair to Allah."

But, as we spoke, behold, up came the blackamoor with other two as they were Ghuls, fouler and more frightful than he, with eyes like red-hot coals; which when we saw, we hurried into the boat and casting off the moorings paddled away and pushed out to sea. As soon as the ogres caught sight of us, they cried out at us and running down to the sea-shore, fell a-pelting us with rocks, whereof some fell amongst us and others fell into the sea. We paddled with all our might till we were beyond their reach, but the most part of us were slain by the rock-throwing, and the winds and waves sported with us and carried us into the midst of the dashing sea, swollen with billows clashing. We knew not whither we went and my fellows died one after another, till there remained but three, myself and two others on board the boat for, as often as one died, we threw him into the sea.

We were sore exhausted for stress of hunger, but we took courage and heartened one another and worked for dear life and paddled with main and might, till the winds cast us upon an island, as we were dead men for fatigue and fear and famine. We landed on the island and walked about it for a while, finding that it abounded in trees and streams and birds; and we ate of the fruits and rejoiced in our escape from the black and our deliverance from the perils of the sea; and thus we did till nightfall, when we lay down and fell asleep for excess of fatigue. But we had hardly closed our eyes before we were aroused by a hissing sound like the sough of wind, and awaking, saw a serpent like a dragon, a seld-seen sight, of monstrous make and belly of enormous bulk which lay in a circle around us. Presently it reared its head and, seizing one of my companions, swallowed him up to his shoulders; then it gulped down the rest of him, and we heard his ribs crack in its belly. Presently it went its way, and we abode in sore amazement and grief for our comrade and mortal fear for ourselves, saying, "By Allah, this is a marvellous thing! Each kind of death that threatened us is more terrible than the last. We were rejoicing in our escape from the black ogre and our deliverance from the perils of the sea; but now we have fallen into that which is worse. There is no Majesty and there is no Might save in Allah! By the Almighty, we have escaped from the blackamoor and from drowning: but how shall we escape from this abominable and viperish monster?"

Then we walked about the island, eating of its fruits and drinking of its streams till dusk, when we climbed up into a high tree and went to sleep there, I being on the topmost bough. As soon as it was dark night, up came the serpent, looking right and left; and, making for the tree whereon we were, climbed up to my comrade and swallowed him down to his shoulders. Then it coiled about the bole with him, whilst I, who could not take my eyes off the sight, heard his bones crack in its belly, and it swallowed him whole, after which it slid down from the tree. When the day broke and the light showed me that the serpent was gone, I came down, as I were a dead man for stress of fear and anguish, and thought to cast myself into the sea and be at rest from the woes of the world; but could not bring myself to this, for verily life is dear. So I took five pieces of wood, broad and long, and bound one crosswise to the soles of my feet and others in like fashion on my right and left sides and over my breast; and the broadest and largest I bound across my head and made them fast with ropes. Then I lay down on the ground on my back, so that I was completely fenced in by the pieces of wood, which enclosed me like a bier. So as soon as it was dark, up came the serpent, as usual, and made towards me, but could not get at me to swallow me for the wood that fenced me in. So it wriggled round me on every side, whilst I looked on, like one dead by reason of my terror; and every now and then it would glide away and come back; but as often as it tried to come at me, it was hindered by the pieces of wood wherewith I had bound myself on every side. It ceased not to beset me thus from sundown till dawn, but when the light of day shone upon the beast it made off, in the utmost fury and extreme disappointment.

Then I put out my hand and unbound myself, well-nigh down among the dead men for fear and suffering; and went down to the island-shore, whence a ship afar off in the midst of the waves suddenly struck my sight. So I tore off a great branch of a tree and made signs with it to the crew, shouting out the while; which when the ship's company saw they said to another, "We must stand in and see what this is; peradventure 'tis a man."

So they made for the island and presently heard my cries, whereupon they took me on board and questioned me of my case. I told them all my adventures from first to last, whereat they marvelled mightily and covered my shame with some of their clothes. Moreover, they set before me somewhat of food and I ate my fill and I drank cold sweet water and was mightily refreshed; and Allah Almighty quickened me after I was virtually dead. So I praised the Most Highest and thanked Him for His favours and exceeding mercies, and my heart revived in me after utter despair, till meseemed as if all I had suffered were but a dream I had dreamed. We sailed on with a fair wind the Almighty sent us till we came to an island, called Al-Salahitah, which aboundeth in sandal-wood. When the captain cast anchor, the merchants and the sailors landed with their goods to sell and to buy.

Then the captain turned to me and said, "Hark'ee, thou art a stranger and a pauper and tellest us that thou hast undergone frightful hardship; wherefore I have a mind to benefit thee with somewhat that may further thee to thy native land, so thou wilt ever bless me and pray for me."

"So be it," answered I; "thou shalt have my prayers."

Quoth he, "Know then that there was with us a man, a traveller, whom we lost, and we know not if he be alive or dead, for we had no news of him; so I purpose to commit his bales of goods to thy charge, that thou mayst sell them in this island. A part of the proceeds we will give thee as an equivalent for thy pains and service, and the rest we will keep till we return to Baghdad, where we will enquire for his family and deliver it to them, together with the unsold goods. Say me then, wilt thou undertake the charge and land and sell them as other merchants do?"

I replied "Hearkening and obedience to thee, O my lord; and great is thy kindness to me," and thanked him; whereupon he bade the sailors and porters bear the bales in question ashore and commit them to my charge.

The ship's scribe asked him, "O master, what bales are these and what merchant's name shall I write upon them?" and he answered, "Write on them the name of Sinbad the Sailor, him who was with us in the ship and whom we lost at the Rukh's island, and of whom we have no tidings; for we mean this stranger to sell them; and we will give him a part of the price for his pains and keep the rest till we return to Baghdad where, if we find the owner we will make it over to him, and if not, to his family."

And the clerk said, "Thy words are apposite and thy rede is right."

Now when I heard the captain give orders for the bales to be inscribed with my name, I said to myself, "By Allah, I am Sinbad the Sailor!"

So I armed myself with courage and patience and waited till all the merchants had landed and were gathered together, talking and chaffering about buying and selling; then I went up to the captain and asked him, "O my lord, knowest thou what manner of man was this Sinbad, whose goods thou hast committed to me for sale?" and he answered, "I know of him naught save that he was a man from Baghdad-city, Sinbad hight the Sailor, who was drowned with many others when we lay anchored at such an island and I have heard nothing of him since then."

At this I cried out with a great cry and said, "O captain, whom Allah keep! know that I am that Sinbad the Sailor and that I was not drowned, but when thou castest anchor at the island, I landed with the rest of the merchants and crew; and I sat down in a pleasant place by myself and ate somewhat of food I had with me and enjoyed myself till I became drowsy and was drowned in sleep; and when I awoke, I found no ship and none near me. These goods are my goods and these bales are my bales; and all the merchants who fetch jewels from the Valley of Diamonds saw me there and will bear me witness that I am the very Sinbad the Sailor; for I related to them everything that had befallen me and told them how you forgot me and left me sleeping on the island, and that betided me which betided me."

When the passengers and crew heard my words, they gathered about me and some of them believed me and others disbelieved; but presently, behold, one of the merchants, hearing me mention the Valley of Diamonds, came up to me and said to them, "Hear what I say, good people! When I related to you the most wonderful thing in my travels, and I told you that, at the time we cast down our slaughtered animals into the Valley of Serpents (I casting with the rest as was my wont), there came up a man hanging to mine, ye believed me not and gave me the lie."

"Yes," quoth they, "thou didst tell us some such tale, but we had no call to credit thee."

He resumed, "Now this is the very man, by token that he gave me diamonds of great value, and high price whose like are not to be found, requiting me more than would have come up sticking to my quarter of meat; and I companied with him to Bassorah-city, where he took leave of us and went on to his native stead, whilst we returned to our own land. This is he; and he told us his name, Sinbad the Sailor, and how the ship left him on the desert island. And know ye that Allah hath sent him hither, so might the truth of my story be made manifest to you. Moreover, these are his goods for, when he first foregathered with us, he told us of them; and the truth of his words is patent."

Hearing the merchant's speech the captain came up to me and considered me straitly awhile, after which he said, "What was the mark on thy bales?"

"Thus and thus," answered I, and reminded him of somewhat that had passed between him and me, when I shipped with him from Bassorah.

Thereupon he was convinced that I was indeed Sinbad the Sailor and took me round the neck and gave me joy of my safety, saying, "By Allah, O my lord, thy case is indeed wondrous and thy tale marvellous; but lauded be Allah who hath brought thee and me together again, and who hath restored to thee thy goods and gear!"

"Alhamdolillah!" quoth the captain, "lauded be Allah who hath restored unto thee thy goods and gear."

Then I disposed of my merchandise to the best of my skill, and profited largely on them whereat I rejoiced with exceeding joy and congratulated myself on my safety and the recovery of my goods. We ceased not to buy and sell at the several islands till we came to the land of Hind, where we bought cloves and ginger and all manner spices; and thence we fared on to the land of Sind, where also we bought and sold. In these Indian seas, I saw wonders without number or count, amongst others a fish like a cow which bringeth forth its young and suckleth them like human beings; and of its skin bucklers are made. There were eke fishes like asses and camels and tortoises twenty cubits wide. And I saw also a bird that cometh out of a sea-shell and layeth eggs and hatcheth her chicks on the surface of the water, never coming up from the sea to the land.

Then we set sail again with a fair wind and the blessing of Almighty Allah; and, after a prosperous voyage, arrived safe and sound at Bassorah. Here I abode a few days and presently returned to Baghdad where I went at once to my quarter and my house and saluted my family and familiars and friends. I had gained on this voyage what was beyond count and reckoning, so I gave alms and largesse and clad the widow and the orphan, by way of thanksgiving for my happy return, and fell to feasting and making merry with my companions and intimates and forgot everything that had befallen me and all the perils and hardships I had suffered.

"These, then, are the most admirable things I sighted on my third voyage, and to-morrow, an it be the will of Allah, you shall come to me and I will relate the adventures of my fourth voyage, which is still more wonderful than those you have already heard" (saith he who telleth the tale).

Then Sinbad the Sailor bade give Sinbad the Landsman an hundred golden dinars as of wont and called for food. So they spread the tables and the company ate the night-meal and went their ways, marvelling at the tale they had heard. The Porter after taking his gold passed the night in his own house, also wondering at what his namesake the Sailor had told him, and as soon as day broke and the morning showed with its sheen and shone, he rose and praying the dawn-prayer betook himself to Sinbad the Sailor, who returned his salute and received him with an open breast and cheerful favour and made him sit with him till the rest of the company arrived, when he caused set on food and they ate and drank and made merry. Then Sinbad the Sailor bespake them and related to them the narrative of

THE FOURTH VOYAGE OF SINBAD THE SAILOR

Know, O my brethren that after my return from my third voyage and foregathering with my friends, and forgetting all my perils and hardships in the enjoyment of ease and comfort and repose, I was visited one day by a company of merchants who sat down with me and talked of foreign travel and traffic, till the old bad man within me yearned to go with them and enjoy the sight of strange countries, and I longed for the society of the various races of mankind and for traffic and profit. So I resolved to travel with them and buying the necessaries for a long voyage, and great store of costly goods, more than ever before, transported them from Baghdad to Bassorah where I took ship with the merchants in question, who were of the chief of the town.

We set out, trusting in the blessing of Almighty Allah; and with a favouring breeze and the best conditions we sailed from island to island and sea to sea, till, one day, there arose against us a contrary wind and the captain cast out his anchors and brought the ship to a standsill, fearing lest she should founder in mid-ocean. Then we all fell to prayer and humbling ourselves before the Most High; but, as we were thus engaged there smote us a furious squall which tore the sails to rags and tatters: the anchor-cable parted and, the ship foundering, we were cast into the sea, goods and all. I kept myself afloat by swimming half the day, till, when I had given myself up for lost, the Almighty threw in my way one of the planks of the ship, whereon I and some others of the merchants scrambled onto a plank with some others of the merchants and, mounting it as we would a horse, paddled with our feet in the sea. We abode thus a day and a night, the wind and waves helping us on, and on the second day shortly before the mid-time between sunrise and noon the breeze freshened and the sea wrought and the rising waves cast us upon an island, well-nigh dead bodies for weariness and want of sleep, cold and hunger and fear and thirst.

We walked about the shore and found abundance of herbs, whereof we ate enough to keep breath in body and to stay our failing spirits, then lay down and slept till morning hard by the sea. And when morning came with its sheen and shone, we arose and walked about the island to the right and left, till we came in sight of an inhabited house afar off. So we made towards it, and ceased not walking till we reached the door thereof when lo! a number of naked men issued from it and without saluting us or a word said, laid hold of us masterfully and carried us to their king, who signed us to sit. So we sat down and they set food before us such as we knew not and whose like we had never seen in all our lives. My companions ate of it, for stress of hunger, but my stomach revolted from it and I would not eat; and my refraining from it was, by Allah's favour, the cause of my being alive till now: for no sooner had my comrades tasted of it than their reason fled and their condition changed and they began to devour it like madmen possessed of an evil spirit. Then the savages gave them to drink of cocoa-nut oil and anointed them therewith; and straightway after drinking thereof, their eyes turned into their heads and they fell to eating greedily, against their wont.

When I saw this, I was confounded and concerned for them, nor was I less anxious about myself, for fear of the naked folk. So I watched them narrowly, and it was not long before I discovered them to be a tribe of Magian cannibals whose King was a Ghul. All who came to their country or whoso they caught in their valleys or on their roads they brought to this King and fed them upon that food and anointed them with that oil, whereupon their stomachs dilated that they might eat largely, whilst their reason fled and they lost the power of thought and became idiots. Then they stuffed them with cocoa-nut oil and the aforesaid food, till they became fat and gross, when they slaughtered them by cutting their throats and roasted them for the King's eating; but, as for the savages themselves, they ate human flesh raw.

When I saw this, I was sore dismayed for myself and my comrades, who were now become so stupefied that they knew not what was done with them and the naked folk committed them to one who used every day to lead them out and pasture them on the island like cattle. And they wandered amongst the trees and rested at will, thus waxing very fat. As for me, I wasted away and became sickly for fear and hunger and my flesh shrivelled on my bones; which when the savages saw, they left me alone and took no thought of me and so far forgot me that one day I gave them the slip and walking out of their place made for the beach which was distant and there espied a very old man seated on a high place, girt by the waters. I looked at him and knew him for the herdsman, who had charge of pasturing my fellows, and with him were many others in like case. As soon as he saw me, he knew me to be in possession of my reason and not afflicted like the rest whom he was pasturing; so signed to me from afar, as who should say, "Turn back and take the right-hand road, for that will lead thee into the King's highway."

So I turned back, as he bade me, and followed the right-hand road, now running for fear and then walking leisurely to rest me, till I was out of the old man's sight. By this time, the sun had gone down and the darkness set in; so I sat down to rest and would have slept, but sleep came not to me that night, for stress of fear and famine and fatigue. When the night was half spent, I rose and walked on, till the day broke in all its beauty and the sun rose over the heads of the lofty hills and athwart the low gravelly plains. Now I was weary and hungry and thirsty; so I ate my fill of herbs and grasses that grew in the island and kept life in body and stayed my stomach, after which I set out again and fared on all that day and the next night, staying my greed with roots and herbs; nor did I cease walking for seven days and their nights, till the morn of the eighth day, when I caught sight of a faint object in the distance. So I made towards it, though my heart quaked for all I had suffered first and last, and behold it was a company of men gathering pepper-grains.

As soon as they saw me, they hastened up to me and surrounding me on all sides, said to me, "Who art thou and whence come?"

I replied, "Know, O folk, that I am a poor stranger," and acquainted them with my case and all the hardships and perils I had suffered. And the men gathering pepper in the island questioned me of my case, when I acquainted them with all the hardships and perils I had suffered and how I had fled from the savages; whereat they marvelled and gave me joy of my safety, saying, "By Allah, this is wonderful! But how didst thou escape from these blacks who swarm in the island and devour all who fall in with them; nor is any safe from them, nor can any get out of their clutches?"

And after I had told them the fate of my companions, they made me sit by them, till they got quit of their work; and fetched me somewhat of good food, which I ate, for I was hungry, and rested awhile, after which they took ship with me and carrying me to their island-home brought me before their King, who returned my salute and received me honourably and questioned me of my case. I told him all that had befallen me, from the day of my leaving Baghdad-city, whereupon he wondered with great wonder at my adventures, he and his courtiers, and bade me sit by him; then he called for food and I ate with him what sufficed me and washed my hands and returned thanks to Almighty Allah for all His favours praising Him and glorifying Him. Then I left the King and walked for solace about the city, which I found wealthy and populous, abounding in market-streets well stocked with food and merchandise and full of buyers and sellers.

So I rejoiced at having reached so pleasant a place and took my ease there after my fatigues; and I made friends with the townsfolk, nor was it long before I became more in honour and favour with them and their King than any of the chief men of the realm. Now I saw that all the citizens, great and small, rode fine horses, high-priced and thorough-bred, without saddles or housings, whereat I wondered and said to the King, "Wherefore, O my lord, dost thou not ride with a saddle? Therein is ease for the rider and increase of power."

"What is a saddle?" asked he: "I never saw nor used such a thing in all my life"; and I answered, "With thy permission I will make thee a saddle, that thou mayest ride on it and see the comfort thereof."

And quoth he, "Do so."

So quoth I to him, "Furnish me with some wood," which being brought, I sought me a clever carpenter and sitting by him showed him how to make the saddle-tree, portraying for him the fashion thereof in ink on the wood. Then I took wool and teased it and made felt of it, and, covering the saddle-tree with leather, stuffed it and polished it and attached the girth and stirrup leathers; after which I fetched a blacksmith and described to him the fashion of the stirrups and bridle-bit. So he forged a fine pair of stirrups and a bit, and filed them smooth and tinned them. Moreover, I made fast to them fringes of silk and fitted bridle-leathers to the bit. Then I fetched one of the best of the royal horses and saddling and bridling him, hung the stirrups to the saddle and led him to the King. The thing took his fancy and he thanked me; then he mounted and rejoiced greatly in the saddle and rewarded me handsomely for my work.

When the King's Wazir saw the saddle, he asked of me one like it and I made it for him. Furthermore, all the grandees and officers of state came for saddles to me; so I fell to making saddles (having taught the craft to the carpenter and blacksmith), and selling them to all who sought, till I amassed great wealth and became in high honour and great favour with the King and his household and grandees. I abode thus till, one day, as I was sitting with the King in all respect and contentment, he said to me, "Know thou, O such an one, thou art become one of us, dear as a brother, and we hold thee in such regard and affection that we cannot part with thee nor suffer thee to leave our city; wherefore I desire of thee obedience in a certain matter, and I will not have thee gainsay me."

Answered I, "O King, what is it thou desirest of me? Far be it from me to gainsay thee in aught, for I am indebted to thee for many favours and bounties and much kindness, and (praised be Allah!) I am become one of thy servants."

Quoth he, "I have a mind to marry thee to a fair, clever and agreeable wife who is wealthy as she is beautiful; so thou mayst be naturalised and domiciled with us: I will lodge thee with me in my palace; wherefore oppose me not neither cross me in this."

When I heard these words I was ashamed and held my peace nor could make him any answer, by reason of my much bashfulness before him.

Asked he, "Why dost thou not reply to me, O my son?"; and I answered saying, "O my master, it is thine to command, O King of the age!" So he summoned the Kazi and the witnesses and married me straightway to a lady of a noble tree and high pedigree; wealthy in moneys and means; the flower of an ancient race; of surpassing beauty and grace, and the owner of farms and estates and many a dwelling-place.

Now after the King my master had married me to this choice wife, he also gave me a great and goodly house standing alone, together with slaves and officers, and assigned me pay and allowances. So I became in all ease and contentment and delight and forgot everything which had befalled me of weariness and trouble and hardship; for I loved my wife with fondest love and she loved me no less, and we were as one and abode in the utmost comfort of life and in its happiness. And I said in myself, "When I return to my native land, I will carry her with me."

But whatso is predestined to a man, that needs must be, and none knoweth what shall befal him. We lived thus a great while, till Almighty Allah bereft one of my neighbours of his wife. Now he was a gossip of mine; so hearing the cry of the keeners I went in to condole with him on his loss and found him in very ill plight, full of trouble and weary of soul and mind. I condoled with him and comforted him, saying, "Mourn not for thy wife who hath now found the mercy of Allah; the Lord will surely give thee a better in her stead and thy name shall be great and thy life shall be long in the land, Inshallah!"

But he wept bitter tears and replied, "O my friend, how can I marry another wife and how shall Allah replace her to me with a better than she, whenas I have but one day left to live?"

"O my brother," said I, "return to thy senses and announce not the glad tidings of thine own death, for thou art well, sound and in good case."

"By thy life, O my friend," rejoined he, "to-morrow thou wilt lose me and wilt never see me again till the Day of Resurrection."

I asked, "How so?" and he answered, "This very day they bury my wife, and they bury me with her in one tomb; for it is the custom with us, if the wife die first, to bury the husband alive with her and in like manner the wife, if the husband die first; so that neither may enjoy life after losing his or her mate."

"By Allah," cried I, "this is a most vile, lewd custom and not to be endured of any!"

Meanwhile, behold, the most part of the townsfolk came in and fell to condoling with my gossip for his wife and for himself. Presently they laid the dead woman out, as was their wont; and, setting her on a bier, carried her and her husband without the city, till they came to a place in the side of the mountain at the end of the island by the sea; and here they raised a great rock and discovered the mouth of a stone-rivetted pit or well, leading down into a vast underground cavern that ran beneath the mountain. Into this pit they threw the corpse, then tying a rope of palm-fibres under the husband's armpits, they let him down into the cavern, and with him a great pitcher of fresh water and seven scones by way of viaticum. When he came to the bottom, he loosed himself from the rope and they drew it up; and, stopping the mouth of the pit with the great stone, they returned to the city, leaving my friend in the cavern with his dead wife.

When I saw this, I said to myself, "By Allah, this fashion of death is more grievous than the first!" And I went in to the King and said to him, "O my lord, why do ye bury the quick with the dead?"

Quoth he, "It hath been the custom, thou must know, of our forbears and our olden Kings from time immemorial, if the husband die first, to bury his wife with him, and the like with the wife, so we may not sever them, alive or dead."

I asked, "O King of the age, if the wife of a foreigner like myself die among you, deal ye with him as with yonder man?" and he answered, "Assuredly, we do with him even as thou hast seen."

When I heard this, my gall-bladder was like to burst, for the violence of my dismay and concern for myself: my wit became dazed; I felt as if in a vile dungeon; and hated their society; for I went about in fear lest my wife should die before me and they bury me alive with her. However, after a while, I comforted myself, saying, "Haply I shall predecease her, or shall have returned to my own land before she die, for none knoweth which shall go first and which shall go last."

Then I applied myself to diverting my mind from this thought with various occupations; but it was not long before my wife sickened and complained and took to her pillow and fared after a few days to the mercy of Allah; and the King and the rest of the folk came, as was their wont, to condole with me and her family and to console us for her loss and not less to condole with me for myself.

Then the women washed her and arraying her in her richest raiment and golden ornaments, necklaces and jewellery, laid her on the bier and bore her to the mountain aforesaid, where they lifted the cover of the pit and cast her in; after which all my intimates and acquaintances and my wife's kith and kin came round me, to farewell me in my lifetime and console me for my own death, whilst I cried out among them, saying, "Almighty Allah never made it lawful to bury the quick with the dead! I am a stranger, not one of your kind; and I cannot abear your custom, and had I known it I never would have wedded among you!"

They heard me not and paid no heed to my words, but laying hold of me, bound me by force and let me down into the cavern, with a large gugglet of sweet water and seven cakes of bread, according to their custom. When I came to the bottom, they called out to me to cast myself loose from the cords, but I refused to do so; so they threw them down on me and, closing the mouth of the pit with the stones aforesaid, went their ways.

I looked about me and found myself in a vast cave full of dead bodies, that exhaled a fulsome and loathsome smell and the air was heavy with the groans of the dying. Thereupon I fell to blaming myself for what I had done, saying, "By Allah, I deserve all that hath befallen me and all that shall befal me! What curse was upon me to take a wife in this city? There is no Majesty and there is no Might save in Allah, the Glorious, the Great! As often as I say, I have escaped from one calamity, I fall into a worse. By Allah, this is an abominable death to die! Would Heaven I had died a decent death and been washed and shrouded like a man and a Moslem. Would I had been drowned at sea or perished in the mountains! It were better than to die this miserable death!" And on such wise I kept blaming my own folly and greed of gain in that black hole, knowing not night from day; and I ceased not to ban the Foul Fiend and to bless the Almighty Friend.

Then I threw myself down on the bones of the dead and lay there, imploring Allah's help and in the violence of my despair, invoking death which came not to me, till the fire of hunger burned my stomach and thirst set my throat aflame when I sat up and feeling for the bread, ate a morsel and upon it swallowed a mouthful of water. After this, the worst night I ever knew, I arose, and exploring the cavern, found that it extended a long way with hollows in its sides; and its floor was strewn with dead bodies and rotten bones, that had lain there from olden time. So I made myself a place in a cavity of the cavern, afar from the corpses lately thrown down and there slept. I abode thus a long while, till my provision was like to give out; and yet I ate not save once every day or second day; nor did I drink more than an occasional draught, for fear my victual should fail me before my death; and I said to myself, "Eat little and drink little; belike the Lord shall vouchsafe deliverance to thee!"

One day, as I sat thus, pondering my case and bethinking me how I should do, when my bread and water should be exhausted, behold, the stone that covered the opening was suddenly rolled away and the light streamed down upon me. Quoth I, "I wonder what is the matter: haply they have brought another corpse."

Then I espied folk standing about the mouth of the pit, who presently let down a dead man and a live woman, weeping and bemoaning herself, and with her an ampler supply of bread and water than usual. I saw her and she was a beautiful woman; but she saw me not; and they closed up the opening and went away. Then I took the leg-bone of a dead man and, going up to the woman, smote her on the crown of the head; and she cried one cry and fell down in a swoon. I smote her a second and a third time, till she was dead, when I laid hands on her bread and water and found on her great plenty of ornaments and rich apparel, necklaces, jewels and gold trinkets; for it was their custom to bury women in all their finery.

I carried the vivers to my sleeping place in the cavern-side and ate and drank of them sparingly, no more than sufficed to keep the life in me, lest the provaunt come speedily to an end and I perish of hunger and thirst. Yet did I never wholly lose hope in Almighty Allah. I abode thus a great while, killing all the live folk they let down into the cavern and taking their provisions of meat and drink; till one day, as I slept, I was awakened by something scratching and burrowing among the bodies in a corner of the cave and said, "What can this be?" fearing wolves or hyaenas.

So I sprang up and seizing the leg-bone aforesaid, made for the noise. As soon as the thing was ware of me, it fled from me into the inward of the cavern, and lo! it was a wild beast. However, I followed it to the further end, till I saw afar off a point of light not bigger than a star, now appearing and then disappearing. So I made for it, and as I drew near, it grew larger and brighter, till I was certified that it was a crevice in the rock, leading to the open country; and I said to myself, "There must be some reason for this opening: either it is the mouth of a second pit, such as that by which they let me down, or else it is a natural fissure in the stonery."

So I bethought me awhile and nearing the light, found that it came from a breach in the back side of the mountain, which the wild beasts had enlarged by burrowing, that they might enter and devour the dead and freely go to and fro. When I saw this, my spirits revived and hope came back to me and I made sure of life, after having died a death. So I went on, as in a dream, and making shift to scramble through the breach found myself on the slope of a high mountain, overlooking the salt sea and cutting off all access thereto from the island, so that none could come at that part of the beach from the city. I praised my Lord and thanked Him, rejoicing greatly and heartening myself with the prospect of deliverance; then I returned through the crack to the cavern and brought out all the food and water I had saved up and donned some of the dead folk's clothes over my own; after which I gathered together all the collars and necklaces of pearls and jewels and trinkets of gold and silver set with precious stones and other ornaments and valuables I could find upon the corpses; and, making them into bundles with the grave clothes and raiment of the dead, carried them out to the back of the mountain facing the sea-shore, where I established myself, purposing to wait there till it should please Almighty Allah to send me relief by means of some passing ship. I visited the cavern daily and as often as I found folk buried alive there, I killed them all indifferently, men and women, and took their victual and valuables and transported them to my seat on the sea-shore. Thus I abode a long while by the sea, pondering my case, till one day I caught sight of a ship passing in the midst of the clashing sea, swollen with dashing billows.

So I took a piece of a white shroud I had with me and, tying it to a staff, ran along the sea-shore, making signals therewith and calling to the people in the ship, till they espied me and hearing my shouts, sent a boat to fetch me off. When it drew near, the crew called out to me, saying, "Who art thou and how camest thou to be on this mountain, whereon never saw we any in our born days?"

I answered, "I am a gentleman and a merchant, who hath been wrecked and saved myself on one of the planks of the ship, with some of my goods; and by the blessing of the Almighty and the decrees of Destiny and my own strength and skill, after much toil and moil I have landed with my gear in this place where I awaited some passing ship to take me off."

155

So they took me in their boat together with the bundles I had made of the jewels and valuables from the cavern, tied up in clothes and shrouds, and rowed back with me to the ship, where the captain said to me, "How camest thou, O man, to yonder place on yonder mountain behind which lieth a great city? All my life I have sailed these seas and passed to and fro hard by these heights; yet never saw I here any living thing save wild beasts and birds."

I repeated to him the story I had told the sailors, but acquainted him with nothing of that which had befallen me in the city and the cavern, lest there should be any of the islandry in the ship. Then I took out some of the best pearls I had with me and offered them to the captain, saying, "O my lord, thou hast been the means of saving me off this mountain. I have no ready money; but take this from me in requital of thy kindness and good offices."

But he refused to accept it of me, saying, "When we find a shipwrecked man on the sea-shore or on an island, we take him up and give him meat and drink, and if he be naked we clothe him; nor take we aught from him; nay, when we reach a port of safety, we set him ashore with a present of our own money and entreat him kindly and charitably, for the love of Allah the Most High."

So I prayed that his life be long in the land and rejoiced in my escape, trusting to be delivered from my stress and to forget my past mishaps; for every time I remembered being let down into the cave with my dead wife I shuddered in horror. Then we pursued our voyage and sailed from island to island and sea to sea, till we arrived at the Island of the Bell, which containeth a city two days' journey in extent, whence after a six days' run we reached the Island Kala, hard by the land of Hind. This place is governed by a potent and puissant King and it produceth excellent camphor and an abundance of the Indian rattan: here also is a lead mine. At last by the decree of Allah, we arrived in safety at Bassorah-town where

I tarried a few days, then went on to Baghdad-city, and, finding my quarter, entered my house with lively pleasure. There I foregathered with my family and friends, who rejoiced in my happy return and gave me joy of my safety. I laid up in my storehouses all the goods I had brought with me, and gave alms and largesse to Fakirs and beggars and clothed the widow and the orphan. Then I gave myself up to pleasure and enjoyment, returning to my old merry mode of life.

"Such, then, be the most marvellous adventures of my fourth voyage, but to-morrow if you will kindly come to me, I will tell you that which befel me in my fifth voyage, which was yet rarer and more marvellous than those which forewent it. And thou, O my brother Sinbad the Landsman, shalt sup with me as thou art wont" (saith he who telleth the tale).

When Sinbad the Sailor had made an end of his story, he called for supper; so they spread the table and the guests ate the evening meal; after which he gave the Porter an hundred dinars as usual, and he and the rest of the company went their ways, glad at heart and marvelling at the tales they had heard. The porter Sinbad passed the night in his own house, in all joy and cheer and wonderment; and, as soon as morning came with its sheen and shone, he prayed the dawn-prayer and repaired to the house of Sinbad the Sailor, who welcomed him and bade him sit with him till the rest of the company arrived, when they ate and drank and made merry and the talk went round amongst them. Presently, their host began the narrative of

THE FIFTH VOYAGE OF SINBAD THE SAILOR

Know, O my brothers, that when I had been awhile on shore after my fourth voyage; and when, in my comfort and pleasures and merry-makings and in my rejoicing over my large gains and profits, I had forgotten all I had endured of perils and sufferings, the carnal man was again seized with the longing to travel and to see foreign countries and islands. Accordingly I bought costly merchandise suited to my purpose and, making it up into bales, repaired to Bassorah, where I walked about the river-quay till I found a fine tall ship, newly builded with gear unused and fitted ready for sea. She pleased me; so I bought her and, embarking my goods in her, hired a master and crew, over whom I set certain of my slaves and servants as inspectors. A number of merchants also brought their outfits and paid me freight and passage-money; then, after reciting the Fatihah we set sail over Allah's pool in all joy and cheer, promising ourselves a prosperous voyage and much profit.

We sailed from city to city and from island to island and from sea to sea viewing the cities and countries by which we passed, and selling and buying in not a few till one day we came to a great uninhabited island, deserted and desolate, whereon was a white dome of biggest bulk half buried in the sands. The merchants landed to examine this dome, leaving me in the ship; and when they drew near, behold, it was a huge Rukh's egg. They fell a-beating it with stones, knowing not what it was, and presently broke it open, whereupon much water ran out of it and the young Rukh appeared within. So they pulled it forth of the shell and cut its throat and took of it great store of meat.

Now I was in the ship and knew not what they did; but presently one of the passengers came up to me and said, "O my lord, come and look at the egg we thought to be a dome."

So I looked and seeing the merchants beating it with stones, called out to them, "Stop, stop! do not meddle with that egg, or the bird Rukh will come out and break our ship and destroy us."

But they paid no heed to me and gave not over smiting upon the egg, when behold, the day grew dark and dun and the sun was hidden from us, as if some great cloud had passed over the firmament. So we raised our eyes and saw that what we took for a cloud was the Rukh poised between us and the sun, and it was his wings that darkened the day. When he came and saw his egg broken, he cried a loud cry, whereupon his mate came flying up and they both began circling about the ship, crying out at us with voices louder than thunder. I called to the Rais and crew, "Put out to sea and seek safety in flight, before we be all destroyed."

So the merchants came on board and we cast off and made haste from the island to gain the open sea. When the Rukhs saw this, they flew off and we crowded all sail on the ship, thinking to get out of their country; but presently the two re-appeared and flew after us and stood over us, each carrying in its claws a huge boulder which it had brought from the mountains. As soon as the he-Rukh came up with us, he let fall upon us the rock he held in his pounces; but the master put about ship, so that the rock missed her by some small matter and plunged into the waves with such violence, that the ship pitched high and then sank into the trough of the sea and the bottom of the ocean appeared to us. Then the she-Rukh let fall her rock, which was bigger than that of her mate, and as Destiny had decreed, it fell on the poop of the ship and crushed it, the rudder flying into twenty pieces; whereupon the vessel foundered and all and everything on board were cast into the main. As for me I struggled for sweet life, till Almighty

Allah threw in my way one of the planks of the ship, to which I clung and bestriding it, fell a-paddling with my feet.

Now the ship had gone down hard by an island in the midst of the main and the winds and waves bore me on till, by permission of the Most High, they cast me up on the shore of the island, at the last gasp for toil and distress and half dead with hunger and thirst. So I landed more like a corpse than a live man and throwing myself down on the beach, lay there awhile, till I began to revive and recover spirits, when I walked about the island and found it as it were one of the garths and gardens of Paradise. Its trees, in abundance dight, bore ripe-yellow fruit for freight; its streams ran clear and bright; its flowers were fair to scent and to sight and its birds warbled with delight the praises of Him to whom belong permanence and all-might. So I ate my fill of the fruits and slaked my thirst with the water of the streams till I could no more and I returned thanks to the Most High and glorified Him; after which I sat till nightfall, hearing no voice and seeing none inhabitant. Then I lay down, well-nigh dead for travail and trouble and terror, and slept without surcease till morning, when I arose and walked about under the trees, till I came to the channel of a draw-well fed by a spring of running water, by which well sat an old man of venerable aspect, girt about with a waist-cloth made of the fibre of palm-fronds. Quoth I to myself, "Haply this Shaykh is one of those who were wrecked in the ship and hath made his way to this island." So I drew near to him and saluted him, and he returned my salam by signs, but spoke not; and I said to him, "O nuncle mine, what causeth thee to sit here?"

He shook his head and moaned and signed to me with his hands as who should say, "Take me on thy shoulders and carry me to the other side of the well-channel."

And quoth I in my mind, "I will deal kindly with him and do what he desireth; it may be I shall win me a reward in Heaven for he may be a paralytic." So I took him on my back and carrying him to the place whereat he pointed, said to him, "Dismount at thy leisure." But he would not get off my back and wound his legs about my neck. I looked at them and seeing that they were like a buffalo's hide for blackness and roughness, was affrighted and would have cast him off; but he clung to me and gripped my neck with his legs, till I was well-nigh choked, the world grew black in my sight and I fell senseless to the ground like one dead. But he still kept his seat and raising his legs drummed with his heels and beat harder than palm-rods my back and shoulders, till he forced me to rise for excess of pain. Then he signed to me with his hand to carry him hither and thither among the trees which bore the best fruits; and if ever I refused to do his bidding or loitered or took my leisure he beat me with his feet more grievously than if I had been beaten with whips. He ceased not to signal with his hand wherever he was minded to go; so I carried him about the island, like a captive slave, and he bepissed and conskited my shoulders and back, dismounting not night nor day; and whenas he wished to sleep he wound his legs about my neck and leaned back and slept awhile, then arose and beat me; whereupon I sprang up in haste, unable to gainsay him because of the pain he inflicted on me. And indeed I blamed myself and sore repented me of having taken compassion on him and continued in this condition, suffering fatigue not to be described, till I said to myself, "I wrought him a weal and he requited me with my ill; by Allah, never more will I do any man a service so long as I live!" And again and again I besought the Most High that I might die, for stress of weariness and misery; and thus I abode a long while till, one day, I came with him to a place wherein was abundance of gourds, many of them dry.

So I took a great dry gourd and, cutting open the head, scooped out the inside and cleaned it; after which I gathered grapes from a vine which grew hard by and squeezed them into the gourd, till it was full of the juice. Then I stopped up the mouth and set it in the sun, where I left it for some days, until it became strong wine; and every day I used to drink of it, to comfort and sustain me under my fatigues with that froward and obstinate fiend; and as often as I drank myself drunk, I forgot my troubles and took new heart. One day he saw me drinking and signed to me with his hand, as who should say, "What is that?"

Quoth I, "It is an excellent cordial, which cheereth the heart and reviveth the spirits."

Then, being heated with wine, I ran and danced with him among the trees, clapping my hands and singing and making merry; and I staggered under him by design. When he saw this, he signed to me to give him the gourd that he might drink, and I feared him and gave it him. So he took it and, draining it to the dregs, cast it on the ground, whereupon he grew frolicsome and began to clap hands and jig to and fro on my shoulders and he made water upon me so copiously that all my dress was drenched. But presently the fumes of the wine rising to his head, he became helplessly drunk and his side-muscles and limbs relaxed and he swayed to and fro on my back. When I saw that he had lost his senses for drunkenness, I put my hand to his legs and, loosing them from my neck, stooped down well-nigh to the ground and threw him at full length. I threw the devil off my shoulders,

hardly crediting my deliverance from him and fearing lest he should shake off his drunkenness and do me a mischief. Then I took up a great stone from among the trees and coming up to him smote him therewith on the head with all my might and crushed in his skull as he lay dead drunk. Thereupon his flesh and fat and blood being in a pulp, he died and went to his desserts, The Fire, no mercy of Allah be upon him!

I then returned, with a heart at ease, to my former station on the sea-shore and abode in that island many days, eating of its fruits and drinking of its waters and keeping a look-out for passing ships; till one day, as I sat on the beach, recalling all that had befallen me and saying, "I wonder if Allah will save me alive and restore me to my home and family and friends!" behold, a ship was making for the island through the dashing sea and clashing waves. Presently, it cast anchor and the passengers landed; so I made for them, and when they saw me all hastened up to me and gathering round me questioned me of my case and how I came thither. I told them all that had betided me, whereat they marvelled with exceeding marvel and said, "He who rode on thy shoulder is called the 'Shaykh al-Bahr' or Old Man of the Sea, and none ever felt his legs on neck and came off alive but thou; and those who die under him he eateth: so praised be Allah for thy safety!" Then they set somewhat of food before me, whereof I ate my fill, and gave me somewhat of clothes wherewith I clad myself anew and covered my nakedness; after which they took me up into the ship, and we sailed days and nights, till fate brought us to a place called the City of Apes, builded with lofty houses, all of which gave upon the sea and it had a single gate studded and strengthened with iron nails.

Now every night, as soon as it is dusk the dwellers in this city use to come forth of the gates and, putting out to sea in boats and ships, pass the night upon the waters in their fear lest the apes should come down on them from the mountains. Hearing this I was sore troubled remembering what I had before suffered from the ape-kind. Presently I landed to solace myself in the city, but meanwhile the ship set sail without me and I repented of having gone ashore, and calling to mind my companions and what had befallen me with the apes, first and after, sat down and fell a-weeping and lamenting. Presently one of the townsfolk accosted me and said to me, "O my lord, meseemeth thou art a stranger to these parts?"

"Yes," answered I, "I am indeed a stranger and a poor one, who came hither in a ship which cast anchor here, and I landed to visit the town; but when I would have gone on board again, I found they had sailed without me."

Quoth he, "Come and embark with us, for if thou lie the night in the city, the apes will destroy thee."

"Hearkening and obedience," replied I, and rising, straightway embarked with him in one of the boats, whereupon they pushed off from shore and anchoring a mile or so from the land, there passed the night.

At daybreak, they rowed back to the city and landing, went each about his business. Thus they did every night, for if any tarried in the town by night the apes came down on him and slew him. As soon as it was day, the apes left the place and ate of the fruits of the gardens, then went back to the mountains and slept there till nightfall, when they again came down upon the city. Now this place was in the farthest part of the country of the blacks, and one of the strangest things that befel me during my sojourn in the city was on this wise.

One of the company with whom I passed the night in the boat, asked me, "O my lord, thou art apparently a stranger in these parts; hast thou any craft whereat thou canst work?" and I answered, "By Allah, O my brother, I have no trade nor know I any handicraft, for I was a merchant and a man of money and substance and had a ship of my own, laden with great store of goods and merchandise; but it foundered at sea and all were drowned excepting me who saved myself on a piece of plank which Allah vouchsafed to me of His favour."

Upon this he brought me a cotton bag and giving it to me, said, "Take this bag and fill it with pebbles from the beach and go forth with a company of the townsfolk to whom I will give a charge respecting thee. Do as they do and belike thou shalt gain what may further thy return voyage to thy native land." Then he carried me to the beach, where I filled my bag with pebbles large and small, and presently we saw a company of folk issue from the town, each bearing a bag like mine, filled with pebbles. To these he committed me, commending me to their care, and saying, "This man is a stranger, so take him with you and teach him how to gather, that he may get his daily bread, and you will earn your reward and recompense in Heaven."

"On our head and eyes be it!" answered they and bidding me welcome, fared on with me till we came to a spacious Wady, full of lofty trees with trunks so smooth that none might climb them.

Now sleeping under these trees were many apes, which when they saw us rose and fled from us and swarmed up among the branches; whereupon my companions began to pelt them with what they had in their bags, and the apes fell to plucking of the fruit of the trees and casting them at the folk. I looked at the fruits they cast at us and found them to be Indian or cocoa-nuts; so I chose out a great tree, full of apes, and going up to it, began to pelt them with stones, and they in return pelted me with nuts, which I collected, as did the rest; so that even before I had made an end of my bagful of pebbles, I had gotten great plenty of nuts; and as soon as my companions had in like manner gotten as many nuts as they could carry, we returned to the city, where we arrived at the fag-end of day. Then I went in to the kindly man who had brought me in company with the nut-gatherers and gave him all I had gotten, thanking him for his kindness; but he would not accept them, saying, "Sell them and make profit by the price"; and presently he added (giving me the key of a closet in his house) "Store thy nuts in this safe place and go thou forth every morning and gather them as thou hast done to-day, and choose out the worst for sale and supplying thyself; but lay up the rest here, so haply thou mayst collect enough to serve thee for thy return home."

"Allah requite thee!" answered I and did as he advised me, going out daily with the cocoa-nut gatherers, who commended me to one another and showed me the best-stocked trees.

Thus did I for some time, till I had laid up great store of excellent nuts, besides a large sum of money, the price of those I had sold. I became thus at my ease and bought all I saw and had a mind to, and passed my time pleasantly greatly enjoying my stay in the city, till, as I stood on the beach, one day, a great ship steering through the heart of the sea presently cast anchor by the shore and landed a company of merchants, who proceeded to sell and buy and barter their goods for cocoa-nuts and other commodities. Then I went to my friend and told him of the coming of the ship and how I had a mind to return to my own country; and he said, "'Tis for thee to decide." So I thanked him for his bounties and took leave of him; then, going to the captain of the ship, I agreed with him for my passage and embarked my cocoa-nuts and what else I possessed.

We weighed anchor the same day and sailed from island to island and sea to sea; and whenever we stopped, I sold and traded with my cocoa-nuts, and the Lord requited me more than I erst had and lost. Amongst other places, we came to an island abounding in cloves and cinnamon and pepper; and the country people told me that by the side of each pepper-bunch groweth a great leaf which shadeth it from the sun and casteth the water off it in the wet season; but, when the rain ceaseth the leaf turneth over and droopeth down by the side of the bunch. Here I took in great store of pepper and cloves and cinnamon, in exchange for cocoa-nuts, and we passed thence to the Island of Al-Usirat, whence cometh the Comorin aloes-wood and thence to another island, five days' journey in length, where grows the Chinese lign-aloes, which is better than the Comorin; but the people of this island are fouler of condition and religion than those of the other, for that they love fornication and wine-bibbing, and know not prayer nor call to prayer. Thence we came to the pearl-fisheries, and I gave the divers some of my cocoa-nuts and said to them, "Dive for my luck and lot!"

They did so and brought up from the deep bight great store of large and priceless pearls; and they said to me, "By Allah, O my master, thy luck is a lucky!"

Then we sailed on, with the blessing of Allah (whose name be exalted!); and ceased not sailing till we arrived safely at Bassorah. There I abode a little and then went on to Baghdad, where I entered my quarter and found my house and foregathered with my family and saluted my friends who gave me joy of my safe return, and I laid up all my goods and valuables in my storehouses. Then I distributed alms and largesse and clothed the widow and the orphan and made presents to my relations and comrades; for the Lord had requited me fourfold that I had lost. After which I returned to my old merry way of life and forgot all I had suffered in the great profit and gain I had made.

"Such, then, is the history of my fifth voyage and its wonderments, and now to supper; and to-morrow, come again and I will tell you what befel me in my sixth voyage; for it was still more wonderful than this" (saith he who telleth the tale).

Then he called for food; and the servants spread the table, and when they had eaten the evening-meal, he bade give Sinbad the porter an hundred golden dinars and the Landsman returned home and lay him down to sleep, much marvelling at all he had heard. Next morning, as soon as it was light, he prayed the dawn-prayer; and, after blessing Mohammed the Cream of all creatures, betook himself to the house of Sinbad the Sailor and wished him a good day. The merchant bade him sit and talked with him, till the rest of the company arrived. Then the servants spread the table and when they had well eaten and drunken and were mirthful and merry, Sinbad the Sailor began in these words the narrative of

THE SIXTH VOYAGE OF SINBAD THE SAILOR

Know, O my brothers and friends and companions all, that I abode some time, after my return from my fifth voyage, in great solace and

satisfaction and mirth and merriment, joyance and enjoyment; and I forgot what I had suffered, seeing the great gain and profit I had made till, one day, as I sat making merry and enjoying myself with my friends, there came in to me a company of merchants whose case told tales of travel, and talked with me of voyage and adventure and greatness of pelf and lucre. Hereupon I remembered the days of my return from abroad, and my joy at once more seeing my native land and foregathering with my family and friends; and my soul yearned for travel and traffic.

So compelled by Fate and Fortune I resolved to undertake another voyage; and, buying me fine and costly merchandise meet for foreign trade, made it up into bales, with which I journeyed from Baghdad to Bassorah. Here I found a great ship ready for sea and full of merchants and notables, who had with them goods of price; so I embarked my bales therein. And we left Bassorah in safety and good spirits under the safeguard of the King, the Preserver, we continued our voyage from place to place and from city to city, buying and selling and profiting and diverting ourselves with the sight of countries where strange folk dwell. And Fortune and the voyage smiled upon us, till one day, as we went along, behold, the captain suddenly cried with a great cry and cast his turband on the deck. Then he buffeted his face like a woman and plucked out his beard and fell down in the waist of the ship well nigh fainting for stress of grief and rage, and crying, "Oh and alas for the ruin of my house and the orphanship of my poor children!"

So all the merchants and sailors came round about him and asked him, "O master, what is the matter?"; for the light had become night before their sight. And he answered, saying, "Know, O folk, that we have wandered from our course and left the sea whose ways we wot, and come into a sea whose ways I know not; and unless Allah vouchsafe us a means of escape, we are all dead men; wherefore pray ye to the Most High, that He deliver us from this strait. Haply amongst you is one righteous whose prayers the Lord will accept."

Then he arose and clomb the mast to see an there were any escape from that strait; and he would have loosed the sails; but the wind redoubled upon the ship and whirled her round thrice and drave her backwards; whereupon her rudder brake and she fell off towards a high mountain. With this the captain came down from the mast, saying, "There is no Majesty and there is no Might save in Allah, the Glorious, the Great; nor can man prevent that which is fore-ordained of fate! By Allah, we are fallen on a place of sure destruction, and there is no way of escape for us, nor can any of us be saved!" Then we all fell a-weeping over ourselves and bidding one another farewell for that our days were come to an end, and we had lost all hopes of life.

Presently the ship struck the mountain and broke up, and all and everything on board of her were plunged into the sea. Some of the merchants were drowned and others made shift to reach the shore and save themselves upon the mountain; I amongst the number, and when we got ashore, we found a great island, or rather peninsula whose base was strewn with wreckage of crafts and goods and gear cast up by the sea from broken ships whose passengers had been drowned; and the quantity confounded compt and calculation. So I climbed the cliffs into the inward of the isle and walked on inland, till I came to a stream of sweet water, that welled up at the nearest foot of the mountains and disappeared in the earth under the range of hills on the opposite side. But all the other passengers went over the mountains to the inner tracts; and, dispersing hither and thither, were confounded at what they saw and became like madmen at the sight of the wealth and treasures wherewith the shores were strewn.

As for me I looked into the bed of the stream aforesaid and saw therein great plenty of rubies, and great royal pearls and all kinds of jewels and precious stones which were as gravel in the bed of the rivulets that ran through the fields, and the sands sparkled and glittered with gems and precious ores. Moreover we found in the island abundance of the finest lign-aloes, both Chinese and Comorin; and there also is a spring of crude ambergris which floweth like wax or gum over the stream-banks, for the great heat of the sun, and runneth down to the sea-shore, where the monsters of the deep come up and swallowing it, return into the sea. But it burneth in their bellies; so they cast it up again and it congealeth on the surface of the water, whereby its color and quantities are changed; and at last, the waves cast it ashore, and the travellers and merchants who know it, collect it and sell it. But as to the raw ambergris which is not swallowed, it floweth over the channel and congealeth on the banks and when the sun shineth on it, it melteth and scenteth the whole valley with a musk-like fragrance: then, when the sun ceaseth from it, it congealeth again. But none can get to this place where is the crude ambergris, because of the mountains which enclose the island on all sides and which foot of man cannot ascend.

We continued thus to explore the island, marvelling at the wonderful works of Allah and the riches we found there, but sore troubled for our own case, and dismayed at our prospects. Now we had picked up on the beach some small matter of victual from the wreck and husbanded it carefully, eating but once every day or two, in our fear lest it should fail us and we die miserably of famine or affright. Moreover, we were weak for colic brought on by sea-sickness and low diet, and my companions deceased, one after other, till there was but a small company of us left. Each that died we washed and shrouded in some of the clothes and linen cast ashore by the tides; and after a little, the rest of my fellows perished, one by one, till I had buried the last of the party and abode alone on the island, with but a little provision left, I who was wont to have so much. And I wept over myself, saying, "Would Heaven I had died before my companions and they had washed and buried me! It had been better than I should perish and none wash me and shroud me and bury me. But there is Majesty and there is no Might save in Allah, the Glorious, the Great!"

Now after I had buried the last of my party and abode alone on the island, I arose and dug me a deep grave on the sea-shore, saying to myself, "Whenas I grow weak and know that death cometh to me, I will cast myself into the grave and die there, so the wind may drift the sand over me and cover me and I be buried therein." Then I fell to reproaching myself for my little wit in leaving my native land and betaking me again to travel, after all I had suffered during my first five voyages, and when I had not made a single one without suffering more horrible perils and more terrible hardships than in its forerunner and having no hope of escape from my present stress; and I repented me of my folly and bemoaned myself, especially as I had no need of money, seeing that I had enough and more than enough and could not spend what I had, no, nor a half of it in all my life. However, after a while Allah sent me a thought and I said to myself, "By God, needs must this stream have an end as well as a beginning; ergo an issue somewhere, and belike its course may lead to some inhabited place; so my best plan is to make me a little boat big enough to sit in, and carry it and launching it on the river, embark therein and drop down the stream. If I escape, I escape, by God's leave; and if I perish, better die in the river than here."

Then, sighing for myself, I set to work collecting a number of pieces of Chinese and Comorin aloes-wood and I bound them together with ropes from the wreckage; then I chose out from the broken-up ships straight planks of even size and fixed them firmly upon the aloes-wood, making me a boat-raft a little narrower than the channel of the stream; and I tied it tightly and firmly as though it were nailed. Then I loaded it with the goods, precious ores and jewels: and the union pearls which were like gravel and the best of the ambergris crude and pure, together with what I had collected on the island and what was left me of victual and wild herbs. Lastly I lashed a piece of wood on either side, to serve me as oars; and launched it, and embarking, did according to the saying of the poet,

> Fly, fly with life whenas evils threat;
> Leave the house to tell of its builder's fate!
> Land after land shalt thou seek and find
> But no other life on thy wish shall wait:
> Fret not thy soul in thy thoughts o' night;
> All woes shall end or sooner or late.
> Whoso is born in one land to die,
> There and only there shall gang his gait:
> Nor trust great things to another wight,
> Soul hath only soul for confederate.

My boat-raft drifted with the stream, I pondering the issue of my affair; and the drifting ceased not till I came to the place where it disappeared beneath the mountain. I rowed my conveyance into the place which was intensely dark; and the current carried the raft with it down the underground channel. The thin stream bore me on through a narrow tunnel where the raft touched either side and my head rubbed against the roof, return therefrom being impossible. Then I blamed myself for having thus risked my life, and said, "If this passage grow any straiter, the raft will hardly pass, and I cannot turn back; so I shall inevitably perish miserably in this place." And I threw myself down upon my face on the raft, by reason of the narrowness of the channel, whilst the stream ceased not to carry me along, knowing not night from day, for the excess of the gloom which encompassed me about and my terror and concern for myself lest I should perish. And in such condition my course continued down the channel which now grew wide and then straiter till, sore aweary by reason of the darkness which could be felt, I fell asleep, as I lay prone on the raft, and I slept knowing not an the time were long or short.

When I awoke at last, I found myself in the light of Heaven and opening my eyes I saw myself in a broad stream and the raft moored to an island in the midst of a number of Indians and Abyssinians. As soon as these blackamoors saw that I was awake, they came up to me and bespoke me in their speech; but I understood not what they said and thought that this was a dream and a vision which had betided me for stress of concern and chagrin. But I was delighted at my escape from the river. When they saw I understood them not and made them no answer, one of them came forward and said to me in Arabic, "Peace be with thee, O my brother! Who art thou and whence faredst thou thither? How camest thou into this river and what manner of land lies behind yonder mountains, for never knew we any one make his way thence to us?"

Quoth I, "And upon thee be peace and the ruth of Allah and his blessing! Who are ye and what country is this?"

"O my brother," answered he, "we are husbandmen and tillers of the soil, who came out to water our fields and plantations; and, finding thee asleep on this raft, laid hold of it and made it fast by us, against thou shouldst awake at thy leisure. So tell us how thou camest hither?"

I answered, "For Allah's sake, O my lord, ere I speak give me somewhat to eat, for I am starving, and after ask me what thou wilt."

So he hastened to fetch me food and I ate my fill, till I was refreshed and my fear was calmed by a good belly-full and my life returned to me. Then I rendered thanks to the Most High for mercies great and small, glad to be out of the river and rejoicing to be amongst them, and I told them all my adventures from first to last, especially my troubles in the narrow channel.

When I landed and found myself amongst the Indians and Abyssinians and had taken some rest, they consulted among themselves and said to one another, "There is no help for it but we carry him with us and present him to our King, that he may acquaint him with his adventures."

So they took me, together with the raft-boat and its lading of monies and merchandise; jewels, minerals and golden gear, and brought me to their King, who was King of Sarandib, telling him what had happened; whereupon he saluted me and bade me welcome. Then he questioned me of my condition and adventures through the man who had spoken Arabic and I repeated to him my story from beginning to end, whereat he marvelled exceedingly and gave me joy of my deliverance; after which I arose and fetched from the raft great store of precious ores and jewels and ambergris and lign-aloes and presented them to the King, who accepted them and entreated me with the utmost honour, appointing me a lodging in his own palace. So I consorted with the chief of the islanders, and they paid me the utmost respect. And I quitted not the royal palace.

Now the Island Sarandib lieth under the equinoctial line, its night and day both numbering twelve hours. It measureth eighty leagues long by a breadth of thirty and its wideth is bounded by a lofty mountain and a deep valley. The mountain is conspicuous from a distance of three days and it containeth many kinds of rubies and other minerals, and spice-trees of all sorts. The surface is covered with emery wherewith gems are cut and fashioned; diamonds are in its rivers and pearls are in its valleys. I ascended that mountain and solaced myself with a view of its marvels which are indescribable and afterwards I returned to the King. Thereupon, all the travellers and merchants who came to the place questioned me of the affairs of my native land and of the Caliph Harun al-Rashid and his rule and I told them of him and of that wherefor he was renowned, and they praised him because of this; whilst I in turn questioned them of the manners and customers of their own countries and got the knowledge I desired.

One day, the King himself asked me of the fashions and form of government of my country, and I acquainted him with the circumstance of the Caliph's sway in the city of Baghdad and the justice of his rule. The King marvelled at my account of his appointments and said, "By Allah, the Caliph's ordinances are indeed wise and his fashions of praiseworthy guise and thou hast made me love him by what thou tellest me; wherefore I have a mind to make him a present and send it by thee."

Quoth I, "Hearkening and obedience, O my lord; I will bear thy gift to him and inform him that thou art his sincere lover and true friend." Then I abode with the King in great honour and regard and consideration for a long while till, one day, as I sat in his palace, I heard news of a company of merchants, that were fitting out a ship for Bassorah, and said to myself, "I cannot do better than voyage with these men." So I rose without stay or delay and kissed the King's hand and acquainted him with my longing to set out with the merchants, for that I pined after my people and mine own land.

Quoth he, "Thou art thine own master; yet, if it be thy will to abide with us, on our head and eyes be it, for thou gladdenest us with thy company."

"By Allah, O my lord," answered I, "thou hast indeed overwhelmed me with thy favours and well-doings; but I weary for a sight of my friends and family and native country." When he heard this, he summoned the merchants in question and commended me to their care, paying my freight and passage-money. Then he bestowed on me great riches from his treasuries and charged me with a magnificent present for the Caliph Harun al-Rashid. Moreover he gave me a sealed letter, saying, "Carry this with thine own hand to the Commander of the Faithful and give him many salutations from us!"

"Hearing and obedience," I replied.

The missive was written on the skin of the Khawi (which is finer than lamb-parchment and of yellow colour), with ink of ultramarine and the contents were as follows. "Peace be with thee from the King of Al-Hind, before whom are a thousand elephants and upon whose palace-crenelles are a thousand jewels. But after (laud to the Lord and praises to His Prophet!): we send thee a trifling gift which be thou pleased to accept. Thou art to us a brother and a sincere friend; and great is the love we bear for thee in heart; favour us therefore with a reply. The gift besitteth not thy dignity: but we beg of thee, O our brother, graciously to accept it and peace be with thee." And the present was a cup of ruby a span high the inside of which was adorned with precious pearls; and a bed covered with the skin of the serpent which swalloweth the elephant, which skin hath spots each like a dinar and whoso sitteth upon it never sickeneth; and an hundred thousand miskals of Indian lign-aloes and a slave-girl like a shining moon.

Then I took leave of him and of all my intimates and acquaintances in the island and embarked with the merchants aforesaid. We sailed with a fair wind, committing ourselves to the care of Allah (be He extolled and exalted!) and by His permission arrived at Bassorah, where I passed a few days and nights equipping myself and packing up my bales. Then I went on to Baghdad-city, the House of Peace, where I sought an audience of the Caliph and laid the King's presents before him. He asked me whence they came and I said to him, "By Allah, O Commander of the Faithful, I know not the name of the city nor the way thither!"

He then asked me, "O Sinbad, is this true which the King writeth?"; and I answered, after kissing the ground, "O my lord, I saw in his kingdom much more than he hath written in his letter. For state processions a throne is set for him upon a huge elephant, eleven cubits high: and upon this he sitteth having his great lords and officers and guests standing in two ranks, on his right hand and on his left. At his head is a man hending in hand a golden javelin and behind him another with a great mace of gold whose head is an emerald a span long and as thick as a man's thumb. And when he mounteth horse there mount with him a thousand horsemen clad in gold brocade and silk; and as the King proceedeth a man precedeth him, crying, 'This is the King of great dignity, of high authority!' And he continueth to repeat his praises in words I remember not, saying at the end of his panegyric, 'This is the King owning the crown whose like nor Solomon nor the Mihraj ever possessed.' Then he is silent and one behind him proclaimeth, saying, 'He will die! Again I say he will die!'; and the other addeth, 'Extolled be the perfection of the Living who dieth not!' Moreover by reason of his justice and ordinance and intelligence, there is no Kazi in his city, and all his lieges distinguish between Truth and Falsehood."

Quoth the Caliph, "How great is this King! His letter hath shown me this; and as for the mightiness of his dominion thou hast told us what thou hast eye-witnessed. By Allah, he hath been endowed with wisdom as with wide rule." Then I related to the Commander of the Faithful all that had befallen me in my last voyage; at which he bade his historians record my story, for the edification of all who might see it. Then he conferred on me exceeding great favours, and I repaired to my quarter and entered my home, where I warehoused all my goods and possessions. Presently, my friends came to me and I distributed presents among my family and gave alms and largesse; after which I yielded myself to joyance and enjoyment, mirth and merry-making, and forgot all that I had suffered.

171

"Such, then, O my brothers, is the history of what befel me in my sixth voyage, and to-morrow, Inshallah! I will tell you the story of my seventh and last voyage, which is still more wondrous and marvellous than that of the first six" (saith he who telleth the tale).

Then he bade lay the table, and the company supped with him; after which he gave the Porter an hundred dinars, as of wont, and they all went their ways, marvelling beyond measure at that which they had heard. When Sinbad the Sailor had related the history of what befel him in his sixth voyage, and all the company had dispersed, Sinbad the Landsman went home and slept as of wont. Next day he rose and prayed the dawn-prayer and repaired to his namesake's house where, after the company was all assembled, the host began to relate

THE SEVENTH VOYAGE OF SINBAD THE SAILOR

Know, O company, that after my return from my sixth voyage, which brought me abundant profit, I resumed my former life in all possible joyance and enjoyment and mirth and making merry day and night; and I tarried some time in this solace and satisfaction till my soul began once more to long to sail the seas and see foreign countries and company with merchants and hear new things. So having made up my mind, I packed up in bales a quantity of precious stuffs suited for sea-trade and repaired with them from Baghdad-city to Bassorah-town, where I found a ship ready for sea, and in her a company of considerable merchants. I shipped with them and becoming friends, we set forth on our venture, in health and safety; and sailed with a fair wind, till we came to a city called Madinat-al-Sin; but after we had left it, as we fared on in all cheer and confidence, devising of traffic and travel, behold, there sprang up a violent head-wind and a tempest of rain fell on us and drenched us and our goods. So we covered the bales with our cloaks and garments and drugget and canvas, lest they be spoiled by the rain, and betook ourselves to prayer and supplication to Almighty Allah and humbled ourselves before Him for deliverance from the peril that was upon us. But the captain arose and tightening his girdle tucked up his skirts and, after taking refuge with Allah from Satan the Stoned, clomb to the mast-head, whence he looked out right and left and gazing at the passengers and crew fell to buffeting his face and plucking out his beard. So we cried to him, "O Rais, what is the matter?"; and he replied saying, "Seek ye deliverance of the Most High from the strait into which we have fallen and bemoan yourselves and take leave of one another; for know that the wind hath gotten the mastery of us and hath driven us into the uttermost of the seas of the world."

Then he came down from the mast-head and opening his sea-chest, pulled out a bag of blue cotton, from which he took a powder like ashes. This he set in a saucer wetted with a little water and, after waiting a short time, smelt and tasted it; and then he took out of the chest a booklet, wherein he read awhile and said weeping, "Know, O ye passengers, that in this book is a marvellous matter, denoting that whoso cometh hither shall surely die, without hope of escape; for that this ocean is called the Sea of the Clime of the King, wherein is the sepulchre of our lord Solomon, son of David (on both be peace!) and therein are serpents of vast bulk and fearsome aspect: and what ship soever cometh to these climes there riseth to her a great fish out of the sea and swalloweth her up with all and everything on board her." Hearing these words from the captain great was our wonder, but hardly had he made an end of speaking, when the ship was lifted out of the water and let fall again and we applied to praying the death-prayer and committing our souls to Allah.

Presently we heard a terrible great cry like the loud-pealing thunder, whereat we were terror-struck and became as dead men, giving ourselves up for lost. Then behold, there came up to us a huge fish, as big as a tall mountain, at whose sight we became wild for affright and, weeping sore, made ready for death, marvelling at its vast size and gruesome semblance; when lo! a second fish made its appearance than which we had seen naught more monstrous. So we bemoaned ourselves of our lives and farewelled one another; but suddenly up came a third fish bigger than the two first; whereupon we lost the power of thought and reason and were

172

stupefied for the excess of our fear and horror. Then the three fish began circling round about the ship and the third and biggest opened his mouth to swallow it, and we looked into its mouth and behold, it was wider than the gate of a city and its throat was like a long valley. So we besought the Almighty and called for succour upon His Apostle (on whom be blessing and peace!), when suddenly a violent squall of wind arose and smote the ship, which rose out of the water and settled upon a great reef, the haunt of sea-monsters, where it broke up and fell asunder into planks and all and everything on board were plunged into the sea.

As for me, I tore off all my clothes but my gown and swam a little way, till I happened upon one of the ship's planks whereto I clung and bestrode it like a horse, whilst the winds and the waters sported with me and the waves carried me up and cast me down; and I was in most piteous plight for fear and distress and hunger and thirst. Then I reproached myself for what I had done and my soul was weary after a life of ease and comfort; and I said to myself, "O Sinbad, O Sailor, thou repentest not and yet thou art ever suffering hardships and travails; yet wilt thou not renounce sea-travel; or, an thou say, 'I renounce,' thou liest in thy renouncement. Endure then with patience that which thou sufferest, for verily thou deservest all that betideth thee!" But when I had bestridden the plank, quoth I to myself, "Thou deservest all that betideth thee. All this is decreed to me of Allah (whose name be exalted!), to turn me from my greed of gain, whence ariseth all that I endure, for I have wealth galore." Then I returned to my senses and said, "In very sooth, this time I repent to the Most High, with a sincere repentance, of my lust for gain and venture; and never will I again name travel with tongue nor in thought." And I ceased not to humble myself before Almighty Allah and weep and bewail myself, recalling my former estate of solace and satisfaction and mirth and merriment and joyance; and thus I abode two days, at the end of which time I came to a great island abounding in trees and streams.

There I landed and ate of the fruits of the island and drank of its waters, till I was refreshed and my life returned to me and my strength and spirits were restored and I recited,

Oft when thy case shows knotty and tangled skein,
Fate downs from Heaven and straightens every ply:
In patience keep thy soul till clear thy lot
For He who ties the knot can eke untie.

Then I walked about, till I found on the further side, a great river of sweet water, running with a strong current; whereupon I called to mind the boat-raft I had made aforetime and said to myself, "Needs must I make another; haply I may free me from this strait. If I escape, I have my desire and I vow to Allah Almighty to foreswear travel; and if I perish I shall be at peace and shall rest from toil and moil." So I rose up and gathered together great store of pieces of wood from the trees (which were all of the finest sanders-wood, whose like is not albe I knew it not), and made shift to twist creepers and tree-twigs into a kind of rope, with which I bound the billets together and so contrived a raft. Then saying, "An I be saved, 'tis of God's grace," I embarked thereon and committed myself to the current, and it bore me on for the first day and the second and the third after leaving the island; whilst I lay in the raft, eating not and drinking, when I was athirst, of the water of the river, till I was weak and giddy as a chicken, for stress of fatigue and famine and fear.

At the end of this time I came to a high mountain, whereunder ran the river; which when I saw, I feared for my life by reason of the straitness I had suffered in my former journey, and I would fain have stayed the raft and landed on the mountain-side; but the current overpowered me and drew it into the subterranean passage like an archway; whereupon I gave myself up for lost and said, "There is no Majesty and there is no Might save in Allah, the Glorious, the Great!"

However, after a little, the raft glided into open air and I saw before me a wide valley, whereinto the river fell with a noise like the rolling of thunder and a swiftness as the rushing of the wind. I held on to the raft, for fear of falling off it, whilst the waves tossed me right and left; and the craft continued to descend with the current nor could I avail to stop it nor turn it shorewards, till it stopped with me at a great and goodly city, grandly edified and containing much people. And when the townsfolk saw me on the raft, dropping down with the current, they threw me out ropes which I had not strength enough to hold; then they tossed a net over the craft and drew it ashore with me, whereupon I fell to the ground amidst them, as I were a dead man, for stress of fear and hunger and lack of sleep.

After awhile, there came up to me out of the crowd an old man of reverend aspect, well stricken in years, who welcomed me and threw over me abundance of handsome clothes, wherewith I covered my nakedness. Then he carried me to the Hammam-bath and brought me cordial sherbets and delicious perfumes; moreover, when I came out, he bore me to his house, where his people made much of me and, seating me in a pleasant place, set rich food before me, whereof I ate my fill and returned thanks to God the Most High for my deliverance. Thereupon his pages fetched me hot water, and I washed my hands, and his handmaids brought me silken napkins, with which I dried them and wiped my mouth. Also the Shaykh set apart for me an apartment in a part of his house and charged his pages and slave-girls to wait upon me and do my will and supply my wants. They were assiduous in my service, and I abode with him in the guest-chamber three days, taking my ease of good eating and good drinking and good scents till life returned to me and my terrors subsided and my heart was calmed and my mind was eased.

On the fourth day the Shaykh, my host, came in to me and said, "Thou cheerest us with thy company, O my son, and praised be Allah for thy safety! Say: wilt thou now come down with me to the beach and the bazar and sell thy goods and take their price? Belike thou mayst buy thee wherewithal to traffic. I have ordered my servants to remove thy stock-in-trade from the sea and they have piled it on the shore."

I was silent awhile and said to myself, "What mean these words and what goods have I?"

Then said he, "O my son, be not troubled nor careful, but come with me to the market and if any offer for thy goods what price contenteth thee, take it; but, an thou be not satisfied, I will lay them up for thee in my warehouse, against a fitting occasion for sale."

So I bethought me of my case and said to myself, "Do his bidding and see what are these goods!" and I said to him, "O my nuncle the Shaykh, I hear and I obey; I may not gainsay thee in aught for Allah's blessing is on all thou dost."

Accordingly he guided me to the market-street, where I found that he had taken in pieces the raft which carried me and which was of sandal-wood and I heard the broker calling it for sale. I found that the Shaykh had taken to pieces my raft which lay on the beach and the broker was crying the sandal-wood for sale. Then the merchants came and opened the gate of bidding for the wood and bid against one another till its price reached a thousand dinars, when they left bidding and my host said to me, "Hear, O my son, this is the current price of thy goods in hard times like these: wilt thou sell them for this or shall I lay them up for thee in my storehouses, till such time as prices rise?"

"O my lord," answered I, "the business is in thy hands: do as thou wilt."

Then asked he, "Wilt thou sell the wood to me, O my son, for an hundred gold pieces over and above what the merchants have bidden for it?" and I answered, "Yes, I have sold it to thee for monies received."

So, he bade his servants transport the wood to his storehouses and, carrying me back to his house, seated me and counted out to me the purchase money; after which he laid it in bags and setting them in a privy place, locked them up with an iron padlock and gave me its key.

Some days after this, the Shaykh said to me, "O my son, I have somewhat to propose to thee, wherein I trust thou wilt do my bidding."

Quoth I, "What is it?"

Quoth he, "I am a very old man and have no son; but I have a daughter who is young in years and fair of favour and endowed with abounding wealth and beauty. Now I have a mind to marry her to thee, that thou mayst abide with her in this our country, and I will make thee master of all I have in hand for I am an old man and thou shalt stand in my stead."

I was silent for shame and made him no answer, whereupon he continued, "Do my desire in this, O my son, for I wish but thy weal; and if thou wilt but do as I say, thou shalt have her at once and be as my son; and all that is under my hand or that cometh to me shall be thine. If thou have a mind to traffic and travel to thy native land, none shall hinder thee, and thy property will be at thy sole disposal; so do as thou wilt."

"By Allah, O my uncle," replied I, "thou art become to me even as my father, and I am a stranger and have undergone many hardships: while for stress of that which I have suffered naught of judgment or knowledge is left to me. It is for thee, therefore, to decide what I shall do."

Hereupon he sent his servants for the Kazi and the witnesses and married me to his daughter making us for a noble marriage-feast and high festival. When I went in to her, I found her perfect in beauty and loveliness and symmetry and grace, clad in rich raiment and covered with a profusion of ornaments and necklaces and other trinkets of gold and silver and precious stones, worth a mint of money, a price none could pay. She pleased me and we loved each other; and I abode with her in solace and delight of life, till her father was taken to the mercy of Allah Almighty. So we shrouded him and buried him, and I laid hands on the whole of his property and all his servants and slaves became mine. Moreover, the merchants installed me in his office, for he was their Shaykh and their Chief; and none of them purchased aught but with his knowledge and by his leave. And now his rank passed on to me.

When I became acquainted with the townsfolk, I found that at the

beginning of each month they were transformed, in that their faces changed
and they became like birds and they put forth wings wherewith they flew
unto the upper regions of the firmament and none remained in the city
save the women and children; and I said in my mind, "When the first of
the month cometh, I will ask one of them to carry me with them, whither
they go."

So when the time came and their complexion changed and their
forms altered, I went in to one of the townsfolk and said to him, "Allah
upon thee! carry me with thee, that I might divert myself with the rest and
return with you."

"This may not be," answered he; but I ceased not to solicit him and I
importuned him till he consented. Then I went out in his company, without
telling any of my family or servants or friends, and he took me on his back
and flew up with me so high in air, that I heard the angels glorifying God in
the heavenly dome, whereat I wondered and exclaimed, "Praised be Allah!
Extolled be the perfection of Allah!"

Hardly had I made an end of pronouncing the Tasbih—praised be
Allah!—when there came out a fire from heaven and all but consumed the
company; whereupon they fled from it and descended with curses upon me
and, casting me down on a high mountain, went away, exceeding wroth
with me, and left me there alone. As I found myself in this plight, I repented
of what I had done and reproached myself for having undertaken that for
which I was unable, saying, "There is no Majesty and there is no Might,
save in Allah, the Glorious, the Great! No sooner am I delivered from one
affliction than I fall into a worse."

And I continued in this case knowing not whither I should go, when
lo! there came up two young men, as they were moons, each using as a staff
a rod of red gold. So I approached them and saluted them; and when they
returned my salam, I said to them, "Allah upon you twain; who are ye and
what are ye?"

Quoth they, "We are of the servants of the Most High Allah, abiding
in this mountain"; and, giving me a rod of red gold they had with them,
went their ways and left me. I walked on along the mountain-ridge staying
my steps with the staff and pondering the case of the two youths, when
behold, a serpent came forth from under the mountain, with a man in
her jaws, whom she had swallowed even to below his navel, and he was
crying out and saying, "Whoso delivereth me, Allah will deliver him from
all adversity!" So I went up to the serpent and smote her on the head with
the golden staff, whereupon she cast the man forth of her mouth.

When I smote the serpent on the head with my golden staff she cast the man forth of her mouth. Then I smote her a second time, and she turned and fled; whereupon he came up to me and said, "Since my deliverance from yonder serpent hath been at thy hands I will never leave thee, and thou shalt be my comrade on this mountain."

"And welcome," answered I; so we fared on along the mountain, till we fell in with a company of folk, and I looked and saw amongst them the very man who had carried me and cast me down there. I went up to him and spake him fair, excusing myself to him and saying, "O my comrade, it is not thus that friend should deal with friend."

Quoth he, "It was thou who well-nigh destroyed us by thy Tasbih and thy glorifying God on my back."

Quoth I, "Pardon me, for I had no knowledge of this matter; but, if thou wilt take me with thee, I swear not to say a word."

So he relented and consented to carry me with him, but he made an express condition that, so long as I abode on his back, I should abstain from pronouncing the Tasbih or otherwise glorifying God. Then I gave the wand of gold to him whom I had delivered from the serpent and bade him farewell, and my friend took me on his back and flew with me as before, till he brought me to the city and set me down in my own house.

My wife came to meet me and saluting me gave me joy of my safety and then said, "Beware of going forth hereafter with yonder folk, neither consort with them, for they are brethren of the devils, and know not how to mention the name of Allah Almighty; neither worship they Him."

"And how did thy father with them?" asked I; and she answered, "My father was not of them, neither did he as they; and as now he is dead methinks thou hadst better sell all we have and with the price buy merchandise and journey to thine own country and people, and I with thee; for I care not to tarry in this city, my father and my mother being dead."

So I sold all the Shaykh's property piecemeal, and looked for one who should be journeying thence to Bassorah that I might join myself to him. And while thus doing I heard of a company of townsfolk who had a mind to make the voyage, but could not find them a ship; so they bought wood and built them a great ship wherein I took passage with them, and paid them all the hire.

Then we embarked, I and my wife, with all our moveables, leaving our houses and domains and so forth, and set sail, and ceased not sailing from island to island and from sea to sea, with a fair wind and a favouring, till we arrived at Bassorah safe and sound. I made no stay there, but freighted another vessel and, transferring my goods to her, set out forthright for Baghdad-city, where I arrived in safety, and entering my quarter and repairing to my house, foregathered with my family and friends and familiars who laid up my goods in my warehouses. When my people who, reckoning the period of my absence on this my seventh voyage, had found it to be seven and twenty years, and had given up all hope of me, heard of my return, they came to welcome me and to give me joy of my safety; and I related to them all that had befallen me; whereat they marvelled with exceeding marvel. Then I forswore travel and vowed to Allah the Most High I would venture no more by land or sea, for that this seventh and last voyage had surfeited me of travel and adventure; and I thanked the Lord (be He praised and glorified!), and blessed Him for having restored me to my kith and kin and country and home.

179

"Consider, therefore, O Sinbad, O Landsman," continued Sinbad the Sailor, "what sufferings I have undergone and what perils and hardships I have endured before coming to my present state." "Allah upon thee, O my Lord!" answered Sinbad the Landsman, "pardon me the wrong I did thee." And they ceased not from friendship and fellowship, abiding in all cheer and pleasures and solace of life till there came to them the Destoyer of delights and the Sunderer of Societies, and the Shatterer of palaces and the Caterer for Cemeteries to wit, the Cup of Death, and glory be to the Living One who dieth not!

And Scheherazade perceived the dawn of day and ceased saying her permitted say. Said the King in himself, "By Allah, I will not slay her until I hear her next story." They rested that night in mutual embrace until dawn: then the King went forth to his Darbar; the Wazirs and troops came in and the audience hall was crowded; so the King gave orders and judged and appointed and deposed and bade and forbade the rest of that day, when the court broke up, and King Shahryar entered his palace; upon which Scheherazade began "The Tale of Prince Sayf al-Muluk."

The Tale of Prince Ṣayf al-Mulūk

Scheherazade continued the following evening,
"It hath reached me, O auspicious King, that…

There was once, in days of old and in ages and times long told, a King in Egypt called Asim bin Safwan, who was a liberal and beneficent sovran, venerable and majestic. He owned many cities and sconces and fortresses and troops and warriors and had a Wazir named Faris bin Salih, and he and all his subjects worshipped the sun and the fire, instead of the All-powerful Sire, the Glorious, the Victorious. Now this King was become a very old man, weakened and wasted with age and sickness and decrepitude; for he had lived an hundred and fourscore years and had no child, male or female, by reason whereof he was ever in cark and care from morning to night and from night to morn.

It so happened that one day of the days, he was sitting on the throne of his Kingship, with his Emirs and Wazirs and Captains and Grandees in attendance on him, according to their custom, in their several stations, and whenever there came in an Emir, who had with him a son or two sons, or haply three who stood at the sides of their sires the King envied him and said in himself, "Every one of these is happy and rejoiceth in his children, whilst

I, I have no child, and to-morrow I die and leave my reign and throne and lands and hoards, and strangers will take them and none will bear me in memory nor will there remain any mention of me in the world." Then he became drowned in the sea of thought and for the much thronging of griefs and anxieties upon his hear, like travellers faring for the well, he shed tears and descending from his throne, sat down upon the floor, weeping and humbling himself before the Lord.

Now when the Wazir and notables of the realm and others who were present in the assembly saw him do thus with his royal person, they feared for their lives and let the poursuivants cry aloud to the lieges, saying, "Hie ye to your homes and rest till the King recover from what aileth him."

So they went away, leaving none in the presence save the Minister who, as soon as the King came to himself, kissed ground between his hands and said, "O King of the Age and the Time, wherefore this weeping and wailing? Tell me who hath transgressed against thee of the Kings or Castellans or Emirs or Grandees, and inform me who hath thwarted thee, O my liege lord, that we may all fall on him and tear his soul from his two sides." But he spake not neither raised his head; whereupon the Minister kissed ground before him a second time and said to him, "O Master, I am even as thy son and thy slave, nay, I have reared thee; yet know I not the cause of thy cark and chagrin and of this thy case; and who should know but I who should stand in my stead between thy hands? Tell me therefore why this weeping and wherefore thine affliction." Nevertheless, the King neither opened his mouth nor raised his head, but ceased not to weep and cry with a loud crying and lament with exceeding lamentation and ejaculate, "Alas!" The Wazir took patience with him awhile, after which he said to him, "Except thou tell me the cause of this thine affliction, I will set this sword to my heart and will slay myself before thine eyes, rather than see thee thus distressed."

Then King Asim raised his head and, wiping away his tears, said, "O Minister of good counsel and experience, leave me to my care and my chagrin, for that which is in my heart of sorrow sufficeth me."

But Faris said, "Tell me, O King, the cause of this thy weeping, haply Allah will appoint thee relief at my hands."

Replied the King, "O Wazir, I weep not for monies nor horses nor kingdoms nor aught else, but that I am become an old man, yea, very old, nigh upon an hundred and fourscore years of age, and I have not been blessed with a child, male or female; so, when I die, they will bury me and my trace will be effaced and my name cut off; the stranger will take my throne and reign and none will ever make mention of my being."

Rejoined the Minister Faris, "O King of the Age, I am older than thou by an hundred years yet have I never been blest with boon of child and cease not day and night from cark and care and concern; so how shall we do, I and thou?"

Quoth Asim, "O Wazir, hast thou no device or shift in this matter?" and quoth the Minister, "Know, O King that I have heard of a Sovran in the land of Saba by name Solomon David-son (upon the twain be the Peace!), who pretendeth to prophetship and avoucheth that he hath a mighty Lord who can do all things and whose kingdom is in the Heavens and who hath dominion over all mankind and birds and beasts and over the wind and the Jinn. Moreover, he kenneth the speech of birds and the language of every other created thing; and withal, he calleth all creatures to the worship of his Lord and discourseth to them of their service. So let us send him a messenger in the King's name and seek of him our need, beseeching him to put up prayer to his Lord, that He vouchsafe each of us boon of issue. If his Faith be soothfast and his Lord Omnipotent, He will assuredly bless each of us with a child male or female, and if the thing thus fall out, we will enter his faith and worship his Lord; else will we take patience and devise us another device."

The King cried, "This is well seen, and my breast is broadened by this thy speech; but where shall we find a messenger befitting this grave matter, for that this Solomon is no Kinglet and the approaching him is no light affair? Indeed, I will send him none, on the like of this matter, save thyself; for thou art ancient and versed in all manner affairs and the like of thee is the like of myself; wherefore I desire that thou weary thyself and journey to him and occupy thyself sedulously with accomplishing this matter, so haply solace may be at thy hand."

The Minister said, "I hear and I obey; but rise thou forthwith and seat thee upon the throne, so the Emirs and Lords of the realm and officers and the lieges may enter applying themselves to thy service, according to their custom; for they all went away from thee, troubled at heart on thine account. Then will I go out and set forth on the Sovran's errand."

So the King arose forthright and sat down on the throne of his kingship, whilst the Wazir went out and said to the Chamberlain, "Bid the folk proceed to their service, as of their wont."

Accordingly the troops and Captains and Lords of the land entered, after they had spread the tables and ate and drank and withdrew as was their wont, after which the Wazir Faris went forth from King Asim and, repairing to his own house, equipped himself for travel and returned to the King,

who opened to him the treasuries and provided him with rarities and things of price and rich stuffs and gear without compare, such as nor Emir nor Wazir hath power to possess. Moreover, King Asim charged him to accost Solomon with reverence, foregoing him with the salam, but not exceeding in speech; "and (continued he) then do thou ask of him thy need, and if he say 'tis granted, return to us in haste, for I shall be awaiting thee."

Accordingly, the Minister kissed hands and took the presents and setting out, fared on night and day, till he came within fifteen days' journey of Saba. Meanwhile Allah (extolled and exalted be He!) inspired Solomon the son of David (the Peace be upon both!) and said to him, "O Solomon, the King of Egypt sendeth unto thee his Chief Wazir, with a present of rarities and such and such things of price; so do thou also despatch thy Counsellor Asaf bin Barkhiya to meet him with honour and with victual at the halting-places; and when he cometh to thy presence, say unto him, 'Verily, thy King hath sent thee in quest of this and that and thy business is thus and thus.' Then do thou propound to him The Saving Faith." Whereupon Solomon bade his Wazir make ready a company of his retainers and go forth to meet the Minister of Egypt with honour and sumptuous provision at the halting-places.

So Asaf made ready all that was needed for their entertainment and setting out, fared on till he fell in with Faris and accosted him with the salam, honouring him and his company with exceeding honour. Moreover, he brought them provaunt and provender at the halting-places and said to them, "Well come and welcome and fair welcome to the coming guests! Rejoice in the certain winning of your wish! Be your souls of good cheer and your eyes cool and clear and your breasts be broadened!"

Quoth Faris in himself, "Who acquainted him with this?"; and he said to Asaf, "O my lord, and who gave thee to know of us and our need?" "It was Solomon son of David (on whom be the Peace!), told us of this!"

"And who told our lord Solomon?" "The Lord of the heaven and the earth told him, the God of all creatures!"

"This is none other than a mighty God!"

"And do ye not worship him?"

"We worship the Sun, and prostrate ourselves thereto."

"O Wazir Faris, the sun is but a star of the stars created by Allah (extolled and exalted be He!), and Allah forbid that it should be a Lord! Because whiles it riseth and whiles it setteth, but our Lord is ever present and never absent and He over all things is Omnipotent!"

Then they journeyed on a little while till they came to the land Saba and drew near the throne of Solomon David-son (upon the twain be

183

peace!), who commanded his hosts of men and Jinn and others to form line on their road. So the beasts of the sea and the elephants and leopards and lynxes and all beasts of the land ranged themselves in espalier on either side of the way, after their several kinds, and similarly the Jinn drew out in two ranks, appearing all to mortal eyes without concealment, in diverse forms grisly and gruesome. So they lined the road on either hand, and the birds bespread their wings over the host of creatures to shade them, warbling one to other in all manner of voices and tongues.

Now when the people of Egypt came to this terrible array, they dreaded it and durst not proceed; but Asaf said to them, "Pass on amidst them and walk forward and fear them not: for they are slaves of Solomon son of David, and none of them will harm you." So saying, he entered between the ranks, followed by all the folk and amongst them the Wazir of Egypt and his company, fearful: and they ceased not faring forwards till they reached the city, where they lodged the embassy in the guest-house and for the space of three days entertained them sumptuously, entreating them with the utmost honour. Then they carried them before Solomon, prophet of Allah (on whom be the Peace!), and when entering they would have kissed the earth before him; but he forbade them, saying, "It befitteth not a man prostrate himself to earth save before Allah (to whom belong Might and Majesty!), Creator of Earth and Heaven and all other things; wherefore, whosoever of you hath a mint to sit let him be seated in my service, or to stand, let him stand, but let none stand to do me worship." So they obeyed him and the Wazir Faris and some of his intimates sat down, whilst certain of the lesser sort remained afoot to wait on him. When they had sat awhile, the servants spread the tables and they all, men and beasts, ate their sufficiency.

Then Solomon bade Faris expound his errand, that it might be accomplished, saying, "Speak and hide naught of that wherefor thou art come; for I know why ye come and what is your errand, which is thus and thus. The King of Egypt who despatched thee, Asim hight, hath become a very old man, infirm, decrepit; and Allah (whose name be exalted!) hath not blessed him with offspring, male or female. So he abode in cark and care and chagrin from morn to night and from night to morn. It so happened that one day of the days as he sat upon the throne of his kingship with his Emirs and Wazirs, and Captains and Grandees in attendance on him, he saw some of them with two sons, others with one, and others even three, who came with their sires to do him service. So he said in himself, of the excess of his sorrow, 'Who shall get my kingdom after my death? Will any save a stranger take it? And thus shall I pass out of being as though I had never been!' On this account he became drowned in the sea of thought, until his eyes were flooded with tears and he covered his face with his kerchief and wept with sore weeping. Then he rose from off his throne and sat down upon the floor wailing and lamenting and none knew what was in heart as he grovelled in the ground save Allah Almighty."

Solomon said to him, "Is this that I have told thee the truth, O Wazir?"

Replied Faris, "O prophet of Allah, this thou hast said is indeed sooth and verity; but when we discoursed of this matter, none was with the King and myself, nor was any ware of our case; who, then told thee of all these things?"

Answered Solomon, "They were told to me by my Lord who knoweth whatso is concealed from the eye and what is hidden in the breasts."

Quoth Faris, "O Prophet of Allah, verily this is none other than a mighty Lord and an omnipotent God!" And he Islamized with all his many.

Then said Solomon to him, "Thou hast with thee such and such presents and rarities"; and Faris replied "Yes." The prophet continued, "I accept them all and give them in free gift unto thee. So do ye rest, thou and thy company, in the place where you have been lodging, till the fatigue of the journey shall cease from you; and to-morrow, Inshallah! thine errand shall be accomplished to the uttermost, if it be the will of Allah the Most High, Lord of heaven and earth and the light which followeth the gloom; Creator of all creatures."

So Faris returned to his quarters and passed the night in deep thought. But when morning morrowed he presented himself before the Lord Solomon, who said to him, "When thou returnest to King Asim bin Safwan and you twain are re-united, do ye both go forth some day armed with bow, bolts and brand, and fare to such a place, where ye shall find a certain tree. Mount upon it and sit silent until the midhour between noon-prayer and that of mid-afternoon, when the noontide heat hath cooled; then descend and look at the foot of the tree, whence ye will see two serpents come forth, one with a head like an ape's and the other with a head like an Ifrit's. Shoot them ye twain with bolts and kill them both; then cut off a span's length from their heads and the like from their tails and throw it away. The rest of the flesh cook and cook well and give it to your wives to eat: then lie with them that night and, by Allah's leave, they shall conceive and bear male children." Moreover, he gave him a seal-ring, a sword, and a wrapper containing two tunics embroidered with gold and jewels, saying, "O Wazir Faris, when your sons grow up to man's estate, give to each of them one of these tunics." Then said he, "In the name of Allah! May the Almighty accomplish your desire! And now nothing remaineth for thee but to depart, relying on the blessing of the Lord the Most High, for the King looketh for thy return night and day and his eye is ever gazing on the road."

So the Wazir advanced to the prophet Solomon son of David (upon both of whom be the Peace!) and farewelled him and fared forth from him after kissing his hands. Rejoicing in the accomplishment of his errand he travelled on with all diligence night and day, and ceased not wayfaring till he drew near to Cairo, when he despatched one of his servants to acquaint King Asim with his approach and the successful issue of his journey; which when the King heard he joyed with exceeding joy, he and his Grandees and Officers and troops especially in the Wazir's safe return. When they met, the Minister dismounted and, kissing ground before the King, gave him the glad news anent the winning of his wish in fullest fashion; after which he expounded the True Faith to him, and the King and all his people embraced Al-Islam with much joy and gladness.

Then said Asim to his Wazir, "Go home and rest this night and a week to boot; then go to the Hammam-bath and come to me, that I may inform thee of what we shall have to consider."

So Faris kissed ground and withdrew, with his suite, pages and eunuchs, to his house, where he rested eight days; after which he repaired to the King and related to him all that had passed between Solomon and himself, adding, "Do thou rise and go forth with me alone."

Then the King and the Minister took two bows and two bolts and repairing to the tree indicated by Solomon, clomb up into it and there sat in silence till the mid-day heat had passed away and it was near upon the hour of mid-afternoon prayer, when they descended and looking about them saw a serpent-couple issue from the roots of the tree. The King gazed at them, marvelling to see them ringed with collars of gold about their necks, and said to Faris, "O Wazir, verily these snakes have golden torques! By Allah, this is forsooth a rare thing! Let us catch them and set them in a cage and keep them to look upon."

But the Minister said, "These hath Allah created for profitable use; so do thou shoot one and I will shoot the other with these our shafts."

Accordingly they shot at them with arrows and slew them; after which they cut off a span's length of their heads and tails and threw it away. Then they carried the rest to the King's palace, where they called the kitchener and giving him the flesh said, "Dress this meat daintily, with onion-sauce and spices, and ladle it out into two saucers and bring them hither at such an hour, without delay!"

The cook took the meat and went with it to the kitchen, where he cooked it and dressed it in skilful fashion with a mighty fine onion-sauce and hot spices; after which he ladled it out into two saucers and set them before the King and the Wazir, who took each a dish and gave their wives to eat of the meat. Then they went in that night unto them and knew them carnally, and by the good pleasure of Allah (extolled and exalted be He!) and His all-might and furtherance, they both conceived on one and the same night.

The King abode three months, troubled in mind and saying in himself, "I wonder whether this thing will prove true or untrue"; till one day, as the lady his Queen was sitting, the child stirred in her womb and she felt a pain and her colour changed. So she knew that she was with child and calling the chief of her eunuchs, gave him this command, "Go to the King, wherever he may be and congratulate him saying, 'O King of the Age, I bring thee the glad tidings that our lady's pregnancy is become manifest, for the child stirreth in her womb.'"

So the eunuch went out in haste, rejoicing, and finding the King alone, with cheek on palm, pondering this thing, kissed ground between his hands and acquainted him with his wife's pregnancy. When the King heard his words, he sprang to his feet and in the excess of his joy, he kissed the eunuch's hands and head and doffing the clothes he had on, gave them to him. Moreover, he said to those who were present in his assembly, "Whoso loveth me, let him bestow largesse upon this man." And they gave him of coin and jewels and jacinths and horses and mules and estates and gardens what was beyond count or calculation.

At that moment in came the Wazir Faris and said to Asim, "O my master, but now I was sitting alone at home and absorbed in thought, pondering the matter of the pregnancy and saying to myself, 'Would I wot an this thing be true and whether my wife Khatun have conceived or not!' when, behold, an eunuch came in to me and brought me the glad tidings that his lady was indeed pregnant, for that her colour was changed and the child stirred in her womb; whereupon, in my joy, I doffed all the clothes I had on and gave them to him, together with a thousand dinars, and made him Chief of the Eunuchs."

Rejoined the King, "O Minister, Allah (extolled and exalted be He!) hath, of His grace and bounty and goodness, and beneficence, made gift to us of the True Faith and brought us out of night into light, and hath been

187

bountiful to us, of His favour and benevolence; wherefore I am minded to solace the folk and cause them to rejoice."

Quoth Faris, "Do what thou wilt," and quoth the King, "O Wazir, go down without stay or delay and set free all who are in the prisons, both criminals and debtors, and whoso transgresseth after this, we will requite as he deserveth even to the striking off of his head. Moreover, we forgive the people three years' taxes, and do thou set up kitchens all around about the city walls and bid the kitcheners hang over the fire all kinds of cooking pots and cook all manner of meats, continuing their cooking night and day, and let all comers, both of our citizens and of the neighbouring countries, far and near, eat and drink and carry to their houses. And do thou command the people to make holiday and decorate the city seven days and shut not the taverns night nor day; and if thou delay I will behead thee!"

So he did as the King bade him and the folk decorated the city and citadel and bulwarks after the goodliest fashion and, donning their richest attire, passed their time in feasting and sporting and making merry, till the days of the Queen's pregnancy were accomplished and she was taken, one night, with labour pains hard before dawn.

Then the King bade summon all the Olema and astronomers, mathematicians and men of learning, astrologers, scientists and scribes in the city, and they assembled and sat awaiting the throwing of a bead into the cup which was to be the signal to the Astrophils, as well as to the nurses and attendants, that the child was born. Presently, as they sat in expectation, the Queen gave birth to a boy like a slice of the moon when fullest and the astrologers fell to calculating and noted his star and nativity and drew his horoscope. Then, on being summoned they rose and, kissing the earth before the King, gave him the glad tidings, saying, "In very sooth the new-born child is of happy augury and born under an auspicious aspect, but" they added, "in the first of his life there will befall him a thing which we fear to name before the King."

Quoth Asim, "Speak and fear not"; so quoth they, "O King, this boy will fare forth from this land and journey in strangerhood and suffer shipwreck and hardship and prisonment and distress, and indeed he hath before him the sorest of sufferings; but he shall free him of them in the end, and win to his wish and live the happiest of lives the rest of his days, ruling over subjects with a strong hand and having dominion in the land, despite enemies and enviers."

Now when the King heard the astrologers' words, he said, "The matter is a mystery; but all that Allah Almighty hath written for the creature of good and bad cometh to pass and needs must betide him from this day to that a thousand solaces."

So he paid no heed to their words or attention to their speeches but bestowed on them robes of honour, as well upon all who were present, and dismissed them; when, behold, in came Faris the Wazir and kissed the earth before the King in huge joy, saying, "Good tidings, O King! My wife hath but now given birth to a son, as he were a slice of the moon."

Replied Asim, "O Wazir, go, bring thy wife and child hither, that she may abide with my wife in my palace, and they shall bring up the two boys together."

So Faris fetched his wife and son and they committed the two children to the nurses wet and dry. And after seven days had passed over them, they brought them before the King and said to him, "What wilt thou name the twain?"

Quoth he, "Do ye name them;" but quoth they, "None nameth the son save his sire."

So he said, "Name my son Sayf al-Muluk, after my grandfather, and the Minister's son Sa'id." Then he bestowed robes of honour on the nurses wet and dry and said to them, "Be ye ruthful over them and rear them after the goodliest fashion."

So they brought up the two boys diligently till they reached the age of five, when the King committed them to a doctor of Sciences who taught them to read the Koran and write. When they were ten years old, King Asim gave them in charge to masters, who instructed them in cavalarice and shooting with shafts and lunging with lance and play of Polo and the like till, by the time they were fifteen years old, they were clever in all manner of martial exercises, nor was there one to view with them in horsemanship, for each of them would do battle with a thousand men and make head against them single handed.

So when they came to years of discretion, whenever King Asim looked on them he joyed in them with exceeding joy; and when they attained their twenty-fifth year, he took Faris his Minister apart one day and said to him, "O Wazir, I am minded to consult with thee concerning a thing I desire to do."

Replied he, "Whatever thou hast a mind to do, do it; for thy judgement is blessed."

Quoth the King, "O Wazir, I am become a very old and decrepit man, sore stricken in years, and I desire to take up my abode in an oratory, that I may worship Allah Almighty and give my kingdom and Sultanate to my son Sayf al-Muluk for that he is grown a goodly youth, perfect in knightly

189

exercises and intellectual attainments, polite letters and gravity, dignity and the art of government. What sayst thou, O Minister, of this project?"

And quoth the counsellor, "Right indeed is thy rede: the idea is a blessed and a fortunate, and if thou do this, I will do the like and my son Sa'id shall be the Prince's Wazir, for he is a comely young man and complete in knowledge and judgment. Thus will the two youths be together, and we will order their affair and neglect not their case, but guide them to goodness and in the way that is straight."

Quoth the King, "Write letters and send them by couriers to all the countries and cities and sconces and fortresses that be under our hands, bidding their chiefs be present on such a day at the Horse-course of the Elephant."

So the Wazir went out without stay or delay and despatched letters of this purport to all the deputies and governors of fortresses and others under King Asim; and he commanded also that all in the city should be present, far and near, high and low. When the appointed time drew nigh, King Asim bade the tent-pitchers plant pavilions in the midst of the Champ-de-Mars and decorate them after the most sumptuous fashion and set up the great throne whereon he sat not but on festivals. And they at once did his bidding. Then he and all his Nabobs and Chamberlains and Emirs sallied forth, and he commanded proclamation be made to the people, saying, "In the name of Allah, come forth to the Maydan!"

So all the Emirs and Wazirs and Governors of provinces and Feudatories came forth to the place of assembly and, entering the royal pavilion, addressed themselves to the service of the King as was their wont, and abode in their several stations, some sitting and others standing, till all the people were gathered together, when the King bade spread the tables and they ate and drank and prayed for him. Then he commanded the Chamberlains to proclaim to the people that they should not depart: so they made proclamation to them, saying, "Let none of you fare hence till he have heard the King's words!"

So they withdrew the curtains of the royal pavilion and the King said, "Whoso loveth me, let him remain till he have heard my speech!"

Whereupon all the folk sat down in mind tranquil after they had been fearful, saying, "Wherefore have we been summoned by the King?"

Then the Sovran rose to his feet, and making them swear that none would stir from his stead, said to them, "O ye Emirs and Wazirs and Lords of the land; the great and the small of you, and all ye who are present of the people; say me, wot ye not that this kingdom was an inheritance to me from my fathers and forefathers?"

Answered they, "Yes, O King we all know that."

And he continued, "I and you, we all worshipped the sun and moon, till Allah (extolled and exalted be He!) vouchsafed us the knowledge of the True Faith and brought us out of darkness unto light, and directed us to the religion of Al-Islam. Know that I am become a very old man, feeble and decrepit, and I desire to take up my abode in a hermitage there to worship Allah Almighty and crave His pardon for past offenses and make this my son Sayf al-Muluk ruler. Ye know full well that he is a comely youth, eloquent, liberal, learned, versed in affairs, intelligent, equitable; wherefore I am minded presently to resign to him my realm and to make him ruler over you and seat him as Sultan in my stead, whilst I give myself to solitude and to the worship of Allah in an oratory, and my son and heir shall judge between you. What say ye then, all of you?"

Thereupon they all rose and kissing ground before him, made answer with "Hearing and obedience," saying, "O our King and our defender an thou should set over us one of thy blackamoor slaves we would obey him and hearken to thy word and accept thy command: how much more then with thy son Sayf al-Muluk? Indeed, we accept of him and approve him on our eyes and heads!"

So King Asim bin Safwan arose and came down from his seat and seating his son on the great throne, took the crown from his own head and set it on the head of Sayf al-Muluk and girt his middle with the royal girdle. Then he sat down beside his son on the throne of his kingship, whilst the Emirs and Wazirs and Lords of the land and all the rest of the folk rose and kissed ground before him, saying, "Indeed, he is worthy of the kingship and hath better right to it than any other."

Then the Chamberlains made proclamation crying, "Aman! Aman! Safety! Safety!" and offered up prayers for his victory and prosperity. And Sayf al-Muluk scattered gold and silver on the heads of the lieges one and all, and conferred robes of honour and gave gifts and largesse.

Then, after a moment, the Wazir Faris arose and kissing ground said, "O Emirs, O Grandees, ye ken that I am Wazir and that my Wazirate dateth from old, before the accession of King Asim bin Safwan, who hath now divested himself of the Kingship and made his son King in his stead?"

Answered they, "Yes, we know that thy Wazirate is from sire after grandsire."

He continued, "And now in my turn I divest myself of office and invest this my son Sa'id, for he is intelligent, quick-witted, sagacious. What say ye all?"

And they replied, "None is worthy to be Wazir to King Sayf al-Muluk but thy son, Sa'id, and they befit each other."

With this Faris arose and taking off his Wazirial turband, set it on his son's head and eke laid his ink-case of office before him, whilst the Chamberlains and the Emirs said, "Indeed, he is deserving of the Wazirship" and the Heralds cried aloud, "Mubarak! Mubarak!—Felix sit et faustus!"

After this, King Asim and Faris the Minister arose and, opening the royal treasuries, conferred magnificent robes of honour on all the Viceroys and Emirs and Wazirs and Lords of the land and other folk and gave salaries and benefactions and wrote them new mandates and diplomas with the signatures of King Sayf al-Muluk and his Wazir Sa'id. Moreover, he made distribution of money to the men-at-arms and gave guerdons, and the provincials abode in the city a full week ere they departed each to his own country and place. Then King Asim carried his son and his Wazir Sa'id back to the palace which was in the city and bade the treasurer bring the seal-ring and signet, sword and wrapper; which being done, he said to the two young men, "O my sons, come hither and let each of you choose two of these things and take them."

The first to make choice was Sayf al-Muluk, who put out his hand and took the ring and the wrapper, whilst Sa'id took the sword and the signet; after which they both kissed the King's hands and went away to their lodging. Now Sayf al-Muluk opened not the wrapper to see what was therein, but threw it on the couch where he and Sa'id slept by night, for it was their habit to lie together. Presently they spread them the bed and the two lay down with a pair of wax candles burning over them and slept till midnight, when Sayf al-Muluk awoke and, seeing the bundle at his head, said in his mind, "I wonder what thing of price is in this wrapper my father gave me!"

So he took it together with a candle and descended from the couch leaving Sa'id sleeping and carried the bundle into a closet, where he opened it and found within a tunic of the fabric of the Jann. He spread it out and saw on the lining of the back, the portraiture wroughten in gold of a girl and marvellous was her loveliness; and no sooner had he set eyes on the figure than his reason fled his head and he became Jinn-mad for love thereof, so that he fell down in a swoon and presently recovering, began to weep and lament, beating his face and breast and kissing her. And he recited these verses:

"Love, at the first, is a spurt of spray
Which Doom disposes and Fates display;

Till, when deep diveth youth in passion-sea
Unbearable sorrows his soul waylay."

And also these two couplets:

"Had I known of Love in what fashion he
Robbeth heart and soul I had guarded me:
But of malice prepense I threw self away
Unwitting of Love what his nature be."

And Sayf al-Muluk ceased not to weep and wail and beat face and breast, till Sa'id awoke and missing him from the bed and seeing but a single candle, said to himself, "Whither is Sayf al-Muluk gone?"

Then he took the other candle and went round about the palace, till he came upon the closet where he saw the Prince lying at full length, weeping with sore weeping and lamenting aloud. So he said to him, "O my brother, for what cause are these tears and what hath befallen thee? Speak to me and tell me the reason thereof."

But Sayf al-Muluk spoke not neither raised his head and continued to weep and wail and beat hand on breast. Seeing him in this case quoth Sa'id, "I am thy Wazir and thy brother, and we were reared together, I and thou; so an thou do not unburden thy breast and discover thy secret to me, to whom shalt thou reveal it and disclose its cause?" And he went on to humble himself and kiss the ground before him a full hour, whilst Sayf al-Muluk paid no heed to him nor answered him a word, but gave not over to weeping.

At last, being affrighted at his case and weary of striving with him, he went out and fetched a sword, with which he returned to the closet, and setting the point to his own breast, said to the Prince, "Rouse thee, O my brother! An thou tell me not what aileth thee, I will slay myself and see thee no longer in this case." Whereupon Sayf al-Muluk raised his head towards the Wazir and answered him, "O my brother, I am ashamed to tell thee what hath betided me"; but Sa'id said, "I conjure thee by Allah, Lord of Lords, Liberator of Necks, Causer of causes, the One, the Ruthful, the Gift-full, the Bountiful, that thou tell me what aileth thee and be not abashed at me, for I am thy slave and thy Minister and counsellor in all thine affairs!"

Quoth Sayf al-Muluk, "Come and look at this likeness."

So Sa'id looked at it awhile and considering it straitly, behold, he saw

193

written, as a crown over its head, in letters of pearl, these words, "This is the counterfeit presentment of Badi'a al-Jamal, daughter of Shahyal bin Sharukh, a King of the Kings of the true-believing Jann who have taken up their abode in the city of Babel and sojourn in the garden of Iram, Son of 'Ad the Greater.'"

When Sa'id, son of the Wazir Faris, had read to Sayf al-Muluk, son of King Asim, the writ on the tunic, which showed the portraiture of Badi'a al-Jamal, daughter of Shahyal bin Sharukh, a King of the Kings of the Moslem Jinns dwelling in Babel-city and in the Garden of Iram, son of 'Ad the Greater,' he cried, "O my brother, knowest thou of what woman this is the presentment, that we may seek for her?"

Sayf al-Muluk replied, "No, by Allah, O my brother, I know her not!" and Sa'id rejoined, "Come, read this writing on the crown."

So Sayf al-Muluk read it and cried out from his heart's core and very vitals, saying, "Alas! Alas! Alas!"

Quoth Sa'id, "O my brother, an the original of the portrait exist and her name be Badi'a al-Jamal, and she abide in the world, I will hasten to seek her, that thou mayst win thy will without delay. But, Allah upon thee, O my brother, leave this weeping and ascend thy throne, that the Officers of the State may come in to do their service to thee, and in the undurn, do thou summon the merchants and fakirs and travellers and pilgrims and paupers and ask of them concerning this city and the garden of Iram; haply by the help and blessing of Allah (extolled and exalted be He!), some one of them shall direct us thither."

So, when it was day, Sayf al-Muluk went forth and mounted the throne, clasping the tunic in his arms, for he could neither stand nor sit without it, nor would sleep visit him save it were with him; and the Emirs and Wazirs and Lords and Officers came in to him. When the Divan was complete all being assembled in their places he said to his Minister, "Go forth to them and tell them that the King hath been suddenly struck by sickness and he, by Allah, hath passed the night in ill case."

So Sa'id fared forth and told the folk what he said; which when old King Asim heard, he was concerned for his son and, summoning the physicians and astrologers, carried them in to Sayf al-Muluk. They looked at him and prescribed him ptisanes and diet-drinks, simples and medicinal waters and wrote him characts and incensed him with Nadd and aloes-wood and ambergris three days' space; but his malady persisted three months, till King Asim was wroth with the leaches and said to them, "Woe to you, O dogs! What? Are all of you impotent to cure my son? Except ye heal him forthright, I will put the whole of you to death."

The Archiater replied, "O King of the Age, in very sooth we know that this is thy son and thou wottest that we fail not of diligence in tending a stranger; so how much more with medicining thy son? But thy son is afflicted with a malady hard to heal, which, if thou desire to know, we will discover it to thee."

Quoth Asim, "What then find ye to be the malady of my son?"; and quoth the leach, "O King of the Age, thy son is in love and he loveth one to whose enjoyment he hath no way of access."

At this the King was wroth and asked, "How know ye that my son is in love and how came love to him?"; they answered, "Enquire of his Wazir and brother Sa'id for he knoweth his case."

The King rose and repaired to his private closet and summoning Sa'id said to him, "Tell me the truth of thy brother's malady."

But Sa'id replied, "I know it not."

So King Asim said to the Sworder, "Take Sa'id and bind his eyes and strike his neck."

Whereupon Sa'id feared for himself and cried, "O King of the Age, grant me immunity."

Replied the King, "Speak and thou shalt have it."

"Thy son is in love."

"With whom is he in love?"

"With a King's daughter of the Jann."

"And where could he have espied a daughter of the Jinns?"

"Her portrait is wroughten on the tunic that was in the bundle given thee by Solomon, prophet of Allah!" When the King heard this, he rose, and going in to Sayf al-Muluk, said to him, "O my son, what hath afflicted thee? What is this portrait whereof thou art enamoured? And why didst thou not tell me."

He replied, "O my sire, I was ashamed to name this to thee and could not bring myself to discover aught thereof to any one at all; but now thou knowest my case, look how thou mayest do to cure me."

Rejoined his father, "What is to be done? Were this one of the daughters of men we might devise a device for coming at her; but she is a King's daughter of the Jinns and who can woo and win her, save it be Solomon David-son, and hardly he? However, O my son, do thou arise forthright and hearten thy heart and take horse and ride out a-hunting or to weapon-play in the Maydan. Divert thyself with eating and drinking and put away cark and care from thy heart, and I will bring thee an hundred

maids of the daughters of Kings; for thou hast no need to the daughters of the Jann, over whom we lack controul and of kind other than ours."

But he said, "I cannot renounce her nor will I seek other than her."

Asked King Asim, "How then shall we do, O my son?"; and Sayf al-Muluk answered, "Bring us all the merchants and travellers and wanderers in the city, that we may question them thereof. Peradventure, Allah will lead us to the city of Babel and the garden of Iram."

So King Asim bade summon all the merchants in the city and strangers and seacaptains and, as each came, enquired of him anent the city of Babel and its peninsula and the garden of Iram; but none of them knew these places nor could any give him tidings thereof. However, when the seance broke up, one of them said, "O King of the Age, an thou be minded to ken this thing, up and hie thee to the land of China; for it hath a vast city and a safe, wherein are store of rarities and things of price and folk of all kinds; and thou shalt not come to the knowledge of this city and garden but from its folk; it may be one of them will direct thee to that thou seekest."

Whereupon quoth Sayf al-Muluk, "O my sire, equip me a ship, that I may fare to the China-land; and do thou rule the reign in my stead."

Replied the old King, "O my son, abide thou on the throne of thy kingship and govern thy commons, and I myself will make the voyage to China and ask for thee of the city of Babel and the garden of Iram."

But Sayf al-Muluk rejoined, "O my sire, in very sooth this affair concerneth me and none can search after it like myself: so, come what will, an thou give me leave to make the voyage, I will depart and wander awhile. If I find trace or tidings of her, my wish will be won, and if not, belike the voyage will broaden my breast and recruit my courage; and haply by foreign travel my case will be made easy to me, and if I live, I shall return to thee safe and sound."

The old King looked at his son and saw nothing for it but to do what he desired; so he gave him the leave he wanted and fitted him forty ships, manned with twenty thousand armed Mamelukes, besides servants, and presented him with great plenty of money and necessaries and warlike gear, as much as he required. When the ships were laden with water and victual, weapons and troops, Sayf al-Muluk's father and mother farewelled him and King Asim said, "Depart, O my son, and travel in weal and health and safety. I commend thee to Him with Whom deposits are not lost."

So the Prince bade adieu to his parents and embarked, with his brother Sa'id and they weighed anchor and sailed till they came to the City of China. When the Chinamen heard of the coming of forty ships, full of armed men and stores, weapons and hoards, they made sure that these were enemies come to battle with them and seige them; so they bolted the gates of the town and made ready the mangonels. But Sayf al-Muluk, hearing of this, sent two of his Chief Mamelukes to the King of China, bidding them say to him, "This is Sayf al-Muluk, son of King Asim of Egypt, who is come to thy city as a guest, to divert himself by viewing thy country awhile, and not for conquest or contention; wherefore, an thou wilt receive him, he will come ashore to thee; and if not he will return and will not disquiet thee nor the people of thy capital."

They presented themselves at the city gates and said, "We are messengers from King Sayf al-Muluk." Whereupon the townsfolk opened the gates and carried them to their King, whose name was Faghfur Shah and between whom and King Asim there had erst been acquaintance. So, when he heard that the new-comer Prince was the son of King Asim, he bestowed robes of honour on the messengers and, bidding open the gates, made ready guest-gifts and went forth in person with the chief officers of his realm, to meet Sayf al-Muluk, and the two Kings embraced.

Then Faghfur said to his guest, "Well come and welcome and fair cheer to him who cometh to us! I am thy slave and the slave of thy sire: my city is between thy hands to command and whatso thou seekest shall be brought before thee."

Then he presented him with the guest-gifts and victual for the folk at their stations; and they took horse, with the Wazir Sa'id and the chiefs of their officers and the rest of their troops, and rode from the sea-shore to the city, which they entered with cymbals clashing and drums beating in token of rejoicing. There they abode in the enjoyment of fair entertainment for forty days, at the end of which quoth the King of China to Sayf al-Muluk, "O son of my brother, how is thy case? Doth my country please thee?" and quoth Sayf al-Muluk, "May Allah Almighty long honour it with thee, O King!"

Said Faghfur, "Naught hath brought thee hither save some need which hath occurred to thee; and whatso thou desirest of my country I will accomplish it to the."

Replied Sayf al-Muluk, "O King, my case is a wondrous," and told him how he had fallen in love with the portrait of Badi'a al-Jamal, and wept bitter tears.

When the King of China heard his story, he wept for pity and solicitude for him and cried, "And what wouldst thou have now, O Sayf al-Muluk?"; and he rejoined, "I would have thee bring me all the wanderers and travellers, the seafarers and sea-captains, that I may question them of the original of this portrait; perhaps one of them may give me tidings of her."

So Faghfur Shah sent out his Nabobs and Chamberlains and body-guards to fetch all the wanderers and travellers in the land, and they brought them before the two Kings, and they were a numerous company. Then Sayf al-Muluk questioned them of the City of Babel and the Garden of Iram, but none of them returned him a reply, whereupon he was bewildered and wist not what to do; but one of the sea-captains said to him, "O auspicious King, an thou wouldst know of this city and that garden, up and hie thee to the Islands of the Indian realm."

Thereupon Sayf al-Muluk bade bring the ships; which being done, they freighted them with vivers and water and all that they needed, and the Prince and his Wazir re-embarked, with all their men, after they had farewelled King Faghfur Shah. They sailed the seas four months with a fair wind, in safety and satisfaction till it chanced that one day of the days there came out upon them a wind and the billows buffeted them from all quarters. The rain and hail descended on them and during twenty days the sea was troubled for the violence of the wind; wherefor the ships drave one against other and brake up, as did the carracks and all on board were drowned, except Sayf al-Muluk and some of his servants, who saved themselves in a little cock-boat.

Then the wind fell by the decree of Allah Almighty and the sun shone out; whereupon Sayf al-Muluk opened his eyes and seeing no sign of the ships nor aught, but sky and sea, said to the Mamelukes who were with him, "Where are the carracks and cock-boats and where is my brother Sa'id?"

They replied, "O King of the Age, there remain nor ships nor boats nor those who were therein; for they are all drowned and become food for fishes."

Now when he heard this, he cried aloud and repeated the saying which whoso saith shall not be confounded, and it is, "There is no Majesty and there is no Might save in Allah, the Glorious, the Great!"

Then he fell to buffeting his face and would have cast himself into the sea, but his Mamelukes withheld him, saying "O King, what will this profit thee? Thou hast brought all this on thyself; for, hadst thou hearkened to thy father's words, naught thereof had betided thee. But this was written from all eternity by the will of the Creator of Souls, that the creature might accomplish that which Allah hath decreed unto him. And indeed, at the time of thy birth, the astrologers assured thy sire that all manner troubles should befal thee. So there is naught for it but patience till Allah deliver us from this our strait."

Replied the Prince, "There is no Majesty and there is no Might save in Allah, the Glorious, the Great! Neither is there refuge nor fleeing from that which He decreeth!" And he sighed and recited these couplets:

"By the Compassionate, I'm dazed about my case for lo!
Troubles and griefs beset me sore; I know not whence
            they grow.
I will be patient, so the folk, that I against a thing
Bitt'rer than very aloes' self, endured have, may know.
Less bitter than my patience is the taste of aloes-juice;
I've borne with patience what's more hot than coals
            with fire aglow.
In this my trouble what resource have I, save to commit
My case to Him who orders all that is, for weal or woe?"

Then he became drowned in the depth of thoughts and his tears ran down upon his cheeks like torrent-rain; and he slept a while of the day, after which he awoke and sought of food somewhat. So they set meat before him and he ate his sufficiency, till they removed the food from before him, whilst the boat drove on with them they knew not whither it was wandering. It drifted with them at the will of the winds and the waves, night and day a great while, till their victual was spent and they saw themselves shent and were reduced to extreme hunger and thirst and exhaustion, when behold, suddenly they sighted an island from afar and the breezes wafted them on, till they came thither. Then, making the cock-boat fast to the coast and leaving one therein to guard it, they fared on into the island, where they found abundance of fruits of all colours and ate of them till they were satisfied. Presently, they saw a person sitting among those trees and he was long-faced, of strange favour and white of beard and body. He called to one of the Mamelukes by his name, saying, "Eat not of these fruits, for they are unripe; but come hither to me, that I may give thee to eat of the best and the ripest."

The slave looked at him and thought that he was one of the shipwrecked, who had made his way to that island; so he joyed with exceeding joy at sight of him and went close up to him, knowing not what was decreed to him in the Secret Purpose nor what was writ upon his brow. But, when he drew near, the stranger in human shape leapt upon him, for he was a Marid, and riding upon his shoulderblades and twisting one of his legs about his neck, let the other hang down upon his back,

199

saying, "Walk on, fellow; for there is no escape for thee from me and thou art become mine ass."

Thereupon the Mameluke fell a-weeping and cried out to his comrades, "Alas, my lord! Flee ye forth of this wood and save yourselves, for one of the dwellers therein hath mounted on my shoulders, and the rest seek you, desiring to ride you like me."

When they heard these words, all fled down to the boat and pushed off to sea; whilst the islanders followed them into the water, saying, "Whither wend ye? Come, tarry with us and we will mount on your backs and give you meat and drink, and you shall be our donkeys."

Hearing this they hastened the more seawards till they left them in the distance and fared on, trusting in Allah Almighty; nor did they leave faring for a month, till another island rose before them and thereon they landed. Here they found fruits of various kinds and busied themselves with eating of them, when behold, they saw from afar, somewhat lying in the road, a hideous creature as it were a column of silver. So they went up to it and one of the men gave it a kick, when lo! it was a thing of human semblance, long of eyes and cloven of head and hidden under one of his ears, for he was wont, whenas he lay down to sleep, to spread on ear under his head, and cover his face with the other ear. He snatched up the Mameluke who had kicked him and carried him off into the middle of the island, and behold, it was all full of Ghuls who eat the sons of Adam. The man cried out to his fellows, "Save yourselves, for this is the island of the man-eating Ghuls, and they mean to tear me to bits and devour me."

When they heard these words they fled back to the boat, without gathering any store of the fruits and putting out to sea, fared on some days till it so happened that they came to another island, where they found a high mountain. So they climbed to the top and there saw a thick copse. Now they were sore anhungered; so they took to eating of the fruits; but, before they were aware, there came upon them from among the trees black men of terrible aspect, each fifty cubits high with eye-teeth protruding from their mouths like elephants' tusks; and, laying hands on Sayf al-Muluk and his company, carried them to their King, whom they found seated on a piece of black felt laid on a rock, and about him a great company of Zanzibar-blacks, standing in his service. The blackamoors who had captured the Prince and his Mamelukes set them before the King and said to him, "We found these birds amoung the trees"; and the King was sharp-set; so he took two of the servants and cut their throats and ate them; which, when Sayf al-Muluk saw, he feared for himself and wept and repeated these verses:

"Familiar with my heart are woes and with them I
Who shunned them; for familiar are great hearts and high.
The woes I suffer are not all of single kind.
I have, thank Allah, varied thousands to aby!"
Then he signed and repeated these also,
"The World hath shot me with its sorrows till
My heart is covered with shafts galore;
And now, when strike me other shafts, must break
Against th'old points the points that latest pour."

When the King heard his weeping and wailing, he said, "Verily these
birds have sweet voices and their song pleaseth me: put them in cages."

So they set them each in his own cage and hung them up at the King's
head that he might listen to their warbling. On this wise Sayf al-Muluk and
his Mamelukes abode and the blackamoors gave them to eat and drink:
and now they wept and now laughed, now spake and now were hushed,
whilst the King of the blacks delighted in the sound of their voices. And
so they continued for a long time. Now this King had a daughter married
in another island who, hearing that her father had birds with sweet voices,
sent a messenger to him seeking of him some of them. So he sent her, by
her Cossid, Sayf al-Muluk and three of his men in four cages; and, when
she saw them, they pleased her and she bade hang them up in a place over
her head. The Prince fell to marvelling at that which had befallen him
and calling to mind his former high and honourable estate and weeping
for himself; and the three servants wept for themselves; and the King's
daughter deemed that they sang. Now it was her wont, whenever any one
from the land of Egypt or elsewhere fell into her hands and he pleased
her, to advance him to great favour with her; and by the decree of Allah
Almighty it befel that, when she saw Sayf al-Muluk she was charmed by his
beauty and loveliness and symmetry and perfect grace, and she commanded
to entreat him and his companions with honour and to loose them from
their cages.

Now one day she took the Prince apart and would have him enjoy
her; but he refused, saying, "O my lady, I am a banisht wight and with
passion for a beloved one in piteous plight, nor with other will I consent
to love-delight." Then she coaxed him and importuned him, but he held
aloof from her, and she could not approach him nor get her desire of him
by any ways and means. At last, when she was weary of courting him in
vain, she waxed wroth with him and his Mamelukes, and commanded that

they should serve her and fetch her wood and water. In such condition they abode four years till Sayf al-Muluk became weary of his life and sent to intercede with the Princess, so haply she might release them and let them wend their ways and be at rest from that their hard labour.

So she sent for him and said to him, "If thou wilt do my desire, I will free thee from this thy durance vile and thou shalt go to thy country, safe and sound." And she wept and ceased not to humble herself to him and wheedle him, but he would not hearken to her words; whereupon she turned from him, in anger, and he and his companions abode on the island in the same plight. The islanders knew them for "The Princess's birds" and durst not work them any wrong; and her heart was at ease concerning them, being assured that they could not escape from the island. So they used to absent themselves from her two and three days at a time and go round about the desert parts in all directions, gathering firewood, which they brought to the Princess's kitchen; and thus they abode five years.

Now one day it so chanced that the Prince and his men were sitting on the sea-shore, devising of what had befallen, and Sayf al-Muluk, seeing himself and his men in such case, bethought him of his mother and father and his brother Sa'id and, calling to mind what high degree he had been in, fell a-weeping and lamenting passing sore, whilst his slaves wept likewise. Then said they to him, "O King of the Age, how long shall we weep? Weeping availeth not; for this thing was written on our brows by the ordinance of Allah, to whom belong Might and Majesty. Indeed, the Pen runneth with that He decreeth and nought will serve us but patience: haply Allah (extolled and exalted be He!) who hath saddened us shall gladden us!"

Quoth he, "O my brothers, how shall we win free from this accursed woman? I see no way of escape for us, save Allah of his grace deliver us from her; but methinks we may flee and be at rest from this hard labour."

And quoth they, "O King of the Age, whither shall we flee? For the whole island is full of Ghuls which devour the Sons of Adam, and whithersoever we go, they will find us there and either eat us or capture and carry us back to that accursed, the King's daughter, who will be wroth with us."

Sayf al-Muluk rejoined, "I will contrive you somewhat, whereby peradventure Allah Almighty shall deliver us and help us to escape from this island."

They asked, "And how wilt thou do?"; and he answered, "Let us cut some of these long pieces of wood, and twist ropes of their bark and bind them one with another, and make of them a raft which we will launch and load with these fruits: then we will fashion us paddles and embark on the raft after breaking our bonds with the axe. It may be that Almighty Allah will make it the means of our deliverance from this accursed woman and vouchsafe us a fair wind to bring us to the land of Hind, for He over all things is Almighty!"

Said they, "Right is thy rede," and rejoiced thereat with exceeding joy.

So they arose without stay or delay and cut with their axes wood for the raft and twisted ropes to bind the logs and at this they worked a whole month. Every day about evening they gathered somewhat of fuel and bore it to the Princess's kitchen, and employed the rest of the twenty-four hours working at the raft.

Sayf al-Muluk and his Mamelukes, having cut the wood and twisted the ropes for their raft, made an end of it and launched it upon the sea; then, after breaking their bonds with the axe, and loading the craft with fruits plucked from the island-trees, they embarked at close of day; nor did any wot of their intent. They put out to sea in their raft and paddled on four months, knowing not whither the craft carried them, till their provaunt failed them and they were suffering the severest extreme of hunger and thirst, when behold, the sea waxed troubled and foamed and rose in high waves, and there came forth upon them a frightful crocodile, which put out its claw and catching up one of the Mamelukes swallowed him. At the sight of this horror Sayf al-Muluk wept bitterly and he and the two men that remained to him pushed off from the place where they had seen the crocodile, sore affrighted.

After this they continued drifting on till one day they espied a mountain terrible tall and spiring high in air, whereat they rejoiced, when presently an island appeared. They made towards it with all their might congratulating one another on the prospect of making land; but hardly had they sighted the island on which was the mountain, when the sea changed face and boiled and rose in big waves and a second crocodile raised its head and putting out its claw caught up the two remaining Mamelukes and swallowed them.

So Sayf al-Muluk abode alone, and making his way to the island, toiled till he reached the mountain-top, where he looked about and found a copse, and walking among the trees fell to eating of the fruits. Presently, he saw among the branches more than twenty great apes, each bigger than a he-mule, whereat he was seized with exceeding fear. The apes came down and surrounded him; then forewent him, signing to him to follow them, and walked on, and he too, till he came to a castle, tall of base and strong of build whose ordinance was one brick of gold and one of silver. The apes entered and he after them, and he saw in the castle all manner of rarities, jewels and precious metals such as tongue faileth to describe. Here also he found a young man, passing tall of stature with no hair on his cheeks, and Sayf al-Muluk was cheered by the sight for there was no human being but he in the castle. The stranger marvelled exceedingly at sight of the Prince and asked him, "What is thy name and of what land art thou and how camest thou hither? Tell me thy tale and hide from me naught thereof."

Answered the Prince, "By Allah, I came not hither of my own consent nor is this place of my intent; yet I cannot but go from place to place till I win my wish."

Quoth the youth, "And what is thy object?"; and quoth the other, "I am of the land of Egypt and my name is Sayf al-Muluk son of King Asim bin Safwan"; and told him all that had passed with him, from first to last. Whereupon the youth arose and stood in his service, saying, "O King of the Age, I was erst in Egypt and heard that thou hadst gone to the land of China; but where is this land and where lies China-land? Verily, this is a wondrous thing and marvellous matter!"

Answered the Prince, "Sooth thou speakest but, when I left China-land, I set out, intending for the land of Hind and a stormy wind arose and the sea boiled and broke all my ships"; brief, he told him all that had befallen him till he came thither; whereupon quoth the other, "O King's son, thou hast had enough of strangerhood and its sufferings; Alhamdolillah— praised be Allah who hath brought thee hither! So now do thou abide with me, that I may enjoy thy company till I die, when thou shalt become King over this island, to which no bound is known, and these apes thou seest are indeed skilled in all manner of crafts; and whatso thou seekest here shalt thou find."

Replied Sayf al-Muluk, "O my brother I may not tarry in any place till my wish be won, albeit I compass the whole world in pursuit thereof and make quest of every one so peradventure Allah may bring me to my desire or my course lead me to the place wherein is the appointed term of my days, and I shall die my death."

Then the youth turned with a sign to one of the apes, and he went out and was absent awhile, after which he returned with other apes girt with silken zones. They brought the trays and set on near an hundred chargers of gold and saucers of silver, containing all manner of meats. Then they stood, after the manner of servants between the hands of Kings, till the youth signalled to the Chamberlains, who sat down, and he whose wont it was to serve stood, whilst the two Princes ate their sufficiency. Then the apes cleared the table and brought basins and ewers of gold, and they washed their hands in rose water; after which they set on fine sugar and nigh forty flagons, in each a different kind of wine, and they drank and took their pleasure and made merry and had a fine time. And all the apes danced and gambolled before them, what while the eaters sat at meat; which when Sayf al-Muluk saw, he marvelled at them and forgot that which had befallen him of sufferings.

At nightfall they lighted waxen candles in candlesticks of gold studded with gems and set on dishes of confections and fruits of sugar-candy. So they ate; and when the hour of rest was come, the apes spread them bedding and they slept. And when morning morrowed, the young man arose, as was his wont, before sunrise and waking Sayf al-Muluk said to him, "Put thy head forth of this lattice and see what standeth beneath it." So he put out his head and saw the wide waste and all the wold filled with apes, whose number none knew save Allah Almighty.

Quoth he, "Here be great plenty of apes, for they cover the whole country: but why are they assembled at this hour?" Quoth the youth, "This is their custom. Every Sabbath, all the apes in the island come hither, some from two and three days' distance, and stand here till I awake from sleep and put forth my head from this lattice, when they kiss ground before me and go about their business."

So saying, he put his head out of the window; and when the apes saw him, they kissed the earth before him and went their way. Sayf al-Muluk abode with the young man a whole month when he farewelled him and departed, escorted by a party of nigh a hundred apes, which the young man bade escort him. They journeyed with him seven days, till they came to the limits of their islands, when they took leave of him and returned to their places, while Sayf al-Muluk fared on alone over mount and hill, desert and plain, four months' journey, one day anhungered and the next satiated, now eating of the herbs of the earth and then of the fruits of the trees, till he repented him of the harm he had done himself by leaving the young man; and he was about to retrace his steps to him, when he saw something black afar off and said to himself, "Is this a city or trees? But I will not turn back till I see what it is."

So he made towards it and when he drew near, he saw that it was a palace tall of base. Now he who built it was Japhet son of Noah (on whom be peace!) and it is of this palace that God the Most High speaketh in His precious Book, whenas He saith, "And an abandoned well and a high-builded palace."

205

Sayf al-Muluk sat down at the gate and said in his mind, "Would I knew what is within yonder palace and what King dwelleth there and who shall acquaint me whether its folk are men or Jinn? Who will tell me the truth of the case?" He sat considering awhile, but, seeing none go in or come out, he rose and committing himself to Allah Almighty entered the palace and walked on, till he had counted seven vestibules; yet saw no one.

Presently looking to his right he beheld three doors, while before him was a fourth, over which hung a curtain. So he went up to this and raising the curtain, found himself in a great hall spread with silken carpets. At the upper end rose a throne of gold whereon sat a damsel, whose face was like the moon, arrayed in royal raiment and beautified as she were a bride on the night of her displaying; and at the foot of the throne was a table of forty trays spread with golden and silvern dishes full of dainty viands. The Prince went up and saluted her, and she returned his salam, saying, "Art thou of mankind or of the Jinn?"

Replied he, "I am a man of the best of mankind; for I am a King, son of a King."

She rejoined, "What seekest thou? Up with thee and eat of yonder food, and after tell me thy past from first to last and how thou camest hither."

So he sat down at the table and removing the cover from a tray of meats (he being hungry), ate till he was full; then washed his right hand and going up to the throne, sat down by the damsel who asked him, "Who art thou and what is thy name and whence comest thou and who brought thee hither?"

He answered, "Indeed my story is a long but do thou first tell me who and what and whence thou art and why thou dwellest in this place alone."

She rejoined, "My name is Daulat Khatun and I am the daughter of the King of Hind. My father dwelleth in the Capital-city of Sarandib and hath a great and goodly garden, there is no goodlier in all the land of Hind or its dependencies; and in this garden is a great tank. One day, I went out into the garden with my slave-women and I stripped me naked and they likewise and, entering the tank, fell to sporting and solacing ourselves therein. Presently, before I could be ware, a something as it were a cloud swooped down on me and snatching me up from amongst my handmaids, soared aloft with me betwixt heaven and earth, saying, 'Fear not, O Daulat Khatun, but be of good heart.' Then he flew on with me a little while, after which he set me down in this palace and straightway without stay or delay became a handsome young man daintily apparelled, who said to me, 'Now dost thou know me?' Replied I, 'No, O my lord'; and he said, 'I am the Blue King, Sovran of the Jann; my father dwelleth in the Castle Al-Kulzum hight, and hath under his hand six hundred thousand Jinn, flyers and divers. It chanced that while passing on my way I saw thee and fell in love with thee for thy lovely form: so I swooped down on thee and snatched thee up from among the slave-girls and brought thee to this the High-builded Castle, which is my dwelling-place. None may fare hither be he man or be he Jinni, and from Hind hither is a journey of an hundred and twenty years: wherefore do thou hold that thou wilt never again behold the land of thy father and thy mother; so abide with me here, in contentment of heart and peace, and I will bring to thy hands whatso thou seekest.' Then he embraced me and kissed me, saying, 'Abide here and fear nothing'; whereupon he went away from me for an hour and presently returned with these tables and carpets and furniture. He comes to me every Third and abideth with me three days and on Friday, at the time of mid-afternoon prayer, he departeth and is absent till the following Third. When he is here, he eateth and drinketh and kisseth and huggeth me, but doth naught else with me, and I am a pure virgin, even as Allah Almighty created me. My father's name is Taj al-Muluk, and he wotteth not what is come of me nor hath he hit upon any trace of me. This is my story: now tell me thy tale."

Answered the Prince, "My story is a long and I fear lest while I am telling it to thee the Ifrit come."

Quoth she "He went out from me but an hour before thy entering and will not return till Third: so sit thee down and take thine ease and hearten thy heart and tell me what hath betided thee, from beginning to end."

And quoth he, "I hear and I obey."

So he fell to telling her all that had befallen him from commencement to conclusion but, when she heard speak of Badi'a al-Jamal, her eyes ran over with railing tears and she cried, "O Badi'a al-Jamal, I had not thought this of thee! Alack for our luck! O Badi'a al-Jamal, dost thou not remember me nor say, 'My sister Daulat Khatun whither is she gone?'" And her weeping redoubled, lamenting for that Badi'a al-Jamal had forgotten her.

Then said Sayf al-Muluk, "O Daulat Khatun, thou art a mortal and she is a Jinniyah: how then can she be thy sister?"

Replied the Princess, "She is my sister by fosterage and this is how it came about. My mother went out to solace herself in the garden, when labour-pangs seized her and she bare me. Now the mother of Badi'a al-Jamal chanced to be passing with her guards, when she also was taken with travail-pains; so she alighted in a side of the garden and there brought forth Badi'a al-Jamal. She despatched one of her women to seek food and childbirth-gear of my mother, who sent her what she sought and invited her to visit her. So she came to her with Badi'a al-Jamal and my mother suckled the child, who with her mother tarried with us in the garden two months. And before wending her ways the mother of Badi'a al-Jamal gave my mother somewhat, saying, 'When thou hast need of me, I will come to thee a middlemost the garden,' and departed to her own land; but she and her daughter used to visit us every year and abide with us awhile before returning home. Wherefore an I were with my mother, O Sayf al-Muluk, and if thou wert with me in my own country and Badi'a al-Jamal and I were together as of wont, I would devise some device with her to bring thee to thy desire of her: but I am here and they know naught of me; for that an they kenned what is become of me, they have power to deliver me from this place; however, the matter is in Allah's hands (extolled and exalteth be He!) and what can I do?"

Quoth Sayf al-Muluk, "Rise and let us flee and go whither the Almighty willeth"; but, quoth she, "We cannot do that: for, by Allah, though we fled hence a year's journey that accursed would overtake us in an hour and slaughter us."

Then said the Prince, "I will hide myself in his way, and when he passeth by I will smite him with the sword and slay him."

Daulat Khatun replied, "Thou canst not succeed in slaying him save thou his soul."

Asked he, "And where is his soul?"; and she answered, "Many a time have I questioned him thereof but he would not tell me, till one day I pressed him and he waxed wroth with me and said to me, 'How often wilt thou ask me of my soul? What hast thou to do with my soul?' I rejoined, 'O Hatim, there remaineth none to me but thou, except Allah; and my life dependeth on thy life and whilst thou livest, all is well for me; so, except I care for thy soul and set it in the apple of this mine eye, how shall I live in thine absence? An I knew where thy soul abideth, I would never cease whilst I live, to hold it in mine embrace and would keep it as my right eye.' Whereupon said he to me, 'What time I was born, the astrologers predicted that I should lose my soul at the hands of the son of a king of mankind. So I took it and set it in the crop of a sparrow, and shut up the bird in a box. The box I set in a casket, and enclosing this in seven other caskets and seven chests, laid the whole in a alabastrine coffer, which I buried within the marge of yon earth-circling sea; for that these parts are far from the world of men and none of them can win hither. So now see I have told thee what thou wouldst know, and do thou tell none thereof, for it is a secret between me and thee.'"

"I rejoined," quoth she, "'To whom should I tell it, seeing that none but thou cometh hither with whom I may talk thereof?' adding, 'By Allah, thou hast indeed set thy soul in the strongest of strongholds to which none may gain access! How should a man win to it, unless the impossible be fore-ordained and Allah decree like as the astrologers predicted?' Thereupon the Jinni, 'Peradventure one may come, having on his finger the seal-ring of Solomon son of David (on the twain be peace!) and lay his hand with the ring on the face of the water, saying, "By the virtue of the names engraven upon this ring, let the soul of such an one come forth!" Whereupon the coffer will rise to the surface and he will break it open and do the like with the chests and caskets, till he come to the little box, when he will take out the sparrow and strangle it, and I shall die.'"

Then said Sayf al-Muluk, "I am the King's son of whom he spake, and this is the ring of Solomon David-son on my finger: so rise, let us go down to the sea-shore and see if his words be leal or leasing!"

Thereupon the two walked down to the sea-shore and the Princess stood on the beach, whilst the Prince waded into the water to his waist and laying his hand with the ring on the surface of the sea, said, "By the virtue of the names and talismans engraven on this ring, and by the might of Sulayman bid Daud (on whom be the Peace!), let the soul of Hatim the Jinni, son of the Blue King, come forth!" Whereat the sea boiled in billows and the coffer of alabaster rose to the surface. Sayf al-Muluk took it and shattered it against the rock and broke open the chests and caskets, till he came to the little box and drew thereout the sparrow.

Then the twain returned to the castle and sat down on the throne; but hardly had they done this, when lo and behold! there arose a dust-cloud terrifying and some huge thing came flying and crying, "Spare me, O King's son, and slay me not; but make me thy freedman, and I will bring thee to thy desire!"

Quoth Daulat Khatun, "The Jinni cometh; slay the sparrow, lest this accursed enter the palace and take it from thee and slaughter me and slaughter thee after me."

So the Prince wrung the sparrow's neck and it died, whereupon the Jinni fell down at the palace-door and became a heap of black ashes. Then said Daulat Khatun, "We are delivered from the hand of yonder accursed; what shall we do now?"; and Sayf al-Muluk replied, "It behoveth us to ask aid of Allah Almighty who hath afflicted us; belike He will direct us and help us to escape from this our strait."

So saying, he arose and pulling up half a score of the doors of the palace, which were of sandal-wood and lign-aloes with nails of gold and silver, bound them together with ropes of silk and floss-silk and fine linen and wrought of them a raft, which he and the Princess aided each other to hale down to the sea-shore. They launched it upon the water till it floated and, making it fast to the beach, returned to the palace, whence they removed all the chargers of gold and saucers of silver and jewels and precious stones and metals and what else was light of load and weighty of worth and freighted the raft therewith. Then they embarked after fashioning two pieces of wood into the likeness of paddles and casting off the rope-moorings, let the raft drift out to sea with them, committing themselves to Allah the Most High, who contenteth those that put their trust in Him and disappointeth not them who rely upon Him. They ceased not faring on thus four months until their victual was exhausted and their sufferings waxed severe and their souls were straitened; so they prayed Allah to vouchsafe them deliverance from that danger. But all this time when they lay down to sleep, Sayf al-Muluk set Daulat Khatun behind him and laid a naked brand at his back, so that, when he turned in sleep the sword was between them.

At last it chanced one night, when Sayf al-Muluk was asleep and Daulat Khatun awake, that behold, the raft drifted landwards and entered a port wherein were ships. The Princess saw the ships and heard a man, he being the chief and head of the captains, talking with the sailors; whereby she knew that this was the port of some city and that they were come to an inhabited country. So she joyed with exceeding joy and waking the Prince said to him, "Ask the captain the name of the city and harbour."

Thereupon Sayf al-Muluk arose and said to the captain, "O my brother, how is this harbour hight and what be the names of yonder city and its King?"

Replied the Captain, "O false face! O frosty beard! an thou knew not the name of this port and city, how camest thou hither?"

Quoth Sayf al-Muluk, "I am a stranger and had taken passage in a merchant ship which was wrecked and sank with all on board; but I saved myself on a plank and made my way hither; wherefore I asked thee the name of the place, and in asking is no offence."

Then said the captain, "This is the city of Amariyah and this harbour is called Kamin al-Bahrayn."

When the Princess heard this she rejoiced with exceeding joy and said, "Praised be Allah!"

He asked, "What is to do?"; and she answered, "O Sayf al-Muluk, rejoice in succour near hand; for the King of this city is my uncle, my father's brother, and his name is Ali al-Muluk," adding, "Say thou then to the captain, 'Is the Sultan of the city, Ali al-Muluk, well?'"

He asked but the captain was wroth with him and cried, "Thou sayest, 'I am a stranger and never in my life came hither.' Who then told thee the name of the lord of the city?"

When Daulat Khatun heard this, she rejoiced and knew him for Mu'in al-Din, one of her father's captains. Now he had fared forth in search of her, after she was lost and finding her not, he never ceased cruising till he came to her uncle's city. Then she bade Sayf al-Muluk say to him, "O Captain Mu'in al-Din, come and speak with thy mistress!"

So he called out to him as she bade, whereat he was wroth with exceeding wrath and answered, "O dog, O thief, O spy, who art thou and how knowest thou me?" Then he said to one of the sailors, "Give me an ash-stave, that I may go to yonder plaguing Arab and break his head."

So he took the stick and made for Sayf al-Muluk, but, when he came to the raft, he saw a something, wondrous, beauteous, which confounded his wits and considering it straitly he made sure that it was Daulat Khatun sitting there, as she were a slice of the moon; whereat he said to the Prince, "Who is that with thee?"

Replied he, "A damsel by name Daulat Khatun."

When the captain heard the Princess's name and knew that she was his mistress and the daughter of his King, he fell down in a fainting-fit, and when he came to himself, he left the raft and whatso was thereon and riding up to the palace, craved an audience of the King; whereupon the chamberlain went in to the presence and said, "Captain Mu'in al-Din is come to bring thee good news; so bid he be brought in."

The King bade admit him; accordingly he entered and kissing ground said to him, "O King, thou owest me a gift for glad tidings; for thy brother's daughter Daulat Khatun hath reached our city safe and sound, and is now on a raft in the harbour, in company with a young man like the moon on the night of its full."

When the King heard this, he rejoiced and conferred a costly robe of honour on the captain. Then he straightway bade decorate the city in honour of the safe return of his brother's daughter, and sending for her and Sayf al-Muluk, saluted the twain and gave them joy of their safety; after which he despatched a messenger to his brother, to let him know that his daughter was found and was with him.

As soon as the news reached Taj al-Muluk he gat him ready and assembling his troops set out for his brother's capital, where he found his daughter and they rejoiced with exceeding joy. He sojourned with his brother a week, after which he took his daughter and Sayf al-Muluk and returned to Sarandib, where the Princess foregathered with her mother and they rejoiced at her safe return; and held high festival and that day was a great day, never was seen its like.

As for Sayf al-Muluk, the King entreated him with honour and said to him, "O Sayf al-Muluk, thou hast done me and my daughter all this good for which I cannot requite thee nor can any requite thee, save the Lord of the three Worlds; but I wish thee to sit upon the throne in my stead and rule the land of Hind, for I offer thee of my throne and kingdom and treasures and servants, all this in free gift to thee."

Whereupon Sayf al-Muluk rose and kissing the ground before the King, thanked him and answered, "O King of the Age, I accept all thou givest me and return it to thee in freest gift; for I, O King of the Age, covet not sovranty nor sultanate nor desire aught but that Allah the Most High bring me to my desire."

Rejoined the King, "O Sayf al-Muluk these my treasures are at thy disposal: take of them what thou wilt, without consulting me, and Allah requite thee for me with all weal!"

Quoth the Prince, "Allah advance the King! There is no delight for me in money or in dominion till I win my wish: but now I have a mind to solace myself in the city and view its thoroughfares and market-streets."

So the King bade bring him a mare of the thoroughbreds, saddled and bridled; and Sayf al-Muluk mounted her and rode through the streets and markets of the city. As he looked about him right and left, lo! his eyes fell on a young man, who was carrying a tunic and crying it for sale at fifteen dinars: so he considered him and saw him to be like his brother Sa'id; and indeed it was his very self, but he was wan of blee and changed for long strangerhood and the travails of travel, so that he knew him not. However, he said to his attendants, "Take yonder youth and carry him to the palace where I lodge, and keep him with you till my return from the ride when I will question him."

But they understood him to say, "Carry him to the prison," and said in themselves "Haply this is some runaway Mameluke of his." So they took him and bore him to the bridewell, where they laid him in irons and left him seated in solitude, unremembered by any.

Presently Sayf al-Muluk returned to the palace, but he forgot his brother Sa'id, and none made mention of him. So he abode in prison, and when they brought out the prisoners, to cut ashlar from the quarries they took Sa'id with them, and he wrought with the rest. He abode a month's space, in this squalor and sore sorrow, pondering his case and saying in himself, "What is the cause of my imprisonment?"; while Sayf al-Muluk's mind was diverted from him by rejoicing and other things; but one day, as he sat, he bethought him of Sa'id and said to his Mamelukes, "Where is the white slave I gave into your charge on such a day?"

Quoth they, "Didst thou not bid us bear him to the bridewell?"; and quoth he, "Nay, I said not so; I bade you carry him to my palace after the ride."

Then he sent his Chamberlains and Emirs for Sa'id and they fetched him in fetters, and loosing him from his irons set him before the Prince, who asked him, "O young man, what countryman art thou?"; and he answered, "I am from Egypt and my name is Sa'id, son of Faris the Wazir."

Now hearing these words Sayf al-Muluk sprang to his feet and throwing himself off the throne and upon his friend, hung on his neck, weeping aloud for very joy and saying, "O my brother, O Sa'id, praise be Allah for King Asim." Then they embraced and shed tears together and all who were present marvelled at them.

After this Sayf al-Muluk bade his people bear Sa'id to the Hammam-bath: and they did so. When he came out, they clad him in costly clothing and carried him back to Sayf al-Muluk who seated him on the throne beside himself. When King Taj al-Muluk heard of the reunion of Sayf al-Muluk and his brother Sa'id, he joyed with joy exceeding and came to them, and the three sat devising of all that had befallen them in the past from first to last.

Then said Sa'id, "O my brother, O Sayf al-Muluk, when the ship sank with all on board I saved myself on a plank with a company of Mamelukes and it drifted with us a whole month, when the wind cast us, by the ordinance of Allah Almighty, upon an island. So we landed and entering among the trees took to eating of the fruits, for we were anhungred. Whilst we were busy eating, there fell on us unawares, folk like Ifrits and springing on our shoulders rode us and said to us, 'Go on with us; for ye are become our asses.'

"So I said to him who had mounted me, 'What art thou and why mountest thou me?' At this he twisted one of his legs about my neck, till I was all but dead, and beat upon my back the while with the other leg, till I thought he had broken my backbone. So I fell to the ground on my face, having no strength left in me for famine and thirst.

"From my fall he knew that I was hungry and taking me by the hand, led me to a tree laden with fruit which was a pear-tree and said to me, 'Eat thy fill of this tree.' So I ate till I had enough and rose to walk against my will; but, ere I had fared afar the creature turned and leaping on my shoulders again drove me on, now walking, now running and now trotting, and he the while mounted on me, laughing and saying, 'Never in my life saw I a donkey like unto thee!'

"We abode thus for years till, one day of the days, it chanced that we saw there great plenty of vines, covered with ripe fruit; so we gathered a quantity of grape-bunches and throwing them into a pit, trod them with our feet, till the pit became a great water-pool. Then we waited awhile and presently returning thither, found that the sun had wroughten on the grape-juice and it was become wine. So we used to drink it till we were drunken and our faces flushed and we fell to singing and dancing and running about in the merriment of drunkenness; whereupon our masters said to us, 'What is it that reddeneth your faces and maketh you dance and sing?'

"We replied, 'Ask us not, what is your quest in questioning us hereof?'

"But they insisted, saying, 'You must tell us so that we may know the truth of the case,' till we told them how we had pressed grapes and made wine.

"Quoth they, 'Give us to drink thereof'; but quoth we, 'The grapes are spent.'

"So they brought us to a Wady, whose length we knew not from its breadth nor its beginning from its end wherein were vines each bunch of grapes on them weighing twenty pounds by the scale and all within easy reach, and they said, 'Gather of these.'

"So we gathered a mighty great store of grapes and finding there a big trench bigger than the great tank in the King's garden we filled it full of fruit. This we trod with our feet and did with the juice as before till it became strong wine, which it did after a month; whereupon we said to them, " 'Tis come to perfection; but in what will ye drink it?'

"And they replied, 'We had asses like unto you; but we ate them and kept their heads: so give us to drink in their skulls.'

"We went to their caves which we found full of heads and bones of the Sons of Adam, and we gave them to drink, when they became drunken and lay down, nigh two hundred of them. Then we said to one another, 'Is it not enough that they should ride us, but they must eat us also? There is no

Majesty and there is no Might save in Allah, the Glorious, the Great! But we will ply them with wine, till they are overcome by drunkenness, when we will slay them and be at rest from them.'

"Accordingly, we awoke them and fell to filling the skulls and gave them to drink, but they said, 'This is bitter.'

"We replied, 'Why say ye 'tis bitter? Whoso saith thus, except he drink of it ten times, he dieth the same day.'

"When they heard this, they feared death and cried to us, 'Give us to drink the whole ten times.'

"So we gave them to drink, and when they swallowed the rest of the ten draughts they waxed drunken exceedingly and their strength failed them and they availed not to mount us. Thereupon we dragged them together by their hands and laying them one upon another, collected great plenty of dry vine-stalks and branches and heaped it about and upon them: then we set fire to the pile and stood afar off, to see what became of them."

"As soon the fire was burnt out, we came back and found them a heap of ashes, wherefore we praised Allah Almighty who had delivered us from them. Then we went forth about the island and sought the sea-shore, where we parted and I and two of the Mamelukes fared on till we came to a thick copse full of fruit and there busied ourselves with eating, and behold, presently up came a man tall of stature, long of beard and lengthy of ear, with eyes like cressets, driving before him and feeding a great flock of sheep. When he saw us he rejoiced and said to us, 'Well come, and fair welcome to you! Draw near me that I may slaughter you an ewe of these sheep and roast it and give you to eat.'

"Quoth we, 'Where is thine abode?'

"And quoth he, 'Hard by yonder mountain; go on towards it till ye come to a cave and enter therein, for you will see many guests like yourselves; and do ye sit with them, whilst we make ready for you the guest-meal.'

"We believed him so fared on, as he bade us, till we came to the cavern, where we found many guests, Sons of Adam like ourselves, but they were all blinded; and when we entered, one said, 'I'm sick'; and another, 'I'm weak.'

"So we cried to them, 'What is this you say and what is the cause of your sickness and weakness?'

"They asked, 'Who are ye?'; and we answered, 'We are guests.'

"Then said they, 'What hath made you fall into the hands of yonder accursed? But there is no Majesty and there is no Might save in Allah, the Glorious, the Great! This is a Ghul who devoureth the Sons of Adam and he hath blinded us and meaneth to eat us.'

"Said we, 'And how did he blind you?' and they replied, 'Even as he will blind yourselves anon.'

"Quoth we, 'And how so?'

"And quoth they, 'He will bring you bowls of soured milk and will say to you, 'Ye are weary with wayfare: take this milk and drink it.' And when ye have drunken thereof, ye will become blind like us.'

"Said I to myself, 'There is no escape for us but by contrivance.' So I dug a hole in the ground and sat over it.

"After an hour or so in came the accursed Ghul with bowls of milk, whereof he gave to each of us, saying, 'Ye come from the desert and are athirst: so take this milk and drink it, whilst I roast you the flesh.'

"I took the cup and carried it to my mouth but emptied it into the hole; then I cried out, 'Alas! my sight is gone and I am blind!' and clapping my hand to my eyes, fell a-weeping and a-wailing, whilst the accursed laughed and said, 'Fear not, thou art now become like mine other guests.'

"But, as for my two comrades, they drank the milk and became blind. Thereupon the Ghul arose and stopping up the mouth of the cavern came to me and felt my ribs, but found me lean and with no flesh on my bones: so he tried another and finding him fat, rejoiced. Then he slaughtered three sheep and skinned them and fetching iron spits, spitted the flesh thereon and set them over the fire to roast. When the meat was done, he placed it before my comrades who ate and he with them; after which he brought a leather-bag full of wine and drank thereof and lay down prone and snored.

"Said I to myself, 'He's drowned in sleep: how shall I slay him?' Then I bethought me of the spits and thrusting two of them into the fire, waited till they were as red-hot coals: whereupon I arose and girded myself and taking a spit in each hand went up to the accursed Ghul and thrust them into his eyes, pressing upon them with all my might. He sprang to his feet for sweet life and would have laid hold of me; but he was blind. So I fled from him into the inner cavern, whilst he ran after me; but I found no place of refuge from him nor whence I might escape into the open country, for the cave was stopped up with stones; wherefore I was bewildered and said to the blind men, 'How shall I do with this accursed?'

"Replied one of them, 'O Sa'id, with a run and a spring mount up to yonder niche and thou wilt find there a sharpened scymitar of copper: bring it to me and I will tell thee what to do.'

"So I clombed to the niche and taking the blade, returned to the blind man, who said to me, 'Smite him with the sword in his middle, and he will die forthright.'

216

"So I rushed after the Ghul, who was weary with running after me and felt for the blind men that he might kill them and, coming up to him smote him with the sword a single stroke across his waist and he fell in twain. then he screamed and cried out to me, 'O man, an thou desire to slay me, strike me a second stroke.' Accordingly, I was about to smite him another cut; but he who had directed me to the niche and the scymitar said, 'Smite him not a second time, for then he will not die, but will live and destroy us.' So I held my hand as he bade me, and the Ghul died.

"Then said the blind man to me, 'Open the mouth of the cave and let us fare forth; so haply Allah may help us and bring us to rest from this place.'

"And I said, 'No harm can come to us now; let us rather abide here and repose and eat of these sheep and drink of this wine, for long is the land.' Accordingly we tarried there two months, eating of the sheep and of the fruits of the island and drinking the generous grape-juice till it so chanced one day, as we sat upon the beach, we caught sight of a ship looming large in the distance; so we made signs for the crew and holla'd to them. They feared to draw near, knowing that the island was inhabited by a Ghul who ate Adamites, and would have sheered off; but we ran down to the marge of the sea and made signs to them, with our turband-ends and shouted to them, whereupon one of the sailors, who was sharp of sight, said to the rest, 'Harkye, comrades, I see these men formed like ourselves, for they have not the fashion of Ghuls.'

"So they made for us, little by little, till they drew near us in the dinghy and were certified that we were indeed human beings, when they saluted us and we returned their salam and gave them the glad tidings of the slaying of the accursed, wherefore they thanked us. Then we carried to the ship all that was in the cave of stuffs and sheep and treasure, together with a viaticum of the island-fruits, such as should serve us days and months, and embarking, sailed on with a fair breeze three days; at the end of which the wind veered round against us and the air became exceeding dark; nor had an hour passed before the wind drave the craft on to a rock, where it broke up and its planks were torn asunder. However, the Great God decreed that I should lay hold of one of the planks, which I bestrode, and it bore me along two days, for the wind had fallen fair again, and I paddled with my feet awhile, till Allah the Most High brought me safe ashore and I landed and came to this city, where I found myself a stranger, solitary, friendless, not knowing what to do; for hunger was sore upon me and I was in great tribulation.

"Thereupon I, O my brother, hid myself and pulling off this my tunic, carried it to the market, saying in my mind, 'I will sell it and live on its price, till Allah accomplish to me whatso he will accomplish.' Then I took the tunic in my hand and cried it for sale, and the folk were looking at it and bidding for it, when, O my brother, thou camest by and seeing me commandedst me to the palace; but thy pages arrested and thrust me into the prison and there I abode till thou bethoughtest thee of me and badst bring me before thee. So now I have told thee what befel me, and Alhamdolillah—Glorified be God—for reunion!"

Much marvelled the two Kings at Sa'id's tale and Taj al-Muluk having made ready a goodly dwelling for Sayf al-Muluk and his Wazir, Daulat Khatun used to visit the Prince there and thank him for his favours and talk with him. One day, he met her and said to her, "O my lady, where is the promise thou madest me, in the palace of Japhet son of Noah, saying, 'Were I with my people, I would make shift to bring thee to thy desire?'"

And Sa'id said to her, "O Princess, I crave thine aid to enable him to win his will."

Answered she, "Yea, verily; I will do my endeavour for him, that he may attain his aim, if it please Allah Almighty."

And she turned to Sayf al-Muluk and said to him, "Be of good cheer and keep thine eyes cool and clear." Then she rose and going in to her mother, said to her, "Come with me forthright and let us purify ourselves and make fumigations that Badi'a al-Jamal and her mother may come and see me and rejoice in me."

Answered the Queen, "With love and goodly gree"; and rising, betook herself to the garden and burnt off these perfumes which she always had by her; nor was it long before Badi'a al-Jamal and her mother made their appearance. The Queen of Hind foregathered with the other Queen and acquainted her with her daughter's safe return, whereat she rejoiced; and rejoiced in each other. Then they pitched the pavilions and dressed dainty viands and made ready the place of entertainment; whilst the two Princesses withdrew to a tent apart and ate together and drank and made merry; after which they sat down to converse, and Badi'a al-Jamal said, "What hath befallen thee in thy strangerhood?" Replied Daulat Khatun, "O my sister how sad is severance and how gladsome is reunion; ask me not what hath befallen me! Oh, what hardships mortals suffer!"

Cried she, "How so?" and the other said to her, "O my sister, I was inmured in the High-builded Castle of Japhet son of Noah, whither the son of the Blue King carried me off, till Sayf al-Muluk slew the Jinni and brought me back to my sire"; and she told her to boot all that the Prince had undergone of hardships and horrors before he came to the Castle.

Badi'a al-Jamal marvelled at her tale and said, "By Allah, O my sister, this is the most wondrous of wonders! This Sayf al-Muluk is indeed a man! But why did he leave his father and mother and betake himself to travel and expose himself to these perils?"

Quoth Daulat Khatun, "I have a mind to tell thee the first part of his history; but shame of thee hindereth me therefrom."

Quoth Badi'a al-Jamal, "Why shouldst thou have shame of me, seeing that thou art my sister and my bosom-friend and there is muchel a matter between thee and me and I know thou willest me naught but well? Tell me then what thou hast to say and be not abashed at me and hide nothing from me and have no fear of consequences."

Answered Daulat Khatun, "By Allah, all the calamities that have betided this unfortunate have been on thine account and because of thee!"

Asked Badi'a al-Jamal, "How so, O my sister?"; and the other answered, "Know that he saw thy portrait wrought on a tunic which thy father sent to Solomon son of David (on the twain be peace!) and he opened it not neither looked at it, but despatched it, with other presents and rarities to Asim bin Safwan, King of Egypt, who gave it, still unopened, to his son Sayf al-Muluk. The Prince unfolded the tunic, thinking to put it on, and seeing thy portrait, became enamoured of it; wherefore he came forth in quest of thee, and left his folk and reign and suffered all these terrors and hardships on thine account."

When Badi'a al-Jamal heard this, she blushed rosy red and was confounded at Daulat Khatun and said, "Verily this may never, never be; for man accordeth not with the Jann." Then Daulat Khatun went on to praise Sayf al-Muluk and extol his comeliness and courage and cavalarice, and ceased not repeating her memories of his prowess and his excellent qualities till she ended with saying, "For the sake of Almighty Allah and of me, O sister mine, come and speak with him, though but one word!"

But Badi'a al-Jamal cried, "By Allah, O sister mine, this that thou sayest I will not hear, neither will I assent to thee therein;" and it was as if she heard naught of what the other said and as if no love of Sayf al-Muluk and his beauty and bearing and bravery had gotten hold upon her heart.

Then Daulat Khatun humbled herself and said, "O Badi'a al-Jamal, by the milk we have sucked, I and thou, and by that which is graven on the seal-ring of Solomon (on whom be peace!) hearken to these my words for I pledged myself in the High-builded Castle of Japhet, to show him thy face. So Allah upon thee, show it to him once, for the love of me, and look thyself on him!"

And she ceased not to weep and implore her and kiss her hands and feet, till she consented and said, "For thy sake I will show him my face once and he shall have a single glance."

With that Daulat Khatun's heart was gladdened and she kissed her hands and feet. Then she went forth and fared to the great pavilion in the garden and bade her slave-women spread it with carpets and set up a couch of gold and place the wine-vessels in order; after which she went into Sayf al-Muluk and to his Wazir Sa'id, whom she found seated in their lodging, and gave the Prince the glad tidings of the winning of his wish, saying, "Go to the pavilion in the garden, thou and thy brother, and hide yourselves there from the eyes of men so none in the palace may espy you, till I come to you with Badi'a al-Jamal."

So they rose and repaired to the appointed pavilion, where they found the couch of gold set and furnished with cushions, and meat and wine ready served. So they sat awhile, whilst Sayf al-Muluk bethought him of his beloved and his breast was straitened and love and longing assailed him: wherefore he rose and walked forth from the vestibule of the pavilion. Sa'id would have followed him, but he said to him, "O my brother, follow me not, but sit in thy stead till I return to thee."

So Sa'id abode seated, whilst Sayf al-Muluk went down into the garden, drunken with the wine of desire and distracted for excess of love-longing and passion-fire: yearning agitated him and transport overcame him and he recited these couplets:

"O passing Fair I have none else but thee;
　Pity this slave in thy love's slavery!
Thou art my search, my joy and my desire!
　None save thyself shall love this heart of me:
Would Heaven I knew thou knewest of my wails
　Night-long and eyelids oped by memory.
Bid sleep to sojourn on these eyen-lids
　Haply in vision I thy sight shall see.
Show favour then to one thus love-distraught:
　Save him from ruin by thy cruelty!
Allah increase thy beauty and thy weal;
　And be thy ransom every enemy!
So shall on Doomsday lovers range beneath
　Thy flag, and beauties 'neath thy banner be."

Then he wept and recited these also:

> "That rarest beauty ever bides my foe
> Who holds my heart and lurks in secresy:
> Speaking, I speak of nothing save her charms
> And when I'm dumb in heart-core woneth she."

Then he wept sore and recited the following:

> "And in my liver higher flames the fire;
> You are my wish and longsome still I yearn:
> To you (none other!) bend I and I hope
> (Lovers long-suffering are!) your grace to earn;
> And that you pity me whose frame by Love
> Is waste and weak his heart with sore concern:
> Relent, be gen'rous, tender-hearted, kind:
> From you I'll ne'er remove, from you ne'er turn!"

221

Then he wept and recited these also:

> "Came to me care when came the love of thee,
> Cruel sleep fled me like thy cruelty:
> Tells me the messenger that thou are wroth:
> Allah forfend what evils told me he!"

Presently Sa'id waxed weary of awaiting him and going forth in quest of him, found him walking in the garden, distraught and reciting these two couplets:

> "By Allah, by th' Almighty, by his right
> Who read the Koran-Chapter 'Fatir' hight;
> Ne'er roam my glances o'er the charms I see;
> Thy grace, rare beauty, is my talk by night."

So he joined him and the twain walked about the garden together solacing themselves and ate of its fruits. Such was their case; but as regards the two Princesses, they came to the pavilion and entering therein after the eunuchs had richly furnished it, according to command, sat down on the couch of gold, beside which was a window that gave upon the garden. The castratos then set before them all manner rich meats and they ate, Daulat Khatun feeding her foster-sister by mouthfuls, till she was satisfied; when she called for divers kinds of sweetmeats, and when the neutrals brought them, they ate what they would of them and washed their hands. After this Daulat Khatun made ready wine and its service, setting on the ewers and bowls and she proceeded to crown the cups and give Badi'a al-Jamal to drink, filling for herself after and drinking in turn. Then Badi'a al-Jamal looked from the window into the garden and gazed upon the fruits and branches that were therein, till her glance fell on Sayf al-Muluk, and she saw him wandering about the parterres, followed by Sa'id, and she heard him recite verses, raining the while railing tears. And that glance of eyes cost her a thousand signs, and she turned to Daulat Khatun and said to her (and indeed the wine sported with her senses), "O my sister, who is that young man I see in the garden, distraught, love-abying, disappointed, sighing?"

Quoth the other, "Dost thou give me leave to bring him hither, that we may look on him?"; and quoth the other, "An thou can avail to bring him, bring him."

So Daulat Khatun called to him, saying "O King's son, come up to us and bring us thy beauty and thy loveliness!"

Sayf al-Muluk recognised her voice and came up to into the pavilion; but no sooner had he set eyes on Badi'a al-Jamal, than he fell down in a swoon; whereupon Daulat Khatun sprinkled on him a little rose-water and he revived. Then he rose and kissed ground before Badi'a al-Jamal who was amazed at his beauty and loveliness; and Daulat Khatun said to her, "Know, O Princess, that this is Sayf al-Muluk, whose hand saved me by the ordinance of Allah Almighty and he it is who hath borne all manner burdens on thine account: wherefore I would have thee look upon him with favour."

Hearing this Badi'a al-Jamal laughed and said, "And who keepeth faith, that this youth should do so? For there is no true love in men."

Cried Sayf al-Muluk, "O Princess, never shall lack of faith be in me, and all men are not created alike." And he wept before her and recited these verses:

> "O thou, Badi'a al-Jamal, show thou some clemency
> To one those lovely eyes opprest with witchery!
> By rights of beauteous hues and tints thy cheeks combine

222

Of snowy white and glowing red anemone,
Punish not with disdain one who is sorely sick
By long, long parting waste hath waxed this frame of me:
This is my wish, my will, the end of my desire,
And Union is my hope an haply this may be!"

Then he wept with violent weeping; and love and longing got the mastery over him and he greeted her with these couplets:

"Peace be to you from lover's wasted love,
All noble hearts to noble favour show:
Peace be to you! Ne'er fail your form my dreams;
Nor hall nor chamber the fair sight forego!
Of you I'm jealous: none may name your name:
Lovers to lovers aye should bend thee low:
So cut not off your grace from him who loves
While sickness wastes and sorrows overthrow.
I watch the flowery stars which frighten me;
While cark and care mine every night foreslow.
Nor Patience bides with me nor plan appears:
What shall I say when questioned of my foe?
God's peace be with you in the hour of need,
Peace sent by lover patient bearing woe!"

Then for the excess of his desire and ecstasy he repeated these couplets also:

"If I to aught save you, O lords of me, incline;
Ne'er may I win of you my wish, my sole design!
Who doth comprise all loveliness save only you?
Who makes the Doomsday dawn e'en now before
        these eyne?
Far be it Love find any rest, for I am one
Who lost for love of you this heart, these vitals mine."

When he had made an end of his verses, he wept with sore weeping and she said to him, "O Prince, I fear to grant myself wholly to thee lest I find in thee nor fondness nor affection; for oftentimes man's fidelity is small and his perfidy is great and thou knowest how the lord Solomon, son of

David (on whom be the Peace!), took Bilkis to his love but, whenas he saw another fairer than she, turned from her thereto."

Sayf al-Muluk replied, "O my eye and O my soul, Allah hath not made all men alike, and I, Inshallah, will keep my troth and die beneath thy feet. Soon shalt thou see what I will do in accordance with my words, and for whatso I say Allah is my warrant." Quoth Badi'a al-Jamal, "Sit and be of good heart and swear to me by the right of thy Faith and let us covenant together that each will not be false to other; and whichever of us breaketh faith may Almighty Allah punish!" At these words he sat down and set his hand in her hand and they sware each to other that neither of them would ever prefer to the other any one, either of man or of the Jann. Then they embraced for a whole hour and wept for excess of their joy, whilst passion overcame Sayf al-Muluk and he recited these couplets:

> "I weep for longing love's own ardency
> To her who claims the heart and soul of me.
> And sore's my sorrow parted long from you,
> And short's my arm to reach the prize I see;
> And mourning grief for what my patience marred
> To blamer's eye unveiled my secresy;
> And waxed strait that whilome was so wide
> Patience nor force remains nor power to dree.
> Would Heaven I knew if God will ever deign to join
> Our lives, and from our cark and care and grief set free!"

After this mutual troth-plighting, Sayf al-Muluk arose and walked in the garden and Badi'a al-Jamal arose also and went forth also afoot followed by a slave-girl bearing somewhat of food and a flask of wine. The Princess sat down and the damsel set the meat and wine before her: nor remained they long ere they were joined by Sayf al-Muluk, who was received with greeting and the two embraced and sat them down awhile to eat and drink.

Then said she to him, "O King's son, thou must now go to the garden of Iram, where dwelleth my grandmother, and seek her consent to our marriage. My slave-girl Marjanah will convey thee thither and as thou farest therein thou wilt see a great pavilion of red satin, lined with green silk. Enter the pavilion heartening thyself and thou wilt see inside it an ancient dame sitting on a couch of red gold set with pearls and jewels. Salute her with respect and courtesy: then look at the foot of the couch, where thou wilt descry a pair of sandals of cloth interwoven with bars of gold, embroidered with jewels. Take them and kiss them and lay them on thy head; then put them under thy right armpit and stand before the old woman, in silence and with thy head bowed down. If she ask thee, 'Who art thou and how camest thou hither and who led thee to this land? And why hast thou taken up the sandals?' make her no answer, but abide silent till Marjanah enter, when she will speak with her and seek to win her aproof for thee and cause her look on thee with consent; so haply Allah Almight may incline her heart to thee and she may grant thee thy wish."

Then she called the handmaid Marjanah hight and said to her, "As thou lovest me, do my errand this day and be not neglectful therein! An thou acccomplish it, thou shalt be a free woman for the sake of Allah Almighty, and I will deal honourably by thee with gifts and there shall be none dearer to me than thou, nor will I discover my secrets to any save thee. So, by my love for thee, fulfil this my need and be not slothful therein."

Replied Marjanah, "O my lady and light of mine eyes, tell me what is it thou requirest of me, that I may accomplish it with both mine eyes."

Badi'a rejoined, "Take this mortal on thy shoulders and bear him to the bloom-garden of Iram and the pavilion of my grandmother, my father's mother, and be careful of his safety. When thou hast brought him into her presence and seest him take the slippers and do them homage, and hearest her ask him, saying, 'Whence art thou and by what road art come and who led thee to this land, and why hast thou taken up the sandals and what is thy need that I give heed to it?' do thou come forward in haste and salute her with the salam and say to her, 'O my lady, I am she who brought him hither and he is the King's son of Egypt. 'Tis he who went to the High-builded Castle and slew the son of the Blue King and delivered the Princess Daulat Khatun from the Castle of Japhet son of Noah and brought her back safe to her father: and I have brought him to thee, that he may give thee the glad tidings of her safety: so deign thou be gracious to him.'

"Then do thou say to her, 'Allah upon thee! is not this young man handsome, O my lady?'

"She will reply, 'Yes'; and do thou rejoin, 'O my lady, indeed he is complete in honour and manhood and valour and he is lord and King of Egypt and compriseth all praiseworthy qualities.'

"An she ask thee, 'What is his need?' do thou make answer, 'My lady saluteth thee and saith to thee, how long shall she sit at home, a maid and unmarried? Indeed, the time is longsome upon her for she is as a magazine wherein wheat is heaped up. What then is thine intent in leaving her without a mate and why dost thou not marry her in thy lifetide and that of her mother, like other girls?'

"If she say, 'How shall we do to marry her? An she have any one in mind, let her tell us of him, and we will do her will as far as may be!' do thou make answer, 'O my lady, thy daughter saith to thee, "Ye were minded aforetime to marry me to Solomon (on whom be peace!) and portrayed him my portrait on a tunic. But he had no lot in me; so he sent the tunic to the King of Egypt and he gave it to his son, who saw my portrait figured thereon and fell in love with me; wherefore he left his father and mother's realm and turning away from the world and whatso is therein, went forth at a venture, a wanderer, love-distraught, and hath borne the utmost hardships and honours for my sake of me."'

"Now thou seest his beauty and loveliness, and thy daughter's heart is enamoured of him; so if ye have a mind to marry her, marry her to this young man and forbid her not from him for he is young and passing comely and King of Egypt, nor wilt thou find a goodlier than he; and if ye will not give her to him, she will slay herself and marry none neither man nor Jinn."

"And," continued Badi'a al-Jamal, "Look thou, O Marjanah, ma mie, how thou mayst do with my grandmother, to win her consent, and beguile her with soft words, so haply she may do my desire."

Quoth the damsel, "O my lady, upon my head and eyes will I serve thee and do what shall content thee."

Then she took Sayf al-Muluk on her shoulders and said to him, "O King's son, shut thine eyes."

He did so and she flew up with him into the welkin; and after awhile she said to him, "O King's son, open thine eyes."

He opened them and found himself in a garden, which was none other than the garden of Iram; and she showed him the pavilion and said, "O Sayf al-Muluk, enter therein!" Thereupon he pronounced the name of Allah Almighty and entering cast a look upon the garden, when he saw the old Queen sitting on the couch, attended by her waiting women. So he drew near her with courtesy and reverence and taking the sandals bussed them and did as Badi'a al-Jamal had enjoined him.

Quoth the ancient dame, "Who art thou and what is thy country; whence comest thou and who brought thee hither and what may be thy wish? Wherefore dost thou take the sandals and kiss them and when didst thou ask of me a favour which I did not grant?"

With this in came Marjanah and saluting her reverently and

worshipfully, repeated to her what Badi'a al-Jamal had told her; which when the old Queen heard, she cried out at her and was wroth with her and said, "How shall there be accord between man and Jinn?"

But Safy al-Muluk replied, "Indeed, I will conform to thy will and be thy page and die in thy love and will keep with thee covenant and regard non but thee: so right soon shalt thou see my truth and lack of falsehood and the excellence of my manly dealing with thee, Inshallah!"

The old woman pondered for a full hour with brow earthwards bent; after which she raised her head and said to him, "O thou beautiful youth, wilt thou indeed keep compact and covenant?"

He replied, "Yes, by Him who raised the heavens and dispread the earth upon the waters, I will indeed keep faith and troth!"

Thereupon quoth she, "I will win for thee thy wish, Inshallah! but for the present go thou into the garden and take thy pleasure therein and eat of its fruits, that have neither like in the world nor equal, whilst I send for my son Shahyal and confabulate with him of the matter. Nothing but good shall come of it, so Allah please, for he will not gainsay me nor disobey my commandment and I will marry thee with his daughter Badi'a al-Jamal. So be of good heart for she shall assuredly be thy wife, O Sayf al-Muluk."

The Prince thanked her for those words and kissing her hands and feet, went forth from her into the garden; whilst she turned to Marjanah and said to her, "Go seek my son Shahyal wherever he is and bring him to me."

So Marjanah went out in quest of King Shahyal and found him and set him before his mother. On such wise fared it with them; but as regards Sayf al-Muluk, whilst he walked in the garden, lo and behold! five Jinn of the people of the Blue King espied him and said to one another, "Whence cometh yonder wight and who brought him hither? Haply 'tis he who slew the son and heir of our lord and master the Blue King"; presently adding, "But we will go about with him and question him and find out all from him."

So they walked gently and softly up to him, as he sat in a corner of the garden, and sitting down by him, said to him, "O beauteous youth, thou didst right well in slaying the son of the Blue King and delivering from him Daulat Khatun; for he was a treacherous hound and had tricked her, and had not Allah appointed thee to her, she had never won free; no, never! But how diddest thou slay him?"

Sayf al-Muluk looked at them and deeming them of the gardenfolk, answered, "I slew him by means of this ring which is on my finger."

Therewith they were assured that it was he who had slain him; so they seized him, two of them holding his hands, whilst other two held his feet and the fifth his mouth, lest he should cry out and King Shahyal's people should hear him and rescue him from their hands. Then they lifted him up and flying away with him ceased not their flight till they came to their King and set him down before him, saying, "O King of the Age, we bring thee the murderer of thy son."

"Where is he?" asked the King and they answered, "This is he."

So the Blue King said to Sayf al-Muluk, "How slewest thou my son, the core of my heart and the light of my sight, without aught of right, for all he had done thee no ill deed?"

Quoth the Prince, "Yea, verily! I slew him because of his violence and frowardness, in that he used to seize Kings' daughters and sever them from their families and carry them to the Ruined Well and the High-builded Castle of Japhet son of Noah and entreat them lewdly by debauching them. I slew him by means of this ring on my finger, and Allah hurried his soul to the fire and the abiding-place dire."

Therewithal the King was assured that this was indeed he who slew his son; so presently he called his Wazirs and said to them, "This is the murtherer of my son sans shadow of doubt: so how do you counsel me to deal with him? Shall I slay him with the foulest slaughter or torture him with the terriblest torments or how?"

Quoth the Chief Minister, "Cut off his limbs, one a day."

Another, "Beat him with a grievous beating every day till he die."

A third, "Cut him across the middle."

A fourth, "Chop off all his fingers and burn him with fire."

A fifth, "Crucify him"; and so on, each speaking according to his rede.

Now there was with the Blue King an old Emir, versed in the vicissitudes and experienced in the exchanges of the times, and he said, "O King of the Age, verily I would say to thee somewhat, and thine is the rede whether thou wilt hearken or not to my say."

Now he was the King's privy Councillor and the Chief Officer of his empire, and the Sovran was wont to give ear to his word and conduct himself by his counsel and gainsay him not in aught. So he rose and kissing ground before his liege lord, said to him, "O King of the Age, if I advise thee in this matter, wilt thou follow my advice and grant me indemnity?"

Quoth the King, "Set forth thine opinion, and thou shalt have immunity."

Then quoth he, "O King of the Age, an thou slay this one nor accept my advice nor hearken to my word, in very sooth I say that his death were now inexpedient, for that he is thy prisoner and in thy power, and under thy protection; so whenas thou wilt, thou mayst lay hand on him and do with him what thou desirest. Have patience, then, O King of the Age, for he hath entered the garden of Iram and is become the betrothed of Badi'a al-Jamal, daughter of King Shahyal, and one of them. Thy people seized him there and brought him hither and he did not hide his case from them or from thee. So an thou slay him, assuredly King Shahyal will seek blood-revenge and lead his host against thee for his daughter's sake, and thou canst not cope with him nor make head against his power."

So the King hearkened to his counsel and commanded to imprison the captive. Thus fared it with Sayf al-Muluk; but as regards the old Queen, grandmother of Badi'a al-Jamal, when her son Shahyal came to her she despatched Marjanah in search of Sayf al-Muluk; but she found him not and returning to her mistress, said, "I found him not in the garden."

So the ancient dame sent for the gardeners and questioned them of the Prince. Quoth they, "We saw him sitting under a tree when behold, five of the Blue King's folk alighted by him and spoke with him, after which they took him up and having gagged him flew away with him."

When the old Queen heard the damsel's words it was no light matter to her and she was wroth with exceeding wrath: so she rose to her feet and said to her son, King Shahyal, "Thou art a King and shall the Blue King's people come to our garden and carry off our guests unhindered, and thou alive?"

And she proceeded to provoke him, saying, "It behoveth not that any transgress against us during thy lifetime."

Answered he, "O mother of me, this man slew the Blue King's son, who was a Jinni and Allah threw him into his hand. He is a Jinni and I am a Jinni: how then shall I go to him and make war on him for the sake of a mortal?"

But she rejoined, "Go to him and demand our guest of him, and if he be still alive and the Blue King deliver him to thee, take him and return; but an he have slain him, take the King and all his children and Harim and household depending on him; then bring them to me alive that I may cut their throats with my own hand and lay in ruins his reign. Except thou go to him and do my bidding, I will not acquit thee of my milk and my rearing of thee shall be counted unlawful."

Thereupon Shahyal rose and assembling his troops, set out, in deference to his mother, desiring to content her and her friends, and in accordance with whatso had been fore-ordained from eternity without beginning; nor did they leave journeying till they came to the land of the

Blue King, who met them with his army and gave them battle. The Blue King's host was put to the rout and the conquerors having taken him and all his sons, great and small, and Grandees and officers bound and brought them before King Shahyal, who said to the captive, "O Azrak, where is the mortal Sayf al-Muluk who whilome was my guest?"

Answered the Blue King, "O Shahyal, thou art a Jinni and I am a Jinni and is't on account of a mortal who slew my son that thou hast done this deed; yea, the murtherer of my son, the core of my liver and solace of my soul. How couldest thou work such work and spill the blood of so many thousand Jinn?"

He replied, "Leave this talk! Knowest thou not that a single mortal is better, in Allah's sight, than a thousand Jinn? If he be alive, bring him to me, and I will set thee free and all whom I have taken of thy sons and people; but an thou have slain him, I will slaughter thee and thy sons."

Quoth the Malik al-Azrak, "O King, is this man of more account with thee than my son?"; and quoth Shahyal, "Verily, thy son was an evildoer who kidnapped Kings' daughters and shut them up in the Ruined Well and the High-builded Castle of Japhet son of Noah and entreated them lewdly." Then said the Blue King, "He is with me; but make thy peace between us." So he delivered the Prince to Shahyal, who made peace between him and the Blue King, and Al-Azrak gave him a bond of absolution for the death of his son.

Then Shahyal conferred robes of honour on them and entertained the Blue King and his troops hospitably for three days, after which he took Sayf al-Muluk and carried him back to the old Queen, his own mother, who rejoiced in him with an exceeding joy, and Shahyal marvelled at the beauty of the Prince and his loveliness and his perfection. Then the Prince related to him his story from beginning to end, especially what did befal him with Badi'a al-Jamal and Shahyal said, "O my mother, since 'tis thy pleasure that this should be, I hear and I obey all that to command it pleaseth thee; wherefore do thou take him and bear him to Sarandib and there celebrate his wedding and marry him to her in all state, for he is a goodly youth and hath endured horrors for her sake." So she and her maidens set out with Sayf al-Muluk for Sarandib and, entering the Garden belonging to the Queen of Hind, foregathered with Daulat Khatun and Badi'a al-Jamal.

Then the lovers met, and the old Queen acquainted the two Princesses with all that had passed between Sayf al-Muluk and the Blue King and how the Prince had been nearhand to a captive's death; but in repetition is no fruition. Then King Taj al-Muluk father of Daulat Khatun assembled the lords of his land and drew up the contract of marriage between Sayf al-Muluk and Badi'a al-Jamal; and he conferred costly robes of honour and gave banquets to the lieges. Then Sayf al-Muluk rose and, kissing ground before the King, said to him, "O King, pardon! I would fain ask of thee somewhat but I fear lest thou refuse it to my disappointment."

Taj al-Muluk replied, "By Allah, though thou soughtest my soul of me, I would not refuse it to thee, after all the kindness thou hast done me!"

Quoth Sayf al-Muluk, "I wish thee to marry the Princess Daulat Khatun to my brother Sa'id, and we will both be thy pages."

"I hear and obey," answered Taj al-Muluk, and assembling his Grandees a second time, let draw up the contract of marriage between his daughter and Sa'id; after which they scattered gold and silver and the King bade decorate the city. So they held high festival and Sayf al-Muluk went in unto Badi'a al-Jamal and Sa'id went in unto Daulat Khatun on the same night. Moreover Sayf al-Muluk abode forty days with Badi'a al-Jamal, at the end of which she said to him, "O King's son, say me, is there left in thy heart any regret for aught?"

And he replied, "Allah forfend! I have accomplished my quest and there abideth no regret in my heart at all: but I would fain meet my father and my mother in the land of Egypt and see if they continue in welfare or not."

So she commanded a company of her slaves to convey them to Egypt, and they carried them to Cairo, where Sayf al-Muluk and Sa'id foregathered with their parents and abode with them a week; after which they took leave of them and returned to Sarandib-city; and from this time forwards, whenever they longed for their folk, they used to go to them and return. Then Sayf al-Muluk and Badi'a al-Jamal abode in all solace of life and its joyance as did Sa'id and Daulat Khatun, till there came to them the Destroyer of delights and Severer of societies; and they all died good Moslems. So glory be to the Living One who dieth not, who createth all creatures and decreeth to them death and who is the First, without beginning, and the Last, without end!

This is all that hath come down to us of the story of Sayf al-Muluk and Badi'a al-Jamal. And Allah alone wotteth the truth. But not less excellent than this tale is the history of "Abu Mohammed Hight Lazybones."

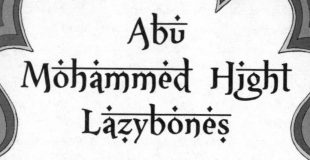

Abu Mohammed Hight Lazybones

"With joy and good will, O auspicious King,"
quoth Scheherazade the next night...

It is told that Harun al-Rashid was sitting one day on the throne of the Caliphate, when there came in to him a youth of his eunuchry, bearing a crown of red gold, set with pearls and rubies and all manner of other gems and jewels, such as money might not buy; and, bussing the ground between his hands, said, "O Commander of the Faithful, the Lady Zubaydah kisseth the earth before thee. Thou knowest she hath bidden make this crown, which lacketh a great jewel for its dome-top; and she hath made search among her treasures, but cannot find a jewel of size to suit her mind."

Quoth the Caliph to his Chamberlains and Viceregents, "Make search for a great jewel, such as Zubaydah desireth."

So they sought, but found nothing befitting her and told the Caliph who, vexed and annoyed thereat, exclaimed, "How am I Caliph and King of the Kings of the earth and cannot find so small a matter as a jewel? Woe to you! Ask of the merchants."

So they enquired of the traders, who replied, "Our lord the Caliph will not find a jewel such as he requireth save with a man of Bassorah, by name Abu Mohammed hight Lazybones."

Thereupon they acquainted the Caliph with this and he bade his Wazir Ja'afar send a note to the Emir Mohammed al-Zubaydi, Governor of Bassorah, commanding him to equip Abu Mohammed Lazybones and bring him into the presence of the Commander of the Faithful. The Minister accordingly wrote a note to that effect and despatched it by Masrur, who set out forthright for the city of Bassorah, and went in to the Emir Mohammed al-Zubaydi, who rejoiced in him and treated him with the high-most honour. Then Masrur read him the mandate of the Prince of True Believers, Harun al-Rashid, to which he replied, "I hear and I obey," and forthwith despatched him, with a company of his followers, to Abu Mohammed's house.

When they reached it, they knocked at the door, whereupon a page came out and Masrur said to him, "Tell thy lord, The Commander of the Faithful summoneth thee."

The servant went in and told his master, who came out and found Masrur, the Caliph's Chamberlain, and a company of the Governor's men at the door. So he kissed ground before Masrur and said, "I hear and obey the summons of the Commander of the Faithful; but first enter ye my house."

They replied, "We cannot do that, save in haste; even as the Prince of True Believers commanded us, for he awaiteth thy coming."

But he said, "Have patience with me a little, till I set my affairs in order."

So after much pressure and abundant persuasion, they entered the house with him and found the vestibule hung with curtains of azure brocade, purfled with red gold, and Abu Mohammed Lazybones bade one of his servants carry Masrur to the private Hammam. Now this bath was in the house and Masrur found its walls and floors of rare and precious marbles, wrought with gold and silver, and its waters mingled with rose-water. Then the servants served Masrur and his company with the perfection of service; and, on their going forth of the Hammam, clad them in robes of honour, brocade-work interwoven with gold. And after leaving the bath Masrur and his men went in to Abu Mohammed Lazybones and found him seated in his upper chamber; and over his head hung curtains of gold-brocade, wrought with pearls and jewels, and the pavilion was spread with cushions, embroidered in red gold. Now the owner was sitting softly upon a quilted cloth covering a settee inlaid with stones of price; and, when he saw Masrur, he went forward to meet him and bidding him welcome, seated him by his side.

Then he called for the food-trays; so they brought them, and when Masrur saw the tables, he exclaimed, "By Allah, never did I behold the like of these appointments in the palace of the Commander of the Faithful!" For indeed the trays contained every manner of meat all served in dishes of gilded porcelain. "So we ate and drank and made merry till the end of the day (quoth Masrur) when the host gave to each and every of us five thousand dinars, and on the morrow he clad us in dresses of honour of green and gold and entreated us with the utmost worship." Then said Masrur to him, "We can tarry no longer for fear of the Caliph's displeasure."

Answered Abu Mohammed Lazybones, "O my lord, have patience with us till the morrow, that we may equip ourselves, and we will then depart with you."

So they tarried with him that day and slept the night; and next morning Abu Mohammed's servants saddled him a she mule with selle and trappings of gold, set with all manner of pearls and stones of price; whereupon quoth Masrur to himself, "I wonder, when Abu Mohammed shall present himself in such equipage, if the Caliph will ask him how he came by all this wealth."

Thereupon they took leave of Al-Zubaydi and, setting out from Bassorah, fared on, without ceasing to fare till they reached Baghdad-city and presented themselves before the Caliph, who bade Abu Mohammed be seated. He sat down and addressed the Caliph in courtly phrase, saying, "O Commander of the Faithful, I have brought with me an humble offering by way of homage: have I thy gracious permission to produce it?"

Al-Rashid replied, "There is no harm in that," whereupon Abu Mohammed bade his men bring in a chest, from which he took a number of rarities, and amongst the rest, trees of gold with leaves of white emeraid, and fruits of pigeon blood rubies and topazes and new pearls and bright. And as the Caliph was struck with admiration he fetched a second chest and brought out of it a tent of brocade, crowned with pearls and jacinths and emeralds and jaspers and other precious stones; its poles were of freshly cut Hindi aloes-wood, and its skirts were set with the greenest smaragds. Thereon were depicted all manner of animals such as beasts and birds, spangled with precious stones, rubies, emeralds, chrysolites and balasses and every kind of precious metal.

Now when Al-Rashid saw these things, he rejoiced with exceeding joy and Abu Mohammed Lazybones said to him, "O Commander of the Faithful, deem not that I have brought these to thee, fearing aught or coveting anything; but I knew myself to be but a man of the people and that such things befitted none save the Commander of the Faithful. And now, with thy leave, I will show thee, for thy diversion, something of what I can do."

Al-Rashid replied, "Do what thou wilt, that we may see."

"To hear is to obey," said Abu Mohammed and, moving his lips, beckoned the palace battlements, whereupon they inclined to him; then he made another sign to them, and they returned to their place. Presently he made a sign with his eye, and there appeared before him closets with closed doors, to which he spoke, and lo! the voices of birds answered him from within.

The Caliph marvelled with passing marvel at this and said to him, "How camest thou by all this, seeing that thou art known only as Abu Mohammed Lazybones, and they tell me that thy father was a cupper serving in a public Hammam, who left thee nothing?"

Whereupon he answered, "O Prince of True Believers, listen to my story, for it is a marvellous and its particulars are wondrous; were it graven with graver-needles upon the eye-corners it were a warner to whose would be warned."

Quoth Al-Rashid, "Let us hear all thou hast to say, O Abu Mohammed!"

So he began "Know then, O Commander of the Faithful (Allah prolong to thee glory and dominion!), the report of the folk; that I am known as the Lazybones and that my father left me nothing, is true; for he was, as thou hast said, nothing but a barber-cupper in a Hammam. And I throughout my youth was the idlest wight on the face of the earth; indeed, so great was my sluggishness that, if I lay at full length in the sultry season and the sun came round upon me, I was too lazy to rise and remove from the sun to the shade. And thus I abode till I reached my fifteenth year, when my father deceased in the mercy of Allah Almighty and left me nothing. However, my mother used to go out a-charing and feed me and give me to drink, whilst I lay on my side.

"Now it came to pass that one day she came in to me with five silver dirhams, and said to me, 'O my son, I hear that Shaykh Abu al-Muzaffar is about to go a voyage to China.' (Now this Shaykh was a good and charitable man who loved the poor.) 'So come, my son, take these five silver bits; and let us both carry them to him and beg him to buy thee therewith somewhat from the land of China; so haply thou mayst make a profit of it by the bounty of Allah, whose name be exalted!'

"I was too idle to move for her; but she swore by the Almighty that, except I rose and went with her, she would bring me neither meat nor drink nor come in to me, but would leave me to die of hunger and thirst. Now when I heard her words, O Commander of the Faithful, I knew she would do as she threatened for her knowledge of my sluggishness; so I said to her, 'Help me to sit up.'

"She did so, and I wept the while and said to her, 'Bring me my shoes.'

"Accordingly, she brought them and I said, 'Put them on my feet.'

"She put them on my feet and I said, 'Lift me up off the ground.'

"So she lifted me up and I said, 'Support me, that I may walk.'

"So she supported me and I continued to fare a foot, at times stumbling over my skirts, till we came to the river bank, where we saluted the Shaykh and I said to him, 'O my uncle, art thou Abu al-Muzaffar?'

"'At thy service,' answered he, and I, 'Take these dirhams and with them buy me somewhat from the land of China: haply Allah may vouchsafe me a profit of it.'

"Quoth the Shaykh to his companions, 'Do ye know this youth?'

"They answered, 'Yes, he is known as Abu Mohammed Lazybones, and we never saw him stir from his house till this moment.'

"Then said he to me, 'O my son, give me the silver with the blessing of Almighty Allah!'

"So he took the money, saying, 'Bismillah in the name of Allah!' and I returned home with my mother.

"Presently Shaykh Abu al-Muzaffar set sail, with a company of merchants, and stayed not till they reached the land of China, where he and his bought and sold; and, having won what they wished, set out on their homeward voyage. When they had been three days at sea, the Shaykh said to his company, 'Stay the vessel!'

"They asked, 'What dost thou want?' and he answered, 'Know that I have forgotten the commission wherewith Abu Mohammed Lazybones charged me; so let us turn back that we may lay out his money on somewhat whereby he may profit.'

"They cried, 'We conjure thee, by Allah Almighty turn not back with us; for we have traversed a long distance and a sore, and while so doing we have endured sad hardship and many terrors.'

"Quoth he, 'There is no help for it but we return'; and they said, 'Take from us double the profit of the five dirhams, and turn us not back.' He agreed to this and they collected for him an ample sum of money.

"Thereupon they sailed on, till they came to an island wherein was much people; when they moored thereto and the merchants went ashore, to buy thence a stock of precious metals and pearls and jewels and so forth.

Presently Abu al-Muzaffar saw a man seated, with many apes before him,
and amongst them one whose hair had been plucked off; and as often as
their owner's attention was diverted from them, the other apes fell upon
the plucked one and beat him and threw him on their master; whereupon
the man rose and bashed them and bound them and punished them for
this; and all the apes were wroth with the plucked ape on this account and
funded him the more.

"When Shaykh Abu al-Muzaffar saw this, he felt for and took
compassion upon the plucked ape and said to his master, 'Wilt thou sell me
yonder monkey?'

"Replied the man, 'Buy,' and Abu al-Muzaffar rejoined, 'I have with me
five dirhams, belonging to an orphan lad. Wilt thou sell it me for that sum?'

"Answered the monkey-merchant, 'It is a bargain; and Allah give
thee a blessing of him!' So he made over the beast and received his
money; and the Shaykh's slaves took the ape and tied him up in the
ship. Then they loosed sail and made for another island, where they cast
anchor; and there came down divers, who plunged for precious stones,
pearls and other gems; so the merchants hired them to dive for money
and they dived.

"Now when the ape saw them doing this, he loosed himself from his
bonds and, jumping off the ship's side, plunged with them, whereupon
quoth Abu al-Muzaffar, 'There is no Majesty and there is no Might, save
in Allah, the Glorious, the Great! The monkey is lost to us with the luck
of the poor fellow for whom we bought him.' And they despaired of him;
but, after a while, the company of divers rose to the surface, and behold,
among them was the ape, with his hands full of jewels of price, which he
threw down before Abu al-Muzaffar.

"The Shaykh marvelled at this and said, 'There is much mystery in
this monkey!'

"Then they cast off and sailed till they came to a third island, called the
Isle of the Zunuj, who are a people of the blacks, which eat the flesh of the
sons of Adam. When the blacks saw them, they boarded them in dug-outs
and, taking all in the vessel, pinioned them and carried them to their King,
who bade slaughter certain of the merchants. So they slaughtered them by
cutting their throats and ate their flesh; and the rest of the traders passed
the night in bonds and were in sore concern. But when it was midnight, the
ape arose and going up to Abu al-Muzaffar, loosed his bonds; and, as the
others saw him free, they said, 'Allah grant our deliverance may be at thy
hands, O Abu al-Muzaffar!'

"But he replied, 'Know that he who delivered me, by leave of Allah Almighty, was none other than this monkey, and I buy my release of him at a thousand dinars!' whereupon the merchants rejoined, 'And we likewise, each and every, will pay him a thousand dinars if he release us.'

With this the ape arose and went up to them and loosed their bonds one by one, till he had freed them all, when they made for the vessel and boarding her, found all safe and nothing missing from her. So they cast off and set sail; and presently Abu al-Muzaffar said to them, 'O merchants, fulfil your promise to the monkey.'

"'We hear and we obey,' answered they; and each one paid him one thousand dinars, whilst Abu al-Muzaffar brought out to him the like sum of his own monies, so that a great heap of coin was collected for the ape.

"Then they fared on till they reached Bassorah-city where their friends came out to meet them; and when they had landed, the Shaykh said, 'Where is Abu Mohammed Lazybones?'

"The news reached my mother, who came to me as I lay asleep and said to me, 'O my son, verily the Shaykh Abu al-Muzaffar hath come back and is now in the city; so rise and go thou to him and salute him and enquire what he hath brought thee; it may be Allah Almighty have opened to thee the door of fortune with somewhat.'

"Quoth I, 'Lift me from the ground and prop me up, whilst I go forth and walk to the river bank.'

"After which I went out and walked on, stumbling over my skirts, till I met the Shaykh, who exclaimed at sight of me, 'Welcome to him whose money hath been the means of my release and that of these merchants, by the will of Almighty Allah.' Then he continued, 'Take this monkey I bought for thee and carry him home and wait till I come to thee.'

"So I took the ape and went off, saying in my mind, 'By Allah, this is naught but rare merchandise!' and led it home, where I said to my mother, 'Whenever I lie down to sleep, thou biddest me rise and trade; see now this merchandise with thine own eyes.'

"Then I sat me down and as I sat, up came the slaves of Abu al-Muzaffar and said to me, 'Art thou Abu Mohammed Lazybones?'

"'Yes' answered I; and behold, Abu al-Muzaffar appeared behind them.

"So I rose up to him and kissed his hands: and he said, 'Come with me to my home.'

"'Hearkening and obedience,' answered I and accompanied him to his house, where he bade his servants bring me what money the monkey had earned for me.

"So they brought it and he said to me, 'O my son, Allah hath blessed thee with this wealth, by way of profit on thy five dirhams.'

Then the slaves set down the treasure in chests, which they had carried on their heads, and Abu al-Muzaffar gave me the keys saying, 'Go before the slaves to thy house; for in sooth all this wealth is thine.'

"So I returned to my mother, who rejoiced in this and said to me, 'O my son, Allah hath blessed thee with all these riches; so put off thy laziness and go down to the bazar and sell and buy.'

"At once I shook off my dull sloth, and opened a shop in the bazar, where the ape used to sit on the same divan with me eating with me when I ate and drinking when I drank. But, every day, he was absent from dawn till noon, when he came back bringing with him a purse of a thousand dinars, which he laid by my side, and sat down; and he ceased not so doing for a great while, till I amassed much wealth, wherewith, O Commander of the Faithful, I purchased houses and lands, and I planted gardens and I bought me white slaves and negroes and concubines.

"Now it came to pass one day, as I sat in my shop, with the ape sitting at my side on the same carpet, behold, he began to turn right and left, and I said to myself, 'What aileth the beast?'

"Then Allah made the ape speak with a ready tongue, and he said to me, 'O Abu Mohammed!' Now when I heard him speak, I was sore afraid; but he said to me, 'Fear not; I will tell thee my case. I am a Marid of the Jinn and came to thee because of thy poor estate; but to-day thou knowest not the amount of thy wealth; and now I have need of thee and if thou do my will, it shall be well for thee.'

"I asked, 'What is it?' and he answered, 'I have a mind to marry thee to a girl like the full moon.'

"Quoth I, 'How so?'; and quoth he, 'To-morrow don thou thy richest dress and mount thy mule, with the saddle of gold and ride to the Haymarket. There enquire for the shop of the Sharif and sit down beside him and say to him, "I come to thee as a suitor craving thy daughter's hand." '

"If he say to thee, 'Thou hast neither cash nor rank nor family'; pull out a thousand dinars and give them to him, and if he ask more, give him more and tempt him with money.

"Whereto I replied, 'To hear is to obey; I will do thy bidding, Inshallah!'

"So on the next morning I donned my richest clothes, mounted my she mule with trappings of gold and rode to the Haymarket where I asked for the Sharif's shop, and finding him there seated, alighted and saluted him and seated myself beside him, and my Mamelukes and negro-slaves stood before me.

"Said the Sharif, 'Haply, thou hast some business with us which we may have pleasure of transacting?'

"Replied I, 'Yes, I have business with thee.'

"Asked he, 'And what is it?'; and I answered, 'I come to thee as a suitor for thy daughter's hand.'

"So he said, 'Thou hast neither cash nor rank nor family'; whereupon I pulled him out a purse of a thousand dinars, red gold, and said to him, 'This is my rank and my family; and he (whom Allah bless and keep!) hath said, "The best of ranks is wealth." And how well quoth the poet:

> "'Whoso two dirhams hath, his lips have learnt
> Speech of all kinds with eloquence bedight:
> Draw near his brethren and crave ear of him,
> And him thou seest haught in pride-full height:
> Were 't not for dirhams wherein glories he,
> Hadst found him 'mid mankind in sorry plight.
> When richard errs in words they all reply,
> "Sooth thou hast spoken and hast said aright!"
> When pauper speaketh truly all reply
> "Thou liest;" and they hold his sayings light.
> Verily dirhams in earth's every stead
> Clothe men with rank and make them fair to sight
> Gold is the very tongue of eloquence;
> Gold is the best of arms for might who'd fight!"'

"Now when the Sharif heard these my words and understood my verse, he bowed his head awhile groundwards then raising it, said, 'If it must be so, I will have of thee other three thousand gold pieces.'

"'I hear and I obey,' answered I, and sent one of my Mamelukes home for the money.

"As soon as he came back with it, I handed it to the Sharif who, when he saw it in his hands, rose, and bidding his servants shut his shop, invited his brother merchants of the bazar the wedding; after which he carried me to his house and wrote out my contract of marriage with his daughter saying to me, 'After ten days, I will bring thee to pay her the first visit.'

"So I went home rejoicing and, shutting myself up with the ape, told

him what had passed; and he said 'Thou hast done well.'

"Now when the time appointed by the Sharif drew near, the ape said to me, 'There is a thing I would have thee do for me; and thou shalt have of me (when it is done) whatso thou wilt.'

"I asked, 'What is that?' and he answered, 'At the upper end of the chamber wherein thou shalt meet thy bride, the Sharif's daughter, stands a cabinet, on whose door is a ring-padlock of copper and the keys under it. Take the keys and open the cabinet in which thou shalt find a coffer of iron with four flags, which are talismans, at its corners; and in its midst stands a brazen basin full of money, wherein is tied a white cock with a cleft comb; while on one side of the coffer are eleven serpents and on the other a knife. Take the knife and slaughter the cock; cut away the flags and upset the chest, then go back to the bride and do away her maidenhead. This is what I have to ask of thee.'

"'Hearkening and obedience,' answered I, and betook myself to the house of the Sharif.

"So as soon as I entered the bride-chamber, I looked for the cabinet and found it even as the ape had described it. Then I went in unto the bride and marvelled at her beauty and loveliness and stature and symmetrical-grace, for indeed they were such as no tongue can set forth. I rejoiced in her with exceeding joy; and in the middle of the night, when my bride slept, I rose and, taking the keys, opened the cabinet. Then I seized the knife and slew the cock and threw down the flags and upset the coffer, whereupon the girl awoke and, seeing the closet open and the cock with cut throat, exclaimed, 'There is no Majesty and there is no Might save in Allah, the Glorious, the Great! The Marid hath got hold of me!'

"Hardly had she made an end of speaking, when the Marid swooped down upon the house and, snatching up the bride, flew away with her; whereupon there arose a mighty clamour and behold, in came the Sharif, buffetting his face and crying, 'O Abu Mohammed, what is this deed thou hast done? Is it thus thou requitest us? I made this talisman in the cabinet fearing for my daughter from this accursed one who, for these six years, hath sought to steal-away the girl, but could not. But now there is no more abiding for thee with us, so wend thy ways.'

"Thereupon I went forth and returned to my own house, where I made search for the ape but could not find him nor any trace of him; whereby I knew that it was he who was the Marid, and that he had carried off my wife and had tricked me into destroying the talisman and the cock, the two things which hindered him from taking her, and I repented, rending my raiment and cuffing my face. And there was no land but was straitened upon me; so I made for the desert forthright and ceased not wandering on till night overtook me, for I knew not whither I was going. And whilst I was deep in sad thought behold, I met two serpents, one tawny and the other white, and they were fighting to kill each other. So I took up a stone and with one cast slew the tawny serpent, which was the aggressor; whereupon the white serpent glided away and was absent for a while, but presently she returned accompanied by ten other white serpents which glided up to the dead serpent and tore her in pieces, so that only the head was left. Then they went their ways and I fell prostrate for weariness on the ground where I stood; but as I lay, pondering my case lo! I heard a Voice though I saw no one and the Voice versified with these two couplets:

> "'Let Fate with slackened bridle fare her pace,
> Nor pass the night with mind which cares an ace
> Between eye-closing and its opening,
> Allah can foulest change to fairest case.'

"Now when I heard this, O Commander of the Faithful, great concern get hold of me and I was beyond measure troubled, and behold, I heard a Voice from behind me extemporise these couplets:

> "'O Moslem! thou whose guide is Alcoran, Joy in what brought
> safe peace to thee, O man.
> Fear not what Satan haply whispered thee,
> And in us see a Truth-believing'

"Then said I, 'I conjure thee, by the truth of Him thou worshippest, let me know who thou art!'

"Thereupon the Invisible Speaker assumed the form of a man and said, 'Fear not; for the report of thy good deed hath reached us, and we are a people of the true-believing Jinn. So, if thou lack aught, let us know it that we may have the pleasure of fulfilling thy want.'

"Quoth I, 'Indeed I am in sore need, for I am afflicted with a grievous affliction and no one was ever afflicted as I am!'

"Quoth he, 'Perchance thou art Abu Mohammed Lazybones?' and I replied, 'Yes.'

"He rejoined, 'I, O Abu Mohammed, am the brother of the white serpent, whose foe thou slewest, we are four brothers by one father and

mother, and we are all indebted to thee for thy kindness. And know thou
that he who played this trick on thee in the likeness of an ape, is a Marid
of the Marids of the Jinn; and had he not used this artifice, he had never
been able to get the girl; for he hath loved her and had a mind to take her
this long while, but he was hindered of that talisman; and had it remained
as it was, he could never have found access to her. However, fret not thyself
for that; we will bring thee to her and kill the Marid; for thy kindness is not
lost upon us.'

"Then he cried out with a terrible outcry in a horrible voice, and behold,
there appeared a troop of the Jinn, of whom he enquired concerning the
ape; and one of them said, 'I know his abiding-place'; and the other asked
'Where abideth he?'

"Said the speaker 'He is in the City of Brass whereon sun riseth not.'

Then said the first Jinni to me, 'O Abu Mohammed, take one of these
our slaves, and he will carry thee on his back and teach thee how thou shalt
get back the girl; but know that this slave is a Marid of the Marids and
beware, whilst he is carrying thee, lest thou utter the name of Allah, or he
will flee from thee and thou wilt fall and be destroyed.'

"'I hear and obey,' answered I and chose out one of the slaves, who
bent down and said to me, 'Mount.'

"So I mounted on his back, and he flew up with me into the firmament,
till I lost sight of the earth and saw the stars as they were the mountains of
earth fixed and firm and heard the angels crying, 'Praise be to Allah,' in
heaven while the Marid held me in converse, diverting me and hindering
me from pronouncing the name of Almighty Allah. But, as we flew, behold,
One clad in green raiment, with streaming tresses and radiant face, holding
in his hand a javelin whence flew sparks of fire, accosted me, saying, 'O
Abu Mohammed, say: "There is no god but *the* God and Mohammed is the
Apostle of God"; or I will smite thee with this javelin.'

"Now already I felt heart-broken by my forced silence as regards
calling on the name of Allah; so I said, 'There is no god but *the* God,
and Mohammed is the Apostle of God.' Whereupon the shining One
smote the Marid with his javelin and he melted away and became ashes;
whilst I was thrown from his back and fell headlong towards the earth,
till I dropped into the midst of a dashing sea, swollen with clashing surge.
And behold I fell hard by a ship with five sailors therein, who seeing me,
made for me and took me up into the vessel; and they began to speak to
me in some speech I knew not; but I signed to them that I understood
not their speech.

243

"So they fared on till the last of the day, when they cast out a net and caught a great fish and they broiled it and gave me to eat; after which they ceased not sailing on till they reached their city and carried me to their King and set me in his presence. So I kissed ground before him, and he bestowed on me a dress of honour and said to me in Arabic (which he knew well), 'I appoint thee one of my officers.'

"Thereupon I asked him the name of the city, and he replied, 'It is called Hanad and is in the land of China.'

"Then he committed me to his Wazir, bidding him show me the city, which was formerly peopled by Infidels, till Almighty Allah turned them into stones; and there I abode a month's space, diverting myself with viewing the place, nor saw I ever greater plenty of trees and fruits than there.

"And when this time had past, one day, as I sat on the bank of a river, behold, there accosted me a horseman, who said to me, 'Art thou not Abu Mohammed Lazybones?'

"'Yes,' answered I; whereupon, he said, 'Fear not, for the report of thy good deed hath reached us.'

"Asked I, 'Who art thou?' and he answered, 'I am a brother of the white serpent, and thou art hard by the place where is the damsel whom thou seekest.'

"So saying, he took off his clothes and clad me therein, saying, 'Fear not, for the slave who perished under thee was one of our slaves.'

"Then the horseman took me up behind him and rode on with me to a desert place, when he said, 'Dismount now and walk on between these two mountains, till thou seest the City of Brass; then halt afar off and enter it not, ere I return to thee and tell thee how thou shalt do.'

"'To hear is to obey,' replied I and, dismounting from behind him, walked on till I came to the city, the walls whereof I found of brass. Then I began to pace round about it, hoping to find a gate, but found none; and presently as I persevered, behold, the serpent's brother rejoined me and gave me a charmed sword which should hinder any from seeing me, then went his way.

"Now he had been gone but a little while, when lo! I heard a noise of cries and found myself in the midst of a multitude of folk whose eyes were in their breasts; and seeing me quoth they, 'Who art thou and what cast thee into this place?'

"So I told them my story, and they said, 'The girl thou seekest is in this city with the Marid; but we know not what he hath done with her. Now we are brethren of the white serpent,' adding, 'Go thou to yonder spring and note where the water entereth, and enter thou with it; for it will bring thee into the city.'

"I did as they bade me, and followed the water-course, till it brought me to a Sardab, a vaulted room under the earth, from which I ascended and found myself in the midst of the city. Here I saw the damsel seated upon a throne of gold, under a canopy of brocade, girt round by a garden full of trees of gold, whose fruits were jewels of price, such as rubies and chrysolites, pearls and coral. And the moment she saw me, she knew me and accosted me with the Moslem salutation, saying, 'O my lord, who guided thee hither?' So I told her all that had passed, and she said, 'Know, that the accursed Marid, of the greatness of his love for me, hath told me what bringeth him bane and what bringeth him gain; and that there is here a talisman by means whereof he could, an he would, destroy the city and all that are therein; and whoso possesseth it, the Ifrits will do his commandment in everything. It standeth upon a pillar.'

"Whereat I asked her, 'And where is the pillar?' and she answered, 'It is in such a place.'

"'And what manner of thing may the talisman be?' said I: said she, 'It is in the semblance of a vulture and upon it is a writing which I cannot read. So go thou thither and seize it, and set it before thee and, taking a chafing dish, throw into it a little musk, whereupon there will arise a smoke which will draw the Ifrits to thee, and they will all present themselves before thee, nor shall one be absent; also they shall be subject to thy word and, whatsoever thou biddest them, that will they do. Arise therefore and fall to this thing, with the blessing of Almighty Allah.'

"I answered, 'Hearkening and obedience' and, going to the column, did as she bade me, where- upon the Ifrits all presented themselves before me saying, 'Here are we, O our lord! Whatsoever thou biddest us, that will we do.'

"Quoth I, 'Bind the Marid who brought the damsel hither from her home.'

"Quoth they, 'We hear and obey,' and off they flew and bound that Marid in straitest bonds and returned after a while, saying, 'We have done thy bidding.'

"Then I dismissed them and, repairing to my wife, told her what had happened and said to her, 'O my bride, wilt thou go with me?'

"'Yes,' answered she. So I carried her forth of the vaulted chamber whereby I had entered the city and we fared on, till we fell in with the folk who had shown me the way to find her.

"So I said to them, 'Point me out a path which shall lead me to my home,' and they did accordingly, and brought us a-foot to the sea-shore and set us aboard a vessel which sailed on before us with a fair wind, till we reached Bassorah-city. And when we entered the house of my father-in-law and her people saw my wife, they rejoiced with exceeding joy. Then I fumigated the vulture with musk and lo! the Ifrits flocked to me from all sides, saying, 'At thy service what wilt thou have us do?' So I bade them transport all that was in the City of Brass of monies and noble metals and stones of price to my house in Bassorah, which they did; and I then ordered them to bring me the ape. They brought him before me, abject and contemptible, and I said to him, 'O accursed, why hast thou dealt thus perfidiously with me?'

"Then I commended the Ifrits to shut him in a brazen vessel so they put him in a brazen cucurbite and sealed it with lead. But I abode with my wife in joy and delight; and now, O Commander of the Faithful, I have under my hand precious things in such measure and rare jewels and other treasure and monies on such wise as neither reckoning may express nor may limits comprise; and, if thou lust after wealth or aught else, I will command the Jinn at once to do thy desire. But all this is of the bounty of Almighty Allah."

Thereupon the Commander of the Faithful wondered greatly and bestowed on him imperial gifts, in exchange for his presents, and entreated him with the favour he deserved.

And Scheherazade perceived the dawn of day and ceased saying her permitted say. Then quoth Dunyazad, "O my sister, how pleasant is thy tale, and how tasteful; how sweet, and how grateful!"

She replied, "And where is this compared with what I could tell thee this coming night, if I live and the King spare me?"

Said the King in himself, "By Allah, I will not slay her until I hear next story, for truly it is wondrous."

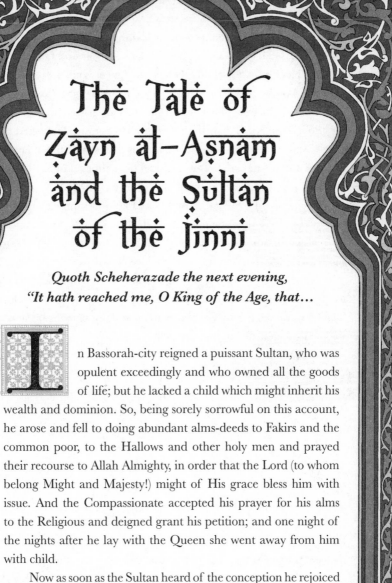

The Tale of Zayn al-Aṣnám and the Sultán of the Jinni

Quoth Scheherazade the next evening,
"It hath reached me, O King of the Age, that…"

In Bassorah-city reigned a puissant Sultan, who was opulent exceedingly and who owned all the goods of life; but he lacked a child which might inherit his wealth and dominion. So, being sorely sorrowful on this account, he arose and fell to doing abundant alms-deeds to Fakirs and the common poor, to the Hallows and other holy men and prayed their recourse to Allah Almighty, in order that the Lord (to whom belong Might and Majesty!) might of His grace bless him with issue. And the Compassionate accepted his prayer for his alms to the Religious and deigned grant his petition; and one night of the nights after he lay with the Queen she went away from him with child.

Now as soon as the Sultan heard of the conception he rejoiced with exceeding great joyance, and when the days of delivery drew near he gathered together all the astrologers and sages who strike the sand-board, and said to them, "'Tis our desire that ye disclose and acquaint us anent the birth which is to be born during the present month whether it shall be male or female, and what shall befal it from the shifts of Time, and what shall proceed from it."

Thereupon the geomantists struck their sand-boards and the astrophils ascertained their ascendants and they drew the horoscope of the babe unborn, and said to the sovran, "O King of the Age and Lord of the Time and the Tide, verily the child to which the Queen shall presently give birth will be a boy and 'twill be right for thee to name him Zayn al-Asnam—Zayn of the Images." Then spake the geomantists, saying, "Know then, Ho though the King, that this little one shall approve him when grown to man's estate valiant and intelligent; but his days shall happen upon sundry troubles and travails, and yet if he doughtily fight against all occurrence he shall become the most opulent of the Kings of the World."

Exclaimed the Sultan, "An the child approve himself valorous, as ye have announced, then the toil and moil which shall be his lot may be held for naught, inasmuch as calamities but train and strengthen the songs of the Kings."

Shortly after this the Queen gave birth to a man-child, and Glory be to Him who fashioned the babe with such peerless beauty and loveliness! The King named his son Zayn al-Asnam, and presently he became even as the poets sang of one of his fellows in semblance,

> He showed; and they cried, "Be Allah blest!"
> And who made him and formed him His might attest!
> This be surely the lord of all loveliness;
> And all others his lieges and thralls be confest.

Then Zayn al-Asnam grew up and increased until his age attained its fifteenth year, when his sire the Sultan appointed for him an experienced governor, one versed in all the sciences and philosophies; who fell to instructing him till such times as he waxed familiar with every branch of knowledge, and in due season he became an adult. Thereupon the Sultan bade summon his son and heir to the presence together with the Lords of his land and the Notables of his lieges and addressed him before them with excellent counsel saying, "O my son, O Zayn al-Asnam, seeing that I be shotten in years and at the present time sick of a sickness which haply shall end my days in this world and which anon shall seat thee in my stead, therefore, I bequeath unto thee the following charge. Beware, O my son, lest thou wrong any man, and incline not to cause the poor complain; but do justice to the injured after the measure of thy might. Furthermore, have a care lest thou trust to every word spoken to thee by the Great; but rather lend thou ever an ear unto the voice of the general; for that thy Grandees will betray thee as they seek only whatso suiteth them, not that which suiteth thy subjects."

A few days after this time the old Sultan's distemper increased and his lifeterm was fulfilled and he died; whereupon his son, Zayn al-Asnam, arose and donned mourning-dress for his father during six days; and on the seventh he went forth to the Divan and took seat upon the throne of his Sultanate. He also held a levee wherein were assembled all the defenders of the realm, and the Ministers and the Lords of the land came forward and condoled with him for the loss of his parent and wished him all good fortune and gave him joy of his kingship and dominion and prayed for his endurance in honour and his permanence in prosperity.

Zayn al-Asnam, seeing himself in this high honour and opulence and he young in years and void of experience, straightway inclined unto lavish expenditure and commerce with the younglings, who were like him and fell to wasting immense wealth upon his pleasures; and neglected his government, nor paid aught of regard to his subjects. Thereupon the Queen-mother began to counsel him, and forbid him from such ill courses, advising him to abandon his perverse inclinations and apply his mind to rule and commandment, and to further the policy of his kingdom, lest the lieges repudiate him and rise up against him and depose him. But he would on no wise hearken to a single of her words and persisted in his ignorant folly; whereat the folk murmured, inasmuch as the Lords of the land had put forth their hands to tyranny and oppression when they saw the King lacking in regard for his Ryots. And presently the commons rose up against Zayn al-Asnam and would have dealt harshly with him had not his mother been a woman of wits and wisdom and contrivance, dearly loved of the general. So she directed the malcontents aright and promised them every good: then she summoned her son Zayn al-Asnam and said to him, "Behold, O my child, that which I foretold for thee, to wit that thou wastest thy realm and lavishest thy life to boot by persevering in what ignorance thou art; for that thou hast placed the governance of thy Kingdom in the hands of inexperienced youth and hast neglected the elders and hast dissipated thy moneys and the moneys of the monarchy, and thou hast lavished all thy treasure upon wilfulness and carnal pleasuring."

Zayn al-Asnam, awaking from the slumber of negligence, forthright accepted his mother's counsel and, faring forth at once to the Diwan, he entrusted the management of the monarchy to certain old officers, men

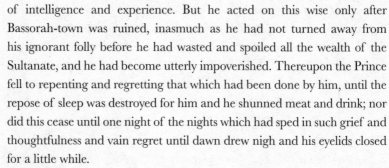

of intelligence and experience. But he acted on this wise only after Bassorah-town was ruined, inasmuch as he had not turned away from his ignorant folly before he had wasted and spoiled all the wealth of the Sultanate, and he had become utterly impoverished. Thereupon the Prince fell to repenting and regretting that which had been done by him, until the repose of sleep was destroyed for him and he shunned meat and drink; nor did this cease until one night of the nights which had sped in such grief and thoughtfulness and vain regret until dawn drew nigh and his eyelids closed for a little while.

Then an old and venerable Shaykh appeared to him in a vision and said to him, "O Zayn al-Asnam, sorrow not; for after sorrow however sore cometh naught but joyance; and, would'st thou win free of this woe, up and hie thee to Egypt where thou shalt find hoards of wealth which shall replace whatso thou hast wasted and will double it more than twofold."

Now when the Prince was aroused from his sleep he recounted to his mother all he had seen in his dream; but his parent began to laugh at him, and he said to her, "Mock me not: there is no help but that I wend Egypt-wards."

Rejoined she, "O my son, believe not in swevens which be mere imbroglios of sleep and lying phantasies;" and retorted saying, "In very sooth my vision is true and the man whom I saw therein is of the Saints of Allah and his words are veridical."

Then on a night of the nights mounting horse alone and privily, he abandoned his Kingdom; and took the highway to Egypt; and he rode day and night until he reached Cairo-city. He entered it and saw it to be a mighty fine capital; then, tethering his steed he found shelter in one of its Cathedral-mosques, and he worn out by weariness; however, when he had rested a little he fared forth and bought himself somewhat of food.

After eating, his excessive fatigue caused him fall asleep in the mosque; nor had he slept long ere the Shaykh appeared to him a second time in vision and said to him, "O Zayn al-Asnam, thou hast obeyed me in whatso I bade thee and I only made trial of thee to test an thou be valiant or a craven. But now I wot thy worth, inasmuch as thou hast accepted my words and thou hast acted upon my advice: so do thou return straightway to thy capital and I will make thee a wealthy ruler, such an one that neither before thee was any king like unto thee nor shall any like unto thee come after thee."

Hereat Zayn al-Asnam awoke and cried "Bismillah—in the name of Allah, the Compassionating, the Compassionate—what be this Shaykh who verily persecuted me until I travelled to Cairo; and I having faith in him and holding that he was either the Apostle (whom Allah save!) or one of the righteous Hallows of God; and there is no Majesty and there is no Might save in Allah, the Glorious, the Great! By the Lord, but I did right well in not relating my dream to any save to my mother, and in warning none of my departure. I had full faith in this oldster; but now, meseemeth, the man is not of those who know the Truth (be He extolled and exalted!); so by Allah I will cast off all confidence in this Shaykh and his doings."

With this resolve the Prince slept that night in the Mosque and on the morrow took horse and after a few days of strenuous travel arrived at his capital Bassorah. Herein he entered by night, and forthright went in to his mother who asked him, "Say me, hast thou won aught of whatso the Shaykh promised thee?" and he answered her by acquainting her with all his adventure.

Then she applied her to consoling and comforting him, saying, "Grieve not, O my son; if Almighty Allah have apportioned unto thee aught thou shalt obtain it without toil and travail. But I would see thee wax sensible and wise, abandoning all these courses which have landed thee in poverty, O my son; and shunning songstresses and commune with the inexperienced and the society of loose livers, male and female. All such pleasures as these are for the sons of the ne'er-do-well, not for the scions of the Kings thy peers."

Herewith Zayn al-Asnam sware an oath to bear in mind all she might say to him, never to gainsay her commandments, nor deviate from them a single hair's breadth; to abandon all she should forbid him, and to fix his thoughts upon rule and goverance. Then he addrest himself to sleep, and as he slumbered, the Shaykh appeared to him a third time in vision, and said, "O Zayn al-Asnam, O thou valorous Prince; this very day, as soon as thou shalt have shaken off thy drowsiness, I will fulfil my covenant with thee. So take with thee a pickaxe, and hie to such a palace of thy sire, and turn up the ground, searching it well in such a place where thou wilt find that which shall enrich thee."

As soon as the Prince awoke, he hastened to his mother in huge joy and told her his tale; but she fell again to laughing at him, and saying, "O my child, indeed this old man maketh mock of thee and naught else; so get thyself clear of him."

But Zayn al-Asnam replied, "O mother mine, verily this Shaykh is soothfast and no liar: for the first time he but tried me and now he proposeth to perform his promise."

Whereto his mother, "At all events, the work is not wearisome; so do thou whatso thou willest even as he bade thee. Make the trial and Inshallah—God willing—return to me rejoicing; yet sore I fear lest thou come back to me and say, 'Sooth thou hast spoken in thy speech, O my mother!'"

However Zayn al-Asnam took up a pickaxe and, descending to that part of the palace where his sire lay entombed, began to dig and to delve; nor had he worked a long while ere, lo and behold! there appeared to him a ring bedded in a marble slab. He removed the stone and saw a ladder-like flight of steps whereby he descended until he found a huge souterrain all pillar'd and propped with columns of marble and alabaster. And when he entered the inner recesses he saw within the cave-like souterrain a pavilion which bewildered his wits, and inside the same stood eight jars of green jasper. So he said in his mind, "What may be these jars and what may be stored therein?" He came forwards and unlidding them found each and every full of antique golden pieces; so he hent a few in hand seen and going to his mother gave of them to her saying, "Hast thou seen, O my mother?"

She marvelled at the matter and made answer, "Beware, O my son, of wasting this wealth as thou dissipatedst other aforetime"; whereupon her son sware to her an oath saying, "Have no care, O my mother, nor be thy heart other than good before me; and I desire that thou also find satisfaction in mine actions."

Presently she arose and went forth with him, and the twain descended into the cavern-like souterrain and entered the pavilion, where the Queen saw that which wildereth the wits; and she made sure with her own eyes that the jars were full of gold. But while they enjoyed the spectacle of the treasure behold, they caught sight of a smaller jar wondrously wrought in green jasper; so Zayn al-Asnam opened it and found therein a golden key; whereupon quoth the Queen-mother, "O my son, needs must this key have some door which it unlocketh."

Accordingly they sought all about the souterrain and the pavilion to find if there be a door or aught like thereto, and presently, seeing a wooden lock fast barred, they knew wherefor the key was intended. Presently the Prince applied it and opened the lock, whereupon the door of a palace gave admittance, and when the twain entered they found it more spacious than the first pavilion and all illumined with a light which dazed the sight; yet not a wax-candle lit it up nor indeed was there a recess for lamps. Hereat they marvelled and meditated and presently they discovered eight images of precious stones, all seated upon as many golden thrones, and each and every was cut of one solid piece; and all the stones were pure and of the finest water and most precious of price.

Zayn al-Asnam was confounded hereat and said to his mother, "Whence could my sire have obtained all these rare things?"

And the twain took their pleasure in gazing at them and considering them and both wondered to see a ninth throne unoccupied, when the Queen espied a silken hanging whereon was inscribed, "O my son, marvel not at this mighty wealth which I have acquired by sore stress and striving travail. But learn also that there existeth a Ninth Statue whose value is twenty-fold greater than these thou seest and, if thou would win it, hie thee again to Cairo-city. There thou shalt find a whilome slave of mine Mubarak hight and he will take thee and guide thee to the Statue; and 'twill be easy to find him on entering Cairo: the first person thou shalt accost will point out the house to thee, for that Mubarak is known throughout the place."

When Zayn al-Asnam had read this writ he cried: "O my mother, 'tis again my desire to wend my way Cairo-wards and seek out this image; so do thou say how seest thou my vision, fact or fiction, after thou assuredst me saying, 'This be an imbroglio of sleep?' However, at all events, O my mother, now there is no help for it but that I travel once more to Cairo."

Replied she, "O my child, seeing that thou be under the protection of the Apostle of Allah (whom may He save and assain!) so do thou fare in safety, while I and thy Wazir will order thy reign in thine absence till such time as thou shalt return."

Accordingly the Prince went forth and gat him ready and rode on till he reached Cairo where he asked for Mubarak's house. The folk answered him saying, "O my lord, this be a man than whom none is wealthier or greater in boon deeds and bounties, and his home is ever open to the stranger."

Then they showed him the way and he followed it till he came to Mubarak's mansion where he knocked at the door and a slave of the black slaves opened to him and asked, "Who art thou and what is it thou wantest?"

The Prince answered, "I am a foreigner from a far country, and I have heard of Mubarak thy lord that he is famed for liberality and generosity; so that I come hither purposing to become his guest."

Thereupon the chattel went in to his lord and, after reporting the matter to him, came out and said to Zayn al-Asnam, "O my lord, a blessing hath descended upon us by thy footsteps. Do thou enter, for my master Mubarak awaiteth thee."

Therewith the Prince passed into a court spacious exceedingly and all beautified with trees and waters, and the slave led him to the pavilion wherein Mubarak was sitting. As the guest came in the host straightway rose up and met him with cordial greeting and cried, "A benediction hath alighted upon us and this night is the most benedight of the nights by reason of thy coming to us! So who are thou, O youth, and whence is thine arrival and whither is thine intent?"

He replied, "I am Zayn al-Asnam and I seek one Mubarak, a slave of the Sultan of Bassorah who deceased a year ago, and I am his son."

Mubarak rejoined, "What sayest thou? Thou the son of the King of Bassorah?" and the other retorted, "Yea, verily I am his son."

Quoth Mubarak, "In good sooth my late lord the King of Bassorah left no son known to me! But what may be thine age, O youth?"

"Twenty years or so," quoth the Prince, presently adding, "But thou, how long is it since thou leftest my sire?"

"I left him eighteen years ago," said the other; "but, O my child Zayn al-Asnam, by what sign canst thou assure me of thy being the son of my old master, the Sovran of Bassorah?"

Said the Prince, "Thou alone knowest that my father laid out beneath his palace a souterrain, and in this he placed forty jars of the finest green jasper, which he filled with pieces of antique gold, also that within a pavilion he built a second palace and set therein eight images of precious stones, each one of a single gem, and all seated upon royal seats of placer-gold. He also wrote upon a silken hanging a writ which I read and which bade me repair to thee and thou wouldst inform me concerning the Ninth Statue whereabouts it may be, assuring me that it is worth all the eight."

Now when Mubarak heard these words, he fell at the feet of Zayn al-Asnam and kissed them exclaiming, "Pardon me, O my lord, in very truth thou art the son of my old master"; adding, presently, "I have spread, O my lord, a feast for all the Grandess of Cairo and I would that thy Highness honour it by thy presence."

The Prince replied, "With love and the best will."

Thereupon Mubarak arose and forewent Zayn al-Asnam to the saloon which was full of the Lords of the land there gathered together, and here he seated himself after stablishing Zayn al-Asnam in the place of honour. Then he bade the tables be spread and the feast be served and he waited upon the Prince with arms crossed behind his back and at times falling upon his knees. So the Grandees of Cairo marvelled to see Mubarak, one of the great men of the city, serving the youth and wondered with extreme wonderment, unknowing whence the stranger was. After this they ate and drank and supped well and were cheered till at last Mubarak turned towards them and said, "O folk, admire not that I wait upon this young man with all worship and honour, for that he is the son of my old lord, the Sultan of Bassorah, who bought me with his money and who died without manumitting me. I am, therefore, bound to do service to his son, this my young lord, and all that my hand possesseth of money and munition belongeth to him nor own I aught thereof at all, at all."

When the Grandees of Cairo heard these words, they stood up before Zayn al-Asnam and salamed to him with mighty great respect and entreated him with high regard and blessed him. Then said the Prince, "O assembly, I am in the presence of your worships, and be ye my witnesses. O Mubarak, thou art now freed and all thou hast of goods, gold and gear erst belonging to us becometh henceforth thine own and thou art endowed with them for good each and every. Eke do thou ask whatso of importance thou wouldst have from me, for I will on no wise let or stay thee in thy requiring it."

With this Mubarak arose and kissed the hand of Zayn al-Asnam and thanked him for his boons, saying, "O my lord, I wish for thee naught save thy weal, but the wealth that is with me is altogether overmuch for my wants."

Then the Prince abode with the Freedman four days, during which all the Grandees of Cairo made act of presence day by day to offer their salams as soon as they heard men say, "This is the master of Mubarak and the monarch of Bassorah."

And whenas the guest had taken his rest he said to his host, "O Mubarak, my tarrying with thee hath been long"; whereto said the other, "Thou wottest, O my lord, that the matter whereinto thou comest to enquire is singular-rare, but that it also involveth risk of death, and I know not if thy valour can make the attainment thereto possible to thee."

Rejoined Zayn al-Asnam, "Know, O Mubarak, that opulence is gained only by blood; nor cometh aught upon mankind save by determination and predestination of the Creator (be He glorified and magnified!); so look to thine own stoutness of heart and take thou no thought of me."

Thereupon Mubarak forthright bade his slaves get them ready for wayfare; so they obeyed his bidding in all things and mounted horse and travelled by light and dark over the wildest of wolds, every day seeing matters and marvels which bewildered their wits, sights they had never seen in all their years, until they drew near unto a certain place. There the party dismounted and Mubarak bade the negro slaves and eunuchs abide on the spot saying to them, "Do ye keep watch and ward over the beasts of burthen and the horses until what time we return to you."

After this the twain set out together afoot and quoth the Freedman to the Prince, "O my lord, here valiancy besitteth, for that now thou art in the land of the Image thou camest to seek."

And they ceased not walking till they reached a lake, a long water and a wide, where quoth Mubarak to his companion, "Know, O my lord, that anon will come to us a little craft bearing a banner of azure tinct and all its planks are of chaunders and lign-aloes of Comorin, the most precious of woods. And now I would charge thee with a charge the which must thou most diligently observe."

Asked the other, "Thou wilt see in that boat a boatman whose fashion is the reverse of man's; but beware, and again I say beware, lest thou utter a word, otherwise he will at once drown us. Learn also that this stead belongeth to the King of the Jinns and that everything thou beholdest is the work of the Jann."

Mubarak and Zayn al-Asnam came upon a lake where, behold, they found a little craft whose planks were of chaunders and lign-aloes of Comorin and therein stood a ferryman with the head of an elephant while the rest of his body wore the semblance of a lion. Presently he approached them and winding his trunk around them lifted them both into the boat and seated them beside himself: then he fell to paddling till he passed through the middle of the lake and he ceased not so doing until he had landed them on the further bank. Here the twain took ground and began to pace forwards, gazing around them the while and regarding the trees which bore for burthen ambergris and lign-aloes, sandal, cloves, and gelsamine, all with flowers and fruits bedrest whose odours broadened the breast and excited the sprite. There also the birds warbled, with various voices, notes ravishing and rapturing the heart by the melodies of their musick.

So Mubarak turned to the Prince and asked him saying, "How seest thou this place, O my lord?" and the other answered, "I deem, O Mubarak, that in very truth this be the Paradise promised to us by the Prophet (whom Allah save and assain!)."

Thence they fared forwards till they came upon a mighty fine palace all builded of emeralds and rubies with gates and doors of gold refined: it was fronted by a bridge one hundred and fifty cubits long to a breadth of fifty, and the whole was one rib of a fish. At the further end thereof stood innumerous hosts of the Jann, all frightful of favour and fear-inspiring of figure and each and every hent in hand javelins of steel which flashed to the sun like December leven.

Thereat quoth the Prince to his companion, "This be a spectacle which ravisheth the wits"; and quoth Mubarak, "It now behoveth that we abide in our places nor advance further lest there happen to us some mishap; and may Allah vouchsafe to us safety!"

Herewith he brought forth his pouch four strips of a yellow silken stuff and zoning himself with one threw the other over his shoulders; and he gave the two remaining pieces to the Prince that he might do with them on like wise. Next he dispread before either of them a waist shawl of white sendal and then he pulled out of his poke sundry precious stones and scents and ambergris and eagle-wood; and, lastly, each took his seat upon his sahs, and when both were ready Mubarak repeated the following words to the Prince and taught him to pronounce them before the King of the Jann, "O my lord, Sovran of the Spirits, we stand within thy precincts and we throw ourselves on thy protection"; whereto Zayn al-Asnam added, "And I adjure him earnestly that he accept of us."

But Mubarak rejoined, "O my lord, by Allah I am in sore fear. Hear me! An he determine to accept us without hurt or harm he will approach us in the semblance of a man rare of beauty and comeliness but, if not, he will assume a form frightful and terrifying. Now an thou see him in his favourable shape do thou arise forthright and salam to him and above all things beware lest thou step beyond this thy coth."

The Prince replied, "To hear is to obey," and the other continued, "And let thy salam to him be thy saying, O King of the Sprites and Sovran of the Jann and Lord of Earth, my sire, the whilome Sultan of Bassorah, whom the Angel of Death hath removed (as is not hidden from thy Highness) was ever taken under thy protection and I, like him, come to thee sueing the same safeguard."

Mubarak fell to lessoning Zayn al-Asnam how he should salute the King of the Jinns, and pursued, "Likewise, O my lord, if he hail us with gladsome face of welcome he will doubtless say thee, 'Ask whatso thou wantest of me!' and the moment he giveth thee his word do thou at once prefer thy petition saying, O my lord, I require of thy Highness the Ninth Statue than which is naught more precious in the world, and thou didst promise my father to vouchsafe me that same."

And after this Mubarak instructed his master how to address the King and crave of him the boon and how to bespeak him with pleasant speech. Then he began his conjurations and fumigations and adjurations and recitations of words not understood of any and but little time elapsed before cold rain down railed and lightning flashed and thunder roared and thick darkness veiled earth's face. Presently came forth a mighty rushing wind and a voice like an earthquake, the quake of earth on Judgment Day. The Prince, seeing these horrors and sighting that which he had never before seen or heard, trembled for terror in every limb; but Mubarak fell to laughing at him and saying, "Fear not, O my lord: for that which thou dreadest is what we seek, for to us it is an earnest of glad tidings and success; so be thou satisfied and hold thyself safe."

After this the skies waxed clear and serene exceedingly while perfumed winds and the purest scents breathed upon them; nor did a long time elapse ere the King of the Jann presented himself under the semblance of a beautiful man who had no peer in comeliness save and excepting Him who lacketh likeness and to Whom be honour and glory! He gazed at Zayn al-Asnam with a gladsome aspect and a riant, whereat the Prince arose forthright and recited the string of benedictions taught to him by his companion and the King said to him with a smiling favour, "O Zayn al-Asnam, verily I was wont to love thy sire, the Sultan of Bassorah and, when he visited me ever, I used to give him an image of those thou sawest, each cut of a single gem; and thou also shalt presently become to me honoured as thy father and yet more. Ere he died I charged him to write upon the silken curtain the writ thou readest and eke I gave promise and made covenant with him to take thee like thy parent under my safeguard and to gift thee as I gifted him with an image, to wit, the ninth, which is of greater worth than all those viewed by thee. So now 'tis my desire to stand by my word and to afford thee my promised aid."

The Lord of the Jann said to the Prince, "I will take thee under my safeguard and the Shaykh thou sawest in thy swevens was myself and I also 'twas who bade thee dig under thy palace down to the souterrain wherein thou sawest the crocks of gold and the figures of fine gems. I also well know wherefore thou art come hither and I am he who caused thee to come and I will give thee what thou seekest, for all that I would not give it to thy sire. But 'tis on condition that thou return unto me bringing a damsel whose age is fifteen, a maiden without rival or likeness in loveliness; furthermore she must be a pure virgin and a clean maid who hath never lusted for male nor hath ever been solicited of man; and lastly, thou must keep faith with me in safeguarding the girl whenas thou returnest hither and beware lest thou play the traitor with her whilst thou bringest her to me."

To this purport the Prince sware a mighty strong oath adding, "O my lord, thou hast indeed honoured me by requiring of me such service, but truly 'twill be right hard for me to find a fair one like unto this; and, grant that I find one perfectly beautiful and young in years after the requirement of thy Highness, how shall I weet if she ever longed for mating with man or that male ever lusted for her?"

Replied the King, "Right thou art, O Zayn al-Asnam, and verily this be a knowledge whereunto the sons of men may on no wise attain. However, I will give thee a mirror of my own whose virtue is this. When thou shalt sight a young lady whose beauty and loveliness please thee, do thou open the glass, and, if thou see therein her image clear and undimmed, do thou learn forthright that she is a clean maid without aught of defect or default and endowed with every praiseworthy quality. But if, contrariwise, the figure be found darkened or clothed in uncleanness, do thou straightway know that damsel is sullied by soil of sex. Shouldst thou find her pure and gifted with all manner good gifts, bring her to me but beware not to offend with her and do villainy, and if thou keep not faith and promise with me bear in mind that thou shalt lose thy life."

Hereupon the Prince made a stable and solemn pact with the King, a covenant of the sons of the Sultans which may never be violated to keep faith with the King of the Jann and never to play traitor thereto, but to bring the maid *en tout bien et tout honneur* to that potentate who made over to him the mirror saying, "O my son, take this looking-glass whereof I bespake thee and depart straightway."

Thereupon the Prince and Mubarak arose and, after blessing him, fared forth and journeyed back until they made the lakelet, where they sat but a little ere appeared the boat which had brought them bearing the Jinni with elephantine head and leonine body, and he was standing up ready for paddling. The twain took passage with him (and this by command of the King of the Jann) until they reached Cairo and returned to their quarters, where they abode whilst they rested from the travails of travel. Then the Prince turned to his companion and said, "Arise with us and wend we to Baghdad-city that we may look for some damsel such as the King describeth!" and Mubarak replied, "O my lord, we be in Cairo, a city of the cities, a wonder of the world, and here no doubt there is but that I shall find such a maiden, nor is there need that we fare therefor to a far country."

Zayn al-Asnam rejoined, "True for thee, O Mubarak, but what be the will and the way whereby to hit upon such a girl, and who shall go about to find her for us?"

Quoth the other, "Be not beaten and broken down, O my lord, by such difficulty: I have by me here an ancient dame (and cursed be the same!) who maketh marriages, and she is past mistress in wiles and guiles; nor will she be hindered by the greatest of obstacles."

So saying, he sent to summon the old trot, and informed her that he wanted a damsel perfect of beauty and not past her fifteenth year, whom he would marry to the son of his lord; and he promised her sumptuous bakhshish and largesse if she would do her very best endeavour. Answered she, "O my lord, be at rest: I will presently contrive to satisfy thy requirement even beyond thy desire; for under my hand are damsels unsurpassable in beauty and loveliness, and all be the daughters of honourable men."

But the old woman, O Lord of the Age, knew naught anent the mirror. So she went forth to wander about the city and work on her well-known ways, and she wandered about town to find a maiden for the Prince Zayn al-Asnam. Whatever notable beauty she saw she would set before Mubarak; but each semblance as it was considered in the mirror showed exceedingly dark and dull, and the inspector would dismiss the girl. This endured until the crone had brought to him all the damsels in Cairo, and not one was found whose reflection in the mirror showed clear-bright and whose honour was pure and clean, in fact such an one as described by the King of the Jann.

Herewith Mubarak, seeing that he had not found one in Cairo to please him, or who proved pure and unsullied as the King of the Jann had required, determined to visit Baghdad: so they rose up and equipped them and set out and in due time they made the City of Peace where they hired them a mighty fine mansion amiddlemost the capital. Here they settled themselves in such comfort and luxury that the Lords of the land would come daily to eat at their table, even the thirsty and those who went forth betimes, and what remained of the meat was distributed to the mesquin and the miserable; also every poor stranger lodging in the Mosques would come to the house and find a meal. Therefore the bruit of them for generosity and liberality went abroad throughout the city and won for them notable name and the fairest of fame; nor did any ever speak of aught save the beneficence of Zayn al-Asnam and his generosity and his opulence.

Now there chanced to be in one of the cathedral-mosques and Imam, Abu Bakr hight, a ghostly man passing jealous and fulsome, who dwelt hard by the manion wherein the Prince and Mubarak abode; and he, when he heard of their lavish gifts and alms deeds, and honourable report, smitten by envy and malice and hatred, fell to devising how he might draw them into some calamity that might despoil the goods they enjoyed and destroy their lives, for it is the wont of envy to fall not save upon the fortunate.

So one day of the days, as he lingered in the Mosque after mid-afternoon prayer, he came forwards amidst the folk and cried, "O ye, my brethren of the Faith which is true and who bear testimony to the unity of the Deity, I would have you to weet that housed in this our quarter are two men which be strangers, and haply ye have heard of them how they lavish and waste immense sums of money, in fact moneys beyond measure, and for my part I cannot but suspect that they are cutpurses and brigands who commit robberies in their own country and who came hither to expend their spoils. O believers of Mohammed, I counsel you in Allah's name that ye guard yourselves against such accurseds; for haply the Caliph shall in coming times hear of these twain and ye also shall fall with them into calamity. I have hastened to caution you, and having warned you I wash my hands of your business, and after this do ye as ye judge fit."

All those present replied with one voice, "Indeed we will do whatso thou wishest us to do, O Abu Bakr!"

But when the Imam heard this from them he arose and, bringing forth ink-case and reed-pen and a sheet of paper, began inditing an address to the Commander of the Faithful, recounting all that was against the two strangers. However, by decree of Destiny, Mubarak chanced to be in the Mosque amongst the crowd when he heard the address of the blameworthy Imam and how he purposed applying by letter to the Caliph. So he delayed not at all but returned home forthright and, taking an hundred dinars and packing up a parcel of costly clothes, silverwrought all, repaired in haste to the reverend's quarters and knocked at the door.

The preacher came and opened to him, but sighting Mubarak he asked him in anger, "What is't thou wantest and who art thou?"

Whereto the other answered, "I am Mubarak and at thy service, O my master the Imam Abu Bakr; and I come to thee from my lord the Emir Zayn al-Asnam who, hearing of and learning thy religious knowledge and right fair repute in this city, would fain make acquaintance with thy Worship and do by thee whatso behoveth him. Also he hath sent me to thee with these garments and this spending-money, hoping excuse of thee for that this be a minor matter compared with your Honour's deserts; but, Inshallah, after this he will not fail in whatever to thee is due."

As soon as Abu Bakr saw the coin and gold and the bundle of clothes, he answered Mubarak saying, "I crave pardon, O my lord, of thy master the Emir for that I have been ashamed of waiting upon him and repentance is right hard upon me for that I have failed to do my devoir by him; wherefore I hope that thou wilt be my deputy in imploring him to pardon my default and, the Creator willing, to-morrow I will do what is incumbent upon me and fare to offer my services and proffer the honour which beseemeth me."

Rejoined Mubarak, "The end of my master's wishes is to see thy worship, O my lord Abu Bakr, and be exalted by thy presence and therethrough to win a blessing."

So saying he bussed the reverend's hand and returned to his own place. On the next day, as Abu Bakr was leading the dawn-prayer of Friday, he took his station amongst the folk amiddlemost the Mosque and cried, "O, our brethren the Moslems great and small and folk of Mohammed one and all, know ye that envy falleth not save upon the wealthy and praiseworthy and never descendeth upon the mean and miserable. I would have you wot, as regards the two strangers whom yesterday I misspake, that one of them is an Emir high in honour and son of most reputable parents, in lieu of being (as I was informed by one of his enviers) a cutpurse and a brigand. Of this matter I have made certain that 'tis a lying report, so beware lest any of you say aught against him or speak evil in regard to the Emir even as I heard yesterday; otherwise you will cast me and cast yourselves into the sorest of calamities with the Prince of True Believers. For a man like this of exalted degree may not possibly take up his abode in our city of Baghdad unbeknown to the Caliph."

Thus Abu Bakr, the Imam, uprooted on such wise from the minds of men the evil which he had implanted by his own words thrown out against the Emir Zayn al-Asnam. But when he had ended congregational prayers and returned to his home, he donned his long gaberdine and made weighty his skirts and lengthened his sleeves, after which he took the road to the mansion of the Prince; and, when he went in, he stood up before the stranger and did him honour with the highmost distinction.

Now Zayn al-Asnam was by nature conscientious albeit young in years; so he returned the Imam Abu Bakr's civilities with all courtesy and, seating himself beside him upon his high-raised divan, bade bring for him ambergris'd coffee. Then the tables were spread for breakfast and the twain ate and drank their sufficiency, whereafter they fell to chatting like boon companions.

Presently the Imam asked the Prince, saying, "O my lord Zayn al-Asnam, doth thy Highness design residing long in this our city of Baghdad?" and the other answered, "Yes indeed, O our lord the Imam; 'tis my intention to tarry here for a while until such time as my requirement shall be fulfilled."

The Imam enquired, "And what may be the requirement of my lord the Emir? Haply when I hear it I may devote my life thereto until I can fulfil it."

Quoth the Prince, "My object is to marry a maiden who must be comely exceedingly, aged fifteen years; pure, chaste, virginal, whom man hath never soiled and who during all her days never lusted for male kind: moreover, she must be unique for beauty and loveliness."

The Imam rejoined, "O my lord, this be a thing hard of finding indeed, hard exceedingly; but I know a damsel of that age who answereth to thy description. Her father, a Wazir who resigned succession and office of his own freewill, now dwelleth in his mansion jealously overwatching his daughter and her education; and I opine that this maiden will suit the fancy of thy Highness, whilst she will rejoice in an Emir such as thyself and eke her parents will be equally well pleased."

The Prince replied, "Inshallah, this damsel whereof thou speakest will suit me and supply my want, and the furtherance of my desire shall be at thy hands. But, O our lord the Imam, 'tis my wish first of all things to look upon her and see if she be pure or otherwise; and, as regarding her singular comeliness, my convicion is that thy word sufficeth and thine avouchment is veridical. Of her purity, however, even thou canst not bear sure and certain testimony in respect to that condition."

Asked the Imam, "How is it possible for you, O my lord the Emir, to learn from her face aught of her and her honour; also whether she be pure or not: indeed, if this be known to your Highness you must be an adept in physiognomy. However, if your Highness be willing to accompany me, I will bear you to the mansion of her sire and make you acquainted with him, so shall he set her before you."

The Imam Abu Bakr took the Prince and passed with him into the mansion of the Wazir; and, when they entered, both salam'd to the housemaster and he rose and received them with greetings especially when he learned that an Emir had visited him and he understood from the Imam that Zayn al-Asnam inclined to wed his daughter. So he summoned her to his presence and she came, whereupon he bade her raise her face-veil; and, when she did his bidding, the Prince considered her and was amazed and perplexed at her beauty and loveliness, he never having seen aught that rivalled her in brightness and brilliancy. So quoth he in his mind, "Would to Heaven I could win a damsel like this, albeit this one be to me unlawful."

Thinking thus he drew forth the mirror from his pouch and considered her image carefully when, lo and behold! the crystal was bright and clean as virgin silver and when he eyed her semblance in the glass he saw it pure as a white dove's. Then sent he forthright for the Kazi and witnesses and they knotted the knot and wrote the writ and the bride was duly throned. Presently the Prince took the Wazir his father-in-law into his own mansion, and to the young lady he sent a present of costly jewels and it was a notable marriage-festival, none like it was ever seen; no, never. Zayn al-Asnam applied himself to inviting the folk right royally and did honour due to Abu Bakr the Imam, giving him abundant gifts, and forwarded to the bride's father offerings of notable rarities.

As soon as the wedding ended, Mubarak said to the Prince, "O my lord, let us arise and wend our ways lest we lose our time in leisure, for that we sought is now found."

Said the Prince, "Right thou art"; and, arising with his companion, the twain fell to equipping them for travel and gat ready for the bride a covered litter to be carried by camels and they set out. Withal Mubarak well knew that the Prince was deep in love to the young lady.

So he took him aside and said to him, "O my lord Zayn al-Asnam, I would warn thee and enjoin thee to keep watch and ward upon thy senses and passions and to observe and preserve the pledge by thee plighted to the King of the Jann."

"O Mubarak," replied the Prince, "an thou knew the love-longing and ecstasy which have befallen me of my love to this young lady, thou wouldst feel ruth for me! indeed I never think of aught else save of taking her to Bassorah and of going in unto her."

Mubarak rejoined. "O my lord, keep thy faith and be not false to thy pact, lest a sore harm betide thee and the loss of thy life as well as that of the young lady. Remember the oath thou swarest nor suffer lust to lay thy reason low and despoil thee of all thy gains and thine honour and thy life."

"Do thou, O Mubarak," retorted the Prince, "become warden over her nor allow me ever to look upon her."

Mubarak, after warning Zayn al-Asnam to protect the virgin-bride against himself, fell also to defending her as his deputy: also he prevented the Prince from even looking upon her. They then travelled along the road unto the Island of the Jann, after they had passed by the line leading unto Misr. But when the bride saw that the wayfare had waxed longsome nor had beheld her bridegroom for all that time since the wedding-night, she turned to Mubarak and said, "Allah upon thee; inform me, O Mubarak, by the life of thy lord the Emir, have we fared this far distance by commandment of my bridegroom Prince Zayn al-Asnam?"

Said he, "Ah, O my lady, sore indeed is thy case to me, yet must I disclose to thee the secret thereof which be this. Thou imaginest that Zayn al-Asnam, the King of Bassorah, is thy bridegroom; but, alas! 'tis not so. He is no husband of thine; nay, the deed he drew up was a mere pretext in the presence of thy parents and thy people; and now thou art going as a bride to the King of the Jann who required thee of the Prince."

When the young lady heard these words, she fell to shedding tears and Zayn al-Asnam wept for her, weeping bitter tears from the excess of his love and affection. Then quoth the young lady, "Ye have nor pity in you nor feeling for me; neither fear ye aught of Allah that, seeing in me a stranger maiden ye cast me into a calamity like this. What reply shall ye return to the Lord on the Day of Reckoning for such treason ye work upon me?" However her words and her weeping availed her naught, for that they stinted not wayfaring with her until they reached the King of the Jann, to whom they forthright on arrival made offer of her.

When he considered the damsel she pleased him, so he turned to Zayn al-Asnam and said to him, "Verily the bride thou broughtest me is exceeding beautiful and passing of loveliness; yet lovelier and more beautiful to me appear thy true faith and the mastery of thine own passions, thy marvellous purity and valiance of heart. So hie thee to thy home and the Ninth Statue, wherefor thou askedst me, by thee shall be found beside the other images, for I will send it by one of my slaves of the Jann."

Hereupon Zayn al-Asnam kissed his hand and marched back with Mubarak to Cairo, where he would not abide long with his companion, but, as soon as he was rested, of his extreme longing and anxious yearning to see the Ninth Statue, he hastened his travel homewards. Withal he ceased not to be thoughtful and sorrowful concerning his maiden-wife and on account of her beauty and loveliness, and he would fall to groaning and crying, "O for my lost joys whose cause wast thou, O singular in every charm and attraction, thou whom I bore away from thy parents and carried to the King of the Jann. Alas, and woe worth the day!" Zayn al-Asnam fell to chiding himself for the deceit and treason which he had practised upon the young lady's parents and for bringing and offering her to the King of the Jann. Then he set out nor ceased travelling till such time as he reached Bassorah, when he entered his palace; and, after saluting his mother, he apprised her of all things that had befallen him.

She replied, "Arise, O my son, that we may look upon the Ninth Statue, for I rejoice with extreme joy at its being in our possession." So both descended into the pavilion where stood the eight images of precious gems and here they found a mighty marvel. 'Twas this: In lieu of seeing the Ninth Statue upon the golden throne, they found seated thereon the young lady whose beauty suggested the sun.

Zayn al-Asnam knew her at first sight and presently she addressed him saying, "Marvel not for that here thou findest me in place of that wherefor thou askedst; and I deem that I thou shalt not regret nor repent when thou acceptest me instead of that thou soughtest."

Said he, "No, by Allah, O life-blood of my heart, verily thou art the end of every wish of me nor would I exchange thee for all the gems of the universe. Would thou knew what was the sorrow which surcharged me on account of our separation and of my reflecting that I took thee from thy parents by fraud and I bore thee as a present to the King of the Jann. Indeed I had well nigh determined to forfeit all my profit of the Ninth Statue and to bear thee away to Bassorah as my own bride, when my comrade and councillor dissuaded me from so doing lest I bring about my death and thy death."

Nor had Zayn al-Asnam ended his words ere they heard the roar of thunderings that would rend a mount and shake the earth, whereat the Queen-mother was seized with mighty fear and affright. But presently appeared the King of the Jinns who said to her, "O my lady, fear not! 'Tis I, the protector of thy son whom I fondly affect for the affection borne to me by his sire. I also am he who manifested myself to him in his sleep; and my object therein was to make trial of his valiance and to learn an he could do violence to his passions for the sake of his promise, or whether the beauty of this lady would so tempt and allure him that he could not keep his promise to me with due regard. Indeed Zayn al-Asnam hath not kept faith and covenant with all nicety as regards the young lady, in that he longed for her to become his wife. However, I am assured that this lapse befel him from man's natural and inherent frailty albeit I repeatedly enjoined him to defend and protect her until he concealed from her his face. I now accept this man's valour and bestow her upon him to wife, for she is the Ninth Statue by me promised to him and she is fairer than all these jewelled images, the like of her not being found in the whole world of men save by the rarest of chances."

Then the King of the Jann turned to the Prince and said to him, "O Emir Zayn al-Asnam, this is thy bride: take her and enjoy her upon the one condition that thou love her only nor choose for thyself another one in addition to her; and I pledge myself that her faith theewards will be of the fairest."

Hereupon the King of the Jann disappeared and the Prince, gladdened and rejoicing, went forth with the maiden and for his love and affection to her he paid to her the first ceremonious visit that same night and he made bride-feasts and banquets throughout his realm and in due time he formally wedded her and went in unto her. Then he stablished himself upon the throne of his kingship and ruled it, bidding and forbidding, and his consort became Queen of Bassorah. His mother left this life a short while afterwards and they both mourned and lamented their loss. Lastly he lived with his wife in all joyance of life till there came to them the Destroyer of delights and the Separator of societies.

Quoth Dunyazad, as was her way, to her sister Scheherazade, "O sister mine, what a rare and delectable tale hast thou told and now prithee favour us with another."

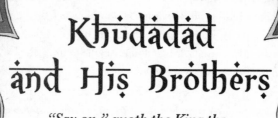

Khudadad and His Brothers

*"Say on," quoth the King the
following evening.
And Scheherazade continued…*

This my tale relateth to the Kingdom of Diyar Bakr in whose capital-city of Harran dwelt a Sultan of illustrious lineage, a protector of the people, a lover of his lieges, a friend of mankind and renowned for being gifted with every good quality. Now Allah Almighty had bestowed upon him all that his heart could desire, save boon of child, for though he had lovely wives within his Harem-door and fair concubines galore, he had been not blessed with a son; wherefor he offered up incessant worship to the Creator.

One night there appeared to him in a dream a man of comely visage and holy of semblance like unto a prophet, who addressed him, saying, "O puissant King, thy vows are at length heard. Arise to-morrow at day-dawn, pray a two-bow prayer and offer up thy petitions; then haste thee to the Chief Gardener of thy palace and require of him a pomegranate whereof do thou eat as many seeds as seemeth best to thee; after which perform another two-bow prayer, and Allah will shower favours and graces upon thy head."

The King, awaking at peep of day, called to mind the vision of the night, and returning thanks to the Almighty, made his orisons and kneeling invoked a benedicite. Then he rose and repaired to the garth, and receiving a pomegranate from the Head-Gardener, counted out and ate fifty grains thereof; to wit, one for each of his wives. After this he lay the night in turn with them all and by the omnipotence of the Creator all gave in due time signs of pregnancy, save one Firuzah hight. So the King conceived a grudge against her, saying in his soul, "Allah holdeth this woman vile and accursed and He willeth not that she become the mother of a Prince, and on this wise hath the curse of barrenness become her lot."

He would have had her done to death but the Grand Wazir made intercession for her and suggested to the Sultan that perchance Firuzah might prove with child and withal not show outward signal thereof, as is the manner of certain women; wherefore to slay her might be to destroy a Prince with the mother. Quoth the King, "So be it! slay her not, but take heed that she abide no longer or at court or in the city, for I cannot support the sight of her."

Replied the Minister, "It shall be done even as thy Highness biddeth: let her be conveyed to the care of thy brother's son, Prince Samir."

The King did according to the counsel of his Wazir and despatched his loathed Queen to Samaria accompanied by a writ with the following purport, to his nephew, "We forward this lady to thy care: entreat her honourably and, shouldest thou remark tokens of pregnancy in her, see that thou acquaint us therewith without stay or delay."

So Firuzah journeyed to Samaria, and when her time was fulfilled she gave birth to a boy babe, and became the mother of a Prince who in favour was resplendent as the sheeny day. Hereat the lord of Samaria sent message by letter to the Sultan of Harran saying, "A Prince hath been borne by the womb of Firuzah: Allah Almighty give thee permanence of prosperity!"

By these tidings the King was filled with joy; and presently he replied to his cousin, Prince Samir, "Each one of my forty-and-nine spouses hath been blessed with issue and it delighteth me beyond bounds that Firuzah hath also given me a son. Let him be named Khudadad—God's gift—do thou have due care of him and whatsoever thou mayest need for his birth-ceremonies shall be counted out to thee without regard to cost."

Accordingly Prince Samir took in hand with all pleasure and delight the charge of Prince Khudadad; and, as soon as the child reached the age for receiving instruction, he caused him to be taught cavalarice and archery and all such arts and sciences which it behoveth the sons of the Kings to learn, so that he became perfect in all manner knowledge. At eighteen years of age he waxed seemly of semblance and such were his strength and valiance that none in the whole world could compare with him.

Presently, feeling himself gifted with unusual vigour and virile character he addressed one day of the days Firuzah his parent, saying, "O mother mine, grant me thy leave to quit Samaria and fare in quest of fortune, especially of some battle-field where I may prove the force and prowess of me. My sire, the Sultan of Harran, hath many foes, some of whom are lusting to wage war with him; and I marvel that at such time he doth not summon me and make me his aid in this mightiest of matters. But seeing that I possess such courage and Allah-given strength it behoveth me not to remain thus idly at home. My father knoweth not of my lustihood, nor forsooth doth he think of me at all; nevertheless 'tis suitable that at such a time I present myself before him, and tender my services until my brothers be fit to fight and to front his foes."

Hereto his mother made answer, "O my dear son, thine absence pleaseth me not, but in truth it becometh thee to help thy father against the enemies who are attacking him on all sides, provided that he send for thine aidance."

Khudadad replied to his mother, "Indeed I am unable to brook delay; moreover such longing have I in heart to look upon the Sultan, my sire, that an I go not and visit him and kiss his feet I shall assuredly die. I will enter his employ as a stranger and all unknown to him, nor will I inform him that I am his son; but I shall be to him as a foreigner or as one of his hired knaves, and with such devotion will I do him suit and service that, when he learneth that I am indeed his child, he may grant me his favour and affection."

Prince Samir also would not suffer him to depart and forbade him therefrom; but one day of the days the Prince suddenly set out from Samaria under pretext that he was about to hunt and chase. He mounted a milk-white steed, whose reins and stirrups were of gold and the saddle and housings were of azure satin dubbed with jewels and fringed with pendants of fresh pearls. His scymitar was hilted with a single diamond, the scabbard of chaunders-wood was crested with rubies and emeralds and it depended from a gemmed waist-belt; while his bow and richly wrought quiver hung by his side. Thus equipped and escorted by his friends and familiars he presently arrived at Harran-city after the fairest fashion; and, when occasion offered itself, he made act of presence before the King and did his obeisance at Darbar.

The Sultan, remarking his beauty and comeliness, or haply by reason of an outburst of natural affection, was pleased to return his salam; and, graciously calling him to his side, asked of him his name and pedigree, whereto Khudadad answered, "O my liege, I am the son of an Emir of Cairo. A longing for travel hath made me quit my native place and wander from clime to clime till at length I have come hither; and, hearing that thou hast matters of importance in hand, I am desirous of approving to thee my valiancy."

The King joyed with exceeding joy to hear this stout and doughty speech, and forthwith gave him a post of command in his army; and Khudadad by careful supervision of the troops soon won the esteem of his officers by his desire to satisfy them and the hearts of his soldiers by reason of his strength and courage, his goodly nature and his kindly disposition. He also brought the host and all its equipments and munitions of warfare into such excellent order and method that the King on inspecting them was delighted and created the stranger Chief Commandant of the forces and made him an especial favourite; while the Wazirs and Emirs, also the Nabobs and the Notables, perceiving that he was highly reputed and regarded, showed him abundant good will and affection.

Presently, the other Princes, who became of no account in the eyes of the King and the lieges, waxed envious of his high degree and dignity. But Khudadad ceased not to please the Sultan his sire, at all times when they conversed together, by his prudence and discretion, his wit and wisdom, and gained his regard ever more and more; and when the invaders, who had planned a raid on the realm, heard of the discipline of the army and of Khudadad's provisions for materials of war, they abstained from all hostile intent. After a while the King committed to Khudadad the custody and education of the forty-nine Princes, wholly relying on his sagesse and skill; and thus, albeit Khudadad was of age like his brothers, he became their master by reason of his sapience and good sense. Whereupon they hated him but the more; and, when taking counsel one day, quoth one to the other, "What be this thing our sire hath done that he should make a stranger-wight his cup-companion and set him to lord it over us? We can do naught save by leave of this our governor, and our condition is past bearing; so contrive we to rid ourselves of this foreigner and at least render him vile and contemptible in the eyes of our sire the Sultan."

Said one, "Let us gather together and slay him in some lonely spot;" and said another, "Not so! to kill him would benefit us naught, for how could we keep the matter hidden from the King? He would become our enemy and Allah only wotteth what evil might befal us. Nay, rather let us crave permission of him and fare a-hunting and then tarry we in some far-off town; and after a while the King will marvel at our absence, then grief

will be sore upon him and at length, waxing displeased and suspicious, he will have this fellow expelled the palace or haply done to death. This is the only sure and safe way of bringing about his destruction."

The forty-and-nine brothers agreed to hold this plan wisest and, presently going together to Khudadad, asked leave of him to ride about the country awhile or fare to the chase, promising they would return by set of sun. He fell into the snare and allowed them to go; whereupon they sallied forth a-hunting but did not come back that day or the next. On the third morning the King who missed them asked Khudadad wherefore it was that none of his sons were to be seen; and he answered that three days before they had gotten leave from him to go a-hunting and had not returned. Hereat the father was perplexed with sore perplexity; and, when sundry days more had passed by and still the Princes appeared not, the old Sultan was much troubled in mind and hardly restraining his rage summoned Khudadad and in hot wrath exclaimed, "O thou neglectful stranger, what courage and over-daring is this of thine that thou didst suffer my sons fare to the chase and didst not ride with them! And now 'tis but right that thou set out and search for them and bring them back; otherwise thou shalt surely die."

Khudadad, hearing these harsh words, was startled and alarmed; however he got him ready and mounted his horse forthwith and left the city in quest of the Princes his brethren, wandering about from country to country, like unto a herd seeking a straying flock of goats. Presently, not finding any trace of them in homestead or on desert-ground, he became sad and sorrowful exceedingly, saying in his soul, "O my brothers, what hath befallen you and where can ye be dwelling? Perchance some mighty foeman hath made you prisoners so that ye cannot escape; and I may never return unto Harran till I find you; for this will be a matter of bitter regret and repine to the King."

So he repented more and more having suffered them to go without his escort and guidance. At length whilst searching for them from plain to plain and forest to forest he chanced come upon a large and spacious prairie in the middlemost whereof rose a castle of black marble; so he rode on at a foot pace and when close under the walls he espied a lady of passing beauty and loveliness who was seated at a window in melancholy plight and with no other ornament than her own charms. Her lovely hair hung down in dishevelled locks; her raiment was tattered and her favour was pale and showed sadness and sorrow.

Withal she was speaking under her breath and Khudadad, giving attentive ear, heard her say these words, "O youth, fly this fatal site, else thou wilt fall into the hands of the monster who dwelleth here: a man-devouring Ethiopian is lord of this palace; and he seizeth all whom Fate sendeth to this prairie and locketh them up in darksome and narrow cells that he may preserve them for food."

Khudadad exclaimed, "O my lady, tell me I pray thee who thou art and whereabouts was thy home;" and she answered, "I am a daughter of Cairo and of the noblest thereof. But lately, as I wended my way to Baghdad, I alighted upon this plain and met that Habashi, who slew all my servants and carrying me off by force placed me in this palace. I no longer cared to live, and a thousand times better were it for me to die; for that this Abyssinian lusteth to enjoy me and albeit to the present time I have escaped the caresses of the impure wretch, to-morrow an I still refuse to gratify his desire he will surely ravish me and do me dead. So I have given up all hope of safety; but thou, why hast thou come hither to perish? Escape without stay or delay, for he hath gone forth in quest of wayfarers and right soon will he return. Moreover he can see far and wide and can descry all who traverse this wold."

Now hardly had the lady spoken these words when the Abyssinian drew in sight; and he was as a Ghul of the Wild, big of bulk, and fearsome of favour and figure, and he mounted a sturdy Tartar steed, brandishing, as he rode, a weighty blade which none save he could wield. Prince Khudadad seeing this monstrous semblance was sore amazed and prayed Heaven that he might be victorious over that devil: then unsheathing his sword he stood awaiting the Abyssinian's approach with courage and steadfastness; but the blackamoor when he drew near deemed the Prince too slight and puny to fight and was minded to seize him alive. Khudadad, seeing how his foe had no intent to combat, struck him with his sword on the knee a stroke so dour that the negro foamed with rage and yelled a yell so loud that the whole prairie resounded with the plaint. Thereupon the brigand, fiery with fury, rose straight in his shovel-stirrups and struck fiercely at Khudadad with his huge sword and, but for the Prince's cunning of fence and the cleverness of his courser, he would have been sliced in twain like unto a cucumber. Though the scymitar whistled through the air, the blow was harmless, and in an eye-twinkling Khudadad dealt him a second cut and struck off his right hand which fell to the ground with the sword hilt it gripped, when the blackamoor losing his balance rolled from the saddle and made earth resound with the fall. Thereupon the Prince sprang from his steed and deftly severing the enemy's head from his body threw it aside.

Now the lady had been looking down at the lattice rigid in prayer for the gallant youth; and, seeing the Abyssinian slain and the Prince victorious, she was overcome with exceeding joy and cried out to her deliverer, "Praise be to Almighty Allah, O my lord, who by thy hand hath defeated and destroyed this fiend. Come now to me within the castle, whose keys are with the Abyssinian; so take them and open the door and deliver me."

Khudadad found a large bunch of keys under the dead man's girdle wherewith he opened the portals of the fort and entered a large saloon in which was the lady; and, no sooner did she behold him than running to meet him she was about to cast herself at his feet and kiss them when Khudadad prevented her. She praised him with highest praise and extolled him for valiancy above all the champions of the world, and he returned the salam to her who, when seen near hand seemed endued with more grace and charms than had appeared from afar. So the Prince joyed with extreme joy and the twain sat down in pleasant converse.

Presently, Khudadad heard shrieks and cries and weeping and wailing with groans and moans and ever loudening lamentations; so he asked the lady, saying, "Whence are these clamours and from whom come these pitiful complaints?"

And, she pointing to a wicket in a hidden corner of the court below, answered, saying, "O my lord, these sounds come therefrom. Many wretches driven by Destiny have fallen into the clutches of the Abyssinian Ghul and are securely locked up in cells, and each day he was wont to roast and eat one of the captives."

"'Twill please me vastly," quoth Khudadad, "to be the means of their deliverance: come, O my lady, and show me where they are imprisoned."

Thereupon the twain drew near to the place and the Prince forthright tried a key upon the lock of the dungeon but it did not fit; then he made essay of another wherewith they opened the wicket. As they were so doing the report of the captives' moaning and groaning increased yet more and more until Khudadad, touched and troubled at their impatience, asked the cause of it.

The lady replied, "O my lord, hearing our footsteps and the rattling of the key in the lock they deem that the cannibal, according to his custom, hath come to supply them with food and to secure one of them for his evening meal. Each feareth lest his turn for roasting be come, so all are affrighted with sore affright and redouble their shouts and cries."

The sounds from that secret place seemed to issue from under ground or from the depths of a draw-well. But when the Prince opened the dungeon door, he espied a steep staircase and descending thereby found himself in a deep pit, narrow and darksome, wherein were penned more than an hundred persons with elbows pinioned and members chained; nor saw he aught of light save through one bull's-eye. So he cried to them, "O ye unfortunates, fear ye no more! I have slain the Abyssinian; and render ye praise to Allah Almighty who hath rid you of your wrong-doer: also I come to strike off your fetters and return you to freedom."

Hearing these glad tidings the prisoners were in raptures of delight and raised a general cry of joy and jubilee. Hereupon Khudadad and the lady began to loose their hands and feet; and each, as he was released from his durance, helped to unchain his fellows: brief, after a moment of time all were delivered from their bonds and bondage. Then each and every kissed Khudadad's feet and gave thanks and prayed for his welfare; and when those whilom prisoners entered the court-yard whereupon the sun was shining sheen, Khudadad recognised amongst them his brothers, in quest of whom he had so long wandered. He was amazed with exceeding amazement and exclaimed, "Laud be to the Lord, that I have found you one and all safe and sound: your father is sorely sad and sorrowful at your absence; and Heaven forfend that this devil hath devoured any from amongst you."

He then counted their number, forty-and-nine, and set them apart from the rest; and all in excess of joy fell upon one another's necks and ceased not to embrace their saviour. After this the Prince spread a feast for the captives, each and every, whom he had delivered; and, when they had eaten and drunken their full, he restored to them the gold and silver, the Turkey carpets and pieces of Chinese silk and brocade and other valuables innumerable which the Abyssinian had plundered from the caravans, as also their own personal goods and chattels, directing each man to claim his own; and what remained he divided equally amongst them. "But," quoth he, "by what means can ye convey these bales to your own countries, and where can ye find beasts of burden in this wild wold?"

Quoth they, "O our Lord, the Abyssinian robbed us of our camels with their loads and doubtless they are in the stables of the castle."

Hereupon Khudadad fared forth with them to the stables and there found tethered and tied not only the camels but also the forty-nine horses of his brothers the princes, and accordingly he gave to each one his own animal. There were moreover in the stables hundreds of Abyssinian slave-boys who, seeing the prisoners released, were certified that their lord the cannibal was slain and fled in dismay to the forest and none thought of giving chase to them. So the merchants loaded their merchandise upon the camels' backs and farewelling the Prince set out for their own countries.

Then quoth Khudadad to the lady, "O thou rare in beauty and chastity, whence camest thou when the Abyssinian seized thee and whither now wouldst thou wend? Inform me thereof that I may restore thee to thy home; haply these Princes, my brethren, sons of the Sultan of Harran, know thine abode; and doubtless they will escort thee thither."

The lady turning to Khudadad presently made answer, "I live far from here and my country, the land of Egypt, is over distant for travel. But thou, O valorous Prince, hast delivered mine honour and my life from the hands of the Abyssinian and hast shown me such favour that 'twould ill become me to conceal from thee my history. I am the daughter of a mighty king; reigning over the Sa'id or upper Nile-land; and when a tyrant foeman seized him and, reaving him of life as well as of his realm, usurped his throne and seized his kingdom, I fled away to preserve my existence and mine honour."

Thereupon Khudadad and his brothers prayed the lady to recount all that had befallen her and reassured her, saying, "Henceforth thou shalt live in solace and luxury: neither toil nor trouble shall betide thee." When she saw that there was no help for her but to tell all her tale, she began in the following words to recount the

HISTORY OF THE PRINCESS OF DARYABAR

In an island of the islands standeth a great city called Daryabar, wherein dwelt a king of exalted degree. But despite his virtue and his valour he was ever sad and sorrowful having naught of offspring, and he offered up without surcease prayers on that behalf. After long years and longsome supplications a half boon was granted to him; to wit, a daughter (myself) was born. My father who grieved sore at first presently rejoiced with joy exceeding at the unfortunate ill-fated birth of me; and, when I came of age to learn, he bade me be taught to read and write; and caused me to be instructed in court-ceremonial and royal duties and the chronicles of the past, to the intent that I might succeed him as heiress to his throne and his kingship.

Now it happened one day that my sire rode out a-hunting and gave chase to a wild ass with such hot pursuit that he found himself at eventide separated from his suite; so, wearied with the chase, he dismounted from his steed and seating himself by the side of a forest-path, he said to himself "The onager will doubtless seek cover in this copse."

276

Suddenly he espied a light shining bright amidst the trees and, thinking that a hamlet might be hard by, he was minded to night there and at day-dawn to determine his further course. Hereupon he arose and walking towards the light he found that it issued from a lonely hut in the forest; then peering into the inside he espied an Abyssinian burly of bulk and in semblance like unto a Satan, seated upon a divan. Before him were ranged many capacious jars full of wine and over a fire of charcoal he was roasting a bullock whole and eating the flesh and ever and anon drinking deep draughts from one of the pitchers. Furthermore the King sighted in that hut a lady of exquisite beauty and comeliness sitting in a corner direly distressed: her hands were fast bound with cords, and at her feet a child of two or three years of age lay beweeping his mother's sorry plight.

Seeing the doleful state of these twain, my sire was filled with ruth and longed to fall upon the ogre sword in hand; however, not being able to cope with him he restrained his wrath and remained on stealthy watch. The giant having drained all the pitchers of wine and devoured half of the barbacued bullock presently addressed himself to the lady and said, "O loveliest of Princesses, how long wilt thou prove thee coy and keep aloof from me? Dost thou not see how desirous I am of winning thy heart and how I am dying for the love of thee? 'Tis therefore only right that thou also shouldst return my affection and know me as thine own, when I will become to thee the kindest of mankind."

"O thou Ghul of the waste," cried the lady, "what be this whereof thou pratest? Never; no, never shalt thou win thy wish of me, however much thou mayest lust therefor. Torment me or, an thou wilt, destroy me downright, but for my part I will on no wise yield me to thy lusts."

At these words the infuriated savage roared aloud, "'Tis enough and more than enough: thy hate breedeth hatred in me and now I desire less to have and hold thee than to do thee die." Then he seized her with one hand, and drawing his sabre with the other, would have struck off her head from her body when my father shot at him a shaft so deftly that it pierced his heart and came out gleaming at his back and he fell to the ground and found instant admission into Jahannam. Hereupon my sire entered the hut and unbinding the lady's bonds enquired of her who she was and by what means that ogre had brought her thither.

Answered she, "Not far from this site there liveth on the sea-shore a race of Saracens, like unto the demons of the desert. Sorely against my will I was wedded to their Prince and the fulsome villain thou hast now slain was one of my husband's chief officers. He fell madly in love to me and he longed with excessive longing to get me into his power and to carry me off from my home. Accordingly, one day of the days when my husband was out of the way and I was in privacy, he carried me off with this my babe from the palace to this wild wood wherein is none save He and where well he wot that all search and labour would be baffled; then, hour after hour he designed guilty designs against me, but by the mercy of Almighty Allah I have ever escaped all carnal soil of that foul monster. This evening, in despair of my safety, I was rejecting his brutal advances when he attempted to take my life and in the attempt he was slain by thy valorous hand. This is then my story which I have told thee."

My father reassured the Princess, saying, "O my lady, let thy heart be at ease; at day-break I will take thee away from this wilderness and escort thee to Daryabar, of which city I am the Sultan; and, shouldst thou become fain of that place, then dwell therein until thy husband shall come in quest of thee."

Quoth the lady, "O my lord, this plan doth not displease me."

So with the earliest light next morning my father took mother and child away from that forest and set forth homewards when suddenly he fell in with his Sirdars and officers who had been wandering hither and thither during the livelong night in search of him. They rejoiced with great joy on seeing the King and marvelled with exceeding marvel at the sight of a veiled one with him, admiring much that so love-some a lady should be found dwelling in a wold so wild. Thereupon the King related to them the tale of the ogre and of the Princess and how he had slain the blackamoor.

Presently they set forth on their homeward way; one of the Emirs seating the dame behind him on his horse's scrupper while another took charge of the child. They reached the royal city, where the King ordered a large and splendid mansion to be built for his guest, the babe also received a suitable education; and thus the mother passed her days in perfect comfort and happiness. After the lapse of some months, when no tidings, however fondly expected, came of her husband, she resigned herself to marrying my father whom she had captivated by her beauty and loveliness and amorous liveliness, whereupon he wedded her, and when the marriage-contract was drawn up (as was customary in those days), they sojourned together in one stead.

As time went on the lad grew up to be a lusty youth of handsome mien; moreover he became perfect in courtly ceremonial and in every art and science that befit Princes. The King and all the Ministers and Emirs highly approved of him, and determined that I should be married to him, and that he should succeed the sovereign as heir to throne and kingship. The youth also was well pleased with such tokens of favour from my father, but chiefly he rejoiced with exceeding joy to hear talk of his union with his protector's only daughter.

One day my sire desired to place my hand in his to the intent that the marriage ceremony should at once take place, but first he would impose upon my suitor certain conditions, whereof one was that he should wed none other but his wife's daughter, that is, myself. This pledge displeased the haughty youth, who forthwith refused his consent thereto, deeming himself by the demand of such condition a despised and contemptible suitor of villain birth. On this wise the wedding was deferred, and this delay became a matter of sore displeasure to the young man, who thought in his heart that my father was his foe. Therefore he ever strove to lure him into his power till one day in a frenzy of rage he slew him and proclaimed himself King of Daryabar. Moreover the murtherer would have entered my chamber to kill me also had not the Wazir, a true and faithful servant of the crown, at the tidings of his liege lord's death speedily taken me away, and hidden me in the house of a friend where he bade me remain concealed.

Two days afterwards, having fitted out a ship, he embarked me therein with a Kahramanah—an old duenna—and set sail for a country whose King was of my father's friends, to the intent that he might consign me to his charge, and obtain from him the aid of an army wherewith he might avenge himself upon the ungrateful and ungracious youth who had proved himself a traitor to the salt. But a few days after our weighing anchor a furious storm began to blow making the captain and crew sore confounded and presently the waves beat upon the vessel with such exceeding violence that she brake up, and the Wazir and the duenna and all who were therein (save myself) were drowned in the billows. But I, albeit well nigh a-swoon, clung to a plank and was shortly after washed ashore by the send of the sea, for Allah of His mighty power had preserved me safe and sound from death-doom by the raging of the ocean, to the end that further troubles might befal me. When I returned to sense and consciousness, I found myself alive on the strand and offered up grateful thanks to Almighty Allah; but not seeing the Wazir or any one of the company I knew that they had perished in the waters.

Presently, calling to remembrance the murther of my father I cried aloud with an exceeding bitter cry and was sore afraid at my lonesome plight, insomuch that I would fain have cast myself again into the sea, when suddenly the voice of man and tramp of horse-hooves fell upon my ears.

Then looking about I descried a band of cavaliers in the midst of whom was a handsome prince: he was mounted upon a steed of purest Rabite blood and was habited in a gold-embroidered surcoat; a girdle studded with diamonds girt his loins and on his head was a crown of gold; in fine it was evident from his garb as from his aspect that he was a born ruler of mankind. Thereupon, seeing me all alone on the sea-shore, the knights marvelled with exceeding marvel; then the Prince detached one of his captains to ascertain my history and acquaint him therewith; but albeit the officer plied me with questions I answered him not a word and shed a flood of tears in the deepest silence. So noting the waifage on the sand they thought to themselves, "Perchance some vessel hath been wrecked upon this shore and its planks and timber have been cast upon the land, and doubtless this lady was in that ship and hath been floated ashore on some plank." Whereupon the cavaliers crowded around me and implored me to relate unto them what had befallen me; nevertheless I still answered them not a word.

Presently the Prince himself drew near to me and, much amazed, sent away his suite from about me and addressed me in these words, "O my lady, fear naught of ill from me nor distress thyself by needless affright. I would convey thee to my home and under my mother's care; wherefore I am curious to know of thee who thou art. The Queen will assuredly befriend thee and keep thee in comfort and happiness." And now understanding that his heart was drawn towards me, I told him all that had betided me, and he on hearing the story of my sad destiny became moved with the deepest emotion and his eyes brimmed with tears. Then he comforted me and carried me with him and committed me to the Queen his mother, who also lent kindly ear to my tale of the past, first and last, and hearing it she also was greatly grieved, and wearied not day or night in tending me and (as far as in her lay) striving to make me happy. Seeing, moreover, that her son was deeply enamoured of me and love-distraught she agreed to my becoming his wife, while I also consented when I looked upon his handsome and noble face and figure and to his proved affection for me and his goodness of heart. Accordingly, in due time the marriage was celebrated with royal pomp and circumstance. But what escape is there from Fate?

On that very night, the night of the wedding, a King of Zanzibar who dwelt hard by that island, and had erewhile practised against the kingdom, seizing his opportunity, attacked us with a mighty army, and having put many to death, bethought him to take me and my husband alive. But we escaped from his hands and fleeing under the murks of night to the sea-shore found there a fisherman's boat, which we entered thanking our stars and launched it and floated far away on the current, unknowing whither Destiny was directing us. On the third day we espied a vessel making us, whereat we rejoiced with joy excessive, deeming her to be some merchantman coming to our aidance. No sooner had it lain alongside, however, than up there sprang five or six pirates, each brandishing a naked brand in hand, and boarding us tied our arms behind us and carried us to their craft. They then tore the veil from my face and forthwith desired to possess me, each saying to other, "I will enjoy this wench."

On this wise wrangling and jangling ensued till right soon it turned to battle and bloodshed, when moment by moment and one by one the ravishers fell dead until all were slain save a single pirate, the bravest of the band. Quoth he to me, "Thou shalt fare with me to Cairo where dwelleth a friend of mine and to him will I give thee, for erewhile I promised him that on this voyage I would secure for him a fair woman for handmaid." Then seeing my husband, whom the pirates had left in bonds he exclaimed, "Who may be this hound? Is he to thee a lover or a friend?" and I made answer, "He is my wedded husband."

"'Tis well," cried he: "in very sooth it behoveth me to release him from the bitter pangs of jealousy and the sight of thee enfolded in another's fond embrace." Whereat the ruffian raised aloft the ill-fated Prince, bound foot and hand, and cast him into the sea, while I shrieked aloud and implored his mercy, but all in vain.

Seeing the Prince struggling and drowning in the waves I cried out and screamed and buffeted my face and tore my hair and would fain have cast myself into the waters but I could not, for he held me fast and lashed me to the mainmast. Then, pursuing our course with favouring winds we soon arrived at a small port-village where he bought camels and boy-slaves and journeyed on towards Cairo; but when several stages of the road were left behind us, the Abyssinian who dwelt in this castle suddenly overtook us. From afar we deemed him to be a lofty tower, and when near us could hardly believe him to be a human being. At once unsheathing his huge sword the Habashi made for the pirate and ordered him to surrender himself prisoner, with me and all his slaves, and with pinioned elbows to accompany him. Hereat the robber with hot courage and heading his followers rushed fiercely on the Abyssinian, and for a long time the fight raged thick and fast, till he and his lay dead upon the field; whereupon the Abyssinian led off the camels and carried me and the pirate's corpse to this castle, and devoured the flesh of his foe at his evening meal. Then turning to me as I wept with bitter weeping he said, "Banish from thy breast this woe and this angry mood; and abide in this castle at perfect ease and in comfort, and solace thyself with my embraces. However, since thou appearest at this present to be in dire distress, I will excuse thee for to-night, but without fail I shall require thee of thyself on the morrow."

He then led me into a separate chamber and locking fast the gates and doors, fell asleep alone in another place. Arising early on the next morning he searched the castle round about, unlocked the wicket which he closed again and sallied forth, according to his custom, in quest of wayfarers. But the caravan escaped him and anon he returned empty-handed when thou didst set upon him and slay him."

On this wise the Princess of Daryabar related her history to Prince Khudadad who was moved with ruth for her: then comforting her he said, "Henceforth fear naught nor be on any wise dismayed. These princes are the sons of the King of Harran; and if it please thee, let them lead thee to his court and stablish thee in comfort and luxury: the King also will guard thee from all evil. Or, shouldest thou be loath to fare with them, wilt thou not consent to take for spouse him who hath rescued thee from so great calamity?"

The Princess of Daryabar consented to wed with him and forthwith the marriage was celebrated with grand display in the castle and here they found meats and drinks of sundry sorts, and delicious fruits and fine wines wherewith the cannibal would regale himself when a-weary of man's flesh. So Khudadad made ready dishes of every colour and feasted his brothers. Next day taking with them such provaunt as was at hand, all set forth for Harran, and at the close of each stage they chose a suitable stead for nighting; and, when but one day's journey lay before them, the Princes supped that night off what was left to them of their viaticum and drained all the wine that remained. But when the drink had mastered their wits, Khudadad thus addressed his brothers, saying, "Hitherto have I withheld from you the secret of my birth, which now I must disclose. Know ye then that I am your brother, for I also am a son of the King of Harran, whom the Lord of Samaria-land brought up and bade educate; and lastly, my mother is the Princess Firuzah." Then to the Princess of Daryabar, "Thou didst not recognize my rank and pedigree and, had I discovered myself erewhile, haply thou hadst been spared the mortification of being wood by a man of vulgar blood. But now ease thy mind for that thy husband is a Prince."

Quoth she, "Albeit thou discoveredst to me naught until this time, still my heart felt assured that thou wast of noble birth and the son of some potent sovereign."

The Princes one and all appeared outwardly well pleased and offered each and every warm congratulations whilst the wedding was celebrating; but inwardly they were filled with envy and sore annoy at such unwelcome issue of events, so much so that when Khudadad retired with the Princess of Daryabar to his tent and slept, those ingrates, forgetful of the service rendered to them by their brother in that he had rescued them when prisoners in the hands of the man-devouring Abyssinian, remained deep in thought and seeking a safe place took counsel one with other to kill him. Quoth the foremost of them, "O my brethren, our father showed him the liveliest affection when he was to us naught save a vagrant and unknown, and indeed made him our ruler and our governor; and now, hearing of his victory won from the ogre and learning that the stranger is his son, will not our sire forthwith appoint this bastard his only heir and give him dominion over us so that we must all be forced to fall at his feet and bear his yoke? My rede is this that we make an end of him in this very spot." Accordingly they stole softly into his tent and dealt him from every side strokes with their swords, so that they slashed him in every limb and fondly thought that they had left him dead on the bed without their awaking the Princess.

Next morning they entered the city of Harran and made their salams to the King, who despaired of sighting them again, so he rejoiced with exceeding joy on seeing them restored to him safe and sound and sane, and asked why they had tarried from him so long. In reply they carefully concealed from him their being thrown into the dungeon by the Ghul of Abyssinia and how Khudadad had rescued them: on the contrary all declared that they had been delayed whilst a-hunting and a-visiting the adjacent cities and countries. So the Sultan gave full credence to their account and held his peace.

Such was their case; but as regards Khudadad, when the Princess of Daryabar awoke in the morning she found her bridegroom lying drowned in blood gashed and pierced with a score of wounds. The Princess, deeming her bridegroom dead, wept at this sight right sore; and, calling to mind his youth and beauty, his valour and his many virtues, she washed his face with her tears and exclaimed, "Well-away and woe is me, O my lover, O Khudadad, do these eyes look upon thee in sudden and violent death? Are these thy brothers (the devils!) whom thy courage hath saved, the destroyers of thee? Nay 'tis I am thy murtheress; I who suffered thee to ally thy Fate with my hapless destiny, a lot that doometh to destruction all who befriend me."

Then considering the body attentively she perceived that breath was slowly coming and going through his nostrils, and that his limbs were yet warm. So she made fast the tent-door and ran city-wards to seek a surgeon, and anon having found a skilful leach, she returned with him, but lo and behold! Khudadad was missing. She wist not what had become of him, but thought in her mind that some wild beast had carried him off; then she wept bitterly and bemoaned her mishap, so that the surgeon was moved to ruth and with words of comfort and consolation offered her house and service; and lastly he bore her to the town and assigned to her a separate dwelling. He also appointed two slave-girls to wait upon her, and albeit he knew naught of her condition he was ever in attendance on her with the honour and homage due to the kings.

One day, she being somewhat less sad of heart, the surgeon, who had now informed himself of her condition, asked her, saying, "O my lady, be pleased to acquaint me with thine estate and thy misfortunes, and as far as in me lieth I will strive to aid and succour thee." And she, observing the leach to be shrewd and trustworthy withal, made known to him her story.

Quoth the surgeon, "An it be thy wish, I would gladly escort thee to thy father-in-law the King of Harran, who is indeed a wise sovereign and a just; and he will rejoice to see thee and will take vengeance on the unnatural Princes, his sons, for the blood of thy husband unjustly shed."

These words pleased well the Princess; so the surgeon hired two dromedaries which they mounted and the twain set forth for the city of Harran. Alighting that same evening at a caravanserai the leach asked what news had come from town; and the Keeper answered, "The King of Harran had a son passing valiant and accomplished who abode with him for some years as a stranger; but lately he was lost, nor doth any know of him whether he be dead or alive. The Princess Firuzah his mother hath sent allwheres in search of him, yet hath she found nor trace nor tidings of him. His parents and indeed all the folk, rich and poor, weep and wail for him and albeit the Sultan hath other forty and nine sons, none of them can compare with him for doughty deeds and skilful craft, nor from any one of them deriveth he aught of comfort or consolation. Full quest and search have been made but hitherto all hath been in vain."

The surgeon thereupon made known these words to the Princess of Daryabar, who was minded to go straightway and acquaint the mother of Khudadad with everything that had befallen her husband; but the surgeon, after full reflection, said, "O Princess, shouldst thou fare with this intent, haply ere thou arrive thither the forty-nine Princes may hear of thy coming; and they, by some means or other, will assuredly do thee die, and thy life will be spent to no purpose. Nay, rather let me go first to Prince Khudadad's mother: I will tell her all thy tale and she doubtless will send for thee. Until such time do thou remain secret in this Serai."

Accordingly the leach rode on leisurely for the city and on the road he met a lady mounted upon a she-mule whose housings were of the richest and finest, while behind her walked confidential servants, followed by a band of horsemen and foot-soldiers and Habashi slaves; and, as she rode along, the people formed espalier, standing on either side to salute her while she passed. The leach also joined the throng and made his obeisance, after which quoth he to a bystander, which was a Darwaysh, "Methinks this lady must be a queen?"

"'Tis even so," quoth the other, "she is the consort of our Sultan and all the folk honour and esteem her above her sister-wives for that in truth she is the mother of Prince Khudadad and of him thou surely hast heard."

Hereupon the surgeon accompanied the cavalcade; and, when the lady dismounted at a cathedral-mosque and gave alms of Ashrafis and gold coins to all around (for the King had enjoined her that until Khudadad's return she should deal charity to the poor with her own hand, and pray for the youth's being restored to his home in peace and safety), the mediciner also mingled with the throng which joined in supplications for their favourite and whispered to a slave saying, "O my brother, it behoveth me that I make known without stay or delay to Queen Firuzah a secret which is with me."

Replied he, "An it be aught concerning Prince Khudadad 'tis well: the King's wife will surely give ear to thee; but an it be other, thou wilt hardly win a hearing, for that she is distraught by the absence of her son and careth not for aught beside."

The surgeon, still speaking low, made reply, "My secret concerneth that which is on her mind."

"If this be so," returned the slave, "do thou follow her train privily till it arrive at the palace gate."

Accordingly, when the Lady Firuzah reached her royal apartments, the man made petition to her, saying, "A stranger would fain tell somewhat to thee in private;" and she deigned give permission and command, exclaiming, "'Tis well, let him be brought hither."

Hereupon the slave presented to her the surgeon whom the Queen with gracious mien bade approach; and he, kissing ground between her

285

hands, made his petition in these words: "I have a long tale to tell thy Highness whereat thou shalt greatly marvel." Then he described to her Khudadad's condition, the villainy of his brothers and his death at their hands and of his corpse having been carried off by wild beasts.

Queen Firuzah hearing of her son's murther fell straight-way a-swooning to the ground, and the attendants ran up and, raising her, besprinkled her face with rose-water until she recovered sense and consciousness. Then she gave orders to the surgeon saying, "Hie thee straightway to the Princess of Daryabar and convey to her greetings and expressions of sympathy both from myself and from his sire"; and as the leach departed she called to mind her son and wept with sore weeping.

By chance the Sultan, who was passing by that way, seeing Firuzah in tears and sobs and breaking out into sore and bitter lamentation, asked of her the reason thereof. She told him all she had heard from the leach, and her husband was filled with hot wrath against his sons. So he rose up and went straightway to the audience-chamber, where the townsfolk had gathered together to petition him and to pray for justice and redress; and they, seeing his features working with rage, were all sore afraid.

Presently the Sultan seated himself on the throne of his kingship and gave an order to his Grand Wazir, saying, "O Wazir Hasan, take with thee a thousand men of the guard which keepeth watch and ward over the palace and do thou bring hither the forty-and-nine Princes, my unworthy sons, and cast them into the prison appointed unto man-slayers and murtherers; and have a heed that none of them escape."

The Wazir did as he was bidden, and seizing the Princes one and all cast them into gaol with the murtherers and other criminals, then reported his action to his liege lord. Hereat the Sultan dismissed sundry claimants and suppliants, saying, "For the space of one full-told month henceforth it besitteth me not to sit in the justice-hall. Depart hence, and, when the thirty days shall have passed away, do ye return hither again."

After this rising from the throne he took with him the Wazir Hasan, and entering the apartment of Queen Firuzah, gave command to the Minister that he bring in all haste and with royal state and dignity from the caravanserai, the Princess of Daryabar and the mediciner. The Wazir straightway took horse accompanied by the Emirs and soldiers; and, leading a fine white she-mule richly adorned with jewelled trappings from out of the royal stables, he rode to the caravanserai wherein abode the Princess of Daryabar. Having told her all that the King had done, he seated her upon the animal and, mounting the surgeon upon a steed of Turcoman blood, all three proceeded with pomp and grandeur to the palace. The shop-keepers and townsfolk ran out to greet the lady as the cavalcade wound its way through the streets; and, when they heard say that she was the wife of Prince Khudadad, they rejoiced with exceeding joy for that they should now receive tidings of his whereabouts.

As soon as the procession reached the palace gates the Princess of Daryabar saw the Sultan, who had come forth to greet her, and she alighted from the mule and kissed his feet. The King then raised her by the hand and conducted her to the chamber wherein sat Queen Firuzah awaiting her visit, and all three fell on one another's necks and wept sore and could on no wise control their grief. But whenas their sorrow was somewhat assuaged, the Princess of Daryabar said to the King, "O my lord the Sultan, I would proffer humble petition that full vengeance may fall upon those, one and all, by whom my husband hath been so foully and cruelly murthered."

Replied the King, "O my lady, rest assured that I will assuredly put to death all those villains in requital for the blood of Khudadad"; presently adding, "'Tis true that the dead body of my brave son hath not been found, still it seemeth but right to me that a tomb be built, a cenotaph whereby his greatness and goodness may be held in everlasting remembrance."

Thereupon he summoned the Grand Wazir and bade that a great Mausoleum of white marble be edified amiddlemost the city and the Minister straightway appointed workmen and made choice of a suitable spot in the very centre of the capital. So there they built a gorgeous cenotaph crowned with a noble dome under which was sculptured a figure of Khudadad; and, when the news of its completion reached the King, he appointed a day for ceremonious mourning and perlections of the Koran. At the appointed time and term the townsfolk gathered together to see the funeral procession and the obsequies for the departed; and the Sultan went in state to the Mausoleum together with all the Wazirs, the Emirs and Lords of the land, and took seat upon carpets of black satin purfled with flowers of gold which were dispread over the marble floor.

After a while a bevy of Knights rode up, with downcast heads and half-closed eyes; and twice circuiting the dome they halted the third time in front of the door, and cried out aloud, "O Prince, O son of our Sultan, could we by the sway of our good swords and the strength of our gallant arms restore thee to life, nor heart nor force would fail us in the endeavour; but before the fiat of Almighty Allah all must bow the neck."

Then the horsemen rode away to the place whence they came, followed by one hundred hermits hoar of head and dwellers of the caves who had passed their lives in solitude and abstinence nor ever held converse with man or womankind, neither did they appear in Harran at any time save for the obsequies of the reigning race. In front came one of these greybeards steadying with one hand a huge and ponderous tome which he bore upon his head.

Presently all the holy men thrice compassed the Mausoleum, then standing on the highway the eldest cried with a loud voice, "O Prince, could we by dint of orisons and devotions bring thee back to life, these hearts and souls of ours would be devoted to quickening thee, and on seeing thee arise once again we would wipe thy feet with our own age-white beards."

And when they also retired came one hundred maidens of wondrous beauty and loveliness, mounted on white barbs whose saddles were richly embroidered and set with jewels: their faces were bare and on their heads they bore golden canisters filled with precious stones, rubies and diamonds. They also rode in circuit round the cenotaph and, halting at the door, the youngest and fairest of them, speaking in the name of her sisterhood, exclaimed, "O Prince, could our youth and our charms avail thee aught, we would present ourselves to thee and become thy handmaids; but alas! thou knowest full well that our beauties are here all in vain nor can our love now warm thy clay." Then they also departed in the deepest grief.

As soon as they had disappeared the Sultan and all with him rose up and walked thrice round the figure that had been set up under the dome; then standing at its feet the father said, "O my beloved son, enlighten these eyes which tears for the stress of separation have thus bedimmed." He then wept bitterly and all his Ministers and Courtiers and Grandees joined in his mourning and lamentations; and, when they had made an end of the obsequies, the Sultan and his suite returned palace-wards and the door of the dome was locked.

The Sultan commanded congregational prayers in all the mosques for a full told week and he ceased not to mourn and weep and wail before the cenotaph of his son for eight days. And as soon as this term was passed he commanded the Grand Wazir that vengeance be meted out for the murther of Prince Khudadad, and that the Princes be brought out from their dungeons and be done to death. The tidings were bruited about the city, and preparations were made for executing the assassins and crowds of folk collected to gaze upon the scaffold, when suddenly came a report that an enemy whom the King had routed in bygone times was marching upon the city with a conquering army. Hereat the Sultan was sore troubled and perplexed and the ministers of state said one to other, "Alas! had Prince

Khudadad been on life he would forthwith have put to flight the forces of
the foe however fierce and fell."

Natheless the Sovran set out from the city with his suite and host,
and eke he made ready for flight to some other land by way of the river
should the enemy's force prove victorious. Then the two powers met in
deadly combat; and the invader, surrounding the King of Harran's many
on every side, would have cut him to pieces with all his warriors, when
behold, an armed force hitherto unseen rode athwart the plain at a pace so
swift and so sure that the two hostile Kings gazed upon them in uttermost
amazement, nor wist any one whence that host came. But when it drew
near, the horsemen charged home on the enemies and in the twinkling of
an eye put them to flight; then hotly pursuing felled them with the biting
sword and the piercing spear.

Seeing this onslaught the King of Harran marvelled greatly and
rendering thanks to heaven said to those around him, "Learn ye the name
of the Captain of yonder host, who he may be and whence came he."

But when all the foemen had fallen upon the field save only a few
who escaped hither and thither and the hostile sultan who had been taken
prisoner, the Captain of the friendly forces returned from pursuit well
pleased to greet the King. And, lo and behold! as the twain drew near one
to other the Sultan was certified that the Captain was none other than his
beloved child, Khudadad, whilome lost and now found. Accordingly, he
rejoiced with joy unspeakable that his enemy had thus been vanquished and
that he had again looked upon his son, Khudadad, who stood before him
alive and safe and sound.

"O my sire," presently exclaimed the Prince, "I am he whom thou
deemest to have been slain; but Allah Almighty hath kept me on life that I
might this day stand thee in good stead and destroy these thine enemies."

"O my beloved son," replied the King, "surely I had despaired and
never hoped again to see thee with these mine eyes." So father and son
dismounted and fell upon each other's necks and quoth the Sultan, clasping
the youth's hand, "Long since have I known of thy valiant deeds, and how
thou didst save thine ill-omened brothers from the hands of the man-
devouring Abyssinian, and of the evil wherewith they requited thee. Go
now to thy mother, of whom naught remaineth, through bitter tears for
thee, save skin and bone: be thou the first to gladden her heart and give her
the good tidings of this thy victory."

As they rode along, the Prince enquired of the Sultan, his sire, how
he had heard tell of the Habashi and of the rescue of the Princes from the

cannibal's clutches. "Hath one of my brothers," added he, "informed thee of this adventure?"

"Not so, O my son," replied the King, "not they, but the Princess of Daryabar told me the miserable tale thereof: she hath dwelt for many days with me and 'twas she who first and foremost demanded vengeance for thy blood."

When Khudadad heard that the Princess his spouse was his father's guest, he rejoiced with exceeding joy and cried, "Suffer me first to see my mother; then will I go to the Princess of Daryabar." The King of Harran hereat struck off the head of his chief enemy and exposed it publicly throughout the streets of his capital, and all the people exulted mightily not only at the victory but also for the return of Khudadad safe and sound; and dancing and feasting were in every household.

Presently Queen Firuzah and the Princess of Daryabar presented themselves before the Sultan and offered their congratulations to him, then they went to see Khudadad both hand in hand and the three falling on one another's necks wept for very joy. After this the King and his Queen and daughter-in-law sat long conversing, and they marvelled much how Khudadad, albeit he was sorely gashed and pierced with the sword, had escaped alive from that wildest of wolds, whereupon the Prince at the bidding of his sire told his tale in these words:

"A peasant mounted on a camel chanced to pass by my pavilion and seeing me sore wounded and weltering in my blood, set me upon his beast and conveyed me to his house; then, choosing some roots of desert-herbs he placed them on the hurts so that they kindly healed, and I speedily recovered strength. After returning thanks to my benefactor and giving him liberal largesse, I set out for the city of Harran and on the road I saw the forces of the foe in countless numbers marching upon thy city. Wherefore I made the matter known to the folk of the townships and villages round about and besought their aid; then collecting a large force I placed myself at the head thereof, and arriving in the nick of time destroyed the invading hosts."

Hereupon the Sultan gave thanks to Allah Almighty and said, "Let all the Princes who conspired against thy life be put to death;" and sent forthright for the Sworder of his vengeance; but Khudadad made request to his sire and said, "In good sooth, O my lord the King, they all deserve the doom thou hast ordained, yet be not these my brethren and eke thine own flesh and blood? I have freely forgiven them their offence against me and I humbly pray thy pardon also, that thou grant them their lives, for that blood ever calleth unto blood."

The Sultan at length consented and forgave their offence. Then, summoning all the Ministers, he declared Khudadad his heir and successor, in presence of the Princes whom he bade bring from the prison house. Khudadad caused their chains and fetters to be stricken off and embraced them one by one, showing them the same fondness and affection as he had shown to them in the castle of the cannibal Habashi. All the folk on hearing of this noble conduct of Prince Khudadad raised shouts of applause and loved him yet more than before. The surgeon who had done such good service to the Princess of Daryabar received a robe of honour and much wealth; and on this wise that which began with mishap had issue in all happiness.

Then quoth Scheherazade, "It is well nigh dawn but, if my life be spared, I will tell thee on the morrow a strange and wonderful history of Aladdin and the Wonderful Lamp."

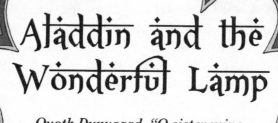

Aladdin and the Wonderful Lamp

Quoth Dunyazad, "O sister mine,
an thou be other than sleepy, tell us one
of thy fair tales, so therewith we may cut
short the waking hours of this our night";
and quoth Scheherazade, "It hath reached me,
O King of the Age, that…

There dwelt in a city of the cities of China a man which was a tailor, withal a pauper, and he had one son, Aladdin hight. Now this boy had been from his babyhood a ne'er-do-well, a scapegrace; and, when he reached his tenth year, his father inclined to teach him his own trade; and, for that he was over indigent to expend money upon his learning other work or craft or apprenticeship, he took the lad into his shop that he might be taught tailoring. But, as Aladdin was a scapegrace and a ne'er-do-well and wont to play at all times with the gutter boys of the quarter, he would not sit in the shop for a single day; nay, he would await his father's leaving it for some purpose, such as to meet a creditor, when he would run off at once and fare forth to the gardens with the other scapegraces and low companions, his fellows. Such was his case; counsel and castigation were of no avail, nor would he obey either parent in aught or learn any trade; and presently, for his sadness and sorrowing because of his son's vicious indolence, the tailor sickened and died. Aladdin continued in his former ill courses and, when his mother saw that her spouse had deceased, and that her son was a scapegrace and good for nothing at all she sold the shop and whatso was to be found therein and fell to spinning cotton yarn. By this toilsome industry she fed herself and found food for her son Aladdin the scapegrace who, seeing himself freed from bearing the severities of his sire, increased in idleness and low habits; nor would he ever stay at home save at meal-hours while his miserable wretched mother lived only by what her hands could spin until the youth had reached his fifteenth year.

It befel, one day of the days, that as he was sitting about the quarter at play with the vagabond boys behold, a Darwaysh from the Maghrib, the Land of the Setting Sun, came up and stood gazing for solace upon the lads and he looked hard at Aladdin and carefully considered his semblance, scarcely noticing his companions the while. Now this Darwaysh was a Moorman from Inner Marocco and he was a magician who could upheap by his magic hill upon hill, and he was also an adept in astrology. So after narrowly considering Aladdin he said in himself, "Verily, this is the lad I need and to find whom I have left my natal land."

Presently he led one of the children apart and questioned him anent the scapegrace saying, "Whose son is he?"

And he sought all information concerning his condition and whatso related to him. After this he walked up to Aladdin and drawing him aside asked, "O my son, haply thou art the child of Such-an-one the tailor?" and the lad answered, "Yes, O my lord, but 'tis long since he died."

The Maghrabi, the Magician, hearing these words threw himself upon Aladdin and wound his arms around his neck and fell to bussing him, weeping the while with tears trickling adown his cheeks. But when the lad saw the Moorman's case he was seized with surprise thereat and questioned him, saying, "What causeth thee weep, O my lord: and how camest thou to know my father?"

"How canst thou, O my son," replied the Moorman, in a soft voice saddened by emotion, "question me with such query after informing me that thy father and my brother is deceased; for that he was my brother-german and now I come from my adopted country and after long exile I rejoiced with exceeding joy in the hope of looking upon him once more and condoling with him over the past; and now thou hast announced to me his demise. But blood hideth not from blood and it hath revealed to me that thou art my nephew, son of my brother, and I knew thee amongst all the lads, albeit thy father, when I parted from him, was yet unmarried."

The Maghrabi, the Magician, said to the tailor's orphan, "O my son Aladdin and I have now failed in the mourning ceremonies and have lost the delight I expected from meeting thy father, my brother, whom after my long banishment I had hoped to see once more ere I die; but far distance wrought me this trouble nor hath the creature aught of asylum from the Creator or artifice against the commandments of Allah Almighty." Then he again clasped Aladdin to his bosom crying, "O my son, I have none to condole with now save thyself; and thou standest in stead of thy sire, thou being his issue and representative and 'whoso leaveth issue dieth not,' O my child!" So saying, the Magician put hand to purse and pulling out ten gold pieces gave them to the lad asking, "O my son, where is your house and where dwelleth she, thy mother, and my brother's widow?"

Presently Aladdin arose with him and showed him the way to their home and meanwhile Quoth the Wizard, "O my son, take these moneys and give them to thy mother, greeting her from me, and let her know that thine uncle, thy father's brother, hath reappeared from his exile and that Inshallah—God willing—on the morrow I will visit her to salute her with the salam and see the house wherein my brother was homed and look upon the place where he lieth buried."

Thereupon Aladdin kissed the Maghrabi's hand, and, after running in his joy at fullest speed to his mother's dwelling, entered to her clean contrariwise to his custom, inasmuch as he never came near her save at meal-times only. And when he found her, the lad exclaimed in his delight, "O my mother, I give thee glad tidings of mine uncle who hath returned from his exile and who now sendeth me to salute thee."

"O my son," she replied, "meseemeth thou mockest me! Who is this uncle and how canst thou have an uncle in the bonds of life?"

He rejoined, "How sayest thou, O my mother, that I have nor living uncles nor kinsmen, when this man is my father's own brother? Indeed he embraced me and bussed me, shedding tears the while, and bade me acquaint thee herewith."

She retorted, "O my son, well I wot thou haddest an uncle, but he is now dead nor am I ware that thou hast other eme."

The Maroccan Magician fared forth next morning and fell to finding out Aladdin, for his heart no longer permitted him to part from the lad; and, as he was to-ing and fro-ing about the city-highways, he came face to face with him disporting himself, as was his wont, amongst the vagabonds and the scapegraces. So he drew near to him and, taking his hand, embraced him and bussed him, then pulled out of his poke two dinars and said, "Hie thee to thy mother and give her these couple of ducats and tell her that thine uncle would eat the evening-meal with you; so do thou take these two gold pieces and prepare for us a succulent supper. But before all things show me once more the way to your home."

"On my head and mine eyes be it, O my uncle," replied the lad and forewent him, pointing out the street leading to the house. Then the Moorman left him and went his ways and Aladdin ran home and, giving the news and the two sequins to his parent, said, "My uncle would sup with us."

So she arose straightway and going to the market-street bought all she required; then, returning to her dwelling she borrowed from the neighbours whatever was needed of pans and platters and so forth and when the meal was cooked and supper time came she said to Aladdin "O my child, the meat is ready but peradventure thine uncle wotteth not the way to our dwelling; so do thou fare forth and meet him on the road."

He replied, "To hear is to obey," and before the twain ended talking a knock was heard at the door. Aladdin went out and opened when, behold, the Maghrabi, the Magician, together with an eunuch carrying the wine and the dessert fruits; so the lad led them in and the slave went about his business.

The Moorman on entering saluted his sister-in-law with the salami then began to shed tears and to question her saying, "Where be the place whereon my brother went to sit?"

She showed it to him, whereat he went up to it and prostrated himself in prayer and kissed the floor crying, "Ah, how scant is my satisfaction and how luckless is my lot, for that I have lost thee, O my brother, O vein of my eye!" And after such fashion he continued weeping and wailing till he swooned away for excess of sobbing and lamentation; wherefor Aladdin's mother was certified of his soothfastness. So coming up to him she raised him from the floor and said, "What gain is there in slaying thyself?"

After consoling him she placed him upon the divan; and, as soon as he was seated at his ease and before the food-trays were served up, he fell to talking with her and saying, "O wife of my brother, it must be a wonder to thee how in all thy days thou never sawest me nor learnedst thou aught of me during the life-time of my brother who hath found mercy. Now the reason is that forty years ago I left this town and exiled myself from my birth-place and wandered forth over all the lands of Al-Hind and Al-Sind and entered Egypt and settled for a long time in its magnificent city, which is one of the world-wonders, till at last I fared to the regions of the Setting Sun and abode for a space of thirty years in the Maroccan interior.

"Now one day of the days, O wife of my brother, as I was sitting alone at home, I fell to thinking of mine own country and of my birth place and of my brother (who hath found mercy); and my yearning to see him waxed excessive and I bewept and bewailed my strangerhood and distance from him. And at last my longings drave me home-wards until I resolved upon travelling to the region which was the falling-place of my head and my homestead, to the end that I might again see my brother. Then Quoth I to myself, 'O man, how long wilt thou wander like a wild Arab from thy place of birth and native stead? Moreover, thou hast one brother and no more; so up with thee and travel and look upon him ere thou die; for who wotteth the woes of the world and the changes of the days? 'Twould be saddest regret an thou lie down to die without beholding thy brother and Allah (laud be to the Lord!) hath vouchsafed thee ample wealth; and belike he may be straitened and in poor case, when thou wilt aid thy brother as well as see him.'

"So I arose at once and equipped me for wayfare and recited the Fatihah; then, whenas Friday prayers ended, I mounted and travelled to this town, after suffering manifold toils and travails which I patiently endured whilst the Lord (to whom be honour and glory!) veiled me with the veil of His protection. So I entered and whilst wandering about the streets, the day before yesterday, I beheld my brother's son Aladdin disporting himself with the boys and, by God the Great, O wife of my brother, the moment I saw him this heart of mine went forth to him (for blood yearneth unto blood!), and my soul felt and informed me that he was my very nephew. So I forgot all my travails and troubles at once on sighting him and I was like to fly for joy; but, when he told me of the dear one's departure to the ruth of Allah Almighty, I fainted for stress of distress and disappointment. Perchance, however, my nephew hath informed thee of the pains which prevailed upon me; but after a fashion I am consoled by the sight of Aladdin the legacy bequeathed to us by him who hath found mercy for that 'whoso leaveth issue is not wholly dead."

And when he looked at his sister-in-law she wept at these his words; so he turned to the lad that he might cause her forget the mention of her mate, as a means of comforting her and also of completing his deceit, and asked him, saying, "O my son Aladdin what hast thou learned in the way of work and what is thy business? Say me, hast thou mastered any craft whereby to earn a livelihood for thyself and for thy mother?"

The lad was abashed and put to shame and he hung down his head and bowed his brow groundwards; but his parent spake out, "How, forsooth? By Allah, he knoweth nothing at all, a child so ungracious as this I never yet saw; no, never! All the day long he idleth away his time with the sons of the quarter, vagabonds like himself, and his father (O regret of me!) died not save of dolour for him. And I also am now in piteous plight: I spin cotton and toil at my distaff, night and day, that I may earn a couple of scones of bread which we eat together. This is his condition, O my brother-in-law; and, by the life of thee, he cometh not near me save at meal-times and none other. Indeed, I am thinking to lock the house-door nor ever open to him again but leave him to go and seek a livelihood whereby he can live, for that I am now grown a woman in years and have no longer strength to toil and go about for a maintenance after this fashion. O Allah, I am compelled to provide him with daily bread when I require to be provided!"

Hereat the Moorman turned to Aladdin and said, "Why is this, O son of my brother, thou goest about in such ungraciousness? 'Tis a disgrace to thee and unsuitable for men like thyself. Thou art a youth of sense, O my son, and the child of honest folk, so 'tis for thee a shame that thy mother, a woman in years, should struggle to support thee. And now that thou hast grown to man's estate it becometh thee to devise thee some device whereby thou canst live, O my child. Look around thee and Alhamdolillah—praise be to Allah—in this our town are many teachers of all manner of crafts and nowhere are they more numerous; so choose thee some calling which may please thee to the end that I establish thee therein; and, when thou growest up, O my son, thou shalt have some business whereby to live. Haply thy father's industry may not be to thy liking; and, if so it be, choose thee some other handicraft which suiteth thy fancy; then let me know and I will aid thee with all I can, O my son."

But when the Maghrabi saw that Aladdin kept silence and made him no reply, he knew that the lad wanted none other occupation than a scapegrace-life, so he said to him, "O son of my brother, let not my words seem hard and harsh to thee, for, if despite all I say, thou still dislike to learn a craft, I will open thee a merchant's store furnished with costliest stuffs and thou shalt become famous amongst the folk and take and give and buy and sell and be well known in the city."

Now when Aladdin heard the words of his uncle the Moorman, and the design of making him a Khwajah—merchant and gentleman—he joyed exceedingly knowing that such folk dress handsomely and fare delicately. So he looked at the Maghrabi smiling and drooping his head groundwards and saying with the tongue of the case that he was content.

The Maghrabi, the Magician, looked at Aladdin and saw him smiling, whereby he understood that the lad was satisfied to become a trader. So he said to him, "Since thou art content that I open thee a merchant's store and make thee a gentleman, do thou, O son of my brother, prove thyself a man and Inshallah—God willing—to-morrow I will take thee to the bazar in the first place and will have a fine suit of clothes cut out for thee, such gear as merchants wear; and, secondly, I will look after a store for thee and keep my word."

Now Aladdin's mother had somewhat doubted the Maroccan being her brother-in-law; but as soon as she heard his promise of opening a merchant's store for her son and setting him up with stuffs and capital and so forth, the woman decided and determined in her mind that this Maghrabi was in very sooth her husband's brother, seeing that no stranger man would do such goodly deed by her son. So she began directing the lad to the right road and teaching him to cast ignorance from out his head and to prove himself a man; moreover she bade him ever obey his excellent uncle as though he were his son and to make up for the time he had wasted in frowardness with his fellows. After this she arose and spread the table, then served up supper; so all sat down and fell to eating and drinking, while the Maghrabi conversed with Aladdin upon matters of business and the like, rejoicing him to such degree that he enjoyed no sleep that night. But when the Moorman saw that the dark hours were passing by, and the wine was drunken, he arose and sped to his own stead; but, ere going, he agreed to return next morning and take Aladdin and look to his suit of merchant's clothes being cut out for him.

And as soon as it was dawn, behold, the Maghrabi rapped at the door which was opened by Aladdin's mother: the Moorman, however, would not enter, but asked to take the lad with him to the market-street. Accordingly Aladdin went forth to his uncle and, wishing him good morning, kissed his hand; and the Maroccan took him by the hand and fared with him to the Bazar. There he entered a clothier's shop containing all kinds of clothes and called for a suit of the most sumptuous; whereat the merchant brought him out his need, all wholly fashioned and ready sewn, and the Moorman said to the lad, "Choose, O my child, whatso pleaseth thee."

Aladdin rejoiced exceedingly seeing that his uncle had given him his choice, so he picked out the suit most to his own liking and the Maroccan paid to the merchant the price thereof in ready money. Presently he led the lad to the Hammam-baths where they bathed; then they came out and drank sherbets, after which Aladdin arose and, donning his new dress in huge joy and delight, went up to his uncle and kissed his hand and thanked him for his favours.

The Maghrabi, the Magician, after leaving the Hammam with Aladdin, took him and trudged with him to the Merchants' bazar; and, having diverted him by showing the market and its sellings and buyings, said to him, "O my son, it besitteth thee to become familiar with the folk, especially with the merchants, so thou mayest learn of them merchant-craft, seeing that the same hath now become thy calling." Then he led him forth and showed him the city and its cathedral-mosques together with all the pleasant sights therein; and, lastly, made him enter a cook's shop. Here dinner was served to them on platters of silver and they dined well and ate and drank their sufficiency, after which they went their ways. Presently the Moorman pointed out to Aladdin the pleasances and noble buildings, and went in with him to the Sultan's Palace and diverted him with displaying all the apartments which were mighty fine and grand; and led him finally to the Khan of stranger merchants where he himself had his abode.

Then the Maroccan invited sundry traders which were in the Caravanserai; and they came and sat down to supper, when he notified to them that the youth was his nephew, Aladdin by name. And after they had eaten and drunken and night had fallen, he rose up and taking the lad with him led him back to his mother, who no sooner saw her boy as he were one of the merchants than her wits took flight and she waxed sad for very gladness. Then she fell to thanking her false connection, the Moorman, for all his benefits and said to him, "O my brother-in-law, I can never say enough though I expressed my gratitude to thee during the rest of thy days and praised thee for the good deeds thou hast done by this my child."

Thereupon quoth the Maroccan, "O wife of my brother, deem this not mere kindness of me, for that the lad is mine own son and 'tis incumbent on me to stand in the stead of my brother, his sire. So be thou fully satisfied!"

And quoth she, "I pray Allah by the honour of the Hallows, the ancients and the moderns, that He preserve thee and cause thee to continue, O my brother-in-law and prolong for me thy life; so shalt thou be a wing over-shadowing this orphan lad; and he shall ever be obedient to thine orders nor shall he do aught save whatso thou biddest him thereunto."

The Maghrabi replied, "O wife of my brother, Aladdin is now a man of sense and the son of goodly folk, and I hope to Allah that he will follow in the footsteps of his sire and cool thine eyes. But I regret that, to-morrow being Friday, I shall not be able to open his shop, as 'tis meeting day when all the merchants, after congregational prayer, go forth to the gardens and pleasances. On the Sabbath, however, Inshallah!—an it please the Creator—we will do our business. Meanwhile to-morrow I will come to thee betimes and take Aladdin for a pleasant stroll to the gardens and pleasances without the city which haply he may hitherto not have beheld. There also he shall see the merchants and notables who go forth to amuse themselves, so shall he become acquainted with them and they with him."

The Maghrabi went away and lay that night in his quarters; and early next morning he came to the tailor's house and rapped at the door. Now Aladdin (for stress of his delight in the new dress he had donned and for the past day's enjoyment in the Hammam and in eating and drinking and gazing at the folk; expecting furthermore his uncle to come at dawn and carry him off on pleasuring to the gardens) had not slept a wink that night, nor closed his eyelids, and would hardly believe it when day broke. But hearing the knock at the door he went out at once in hot haste, like a spark of fire, and opened and saw his uncle, the Magician, who embraced him and kissed him. Then, taking his hand, the Moorman said to him as they fared forth together, "O son of my brother, this day will I show thee a sight thou never sawest in all thy life," and he began to make the lad laugh and cheer him with pleasant talk. So doing they left the city-gate, and the Maroccan took to promenading with Aladdin amongst the gardens and to pointing out for his pleasure the mighty fine pleasances and the marvellous high-builded pavilions. And whenever they stood to stare at a garth or a mansion or a palace the Maghrabi would say to his companion, "Doth this please thee, O son of my brother?"

Aladdin was nigh to fly with delight at seeing sights he had never seen in all his born days; and they ceased not to stroll about and solace themselves until they waxed aweary, when they entered a mighty grand garden which was nearhand, a place that the heart delighted and the sight belighted; for that its swift-running rills flowed amidst the flowers and the waters jetted from the jaws of lions moulded in yellow brass like unto gold. So they took seat over against a lakelet and rested a little while, and Aladdin enjoyed himself with joy exceeding and fell to jesting with his uncle and making merry with him as though the Magician were really his father's brother. Presently the Maghrabi arose and loosing his girdle drew forth from thereunder a bag full of victual, dried fruits and so forth, saying to Aladdin, "O my nephew, haply thou art become anhungered; so come forward and eat what thou needest." Accordingly the lad fell upon the food and the Moorman ate with him and they were gladdened and cheered by rest and good cheer.

Then Quoth the Magician, "Arise, O son of my brother, an thou be reposed and let us stroll onwards a little and reach the end of our walk."

Thereupon Aladdin arose and the Maroccan paced with him from garden to garden until they left all behind them and reached the base of a high and naked hill; when the lad who, during all his days, had never issued from the city-gate and never in his life had walked such a walk as this, said to the Maghrabi, "O uncle mine, whither are we wending? We have left the gardens behind us one and all and have reached the barren hill-country; and, if the way be still long, I have no strength left for walking: indeed I am ready to fall with fatigue. There are no gardens before us, so let us hark back and return to town."

Said the Magician, "No, O my son; this is the right road, nor are the gardens ended for we are going to look at one which hath ne'er its like amongst those of the Kings and all thou hast beheld are naught in comparison therewith. Then gird thy courage to walk; thou art now a man, Alhamdolillah—praise be to Allah!"

Then the Maghrabi fell to soothing Aladdin with soft words and telling him wondrous tales, lies as well as truth, until they reached the site intended by the African Magician who had travelled from the Sunset-land to the regions of China for the sake thereof. And when they made the place, the Moorman said to Aladdin, "O son of my brother, sit thee down and take thy rest, for this is the spot we are now seeking and, Inshallah, soon will I divert thee by displaying marvel-matters whose like not one in the world ever saw; nor hath any solaced himself with gazing upon that which thou art about to behold. No one of created beings hath enjoyed the sights thou art about to see. But when thou art rested, arise and seek some wood-chips and fuel sticks which be small and dry, wherewith we may kindle a fire: then will I show thee, O son of my brother, matters beyond the range of matter."

Now, when the lad heard these words, he longed to look upon what his uncle was about to do and, forgetting his fatigue, he rose forthright and fell to gathering small wood-chips and dry sticks, and continued until the Moorman cried to him, "Enough, O son of my brother!"

Presently the Magician brought out from his breast-pocket a casket which he opened, and drew from it all he needed of incense; then he fumigated and conjured and adjured, muttering words none might understand. And the ground straightway clave asunder after thick gloom and quake of earth and bellowings of thunder. Hereat Aladdin was startled and so affrighted that he tried to fly; but, when the African Magician saw his design, he waxed wroth with exceeding wrath, for that without the lad his work would profit him naught, the hidden hoard which he sought to open being not to be opened save by means of Aladdin. So noting this attempt to run away, the Magician arose and raising his hand smote Aladdin on the head a buffet so sore that well nigh his back-teeth were knocked out, and he fell swooning to the ground. But after a time he revived by the magic of the Magician, and cried, weeping the while, "O my uncle, what have I done that deserveth from thee such a blow as this?"

Hereat the Maghrabi fell to soothing him, and said, "O my son, 'tis my intent to make thee a man; therefore, do thou not gainsay me, for that I am thine uncle and like unto thy father. Obey me, therefore, in all I bid thee, and shortly thou shalt forget all this travail and toil whenas thou shalt look upon the marvel-matters I am about to show thee." And soon after the ground had cloven asunder before the Maroccan it displayed a marble slab wherein was fixed a copper ring. The Maghrabi, striking a geomantic table turned to Aladdin, and said to him, "An thou do all I shall bid thee, indeed thou shalt become wealthier than any of the kings, and for this reason, O my son, I struck thee, because here lieth a hoard which is stored in thy name; and yet thou designedst to leave it and to levant. But now collect thy thoughts, and behold how I opened earth by my spells and adjurations. Under yon stone wherein the ring is set lieth the treasure wherewith I acquainted thee: so set thy hand upon the ring and raise the slab, for that none other amongst the folk, thyself excepted, hath power to open it, nor may any of mortal birth, save thyself, set foot within this Enchanted Treasury which hath been kept for thee. But 'tis needful that thou learn of me all wherewith I would charge thee; nor gainsay e'en a single syllable of my words. All this, O my child, is for thy good; the hoard being of immense value, whose like the kings of the world never accumulated, and do thou remember that 'tis for thee and me."

So poor Aladdin forgot his fatigue and buffet and tear-shedding, and he was dumbed and dazed at the Maghrabi's words and rejoiced that he was fated to become rich in such measure that not even the Sultans would be richer than himself. Accordingly, he cried, "O my uncle, bid me do all thou pleasest, for I will be obedient unto thy bidding."

The Maghrabi replied, "O my nephew, thou art to me as my own child and even dearer, for being my brother's son and for my having none other kith and kin except thyself; and thou, O my child, art my heir and successor." So saying, he went up to Aladdin and kissed him and said, "For whom do I intend these my labours? Indeed, each and every are for thy sake, O my son, to the end that I may leave thee a rich man and one of the very greatest. So gainsay me not in all I shall say to thee, and now go up to yonder ring and uplift it as I bade thee."

Aladdin answered, "O uncle mine, this ring is over heavy for me: I cannot raise it single-handed, so do thou also come forward and lend me strength and aidance towards uplifting it, for indeed I am young in years."

The Moorman replied, "O son of my brother, we shall find it impossible to do aught if I assist thee, and all our efforts would be in vain. But do thou set thy hand upon the ring and pull it up, and thou shalt raise the slab forth-right, and in very sooth I told thee that none can touch it save thyself. But whilst haling at it cease not to pronounce thy name and the names of thy father and mother, so 'twill rise at once to thee nor shalt thou feel its weight."

Thereupon the lad mustered up strength and girt the loins of resolution and did as the Maroccan had bidden him, and hove up the slab with all ease when he pronounced his name and the names of his parents, even as the Magician had bidden him. And as soon as the stone was raised he threw it aside.

After Aladdin had raised the slab from over the entrance to the Hoard there appeared before him a Sardab, a souterrain, whereunto led a case of some twelve stairs and the Maghrabi said, "O Aladdin, collect thy thoughts and do whatso I bid thee to the minutest detail nor fail in aught thereof. Go down with all care into yonder vault until thou reach the bottom and there shalt thou find a space divided into four halls, and in each of these thou shalt see four golden jars and others of virgin or and silver. Beware, however, lest thou take aught therefrom or touch them, nor allow thy gown or its skirts even to brush the jars or the walls. Leave them and fare forwards until thou reach the fourth hall without lingering for a single moment on the way; and, if thou do aught contrary thereto thou wilt be at once transformed and become a black stone. When reaching the fourth hall thou wilt find therein a door which do thou open, and pronouncing the names thou spakest over the slab, enter there through into a garden adorned everywhere with fruit-bearing trees. This thou must traverse by a path thou wilt see in front of thee measuring some fifty cubits long, beyond which thou wilt come upon an open saloon and therein a ladder of some thirty rungs. And thou shalt also see hanging from its ceiling; so mount the ladder and take that Lamp and place it in thy breast-pocket after pouring out its contents; nor fear evil from it for thy clothes because its contents are

303

not common oil. And on return thou art allowed to pluck from the trees whatso thou pleasest, for all is thine so long as the Lamp is in thy hand."

Now when the Moorman ended his charge to Aladdin, he drew off a seal-ring and put it upon the lad's forefinger saying, "O my son, verily this signet shall free thee from all hurt and fear which may threaten thee, but only on condition that thou bear in mind all I have told thee. So arise straightway and go down the stairs, strengthening thy purpose and girding the loins of resolution: moreover fear not for thou art now a man and no longer a child. And in shortest time, O my son, thou shalt win thee immense riches and thou shalt become the wealthiest of the world."

Accordingly, Aladdin arose and descended into the souterrain, where he found the four halls, each containing four jars of gold and these he passed by, as the Maroccan had bidden him, with the utmost care and caution. Thence he fared into the garden and walked along its length until he entered the saloon, where he mounted the ladder and took the Lamp which he extinguished, pouring out the oil which was therein, and placed it in his breast-pocket. Presently, descending the ladder he returned to the garden where he fell to gazing at the trees whereupon sat birds glorifying with loud voices their great Creator.

Now he had not observed them as he went in, but all these trees bare for fruitage costly gems; moreover each had its own kind of growth and jewels of its peculiar sort; and these were of every colour, green and white; yellow, red and other such brilliant hues and the radiance flashing from these gems paled the rays of the sun in forenoon sheen. Furthermore the size of each stone so far surpassed description that no King of the Kings of the world owned a single gem equal to the larger sort nor could boast of even one half the size of the smaller kind of them. Aladdin walked amongst the trees and gazed upon them and other things which surprised the sight and bewildered the wits; and, as he considered them, he saw that in lieu of common fruits the produce was of mighty fine jewels and precious stones, such as emeralds and diamonds; rubies, spinels and balasses, pearls and similar gems astounding the mental vision of man. And forasmuch as the lad had never beheld things like these during his born days nor had reached those years of discretion which would teach him the worth of such valuables (he being still but a little lad), he fancied that all these jewels were of glass or crystal. So he collected them until he had filled his breast-pockets and began to certify himself if they were or were not common fruits, such as grapes, figs and such like edibles. But seeing them of glassy substance, he, in his ignorance of precious stones and their prices, gathered into his breast-pockets every kind of growth the trees afforded; and, having failed of his purpose in finding them food, he said in his mind, "I will collect a portion of these glass fruits for playthings at home."

So he fell to plucking them in quantities and cramming them in his pokes and breast-pockets till these were stuffed full; after which he picked others which he placed in his waist-shawl and then, girding himself therewith, carried off all he availed to, purposing to place them in the house by way of ornaments and, as hath been mentioned, never imagining that they were other than glass. Then he hurried his pace in fear of his uncle, the Maghrabi, until he had passed through the four halls and lastly on his return reached the souterrain where he cast not a look at the jars of gold, albeit he was able and allowed to take of the contents on his way back. But when he came to the souterrain-stairs and clomb the steps till naught remained but the last; and, finding this higher than all the others, he was unable alone and unassisted, burthened moreover as he was, to mount it.

So he said to the Maghrabi, "O my uncle, lend me thy hand and aid me to climb;" but the Moorman answered, "O my son, give me the Lamp and lighten thy load; belike 'tis that weigheth thee down."

The lad rejoined, "O my uncle, 'tis not the Lamp downweigheth me at all; but do thou lend me a hand and as soon as I reach ground I will give it to thee."

Hereat the Maroccan, the Magician, whose only object was the Lamp and none other, began to insist upon Aladdin giving it to him at once; but the lad (forasmuch as he had placed it at the bottom of his breast-pocket and his other pouches being full of gems bulged outwards) could not reach it with his fingers to hand it over, so the wizard after much vain persistency in requiring what his nephew was unable to give, fell to raging with furious rage and to demanding the Lamp whilst Aladdin could not get at it. Yet had the lad promised truthfully that he would give it up as soon as he might reach ground, without lying thought or ill-intent. But when the Moorman saw that he would not hand it over, he waxed wroth with wrath exceeding and cut off all his hopes of winning it; so he conjured and adjured and cast incense amiddlemost the fire, when forthright the slab made a cover of itself, and by the might of magic ridded the entrance; the earth buried the stone as it was aforetime and Aladdin, unable to issue forth, remained underground.

Now the Sorcerer was a stranger, and, as we have mentioned, no uncle of Aladdin's, and he had misrepresented himself and preferred a lying claim, to the end that he might obtain the Lamp by means of the lad

for whom his Hoard had been upstored. So the Accursed heaped the earth over him and left him to die of hunger. For this Maghrabi was an African of Afrikiyah proper, born in the Inner Sunset-land, and from his earliest age upwards he had been addicted to witchcraft and had studied and practiced every manner of occult science, for which unholy lore the city of Africa is notorious. And he ceased not to read and hear lectures until he had become a past-master in all such knowledge. And of the abounding skill in spells and conjurations which he had acquired by the perusing and the lessoning of forty years, one day of the days he discovered by devilish inspiration that there lay in an extreme city of the cities of China, named Al-Kal'as, an immense Hoard, the like whereof none of the Kings in this world had ever accumulated: moreover, that the most marvellous article in this Enchanted Treasure was a wonderful Lamp which, whoso possessed, could not possibly be surpassed by any man upon earth, either in high degree or in wealth and opulence; nor could the mightiest monarch of the universe attain to the all-sufficiency of this Lamp with its might of magical means.

When the Maghrabi assured himself by his science and saw that this Hoard could be opened only by the presence of a lad named Aladdin, of pauper family and abiding in that very city, and learnt how taking it would be easy and without hardships, he straightway and without stay or delay equipped himself for a voyage to China (as we have already told) and he did what he did with Aladdin fancying that he would become Lord of the Lamp. But his attempt and his hopes were baffled and his work was clean wasted; whereupon, determining to do the lad die, he heaped up the earth over him by gramarye to the end that the unfortunate might perish, reflecting that "The live man hath no murtherer."

Secondly, he did so with the design that, as Aladdin could not come forth from underground, he would also be impotent to bring out the Lamp from the souterrain. So presently he wended his ways and retired to his own land, Africa, a sadder man and disappointed of all his expectations.

Such was the case with the Wizard; but as regards Aladdin when the earth was heaped over him, he began shouting to the Moorman whom he believed to be his uncle, and praying him to lend a hand that he might issue from the souterrain and return to earth's surface; but, however loudly he cried, none was found to reply.

At that moment he comprehended the sleight which the Maroccan had played upon him, and that the man was no uncle but a liar and a wizard. Then the unhappy despaired of life, and learned to his sorrow that there was no escape for him; so he fell to beweeping with sore weeping the calamity had befallen him; and after a little while he stood up and descended the stairs to see if Allah Almighty had lightened his grief-load by leaving a door of issue. So he turned him to the right and to the left but he saw naught save darkness and four walls closed upon him, for that the Magician had by his magic locked all the doors and had shut up even the garden, wherethrough the lad erst had passed, lest it offer him the means of issuing out upon earth's surface, and that he might surely die.

Then Aladdin's weeping waxed sorer, and his wailing louder whenas he found all the doors fast shut, for he had thought to solace himself awhile in the garden. But when he felt that all were locked, he fell to shedding tears and lamenting like unto one who hath lost his every hope, and he returned to sit upon the stairs of the flight whereby he had entered the souterrain, weeping and wailing and wanting all hopes. But it is a light matter for Allah (be He exalted and extolled!) whenas He designeth aught to say, "Be" and it becometh; for that He createth joy in the midst of annoy; and on this wise it was with Aladdin.

Whilst the Maghrabi, the Magician, was sending him down into the souterrain he set upon his finger by way of gift, a seal ring and said, "Verily, this signet shall save thee from every strait an thou fall into calamity and ill shifts of time; and it shall remove from thee all hurt and harm, and aid thee with a strong arm whereso thou mayest be set." Now this was by destiny of God the Great, that it might be the means of Aladdin's escape; for whilst he sat wailing and weeping over his case and cast away all hope of life, and utter misery overwhelmed him, he rubbed his hands together for excess of sorrow, as is the wont of the woeful; then, raising them in supplication to Allah, he cried, "I testify that there is no God save Thou alone, The Most Great, the Omnipotent, the All-Conquering, Quickener of the dead, Creator of man's need and Granter thereof, Resolver of his difficulties and duresse and Bringer of joy not of annoy. Thou art my sufficiency and Thou art the Truest of Trustees. And I bear witness that Mohammed is Thy servant and Thine Apostle and I supplicate Thee, O my God, by his favour with Thee to free me from this my foul plight."

And whilst he implored the Lord and was chafing his hands in the soreness of his sorrow for that had befallen him of calamity, his fingers chanced to rub the Ring when, lo and behold! forthright its Familiar rose upright before him and cried, "Adsum; thy slave between thy hands is come! Ask whatso thou wantest, for that I am the thrall of him on whose hand is the Ring, the Signet of my lord and master."

Hereat the lad looked at him and saw standing before him a Marid like unto an Ifrit of our lord Solomon's Jinns. He trembled at the terrible sight; but, hearing the Slave of the Ring say, "Ask whatso thou wantest, verily, I am thy thrall, seeing that the signet of my lord be upon thy finger," he recovered his spirits and remembered the Moorman's saying when giving him the Ring. So he rejoiced exceedingly and became brave and cried, "Ho thou; Slave of the Lord of the Ring, I desire thee to set me upon the face of earth."

And hardly had he spoken this speech when suddenly the ground clave asunder and he found himself at the door of the Hoard and outside it in full view of the world. Now for three whole days he had been sitting in the darkness of the Treasury underground and when the sheen of day and the thine of sun smote his face he found himself unable to keep his eyes open; so he began to unclose the lids á little and to close them a little until his eyeballs regained force and got used to the light and were purged of the noisome murk. Withal he was astounded at finding himself without the Hoard-door whereby he had passed in when it was opened by the Maghrabi, the Magician; especially as the adit had been lidded and the ground had been smoothed, showing no sign whatever of entrance. Thereat his surprise increased until he fancied himself in another place, nor was his mind convinced that the stead was the same until he saw the spot whereupon they had kindled the fire of wood-chips and dried sticks, and where the African Wizard had conjured over the incense. Then he turned him rightwards and leftwards and sighted the gardens from afar and his eyes recognized the road whereby he had come. So he returned thanks to Allah Almighty who had restored him to the face of earth and had freed him from death after he had cut off all hopes of life.

Presently he arose and walked along the way to the town, which now he well knew, until he entered the streets and passed on to his own home. Then he went in to his mother and on seeing her, of the overwhelming stress of joy at his escape and the memory of past affright and the hardships he had borne and the pangs of hunger, he fell to the ground before his parent in a fainting-fit. Now his mother had been passing sad since the time of his leaving her and she found her moaning and crying about him; however on sighting him enter the house she joyed with exceeding joy, but soon was overwhelmed with woe when he sank upon the ground swooning before her eyes. Still, she did not neglect the matter or treat it lightly, but at once hastened to sprinkle water upon his face and after she asked of the neighbours some scents which she made him snuff up. And when he came round a little, he prayed her to bring him somewhat of food saying, "O my mother 'tis now three days since I ate anything at all."

Thereupon she arose and brought him what she had by her; then, setting it before him, said, "Come forward, O my son; eat and be cheered and, when thou shalt have rested, tell me what hath betided and affected thee, O my child; at this present I will not question thee for thou art aweary in very deed."

Aladdin ate and drank and was cheered and after he had rested and had recovered spirits he cried, "Ah, O my mother, I have a sore grievance against thee for leaving me to that accursed wight who strave to compass my destruction and designed to take my life. Know that I beheld Death with mine own eyes at the hand of this damned wretch, whom thou didst certify to be my uncle; and, had not Almighty Allah rescued me from him, I and thou, O my mother, had been cozened by the excess of this Accursed's promises to work my welfare, and by the great show of affection which he manifested to us. Learn, O my mother, that this fellow is a sorcerer, a Moorman, an accursed, a liar, a traitor, a hypocrite; nor deem I that the devils under the earth are damnable as he. Allah abase him in his every book! Hear then, O my mother, what this abominable one did, and all I shall tell thee will be soothfast and certain. See how the damned villain brake every promise he made, certifying that he would soon work all good with me; and do thou consider the fondness which he displayed to me and the deeds which he did by me; and all this only to win his wish, for his design was to destroy me; and Alhamdolillah—laud to the Lord—for my deliverance. Listen and learn, O my mother, how this Accursed entreated me."

Then Aladdin informed his mother of all that had befallen him (weeping the while for stress of gladness); how the Maghrabi had led him to a hill wherein was hidden the Hoard and how he had conjured and fumigated, adding, "After which, O my mother, mighty fear get hold of me when the hill split and the earth gaped before me by his wizardry; and I trembled with terror at the rolling of thunder in mine ears and the murk which fell upon us when he fumigated and muttered spells. Seeing these horrors I in mine affright designed to fly; but, when he understood mine intent he reviled me and smote me a buffet so sore that it caused me to swoon. However, inasmuch as the Treasury was to be opened only by means of me, O my mother, he could not descend therein himself, it being in my name and not in his; and, for that he is an ill-omened magician, he understood that I was necessary to him and this was his need of me.

"After he had buffetted me, he judged it advisable to soothe me in order that he might send me down into the Enchanted Treasury; and first he drew from his finger a Ring which he placed upon mine. So I descended and found four halls all full of gold and silver which counted as naught, and the Accursed had charged me not to touch aught thereof. Then I entered a mighty fine flower-garden everywhere bedecked with tall trees whose foliage and fruitage bewildered the wits, for all, O my mother, were of vari-coloured glass, and lastly I reached the Hall wherein hung this Lamp. So I took it straightway and put it out and poured forth its contents."

And so saying Aladdin drew the Lamp from his breast-pocket and showed it to his mother, together with the gems and jewels which he had brought from the garden; and there were two large bag-pockets full of precious stones, whereof not one was to be found amongst the kings of the world. But the lad knew naught anent their worth deeming them glass or crystal; and presently he resumed, "After this, O mother mine, I reached the Hoard-door carrying the Lamp and shouted to the accursed Sorcerer, which called himself my uncle, to lend me a hand and hale me up, I being unable to mount of myself the last step for the over weight of my burthen. But he would not and said only, 'First hand me the Lamp!' As, however, I had placed it at the bottom of my breast- pocket and the other pouches bulged out beyond it, I was unable to get at it and said, 'O my uncle, I cannot reach thee the Lamp, but I will give it to thee when outside the Treasury.' His only need was the Lamp and he designed, O my mother, to snatch it from me and after that slay me, as indeed he did his best to do by heaping the earth over my head. Such then is what befel me from this foul Sorcerer."

Hereupon Aladdin fell to abusing the Magician in hot wrath and with a burning heart and crying, "Well-away! I take refuge from this damned wight, the ill-omened, the wrongdoer, the forswearer, the lost to all humanity, the arch-traitor, the hypocrite, the annihilator of ruth and mercy."

When Aladdin's mother heard his words and what had befallen him from the Maghrabi, the Magician, she said, "Yea, verily, O my son, he is a miscreant, a hypocrite who murthereth the folk by his magic; but 'twas the grace of Allah Almighty, O my child, that saved thee from the tricks and the treachery of this accursed Sorcerer whom I deemed to be truly thine uncle." Then, as the lad had not slept a wink for three days and found himself nodding, he sought his natural rest, his mother doing on like wise; nor did he awake till about noon on the second day.

As soon as he shook off slumber he called for somewhat of food being sore anhungered, but said his mother, "O my son, I have no victual for thee inasmuch as yesterday thou atest all that was in the house. But wait patiently a while: I have spun a trifle of yarn which I will carry to the market-street and sell it and buy with what it may be worth some victual for thee."

"O my mother," said he, "keep your yarn and sell it not; but fetch me the Lamp I brought hither that I may go vend it and with its price purchase provaunt, for that I deem 'twill bring more money than the spinnings."

So Aladdin's mother arose and fetched the Lamp for her son; but, while so doing, she saw that it was dirty exceedingly; so she said, "O my son, here is the Lamp, but 'tis very foul: after we shall have washed it and polished it 'twill sell better."

Then, taking a handful of sand she began to rub therewith, but she had only begun when appeared to her one of the Jann whose favour was frightful and whose bulk was horrible big, and he was gigantic as one of the Jababirah. And forthright he cried to her, "Say whatso thou wantest of me? Here am I, thy Slave and Slave to whoso holdeth the Lamp; and not I alone, but all the Slaves of the Wonderful Lamp which thou hendest in hand."

She quaked and terror was sore upon her when she looked at that frightful form and her tongue being tied she could not return aught reply, never having been accustomed to espy similar semblances; nay, she fell to the ground oppressed by her affright.

Now her son was standing afar off and he had already seen the Jinni of the Ring which he had rubbed within the Treasury; so when he heard the Slave speaking to his parent, he hastened forwards and snatching the Lamp from her hand, said, "O Slave of the Lamp, I am unhungered and 'tis my desire that thou fetch me somewhat to eat and let it be something toothsome beyond our means."

The Jinni disappeared for an eye-twinkle and returned with a mighty fine tray and precious of price, for that 'twas all in virginal silver and upon it stood twelve golden platters of meats manifold and dainties delicate, with bread snowier than snow; also two silvern cups and as many black jacks full of wine clear-strained and long-stored. And after setting all these before Aladdin, he evanished from vision.

Thereupon the lad went and sprinkled rose water upon his mother's face and caused her snuff up perfumes pure and pungent and said to her when she revived, "Rise, O mother mine, and let us eat of these meats wherewith Almighty Allah hath eased our poverty."

But when she saw that mighty fine silvern tray she fell to marvelling at the matter and quoth she, "O my son, who be this generous, this beneficent one who hath abated our hunger-pains and our penury? We are indeed under obligation to him and, meseemeth, 'tis the Sultan who, hearing of our mean condition and our misery, hath sent us this food tray."

Quoth he, "O my mother, this be no time for questioning: arouse thee and let us eat for we are both a-famished."

Accordingly, they sat down to the tray and fell to feeding when Aladdin's mother tasted meats whose like in all her time she had never touched; so they devoured them with sharpened appetites and all the capacity engendered by stress of hunger; and, secondly, the food was such as that marked the tables of the Kings. But neither of them knew whether the tray was or was not valuable, for never in their born days had they looked upon aught like it.

As soon as they had finished the meal (withal leaving victual enough for supper and eke for the next day), they arose and washed their hands and sat at chat, when the mother turned to her son and said, "Tell me, O my child, what befel thee from the Slave, the Jinni, now that Alhamdolillah— laud to the Lord!—we have eaten our full of the good things wherewith He hath favoured us and thou hast no pretext for saying to me, 'I am anhungered.'"

So Aladdin related to her all that took place between him and the Slave what while she had sunk upon the ground aswoon for sore terror; and at this she, being seized with mighty great surprise, said, "'tis true; for the Jinns do present themselves before the Sons of Adam but I, O my son, never saw them in all my life and meseemeth that this be the same who saved thee when thou west within the Enchanted Hoard."

"This is not he, O my mother: this who appeared before thee is the Slave of the Lamp!"

"Who may this be, O my son?"

"This be a Slave of sort and shape other than he; that was the Familiar of the Ring and this his fellow thou sawest was the Slave of the Lamp thou hentest in hand. Verily, O my mother, the Jinni who appeared to thee was the Slave of the Lamp."

And when his parent heard these words she cried, "There! there! so this Accursed, who showed himself to me and went nigh unto killing me with affright, is attached to the Lamp."

"Yes," he replied, and she rejoined, "Now I conjure thee, O my son, by the milk wherewith I suckled thee, to throw away from thee this Lamp and this Ring; because they can cause us only extreme terror and I especially can never abear a second glance at them. Moreover all intercourse with them is unlawful, for that the Prophet (whom Allah save and assain!) warned us against them with threats."

He replied, "Thy commands, O my mother, be upon my head and mine eyes; but, as regards this saying thou saidest, 'tis impossible that I part or with Lamp or with Ring. Thou thyself hast seen what good the Slave wrought us whenas we were famishing; and know, O my mother, that the Maghrabi, the liar, the Magician, when sending me down into the Hoard, sought nor the silver nor the gold wherewith the four halls were fulfilled, but charged me to bring him only the Lamp (naught else), because in very deed he had learned its priceless value; and, had he not been certified of it, he had never endured such toil and trouble nor had he travelled from his own land to our land in search thereof; neither had he shut me up in the Treasury when he despaired of the Lamp which I would not hand to him. Therefore it besitteth us, O my mother, to keep this Lamp and take all care thereof nor disclose its mysteries to any; for this is now our means of livelihood and this it is shall enrich us. And likewise as regards the Ring, I will never withdraw it from my finger inasmuch as but for this thou hadst nevermore seen me on life nay I should have died within the Hoard underground. How then can I possibly remove it from my finger? And who wotteth that which may betide me by the lapse of Time, what trippings or calamities or injurious mishaps wherefrom this Ring may deliver me? However, for regard to thy feelings I will stow away the Lamp nor ever suffer it to be seen of thee hereafter."

Now when his mother heard his words and pondered them she knew they were true and said to him, "Do, O my son, whatso thou wiliest for my part I wish never to see them nor ever sight that frightful spectacle I erst saw."

Aladdin and his mother continued eating of the meats brought them by the Jinni for two full told days till they were finished; but when he learned that nothing of food remained for them, he arose and took a platter of the platters which the Slave had brought upon the tray. Now they were all of the finest gold but the lad knew naught thereof; so he bore it to the Bazar and there, seeing a man which was a peddler, a viler than the Satans, offered it to him for sale. When the peddler espied it he took the lad aside that none might see him, and he looked at the platter and considered it till he was certified that it was of gold refined. But he knew not whether Aladdin was acquainted with its value or he was in such matters a raw laddie, so he asked him, "For how much, O my lord, this platter?" and the other answered, "Thou wottest what be its worth."

The peddler debated with himself as to how much he should offer, because Aladdin had returned him a craftsman-like reply; and he thought of the smallest valuation; at the same time he feared lest the lad, haply knowing its worth, should expect a considerable sum. So he said in his mind, "Belike the fellow is an ignoramus in such matters nor is ware of the price of the platter." Whereupon he pulled out of his pocket a dinar, and Aladdin eyed the gold piece lying in his palm and hastily taking it went his way; whereby the peddler was certified of his customer's innocence of all such knowledge, and repented with entire repentance that he had given him a golden dinar in lieu of a copper carat, a bright-polished groat.

However, Aladdin made no delay but went at once to the baker's where he bought him bread and changed the ducat; then, going to his mother, he gave her the scones and the remaining small coin and said, "O my mother, hie thee and buy thee all we require." So she arose and walked to the Bazar and laid in the necessary stock; after which they ate and were cheered. And whenever the price of the platter was expended, Aladdin would take another and carry it to the accursed peddler who bought each and every at a pitiful price; and even this he would have minished but, seeing how he had paid a dinar for the first, he feared to offer a lesser sum, lest the lad go and sell to some rival in trade and thus lose his usurious gains.

Now when all the golden platters were sold, there remained only the silver tray whereupon they stood; and, for that it was large and weighty, Aladdin brought the peddler to his house and produced the article, when the buyer, seeing its size gave him ten dinars and these being accepted went his ways. Aladdin and his mother lived upon the sequins until they were spent; then he brought out the Lamp and rubbed it and straightway appeared the Slave who had shown himself aforetime.

The Slave of the Lamp, on appearing to Aladdin said, "Ask, O my lord, whatso thou wantest for I am thy Slave and the thrall of whoso hath the Lamp"; and said the lad, "I desire that thou bring me a tray of food like unto that thou broughtest me erewhiles, for indeed I am famisht." Accordingly, in the glance of an eye the Slave produced a similar tray supporting twelve platters of the most sumptuous, furnished with requisite cates; and thereon stood clean bread and sundry glass bottles of strained wine.

Now Aladdin's mother had gone out when she knew he was about to rub the Lamp that she might not again look upon the Jinni; but after a while she returned and, when she sighted the tray covered with silvern platters and smelt the savour of the rich meats diffused over the house, she marvelled and rejoiced. Thereupon quoth he, "Look, O my mother! Thou badest me throw away the Lamp, see now its virtues"; and quoth she, "O my son, Allah increase his weal, but I would not look upon him."

Then the lad sat down with his parent to the tray and they ate and drank until they were satisfied; after which they removed what remained for use on the morrow. As soon as the meats had been consumed, Aladdin arose and stowed away under his clothes a platter of the platters and went forth to find the peddler, purposing to sell it to him; but by fiat of Fate he passed by the shop of an ancient jeweller, an honest man and a pious who feared Allah. When the Shaykh saw the lad, he asked him saying, "O my son, what dost thou want? for that times manifold have I seen thee passing hereby and having dealings with a Jewish man; and I have espied thee handing over to him sundry articles; now also I fancy thou hast somewhat for sale and thou seekest him as a buyer thereof. But thou wottest not, O my child, that the Jews ever hold lawful to them the good of Moslems, the Confessors of Allah Almighty's unity, and, always defraud them; especially this accursed Jew with whom thou hast relations and into whose hands thou hast fallen. If then, O my son, thou have aught thou wouldest sell show the same to me and never fear, for I will give thee its full price by the truth of Almighty Allah."

Thereupon Aladdin brought out the platter which when the ancient goldsmith saw, he took and weighed it in his scales and asked the lad saying, "Was it the fellow of this thou soldest to the Jew?"

"Yes, its fellow and its brother," he answered, and quoth the old man, "What price did he pay thee?"

Quoth the lad, "One dinar."

The ancient goldsmith cried, "Ah! I take refuge from this Accursed who cozeneth the servants of Allah Almighty!" Then, looking at the lad, he exclaimed, "O my son, verily yon tricksy Jew hath cheated thee and laughed at thee, this platter being pure silver and virginal. I have weighed it and found it worth seventy dinars; and, if thou please to take its value, take it."

Thereupon the Shaykh counted out to him seventy gold pieces, which he accepted and presently thanked him for his kindness in exposing the Jew's rascality. And after this, whenever the price of a platter was expended, he would bring another, and on such wise he and his mother were soon in better circumstances; yet they ceased not to live after their olden fashion as middle class folk without spending on diet overmuch or squandering money.

315

But Aladdin had now thrown off the ungraciousness of his boyhood; he shunned the society of scapegraces and he began to frequent good men and true, repairing daily to the market-street of the merchants and there companying with the great and the small of them, asking about matters of merchandise and learning the price of investments and so forth; he likewise frequented the Bazars of the Goldsmiths and the Jewellers where he would sit and divert himself by inspecting their precious stones and by noting how jewels were sold and bought therein. Accordingly, he presently became ware that the tree-fruits, wherewith he had filled his pockets what time he entered the Enchanted Treasury, were neither glass nor crystal but gems rich and rare; and he understood that he had acquired immense wealth such as the Kings never can possess. He then considered all the precious stones which were in the Jewellers' Quarter, but found that their biggest was not worth his smallest. On this wise he ceased not every day repairing to the Bazar and making himself familiar with the folk and winning their loving will; and enquiring anent selling and buying, giving and taking, the dear and the cheap, until one day of the days when, after rising at dawn and donning his dress he went forth, as was his wont, to the Jewellers' Bazar; and, as he passed along it he heard the crier crying as follows:

"By command of our magnificent master, the King of the Time and the Lord of the Age and the Tide, let all the folk lock up their shops and stores and retire within their houses, for that the Lady Badr al-Budur, daughter of the Sultan, designeth to visit the Hammam; and whoso gainsayeth the order shall be punished with death-penalty and be his blood upon his own neck!"

But when Aladdin heard the proclamation, he longed to look upon the King's daughter and said in his mind, "Indeed all the lieges talk of her beauty and loveliness and the end of my desires is to see her."

Aladdin fell to contriving some means whereby he might look upon the Princess Badr al-Budur and at last judged best to take his station behind the Hammam door whence he might see her face as she entered. Accordingly, without stay or delay he repaired to the Baths before she was expected and stood a-rear of the entrance, a place whereat none of the folk happened to be looking. Now when the Sultan's daughter had gone the rounds of the city and its main streets and had solaced herself by sight-seeing, she finally reached the Hammam and whilst entering she raised her veil, when her face rose before sight as it were a pearl of price or a sheeny sun, and she was as one of whom the describer sang:

316

"Magic Kohl enchanteth the glances so bright of her:
We pluck roses in posies from cheeks rosy bright of her:
Of night's gloomiest hue is the gloom of the hair of her
And her bright brow uplighteth the murks of the night of her."

(Quoth the reciter) when the Princess raised from her face the veil and Aladdin saw her favour he said, "In very truth her fashion magnifieth her Almighty Fashioner and glory be to Him who created her and adorned her with this beauty and loveliness."

His strength was struck down from the moment he saw her and his thoughts were distraught; his gaze was dazed, the love of her get hold of the whole of his heart; and, when he returned home to his mother, he was as one in ecstasy. His parent addressed him, but he neither replied nor denied; and, when she set before him the morning meal he continued in like case; so quoth she, "O my son, what is't may have befallen thee? Say me, doth aught ail thee? Let me know what ill hath betided thee for, unlike thy custom, thou speakest not when I bespeak thee."

Thereupon Aladdin (who used to think that all women resembled his mother and who, albeit he had heard of the charms of Badr al-Budur, daughter of the Sultan, yet knew not what "beauty" and "loveliness" might signify) turned to his parent and exclaimed, "Let me be!"

However, she persisted in praying him to come forwards and eat, so he did her bidding but hardly touched food; after which he lay at full length on his bed all the night through in cogitation deep until morning morrowed. The same was his condition during the next day, when his mother was perplexed for the case of her son and unable to learn what had happened to him. So, thinking that belike he might be ailing she drew near him and asked him saying, "O my son, an thou sense aught of pain or such like, let me know that I may fare forth and fetch thee the physician; and to-day there be in this our city a leach from the Land of the Arabs whom the Sultan hath sent to summon and the bruit abroad reporteth him to be skillful exceedingly. So, an be thou ill let me go and bring him to thee."

Aladdin, hearing his parent's offer to summon the mediciner, said, "O my mother, I am well in body and on no wise ill. But I ever thought that all women resembled thee until yesterday, when I beheld the Lady Badr al-Budur daughter of the Sultan, as she was faring for the Baths." Then he related to her all and everything that had happened to him adding, "Haply thou also hast heard the crier a-crying, 'Let no man open shop or stand in street that the Lady Badr al-Budur may repair to the Hammam without eye seeing her.' But I have looked upon her even as she is, for she raised her veil at the door and, when I viewed her favour and beheld that noble work of the Creator, a sore fit of ecstasy, O my mother, fell upon me for love of her and firm resolve to win her hath opened its way into every limb of me, nor is repose possible for me except I win her. Wherefor I purpose asking her to wife from the Sultan her sire in lawful wedlock."

When Aladdin's mother heard her son's words, she belittled his wits and cried, "O my child, the name of Allah upon thee! meseemeth thou hast lost thy senses. But be thou rightly guided, O my son, nor be thou as the men Jinn-maddened!"

He replied, "Nay, O mother mine, I am not out of my mind nor am I of the maniacs; nor shall this thy saying alter one jot of what is in my thoughts, for rest is impossible to me until I shall have won the dearling of my heart's core, the beautiful Lady Badr al-Budur. And now I am resolved to ask her of her sire the Sultan."

She rejoined, "O my son, by my life upon thee speak not such speech, lest any overhear thee and say thou be insane: so cast away from thee such nonsense! Who shall undertake a matter like this or make such request to the King? Indeed, I know not how, supposing this thy speech to be soothfast, thou shalt manage to crave such grace of the Sultan or through whom thou desirest to propose it."

He retorted, "Through whom shall I ask it, O my mother, when thou art present? And who is there fonder and more faithful to me than thyself? So my design is that thou thy self shalt proffer this my petition."

Quoth she, "O my son, Allah remove me far therefrom! What! have I lost my wits like thyself? Cast the thought away and a long way from thy heart. Remember whose son thou art, O my child, the orphan boy of a tailor, the poorest and meanest of the tailors toiling in this city; and I, thy mother, am also come of pauper folk and indigent. How then durst thou ask to wife the daughter of the Sultan, whose sire would not deign marry her with the sons of the Kings and the Sovrans, except they were his peers in honour and grandeur and majesty; and, were they but one degree lower, he would refuse his daughter to them."

Quoth he, "O my mother, everything thou hast called to mind is known to me; moreover 'tis thoroughly well known to me that I am the child of pauper parents; withal do not these words of thee divert me from my design at all, at all. Nor the less do I hope of thee, an I be thy son and thou truly love me, that thou grant me this favour, otherwise thou wilt destroy me; and present Death hovereth over my head except I win my will of my heart's dearling; and I, O my mother, am in every case thy child."

Hearing these words, his parent wept of her sorrow for him and said, "O my child! Yes, in very deed I am thy mother, nor have I any son or life's blood of my liver except thyself, and the end of my wishes is to give thee a wife and rejoice in thee. But suppose that I would seek a bride of our likes and equals, her people will at once ask an thou have any land or garden, merchandise or handicraft, wherewith thou canst support her; and what is the reply I can return? Then, if I cannot possibly answer the poor like ourselves, how shall I be bold enough, O my son, to ask for the daughter of the Sultan of China-land who hath no peer or behind or before him? Therefore do thou weigh this matter in thy mind. Also who shall ask her to wife for the son of a snip? Well indeed I wot that my saying aught of this kind will but increase our misfortunes; for that it may be the cause of our incurring mortal danger from the Sultan; peradventure even death for thee and me. And, as concerneth myself, how shall I venture upon such rash deed and perilous, O my son? and in what way shall I ask the Sultan for his daughter to be thy wife; and, indeed, how ever shall I even get access to him? And should I succeed therein, what is to be my answer an they ask me touching thy means? Haply the King will hold me to be a madwoman. And, lastly, suppose that I obtain audience of the Sultan, what offering is there I can submit to the King's majesty?

"'Tis true, O my child, that the Sultan is mild and merciful, never rejecting any who approach him to require justice or ruth or protection, nor any who pray him for a present; for he is liberal and lavisheth favour upon near and far. But he dealeth his boons to those deserving them, to men who have done some derring-do in battle under his eyes or have rendered as civilians great service to his estate. But thou! do thou tell me what feat thou hast performed in his presence or before the public that thou meritest from him such grace? And, secondly, this boon thou ambitionest is not for one of our condition, nor is it possible that the King grant to thee the bourne of thine aspiration; for whoso goeth to the Sultan and craveth of him a favour, him it besitteth to take in hand somewhat that suiteth the royal majesty, as indeed I warned thee aforetime. How, then, shalt thou risk thyself to stand before the Sultan and ask his daughter in marriage, when thou hast with thee naught to offer him of that which beseemeth his exalted station?"

Hereto Aladdin replied, "O my mother, thou speakest to the point and hast reminded me aright and 'tis meet that I revolve in mind the whole of thy remindings. But, O my mother, the love of Princess Badr al-Budur hath entered into the core of my heart; nor can I rest without I win her. However, thou hast also recalled to me a matter which I forgot and 'tis this emboldeneth me to ask his daughter of the King. Albeit thou, O my mother, declarest that I have no gift which I can submit to the Sultan, as is the wont of the world, yet in very sooth I have an offering and a present whose equal, O my mother, I hold none of the Kings to possess; no, nor even aught like it. Because verily that which I deemed glass or crystal was nothing but precious stones and I hold that all the Kings of the World have never possessed any thing like one of the smallest thereof. For, by frequenting the jeweller-folk, I have learned that they are the costliest gems and these are what I brought in my pockets from the Hoard, whereupon, an thou please, compose thy mind. We have in our house a bowl of China porcelain; so arise thou and fetch it, that I may fill it with these jewels, which thou shalt carry as a gift to the King, and thou shalt stand in his presence and solicit him for my requirement. I am certified that by such means the matter will become easy to thee; and, if thou be unwilling, O my mother, to strive for the winning of my wish as regards the lady Badr al-Budur, know thou that surely I shall die. Nor do thou imagine that this gift is of aught save the costliest of stones and be assured, O my mother, that in my many visits to the Jewellers' Bazar I have observed the merchants selling for sums man's judgment may not determine jewels whose beauty is not worth one quarter carat of what we possess; seeing which I was certified that ours are beyond all price. So arise, O my mother, as I bade thee and bring me the porcelain bowl aforesaid, that I may arrange therein some of these gems and we will see what semblance they show."

So she brought him the China bowl saying in herself, "I shall know what to do when I find out if the words of my child concerning these jewels be soothfast or not;" and she set it before her son who pulled the stones out of his pockets and disposed them in the bowl and ceased not arranging therein gems of sorts till such time as he had filled it. And when it was brimful she could not fix her eyes firmly upon it; on the contrary, she winked and blinked for the dazzle of the stones and their radiance and excess of lightning like glance; and her wits were bewildered thereat; only she was not certified of their value being really of the enormous extent she had been told. Withal she reflected that possibly her son might have spoken aright when he declared that their like was not to be found with the Kings.

Then Aladdin turned to her and said, "Thou hast seen, O my mother, that this present intended for the Sultan is magnificent, and I am certified that it will procure for thee high honour with him and that he will receive thee with all respect. And now, O my mother, thou hast no excuse; so compose thy thoughts and arise; take thou this bowl and away with it to the palace."

His mother rejoined, "O my son, 'tis true that the present is high-priced exceedingly and the costliest of the costly; also that according to thy word none owneth its like. But who would have the boldness to go and ask the Sultan for his daughter, the Lady Badr al-Badur? I indeed dare not say to him, 'I want thy daughter!' when he shall ask me, 'What is thy want?' for know thou, O my son, that my tongue will be tied. And, granting that Allah assist me and I embolden myself to say to him, 'My wish is to become a connection of thine through the marriage of thy daughter, the Lady Badr al-Budur, to my son Aladdin,' they will surely decide at once that I am demented and will thrust me forth in disgrace and despised. I will not tell thee that I shall thereby fall into danger of death, for 'twill not only be I but thou likewise. However, O my son, of my regard for thine inclination, I needs must embolden myself and hie thither; yet, O my child, if the King receive me and honour me on account of the gift and enquire of me what thou desirest."

Aladdin's mother said to her son, "And in reply I ask of him that which thou desirest in the matter of thy marriage with his daughter, how shall I answer him an he ask me, as is man's wont, What estates hast thou, and what income? And perchance, O my son, he will question me of this before questioning me of thee." Aladdin replied, "'tis not possible that the Sultan should make such demand what time he considereth the jewels and their magnificence; nor is it meet to think of such things as these which may never occur. Now do thou but arise and set before him this present of precious stones and ask of him his daughter for me, and sit not yonder making much of the difficulty in thy fancy. Ere this thou hast learned, O mother mine, that the Lamp which we possess hath become to us a stable income and that whatso I want of it the same is supplied to me; and my hope is that by means thereof I shall learn how to answer the Sultan should he ask me of that thou sayest."

Then Aladdin and his mother fell to talking over the subject all that night long and when morning morrowed, the dame arose and heartened her heart, especially as her son had expounded to her some little of the powers of the Lamp and the virtues thereof; to wit, that it would supply all they required of it.

Aladdin, however, seeing his parent take courage when he explained to her the workings of the Lamp, feared lest she might tattle to the folk thereof; so he said to her, "O my mother, beware how thou talk to any of the properties of the Lamp and its profit, as this is our one great good. Guard thy thoughts lest thou speak over much concerning it before others, whoso they be; haply we shall lose it and lose the boon fortune we possess and the benefits we expect, for that 'tis of him."

His mother replied, "Fear not, therefor, O my son," and she arose and took the bowl full of jewels, which she wrapped up in a fine kerchief, and went forth betimes that she might reach the Divan ere it became crowded. When she passed into the Palace, the levee not being fully attended, she saw the Wazirs and sundry of the Lords of the land going into the presence-room and after a short time, when the Divan was made complete by the Ministers and high Officials and Chieftains and Emirs and Grandees, the Sultan appeared and the Wazirs made their obeisance and likewise did the Nobles and the Notables. The King seated himself upon the throne of his kingship, and all present at the levee stood before him with crossed arms awaiting his commandment to sit; and, when they received it, each took his place according to his degree; then the claimants came before the Sultan who delivered sentence, after his wonted way, until the Divan was ended, when the King arose and withdrew into the palace and the others all went their ways.

Aladdin's mother, having come the earliest of all, found means of entering without any addressing her or offering to lead her to the presence; and she ceased not standing there until the Divan ended, when the Sultan arose and withdrew into the palace and the others all went about their business. And when she saw the throne empty and the King passing into his Harem, she also wended her ways and returned home. But as soon as her son espied her, bowl in hand, he thought that haply something untoward had befallen her, but he would not ask of aught until such time as she had set down the bowl, when she acquainted him with that which had occurred and ended by adding, "Alhamdolillah—laud to the Lord!—O my child, that I found courage enough and secured for myself standing place in the levee this day; and, albe I dreaded to bespeak the King yet (Inshallah!) on the morrow I will address him. Even to-day were many who, like myself, could not get audience of the Sultan. But be of good cheer, O my son, and to-morrow needs must I bespeak him for thy sake; and what happened not may happen."

When Aladdin heard his parent's words, he joyed with excessive joy; and, although he expected the matter to be managed hour by hour, for excess of his love and longing to the Lady Badr al-Budur, yet he possessed his soul in patience. They slept well that night and betimes next morning the mother of Aladdin arose and went with her bowl to the King's court which she found closed. So she asked the people and they told her that the Sultan did not hold a levee every day but only thrice in the se'nnight; wherefor she determined to return home; and, after this, whenever she saw the court open she would stand before the King until the reception ended and when it was shut she would go to make sure thereof; and this was the case for the whole month. The Sultan was wont to remark her presence at every levee, but, on the last day when she took her station, as was her wont, before the Council, she allowed it to close and lacked boldness to come forwards and speak even a syllable.

Now as the King having risen was making for his Harem accompanied by the Grand Wazir, he turned to him and said, "O Wazir, during the last six or seven levee days I see yonder old woman present herself at every reception and I also note that she always carrieth a something under her mantilla. Say me, hast thou, O Wazir, any knowledge of her and her intention?"

"O my lord the Sultan," said the other, "verily women be weakly of wits, and haply this goodwife cometh hither to complain before thee against her goodman or some of her people." But this reply was far from satisfying the Sultan; nay, be bade the Wazir, in case she should come again, set her before him; and forthright the Minister placed hand on head and exclaimed, "To hear is to obey, O our lord the Sultan!"

Mother of Aladdin made a practice of repairing to the Divan every day and passing into the room and standing opposite the King, albeit she was sorrowful and sore aweary, withal for her son's sake she endeavored to make easy all her difficulties. Now one day of the days, when she did according to her custom, the Sultan cast his eyes upon her as she stood before him, and said to his Grand Wazir, "This be the very woman whereof I spake to thee yesterday, so do thou straightway bring her before me, that I may see what be her suit and fulfil her need."

Accordingly, the Minister at once introduced her and when in the presence she saluted the King by kissing her finger tips and raising them to her brow; and, praying for the Sultan's glory and continuance and the permanence of his prosperity, bussed ground before him. Thereupon, quoth he "O woman, for sundry days I have seen thee attend the levee sans a word said; so tell me an thou have any requirement I may grant."

She kissed ground a second time and after blessing him, answered, "Yea, verily, as thy head liveth, O King of the Age, I have a want; but first of all, do thou deign grant me a promise of safety that I may prefer my suit to the ears of our lord the Sultan; for haply thy Highness may find it a singular."

The King, wishing to know her need, and being a man of unusual mildness and clemency, gave his word for her immunity and bade forthwith dismiss all about him, remaining without other but the Grand Wazir. Then he turned towards his suppliant and said, "Inform me of thy suit: thou hast the safeguard of Allah Almighty."

"O King of the Age," replied she, "I also require of thee pardon;" and quoth he, "Allah pardon thee even as I do."

Then, quoth she, "O our lord the Sultan, I have a son, Aladdin hight; and he, one day of the days, having heard the crier commending all men to shut shop and shun the streets, for that the Lady Badr al-Budur, daughter of the Sultan, was going to the Hammam, felt an uncontrollable longing to look upon her, and hid himself in a stead whence he could sight her right well, and that place was behind the door of the Baths. When she entered he beheld her and considered her as he wished, and but too well; for, since the time he looked upon her, O King of the Age, unto this hour, life hath not been pleasant to him. And he hath required of me that I ask her to wife for him from thy Highness, nor could I drive this fancy from his mind because love of her hath mastered his vitals and to such degree that he said to me, 'Know thou, O mother mine, that an I win not my wish surely I shall die.' Accordingly I hope that thy Highness will deign be mild and merciful and pardon this boldness on the part of me and my child and refrain to punish us therefor."

When the Sultan heard her tale he regarded her with kindness and, laughing aloud, asked her, "What may be that thou carriest and what be in yonder kerchief?" And she seeing the Sultan laugh in lieu of waxing wroth at her words, forthright opened the wrapper and set before him the bowl of jewels, whereby the audience-hall was illumined as it were by lustres and candelabra; and he was dazed and amazed at the radiance of the rare gems, and he fell to marvelling at their size and beauty and excellence.

When the King saw the gems he was seized by surprise and cried, "Never at all until this day saw I anything like these jewels for size and beauty and excellence: nor deem I that there be found in my treasury a single one like them." Then he turned to his Minister and asked, "What sayest thou, seen in thy time such mighty fine jewels as these?"

The other answered, "Never saw I such, O our lord the Sultan, nor do I think that there be in the treasures of my lord the Sultan the fellow of the least thereof."

The King resumed, "Now indeed whoso hath presented to me such jewels meriteth to become bridegroom to my daughter, Badr al-Budur; because, as far as I see, none is more deserving of her than he."

When the Wazir heard the Sultan's words he was tongue-tied with concern and he grieved with sore grief, for the King had promised to give the Princess in marriage to his son; so after a little while he said, "O King of the Age, thy Highness deigned promise me that the Lady Badr al-Budur should be spouse to my son; so 'tis but right that thine exalted Highness vouchsafe us a delay of three months, during which time, Inshallah! my child may obtain and present an offering yet costlier than this."

Accordingly the King, albeit he knew that such a thing could not be done, or by the Wazir or by the greatest of his Grandees, yet of his grace and kindness granted him the required delay. Then he turned to the old woman, Aladdin's mother, and said, "Go to thy son and tell him I have pledged my word that my daughter shall be in his name; only 'tis needful that I make the requisite preparations of nuptial furniture for her use; and 'tis only meet that he take patience for the next three months."

Receiving this reply, Aladdin's mother thanked the Sultan and blessed him; then, going forth in hottest haste, as one flying for joy, she went home; and when her son saw her entering with a smiling face, he was gladdened at the sign of good news, especially because she had returned without delay as on the Fast days, and had not brought back the bowl. Presently he asked her saying, "Inshallah, thou bearest me, O my mother, glad tidings; and peradventure the jewels and their value have wrought their work and belike thou hast been kindly received by the King and he hath shown thee grace and hath given ear to thy request?"

So she told him the whole tale, how the Sultan had entreated her well and had marvelled at the extraordinary size of the gems and their surpassing water as did also the Wazir, adding, "And he promised that his daughter should be thine. Only, O my child, the Wazir spake of a secret contract made with him by the Sultan before he pledged himself to me and, after speaking privily, the King put me off to the end of three months: therefore I have become fearful lest the Wazir be evilly disposed to thee and perchance he may attempt to change the Sultan's mind."

When Aladdin heard his mother's words and how the Sultan had promised him his daughter, deferring, however, the wedding until after the third month, his mind was gladdened and he rejoiced exceedingly and said, "Inasmuch as the King hath given his word after three months (well, it *is* a long time!), at all events my gladness is mighty great."

Then he thanked his parent, showing her how her good work had exceeded her toil and travail; and said to her, "By Allah, O my mother, hitherto I was as 'twere in my grave and therefrom thou hast withdrawn me; and I praise Allah Almighty because I am at this moment certified that no man in the world is happier than I or more fortunate."

Then he took patience until two of the three months had gone by. Now one day of the days his mother fared forth about sundown to the Bazar that she might buy somewhat of oil; and she found all the market shops fast shut and the whole city decorated, and the folk placing waxen tapers and flowers at their casements; and she beheld the soldiers and household troops and Aghas riding in procession and flambeaux and lustres flaming and flaring, and she wondered at the marvellous sight and the glamour of the scene.

So she went in to an oilman's store which stood open still and bought her need of him and said, "By thy life, O uncle, tell me what be the tidings in town this day, that people have made all these decorations and every house and market-street are adorned and the troops all stand on guard?"

The oilman asked her, "O woman, I suppose thou art a stranger and not one of this city?" and she answered, "Nay, I am thy townswoman."

He rejoined, "Thou a townswoman, and yet wottest not that this very night the son of the Grand Wazir goeth in to the Lady Badr al-Budur, daughter of the Sultan! He is now in the Hammam and all this power of soldiery is on guard and standing under arms to await his coming forth, when they will bear him in bridal procession to the palace where the Princess expecteth him."

As the mother of Aladdin heard these words, she grieved and was distraught in thought and perplexed how to inform her son of this sorrowful event, well knowing that the poor youth was looking, hour by hour, to the end of the three months. But she returned straightway home to him and when she had entered she said, "O my son, I would give thee certain tidings, yet hard to me will be the sorrow they shall occasion thee."

He cried, "Let me know what be thy news"; and she replied, "Verily the Sultan hath broken his promise to thee in the matter of the Lady Badr al-Budur, and this very night the Grand Wazir's son goeth in to her. And for some time, O my son, I have suspected that the Minister would change the King's mind, even as I told thee how he had spoken privily to him before me."

Aladdin asked, "How learnedst thou that the Wazir's son is this night to pay his first visit to the Princess?"

So she told him the whole tale, how when going to buy oil she had found the city decorated and the eunuch-officials and Lords of the land with the troops under arms awaiting the bridegroom from the Baths; and that the first visit was appointed for that very night. Hearing this Aladdin was seized with a fever of jealousy brought on by his grief: however, after a short while he remembered the Lamp and, recovering his spirits said, "By thy life, O my mother, do thou believe that the Wazir's son will not enjoy her as thou thinkest. But now leave we this discourse and arise thou and serve up supper and after eating let me retire to my own chamber and all will be well and happy."

Aladdin, after he had supped, retired to his chamber and, locking the door, brought out the Lamp and rubbed it, whenas forthright appeared to him its Familiar who said, "Ask whatso thou wantest, for I am thy Slave and Slave to him who holdeth the Lamp in hand; I and all the Slaves of the Lamp."

He replied, "Hear me! I prayed the Sultan for his daughter to wife and he plighted her to me after three months; but he hath not kept his word; nay, he hath given her to the son of the Wazir and this very night the bridegroom will go in to her. Therefore I command thee (an thou be a trusty Servitor to the Lamp) when thou shalt see bride and bridegroom bedded together this night, at once take them up and bear them hither abed; and this be what I want of thee."

The Marid replied, "Hearing and obeying; and if thou have other service but this, do thou demand of me all thou desirest."

Quoth Aladdin, "At the present time I require naught save that I bade thee do."

Hereupon the Slave disappeared and Aladdin returned to pass the rest of the evening with his mother. But at the hour when he knew that the Servitor would be coming, he arose and retired to his chamber and after a little while, behold, the Marid came bringing to him the newly-wedded couple upon their bridal-bed. Aladdin rejoiced to see them with exceeding joy; then he cried to the Slave, "Carry yonder gallows-bird hence and lay him at full length in the privy."

His bidding was done straightway; but, before leaving him, the Slave blew upon the bridegroom a blast so cold that it shrivelled him and the plight of the Wazir's son became piteous. Then the Servitor returning to Aladdin said to him, "An thou require aught else, inform me thereof"; and said the other, "Return a-morn that thou mayest restore them to their stead;" whereto, "I hear and obey," quoth the Marid and evanished.

Presently Aladdin arose, hardly believing that the affair had been such a success for him; but whenas he looked upon the Lady Badr al-Budur lying under his own roof, albeit he had long burned with her love yet he preserved respect for her and said, "O Princess of fair ones, think not that I brought thee hither to minish thy honour. Heaven forfend! Nay 'twas only to prevent the wrong man enjoying thee, for that thy sire the Sultan promised thee to me. So do thou rest in peace."

When the Lady Badr al-Budur, daughter of the Sultan, saw herself in that mean and darksome lodging, and heard Aladdin's words, she was seized with fear and trembling and waxed clean distraught; nor could she return aught of reply. Presently the youth arose and stripping off his outer dress placed a scymitar between them and lay upon the bed beside the Princess; and he did no villain deed, for it sufficed him to prevent the consummation of her nuptials with the Wazir's son. On the other hand the Lady Badr al-Budur passed a night the evillest of all nights; nor in her born days had she seen a worse; and the same was the case with the Minister's son who lay in the chapel of ease and who dared not stir for the fear of the Jinni which overwhelmed him.

As soon as it was morning the Slave appeared before Aladdin, without the Lamp being rubbed, and said to him, "O my lord, an thou require aught, command me therefor, that I may do it upon my head and mine eyes."

Said the other, "Go, take up and carry the bride and bridegroom to their own apartment"; so the Servitor did his bidding in an eye-glance and bore away the pair, and placed them in the palace as whilome they were and without their seeing any one; but both died of affright when they found themselves being transported from stead to stead. And the Marid had barely time to set them down and wend his ways ere the Sultan came on a visit of congratulation to his daughter; and, when the Wazir's son heard the doors thrown open, he sprang straightway from his couch and donned his dress for he knew that none save the King could enter at that hour. Yet it was exceedingly hard for him to leave his bed wherein he wished to warm himself a trifle after his cold night in the water closet which he had lately left.

The Sultan went in to his daughter Badr al-Budur and kissing her between the eyes gave her good morning and asked her of her bridegroom and whether she was pleased and satisfied with him. But she returned no reply whatever and looked at him with the eye of anger and, although he repeated his words again and again, she held her peace nor bespake him with a single syllable. So the King quitted her and, going to the Queen, informed her of what had taken place between him and his daughter; and the mother, unwilling to leave the Sultan angered with their child, said to him, "O King of the Age, this be the custom of most newly-married couples at least during their first days of marriage, for that they are bashful and somewhat coy. So deign thou excuse her and after a little while she will again become herself and speak with the folk as before, whereas now her shame, O King of the Age, keepeth her silent. However 'tis my wish to fare forth and see her."

Thereupon the Queen arose and donned her dress; then, going to her daughter, wished her good morning and kissed her between the eyes. Yet would the Princess make no answer at all, whereat quoth the Queen to herself, "Doubtless some strange matter hath occurred to trouble her with such trouble as this." So she asked her saying "O my daughter, what hath caused this thy case? Let me know what hath betided thee that, when I come and give thee good morning, thou hast not a word to say to me?"

Thereat the Lady Badr al-Budur raised her head and said, "Pardon me O my mother, 'twas my duty to meet thee with all respect and worship, seeing that thou hast honoured me by this visit. However, I pray thee to hear the cause of this my condition and see how the night I have just spent hath been to me the evillest of the nights. Hardly had we lain down, O my mother, than one whose form I wot not uplifted our bed and transported it to a darksome place, fulsome and mean." Then the Princess related to the Queen-mother all that had befallen her that night; how they had taken away her bridegroom, leaving her lone and lonesome, and how after a while came another youth who lay beside her, in lieu of her bridegroom, after placing his scymitar between her and himself; "and in the morning" (she continued) "he who carried us off returned and bore us straight back to our own stead. But at once when he arrived hither he left us and suddenly my sire the Sultan entered at the hour and moment of our coming and I had nor heart nor tongue to speak him withal, for the stress of the terror and trembling which came upon me. Haply such lack of duty may have proved sore to him, so I hope, O my mother, that thou wilt acquaint him with the cause of this my condition and that he will pardon me for not answering him and blame me not, but rather accept my excuses."

When the Queen heard these words of Princess Badr al-Budur, she said to her, "O my child, compose thy thoughts. An thou tell such tale before any, haply shall he say, 'Verily, the Sultan's daughter hath lost her wits.' And thou hast done right well in not choosing to recount thine adventure to thy father; and beware and again I say beware, O my daughter, lest thou inform him thereof."

The Princess replied, "O my mother, I have spoken to thee like one sound in senses nor have I lost my wits: this be what befel me and, if thou believe it not because coming from me, ask my bridegroom."

To which the Queen replied, "Rise up straightway, O my daughter, and banish from thy thoughts such fancies as these; and robe thyself and come forth to glance at the bridal feasts and festivities they are making in the city for the sake of thee and thy nuptials; and listen to the drumming and the singing and look at the decorations all intended to honour thy marriage, O my daughter."

So saying, the Queen at once summoned the tirewomen who dressed and prepared the Lady Badr al-Budur; and presently she went in to the Sultan and assured him that their daughter had suffered during all her wedding-night from swevens and nightmare and said to him, "Be not severe with her for not answering thee."

Then the Queen sent privily for the Wazir's son and asked of the matter, saying, "Tell me, are these words of the Lady Badr al-Budur soothfast or not?"

But he, in his fear of losing his bride out of hand, answered, "O my lady, I have no knowledge of that whereof thou speakest." Accordingly the mother made sure that her daughter had seen visions and dreams.

The marriage-feasts lasted throughout that day with Almahs and singers and the smiting of all manner instruments of mirth and merriment, while the Queen and the Wazir and his son strave right strenuously to enhance the festivities that the Princess might enjoy herself; and that day they left nothing of what exciteth to pleasure unrepresented in her presence, to the end that she might forget what was in her thoughts and derive increase of joyance. Yet did naught of this take any effect upon her; nay, she sat in silence, sad of thought, sore perplexed at what had befallen her during the last night. It is true that the Wazir's son had suffered even more because he had passed his sleeping hours lying in the water-closet: he, however, had falsed the story and had cast out remembrance of the night in the first place for his fear of losing his bride and with her the honour of a connection which brought him such excess of consideration and for which men envied him so much; and, secondly, on account of the wondrous loveliness of the Lady Badr al-Budur and her marvellous beauty.

Aladdin also went forth that day and looked at the merry-makings which extended throughout the city as well as the palace and he fell a-laughing, especially when he heard the folk prating of the high honour which had accrued to the son of the Wazir and the prosperity of his fortunes in having become son-in-law to the Sultan and the high consideration shown by the wedding fetes. And he said in his mind, "Indeed ye wot not, O ye miserables, what befel him last night that ye envy him!" But after darkness fell and it was time for sleep, Aladdin arose and, retiring to his chamber, rubbed the Lamp, whereupon the Slave incontinently appeared.

When the Slave appeared in presence of Aladdin, he was bidden to bring him the Sultan's daughter together with her bridegroom as on the past night ere the Wazir's son could abate her maidenhead. So the Marid without stay or delay evanished for a little while until the appointed time, when he returned carrying the bed whereon lay the Lady Badr al-Budur and the Wazir's son; and he did with the bridegroom as he had done before, to wit, he took him up and lay him at full length in the jakes and there left him dried up for excess of fear and trembling. Then Aladdin arose, and placing the scymitar between himself and the Princess, lay down beside her; and when day broke the Slave restored the pair to their own place, leaving Aladdin filled with delight at the state of the Minister's son.

Now when the Sultan woke up amorn he resolved to visit his daughter and see if she would treat him as on the past day; so shaking off his sleep he sprang up and arrayed himself in his raiment and, going to the apartment of the Princess bade open the door. Thereat the son of the Wazir arose forthright and came down from his bed and began donning his dress whilst his ribs were wrung with cold; for when the King entered the Slave had but just brought him back. The Sultan, raising the arras, drew near his daughter as she lay abed and gave her good morning; then kissing her between the eyes, he asked her of her case. But he saw her looking sour and sad and she answered him not at all, only glowering at him as one in anger and her plight was pitiable. Hereat the Sultan waxed wroth with her for that she would not reply and he suspected that something evil had befallen her, whereupon he bared his blade and cried to her, brand in hand, saying, "What be this hath betided thee? Either acquaint me with what happened or this very moment I will take thy life! Is such conduct the token of honour and respect I expect of thee, that I address thee and thou answerest me not a word?"

When the Lady Badar al-Badur saw her sire in high dudgeon and the naked glaive in his grip, she was freed from her fear of the past, so she raised her head and said to him, "O my beloved father, be not wroth with me nor be hasty in thy hot passion for I am excusable in what thou shalt see of my case. So do thou lend an ear to what occurred to me and well I wot that after hearing my account of what befel to me during these two last nights, thou wilt pardon me and thy Highness will be softened to pitying me even as I claim of thee affection for thy child." Then the Princess informed her father of all that had betided her adding, "O my sire, an thou believe me not, ask my bridegroom and he will recount to thy Highness the whole adventure, nor did I know either what they would do with him when they bore him away from my side or where they would place him."

When the Sultan heard his daughter's words, he was saddened and his eyes brimmed with tears, then he sheathed his sabre and kissed her saying, "O my daughter wherefore didst thou not tell me what happened on the past night that I might have guarded thee from this torture and terror which visited thee a second time? But now 'tis no matter. Rise and cast out all such care and to-night I will set a watch to ward thee nor shall any mishap again make thee miserable."

Then the Sultan returned to his palace and straightway bade summon the Grand Wazir and asked him, as he stood before him in his service, "O Wazir how dost thou look upon this matter? Haply thy son hath informed thee of what occurred to him and to my daughter."

The Minister replied, "O King of the Age, I have not seen my son or yesterday or to-day."

Hereat the Sultan told him all that had afflicted the Princess, adding, "'tis my desire that thou at once seek tidings of thy son concerning the facts of the case: peradventure of her fear my daughter may not be fully aware of what really befel her; withal I hold all her words to be truthful." So the Grand Wazir arose and, going forth, bade summon his son and asked him anent all his lord had told him whether it be true or untrue.

The youth replied, "O my father the Wazir, Heaven forbid that the Lady Badr al-Budur speak falsely: indeed all she said was sooth and these two nights proved to us the evillest of our nights instead of being nights of pleasure and marriage-joys. But what befel me was the greater evil because, instead of sleeping abed with my bride, I lay in the wardrobe, a black hole, frightful, noisome of stench, truly damnable; and my ribs were bursten with cold." In fine the young man told his father the whole tale, adding as he ended it, "O dear father mine, I implore thee to speak with the Sultan that he may set me free from this marriage. Yes, indeed 'tis a high honour for me to be the Sultan's son-in-law and especially the love of the Princess hath gotten hold of my vitals; but I have no strength left to endure a single night like unto these two last."

The Wazir, hearing the words of his son, was saddened and sorrowful exceedingly, for it was his design to advance and promote his child by making him son-in-law to the Sultan. So he became thoughtful and perplexed about the affair and the device whereby to manage it, and it was sore grievous for him to break off the marriage, it having been a rare enjoyment to him that he had fallen upon such high good fortune. Accordingly he said, "Take patience, O my son, until we see what may happen this night, when we will set watchmen to ward you; nor do thou give up the exalted distinction which hath fallen to none save to thyself."

Then the Wazir left him and, returning to the sovran, reported that all told to him by the Lady Badr al-Budur was a true tale; whereupon quoth the Sultan, "Since the affair is on this wise, we require no delay," and he at once ordered all the rejoicings to cease and the marriage to be broken off. This caused the folk and the citizen to marvel at the matter, especially when they saw the Grand Wazir and his son leaving the palace in pitiable plight for grief and stress of passion; and the people fell to asking, "What hath happened and what is the cause of the wedding being made null and void?" Nor did any know aught of the truth save Aladdin the lover who claimed the Princess's hand, and he laughed in his sleeve. But even after the marriage was dissolved, the Sultan forgot nor even recalled to mind his promise made to Aladdin's mother; and the same was the case with the Grand Wazir, while neither had any inkling of whence befel them that which had befallen.

So Aladdin patiently awaited the lapse of the three months after which the Sultan had pledged himself to give him to wife his daughter; but, as soon as ever the term came, he sent his mother to the Sultan for the purpose of requiring him to keep his covenant. So she went to the palace and when the King appeared in the Divan and saw the old woman standing before him, he remembered his promise to her concerning the marriage after a term of three months, and he turned to the Minister and said "O Wazir, this be the ancient dame who presented me with the jewels and to whom we pledged our word that when the three months had elapsed we would summon her to our presence before all others."

So the Minister went forth and fetched her and when she went in to the Sultan's presence she saluted him and prayed for his glory and permanence of prosperity. Hereat the King asked her if she needed aught, and she answered, "O King of the Age, the three months' term thou assignedst to me is finished, and this is thy time to marry my son Aladdin with thy daughter, the Lady Badr al-Budur."

The Sultan was distraught at this demand, especially when he saw the old woman's pauper condition, one of the meanest of her kind; and yet the

333

offering she had brought to him was of the most magnificent, far beyond his power to pay the price. Accordingly, he turned to the Grand Wazir and said, "What device is there with thee? In very sooth I did pass my word, yet meseemeth that they be pauper folk and not persons of high condition."

The Grand Wazir who was dying of envy and who was especially saddened by what had befallen his son, said to himself, "How shall one like this wed the King's daughter and my son lose this highmost honour?" Accordingly, he answered his Sovran speaking privily, "O my lord, 'tis an easy matter to keep off a poor devil such as this, for he is not worthy that thy Highness give his daughter to a fellow whom none knoweth what he may be."

"By what means," enquired the Sultan, "shall we put off the man when I pledged my promise; and the word of the Kings is their bond?"

Replied the Wazir, "O my lord, my rede is that thou demand of him forty platters made of pure sand-gold and full of gems (such as the woman brought thee aforetime), with forty white slave-girls to carry the platters and forty black eunuch-slaves."

The King rejoined, "By Allah, O Wazir, thou hast spoken to the purpose, seeing that such thing is not possible and by this way we shall be freed." Then quoth he to Aladdin's mother, "Do thou go and tell thy son that I am a man of my word even as I plighted it to him, but on condition that he have power to pay the dower of my daughter; and that which I require of him is a settlement consisting of two score platters of virgin gold, all brimming with gems the like of those thou broughtest to me, and as many white handmaids to carry them and two score black eunuch-slaves to serve and escort the bearers. An thy son avail hereto I will marry him with my daughter."

Thereupon she returned home wagging her head and saying in her mind, "Whence can my poor boy procure these platters and such jewels? And granted that he return to the Enchanted Treasury and pluck them from the trees which, however, I hold impossible; yet given that he bring them whence shall he come by the girls and the blacks?" Nor did she leave communing with herself till she reached her home, where she found Aladdin awaiting her, and she lost no time in saying "O my son, did I not tell thee never to fancy that thy power would extend to the Lady Badr al-Budur, and that such a matter is not possible to folk like ourselves?"

"Recount to me the news," quoth he; so quoth she, "O my child, verily the Sultan received me with all honour according to his custom and, meseemeth his intentions towards us be friendly. But thine enemy is that accursed Wazir; for, after I addressed the King in thy name as thou badest me say, 'In very sooth the promised term is past,' adding ''Twere well an thy Highness would deign issue commandment for the espousals of thy daughter the Lady Badr al-Budur to my son Aladdin' he turned to and addressed the Minister who answered privily, after which the Sultan gave me his reply." Then she enumerated the King's demands and said, "O my son, he indeed expecteth of thee an instant reply but I fancy that we have no answer for him."

When Aladdin heard these words he laughed and said, "O my mother, thou affirmeth that we have no answer and thou deemest the case difficult exceedingly; but compose thy thoughts and arise and bring me somewhat we may eat; and, after we have dined, an the Compassionate be willing, thou shalt see my reply. Also the Sultan thinketh like thyself that he hath demanded a prodigious dower in order to divert me from his daughter, whereas the fact is that he hath required of me a matter far less than I expected. But do thou fare forth at once and purchase the provision and leave me to procure thee a reply."

So she went out to fetch her needful from the Bazar and Aladdin retired to his chamber and taking the Lamp rubbed it, when forthright appeared to him its Slave and said, "Ask, O my lord, whatso thou wantest."

The other replied, "I have demanded of the Sultan his daughter to wife and he hath required of me forty bowls of purest gold each weighing ten pounds and all to be filled with gems such as we find in the Gardens of the Hoard; furthermore, that they be borne on the heads of as many white handmaids, each attended by her black eunuch-slave, also forty in full rate; so I desire that thou bring all these into my presence."

"Hearkening and obeying, O my lord," quoth the Slave and, disappearing for the space of an hour or so, presently returned bringing the platters and jewels, handmaids and eunuchs; then, setting them before him the Marid cried, "This be what thou demandest of me: declare now an thou want any matter or service other than this."

Aladdin rejoined, "I have need of naught else; but, an I do, I will summon thee and let thee know."

The Slave now disappeared and, after a little while, Aladdin's mother returned home and, on entering the house, saw the blacks and the handmaids. Hereat she wondered and exclaimed, "All this proceedeth from the Lamp which Allah perpetuate to my son!"

But ere she doffed her mantilla Aladdin said to her, "O my mother, this be thy time before the Sultan enter his Serraglio-palace; do thou carry to him what he required and wend thou with it at once, so may he know that I avail to supply all he wanteth and yet more; also that he is beguiled by his Grand Wazir and the twain imagined vainly that they would baffle me."

Then he arose forthright and opened the house-door, when the handmaids and blackamoors paced forth in pairs, each girl with her eunuch beside her, until they crowded the quarter, Aladdin's mother foregoing them. And when the folk of that ward sighted such mighty fine sight and marvellous spectacle, all stood at gaze and they considered the forms and figures of the handmaids marvelling at their beauty and loveliness, for each and every wore robes inwrought with gold and studded with jewels, no dress being worth less than a thousand dinars. They stared as intently at the bowls and albeit these were covered with pieces of brocade, also orfrayed and dubbed with precious stones, yet the sheen outshot from them dulled the shine of sun.

The folk and especially the people of the quarter stood a marvelling at this singular scene. Then Aladdin's mother walked forwards and all the handmaids and eunuchs paced behind her in the best of ordinance and disposition, and the citizens gathered to gaze at the beauty of the damsels, glorifying God the Most Great, until the train reached the palace and entered it accompanied by the tailor's widow. Now when the Aghas and Chamberlains and Army-officers beheld them, all were seized with surprise, notably by seeing the handmaids who each and every would ravish the reason of an anchorite. And albeit the royal Chamberlains and Officials were men of family, the sons of Grandees and Emirs, yet they could not but especially wonder at the costly dresses of the girls and the platters borne upon their heads; nor could they gaze at them open-eyed by reason of the exceeding brilliance and radiance. Then the Nabobs went in and reported to the King who forthright bade admit them to the presence chamber, and Aladdin's mother went in with them. When they stood before the Sultan, all saluted him with every sign of respect and worship and prayed for his glory and prosperity; then they set down from their heads the bowls at his feet and, having removed the brocade covers, rested with arms crossed behind them.

The Sultan wondered with exceeding wonder and was distraught by the beauty of the handmaids and their loveliness which passed praise; and his wits were wildered when he considered the golden bowls brimful of gems which captured man's vision, and he was perplexed at the marvel until he became, like the dumb, unable to utter a syllable for the excess of his wonder. Also his sense was stupefied the more when he bethought him that within a hour or so all these treasures had been collected. Presently he commended the slave-girls to enter, with what loads they bore, the dower of the Princess; and, when they had done his bidding Aladdin's mother came forward and said to the Sultan, "O my lord, this be not much wherewith to honour the Lady Badr al-Budur, for that she meriteth these things multiplied times manifold."

Hereat the Sovran turned to the Minister and asked, "What sayest thou, O Wazir? is not he who could produce such wealth in a time so brief, is he not, I say, worthy to become the Sultan's son-in-law and take the King's daughter to wife?"

Then the Minister (although he marvelled at these riches even more than did the Sultan), whose envy was killing him and growing greater hour by hour, seeing his liege lord satisfied with the moneys and the dower and yet being unable to fight against fact, made answer, "'Tis not worthy of her." Withal he fell to devising a device against the King that he might withhold the Lady Badr al-Budur from Aladdin and accordingly he continued, "O my liege, the treasures of the universe all of them are not worth a nail-paring of thy daughter: indeed thy Highness hath prized these things overmuch in comparison with her."

When the King heard the words of his Grand Wazir, he knew that the speech was prompted by excess of envy; so turning to the mother of Aladdin he said, "O woman, go to thy son and tell him that I have accepted of him the dower and stand to my bargain, and that my daughter be his bride and he my son-in-law: furthermore, bid him at once make act of presence that I may become familiar with him: he shall see naught from me save all honour and consideration, and this night shall be the beginning of the marriage-festivities. Only, as I said to thee, let him come to me and tarry not."

Thereupon Aladdin's mother returned home with the speed of the stormwinds that she might hasten her utmost to congratulate her son; and she flew with joy at the thought that her boy was about to become son-in-law to the Sultan. After her departure the King dismissed the Divan and, entering the palace of the Princess, bade them bring the bowls and the handmaids before him and before her, that she also might inspect them. But when the Lady Badr al-Budur considered the jewels, she waxed distraught and cried, "Meseemeth that in the treasuries of the world there be not found one jewel rivalling these jewels." Then she looked at the handmaids and marvelled at their beauty and loveliness, and knew that all this came from her new bridegroom who had sent them in her service. So she was gladdened, albeit she had been grieved and saddened on account of her former husband, the Wazir's son, and she rejoiced with exceeding joy when she gazed upon the damsels and their charms; nor was her sire, the Sultan, less pleased and inspirited when he saw his daughter relieved of all her mourning and melancholy and his own vanished at the sight of her enjoyment.

Then he asked her, "O my daughter, do these things divert thee? Indeed I deem that this suitor of thine be more suitable to thee than the son of the Wazir; and right soon (Inshallah!), O my daughter, shalt thou have fuller joy with him."

Such was the case with the King; but as regards Aladdin, as soon as he saw his mother entering the house with face laughing for stress of joy he rejoiced at the sign of glad tidings and cried, "To Allah alone be lauds! Perfected is all I desired."

Rejoined his mother, "Be gladdened at my good news, O my son, and hearten thy heart and cool thine eyes for the winning of thy wish. The Sultan hath accepted thine offering, I mean the moneys and the dower of the Lady Badr al-Budur, who is now thine affianced bride; and, this very night, O my child, is your marriage and thy first visit to her; for the King, that he might assure me of his word, hath proclaimed to the world thou art his son-in-law and promised this night to be the night of going in. But he also said to me, 'Let thy son come hither forthright that I may become familiar with him and receive him with all honour and worship.' And now here am I, O my son, at the end of my labours; happen whatso may happen the rest is upon thy shoulders."

Thereupon Aladdin arose and kissed his mother's hand and thanked her, enhancing her kindly service: then he left her and entering his chamber took the Lamp and rubbed it when, lo and behold! its Slave appeared and cried, "Adsum! Ask whatso thou wantest."

The young man replied, "'tis my desire that thou take me to a Hammam whose like is not in the world; then, fetch me a dress so costly and kingly that no royalty ever owned its fellow."

The Marid replied, "I hear and I obey," and carried him to Baths such as were never seen by the Kings of the Chosroes, for the building was all of alabaster and carnelian and it contained marvellous limnings which captured the sight; and the great hall was studded with precious stones. Not a soul was therein but, when Aladdin entered, one of the Jann in human shape washed him and bathed him to the best of his desire.

Aladdin, after having been washed and bathed, left the Baths and went into the great hall where he found that his old dress had been removed and replaced by a suit of the most precious and princely. Then he was served with sherbets and ambergris'd coffee and, after drinking, he arose and a party of black slaves came forwards and clad him in the costliest of clothing, then perfumed and fumigated him. It is known that Aladdin was the son of a tailor, a pauper, yet now would none deem him to be such; nay, all would say, "This be the greatest that is of the progeny of the Kings: praise be to Him who changeth and who is not changed!"

Presently came the Jinni and lifting him up bore him to his home and asked, "O my lord, tell me hast thou aught of need?"

He answered, "Yes, 'tis my desire that thou bring me eight and forty Mamelukes, of whom two dozen shall forego me and the rest follow me, the whole number with their war-chargers and clothing and accoutrements; and all upon them and their steeds must be of naught save of highest worth and the costliest, such as may not be found in treasuries of the Kings. Then fetch me a stallion fit for the riding of the Chosroes and let his furniture, all thereof, be of gold crusted with the finest gems: fetch me also eight and forty thousand dinars that each white slave may carry a thousand gold pieces. 'Tis now my intent to fare to the Sultan, so delay thou not, for that without all these requisites whereof I bespake thee I may not visit him. Moreover set before me a dozen slave-girls unique in beauty and dight with the most magnificent dresses, that they wend with my mother to the royal palace; and let every handmaid be robed in raiment that befitteth Queen's wearing."

The Slave replied, "To hear is to obey"; and, disappearing for an eye-twinkling, brought all he was bidden bring and led by hand a stallion whose rival was not amongst the Arabian Arabs, and its saddle cloth was of splendid brocade gold-inwrought.

Thereupon, without stay or delay, Aladdin sent for his mother and gave her the garments she should wear and committed to her charge the twelve slave-girls forming her suite to the palace. Then he sent one of the Mamelukes, whom the Jinni had brought, to see if the Sultan had left the Serraglio or not. The white slave went forth lighter than the lightning and returning in like haste, said, "O my lord, the Sultan awaiteth thee!"

Hereat Aladdin arose and took horse, his Mamelukes riding a-van and a-rear of him, and they were such that all must cry, "Laud to the Lord who created them and clothed them with such beauty and loveliness." And they scattered gold amongst the crowd in front of their master who surpassed them all in comeliness and seemlihead nor needst thou ask concerning the sons of the Kings—praise be to the Bountiful, the Eternal! All this was of the virtues of the Wonderful Lamp, which, whoso possessed, him it gifted with fairest favour and finest figure, with wealth and with wisdom. The folk admired Aladdin's liberality and exceeding generosity and all were distraught seeing his charms and elegance, his gravity and his good manners, they glorified the Creator for this noble creation, they blessed him each and every and, albeit they knew him for the son of Such-an-one, the tailor, yet no man envied him; nay, all owned that he deserved his great good fortune. The people were bewildered at Aladdin and his liberality and generosity; and all blessed and prayed for him, high and low, as he rode palace-wards with the Mamelukes before and behind him, scattering gold upon the heads of the folk.

Now the Sultan had assembled the Lords of the land and, informing them of the promise he had passed to Aladdin, touching the marriage of his daughter, had bidden them await his approach and then go forth, one and all, to meet him and greet him. Hereupon the Emirs and Wazirs, the Chamberlains, the Nabobs and the Army-officers took their stations expecting him at the palace gate. Aladdin would fain have dismounted at the outer entrance; but one of the Nobles, whom the King had deputed for such duty, approached him and said, "O my lord, 'tis the Royal Command that thou enter riding thy steed nor dismount except at the Divan-door."

Then they all forewent him in a body and conducted him to the appointed place where they crowded about him, these to hold his stirrup and those supporting him on either side whilst others took him by the hands and helped him dismount; after which all the Emirs and Nobles preceded him into the Divan and led him close up to the royal throne. Thereupon the Sultan came down forthright from his seat of estate and, forbidding him to buss the carpet, embraced and kissed and seated him to the right of and beside himself. Aladdin did whatso is suitable, in the case of the Kings, of salutation and offering of blessings, and said, "O our lord the Sultan, indeed the generosity of thy Highness demanded that thou deign vouchsafe to me the hand of thy daughter, the Lady Badr al-Budur, albeit I undeserve the greatness of such gift, I being but the humblest of thy slaves I pray Allah grant thee prosperity and perpetuance; but in very sooth, O King, my tongue is helpless to thank thee for the fullness of the favour, passing all measure, which thou hast bestowed upon me. And I hope of thy Highness that thou wilt give me a piece of ground fitted for a pavilion which shall besit thy daughter, the Lady Badr al-Budur."

The Sultan was struck with admiration when he saw Aladdin in his princely suit and looked upon him and considered his beauty and loveliness, and noted the Mamelukes standing to serve him in their comeliness and seemlihead; and still his marvel grew when the mother of Aladdin approached him in costly raiment and sumptuous, clad as though she were a Queen, and when he gazed upon the twelve handmaids standing before her with crossed arms and with all worship and reverence doing her service. He also considered the eloquence of Aladdin and his delicacy of speech and he was astounded thereat, he and all his who were present at the levee. Thereupon fire was kindled in the Grand Wazir's heart for envy of Aladdin until he was like to die: and it was worse when the Sultan, after hearing the youth's succession of prayers and seeing his high dignity of demeanour, respectful withal, and his eloquence and elegance of language, clasped him to his bosom and kissed him and cried, "Alas, O my son, that I have not enjoyed thy converse before this day!"

When the Sultan beheld Aladdin after such fashion, he rejoiced in him with mighty great joy and straightway bade the music and the bands strike up; then he arose and, taking the youth led him into the palace where supper had been prepared and the Eunuchs at once laid the tables. So the Sovran sat down and seated his son-in-law on his right side and the Wazirs and high officials and Lords of the land took places each according to his degree, whereupon the bands played and a mighty fine marriage-feast was dispread in the palace. The King now applied himself to making friendship with Aladdin and conversed with the youth, who answered him with all courtesy and eloquence, as though he had been bred in the palaces of the kings or he had lived with them his daily life. And the more the talk was prolonged between them, the more did the Sultan's pleasure and delight increase, hearing his son-in-law's readiness of reply and his sweet flow of language.

But after they had eaten and drunken and the trays were removed, the King bade summon the Kazis and witnesses who presently attended and knitted the knot and wrote out the contract-writ between Aladdin and the Lady Badr al-Budur. And presently the bridegroom arose and would have fared forth, when his father-in-law withheld him and asked, "Whither away, O my child? The bride-fetes have begun and the marriage is made and the tie is tied and the writ is written."

He replied, "O my lord the King, 'tis my desire to edify, for the Lady Badr al-Budur, a pavilion befitting her station and high degree, nor can I visit her before so doing. But, Inshallah! the building shall be finished within the shortest time, by the utmost endeavor of thy slave and by the kindly regard of thy Highness, and, although I do (yes indeed!) long to enjoy the society of the Lady Badr al-Budur, yet 'tis incumbent on me first to serve her and it becometh me to set about the work forthright."

"Look around thee, O my son," replied the Sultan, "for what ground thou deemest suitable to thy design and do thou take all things into thy hands; but I deem the best for thee will be yonder broad plain facing my palace; and, if it please the build thy pavilion thereupon."

"And this," answered Aladdin "is the sum of my wishes that I may be nearhand to thy Highness." So saying he farewelled the King and took horse, with his Mamelukes riding before him and behind him, and all the world blessed him and cried, "By Allah he is deserving," until such time as he reached his home.

Then he alighted from his stallion and repairing to his chamber, rubbed the Lamp and behold, the Slave stood before him and said, "Ask, O my lord whatso thou wantest;" and Aladdin rejoined, "I require thee of a service grave and important which thou must do for me, and 'tis that thou build me with all urgency a pavilion fronting the palace of the Sultan; and it must be a marvel for it shall be provided with every requisite, such as royal furniture and so forth."

The Slave replied, "To hear is to obey." The Slave evanished and, before the next dawn brake, returned to Aladdin and said, "O my lord, the pavilion is finished to the fullest of thy fancy; and, if thou wouldst inspect it, arise forthright and fare with me."

Accordingly, he rose up and the Slave carried him in the space of an eye-glance to the pavilion which, when Aladdin looked upon it struck him with surprise at such building, all its stones being of jasper and alabaster, Sumaki marble and mosaic-work. Then the Slave led him into the treasury which was full of all manner of gold and silver and costly gems, not to be counted or computed, priced or estimated. Thence to another place, where Aladdin saw all requisites for the tables, plates and dishes, spoons and ladles, basins and covers, cups and tasses, the whole of precious metal: thence to the kitchen, where they found the kitcheners provided with their needs and cooking batteries, likewise golden and silvern; thence to a warehouse piled up with chests full-packed of royal raiment, stuffs that captured the reason, such as gold-wrought brocades from India and China and kimcobs or orfrayed cloths; thence to many apartments replete with appointments which beggar description; thence to the stables containing coursers whose like was not to be met with amongst the kings of the universe; and, lastly, they went to the harness-rooms all hung with housings, costly saddles and other furniture, everywhere studded with pearls and precious stones. And all this was the work of one night.

Aladdin was wonder-struck and astounded by that magnificent display of wealth which not even the mightiest monarch on earth could produce; and more so to see his pavilion fully provided with eunuchs and handmaids whose beauty would seduce a saint. Yet the prime marvel of the pavilion was an upper kiosque or belvedere of four-and-twenty windows all made of emeralds and rubies and other gems; and one window remained unfinished at the requirement of Aladdin that the Sultan might prove him impotent to complete it.

When the youth had inspected the whole edifice, he was pleased and gladdened exceedingly: then, turning to the Slave he said, "I require of thee still one thing which is yet wanting and whereof I had forgotten to tell thee."

"Ask, O my lord, thy want," quoth the Servitor; and quoth the other, "demand of thee a carpet of the primest brocade all gold-inwrought which, when unrolled and outstretched, shall extend hence to the Sultan's palace in order that the Lady Badr al-Budur may, when coming hither, pace upon it and not tread common earth." The Slave departed for a short while and said on his return, "O my lord verily that which thou demandest is here." Then he took him and showed him a carpet which wildered the wits, and it extended from palace to pavilion; and after this the Servitor bore off Aladdin and set him down in his own home.

The Slave, after displaying the Carpet to Aladdin, bore him home. Now day was brightening so the Sultan rose from his sleep and throwing open the casement looked out and espied, opposite his palace, a palatial pavilion ready edified. Thereupon he fell to rubbing his eyes and opening them their widest and considering the scene, and he soon was certified that the new edifice was mighty fine and grand enough to bewilder the wits. Moreover, with amazement as great he saw the carpet dispread between palace and pavilion: like their lord also the royal door-keepers and the household, one and all, were dazed and amazed at the spectacle.

Meanwhile the Wazir came in and, as he entered, espied the newly builded pavilion and the carpet, whereat he also wondered; and, when he went in to the Sultan the twain fell to talking on this marvellous matter with great surprise at a sight which distracted the gazer and attracted the heart. They said finally, "In very truth, of this pavilion we deem that none of the royalties could build its fellow"; and the King, turning to the Minister, asked him, "Hast thou seen now that Aladdin is worthy to be the husband of the Princess my daughter? Hast thou looked upon and considered this right royal building, this magnificence of opulence, which thought of man can not contain?"

But the Wazir in his envy of Aladdin replied, "O King of the Age, indeed this foundation and this building and this opulence may not be save by means of magic nor can any man in the world, be he the richest in good or the greatest in governance, avail to found and finish in a single night such edifice as this."

The Sultan rejoined, "I am surprised to see in thee how thou dost continually harp on evil opinion of Aladdin; but I hold that 'tis caused by thine envy and jealousy. Thou wast present when I gave him the ground at his own prayer for a place whereon he might build a pavilion wherein to lodge my daughter, and I myself favoured him with a site for the same and that too before thy very face. But however that be, shall one who could send me as dower for the Princess such store of such stones whereof the kings never obtained even a few, shall he, I say, be unable to edify an edifice like this?"

When the Wazir heard the Sultan's words, he knew that his lord loved Aladdin exceedingly; so his envy and malice increased; only, as he could do nothing against the youth, he sat silent and impotent to return a reply. But Aladdin seeing that it was broad day, and the appointed time had come for his repairing to the palace (where his wedding was being celebrated and the Emirs and Wazirs and Grandees were gathered together about the Sultan to be present at the ceremony), arose and rubbed the Lamp, and when its Slave appeared and said, "O my lord, ask whatso thou wantest, for I stand before thee and at thy service," said he, "I mean forthright to seek the palace, this day being my wedding-festival and I want thee to supply me with ten thousand dinars."

The Slave evanished for an eye-twinkling and returned bringing the moneys, when Aladdin took horse with his Mamelukes a-van and a-rear and passed on his way, scattering as he went gold pieces upon the lieges until all were fondly affected towards him and his dignity was enhanced. But when he drew near the palace, and the Emirs and Aghas and Army-officers who were standing to await him noted his approach, they hastened straightway to the King and gave him the tidings thereof; whereupon the Sultan rose and met his son-in-law and after embracing and kissing him, led him still holding his hand into his own apartment where he sat down and seated him by his right side.

The city was all decorated and music rang through the palace and the singers sang until the King bade bring the noon-meal, when the eunuchs and Mamelukes hastened to spread the tables and trays which are such as are served to the kings. Then the Sultan and Aladdin and the Lords of the land and the Grandees of the realm took their seats and ate and drank until they were satisfied. And it was a mighty fine wedding in city and palace and the high nobles all rejoiced therein and the commons of the kingdom were equally gladdened, while the Governors of provinces and Nabobs of districts flocked from far regions to witness Aladdin's marriage and its processions and festivities. The Sultan also marvelled in his mind to look at Aladdin's mother and recall to mind how she was wont to visit him in pauper plight, while her son could command all this opulence and magnificence. And when the spectators, who crowded the royal palace to enjoy the wedding-feasts, looked upon Aladdin's pavilion and the beauties of the building, they were seized with an immense surprise that so vast an edifice as this could be reared on high during a single night; and they blessed the youth and cried, "Allah gladden him! By Allah, he deserveth all this! Allah bless his days!"

When dinner was done, Aladdin rose and, farewelling the Sultan, took horse with his Mamelukes and rode to his own pavilion that he might prepare to receive therein his bride, the Lady Badr al-Budur. And as he passed, all the folk shouted their good wishes with one voice and their words were, "Allah gladden thee! Allah increase thy glory. Allah grant thee length of life!" while immense crowds of people gathered to swell the marriage procession and they conducted him to his new home, he showering gold upon them during the whole time.

When he reached his pavilion, he dismounted and walked in and sat him down on the divan, whilst his Mamelukes stood before him with arms afolded; also after a short delay they brought him sherbets and, when these were drunk, he ordered his white slaves and handmaids and eunuchs and all who were in the pavilion to make ready for meeting the Lady Badr al-Budur. Moreover, as soon as mid-afternoon came and the air had cooled and the great heat of the sun was abated, the Sultan bade his Army-officers and Emirs and Wazirs go down into the Maydan plain whither he likewise rode. And Aladdin also took horse with his Mamelukes, he mounting a stallion whose like was not among the steeds of the Arab al-Arba, and he showed his horsemanship in the hippodrome and so played with the Jarid that none could withstand him, while his bride sat gazing upon him from the latticed balcony of her bower and, seeing in him such beauty and cavalarice, she fell headlong in love of him and was like to fly for joy. And after they had ringed their horses on the Maydan and each had displayed whatso he could of horsemanship, Aladdin proving himself the best man of all, they rode in a body to the Sultan's palace and the youth also returned to his own pavilion.

But when it was evening, the Wazirs and Nobles took the bridegroom and, falling in, escorted him to the royal Hammam (known as the Sultani), when he was bathed and perfumed. As soon as he came out he donned a dress more magnificent than the former and took horse with the Emirs and the soldier-officers riding before him and forming a grand cortege, wherein four of the Wazirs bore naked swords round about him. All the citizens and the strangers and the troops marched before him in ordered throng carrying wax-candles and kettle drums and pipes and other instruments of mirth and merriment, until they conducted him to his pavilion. Here he alighted and walking in took his seat and seated the Wazirs and Emirs who had escorted him, and the Mamelukes brought sherbets and sugared drinks, which they also passed to the people who had followed in his train. It was a world of folk whose tale might not be told; withal Aladdin bade his Mamelukes stand without the pavilion-doors and shower gold upon the crowd.

When the Sultan returned from the Maydan-plain to his palace he ordered the household, men as well as women, straightway to form a cavalcade for his daughter, with all ceremony, and bear her to her bridegroom's pavilion. So the nobles and soldier-officers, who had followed and escorted the bridegroom, at once mounted, and the handmaids and eunuchs went forth with wax-candles and made a mighty fine procession for the Lady Badr al-Budur and they paced on preceding her till they entered the pavilion of Aladdin whose mother walked beside the bride. In front of the Princess also fared the wives of the Wazirs and Emirs, Grandees and Notables, and in attendance on her were the eight and forty slave-girls presented to her aforetime by her bridegroom, each hending in hand a huge cierge scented with camphor and ambergris and set in a candlestick of gem-studded gold. And reaching Aladdin's pavilion they led her to her bower in the upper storey and changed her robes and enthroned her; then, as soon as the displaying was ended, they accompanied her to Aladdin's apartments and presently he paid her the first visit.

Now his mother was with the bride and, when the bridegroom came up and did off her veil, the ancient dame fell to considering the beauty of the Princess and her loveliness; and she looked around at the pavilion which was all litten up by gold and gems besides the manifold candelabra of precious metals encrusted with emeralds and jacinths; so she said in her mind, "Once upon a time I thought the Sultan's palace mighty fine, but this pavilion is a thing apart; nor do I deem that any of the greatest Kings of Chosroes attained in his day to aught like thereof; also am I certified that all the world could not build anything evening it." Nor less did the lady Badr al-Budur fall to gazing at the pavilion and marvelling for its magnificence.

Then the tables were spread and they all ate and drank and were gladdened; after which fourscore damsels came before them each holding in hand an instrument of mirth and merriment; then they deftly moved their fingertips and touched the strings smiting them into song, most musical, most melancholy, till they rent the hearts of the hearers. Hereat the Princess increased in marvel and quoth she to herself, "In all my life ne'er heard I songs like these," till she forsook food, the better to listen. And at last Aladdin poured out for her wine and passed it to her with his own hand; so great joy and jubilee went round amongst them and it was a notable night, such an one as Iskander, Lord of the Two Horns, had never spent in his time.

When they had finished eating and drinking and the tables were removed from before them, Aladdin arose and went in to his bride. As soon as morning morrowed he left his bed and the treasurer brought him a costly suit and a mighty fine, of the most sumptuous robes worn by the kings. Then, after drinking coffee devoured with ambergris, he ordered the horses be saddled and, mounting with his Mamelukes before and behind him, rode to the Sultan's palace and on his entering its court the eunuchs went in and reported his coming to their lord.

When the Sultan heard of Aladdin's approach, he rose up forthright to receive him and embraced and kissed him as though he were his own son: then, seating him on his right, he blessed and prayed for him, as did the Wazirs and Emirs, the Lords of the land and the Grandees of the realm. Presently, the King commanded bring the morning-meal which the attendants served up and all broke their fast together, and when they had eaten and drunken their sufficiency and the tables were removed by the eunuchs, Aladdin turned to the Sultan and said, "O my lord, would thy Highness deign honour me this day at dinner, in the house of the Lady Badr al-Budur thy beloved daughter, and come accompanied by all thy Ministers and Grandees of the reign?"

The King replied (and he was delighted with his son-in-law), "Thou art surpassing in liberality, O my son!" Then he gave orders to all invited and rode forth with them (Aladdin also riding beside him) till they reached the pavilion and as he entered it and considered its construction, its architecture and its stonery, all jasper and carnelian, his sight was dazed and his wits were amazed at such grandeur and magnificence of opulence. Then turning to the Minister he thus addressed him, "What

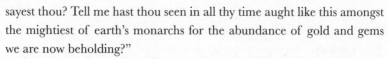

sayest thou? Tell me hast thou seen in all thy time aught like this amongst the mightiest of earth's monarchs for the abundance of gold and gems we are now beholding?"

The Grand Wazir replied, "O my lord the King, this be a feat which cannot be accomplished by might of monarch amongst Adam's sons; nor could the collected peoples of the universal world build a palace like unto this; nay, even builders could not be found to make aught resembling it, save (as I said to thy Highness) by force of sorcery."

These words certified the King that his Minister spake not except in envy end jealousy of Aladdin, and would stablish in the royal mind that all this splendour was not made of man but by means of magic and with the aid of the Black Art. So quoth he to him, "Suffice thee so much, O Wazir: thou hast none other word to speak and well I know what cause urgeth thee to say this say."

Then Aladdin preceded the Sultan till he conducted him to the upper Kiosque where he saw its skylights, windows and latticed casements and jalousies wholly made of emeralds and rubies and other costly gems; whereat his mind was perplexed and his wits were bewildered and his thoughts were distraught. Presently he took to strolling round the Kiosque and solacing himself with these sights which captured the vision, till he chanced to cast a glance at the window which Aladdin by design had left unwrought and not finished like the rest; and, when he noted its lack of completion, he cried, "Woe and well away for thee, O window, because of thine imperfection"; and, turning to his Minister he asked, "Knowest thou the reason of leaving incomplete this window and its framework?"

The Wazir said to the Sultan, "O my lord, I conceive that the want of finish in this window resulteth from thy Highness having pushed on Aladdin's marriage and he lacked the leisure to complete it."

Now at that time, Aladdin had gone in to his bride, the Lady Badr al-Budur, to inform her of her father's presence; and, when he returned, the King asked him, "O my son what is the reason why the window of this Kiosque was not made perfect?"

"O King of the Age, seeing the suddenness of my wedding," answered he, "I failed to find artists for finishing it."

Quoth the Sultan, "I have a mind to complete it myself;" and quoth Aladdin, "Allah perpetuate thy glory, O thou the King; so shall thy memory endure in thy daughter's pavilion."

The Sultan forthright bade summon jewellers and goldsmiths and ordered them be supplied from the treasury with all their needs of gold

and gems and noble ores; and, when they were gathered together he commanded them to complete the work still wanting in the Kiosque-window. Meanwhile the Princess came forth to meet her sire the Sultan who noticed, as she drew near, her smiling face; so he embraced her and kissed her, then led her to the pavilion and all entered in a body.

Now this was the time of the noon-day meal and one table had been spread for the Sovran, his daughter and his son-in-law and a second for the Wazirs, the Lords of the land, the Grandees of the realm, the Chief Officers of the host, the Chamberlains and the Nabobs. The King took seat between the Princess and her husband; and, when he put forth his hand to the food and tasted it, he was struck with surprise by the flavour of the dishes and their savoury and sumptuous cooking. Moreover, there stood before him the fourscore damsels each and every saying to the full moon, "Rise that I may seat myself in thy stead!"

All held instruments of mirth and merriment and they tuned the same and deftly moved their fingertips and smote the strings into song most musical, most melodious, which expanded the mourner's heart. Hereby the Sultan was gladdened and time was good to him and for high enjoyment he exclaimed, "In very sooth the thing is beyond the compass of King and Kaysar." Then they fell to eating and drinking; and the cup went round until they had drunken enough, when sweetmeats and fruits of sorts and other such edibles were served, the dessert being laid out in a different salon whither they removed and enjoyed of these pleasures their sufficiency.

Presently the Sultan arose that he might see if the produce of his jewellers and goldsmiths favoured that of the pavilion; so he went upstairs to them and inspected their work and how they had wrought; but he noted a mighty great difference and his men were far from being able to make anything like the rest of Aladdin's pavilion.

After the King had inspected the work of his jewellers and goldsmiths, they informed him how all the gems stored in the Lesser Treasury had been brought to them and used by them but that the whole had proved insufficient; wherefor he bade open the Greater Treasury and gave the workmen all they wanted of him. Moreover he allowed them, an it sufficed not, to take the jewels wherewith Aladdin had gifted him. They carried off the whole and pushed on their labours but they found the gems fail them, albeit had they not yet finished half the part wanting to the Kiosque-window. Herewith the King commended them to seize all the precious stones owned by the Wazirs and Grandees of the realm; but, although they did his bidding, the supply still fell short of their requirements.

Next morning Aladdin arose to look at the jeweller's work and remarked
that they had not finished a moiety of what was wanting to the Kiosque-window: so he at once ordered them to undo all they had done and restore the
jewels to their owners. Accordingly, they pulled out the precious stones and
sent the Sultan's to the Sultan and the Wazirs' to the Wazirs. Then the jewellers
went to the King and told him of what Aladdin had bidden; so he asked them,
"What said he to you, and what was his reason and wherefore was he not content that the window be finished and why did he undo the work ye wrought?"

They answered, "O our lord, we know not at all, but he bade us deface
whatso we had done."

Hereupon the Sultan at once called for his horse, and mounting, took
the way pavilion-wards, when Aladdin, after dismissing the goldsmiths
and jewellers had retired into his closet and had rubbed the Lamp. Hereat
straightway its Servitor appeared to him and said, "Ask whatso thou
wantest: thy Slave is between thy hands"; and said Aladdin, "'tis my desire
that thou finish the window which was left unfinished."

The Marid replied, "On my head be it and also upon mine eyes!" then
he vanished and after a little while returned saying, "O my lord, verily that
thou commandedst me do is completed."

So Aladdin went upstairs to the Kiosque and found the whole window
in wholly finished state; and, whilst he was still considering it, behold, a
castrato came in to him and said, "O my lord, the Sultan hath ridden forth
to visit thee and is passing through the pavilion-gate." So Aladdin at once
went down and received his father-in-law.

The Sultan, on sighting his son-in-law, cried to him, "Wherefore, O my
child, hast thou wrought on this wise and sufferedst not the jewellers to complete the Kiosque-window leaving in the pavilion an unfinished place?"

Aladdin replied "O King of the Age, I left it not imperfect save for a
design of mine own; nor was I incapable of perfecting it nor could I purpose
that thy Highness should honour me with visiting a pavilion wherein was
aught of deficiency. And, that thou mayest know I am not unable to make
it perfect, let thy Highness deign walk upstairs with me and see if anything
remain to be done therewith or not."

So the Sultan went up with him and, entering the Kiosque, fell to
looking right and left, but he saw no default at all in any of the windows; nay,
he noted that all were perfect. So he marvelled at the sight and embraced
Aladdin and kissed him, saying, "O my son, what be this singular feat?
Thou canst work in a single night what in months the jewellers could not
do. By Allah, I deem thou hast nor brother nor rival in this world."

Quoth Aladdin, "Allah prolong thy life and preserve thee to perpetuity! thy slave deserveth not this encomium"; and quoth the King, "By Allah, O my child, thou meritest all praise for a feat whereof all the artists of the world were incapable." Then the Sultan came down and entered the apartments of his daughter the Lady Badr al-Budur, to take rest beside her, and he saw her joyous exceedingly at the glory and grandeur wherein she was; then, after reposing awhile he returned to his palace.

Now Aladdin was wont every day to thread the city-streets with his Mamelukes riding a-van and a-rear of him showering rightwards and leftwards gold upon the folk; and all the world, stranger and neighbour, far and near, were fulfilled of his love for the excess of his liberality and generosity. Moreover he increased the pensions of the poor Religious and the paupers and he would distribute alms to them with his own hand; by which good deed, he won high renown throughout the realm and most of the Lords of the land and Emirs would eat at his table; and men swore not at all save by his precious life. Nor did he leave faring to the chase and the Maydan-plain and the riding of horses and playing at javelin-play in presence of the Sultan; and, whenever the Lady Badr al-Budur beheld him disporting himself on the backs of steeds, she loved him much the more, and thought to herself that Allah had wrought her abundant good by causing to happen whatso happened with the son of the Wazir and by preserving her virginity intact for her true bridegroom, Aladdin.

Aladdin won for himself day by day a fairer fame and a rarer report, while affection for him increased in the hearts of all the lieges and he waxed greater in the eyes of men. Moreover it chanced that in those days certain enemies took horse and attacked the Sultan, who armed and accoutred an army to repel them and made Aladdin commander thereof. So he marched with his men nor ceased marching until he drew near the foe whose forces were exceeding many; and, presently, when the action began he bared his brand and charged home upon the enemy. Then battle and slaughter befel and violent was the hurry-burly, but at last Aladdin broke the hostile host and put all to flight, slaying the best part of them and pillaging their coin and cattle, property and possessions; and he despoiled them of spoils that could not be counted nor computed. Then he returned victorious after a noble victory and entered the capital which had decorated herself in his honour, of her delight in him; and the Sultan went forth to meet him and giving him joy embraced him and kissed him; and throughout the kingdom was held high festival with great joy and gladness.

Presently, the Sovran and his son-in-law repaired to the pavilion where they were met by the Princess Badr al-Budur who rejoiced in her husband and, after kissing him between the eyes, led him to her apartments. After a time the Sultan also came and they sat down while the slave-girls brought them sherbets and confections which they ate and drank. Then the Sultan commanded that the whole kingdom be decorated for the triumph of his son-in-law and his victory over the invader; and the subjects and soldiery and all the people knew only Allah in heaven and Aladdin on earth; for that their love, won by his liberality, was increased by his noble horsemanship and his successful battling for the country and putting to flight the foe.

Such then was the high fortune of Aladdin; but as regards the Maghrabi, the Magician, after returning to his native country, he passed all this space of time in bewailing what he had borne of toil and travail to win the Lamp and mostly that his trouble had gone vain and that the morsel when almost touching his lips had flown from his grasp. He pondered all this and mourned and reviled Aladdin for the excess of his rage against him and at times he would exclaim, "For this bastard's death underground I am well satisfied and hope only that some time or other I may obtain the Lamp, seeing how 'tis yet safe."

Now one day of the days he struck a table of sand and dotted down the figures and carefully considered their consequence; then he transferred them to paper that he might study them and make sure of Aladdin's destruction and the safety of the Lamp preserved beneath the earth. Presently, he firmly stablished the sequence of the figures, mothers as well as daughters, but still he saw not the Lamp. Thereupon rage overrode him and he made another trial to be assured of Aladdin's death; but he saw him not in the Enchanted Treasure. Hereat his wrath still grew, and it waxed greater when he ascertained that the youth had issued from underground and was now upon earth's surface alive and alert: furthermore, that he had become owner of the Lamp, for which he had himself endured such toil and travail and troubles as man may not bear save for so great an object.

Accordingly quoth he to himself, "I have suffered sore pains and penalties which none else could have endured for the Lamp's sake in order that other than I may carry it off; and this Accursed hath taken it without difficulty. And who knoweth an he wot the virtues of the Lamp, than whose owner none in the world should be wealthier?"

The Maghrabi, the Magician, having considered and ascertained that Aladdin had escaped from the souterrain and had gotten the boon of the Lamp, said to himself, "There is no help but that I work for his destruction." He then struck another geomantic table and examining the figures saw that the lad had won for himself unmeasurable riches and had wedded the daughter of his King; so of his envy and jealousy he was fired with the flame of wrath; and, rising without let or stay, he equipped himself and set forth for China-land, where he arrived in due season.

Now when he had reached the King's capital wherein was Aladdin, he alighted at one of the Khans; and, when he had rested from the weariness of wayfare, he donned his dress and went down to wander about the streets, where he never passed a group without hearing them prate about the pavilion and its grandeur and vaunt the beauty of Aladdin and his lonesomeness, his liberality and generosity, his fine manners and his good morals. Presently he entered an establishment wherein men were drinking a certain warm beverage; and, going up to one of those who were loud in their lauds, he said to him, "O fair youth, who may be the man ye describe and commend?"

"Apparently thou art a foreigner, O man," answered the other, "and thou comest from a far country; but, even this granted, how happeneth it thou hast not heard of the Emir Aladdin whose renown, I fancy, hath filled the universe and whose pavilion, known by report to far and near, is one of the Wonders of the World? How, then, never came to thine ears aught of this or the name of Aladdin (whose glory and enjoyment our Lord increase!) and his fame?"

The Moorman replied, "The sum of my wishes is to look upon this pavilion and, if thou wouldest do me a favour, prithee guide me thereunto, for I am a foreigner."

The man rejoined, "To hear is to obey"; and, foregoing him pointed out Aladdin's pavilion, whereupon the Maroccan fell to considering it and at once understood that it was the work of the Lamp. So he cried, "Ah! Ah! needs must I dig a pit for this Accursed, this son of a snip, who could not earn for himself even an evening meal: and, if the Fates abet me, I will assuredly destroy his life and send his mother back to spinning at her wheel, e'en as she was wont erewhiles to do." So saying, he returned to his caravanserai in a sore state of grief and melancholy and regret bred by his envy and hate of Aladdin.

When the Maghrabi, the Magician, reached his caravanserai, he took his astrological gear and geomantic table to discover where might be the Lamp; and he found that it was in the pavilion and not upon Aladdin's person. So he rejoiced thereat with joy exceeding and exclaimed, "Now indeed 'twill be an easy task to take the life of this Accursed and I see my way to getting the Lamp."

Then he went to a coppersmith and said to him, "Do thou make me a set of lamps and take from me their full price and more; only I would have thee hasten to finish them."

Replied the smith, "Hearing and obeying," and fell aworking to keep his word; and when they were ready the Moorman paid him what price he required; then taking them he carried them to the Khan and set them in a basket. Presently he began wandering about the highways and market-streets of the capital crying aloud, "Ho! who will exchange old lamps for new lamps?"

But when the folk heard him cry on this wise, they derided him and said, "Doubtless this man is Jinn-mad, for that he goeth about offering new for old;" and a world followed him and the children of the quarter caught him up from place to place, laughing at him the while, nor did he forbid them or care for their maltreatment. And he ceased not strolling about the streets till he came under Aladdin's pavilion, where he shouted with his loudest voice and the boys screamed at him, "A madman! A madman!"

Now Destiny had decreed that the Lady Badr al-Budur be sitting in her Kiosque whence she heard one crying like a crier, and the children bawling at him; only she understood not what was going on; so she gave orders to one of her slave-girls saying, "Go thou and see who 'tis that crieth and what be his cry?"

The girl fared forth and looked on when she beheld a man crying, "Ho! who will exchange old lamps for new lamps?" and the little ones pursuing and laughing at him; and as loudly laughed the Princess when this strange case was told to her.

Now Aladdin had carelessly left the Lamp in his pavilion without hiding it and locking it up in his strong box; and one of the slave-girls who had seen it said, "O my lady, I think to have noticed, in the apartment of my lord Aladdin, an old lamp: so let us give it in change for a new lamp to this man, and see if his cry be truth or lie."

Hereupon the Princess said to the slave-girl, "Bring the old lamp which thou saidst to have seen in thy lord's apartment." Now the Lady Badr al-Budur knew naught of the Lamp and of the specialties thereof which had raised Aladdin her spouse to such high degree and grandeur; and her only end and aim was to understand by experiment the mind of a man who would give in exchange the new for the old. So the handmaid fared forth and went up to Aladdin's apartment and returned with the Lamp to her lady who, like all the others, knew nothing of the Maghrabi's cunning tricks and his crafty device.

Then the Princess bade an Agha of the eunuchry go down and barter the old Lamp for a new lamp. So he obeyed her bidding and, after taking a new lamp from the man, he returned and laid it before his lady who looking at it and seeing that it was brand-new, fell to laughing at the Moorman's wits. But the Maroccan, when he held the article in hand and recognised it for the Lamp of the Enchanted Treasury, at once placed it in his breast-pocket and left all the other lamps to the folk who were bartering of him. Then he went forth running till he was clear of the city, when he walked leisurely over the level grounds and he took patience until night fell on him in desert ground where was none other but himself. There he brought out the Lamp when suddenly appeared to him the Marid who said, "Adsum! thy slave between thy hands is come: ask of me whatso thou wantest."

"'Tis my desire," the Moorman replied, "that thou upraise from its present place Aladdin's pavilion with its inmates and all that be therein, not forgetting myself, and set it down upon my own land, Africa. Thou knowest my town and I want the building placed in the gardens hard by it."

The Marid-slave replied, "Hearkening and obedience: close thine eyes and open thine eyes whenas thou shalt find thyself together with the pavilion in thine own country." This was done; and, in an eye-twinkling, the Maroccan and the pavilion with all therein were transported to the African land.

Such then was the work of the Maghrabi, the Magician; but now let us return to the Sultan and his son-in-law. It was the custom of the King, because of his attachment to and his affection for his daughter, every morning when he had shaken off sleep, to open the latticed casement and look out therefrom that he might catch sight of her abode. So that day he arose and did as he was wont.

When the Sultan drew near the latticed casement of his palace and looked out at Aladdin's pavilion he saw naught; nay, the site was smooth as a well-trodden highway and like unto what it had been aforetime; and he could find nor edifice nor offices. So astonishment clothed him as with a garment, and his wits were wildered and he began to rub his eyes, lest they be dimmed or darkened, and to gaze intently; but at last he was certified that no trace of the pavilion remained nor sign of its being; nor wist he the why and the wherefore of its disappearance. So his surprise increased and he smote hand upon hand and the tears trickled down his cheeks over his beard, for that he knew not what had become of his daughter. Then he sent out officials forthright and summoned the Grand Wazir who at once attended; and, seeing him in this piteous plight said,

"Pardon, O King of the Age, may Allah avert from thee every ill! Wherefore art thou in such sorrow?"

Exclaimed the Sovran, "Methinketh thou wottest not my case?" and quoth the Minister, "On no wise. O our lord: by Allah, I know of it nothing at all."

"Then," resumed the Sultan, "'tis manifest thou hast not looked this day in the direction of Aladdin's pavilion." "True, O my lord," quoth the Wazir, "it must still be locked and fast shut"; and quoth the King, "Forasmuch as thou hast no inkling of aught, arise and look out at the window and see Aladdin's pavilion whereof thou sayest 'tis locked and fast shut."

The Minister obeyed his bidding but could not see anything, or pavilion or other place; so with mind and thoughts sore perplexed he returned to his liege lord who asked him, "Hast now learned the reason of my distress and noted yon locked-up palace and fast shut?"

Answered the Wazir, "O King of the Age erewhile I represented to thy Highness that this pavilion and these matters be all magical."

Hereat the Sultan, fired with wrath, cried, "Where be Aladdin?" and the Minister replied, "He hath gone a-hunting," when the King commanded without stay or delay sundry of his Aghas and Army-officers to go and bring to him his son-in-law chained and with pinioned elbows.

So they fared forth until they found Aladdin when they said to him, "O our lord Aladdin, excuse us nor be thou wroth with us; for the King hath commanded that we carry thee before him pinioned and fettered, and we hope pardon from thee because we are under the royal orders which we cannot gainsay."

Aladdin, hearing these words, was seized with surprise and not knowing the reason of this remained tongue-tied for a time, after which he turned to them and asked, "O assembly, have you naught of knowledge concerning the motive of the royal mandate? Well I wot my soul to be innocent and that I never sinned against king or against kingdom."

"O our lord," answered they, "we have no inkling whatever."

So Aladdin alighted from his horse and said to them, "Do ye whatso the Sultan bade you do, for that the King's command is upon the head and the eyes."

The Aghas, having bound Aladdin in bonds and pinioned his elbows behind his back, haled him in chains and carried him into the city. But when the lieges saw him pinioned and ironed, they understood that the Sultan purposed to strike off his head; and, forasmuch as he was loved of them exceedingly, all gathered together and seized their weapons; then, swarming out of their houses, followed the soldiery to see what was to do. And when the troops arrived with Aladdin at the palace, they went in and informed the Sultan of this, whereat he forthright commanded the Sworder to cut off the head of his son-in-law.

Now as soon as the subjects were aware of this order, they barricaded the gates and closed the doors of the palace and sent a message to the King saying, "At this very moment we will level thine abode over the heads of all it containeth and over thine own, if the least hurt or harm befal Aladdin."

So the Wazir went in and reported to the Sultan, "O King of the Age, thy commandment is about to seal the roll of our lives; and 'twere more suitable that thou pardon thy son-in-law lest there chance to us a sore mischance; for that the lieges do love him far more than they love us."

Now the Sworder had already dispread the carpet of blood and, having seated Aladdin thereon, had bandaged his eyes; moreover he had walked round him several times awaiting the last orders of his lord, when the King looked out of the window and saw his subjects, who had suddenly attacked him, swarming up the walls intending to tear them down. So forthright he bade the Sworder stay his hand from Aladdin and commanded the crier fare forth to the crowd and cry aloud that he had pardoned his son-in-law and received him back into favour. But when Aladdin found himself free and saw the Sultan seated on his throne, he went up to him and said, "O my lord, inasmuch as thy Highness hath favoured me throughout my life, so of thy grace now deign let me know the how and the wherein I have sinned against thee?"

"O traitor," cried the King, "unto this present I knew not any sin of thine;" then, turning to the Wazir he said, "Take him and make him look out at the window and after let him tell us where be his pavilion."

And when the royal order was obeyed Aladdin saw the place level as a well trodden road, even as it had been ere the base of the building was laid, nor was there the faintest trace of edifice. Hereat he was astonished and perplexed knowing not what had occurred; but, when he returned to the presence, the King asked him, "What is it thou hast seen? Where is thy pavilion and where is my daughter, the core of my heart, my only child, than whom I have none other?"

Aladdin answered "O King of the Age, I wot naught thereof nor aught of what hath befallen," and the Sultan rejoined, "Thou must know, O Aladdin, I have pardoned thee only that thou go forth and look into this affair and enquire for me concerning my daughter; nor do thou ever show thyself in my presence except she be with thee; and, if thou bring her not, by the life of my head, I will cut off the head of thee."

The other replied, "To hear is to obey: only vouchsafe me a delay and respite of some forty days; after which, an I produce her not, strike off my head and do with me whatso thou wishes."

The Sultan said to Aladdin, "Verily I have granted thee thy request, a delay of forty days; but think not thou canst fly from my hand, for I would bring thee back even if thou wert above the clouds instead of being only upon earth's surface."

Replied Aladdin, "O my lord the Sultan, as I said to thy Highness, an I fail to bring her within the term appointed, I will present myself for my head to be stricken off."

Now when the folk and the lieges all saw Aladdin at liberty, they rejoiced with joy exceeding and were delighted for his release; but the shame of his treatment and bashfulness before his friends and the envious exultation of his foes had bowed down Aladdin's head; so he went forth a wandering through the city ways and he was perplexed concerning his case and knew not what had befallen him. He lingered about the capital for two days, in saddest state, wotting not what to do in order to find his wife and his pavilion, and during this time sundry of the folk privily brought him meat and drink.

When the two days were done he left the city to stray about the waste and open lands outlying the walls, without a notion as to whither he should wend; and he walked on aimlessly until the path led him beside a river where, of the stress of sorrow that overwhelmed him, he abandoned himself to despair and thought of casting himself into the water. Being, however, a good Moslem who professed the unity of the God-head, he feared Allah in his soul; and, standing upon the margin he prepared to perform the Wuzu-ablution. But as he was baling up the water in his right hand and rubbing his fingers, it so chanced that he also rubbed the Ring. Hereat its Marid appeared and said to him, "Adsum! thy thrall between thy hands is come: ask of me whatso thou wantest."

Seeing the Marid, Aladdin rejoiced with exceeding joy and cried, "O Slave, I desire of thee that thou bring before me my pavilion and therein my wife, the Lady Badr al-Budur, together with all and everything it containeth."

"O my lord," replied the Marid, "'tis right hard upon me that thou demandest a service whereto I may not avail: this matter dependeth upon the Slave of the Lamp nor dare I even attempt it."

Aladdin rejoined, "Forasmuch as the matter is beyond thy competence, I require it not of thee, but at least do thou take me up and set me down beside my pavilion in what land soever that may be."

The Slave exclaimed, "Hearing and obeying, O my lord;" and, uplifting him high in air, with in the space of an eye-glance set him down beside his pavilion in the land of Africa and upon a spot facing his wife's apartment.

Now this was at fall of night yet one look enabled him to recognise his home; whereby his cark and care were cleared away and he recovered trust in Allah after cutting off all his hope to look upon his wife once more. Then he fell to pondering the secret and mysterious favours of the Lord (glorified be His omnipotence!); and how, after despair had mastered him, the Ring had come to gladden him and how, when all his hopes were cut off Allah had deigned bless him with the services of its Slave. So he rejoiced and his melancholy left him; then, as he had passed four days without sleep for the excess of his cark and care and sorrow and stress of thought, he drew near his pavilion and slept under a tree hard by the building which (as we mentioned) had been set down amongst the gardens outlying the city of Africa.

Aladdin lay that night under a tree beside his pavilion in all restfulness; but whoso weareth head hard by the headsman may not sleep o' nights save whenas slumber prevail over him. He slumbered till Morning showed her face and, when awakened by the warbling of the small birds, he arose and went down to the bank of the river which flowed thereby into the city; and here he again washed hands and face and after finished his Wuzu-ablution. Then he prayed the dawn-prayer, and when he had ended his orisons he returned and sat down under the windows of the Princess's bower.

Now the Lady Badr al-Budur, of her exceeding sorrow for severance from her husband and her sire the Sultan, and for the great mishap which had happened to her from the Maghrabi, the Magician, the Accursed, was wont to rise during the murk preceding dawn and to sit in tears inasmuch as she could not sleep o' nights, and had forsworn meat and drink. Her favourite slave-girl would enter her chamber at the hour of prayer-salutation in order to dress her; and this time, by decree of Destiny, when she threw open the window to let her lady comfort and console herself by looking upon the trees and rills, and she herself peered out of the lattice, she caught sight of her master sitting below, and informed the Princess of this, saying, "O my lady! O my lady! here's my lord Aladdin seated at the foot of the wall."

So her mistress arose hurriedly and gazing from the casement saw him; and her husband raising his head saw her; so she saluted him and he saluted her, both being like to fly for joy. Presently quoth she, "Up and come in to me by the private postern, for now the Accursed is not here"; and she gave orders to the slave-girl who went down and opened for him. Then Aladdin passed through it and was met by his wife, when they embraced and exchanged kisses with all delight until they wept for overjoy.

After this they sat down and Aladdin said to her, "O my lady, before all things 'tis my desire to ask thee a question. 'Twas my wont to place an old copper lamp in such a part of my pavilion, what became of that same?"

When the Princess heard these words she sighed and cried, "O my dearling, 'twas that very Lamp which garred us fall into this calamity!"

Aladdin asked her, "How befel the affair?" and she answered by recounting to him all that passed, first and last, especially how they had given in exchange an old lamp for a new lamp, adding, "And next day we hardly saw one another at dawn before we found ourselves in this land, and he who deceived us and took the lamp by way of barter informed me that he had done the deed by might of his magic and by means of the Lamp; that he is a Moorman from Africa, and that we are now in his native country."

When the Lady Badr al-Budur ceased speaking, Aladdin resumed, "Tell me the intent of this Accursed in thy respect, also what he sayeth to thee and what be his will of thee?"

She replied, "Every day he cometh to visit me once and no more: he would woo me to his love and he sueth that I take him to spouse in lieu of thee and that I forget thee and be consoled for the loss of thee. And he telleth me that the Sultan my sire hath cut off my husband's head, adding that thou, the son of pauper parents, wast by him enriched. And he sootheth me with talk, but he never seeth aught from me save weeping and wailing; nor hath he heard from me one sugar-sweet word."

Quoth Aladdin, "Tell me where he hath placed the Lamp an thou know anything thereof:" and quoth she, "He beareth it about on his body alway, nor is it possible that he leave it for a single hour; moreover once when he related what I have now recounted to thee, he brought it out of his breast-pocket and allowed me to look upon it."

When Aladdin heard these words, he joyed with exceeding joy and said, "O my lady, do thou lend ear to me. 'Tis my design to go from thee forthright and to return only after doffing this my dress; so wonder not when thou see me changed, but direct one of thy women to stand by the private pastern alway and, whenever she espy me coming, at once to open. And now I will devise a device whereby to slay this damned loon."

Herewith he arose and, issuing from the pavilion door, walked till he met on the way a Fellah to whom he said, "O man, take my attire and give me thy garments." But the peasant refused, so Aladdin stripped him of his dress perforce and donned it, leaving to the man his own rich gear by way of gift. Then he followed the highway leading to the neighbouring city and entering it went to the Perfumers' Bazar where he bought of one some rarely potent Bhang, the son of a minute, paying two dinars for two drachms thereof and he returned in disguise by the same road till he reached the pavilion. Here the slave-girl opened to him the private pastern wherethrough he went in to the Lady Badr al-Budur.

When Aladdin went in disguised to his wife he said, "Hear me! I desire of thee that thou dress and dight thyself in thy best and thou cast off all outer show and semblance of care; also when the Accursed, the Maghrabi, shall visit thee, do thou receive him with a 'Welcome and fair welcome,' and meet him with smiling face and invite him to come and sup with thee. Moreover, let him note that thou hast forgotten Aladdin thy beloved, likewise thy father; and that thou hast learned to love him with exceeding love, displaying to him all manner joy and pleasure. Then ask him for wine which must be red and pledge him to his secret in a significant draught; and, when thou hast given him two to three cups full and hast made him wax careless, then drop these drops into his cup and fill it up with wine: no sooner shall he drink of it than he will fall upon his back senseless as one dead."

Hearing these words, the Princess exclaimed, "'Tis exceedingly sore to me that I do such deed; withal must I do it that we escape the defilement of this Accursed who tortured me by severance from thee and from my sire. Lawful and right therefore is the slaughter of this Accursed."

Then Aladdin ate and drank with his wife what hindered his hunger; then, rising without stay or delay, fared forth the pavilion. So the Lady Badr al-Budur summoned the tirewoman who robed and arrayed her in her finest raiment and adorned her and perfumed her; and, as she was thus, behold, the accursed Maghrabi entered. He joyed much seeing her in such case and yet more when she confronted him, contrary to her custom, with a laughing face; and his love-longing increased and his desire to have her.

Then she took him and, seating him beside her, said, "O my darling, do thou (an thou be willing) come to me this night and let us sup together. Sufficient to me hath been my sorrow for, were I to sit mourning through a thousand years or even two thousand, Aladdin would not return to me from the tomb; and I depend upon thy say of yesterday, to wit, that my sire the Sultan slew him in his stress of sorrow for severance from me. Nor wonder thou an I have changed this day from what I was yesterday; and the reason thereof is I have determined upon taking thee to friend and playfellow in lieu of and succession to Aladdin, for that now I have none other man but thyself. So I hope for thy presence this night, that we may sup together and we may carouse and drink somewhat of wine each with other; and especially 'tis my desire that thou cause me taste the wine of thy natal soil, the African land, because belike 'tis better than aught of the wine of China we drink: I have with me some wine but 'tis the growth of my country and I vehemently wish to taste the wine produced by thine."

When the Maghrabi saw the love lavisht upon him by the Lady Badr al-Budur, and noted her change from the sorrowful, melancholy woman she was wont to be, he thought that she had cut off her hope of Aladdin and he joyed exceedingly and said to her, "I hear and obey, O my lady, whatso thou wishest and all thou biddest. I have at home a jar of our country wine, which I have carefully kept and stored deep in earth for a space of eight years; and I will now fare and fill from it our need and will return to thee in all haste."

But the Princess, that she might wheedle him the more and yet more, replied "O my darling, go not thou, leaving me alone, but send one of the eunuchs to fill for us thereof and do thou remain sitting beside me, that I may find in thee my consolation." He rejoined, "O my lady, none wotteth where the jar be buried save myself nor will I tarry from thee." So saying, the Moorman went out and after a short time he brought back as much wine as they wanted whereupon quoth the Princess to him, "Thou hast been at pains and trouble to serve me and I have suffered for thy sake, O my beloved."

Quoth he, "On no wise, O eyes of me; I hold myself enhonoured by thy service."

Then the Lady Badr al-Budur sat with him at table, and the twain fell to eating and presently the Princess expressed a wish to drink, when the handmaid filled her a cup forthright and then crowned another for the Maroccan. So she drank to his long life and his secret wishes and he also drank to her life; then the Princess, who was unique in eloquence and delicacy of speech, fell to making a cup companion of him and beguiled him by addressing him in the sweetest terms full of hidden meaning. This was done only that he might become more madly enamoured of her, but the Maghrabi thought that it resulted from her true inclination for him; nor knew that it was a snare set up to slay him. So his longing for her increased, and he was dying of love for her when he saw her address him in such tenderness of words and thoughts, and his head began to swim and all the world seemed as nothing in his eyes.

But when they came to the last of the supper and the wine had mastered his brains and the Princess saw this in him, she said, "With us there be a custom throughout our country, but I know not an it be the usage of yours or not."

The Moorman replied, "And what may that be?"

So she said to him, "At the end of supper each lover in turn taketh the cup of the beloved and drinketh it off"; and at once she crowned one with wine and bade the handmaid carry to him her cup wherein the drink was blended with the Bhang.

Now she had taught the slave-girl what to do and all the handmaids and eunuchs in the pavilion longed for the Sorcerer's slaughter and in that matter were one with the Princess. Accordingly the damsel handed him the cup and he, when he heard her words and saw her drinking from his cup and passing hers to him noted all that show of love, fancied himself Iskander, Lord of the Two Horns.

Then said she to him, the while swaying gracefully to either side and putting her hand within his hand, "O my life, here is thy cup with me and my cup with thee, and on this wise do lovers drink from each other's cups."

Then she bussed the brim and drained it to the dregs and again she kissed its lip and offered it to him. Thereat he hew for joy and meaning to do the like, raised her cup to his mouth and drank off the whole contents, without considering whether there was therein aught harmful or not. And forthright he rolled upon his back in deathlike condition and the cup dropped from his grasp, whereupon the Lady Badr al-Budur and the slave-girls ran hurriedly and opened the pavilion door to their lord Aladdin who, disguised as a Fellah, entered therein.

Aladdin entering his pavilion, went up to the apartment of his wife, whom he found still sitting at table; and facing her lay the Maghrabi as one slaughtered; so he at once drew near to her and kissed her and thanked her for this. Then rejoicing with joy exceeding he turned to her and said "Do thou with thy handmaids betake thyself to the inner-rooms and leave me alone for the present that I may take counsel touching mine affair."

The Princess hesitated not but went away at once, she and her women; then Aladdin arose and after locking the door upon them, walked up to the Moorman and put forth his hand to his breast-pocket and thence drew the

Lamp; after which he unsheathed his sword and slew the villain. Presently he rubbed the Lamp and the Marid-slave appeared and said, "Adsum, O my lord, what is it thou wantest?"

"I desire of thee," said Aladdin, "that thou take up my pavilion from this country and transport it to the land of China and there set it down upon the site where it was whilome, fronting the palace of the Sultan."

The Marid replied, "Hearing and obeying, O my lord."

Then Aladdin went and sat down with his wife and throwing his arms round her neck kissed her and she kissed him, and they sat in converse, what while the Jinni transported the pavilion and all therein to the place appointed. Presently Aladdin bade the handmaids spread the table before him and he and the Lady Badr al-Budur took seat thereat and fell to eating and drinking, in all joy and gladness, till they had their sufficiency when, removing to the chamber of wine and cup-converse, they sat there and caroused in fair companionship and each kissed other with all love-liesse. The time had been long and longsome since they enjoyed aught of pleasure; so they ceased not doing thus until the wine-sun arose in their heads and sleep get hold of them, at which time they went to their bed in all ease and comfort.

Early on the next morning Aladdin woke and awoke his wife, and the slave-girls came in and donned her dress and prepared her and adorned her whilst her husband arrayed himself in his costliest raiment and the twain were ready to fly for joy at reunion after parting. Moreover the Princess was especially joyous and gladsome because on that day she expected to see her beloved father.

Such was the case of Aladdin and the Lady Badr al-Budur; but as regards the Sultan, after he drove away his son-in-law he never ceased to sorrow for the loss of his daughter; and every hour of every day he would sit and weep for her as women weep, because she was his only child and he had none other to take to heart. And as he shook off sleep, morning after morning, he would hasten to the window and throw it open and peer in the direction where formerly stood Aladdin's pavilion and pour forth tears until his eyes were dried up and their lids were ulcered.

Now on that day he arose at dawn and, according to his custom, looked out when, lo and behold! he saw before him an edifice; so he rubbed his eyes and considered it curiously when he became certified that it was the pavilion of his son-in-law. So he called for a horse without let or delay; and as soon as his beast was saddled, he mounted and made for the place; and Aladdin, when he saw his father-in-law approaching, went down and met him half way: then, taking his hand, aided him to step upstairs to the apartment of his daughter. And the Princess, being as earnestly desirous to see her sire, descended and greeted him at the door of the staircase fronting the ground-floor hall. Thereupon the King folded her in his arms and kissed her, shedding tears of joy; and she did likewise till at last Aladdin led them to the upper saloon where they took seats and the Sultan fell to asking her case and what had betided her.

The Lady Badr al-Budur began to inform the Sultan of all which had befallen her, saying, "O my father, I recovered not life save yesterday when I saw my husband, and he it was who freed me from the thraldom of that Maghrabi, that Magician, that Accursed, than whom I believe there be none viler on the face of earth; and, but for my beloved, I had never escaped him nor hadst thou seen me during the rest of my days. But mighty sadness and sorrow get about me, O my father, not only for losing thee but also for the loss of a husband, under whose kindness I shall be all the length of my life, seeing that he freed me from that fulsome sorcerer." Then the Princess began repeating to her sire every thing that happened to her, and relating to him how the Moorman had tricked her in the guise of a lamp-seller who offered in exchange new for old; how she had given him the Lamp whose worth she knew not, and how she had bartered it away only to laugh at the lampman's folly. "And next morning, O my father," she continued, "we found ourselves and whatso the pavilion contained in Africa-land, till such time as my husband came to us and devised a device whereby we escaped: and, had it not been for Aladdin's hastening to our aid, the Accursed was determined to enjoy me perforce." Then she told him of the Bhang-drops administered in wine to the African and concluded, "Then my husband returned to me and how I know not, but we were shifted from Africa land to this place."

Aladdin in his turn recounted how, finding the wizard dead drunken, he had sent away his wife and her women from the polluted place into the inner apartments; how he had taken the Lamp from the Sorcerer's breast-pocket whereto he was directed by his wife; how he had slaughtered the villain and, finally how, making use of the Lamp, he had summoned its Slave and ordered him to transport the pavilion back to its proper site, ending his tale with, "And, if thy Highness have any doubt anent my words, arise with me and look upon the accursed Magician."

The King did accordingly and, having considered the Moorman, bade the carcase be carried away forthright and burned and its ashes scattered in air. Then he took to embracing Aladdin and kissing him said, "Pardon me, O my son, for that I was about to destroy thy life through the foul deeds of this damned enchanter, who cast thee into such pit of peril; and I may be excused, O my child, for what I did by thee, because I found myself forlorn of my daughter; my only one, who to me is dearer than my very kingdom. Thou knowest how the hearts of parents yearn unto their offspring, especially when like myself they have but one and none other to love." And on this wise the Sultan took to excusing himself and kissing his son-in-law.

Aladdin said to the Sultan, "O King of the Time, thou didst naught to me contrary to Holy Law, and I also sinned not against thee; but all the trouble came from that Maghrabi, the impure, the Magician."

Thereupon the Sultan bade the city be decorated and they obeyed him and held high feast and festivities. He also commanded the crier to cry about the streets saying, "This day is a mighty great fete, wherein public rejoicings must be held throughout the realm, for a full month of thirty days, in honour of the Lady Badr al-Budur and her husband Aladdin's return to their home."

On this wise befel it with Aladdin and the Maghrabi; but withal the King's son-in-law escaped not wholly from the Accursed, albeit the body had been burnt and the ashes scattered in air. For the villain had a brother yet more villainous than himself, and a greater adept in necromancy, geomancy and astromancy; and, even as the old saw saith "A bean and 'twas split"; so each one dwelt in his own quarter of the globe that he might fill it with his sorcery, his fraud and his treason.

Now, one day of the days it fortuned that the Moorman's brother would learn how it fared with him, so he brought out his sandboard and dotted it and produced the figures which, when he had considered and carefully studied them, gave him to know that the man he sought was dead and housed in the tomb. So he grieved and was certified of his decease, but he dotted a second time seeking to learn the manner of the death and where it had taken place; so he found that the site was the China-land and that the mode was the foulest of slaughter; furthermore, that he who did him die was a young man Aladdin hight. Seeing this he straightway arose and equipped himself for wayfare; then he set out and cut across the wilds and words and heights for the space of many a month until he reached China and the capital of the Sultan wherein was the slayer of his brother. He alighted at the so-called Strangers' Khan and, hiring himself a cell, took rest therein for a while; then he fared forth and wandered about the highways that he might discern some path which would aid him unto the winning of his ill-minded wish, to wit, of wreaking upon Aladdin blood-revenge for his brother.

Presently he entered a coffee-house, a fine building which stood in the market-place and which collected a throng of folk to play, some at the mankalah, others at the backgammon and others at the chess and what not else. There he sat down and listened to those seated beside him and they chanced to be conversing about an ancient dame and a holy, by name Fatimah, who dwelt alway at her devotions in a hermitage without the town, and this she never entered save only two days each month. They mentioned also that she had performed many saintly miracles which, when the Maghrabi, the Necromancer, heard he said in himself, "Now have I found that which I sought: Inshallah—God willing—by means of this crone will I win to my wish."

The Maghrabi, the Necromancer, went up to the folk who were talking of the miracles performed by the devout old woman and said to one of them, "O my uncle, I heard you all chatting about the prodigies of a certain saintess named Fatimah: who is she and where may be her abode?"

"Marvellous!" exclaimed the man: "How canst thou be in our city and yet never have heard about the miracles of the Lady Fatimah? Evidently, O thou poor fellow, thou art a foreigner, since the fastings of this devotee and her asceticism in worldly matters and the beauties of her piety never came to thine ears."

The Moorman rejoined, "'Tis true, O my lord: yes, I am a stranger and came to this your city only yesternight; and I hope thou wilt inform me concerning the saintly miracles of this virtuous woman and where may be her wone, for that I have fallen into a calamity, and 'tis my wish to visit her and crave her prayers, so haply Allah (to whom be honour and glory!) will, through her blessings, deliver me from mine evil." Hereat the man recounted to him the marvels of Fatimah the Devotee and her piety and the beauties of her worship; then, taking him by the hand went with him without the city and showed him the way to her abode, a cavern upon a hillock's head. The Necromancer acknowledged his kindness in many words and, thanking him for his good offices, returned to his cell in the caravanserai.

Now by the fiat of Fate on the very next day Fatimah came down to the city, and the Maghrabi, the Necromancer, happened to leave his hostelry a-morn, when he saw the folk swarming and crowding; wherefore he went up to discover what was to do and found the Devotee standing amiddlemost the throng, and all who suffered from pain or sickness flocked to her soliciting a blessing and praying for her prayers; and each and every she touched became whole of his illness. The Maroccan, the Necromancer, followed her about until she returned to her antre; then, awaiting till the evening evened, he arose and repaired to a vintner's store where he drank a cup of wine. After this he fared forth the city and finding the Devotee's cavern, entered it and saw her lying prostrate with her back upon a strip of matting. So he came for ward and mounted upon her belly; then he drew his dagger and shouted at her; and, when she awoke and opened her eyes, she espied a Moorish man with an unsheathed poniard sitting upon her middle as though about to kill her. She was troubled and sore terrified, but he said to her, "Hearken! an thou cry out or utter a word I will slay thee at this very moment: arise now and do all I bid thee."

Then he sware to her an oath that if she obeyed his orders, whatever they might be, he would not do her die. So saying, he rose up from off her and Fatimah also arose, when he said to her, "Give me thy gear and take thou my habit"; whereupon she gave him her clothing and head-fillets, her face-kerchief and her mantilla. Then quoth he, "'tis also requisite that thou anoint me with somewhat shall make the colour of my face like unto thine."

Accordingly she went into the inner cavern and, bringing out a gallipot of ointment, spread somewhat thereof upon her palm and with it besmeared his face until its hue favoured her own; then she gave him her staff and, showing him how to walk and what to do when he entered the city, hung her rosary around his neck. Lastly she handed to him a mirror and said, "Now look! Thou differest from me in naught"; and he saw himself Fatimah's counterpart as though she had never gone or come. But after obtaining his every object he falsed his oath and asked for a cord which she brought to him; then he seized her and strangled her in the cavern; and, presently, when she was dead, haled the corpse outside and threw it into a pit hard by.

The Maghrabi, after murthering Fatimah, threw her body into a pit and went back to sleep in her cavern; and, when broke the day, he rose and repairing to the town took his stand under the walls of Aladdin's pavilion. Hereupon flocked the folk about him, all being certified that he was Fatimah the Devotee and he fell to doing whatso she was wont to do: he laid hands on these in pain and recited for those a chapter of the Koran and made orisons for a third.

Presently the thronging of the folk and the clamouring of the crowd were heard by the Lady Badr al-Budur, who said to her handmaidens, "Look what is to do and what be the cause of this turmoil!"

Thereupon the Agha of the eunuchry fared forth to see what might be the matter and presently returning said, "O my lady, this clamour is caused by the Lady Fatimah, and if thou be pleased to command, I will bring her to thee; so shalt thou gain through her a blessing."

The Princess answered, "Go bring her, for since many a day I am always hearing of her miracles and her virtues, and I do long to see her and get a blessing by her intervention, for the folk recount her manifestations in many cases of difficulty."

The Agha went forth and brought in the Maroccan, the Necromancer, habited in Fatimah's clothing; and, when the wizard stood before the Lady Badr al-Budur, he began at first sight to bless her with a string of prayers; nor did any one of those present doubt at all but that he was the Devotee herself. The Princess arose and salam'd to him then seating him beside her, said, "O my Lady Fatimah, 'tis my desire that thou abide with me alway, so might I be blessed through thee, and also learn of thee the paths of worship and piety and follow thine example making for salvation."

Now all this was a foul deceit of the accursed African and he designed furthermore to complete his guile, so he continued, "O my Lady, I am a poor woman and a religious that dwelleth in the desert; and the like of me deserveth not to abide in the palaces of the kings."

But the Princess replied, "Have no care whatever, O my Lady Fatimah; I will set apart for thee an apartment of my pavilion, that thou mayest worship therein and none shall ever come to trouble thee; also thou shalt avail to worship Allah in my place better than in thy cavern."

The Maroccan rejoined, "Hearkening and obedience, O my lady; I will not oppose thine order for that the commands of the children of the kings may not be gainsaid nor renounced. Only I hope of thee that my eating and drinking and sitting may be within my own chamber which shall be kept wholly private; nor do I require or desire the delicacies of diet, but do thou favour me by sending thy handmaid every day with a bit of bread and a sup of water; and, when I feel fain of food, let me eat by myself in my own room."

Now the Accursed hereby purposed to avert the danger of haply raising his face-kerchief at meal-times, when his intent might be baffled by his beard and mustachios discovering him to be a man. The Princess replied, "O my Lady Fatimah, be of good heart; naught shall happen save what thou wishest. But now arise and let me show thee the apartment in the palace which I would prepare for thy sojourn with us."

The Lady Badr al-Budur arose and taking the Necromancer who had disguised himself as the Devotee, ushered him in to the place which she had kindly promised him for a home and said, "O my Lady Fatimah, here thou shalt dwell with every comfort about thee and in all privacy and repose; and the place shall be named after thy name"; whereupon the Maghrabi acknowledged her kindness and prayed for her.

Then the Princess showed him the jalousies and the jewelled Kiosque with its four and twenty windows and said to him, "What thinkest thou, O my Lady Fatimah, of this marvellous pavilion?"

The Moorman replied, "By Allah, O my daughter, 'tis indeed passing fine and wondrous exceedingly; nor do I deem that its fellow is to be found in the whole universe; but alas for the lack of one thing which would enhance its beauty and decoration!"

The Princess asked her, "O my Lady Fatimah, what lacketh it and what be this thing would add to its adornment? Tell me thereof, inasmuch as I was wont to believe it wholly perfect."

The Maroccan answered, "O my lady, all it wanteth is that there be hanging from the middle of the dome the egg of a fowl called the Rukh; and, were this done, the pavilion would lack its peer all the world over."

The Princess asked, "What be this bird and where can we find her egg?" and the Maroccan answered, "O my lady, the Rukh is indeed a giant fowl which carrieth off camels and elephants in her pounces and flieth away with them, such is her stature and strength; also this fowl is mostly found in Mount Kaf; and the architect who built this pavilion is able to bring thee one of her eggs."

They then left such talk as it was the hour for the noon day meal and, when the handmaid had spread the table, the Lady Badr al-Budur sent down to invite the Accursed African to eat with her. But he accepted not and for a reason he would on no wise consent; nay, he rose and retired to the room which the Princess had assigned to him and whither the slave-girls carried his dinner. Now when evening evened, Aladdin returned from the chase and met his wife who salam'd to him and he clasped her to his bosom and kissed her.

Presently, looking at her face he saw thereon a shade of sadness and he noted that contrary to her custom, she did not laugh; so he asked her, "What hath betided thee, O my dearling? tell me, hath aught happened to trouble thy thoughts!"

"Nothing whatever," answered she, "but, O my beloved, I fancied that our pavilion lacked naught at all; however, O eyes of me, O Aladdin, were the dome of the upper story hung with an egg of the fowl called Rukh, there would be naught like it in the universe."

Her husband rejoined, "And for this trifle thou art saddened when 'tis the easiest of all matters to me! So cheer thyself; and, whatever thou wantest, 'tis enough thou inform me thereof, and I will bring it from the abysses of the earth in the quickest time and at the earliest hour."

Aladdin after refreshing the spirits of his Princess by promising her all she could desire, repaired straight way to his chamber and taking the Lamp rubbed it, when the Marid appeared without let or delay saying, "Ask whatso thou wantest."

Said the other, "I desire thee to fetch me an egg of the bird Rukh and do thou hang it to the dome-crown of this my pavilion."

But when the Marid heard these words, his face waxed fierce and he shouted with a mighty loud voice and a frightful, and cried, "O denier of kindly deeds, sufficeth it not for thee that I and all the Slaves of the Lamp are ever at thy service, but thou must also require me to bring thee our Liege Lady for thy pleasure, and hang her up at thy pavilion dome for the enjoyment of thee and thy wife! Now by Allah, ye deserve, thou and she, that I reduce you to ashes this very moment and scatter you upon the air; but, inasmuch as ye twain be ignorant of this matter, unknowing its inner from its outer significance, I will pardon you for indeed ye are but innocents. The offence cometh from that accursed Necromancer, brother to the Maghrabi, the Magician, who abideth here representing himself to be Fatimah, the Devotee, after assuming her dress and belongings and murthering her in the cavern: indeed he came hither seeking to slay thee by way of blood-revenge for his brother; and 'tis he who taught thy wife to require this matter of me."

So saying the Marid evanished. But when Aladdin heard these words, his wits fled his head and his joints trembled at the Marid's terrible shout; but he empowered his purpose and, rising forthright, issued from his chamber and went into his wife's. There he affected an ache of head, for that he knew how famous was Fatimah for the art and mystery of healing all such pains; and, when the Lady Badr al-Budur saw him sitting hand to head and complaining of unease, she asked him the cause and he answered, "I know of none other save that my head acheth exceedingly."

Hereupon she straightway bade summon Fatimah that the Devotee might impose her hand upon his head; and Aladdin asked her, "Who may this Fatimah be?"

So she informed him that it was Fatimah the Devotee to whom she had given a home in the pavilion. Meanwhile the slave-girls had fared forth and summoned the Maghrabi, and when the Accursed made act of presence, Aladdin rose up to him and, acting like one who knew naught of his purpose, salam'd to him as though he had been the real Fatimah and, kissing the hem of his sleeve, welcomed him and entreated him with honour and said, "O my Lady Fatimah, I hope thou wilt bless me with a boon, for well I wot thy practice in the healing of pains: I have gotten a mighty ache in my head." The Moorman, the Accursed, could hardly believe that he heard such words, this being all that he desired.

The Maghrabi, the Necromancer, habited as Fatimah the Devotee, came up to Aladdin that he might place hand upon his head and heal his ache; so he imposed one hand and, putting forth the other under his gown, drew a dagger wherewith to slay him. But Aladdin watched him and, taking patience till he had wholly unsheathed the weapon, seized him with a forceful grip; and, wrenching the dagger from his grasp plunged it deep into his heart. When the Lady Badr al-Budur saw him do on this wise, she shrieked and cried out, "What hath this virtuous and holy woman done that thou hast charged thy neck with the heavy burthen of her blood shed wrongfully? Hast thou no fear of Allah that thou killest Fatimah, this saintly woman, whose miracles are far-famed?"

"No," replied Aladdin "I have not killed Fatimah. I have slain only Fatimah's slayer, he that is the brother of the Maghrabi, the Accursed, the Magician, who carried thee off by his black art and transported my pavilion to the Africa-land; and this damnable brother of his came to our city and wrought these wiles, murthering Fatimah and assuming her habit, only that he might avenge upon me his brother's blood; and he also 'twas who taught thee to require of me a Rukh's egg, that my death might result from such requirement. But, an thou doubt my speech, come forwards and consider the person I have slain."

Thereupon Aladdin drew aside the Moorman's face-kerchief and the Lady Badr al-Budur saw the semblance of a man with a full beard that well nigh covered his features. She at once knew the truth and said to her husband, "O my beloved, twice have I cast thee into death-risk!" but he rejoined, "No harm in that, O my lady, by the blessing of your loving eyes: I accept with all joy all things thou bringest me."

The Princess, hearing these words, hastened to fold him in her arms and kissed him saying, "O my dearling, all this is for my love to thee and I knew naught thereof; but indeed I do not deem lightly of thine affection."

So Aladdin kissed her and strained her to his breast; and the love between them waxed but greater. At that moment the Sultan appeared and they told him all that had happened, showing him the corpse of the Maghrabi, the Necromancer, when the King commanded the body to be burned and the ashes scattered on air, even as had befallen the Wizard's brother. And Aladdin abode with his wife, the Lady Badr al-Budur, in all pleasure and joyance of life and thenceforward escaped every danger; and, after a while, when the Sultan deceased, his son-in-law was seated upon the throne of the Kingdom; and he commanded and dealt justice to the lieges so that all the folk loved him, and he lived with his wife in all solace and happiness until there came to him the Destroyer of delights and the Severer of societies.

When Queen Scheherazade ended this story she said to Shahryar, "O my lord, thou art doubtless astonished at the audacity of Aladdin, but I am assured that thou wilt be the more surprised on hearing the story of the curious adventures of Harun al-Rashid."

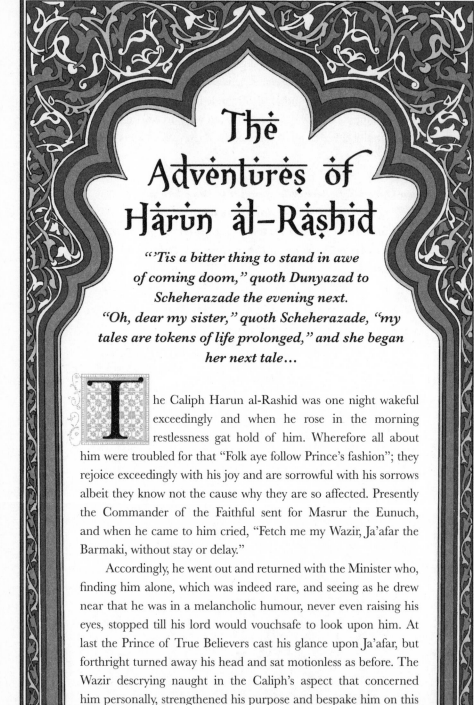

The Adventures of Harun al-Rashid

*"'Tis a bitter thing to stand in awe
of coming doom," quoth Dunyazad to
Scheherazade the evening next.
"Oh, dear my sister," quoth Scheherazade, "my
tales are tokens of life prolonged," and she began
her next tale…*

The Caliph Harun al-Rashid was one night wakeful exceedingly and when he rose in the morning restlessness gat hold of him. Wherefore all about him were troubled for that "Folk aye follow Prince's fashion"; they rejoice exceedingly with his joy and are sorrowful with his sorrows albeit they know not the cause why they are so affected. Presently the Commander of the Faithful sent for Masrur the Eunuch, and when he came to him cried, "Fetch me my Wazir, Ja'afar the Barmaki, without stay or delay."

Accordingly, he went out and returned with the Minister who, finding him alone, which was indeed rare, and seeing as he drew near that he was in a melancholic humour, never even raising his eyes, stopped till his lord would vouchsafe to look upon him. At last the Prince of True Believers cast his glance upon Ja'afar, but forthright turned away his head and sat motionless as before. The Wazir descrying naught in the Caliph's aspect that concerned him personally, strengthened his purpose and bespake him on this wise, "O Commander of the Faithful, wilt thine Highness deign suffer me to ask whence cometh this sadness?" and the Caliph answered with a clearer brow, "Verily, O Wazir, these moods have of late become troublesome to me, nor are they to be moved save by hearing strange tales and verses; and, if thou come not hither on a pressing affair, thou wilt gladden me by relating somewhat to dispel my sadness."

Replied the Wazir, "O Commander of the Faithful, my office compelleth me to stand on thy service, and I would fain remind thee that this is the day appointed for informing thyself of the good governance of thy capital and its environs, and this matter shall, Inshallah, divert thy mind and dispel its gloom."

The Caliph answered, "Thou dost well to remind me, for that I had wholly forgotten it; so fare forth and change thy vestments while I do the same with mine."

Presently the twain donned habits of stranger merchants and issued out by a private postern of the palace-garden, which led them into the fields. After they had skirted the city, they reached the Euphrates' bank at some distance from the gate opening on that side, without having observed aught of disorder; then they crossed the river in the first ferry-boat they found, and, making a second round on the further side, they passed over the bridge that joined the two halves of Baghdad-town. At the bridge-foot they met with a blind old man who asked alms of them; and the Caliph turned about and crossed his palm with a dinar, whereupon the beggar caught hold of his hand, and held him fast, saying, "O beneficent man, whoso thou ever may be, whom Allah hath inspired to bestow an alms upon me, refuse not the favour I crave of thee, which is, to strike me a buffet upon the ear, for that I deserve such punishment and a greater still." After these words he quitted his hold of the Caliph's hand that it might smite him, yet for fear lest the stranger pass on without so doing he grasped him fast by his long robe.

The Caliph, surprised by the blind man's words and deeds said, "I may not grant thy request nor will I minish the merit of my charity, by treating thee as thou wouldst have me entreat thee."

Saying these words, he strove to get away from the blind man, but he who after his long experience expected this refusal of his benefactor, did his utmost to keep hold of him, and cried, "O my lord, forgive my audacity and my persistency; and I implore thee either give me a cuff on the ear, or take back thine alms, for I may not receive it save on that condition, without falsing a solemn oath I have sworn before the face of Allah; and, if thou knew the reason, thou wouldst accord with me that the penalty is light indeed." Then the Caliph not caring to be delayed any longer, yielded to the blind man's importunity, and gave him a slight cuff: whereupon he loosed him forthright and thanked him and blessed him.

When the Caliph and his Wazir had walked some way from the blind man, the former exclaimed, "This blind beggar must assuredly have some right good cause for behaving himself in such manner to all who give him alms, and I would fain know it. Do thou return to him and tell him who I am, and bid him fail not to appear at my palace about mid-afternoon prayer time that I may converse with him, and hear whatso he hath to say." Hereupon Ja'afar went back and bestowed alms on the blind man giving him another cuff on the ear and apprised him of the Caliph's command, and returned forthright to his lord.

Presently, when the twain reached the town, they found in a square a vast crowd of folk gazing at a handsome youth and a well shaped, who was mounted on a mare which he rode at fullest speed round the open space, spurring and whipping the beast so cruelly that she was covered with sweat and blood. Seeing this the Caliph, amazed at the youth's brutality, stopped to ask the by-standers an they knew why he tortured and tormented the mare on such wise; but he could learn naught save that for some while past, every day at the same time, he had entreated her after the same fashion.

Hereat as they walked along, the Caliph bid his Wazir especially notice the place and order the young man to come without failing on the next day, at the hour appointed for the blind man. But ere the Caliph reached his palace, he saw in a street, which he had not passed through for many months, a newly built mansion, which seemed to him the palace of some great lord of the land. He asked the Wazir, an he knew its owner; and Ja'afar answered he did not but would make inquiry. So he consulted a neighbour who told him that the house owner was one Khwajah Hasan surnamed Al-Habbal from his handicraft, rope-making; that he himself had seen the man at work in the days of his poverty, that he knew not how Fate and Fortune had befriended him, yet that the same Khwajah had gotten such exceeding wealth that he had been enabled to pay honourably and sumptuously all the expenses he had incurred when building his palace.

Then the Wazir returned to the Caliph and gave him a full account of whatso he had heard, whereat cried the Prince of True Believers, "I must see this Khwajah Hasan al-Habbal: do thou therefore, O Wazir, go and tell him to come to my palace, at the same hour thou hast appointed for the other twain."

The Minister did his lord's bidding and the next day, after mid-afternoon prayers, the Caliph retired to his own apartment and Ja'afar introduced the three persons whereof we have been speaking and presented them to the Caliph. All prostrated themselves at his feet and when they rose up, the Commander of the Faithful asked his name of the blind man, who answered he was hight Baba Abdullah.

"O Servant of Allah," cried the Caliph, "thy manner of asking alms yesterday seemed so strange to me that, had it not been for certain considerations I should not have granted thy petition; nay, I would have prevented thy giving further offence to the folk. And now I have bidden thee hither that I may know from thyself what impelled thee to swear that rash oath whereof thou toldest me, that I may better judge whether thou have done well or ill, and if I should suffer thee to persist in a practice which meseemeth must set so pernicious an example. Tell me openly how such mad thought entered into thy head, and conceal not aught, for I will know the truth and the full truth."

Baba Abdullah, terrified by these words, cast himself a second time at the Caliph's feet with his face prone to the ground, and when he rose again, said, "O Commander of the Faithful, I crave pardon of thy Highness for my audacity, in that I dared require, and well nigh compelled thee to do a thing which verily seemeth contrary to sound sense. I acknowledge mine offence; but as I knew not thy Highness at that time, I implore thy clemency, and I pray thou wilt consider my ignorance of thine exalted degree. And now as to the extravagance of my action, I readily admit that it must be strange to the sons of Adam; but in the eye of Allah 'tis but a slight penance wherewith I have charged myself for an enormous crime of which I am guilty, and wherefor, an all the people in the world were each and every to give me a cuff on the ear 'twould not be sufficient atonement. Thy Highness shall judge of it thyself, when I, in telling my tale according to thy commandment, will inform thee of what was my offence." And here he began to relate

The Story of the Blind Man, Baba Abdullah

O my lord the Caliph, I, the humblest of thy slaves, was born in Baghdad, where my father and mother, presently dying within a few days of each other, left me a fortune large enough to last me throughout my lifetime. But I knew not its value and soon I had squandered it in luxury and loose living and I cared naught for thrift or for increasing my store. But when little was left to me of my substance, I repented of my evil courses and toiled and laboured hard by day and night to increase my remaining stock of money. It is truly said, "After waste cometh knowledge of worth." Thus little by little I got together fourscore camels, which I let on hire to merchants, and thus I made goodly gain each time I found occasion: moreover I was wont to engage myself together with my beasts and on this wise I journeyed over all the dominions and domains of thy Highness. Brief, I hoped ere long to reap an abundant crop of gold by the hiring out of my baggage animals.

Once I had carried merchants' stuffs to Bassorah for shipping India-wards and I was returning to Baghdad with my beasts unladen. Now as I fared homewards I chanced pass across a plain of excellent pasturage lying fallow and far from any village, and there unsaddled the camels which I hobbled and tethered together that they might crop the luxuriant herbs and thorns and yet not fare astray. Presently appeared a Darwaysh who was travelling afoot for Bassorah, and he took seat beside me to enjoy ease after unease; whereat I asked him whence he wayfared and whither he was wending. He also asked me the same question and when we had told each to other our own tales, we produced our provisions and brake our fast together, talking of various matters as we ate.

Quoth the Darwaysh, "I know a spot hard by which enholdeth a hoard and its wealth is so wonder-great that shouldst thou load upon thy fourscore camels the heaviest burthens of golden coins and costly gems from that treasure there will appear no minishing thereof."

Hearing these words I rejoiced with exceeding joy and gathering from his mien and demeanour that he did not deceive me, I arose forthright and falling upon his neck, exclaimed, "O Hallow of Allah, who cares naught for this world's goods and hast renounced all mundane lusts and luxuries, assuredly thou hast full knowledge of this treasure, for naught remaineth hidden from holy men as thou art. I pray thee tell me where it may be found that I may load my fourscore beasts with bales of Ashrafis and jewels: I wot full well that thou hast no greed for the wealth of this world, but take, I pray thee, one of these my fourscore camels as recompense and reward for the favour."

Thus spake I with my tongue but in my heart I sorely grieved to think that I must part with a single camel-load of coins and gems; withal I reflected that the other three-score and nineteen camel-loads would contain riches to my heart's content. Accordingly, as I wavered in mind, at one moment consenting and at the next instant repenting, the Darwaysh noting my greed and covetise and avarice, replied, "Not so, O my brother: one camel doth not suffice me that I should shew thee all this hoard. On a single condition only will I tell thee of the place; to wit, that we twain lead the animals thither and lade them with the treasure, then shalt thou give me one half thereof and take the other half to thyself. With forty camels' load of costly ores and minerals forsure thou canst buy thousands more of camels."

Then, seeing that refusal was impossible, I cried "So be it! I agree to thy proposal and I will do as thou desires"; for in my heart I had conned the matter over and well I wist that forty camel-loads of gold and gems would suffice me and many generations of my descendants; and I feared lest an I gain say him I should repent for ever and ever having let so great a treasure slip out of hand. Accordingly, giving full consent to all be said, I got together every one of my beasts and set me a-wayfaring along with the Fakir. After travelling over some short distance we came upon a gorge between two craggy mountain-walls towering high in crescent form and the pass was exceeding narrow so that the animals were forced to pace in single file, but further on it flared out and we could thread it without difficulty into the broad Wady below. No human being was anywhere to be seen or heard in this wild land, so we were undisturbed and easy in our minds nor feared aught.

I did as the Darwaysh had bidden me; and, nakhing all the camels, I followed in wake of him. After walking a short way from the halting-place he produced a flint and steel and struck fire therewith and lit some sticks he had gotten together; then, throwing a handful of strong-smelling incense upon the flames, he muttered words of incantation which I could by no means understand. At once a cloud of smoke arose, and spireing upwards veiled the mountains; and presently, the vapour clearing away, we saw a huge rock with pathway leading to its perpendicular face. Here the precipice showed an open door, wherethrough appeared in the bowels of the mountain a splendid palace, the workmanship of the Jinns, for no man had power to build aught like it. In due time, after sore toil, we entered therein and found an endless treasure, ranged in mounds with the utmost ordinance and regularity.

Seeing a heap of Ashrafis I pounced upon it as a vulture swoopeth upon her quarry, the carrion, and fell to filling the sacks with golden coin to my heart's content. The bags were big, but I was constrained to stuff them only in proportion to the strength of my beasts. The Darwaysh, too, busied himself in like manner, but he charged his sacks with gems and jewels only, counselling me the while to do as he did. So I cast aside the ducats and filled my bags with naught save the most precious of the stonery.

When we had wrought our best, we set the well-stuffed sacks upon the camels' backs and we made ready to depart; but, before we left the treasure-house wherein stood ranged thousands of golden vessels, exquisite in shape and workmanship, the Darwaysh went into a hidden chamber and brought from out a silvern casket a little golden box full of some unguent, which he showed to me, and then he placed it in his pocket. Presently, he again threw incense upon the fire and recited his incantations and conjurations, whereat the door closed and the rock became as before. We then divided the camels, he taking one half and I the other; and, passing through the strait and gloomy gorge in single file, we came out upon the open plain. Here our way parted, he wending in the direction of Bassorah and I Baghdad-wards; and when about to leave him I showered thanks upon the Darwaysh who had obtained me all this wealth and riches worth a thousand thousand of gold coins; and farewelled him with deep emotions of gratitude; after which we embraced and wended our several ways.

But hardly had I bidden adieu to the Fakir and had gone some little distance from him with my file of camels than the Shaytan tempted me with greed of gain so that I said to myself, "The Darwaysh is alone in the world, without friends or kinsman, and is wholly estranged from matters mundane. What will these camel-loads of filthy lucre advantage him? Moreover, engrossed by the care of the camels, not to speak of the deceitfulness of riches, he may neglect his prayer and worship: therefore it behoveth me to take back from him some few of my beasts."

With this resolve I made the camels halt and tying up their forelegs ran back after the holy man and called out his name. He heard my loud shouts and awaited me forthright; and, as soon as I approached him I said, "When I had quitted thee a thought came into my mind; to wit, that thou art a recluse who keepest thyself aloof from earthly things, pure in heart and busied only with orison and devotion. Now care of all these camels will cause thee only toil and moil and trouble and waste of precious time: 'twere better then to give them back and not run the risk of these discomforts and dangers."

The Darwaysh replied, "O my son, thou speakest sooth. The tending of all these animals will bring me naught save ache of head, so do thou take of them as many as thou listest. I thought not of the burthen and posher till thou drewest my attention thereto; but now I am forewarned thereof; so may Almighty Allah keep thee in His holy keeping!"

Accordingly, I took ten camels of him and was about to gang my gait when suddenly it struck me, "This Fakir was unconcerned at giving up ten camels, so 'twere better I ask more of him." Thereupon I drew nearer to him and said, "Thou canst hardly manage thirty camels; do give me, I pray thee, other ten." Said he, "O my son, do whatso thou wishest! Take thee other ten camels; twenty will suffice me." I did his bidding and driving off the twenty added them to my forty.

Then the spirit of concupiscence possessed me, and I bethought me more and more to get yet other ten camels from his share; so I retraced my steps for the third time and asked him for another ten, and of these, as also the remaining ten, I wheedled him. The Darwaysh gladly gave up the last of his camels, and, shaking out his skirts, made ready to depart; but still my accursed greed stuck to me. Albeit I had got the fourscore beasts laden with Ashrafis and jewels, and I might have gone home happy and content, with wealth for fourscore generations, Satan tempted me still more, and urged me also to take the box of ointment, which I supposed to contain something more precious than rubies.

So when I had again farewelled and embraced him I paused awhile and said, "What wilt thou do with the little box of salve thou hast taken to thy portion? I pray thee give me that also." The Fakir would by no means part with it, whereupon I lusted the more to possess it, and resolved in my mind that, should the holy man give it up of his free will, then well and good, but if not I would force it from him.

Seeing my intent he drew the box from out his breast-pocket and handed it to me saying, "O my son, an thou wouldst have this box of ointment, then freely do I give it to thee; but first it behoveth thee to learn the virtue of the unguent it containeth."

Hearing these words I said, "Forasmuch as thou hast shown me all this favour, I beseech thee tell me of this ointment and what of properties it possesseth."

Quoth he, "The wonders of this ointment are passing strange and rare. An thou close thy left eye and rub upon the lid the smallest bit of the salve then all the treasures of the world now concealed from thy gaze will come to sight; but an thou rub aught thereof upon thy right eye thou shalt straightway become stone blind of both."

Thereat I bethought me of putting this wondrous unguent to the test and placing in his hand the box I said, "I see thou understandest this matter right well; so now I pray thee apply somewhat of the ointment with thine own hand to my left eyelid."

The Darwaysh thereupon closed my left eye and with his finger rubbed a little of the unguent over the lid; and when I opened it and looked around

381

I saw the hidden hoards of the earth in countless quantities even as the Fakir had told me I should see them. Then closing my right eyelid, I bade him apply some of the salve to that eye also. Said he, "O my son, I have forewarned thee that if I rub it upon thy right eyelid thou shalt become stone blind of both. Put far from thee this foolish thought: why shouldst thou bring this evil to no purpose on thyself?"

He spake sooth indeed, but by reason of my accursed ill-fate I would not heed his words and considered in my mind, "If applying the salve to the left eyelid hath produced such effect, assuredly far more wondrous still shall be the result when rubbed on the right eye. This fellow doth play me false and keepeth back from me the truth of the matter." When I had thus determined in my mind I laughed and said to the holy man, "Thou art deceiving me to the intent that I should not advantage myself by the secret, for that rubbing the unguent upon the right eyelid hath some greater virtue than applying it to the left eye, and thou wouldst withhold the matter from me. It can never be that the same ointment hath qualities so contrary and virtues so diverse."

Replied the other, "Allah Almighty is my witness that the marvels of the ointment be none other save these whereof I bespake thee; O dear my friend, have faith in me, for naught hath been told thee save what is sober sooth."

Still would I not believe his words, thinking that he dissembled with me and kept secret from me the main virtue of the unguent. Wherefore filled with this foolish thought I pressed him sore and begged that he rub the ointment upon my right eyelid; but he still refused and said, "Thou seest how much of favour I have shown to thee: wherefore should I now do thee so dire an evil? Know for a surety that it would bring thee lifelong grief and misery; and I beseech thee, by Allah the Almighty, abandon this thy purpose and believe my words."

But the more he refused so much the more did I persist; and in fine I made oath and sware by Allah, saying, "O Darwaysh, what things soever I have asked of thee thou gayest freely unto me and now remaineth only this request for me to make. Allah upon thee, gainsay me not and grant me this last of thy boons: and whatever shall betide me I will not hold thee responsible therefor. Let Destiny decide for good or for evil."

When the holy man saw that his denial was of no avail and that I irked him with exceeding persistence, he put the smallest bit of ointment on my right lid and, as I opened wide my eyes, lo and behold! both were stone-blind: naught could I see for the black darkness before them and ever since that day have I been sightless and helpless as thou foundest me. When

I knew that I was blinded, I exclaimed, "O Darwaysh of ill-omen, what thou didst fore tell hath come to pass;" and I fell to cursing him and saying "O would to Heaven thou hadst never brought me to the hoard or hadst given me such wealth. What now avail me all this gold and jewels? Take back thy forty camels and make me whole again."

Replied he, "What evil have I done to thee? I showed thee favours more than any man hath ever dealt to another. Thou wouldst not heed my rede, but didst harden thy heart and lustedst to obtain this wealth and to pry into the hidden treasures of the earth. Thou wouldst not be content with what thou hadst and thou didst misdoubt my words thinking that I would play thee false. Thy case is beyond all hope, for never more wilt thou regain thy sight; no, never." Then said I with tears and lamentations, "O Fakir, take back thy fourscore camels laden with gold and precious stones and wend thy way: I absolve thee from all blame, natheless I beseech thee by Allah Almighty to restore my sight an thou art able."

He answered not a word, but leaving me in miserable plight presently took the load to Bassorah, driving before him the fourscore camels laden with wealth. I cried aloud and besought him to lead me with him away from the life destroying wilderness, or to put me on the path of some caravan, but he regarded not my cries and abandoned me there.

So when the Darwaysh departed from me, I had well nigh died of grief and wrath at the loss of my sight and of my riches, and from the pangs of thirst and hunger. Next day by good fortune a caravan from Bassorah passed that way; and, seeing me in such a grievous condition, the merchants had compassion on me and made me travel with them to Baghdad. Naught could I do save beg my bread in order to keep myself alive; so I became a mendicant and made this vow to Allah Almighty that, as a punishment for this my unlucky greed and cursed covetise, I would require a cuff upon my ear from everyone who might take pity on my case and give an alms. On this wise it was that yesterday I pursued thee with such pertinacity.

When the blind man made an end of his story the Caliph said, "O Baba Abdullah! thine offence was grievous; may Allah have mercy on thee therefor. It now remaineth to thee to tell thy case to devotees and anchorites that they may offer up their potent prayers in thy behalf. Take no thought for thy daily wants: I have determined that for thy living thou shalt have a dole of four dirhams a day from my royal treasury according to thy need as long as thou mayest live. But see that thou go no more to ask for alms about my city."

So Baba Abdullah returned thanks to the Prince of True Believers, saying, "I will do according to thy bidding."

Now when the Caliph Harun al-Rashid had heard the story of Baba Abdullah and the Darwaysh, he turned to and addressed the young man whom he had seen riding at fullest speed upon the mare and savagely lashing and ill-treating her. "What is thy name?" quoth he, and quoth the youth, bowing his brow groundwards, "My name, O Commander of the Faithful, is Sidi Nu'uman."

Then said the Caliph, "Hearken now, O Sidi Nu'uman! Ofttimes have I watched the horsemen exercise their horses, and I myself have often done likewise, but never saw I any who rode so mercilessly as thou didst ride thy mare, for thou didst ply both whip and shovel-iron in cruellest fashion. The folk all stood to gaze with wonderment, but chiefly I, who was constrained against my wish to stop and ask the cause of the bystanders. None, however, could make clear the matter, and all men said that thou art wont each day to ride the mare in this most brutal fashion, whereat my mind marvelled all the more. I now would ask of thee the cause of this thy ruthless savagery, and see that thou tell me every whit and leave not aught unsaid."

Sidi Nu'uman, hearing the order of the Commander of the Faithful, became aware he was fully bent upon hearing the whole matter and would on no wise suffer him to depart until all was explained. So the colour of his countenance changed and he stood speechless like a statue through fear and trepidation; whereat said the Prince of True Believers, "O Sidi Nu'uman, fear naught but tell me all thy tale. Regard me in the light of one of thy friends and speak without reserve, and explain to me the matter fully as thou wouldst do hadst thou been speaking to thy familiars. Moreover, an thou art afraid of any matter which thou shalt confide to me and if thou dread my indignation, I grant thee immunity and a free pardon."

At these comforting words of the Caliph, Sidi Nu'uman took courage, and with clasped hands replied, "I trust I have not in this matter done aught contrary to thy Highness's law and custom, and therefore will I willingly obey thy bidding and relate to thee all my tale. If I have offended in anything then am I worthy of thy punishment. 'Tis true that I have daily exercised the mare and ridden her at speed around the hippodrome as thou sawest me do; and I lashed and gored her with all my might. Thou hadst compassion on the mare and didst deem me cruel hearted to entreat her thus, but when thou shalt have heard all my adventure thou wilt admit, Inshallah—God willing—that this be only a trifling penalty for her offence, and that not she but I deserve thy pity and pardon! With thy permission

I will now begin my story."

The Caliph Harun al-Rashid accorded the youth permission to speak and that the rider of the mare began in these words

THE HISTORY OF SIDI NU'UMAN

O Lord of beneficence and benevolence, my parents were possessed of wealth and riches sufficient to provide their son when they died with ample means for a life long livelihood so that he might pass his days like a Grandee of the land in ease and joyance and delight. I—their only child— had nor care nor trouble about any matter until one day of the days, when in the prime of manhood, I was a minded to take unto me a wife, a woman winsome and comely to look upon, that we might live together in mutual love and double blessedness. But Allah Almighty willed not that a model helpmate become mine; nay, Destiny wedded me to grief and the direst misery. I married a maid who in outward form and features was a model of beauty and loveliness without, however, one single gracious gift of mind or soul; and on the very second day after the wedding her evil nature began to manifest itself.

Thou art well aware, O Prince of True Believers, that by Moslem custom none may look upon the face of his betrothed before the marriage contract? nor after wedlock can he complain should his bride prove a shrew or a fright: he must needs dwell with her in such content as he may and be thankful for his fate, be it fair or unfair. When I saw first the face of my bride and learnt that it was passing comely, I joyed with exceeding joy and gave thanks to Almighty Allah that He had bestowed on me so charming a mate. That night I slept with her in joy and love-delight; but next day when the noon meal was spread for me and her I found her not at table and sent to summon her; and after some delay, she came and sat her down. I dissembled my annoyance and forbore for this late coming to find fault with her which I soon had ample reason to do. It so happened that amongst the many dishes which were served up to us was a fine pilaff, of which I, according to the custom in our city, began to eat with a spoon; but she, in lieu of it pulled out an ear pick from her pocket and therewith fell to picking up the rice and ate it grain by grain.

Seeing this strange conduct I was sore amazed and fuming inwardly said in sweet tones, "O my Aminah, what be this way of eating? hast thou learnt it of thy people or art thou counting grains of rice purposing to make a hearty meal here after? Thou hast eaten but ten or twenty during all this time. Or haply thou art practicing thrift: if so I would have thee know that Allah Almighty hath given me abundant store and fear not on that account; but do thou, O my dearling, as all do and eat as thou seest thy husband eat." I fondly thought that she would assuredly vouchsafe some words of thanks, but never a syllable spake she and ceased not picking up grain after grain: nay more, in order to provoke me to greater displeasure, she paused for a long time between each.

Now when the next course of cakes came on she idly brake some bread and tossed a crumb or two into her mouth; in fact she ate less than would satisfy the stomach of a sparrow. I marvelled much to see her so obstinate and self-willed but I said to myself, in mine innocence, "May be she hath not been accustomed to eat with men, and especially she may be too shame faced to eat heartily in presence of her husband: she will in time do whatso do other folk." I thought also that perchance she hath already broken her fast and lost appetite, or haply it hath been her habit to eat alone. So I said nothing and after dinner went out to smell the air and play the Jarid and thought no more of the matter. When, however, we two sat again at meat my bride ate after the same fashion as before; nay, she would ever persist in her perversity; whereat I was sore troubled in mind, and marvelled how without food she kept herself alive.

One night it chanced that deeming me fast asleep she rose up in stealth from my side, I being wide awake: when I saw her step cautiously from the bed as one fearing lest she might disturb me. I wondered with exceeding wonder why she should arise from sleep to leave me thus and methought I would look into the matter. Wherefore I still feigned sleep and snored but watched her as I lay, and presently saw her dress herself and leave the room; I then sprang off the bed and throwing on my robe and slinging my sword across my shoulder looked out of the window to spy whither she went. Presently she crossed the courtyard and opening the street-door fared forth; and I also ran out through the entrance which she had left unlocked; then followed her by the light of the moon until she entered a cemetery hard by our home.

When I beheld Aminah my bride enter the cemetery, I stood without and close to the wall over which I peered so that I could espy her well but she could not discover me. Then what did I behold but Aminah sitting with a Ghul! Thy Highness wotteth well that Ghuls be of the race of devils; to wit, they are unclean spirits which inhabit ruins and which terrify solitary wayfarers and at times seizing them feed upon their flesh; and if by day they find not any traveller to eat they go by night to the graveyards and dig out and devour dead bodies. So I was sore amazed and terrified to see my wife thus seated with a Ghul.

Then the twain dug up from the grave a corpse which had been newly buried, and the Ghul and my wife Aminah tore off pieces of the flesh which she ate making merry the while and chatting with her companion but inasmuch as I stood at some distance I could not hear what it was they said. At this sight I trembled with exceeding fear. And when they had made an end of eating they cast the bones into the pit and thereover heaped up the earth e'en as it was before. Leaving them thus engaged in their foul and fulsome work, I hastened home; and, allowing the street-door to remain half-open as my bride had done, I reached my room, and throwing myself upon our bed feigned sleep.

Presently Aminah came and doffing her dress calmly lay beside me, and I knew by her manner that she had not seen me at all, nor guessed that I had followed her to the cemetery. This gave me great relief of mind, withal I loathed to bed beside a cannibal and a corpse-eater; howbeit I lay still despite extreme misliking till the Muezzin's call for dawn-prayers, when getting up I busied myself with the Wuzu-ablution and set forth mosque-wards. Then having said my prayers and fulfilled my ceremonial duties, I strolled about the gardens, and during this walk having turned over the matter in my mind, determined that it behoved me to remove my bride from such ill companionship, and wean her from the habit of devouring dead bodies.

With these thoughts I came back home at dinner-time, when Aminah on seeing me return bade the servants serve up the noontide meal and we twain sat at table; but as before she fell to picking up the rice grain by grain. Thereat said I to her, "O my wife, it irketh me much to see thee picking up each grain of rice like a hen. If this dish suit not thy taste see there are, by Allah's grace and the Almighty's favour, all kinds of meats before us. Do thou eat of that which pleaseth thee most; each day the table is bespread with dishes of different kinds and if these please thee not, thou hast only to order whatsoever food thy soul desireth. Yet I would ask of thee one question: Is there no meat upon the table as rich and toothsome as man's flesh, that thou refuseth every dish they set before thee?"

Ere I had finished speaking my wife became assured that I was aware of her night adventure: she suddenly waxed wroth with exceeding wrath, her face flushed red as fire, her eyeballs started out from their sockets and she foamed at the mouth with ungovernable fury. Seeing her in this mood I was terrified and my sense and reason fled by reason of my affright; but presently in the madness of her passion she took up a tasse of water which stood beside her and dipping her fingers in the contents muttered some words which I could not understand; then sprinkling some drops over me, cried, "Accursed that thou art! for this thine insolence and betrayal do thou be straightway turned into a dog."

At once I became transmewed and she, picking up a staff began to ribroast me right mercilessly and well nigh killed me. I ran about from room to room but she pursued me with the stick, and tunded and belaboured me with might and main, till she was clean exhausted. She then threw the street-door half open and, as I made for it to save my life, attempted violently to close it, so as to squeeze my soul out of my body; but I saw her design and baffled it, leaving behind me, however, the tip of my tail; and piteously yelping hereat I escaped further basting and thought myself lucky to get away from her without broken bones. When I stood in the street still whining and ailing, the dogs of the quarter seeing a stranger, at once came rushing at me barking and biting; and I with tail between my legs tore along the market place and ran into the shop of one who sold sheeps' and goats' heads and trotters; and there crouching low hid me in a dark corner.

The shopkeeper, despite his scruples of conscience, which caused him to hold all dogs impure, hath ruth upon my sorry plight and drove away the yelling and grinning curs that would have followed me into his shop; and I, escaping this danger of doom, passed all the night hid in my corner. Early next morning the butcher sallied forth to buy his usual wares, sheeps' heads and hooves, and, coming back with a large supply, he began to lay them out for sale within the shop, when I, seeing that a whole pack of dogs had gathered about the place attracted by the smell of flesh, also joined them. The owner noticed me among the ragged tykes and said to himself, "This dog hath tasted naught since yesterday when it ran yelping hungrily and hid within my shop." He then threw me a fair sized piece of meat, but I refused it and went up to him and wagged my tail to the end that he might know my wish to stay with him and be protected by his stall: he, however, thought that I had eaten my sufficiency, and, picking up a staff frightened me away.

So when I saw how the butcher heeded not my case, I trotted off and wandering to and fro presently came to a bakery and stood before the door wherethrough I espied the baker at breakfast. Albeit I made no sign as though I wanted aught of food, he threw me a bittock of bread; and I, in lieu of snapping it up and greedily swallowing it, as is the fashion with all dogs the gentle and simple of them, approached him with it and gazed in his face

and wagged my tail by way of thanks. He was pleased by this my well bred behaviour and smiled at me; whereat I albeit not one whit anhungered, but merely to humour him, fell to eating the bread, little by little and leisurely, to testify my respect. He was yet more satisfied with my manners and wished to keep me in his shop; and I, noting his intent, sat by the door and looked wistfully at him, whereby he knew that I desired naught of him save his protection. He then caressed me and took charge of me and kept me to guard his store, but I would not enter his house till after he had led the way; he also showed me where to lie o'nights and fed me well at every meal and entreated me right hospitably. I likewise would watch his every movement and always lay down or rose up even as he bade me; and whenas he left his lodging or walked anywhither he took me with him. If ever when I lay asleep he went outside and found me not, he would stand still in the street and call to me crying, "Bakht! Bakht!" an auspicious name he had given to me; and straightway on hearing him I would rush about and frisk before the door; and when he set out to taste the air I paced beside him now running on ahead, now following at his heels and ever and anon looking up in his face.

Thus some time passed during which I lived with him in all comfort; till one day of the days it so chanced that a woman came to the bakery to buy her bread and gave the owner several dirhams to its price, whereof one was bad coin whilst the others were good. My master tested all the silvers and, finding out the false bit, returned it demanding a true dirham in exchange; but the woman wrangled and would not take it back and swore that it was sound. Quoth the baker, "The dirham is beyond all doubt a worthless: see yonder dog of mine, he is but a beast, yet mark me he will tell thee whether it be true or false silver."

So he called me by my name, "Bakht! Bakht!" whereat I sprang up and ran towards him and he, throwing all the moneys upon the ground before me, cried, "Here, look these dirhams over and if there be a false coin among them separate it from all the others."

I inspected the silvers each by each and found the counterfeit: then, putting it on one side and all the others on another, I placed my paw upon the false silver and wagging what remained of my tail looked up at my master's face. The baker was delighted with my sagacity, and the woman also, marvelling with excessive marvel at what had happened, took back her bad dirham and paid another in exchange. But when the buyer fared forth, my master called together his neighbours and gossips and related to them this matter; so they threw down on the ground before me coins both good and bad, in order that they might test me and see with their own eyes an I were

as clever as my master had said I was. Many times in succession I picked out the false coins from amongst the true and placed my paw upon them without once failing; so all went away astounded and related the case to each and every one they saw and thus the bruit of me spread abroad throughout the city. That live long day I spent in testing dirhams fair and foul.

From that day forward the baker honoured me yet more highly, and all his friends and familiars laughed and said, "Forsooth thou hast in this dog a mighty good Shroff." And some envied my master his luck in having me within the shop, and tried ofttimes to entice me away, but the baker kept me with him nor would he ever allow me to leave his side; for the fame of me brought him a host of customers from every quarter of the town even the farthest.

Not many days after there came another woman to buy loaves at our shop and paid the baker six dirhams whereof one was worthless. My master passed them over to me for test and trial, and straightway I picked out the false one, and placing paw thereon looked up in the woman's face. Hereat she waxed confused and confessed that it was miscoined and praised me for that I had found it out; then, going forth the same woman made signs to me that I should follow her unbeknown to the baker.

Now I had not ceased praying Allah that somehow He would restore me to my human form and hoped that some good follower of the Almighty would take note of this my sorry condition and vouchsafe me succour. So as the woman turned several times and looked at me, I was persuaded in my mind that she had knowledge of my case; I therefore kept my eyes upon her; which seeing she came back ere she had stepped many paces, and beckoned me to accompany her. I understood her signal and sneaking out of the presence of the baker, who was busy heating his oven, followed in her wake. Pleased beyond all measure to see me obey her, she went straight way home with me, and entering she locked the door and led me into a room where sat a fair maid in embroidered dress whom I judged by her favour to be the good woman's daughter. The damsel was well skilled in arts magical; so the mother said to her, "O my daughter, here is a dog which telleth bad dirhams from good dirhams. When first I heard the marvel I bethought me that the beastie must be a man whom some base wretch and cruel hearted had turned into a dog. Methought that to day I would see this animal and test it when buying loaves at the booth of yonder baker and behold, it hath acquitted itself after the fairest of fashions and hath stood the test and trial. Look well, O my daughter, at this dog and see whether it be indeed an animal or a man transformed into a beast by gramarye."

The young lady, who had veiled her face, hereupon considered me attentively and presently cried, "O my mother, 'tis even as thou sayest, and this I will prove to thee forthright."

Then rising from her seat she took a basin of water and dipping hand therein sprinkled some drops upon me saying, "An thou wert born a dog then do thou abide a dog, but an thou wert born a man then, by virtue of this water, resume thine human favour and figure."

Immediately I was transformed from the shape of a dog to human semblance and I fell at the maiden's feet and kissed the ground before her giving her thanks; then, bussing the hem of her garment, I cried, "O my lady, thou hast been exceeding gracious unto one unbeknown to thee and a stranger. How can I find words wherewith to thank thee and bless thee as thou deserves?"

"Tell me now, I pray thee, how and whereby I may shew my gratitude to thee? From this day forth I am beholden to thy kindness and am become thy slave." Then I related all my case and told her of Aminah's wickedness and what of wrongs she had wrought me; and I made due acknowledgment to her mother for that she had brought me to her home.

Herewith quoth the damsel to me, "O Sidi Nu'uman, I pray thee bestow not such exceeding thanks upon me, for rather am I glad and grateful in conferring this service upon one so well-deserving as thou art. I have been familiar with thy wife Aminah for a long time before thou didst marry her; I also knew that she had skill in witchcraft and she likewise knoweth of my art, for we twain learnt together of one and the same mistress in the science. We met ofttimes at the Hammam as friends but, in asmuch as she was ill-mannered and ill-tempered, I declined further intimacy with her. Think not that it sufficeth me to have made thee recover thy form as it was aforetime; nay, verily needs must I take due vengeance of her for the wrong she hath done thee. And this will I do at thy hand, so shalt thou have mastery over her and find thyself lord of thine own house and home. Tarry here awhile until I come again." So saying the damsel passed into another room and I remained sitting and talking with her mother and praised her excellence and kindness towards me.

The ancient dame also related strange and rare deeds of wonder done by her with pure purpose and lawful means, till the girl returned with an ewer in hand and said, "O Sidi Nu'uman, my magical art doth tell me that Aminah is at this present away from home but she will return thither presently. Meanwhile she dissembleth with the domestics and feigneth grief at severance from thee; and she hath pretended that, as thou sattest at meat with her, thou didst suddenly arise and fare forth on some weighty matter, when presently a dog rushed through the open door into the room and she drove it away with a staff." Then giving me a gugglet full of the water the maiden resumed, "O Sidi Nu'uman, go now to thine own house and, keeping this gugglet by thee, await patiently Aminah's coming. Anon she will return and seeing thee will be sore perplexed and will hasten to escape from thee; but before she go forth sprinkle some drops from this gugglet upon her and recite these spells which I shall teach thee. I need not tell thee more; thou wilt espy with thine own eyes what shall happen."

Having said these words the young lady taught me magical phrases which I fixed in my memory full firmly, and after this I took my leave and farewelled them both. When I reached home it happened even as the young magician had told me; and I had tarried but a short time in the house when Aminah came in. I held the gugglet in hand and she seeing me trembled with sore trembling and would fain have run away; but I hastily sprinkled some drops upon her and repeated the magical words, whereat she was turned into a mare—the animal thy Highness deigned remark but yesterday. I marvelled greatly to sight this transformation and seizing the mare's mane led her to the stable and secured her with a halter.

When I had secured the mare, I loaded her with reproaches for her wickedness and her base behaviour, and lashed her with a whip till my forearm was tired. Then I resolved within myself that I would ride her at full speed round the square each day and thus inflict upon her the justest penalty.

Herewith Sidi Nu'uman held his peace, having made an end of telling his tale; but presently he resumed, "O Commander of the Faithful, I trow thou art not displeased at this my conduct, nay rather thou wouldst punish such a woman with a punishment still greater than this."

He then kissed the hem of the Caliph's robe and kept silence; and Harun al-Rashid, perceiving that he had said all his say, exclaimed, "In very sooth thy story is exceeding strange and rare. The wrong doing of thy wife hath no excuse and thy requital is methinks in due measure and just degree, but I would ask thee one thing—How long wilt thou chastise her thus, and how long will she remain in bestial guise? 'Twere better now for thee to seek the young lady by whose magical skill thy wife was transformed and beg that she bring her back to human shape. And yet I fear me greatly lest perchance whenas this sorceress, this Ghulah, shall find herself restored to woman's form and resumeth her conjurations and incantations she may—who knoweth?—

requite thee with far greater wrong than she hath done thee heretofore, and from this thou wilt not be able to escape."

After this the Prince of True Believers forbore to urge the matter, albeit he was mild and merciful by nature, and addressing the third man whom the Wazir had brought before him said, "As I was walking in such a quarter I was astonished to see thy mansion, so great and so grand is it; and when I made enquiry of the townsfolk they answered each and every, that the palace belongeth to one (thyself) whom they called Khwajah Hasan. They added that thou west erewhile exceeding poor and in straitened case, but that Allah Almighty had widened thy means and had now sent thee wealth in such store that thou hast builded the finest of buildings; moreover, that albeit thou hast so princely a domicile and such abundance of riches, thou art not unmindful of thy former estate, and thou dost not waste thy substance in riotous living but thou addest thereto by lawful trade. The neighbourhood all speaketh well of thee and not a wight of them hath aught to say against thee; so I now would know of thee the certainty of these things and hear from thine own lips how thou didst gain this abundant wealth. I have summoned thee before me that I might be assured of all such matters by actual hearsay: so fear not to tell me all thy tale; I desire naught of thee save knowledge of this thy case. Enjoy thou to thy heart's content the opulence that Almighty Allah deigned bestow upon thee, and let thy soul have pleasure therein."

Thus spake the Caliph and the gracious words reassured the man. Then Khwajah Hasan threw himself before the Commander of the Faithful and, kissing the carpet at the foot of the throne, exclaimed, "O Prince of True Believers, I will relate to thee a faithful relation of my adventure, and Almighty Allah be my witness that I have not done aught contrary to thy laws and just commandments, and that all this my wealth is by the favour and goodness of Allah alone." Harun al-Rashid hereupon again bade him speak out boldly and forthwith he began to recount in the following words

THE HISTORY OF KHWAJAH HASAN AL-HABBAL

O Lord of beneficence! obedient to thy royal behest, I will now inform thy Highness of the means and the measures whereby Destiny cowered me with such wealth; but first I would thou hear somewhat of two amongst my friends who abode in the House of Peace, Baghdad. They twain are yet alive and both well know the history which thy slave shall now relate. One of them, men call Sa'd, the other Sa'di. Now Sa'di opined that without riches no one in this world could be happy and independent; moreover that without hard toil and trouble and wariness and wisdom withal it were impossible to become wealthy. But Sa'd differing therefrom would affirm that affluence cometh not to any save by decree of Destiny and fiat of Fate and Fortune. Sa'd was a poor man while Sa'di had great store of good; yet there sprang up a firm friendship between them and fond affection each for other; nor were they ever wont to differ upon any matter save only upon this; to wit, that Sa'di relied solely upon deliberation and forethought and Sa'd upon doom and man's lot.

It chanced one day that, as they sat talking together on this matter, quoth Sa'di, "A poor man is he who either is born a pauper and passeth all his days in want and penury, or he who having been born to wealth and comfort, doth in the time of manhood squander all he hath and falleth into grievous need; then lacketh he the power to regain his riches and to live at ease by wit and industry."

Sa'd made answer, saying, "Nor wit nor industry availeth aught to any one, but Fate alone enableth him to acquire and to preserve riches. Misery and want are but accidents and deliberation is naught. Full many a poor man hath waxed affluent by favour of Fate and richards manifold have, despite their skill and store, been reduced to misery and beggary."

Quoth Sa'di, "Thou speakest foolishly. Howbeit put we the matter to fair test and find out for ourselves some handicraftsman scanty of means and living upon his daily wage; him let us provide with money, then will he without a doubt increase his stock and abide in ease and comfort, and so shalt thou be persuaded that my words be true."

Now as they twain were walking on, they passed through the lane wherein stood my lodging and saw me a twisting ropes, which craft my father and grandfather and many generations before me had followed. By the condition of my home and dress they judged that I was a needy man; where upon Sa'd pointing me out to Sa'di said, "An thou wouldst make trial of this our matter of dispute, see yonder wight. He hath dwelt here for many years and by this trade of rope making cloth gain a bare subsistence for himself and his. I know his case right well of old; he is a worthy subject for the trial; so do thou give him some gold pieces and test the matter."

"Right willingly," replied Sa'di, "but first let us take full cognizance of him." So the two friends came up to me, whereat I left my work and saluted them. They returned my salam after which quoth Sa'di, "Prithee what be thy name?"

Quoth I, "My name is Hasan, but by reason of my trade of rope making all men call me Hasan al-Habbal."

Thereupon Sa'di asked me, "How farest thou by this industry? Me thinks thou art blithe and quite content therewith. Thou hast worked long and well and doubtless thou hast laid by large store of hemp and other stock. Thy forbears carried on this craft for many years and must have left thee much of capital and property which thou hast turned to good account and on this wise thou hast largely increased thy wealth."

Quoth I, "O my lord, no money have I in pouch whereby I may live happy or even buy me enough to eat. This is my case that every day, from dawn till eve I spend in making ropes, nor have I one single moment wherein to take rest; and still I am sore straitened to provide even dry bread for myself and family. A wife have I and five small children, who are yet too young to help me ply this business: and 'tis no easy matter to supply their daily wants; how then canst thou suppose that I am enabled to put by large store of hemp and stock? What ropes I twist each day I sell straightway, and of the money earned thereby I spend part upon our needs and with the rest I buy hemp wherewith I twist ropes on the next day. However, praise be to Almighty Allah that, despite this my state of penury He provideth us with bread sufficing our necessity."

When I had made known all my condition Sa'di replied, "O Hasan, now I am certified of thy case and indeed 'tis other than I had supposed; and, given that I gave thee a purse of two hundred Ashrafis, assuredly thou shalt therewith greatly add to thy gains and be enabled to live in ease and affluence: what sayest thou thereto?"

Said I, "An thou favour me with such bounty I should hope to grow richer than all and every of my fellow-craftsmen, albeit Baghdad-town is prosperous as it is populous." Then Sa'di, deeming me true and trustworthy, pulled out of his pocket a purse of two hundred gold pieces and handing them to me said, "Take these coins and trade therewith. May Allah advance thee but see to it that thou use this money with all heed, and waste it not in folly and ungraciousness. I and my friend Sa'd will rejoice with all joy to hear of thy well being; and, if hereafter we come again and find thee in flourishing condition, 'twill be matter of much satisfaction to us both."

Accordingly, O Commander of the Faithful, I took the purse of gold with much gladness and a grateful heart and, placing it in my pocket, thanked Sa'di kissing his garment-hem, whereupon the two friends fared forth. And I, O Prince of True Believers, seeing the twain depart, went on working, but was sore puzzled and perplexed as to where I might bestow the purse; for my house contained neither cupboard nor locker. Howbeit I took it home and kept the matter hidden from my wife and children and when alone and unobserved I drew out ten gold coins by way of spending money; then, binding the purse mouth with a bit of string I tied it tightly in the folds of my turband and wound the cloth around my head.

Presently, I went off to the market street and bought me a stock of hemp and coming homewards I laid in some meat for supper, it being now a long while since we had tasted flesh. But as I trudged along the road, meat in hand, a kite came suddenly swooping down, and would have snatched the morsel from out my hand had I not driven off the bird with the other hand. Then it had fain pounced upon the flesh on the left side but again I scared it away and thus, whilst exerting myself with frantic efforts to ward off the bird, by ill luck my turband fell to the ground. At once that accursed kite swooped down and flew off with it in its talons; and I ran pursuing it and shouted aloud.

Hearing my cries the Bazar-folk, men and women and a rout of children, did what they could to scare it away and make the beastly bird drop its prey, but they shouted and cast stones in vain: the kite would not let drop the turband and presently flew clean out of sight. I was sore distressed and heavy hearted to lose the Ashrafis as I tried me home bearing the hemp and what of food I had bought, but chiefly was I vexed and grieved in mind, and ready to die of shame at the thought of what Sa'di would say; especially when I reflected how he would misdoubt my words, nor deem the tale true when I should tell him that a kite had carried off my turband with the gold pieces, but rather would he think that I had practised some deceit and had devised some amusing fable by way of excuse. Howbeit I hugely enjoyed what had remained of the ten Ashrafis and with my wife and children fared sumptuously for some days.

Presently, when all the gold was spent and naught remained thereof, I became as poor and needy as before, withal I was content and thankful to Almighty Allah nor blamed my lot. He had sent in his mercy this purse of gold to me unawares and now He had taken it away, wherefore I was grateful and satisfied, for what He doeth is ever well done.

My wife, who knew not of the matter of the Ashrafis, presently perceived that I was ill at ease and I was compelled for a quiet life to let her know my secret; moreover the neighbours came round to ask me of my case: but I was right loath to tell them all that had betided; they could not bring back what was gone and they would assuredly rejoice at my calamity. However, when they pressed me close I told them every whit; and some thought that I had spoken falsely and derided me and others that I was daft and hare-brained and my words were the wild pratings of an idiot or the drivel of dreams. The youngsters made abundant fun of me and laughed to think that I, who never in my born days had sighted a golden coin, should tell how I had gotten so many Ashrafis, and how a kite had flown away with them. My wife, however, gave full credence to my tale and wept and beat her breast for sorrow.

Thus six months passed over us, when it chanced one day that the two friends, to wit, Sa'di and Sa'd, came to my quarter of the town, when quoth Sa'd to Sa'di, "Lo, yonder is the street where dwelleth Hasan al-Habbal. Come let us go and see how he hath added to his stock and how far he hath prospered by means of the two hundred Ashrafis thou gavest him."

Sa'di rejoined, "'Tis well said; indeed, we have not seen him for many days: I would fain visit him and I should rejoice to hear that he hath prospered." So the twain walked along towards my house, Sa'd saying to Sa'di, "Forsooth I perceive that he appeareth the same in semblance, poor and ill-conditioned as before; he weareth old and tattered garments, save that his turband seemeth somewhat newer and cleaner. Look well and judge thyself and 'tis even as I said."

Thereupon Sa'di came up closer to me and he also understood that my condition was unaltered; and presently the two friends addressed me. After the usual salutetion Sa'd asked, "O Hasan, how fareth it with thee, and how goeth it with thy business and have the two hundred Ashrafis stood thee in good stead and amended thy trade?"

To this answered I, "O my lords, how can I tell you of the sad mishap that hath befallen me? I dare not speak for very shame, yet cannot I keep the adventure concealed. Verily a marvellous matter and a wondrous hath happened to me, the tale whereof will fill you with wonderment and suspicion, for I wot full well that ye will not believe it, and that I shall be to you as one that dealeth in lies; withal needs must I tell you the whole however unwillingly."

Hereat I recounted to them every whit that had betided me first and last, especially that which had befallen me from the kite; but Sa'di misdoubted me and mistrusted me and cried, "O Hasan, thou speakest but in jest and dost dissemble with us. 'Tis hard to believe the tale thou tellest. Kites are not wont to fly off with turbands, but only with such things as they can eat. Thou wouldst but outwit us and thou art of those who, when some good fortune cometh to them unforeseen, do straightways abandon their work or their business and, wasting all in pleasuring, become once

more poor and thereafter must nilly-willy eke out a living as best they may. This methinks be especially the case with thee; thou hast squandered our gift with all speed and now art needy as before."

"O good my lord, not so," cried I; "this blame and these hard words ill befit my deserts, for I am wholly innocent of all thou imputest to me. The strange mishap whereof I told thee is the truest of truths; and to prove that it is no lie all the town-folk have knowledge thereof and in good sooth I do not play thee false. 'Tis certain that kites do not fly away with turbands; but such mishaps, wondrous and marvellous, may betide mankind especially the miserable of lot."

Sa'd also espoused my cause and said, "O Sa'di, ofttimes have we seen and heard how kites carry off many things besides comestibles; and his tale may not be wholly contrary to reason."

Then Sa'di pulled out from his pocket a purseful of gold pieces and counted out and gave me another two hundred, saying, "O Hasan, take these Ashrafis, but see that thou keep them with all heed and diligence and beware, and again I say beware, lest thou lose them like the others. Expend them in such fashion that thou mayst reap full benefit therefrom and prosper even as thou seest thy neighbours prosper."

I took the money from him and poured out thanks and blessings upon his head, and when they went their ways I returned to my rope-walk and thence in due time straight home. My wife and children were abroad, so again I took ten gold coins of the two hundred and securely tied up the remainder in a piece of cloth then I looked around to find a spot wherein to hide my hoard so that my wife and youngsters might not come to know of it and lay hands thereon. Presently, I espied a large earthen jar full of bran standing in a corner of the room, so herein I hid the rag with the gold coins and I misdeemed that it was safely concealed from wife and wees.

When I had put the Ashrafis a bottom the jar of bran, my wife came in and I said naught to her of the two friends or of aught had happened, but I set out for the Bazar to buy hemp.

Now as soon as I had left the house there came, by evil fate impelled, a man who sold Tafl, or fuller's earth, wherewith the poorer sort of women are wont to wash their hair. My wife would fain have bought some but not a single Kauri or almond had she. Then she took thought and said to herself, "This jar of bran is here to no purpose, I will exchange it for the clay," and he also, the Tafl seller, agreed to this proposal and went off taking the jar of bran as the price of the washing earth.

Anon I came back with a load of hemp upon my head and other five on the heads of as many porters who accompanied me; and I helped them off with their burthens and, after storing the stuff in a room, I paid and dismissed them. Then I stretched me out upon the floor to take rest awhile and looking towards the corner where once stood the jar of bran I found it gone. Words fail me, O Prince of True Believers, to describe the tumult of feelings which filled my heart at the sight. I sprang up with all speed and calling to my wife enquired of her whither the jar had been carried; and she replied that she had exchanged its contents for a trifle of washing clay.

Then cried I aloud, "O wretched, O miserable, what hast thou done? thou hast ruined me and thy children; thou hast given away great wealth to that clay-selling fellow!"

Then I told her all that had betided me, of the coming of the two friends and how I had hidden the hundred and ninety Ashrafis within the bran-jar; and she, on hearing this wept sore and beat her breast and tore her hair crying, "Where now shall I find that clay-seller? The wight is a stranger, never before did I see him about this quarter or this street." Then turning to me she continued, "Herein thou hast dealt right foolishly, for that thou didst not tell me of the matter, nor didst place any trust in me; otherwise this mishap would never have happened to us; no, never."

And she lamented with loud lamentation and bitter whereat I said, "Make not such hubbub nor display such trouble, lest our neighbours overhear thee, and learning of our mishap peradventure laugh at us and call us fools. It behoveth us to rest content with the will of Almighty Allah."

However the ten Ashrafis which I had taken from the two hundred sufficed me to carry on my trade and to live with more of ease for some short while; but I ever grieved and I marvelled much anent what could be said to Sa'di when he should come again; for inasmuch as he believed me not the first time I was assured in my mind that now he would denounce me aloud as a cheat and a liar.

One day of the days the twain, to wit, Sa'd and Sa'di, came strolling towards my house conversing and, as usual, arguing about me and my case; and I seeing them from afar left off working that I might hide myself, as I could not for very shame come forth and accost them. Seeing this and not guessing the reason they entered my dwelling and, saluting me with the salam, asked me how I had fared. I durst not raise my eyes so abashed and mortified was I, and with bended brow returned the greeting; when they, noting my sorry plight, marvelled saying, "Is all well with thee? Why art thou in this state? Hast thou not made good use of the gold or hast thou wasted thy wealth in lewd living?"

Quoth I, "O my lords, the story of the Ashrafis is none other than this. When ye departed from me I went home with the purse of money and, finding no one was in the house for all had gone out somewhere, I took out therefrom ten gold pieces. Then I put the rest together with the purse within a large earthen jar filled full of bran which had long stood in one corner of the room, so might the matter be kept privy from my wife and children. But whilst I was in the market buying me some hemp, my wife returned home; and at that moment there came in to her a man which sold fuller's earth for washing hair. She had need thereof withal naught to pay with; so she went out to him and said, 'I am clean without coin, but I have a quantity of bran; say me, wilt thou have that in change for thy clay?' The man agreed and accordingly my wife took the earth of him, and gave him in exchange the jarful of bran which he carried away with him and ganged his gait. An ye ask, 'Wherefore didst thou not confide the matter to thy spouse and tell her that thou hadst put the money in the jar?' I on my side answer, that ye gave me strict injunctions to keep the money this time with the utmost heed and caution. Methought that stead was the safest wherein to store the gold and I was loath to trust my wife lest haply she take some coin therefrom and expend it upon her household. O my lords, I am certified of your goodness and graciousness, but poverty and penury are writ in my Book of Fate; how then can I aspire to possessions and prosperity? Withal, never while I breathe the breath of life, shall I be forgetful of this your generous favour."

Quoth Sa'di, "Meseemeth I have disbursed four hundred Ashrafis to no purpose in giving them to thee; yet the intent wherewith they were given was that thou shouldst benefit thereby, not that I claim thy praise and thanksgiving."

So they twain compassionated and condoled with me in my misfortune; and presently Sa'd, an upright man and one who had acquaintance with me since many a year, produced a leaden coin which he had picked up from the path and was still carrying in his pocket; and, after shewing it to Sa'di, said to me, "Seest thou this bit of lead? Take it and by favour of Fate thou shalt find out what blessings it will bring to thee."

Sa'di on espying it laughed aloud and made jest of the matter and flouting said, "What advantage will there be to Hasan from this mite of lead and in what way shall he use it?" Sa'd handing me the leaden coin retorted in reply, "Give no heed to whatso Sa'di may say, but keep this by thee. Let him laugh an he please. One day haply shall come to pass, Inshallah—an it be the will of Almighty Allah—that thou shalt by means thereof become a wealthy man and a magnifico." I took the bit of lead and put it in my pocket, and the twain bade me farewell and went their way.

As soon as Sa'd and Sa'di had departed, I went on rope-twisting until night came and when doffing my dress to go to bed the bit of lead which Sa'd had given me fell out of my pocket; so I picked it up and set it carelessly in a small niche in the wall. Now that very night so it happened that a fisherman, one of my neighbours, stood in need of a small coin wherewith to buy some twine for mending his drag-net, as he was wont to do during the dark hours, in order that he might catch the fish ere dawn of day and selling his quarry, buy victuals for himself and his household. So, as he was accustomed to rise while yet somewhat of night remained, he bade his wife go round about to all the neighbours and borrow a copper that he might buy the twine required; and the woman went everywhere, from house to house, but nowhere could she get loan of a farthing, and at last she came home weary and disappointed.

Quoth the fisherman to her, "Hast thou been to Hasan al-Habbal?" and quoth she, "Nay, I have not tried at his place. It is the furthest of all the neighbours' houses and fanciest thou, even had I gone there, I could thence have brought back aught?"

"Off with thee, O laziest of hussies and good for nothing of baggages," cried the fisherman, "away with thee this instant; perchance he hath a copper to lend us."

Accordingly the woman, grumbling and muttering, fared forth and coming to my dwelling knocked at the door, saying, "O Hasan al-Habbal, my husband is in sore need of a pice wherewith to buy some twine for mending his nets."

Minding me of the coin which Sa'd had given me and where it had been put away, I shouted out to her, "Have patience, my spouse will go forth to thee and give thee what thou needest."

My wife, hearing all this hubbub, woke from sleep, and I told her where to find the bit of money, whereupon she fetched it and gave it to the woman, who joyed with exceeding joy, and said, "Thou and thy husband have shown great kindness to my man, wherefore I promise thee that whatsoever fish he may chance to catch at the first throw of the net shall be thine; and I am assured that my goodman, when he shall hear of this my promise, will consent thereto."

Accordingly when the woman took the money to her husband and told him of what pledge she had given, he was right willing, and said to her, "Thou hast done well and wisely in that thou madest this covenant."

Then having bought some twine and mended all the nets he rose before dawn and hastened riverwards to catch fish according to his custom. But when he cast the net into the stream for the first throw and haled it in, he found that it contained but one fish and that a full span or so in thickness, which he placed apart as my portion. Then he threw the net again and again and at each cast he caught many fishes both small and great, but none reached in size that he first had netted.

As soon as he returned home the fisherman came at once to me and brought the fish he had netted in my name, and said, "O our neighbour, my wife promised over night that thou shouldst have whatever fishes should come to ground at the first net throw; and this fish is the only one I caught. Here it is, prithee take it as a thanks offering for the kindness of last night, and as fulfilment of the promise. If Allah Almighty had vouchsafed to me of fish a seine-full, all had been thine but 'tis thy fate that only this one was landed at the first cast."

Said I, "The mite I gave thee yesternight was not of such value that I should look for somewhat in return"; and refused to accept it. But after much "say and said" he would not take back the fish, and he insisted that it was mine: wherefore I agreed to keep it and gave it to my wife, saying, "O woman, this fish is a return for the mite I gave last night to the fisherman our neighbour. Sa'd hath declared that by means of that coin I shall attain to much riches and abundant opulence."

Then I recounted to my wife how my two friends had visited me and what they said and did, and all concerning the leaden coin which Sa'd had given to me. She wondered at seeing but a single fish and said, "How shall I cook it? Meseemeth 'twere best to cut it up and broil it for the children, especially as we have naught of spices and condiments wherewith to dress it otherwise."

Then, as she sliced and cleansed the fish she found within its belly a large diamond which she supposed to be a bit of glass or crystal; for she oft had heard tell of diamonds but never with her own eyes had she beheld one. So she gave it to the youngest of the children for a plaything and when the others saw it, by reason of its brightness and brilliancy all desired to have and each kept it in turn awhile; moreover when night came and the lamp was lighted they crowded round the stone and gazed upon its beauty, and screamed and shouted with delight. When my wife had spread the table we sat down to supper and the eldest boy set the diamond upon the tray, and as soon as we all had finished eating, the children fought and scrambled as before for it. At first I paid no heed to their noise and hubbub, but when it waxed exceeding loud and irksome I asked my eldest lad the cause why they quarrelled and made such turmoil.

Quoth he, "The trouble and dispute are about a piece of glass which giveth forth a light as bright as the lamp."

Whereat I told him to produce it and marvelled greatly to see its sparkling water, and enquired of my wife whence she had gotten the piece of crystal.

Quoth she, "This I found within the belly of the fish as I was gutting it."

Still I did not suppose it to be aught but glass. Presently I bade my wife hide the lamp behind the hearth.

And when my wife had hidden the lamp from view, such was the brightness of the diamond that we could see right well without other light; wherefore I placed it upon the hearth that we might work by it, and said within myself, "The coin that Sa'd left with me hath produced this benefit that we no longer stand in need of a lamp: at least it saveth us oil." When the youngsters saw me put out the lamp and use the glass in its stead they jumped and danced for joy, and screamed and shouted with glee so that all the neighbours round about could hear them when I chid them and sent them to bed; we also went to rest and right soon fell asleep.

Next day I woke betimes and went on with my work and thought not of the piece of glass. Now there dwelt hard by us a wealthy Jew, a jeweller who bought and sold all kinds of precious stones; and, as he and his wife essayed to sleep that night, by reason of the noise and clamour of the children they were disturbed for many hours and slumber visited not their eyes. And when morn appeared, the jeweller's wife came to our house to make complaint both for herself and her husband anent the hubbub and shouting. Ere she could say a word of blame my wife, guessing the intent wherewith she came, addressed her saying, "O Rahil, I fear me that my children pestered thee last night with their laughing and crying. I crave thine indulgence in this matter; well thou must wot how children now cry now laugh at trifles. Come in and see the cause of all their excitement wherefor thou wouldst justly call me to account."

She did accordingly and saw the bit of glass about which the youngsters had made such din and uproar; and when she, who had long experience of all manner precious stones, beheld the diamond she was filled with wonderment. My wife then told her how she had found it in the fish's belly,

whereupon quoth the Jewess, "This bit of glass is more excellent than all other sorts of glass. I too have such an one as this which I am wont to wear sometimes; and wouldst thou sell it I will buy this thing of thee." Hearing her words the children began to cry and said, "O mother dear, an thou wilt not sell it we promise henceforth to make no noise."

Understanding that they would by no means part with it, the women held their peace and presently the Jewess fared forth, but ere she took her leave she whispered my wife, "See that thou tell the matter to none; and, if thou have a mind to sell it at once send me word."

Now the Jew was sitting in his shop when his wife went to him and told him of the bit of glass. Quoth he, "Go straightway back and offer a price for it, saying that 'tis for me. Begin with some small bidding, then raise the sum until thou get it."

The Jewess thereupon returned to my house and offered twenty Ashrafis, which my wife deemed a large sum to give for such a trifle; however, she would not close the bargain. At that moment I happened to leave my work and, coming home to our noon meal, saw the two women talking on the threshold; and my wife stopped me, saying, "This neighbour biddeth twenty Ashrafis to price for the piece of glass, but I have as yet given her no reply. What sayest thou?"

Then I bethought me of what Sa'd had told me; to wit, that much wealth would come to me by virtue of his leaden coin. The Jewess seeing how I hesitated bethought her that I would not consent to the price; so quoth she, "O neighbour, an thou wilt not agree to part with the bit of glass for twenty pieces of gold, I will e'en give thee fifty."

Hereat I reflected that whereas the Jewess raised her offer so readily from twenty golden pieces to fifty, this glass must surely be of great value; so I kept silence and answered her not a word. Then noting that I still held my peace she cried, "Take then one hundred: this be its full value; nay I know not in very deed if my husband will consent to so high a price."

Said I in reply, "O my good woman, why talk so foolishly? I will not sell it for aught less than an hundred thousand gold coins; and thou mayest take it at that price but only because thou art neighbour to us."

The Jewess raised her offer coin by coin to fifty thousand Ashrafis and said, "I pray thee wait till morning and sell it not till then, so that my man may come round and see it." "Right willingly," quoth I; "by all manner of means let thy husband drop in and inspect it."

Next day the Jew came to my house and I drew forth and showed to him the diamond which shone and glittered in my palm with light as bright as any lamp's. Presently, assured that all which his wife had told him of its water and lustre was strictly true, he took it in hand and, examining it and turning it about, marvelled with mighty marvel at its beauty saying, "My wife made offer of fifty thousand gold pieces: see now I will give thee yet another twenty thousand."

Said I, "Thy wife hath surely named to thee what sum I fixed to wit, one hundred thousand Ashrafis and naught less: I shall not abate one jot or tittle of this price." The Jew did all he could to buy it for a lesser sum; but I answered only, "It mattereth naught; an thou desire not to come to my terms I must needs sell it to some other jeweller."

At length he consented and weighed me out two thousand gold pieces by way of earnest-money, saying, "To-morrow I will bring the amount of my offer and carry off my diamond."

To this I gave assent and so, on the day following, he came to me and weighed out the full sum of one hundred thousand Ashrafis, which he had raised amongst his friends and partners in business. Then I gave him the diamond which had brought me such exceeding wealth, and offered thanks to him and praises unto Almighty Allah for this great good Fortune gotten unawares, and much I hoped soon to see my two friends, Sa'd and Sa'di, and to thank them likewise. So first I set my house in order and gave spending-money to my wife for home necessaries and for clothing herself and children; moreover, I also bought me a fine mansion and furnished it with the best.

Then said I to my wife, who thought of nothing save rich clothes and high diet and a life of ease and enjoyment, "It behoveth us not to give up this our craft: we must needs put by some coin and carry on the business." Accordingly, I went to all the rope-makers of the city and buying with much money several manufactories put them to work, and over each establishment I set an overseer, an intelligent man and a trustworthy, so that there is not now throughout Baghdad-city a single ward or quarter that hath not walks and workshops of mine for rope making. Nay, further, I have in each town and every district of Al-Irak warehouses, all under charge of honest supervisors; and thus it is that I have amassed such a muchel of wealth. Lastly, for my own especial place of business I bought another house, a ruined place with a sufficiency of land adjoining; and, pulling down the old shell, I edified in lieu thereof the new and spacious edifice which thy Highness hath deigned yesterday to look upon. Here all my workmen are lodged and here also are kept my office-books and accounts; and besides my warehouse it containeth apartments fitted with furniture in simple style all sufficient for myself and my family.

After some time I quitted my old home, wherein Sa'd and Sa'di had seen me working, and went and lived in the new mansion and not long after this removal my two friends and benefactors bethought them that they would come and visit me. They marvelled much when, entering my old workshop, they found me not, and they asked the neighbours, "Where dwelleth such and such a rope-maker? Is he alive or dead?"

Quoth the folk "He now is a rich merchant; and men no longer call him simply 'Hasan,' but entitle him 'Master Hasan the Rope-maker.' He hath built him a splendid building and he dwelleth in such and such a quarter."

Whereupon the two familiars set forth in search of me; and they rejoiced at the good report; albeit Sa'di would by no means be convinced that all my wealth had sprung (as Sa'd contended) from its root, that small leaden coin. Presently, conning the matter over in his mind he said to his comrade, "It delighteth me much to hear of all this good fortune which hath betided Hasan, despite that he twice deceived me and took from me four hundred gold pieces, whereby he hath gotten to himself these riches; for it is absurd to think that it hath come from the leaden coin thou gavest him. Withal I do forgive him and owe him no grudge."

Replied the other, "Thou art mistaken. I know Hasan of old to be a good man and true: he would not delude thee and what he told us is simple sooth. I am persuaded in my mind that he hath won all his wealth and opulence by the leaden coin: however we shall hear anon what he may have to say."

Conversing thus they came into the street wherein I now dwell and, seeing a large and magnificent mansion and a new made, they guessed it was mine. So they knocked and, on the porter opening, Sa'di marvelled to see such grandeur and so many folk sitting within, and feared lest haply they had unwittingly entered the house of some Emir. Then plucking courage he enquired of the porter, "Is this the dwelling place of Khwajah Hasan al-Habbal?"

The porter made reply, "This is verily the house of Khwajah Hasan al-Habbal; he is within and he sitteth in his office. I pray thee enter and one of the slaves will make known thy coming to him." Hereupon the two friends walked in, and as soon as I saw them I recognised them, and rising up to them I ran and kissed the hems of their garments. They would fain have fallen on my neck and embraced me, but with meekness of mind I would not suffer them so to do; and presently I led them into a large and spacious saloon, and bade them sit upon the highmost seats of honour. They would have constrained me to take the best place, but I exclaimed,

"O my lords, I am on no wise better than the poor rope-maker Hasan, who not unmindful of your worth and goodness ever prayeth for your welfare, and who deserveth not to sit in higher stead than you."

Then they took seat and I opposite them, when quoth Sa'di, "My heart rejoiceth with exceeding joy to see thee in this condition, for that Allah hath given thee all even as thou wishedst. I doubt not thou has gotten all this abundance and opulence by means of the four hundred gold pieces which I gave to thee; but say me truly wherefore didst thou twice deceive me and bespeak me falsely?"

Sa'd listened to these words with silent indignation, and ere I could make reply he broke out saying, "O Sa'di, how often have I assured thee that all which Hasan said aforetime anent the losing of the Ashrafis is very sooth and no leasing?"

Then they began to dispute each with other; when I, recovering from my surprise, exclaimed, "O my lords, of what avail is this contention? Be not at variance, I beseech you, on my account. All that had befallen me I made known to you; and, whether ye believe my words or ye believe them not, it mattereth but little. Now hearken to the whole truth of my tale."

Then I made known to them the story of the piece of lead which I had given to the fisherman and of the diamond found in the fish's belly; brief, I told them every whit even as I have now related to thy Highness. On hearing all my adventure Sa'di said, "O Khwajah Hasan, it seemeth to me passing strange that so great a diamond should be found in the belly of a fish; and I deem it a thing impossible that a kite should fly off with thy turband, or that thy wife should give away the jar of bran in exchange for fuller's earth. Thou sayest the tale is true, still can I not give credit to thy words, for I know full well that the four hundred gold pieces have gotten thee all this wealth."

But when they twain rose up to take their leave, I also arose and said, "O my lords, ye have shown favour to me in that ye have thus deigned visit me in my poor home. I beseech you now to taste of my food and to tarry here this night under your servant's roof; as to-morrow I would fain take you by the way of the river to a country house which I have lately bought."

Hereto they consented with some objections; and I, after giving orders for the evening meal, showed them about the house and displayed the furniture and entertained them with pleasing words and pleasant converse, till a slave came and announced that supper was served. So I led them to the saloon wherein were ranged the trays loaded with many kinds of meats; on all sides stood camphorated wax candles, and before the table were

gathered musicians singing and playing on various instruments of mirth and merriment, whilst in the upper part of the saloon men and women were dancing and making much diversion.

When we had supped we went to bed, and rising early we prayed the dawn-prayer, and presently embarked on a large and well-appointed boat, and the rowers rowing with a flowing tide soon landed us at my country seat. Then we strolled in a body about the grounds and entered the house, when I showed them our new buildings and displayed to them all that appertained thereto; and hereat they marvelled with great marvel. Thence we repaired to the garden and saw, planted in rows along the walks, fruit-trees of all kinds with ripe fruit bowed down, and watered with water from the river by means of brick-work channels. All round were flowering shrubs whose perfume gladdened the Zephyr; here and there fountains and jets of water shot high in air; and sweet-voiced birds made melody amid the leafy branches hymning the One, the Eternal; in short, the sights and scents on every side filled the soul with joy and gladness. My two friends walked about in joyance and delight, and thanked me again and again for bringing them to so lovely a site and said, "Almighty Allah prosper thee in house and garth."

At last I led them to the foot of a tall tree near to one of the garden walls and shewed them a little summer-house wherein I was wont to take rest and refreshment; and the room was furnished with cushions and divans and pillows purfled with virgin gold.

Now so it happened that, as we sat at rest within that summer house, two sons of mine, whom I had sent together with their governor to my country place for change of water and air, were roaming about the garden seeking birds' nests. Presently they came across a big one upon the top most boughs and tried to swarm up the trunk and carry it off, but by reason of their lack of strength and little practice they durst not venture so high; whereupon they bade a slave boy who ever attended on them, climb the tree. He did their bidding, but when looking into the nest he was amazed with exceeding amazement to see it mainly made of an old turband. So he brought down the stuff and handed it to the lads.

My eldest son took it from his hands and carried it to the arbour for me to see, and set it at my feet saying in high glee, "O my father, look here; this nest is made of cloth."

Sa'd and Sa'di wondered with all wonderment at the sight and the marvel grew the greater when I, after considering it closely, recognised it for the very turband whereon the kite had swooped and which had been borne off by the bird. Then quoth I to my two friends "Examine well this turband

and certify yourselves that it is the selfsame one worn upon my head when first ye honoured me with your presence."

Quoth Sa'd, "I know it not," and quoth Sa'di, "An thou find within it the hundred and ninety gold pieces, then shalt thou be assured that is thy turband in very sooth."

I said, "O my lord, this is, well I wot, that very turband."

And as I held it in my hand, I found it heavy of weight, and opening out the folds felt somewhat tied up in one of the corners of the cloth; so I unrolled the swathes when lo and behold! I came upon the purse of gold pieces.

Hereat, shewing it to Sa'di, I cried, "Canst thou not recognise this purse?" and he replied, "'Tis in truth the very purse of Ashrafis which I gave thee when first we met."

Then I opened the mouth and, pouring out the gold in one heap upon the carpet, bade him count his money; and he turned it over coin by coin and made the sum there of one hundred and ninety Ashrafis. Hereat waxing sore ashamed and confounded, he exclaimed, "Now do I believe thy words: nevertheless must thou admit that thou hast earned one half of this thy prodigious wealth with the two hundred gold pieces I gave thee after our second visit, and the other half by means of the mite thou gottest from Sa'd."

To this I made no answer, but my friends ceased not to dispute upon the matter. We then sat down to meat and drink, and when we had eaten our sufficiency, I and my two friends went to sleep in the cool arbour; after which when the sun was well nigh set we mounted and rode off to Baghdad leaving the servants to follow. However, arrived at the city we found all the shops shut and nowhere could we get grain and forage for the horses, and I sent off two slave boys who had run alongside of us to search for provender. One of them found a jar of bran in the shop of a corn-dealer and paying for the provision brought it, together with the jar, under promise that on the morrow he would carry back the vessel. Then he began to take out the bran by handfuls in the dark and to set it before the horses.

So as the slave boy took out the bran by handfuls and set it before the horses, suddenly his hand came upon a piece of cloth wherein was somewhat heavy. He brought it to me even as he found it and said, "See, is not this cloth the very one of whose loss thou hast ofttimes spoken to us?" I took it and wondering with great wonder knew it was the self same piece of stuff wherein I had tied up the hundred and four-score and ten Ashrafis before hiding them in the jar of bran.

Then said I to my friends, "O my lords, it hath pleased Almighty Allah, ere we parted, I and you, to bear me witness of my words and to stablish that I told you naught save whatso was very sooth."

And I resumed, addressing Sa'di, "See here the other sum of money, that is, the hundred and ninety Ashrafis which thou gayest me and which I tied up in this very piece of cloth I now recognise."

Then I sent for the earthen jar that they might see it, and also bade carry it to my wife that she also might bear witness, an it be or be not the very bran-jar which she gave in exchange for fuller's earth. Anon she sent us word and said, "Yea verily I know it well. 'Tis the same jar which I had filled with bran."

Accordingly Sa'di owned that he was wrong and said to S'ad, "Now I know that thou speakest truth, and am convinced that wealth cometh not by wealth; but only by the grace of Almighty Allah doth a poor man become a rich man." And he begged pardon for his mistrust and unbelief.

We accepted his excuses whereupon we retired to rest and early on the morrow my two friends bade me adieu and journeyed home wards with full persuasion that I had done no wrong and had not squandered the moneys they had given me.

Now when the Caliph Harun al-Rashid had heard the story of Khwajah Hasan to the end, he said, "I have known thee of old by fair report of thee from the folk who, one and all, declare that thou art a good man and true. Moreover the self same diamond whereby thou hast attained to so great riches is now in my treasury; so I would fain send for Sa'di forthright that he may see it with his own eyes, and weet for certain that not by means of money do men become or rich or poor."

The Prince of True Believers said moreover to Khwajah Hasan al-Habbal, "Go now and tell thy tale to my treasurer that he may take it down in writing for an everlasting memorial, and place the writ in the treasury together with the diamond."

Then the Caliph with a nod dismissed Khawajah Hasan; and Sidi Nu'uman and Baba Abdullah also kissed the foot of the throne and departed.

So when Queen Scheherazade had made an end of relating this history she was about to begin the story of "Ali Baba and the Forty Thieves," but King Shahryar prevented her, saying, "O Scheherazade I am well pleased with this thy tale, but now the dawn appeareth and the chanticleer of morn doth sound his shrill clarion. This day also I spare thy life, to the intent that I may listen at my ease to this new history of thine at the end of the coming night." Hereupon the three took their rest until the fittest time drew near.

411

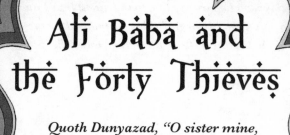

Ali Baba and the Forty Thieves

Quoth Dunyazad, "O sister mine,
an thou be other than sleepy, tell us one
of thy fair tales, so therewith we may cut
short the waking hours of this our night";
and quoth Scheherazade...

I n days of yore and in times and tides long gone before there dwelt in a certain town of Persia two brothers one named Kasim and the other Ali Baba, who at their father's demise had divided the little wealth he had left to them with equitable division, and had lost no time in wasting and spending it all. The elder, however, presently took to himself a wife, the daughter of an opulent merchant; so that when his father-in-law fared to the mercy of Almighty Allah, he became owner of a large shop filled with rare goods and costly wares and of a storehouse stocked with precious stuffs; likewise of much gold that was buried in the ground. Thus was he known throughout the city as a substantial man. But the woman whom Ali Baba had married was poor and needy; they lived, therefore, in a mean hovel and Ali Baba eked out a scanty livelihood by the sale of fuel which he daily collected in the jungle and carried about the town to the Bazar upon his three asses.

Now it chanced one day that Ali Baba had cut dead branches and dry fuel sufficient for his need, and had placed the load upon his beasts when suddenly he espied a dust-cloud spireing high in air to his right and moving rapidly towards him; and when he closely considered it he descried a troop of horsemen riding on amain and about to reach him. At this sight he was sore alarmed, and fearing lest perchance they were a band of bandits who would slay him and drive off his donkeys, in his affright he began to run; but forasmuch as they were near hand and he could not escape from out the forest, he drove his animals laden with the fuel into a bye-way of the bushes and swarmed up a thick trunk of a huge tree to hide himself therein; and he sat upon a branch whence he could descry everything beneath him whilst none below could catch a glimpse of him above; and that tree grew close beside a rock which towered high above head. The horsemen, young, active, and doughty riders, came close up to the rock-face and all dismounted; whereat Ali Baba took good note of them and soon he was fully persuaded by their mien and demeanour that they were a troop of highwaymen who, having fallen upon a caravan had despoiled it and carried off the spoil and brought their booty to this place with intent of concealing it safely in some cache. Moreover he observed that they were forty in number.

Ali Baba saw the robbers each unbridle his horse and hobble it; then all took off their saddle-bags which proved to be full of gold and silver. The man who seemed to be the captain presently pushed forwards, load on shoulder, through thorns and thickets, till he came up to a certain spot where he uttered these strange words, "Open, O Simsim!" and forthwith appeared a wide doorway in the face of the rock. The robbers went in and last of all their Chief and then the portal shut of itself.

Long while they stayed within the cave whilst Ali Baba was constrained to abide perched upon the tree, reflecting that if he came down peradventure the band might issue forth that very moment and seize him and slay him. At last he had determined to mount one of the horses and driving on his asses to return townwards, when suddenly the portal dew open. The robber-chief was first to issue forth; then, standing at the entrance, he saw and counted his men as they came out, and lastly he spake the magical words, "Shut, O Simsim!" whereat the door closed of itself. When all had passed muster and review, each slung on his saddle-bags and bridled his own horse and as soon as ready they rode off, led by the leader, in the direction whence they came.

Ali Baba remained still perched on the tree and watched their departure; nor would he descend until what time they were clean gone out of sight, lest perchance one of them return and look around and descry

him. Then he thought within himself, "I too will try the virtue of those magical words and see if at my bidding the door will open and close." So he called out aloud, "Open, O Simsim!" And no sooner had he spoken than straightway the portal flew open and he entered within.

He saw a large cavern and a vaulted, in height equalling the stature of a full-grown man and it was hewn in the live stone and lighted up with light that came through air-holes and bullseyes in the upper surface of the rock which formed the roof. He had expected to find naught save outer gloom in this robbers' den, and he was surprised to see the whole room filled with bales of all manner stuffs, and heaped up from sole to ceiling with camel-loads of silks and brocades and embroidered cloths and mounds on mounds of vari-coloured carpetings; besides which he espied coins golden and silvern without measure or account, some piled upon the ground and others bound in leathern bags and sacks. Seeing these goods and moneys in such abundance, Ali Baba determined in his mind that not during a few years only but for many generations thieves must have stored their gains and spoils in this place.

When he stood within the cave, its door had closed upon him, yet he was not dismayed since he had kept in memory the magical words; and he took no heed of the precious stuffs around him, but applied himself only and wholly to the sacks of Ashrafis. Of these he carried out as many as he judged sufficient burthen for the beasts; then he loaded them upon his animals, and covered this plunder with sticks and fuel, so none might discern the bags, but might think that he was carrying home his usual ware. Lastly he called out, "Shut, O Simsim!" and forthwith the door closed, for the spell so wrought that whensoever any entered the cave, its portal shut of itself behind him; and, as he issued therefrom, the same would neither open nor close again till he had pronounced the words, "Shut, O Simsim!"

Presently, having laden his asses Ali Baba urged them before him with all speed to the city and reaching home he drove them into the yard; and, shutting close the outer door, took down first the sticks and after the bags of gold which he carried in to his wife. She felt them and finding them full of coin suspected that Ali Baba had been robbing and fell to berating and blaming him for that he should do so ill a thing.

Quoth Ali Baba to his wife: "Indeed I am no robber and rather do thou rejoice with me at our good fortune." Hereupon he told her of his adventure and began to pour the gold from the bags in heaps before her, and her sight was dazzled by the sheen and her heart delighted at his recital and adventures. Then she began counting the gold, whereat quoth Ali Baba,

"O silly woman how long wilt thou continue turning over the coin? now let me dig a hole wherein to hide this treasure that none may know its secret."

Quoth she, "Right is thy rede! still would I weigh the moneys and have some inkling of their amount;" and he replied, "As thou pleasest, but see thou tell no man."

So she went off in haste to Kasim's home to borrow weights and scales wherewith she might balance the Ashrafis and make some reckoning of their value; and when she could not find Kasim she said to his wife, "Lend me, I pray thee, thy scales for a moment."

Replied her sister-in-law, "Hast thou need of the bigger balance or the smaller?" and the other rejoined, "I need not the large scales, give me the little"; and her sister-in-law cried, "Stay here a moment whilst I look about and find thy want."

With this pretext Kasim's wife went aside and secretly smeared wax and suet over the pan of the balance, that she might know what thing it was Ali Baba's wife would weigh, for she made sure that whatso it be some bit thereof would stick to the wax and fat. So the woman took this opportunity to satisfy her curiosity, and Ali Baba's wife suspecting naught thereof carried home the scales and began to weigh the gold, whilst Ali Baba ceased not digging; and, when the money was weighed, they twain stowed it into the hole which they carefully filled up with earth.

Then the good wife took back the scales to her kinswoman, all unknowing that an Ashrafi had adhered to the cup of the scales; but when Kasim's wife espied the gold coin she fumed with envy and wrath saying to herself, "So ho! they borrowed my balance to weigh out Ashrafis?" and she marvelled greatly whence so poor a man as Ali Baba had gotten such store of wealth that he should be obliged to weigh it with a pair of scales.

Now after long pondering the matter, when her husband returned home at eventide, she said to him, "O man, thou deemest thyself a wight of wealth and substance, but lo, thy brother Ali Baba is an Emir by the side of thee and richer far than thou art. He hath such heaps of gold that he must needs weigh his moneys with scales, whilst thou, forsooth, art satisfied to count thy coin."

"Whence knowest thou this?" asked Kasim, and in answer his wife related all anent the pair of scales and how she found an Ashrafi stuck to them, and shewed him the gold coin which bore the mark and superscription of some ancient king. No sleep had Kasim all that night by reason of his envy and jealousy and covetise; and next morning he rose betimes and going to Ali Baba said, "O my brother, to all appearance thou art poor and needy; but in effect thou hast a store of wealth so abundant that perforce thou must weigh thy gold with scales."

Quoth Ali Baba, "What is this thou sayest? I understand thee not; make clear thy purport;" and quoth Kasim with ready rage, "Feign not that thou art ignorant of what I say and think not to deceive me." Then showing him the Ashrafi he cried, "Thousands of gold coins such as these thou hast put by; and meanwhile my wife found this one stuck to the cup of the scales."

Then Ali Baba understood how both Kasim and his wife knew that he had store of Ashrafis, and said in his mind that it would not avail him to keep the matter hidden, but would rather cause ill-will and mischief; and thus he was induced to tell his brother every whit concerning the bandits and also of the treasure trove in the cave. When he had heard the story, Kasim exclaimed, "I would fain learn of thee the certainty of the place where thou foundest the moneys; also the magical words whereby the door opened and closed; and I forewarn thee an thou tell me not the whole truth, I will give notice of those Ashrafis to the Wali; then shalt thou forfeit all thy wealth and be disgraced and thrown into gaol."

Thereupon Ali Baba told him his tale not forgetting the magical words; and Kasim who kept careful heed of all these matters next day set out, driving ten mules he had hired, and readily found the place which Ali Baba had described to him. And when he came to the afore said rock and to the tree whereon Ali Baba had hidden himself and he had made sure of the door he cried in great joy, "Open, O Simsim!" The portal yawned wide at once and Kasim went within and saw the piles of jewels and treasures lying ranged all around; and, as soon as he stood amongst them the door shut after him as wont to do.

He walked about in ecstasy marvelling at the treasures, and when weary of admiration he gathered together bags of Ashrafis, a sufficient load for his ten mules, and placed them by the entrance in readiness to be carried outside and set upon the beasts. But by the will of Allah Almighty he had clean forgotten the cabalistic words and cried out, "Open, O Barley!" whereat the door refused to move. Astonished and confused beyond measure he named the names of all manner of grains save sesame, which had slipped from his memory as though he had never heard the word; whereat in his dire distress he heeded not the Ashrafis that lay heaped at the entrance and paced to and fro, backwards and forwards, within the cave sorely puzzled and perplexed. The wealth whose sight had erewhile filled his heart with joy and gladness was now the cause of bitter grief and sadness.

Kasim gave up all hope of the life which he by his greed and envy had so sore imperilled. It came to pass that at noontide the robbers, returning by that way, saw from afar some mules standing beside the entrance and much they marvelled at what had brought the beasts to that place; for, inasmuch as Kasim by mischance had failed to tether or hobble them, they had strayed about the jungle and were browsing hither and thither. However, the thieves paid scant regard to the estrays nor cared they to secure them, but only wondered by what means they had wandered so far from the town. Then, reaching the cave the Captain and his troop dismounted and going up to the door repeated the formula and at once it flew open.

Now Kasim had heard from within the cave the horse hooves drawing nigh and yet nigher; and he fell down to the ground in a fit of fear never doubting that it was the clatter of the banditti who would slaughter him without fail. Howbeit he presently took heart of grace and at the moment when the door flew open he rushed out hoping to make good his escape. But the unhappy ran full tilt against the Captain who stood in front of the band, and felled him to the ground; where upon a robber standing near his chief at once bared his brand and with one cut crave Kasim clean in twain. Thereupon the robbers rushed into the cavern, and put back as they were before the bags of Ashrafis which Kasim had heaped up at the doorway ready for taking away; nor recked they aught of those which Ali Baba had removed, so dazed and amazed were they to discover by what means the strange man had effected an entrance. All knew that it was not possible for any to drop through the skylights so tall and steep was the rock's face, withal slippery of ascent; and also that none could enter by the portal unless he knew the magical words whereby to open it. However they presently quartered the dead body of Kasim and hung it to the door within the cavern, two parts to the right jamb and as many to the left that the sight might be a warning of approaching doom for all who dared enter the cave. Then coming out they closed the hoard door and rode away upon their wonted work.

417

Now when night fell and Kasim came not home, his wife waxed uneasy in mind and running round to Ali Baba said, "O my brother, Kasim hath not returned: thou knowest whither he went, and sore I fear me some misfortune hath betided him."

Ali Baba also divined that a mishap had happened to prevent his return; not the less, however, he strove to comfort his sister-in-law with words of cheer and said, "O wife of my brother, Kasim haply exerciseth discretion and, avoiding the city, cometh by a roundabout road and will be here anon. This, I do believe, is the reason why he tarrieth." Thereupon comforted in spirit Kasim's wife fared homewards and sat awaiting her husband's return; but when half the night was spent and still he came not, she was as one distraught. She feared to cry aloud for her grief, lest haply the neighbours hearing her should come and learn the secret; so she wept in silence and upbraiding herself fell to thinking, "Wherefore did I disclose this secret to him and beget envy and jealousy of Ali Baba? this be the fruit thereof and hence the disaster that hath come down upon me." She spent the rest of the night in bitter tears and early on the morrow tried in hottest hurry to Ali Baba and prayed that he would go forth in quest of his brother; so he strove to console her and straightway set out with his asses for the forest.

Presently, reaching the rock he wondered to see stains of blood freshly shed and not finding his brother or the ten mules he forefelt a calamity from so evil a sign. He then went to the door and saying, "Open, O Simsim!" he pushed in and saw the dead body of Kasim, two parts hanging to the right, and the rest to the left of the entrance. Albeit he was affrighted beyond measure of affright he wrapped the quarters in two cloths and laid them upon one of his asses, hiding them carefully with sticks and fuel that none might see them. Then he placed the bags of gold upon the two other animals and likewise covered them most carefully; and, when all was made ready he closed the cave door with the magical words, and set him forth wending homewards with all ward and watchfulness. The asses with the load of Ashrafis he made over to his wife and bade her bury the bags with diligence; but he told her not the condition in which he had come upon his brother Kasim. Then he went with the other ass, to wit, the beast whereon was laid the corpse to the widow's house and knocked gently at the door.

Now Kasim had a slave-girl shrewd and sharp witted, Morgiana hight. She as softly undid the bolt and admitted Ali Baba and the ass into the courtyard of the house, when he let down the body from the beast's back and said, "O Morgiana, haste thee and make thee ready to perform the rites for the burial of thy lord: I now go to tell the tidings to thy mistress and I will quickly return to help thee in this matter."

At that instant Kasim's widow seeing her brother-in-law, exclaimed, "O Ali Baba, what news bringest thou of my spouse? Alas, I see grief tokens written upon thy countenance. Say quickly what hath happened." Then he recounted to her how it had fared with her husband and how he had been slain by the robbers and in what wise he had brought home the dead body.

Ali Baba pursued: "O my lady, what was to happen hath happened but it behoveth us to keep this matter secret, for that our lives depend upon privacy."

She wept with sore weeping and made answer, "It hath fared with my husband according to the fiat of Fate; and now for thy safety's sake I give thee my word to keep the affair concealed."

He replied, "Naught can avail when Allah hath decreed. Rest thee in patience; until the days of thy widow-hood be accomplisht; after which time I will take thee to wife, and thou shalt live in comfort and happiness; and fear not lest my first spouse vex thee or show aught of jealousy, for that she is kindly and tender of heart."

The widow lamenting her loss noisily, cried, "Be it as e'en thou please."

Then Ali Baba farewelled her, weeping and wailing for her husband; and joining Morgiana took counsel with her how to manage the burial of his brother. So, after much consultation and many warnings, he left the slave-girl and departed home driving his ass before him.

As soon as Ali Baba had fared forth Morgiana went quickly to a druggist's shop; and, that she might the better dissemble with him and not make known the matter, she asked of him a drug often administered to men when diseased with dangerous dis-temper. He gave it saying, "Who is there in thy house that lieth so ill as to require this medicine?" and said she, "My Master Kasim is sick well nigh unto death: for many days he hath nor spoken nor tasted aught of food, so that almost we despair of his life."

Next day Morgiana went again and asked the druggist for more of medicine and essences such as are adhibited to the sick when at door of death, that the moribund may haply rally before the last breath. The man gave the potion and she taking it sighed aloud and wept, saying, "I fear me he may not have strength to drink this draught: methinks all will be over with him ere I return to the house."

Meanwhile Ali Baba was anxiously awaiting to hear sounds of wailing and lamentation in Kasim's home that he might at such signal hasten thither and take part in the ceremonies of the funeral. Early on the second day Morgiana went with veiled face to one Baba Mustafa, a tailor well shotten in years whose craft was to make shrouds and cerecloths; and as soon as she saw him open his shop she gave him a gold piece and said, "Do thou bind a bandage over thine eyes and come along with me." Mustafa made as though he would not go, whereat Morgiana placed a second gold coin in his palm and entreated him to accompany her. The tailor presently consented for greed of gain, so tying a kerchief tightly over his eyes she led him by the hand to the house wherein lay the dead body of her master. Then, taking off the bandage in the darkened room she bade him sew together the quarters of the corpse, limb to its limb; and, casting a cloth upon the body, said to the tailor "Make haste and sew a shroud according to the size of this dead man and I will give thee therefor yet another ducat." Baba Mustafa quickly made the cerecloth of fitting length and breadth, and Morgiana paid him the promised Ashrafi; then once more bandaging his eyes led him back to the place whence she had brought him.

After this she returned hurriedly home and with the help of Ali Baba washed the body in warm water and donning the shroud lay the corpse upon a clean place ready for burial. This done Morgiana went to the mosque and gave notice to an Imam that a funeral was awaiting the mourners in a certain household, and prayed that he would come to read the prayers for the dead; and the Imam went back with her. Then four neighbours took up the bier and bore it on their shoulders and fared forth with the Imam and others who were wont to give assistance at such obsequies. After the funeral prayers were ended four other men carried off the coffin; and Morgiana walked before it bare of head, striking her breast and weeping and wailing with exceeding loud lament, whilst Ali Baba and the neighbours came behind. In such order they entered the cemetery and buried him; then, leaving him to Munkar and Nakir the Questioners of the Dead all wended their ways.

Presently the women of the quarter, according to the custom of the city, gathered together in the house of mourning and sat an hour with Kasim's widow comforting and condoling, presently leaving her somewhat resigned and cheered. Ali Baba stayed forty days at home in ceremonial lamentation for the loss of his brother; so none within the town save himself and his wife (Kasim's widow) and Morgiana knew aught about the secret. And when the forty days of mourning were ended Ali Baba removed to his own quarters all the property belonging to the deceased and openly married the widow; then he appointed his nephew, his brother's eldest son, who had lived a long time with a wealthy merchant and was perfect of knowledge in all matters of trade, such as selling and buying, to take charge of the defunct's shop and to carry on the business.

It so chanced one day when the robbers, as was their wont, came to the treasure-cave that they marvelled exceedingly to find nor sign nor trace of Kasim's body whilst they observed that much of gold had been carried off. Quoth the Captain, "Now it behoveth us to make enquiry in this matter; else shall we suffer much of loss and this our treasure, which we and our forefathers have amassed during the course of many years, will little by little be wasted and spoiled." Hereto all assented and with single mind agreed that he whom they had slain had knowledge of the magical words whereby the door was made to open; moreover that some one beside him had cognizance the spell and had carried off the body, and also much of gold; wherefore they needs must make diligent research and find out who the man ever might be.

They then took counsel and determined that one amongst them, who should be sagacious and deft of wit, must don the dress of some merchant from foreign parts; then, repairing to the city he must go about from quarter to quarter and from street to street, and learn if any townsman had lately died and if so where he wont to dwell, that with this clue they might be enabled to find the wight they sought. Hereat said one of the robbers, "Grant me leave that I fare and find out such tidings in the town and bring thee word anon; and if I fail of my purpose I hold my life in forfeit." Accordingly that bandit, after disguising himself by dress, pushed at night into the town and next morning early he repaired to the market square and saw that none of the shops had yet been opened, save only that of Baba Mustafa the tailor, who thread and needle in hand sat upon his working stool. The thief bade him good day and said, "'Tis yet dark: how canst thou see to sew?"

Said the tailor, "I perceive thou art a stranger. Despite my years my eyesight is so keen that only yesterday I sewed together a dead body whilst sitting in a room quite darkened."

Quoth the bandit thereupon to himself, "I shall get somewhat of my want from this snip;" and to secure a further clue he asked, "Meseemeth thou wouldst jest with me and thou meanest that a cerecloth for a corpse was stitched by thee and that thy business is to sew shrouds."

Answered the tailor, "It mattereth not to thee: question me no more questions."

Thereupon the robber placed an Ashrafi in his hand and continued, "I desire not to discover aught thou hidest, albeit my breast like every honest man's is the grave of secrets; and this only would I learn of thee, in what house didst thou do that job? Canst thou direct me thither, or thyself conduct me thereto?"

The tailor took the gold with greed and cried, "I have not seen with my own eyes the way to that house. A certain bondswoman led me to a place which I know right well and there she bandaged my eyes and guided me to some tenement and lastly carried me into a darkened room where lay

the dead body dismembered. Then she unbound the kerchief and bade me sew together first the corpse and then the shroud, which having done she again blindfolded me and led me back to the stead whence she had brought me and left me there. Thou seest then I am not able to tell thee where thou shalt find the house."

Quoth the robber, "Albeit thou knowest not the dwelling whereof thou speakest, still canst thou take me to the place where thou west blindfolded; then I will bind a kerchief over thine eyes and lead thee as thou west led: on this wise per chance thou mayest hit upon the site. An thou wilt do this favour by me, see here another golden ducat is thine." There upon the bandit slipped a second Ashrafi into the tailor's palm, and Baba Mustafa thrust it with the first into his pocket; then, leaving his shop as it was, he walked to the place where Morgiana had tied the kerchief around his eyes, and with him went the robber who, after binding on the bandage, led him by the hand. Baba Mustafa, who was clever and keen-witted, presently striking the street whereby he had fared with the handmaid, walked on counting step by step; then, halting suddenly, he said, "Thus far I came with her"; and the twain stopped in front of Kasim's house wherein now dwelt his brother Ali Baba.

The robber then made marks with white chalk upon the door to the end that he might readily find it at some future time, and removing the bandage from the tailor's eyes said, "O Baba Mustafa, I thank thee for this favour: and Almighty Allah guerdon thee for thy goodness. Tell me now, I pray thee, who dwelleth in yonder house?"

Quoth he, "In very sooth I wot not, for I have little knowledge concerning this quarter of the city"; and the bandit, understanding that he could find no further clue from the tailor, dismissed him to his shop with abundant thanks, and hastened back to the tryst place in the jungle where the band awaited his coming.

Not long after it so fortuned that Morgiana, going out upon some errand, marvelled exceedingly at seeing the chalk-marks showing white in the door; she stood awhile deep in thought and presently divined that some enemy had made the signs that he might recognize the house and play some sleight upon her lord. She therefore chalked the doors of all her neighbours in like manner and kept the matter secret, never entrusting it or to master or to mistress.

Meanwhile the robber told his comrades his tale of adventure and how he had found the clue; so the Captain and with him all the band went one after other by different ways till they entered the city; and he who had placed the mark on Ali Baba's door accompanied the Chief to point out the place. He conducted him straightway to the house and strewing the sign exclaimed, "Here dwelleth he of whom we are in search!"

But when the Captain looked around him he saw that all the dwellings bore chalk-marks after like fashion and he wondered saying, "By what manner of means knowest thou which house of all these houses that bear similar signs is that whereof thou spakest?"

Hereat the robber-guide was confounded beyond measure of confusion, and could make no answer; then with an oath he cried, "I did assuredly set a sign upon a door, but I know not whence came all the marks upon the other entrances; nor can I say for a surety which it was I chalked."

Thereupon the Captain returned to the marketplace and said to his men, "We have toiled and laboured in vain, nor have we found the house we went forth to seek. Return we now to the forest our rendezvous: I also will fare thither." Then all trooped off and assembled together within the treasure-cave; and, when the robbers had all met, the Captain judged him worthy of punishment who had spoken falsely and had led them through the city to no purpose. So he imprisoned him in presence of them all; and then said he, "To him amongst you will I show special favour who shall go to town and bring me intelligence whereby we may lay hands upon the plunderer of our property."

Hereat another of the company came forward and said, "I am ready to go and enquire into the case, and 'tis I who will bring thee to thy wish."

The Captain after giving him presents and promises despatched him upon his errand; and by the decree of Destiny which none may gainsay, this second robber went first to the house of Baba Mustafa the tailor, as had done the thief who had foregone him. In like manner he also persuaded the snip with gifts of golden coin that he be led hood-winked and thus too he was guided to Ali Baba's door. Here noting the work of his predecessor, he affixed to the jamb a mark with red chalk the better to distinguish it from the others whereon still showed the white. Then tried he back in stealth to his company; but Morgiana on her part also descried the red sign on the entrance and with subtle forethought marked all the others after the same fashion; nor told she any what she had done.

Meanwhile the bandit rejoined his band and vauntingly said, "O our Captain, I have found the house and thereon put a mark whereby I shall distinguish it clearly from all its neighbours."

The Captain despatched another of his men to the city and he found the place, but, as aforetime, when the troop repaired thither they saw each and every house marked with signs of red chalk. So they returned disappointed and the Captain, waxing displeased exceedingly and distraught, clapped also this spy into gaol. Then said the chief to himself, "Two men have failed in their endeavour and have met their rightful meed of punishment; and I trow that none other of my band will essay to follow up their research; so I myself will go and find the house of this wight." Accordingly he fared along and aided by the tailor Baba Mustafa, who had gained much gain of golden pieces in this matter, he hit upon the house of Ali Baba; and here he made no outward show or sign, but marked it on the tablet of his heart and impressed the picture upon the page of his memory.

Then returning to the jungle he said to his men, "I have full cognizance of the place and have limned it clearly in my mind; so now there will be no difficulty in finding it. Go forth straightways and buy me and bring hither nineteen mules together with one large leathern jar of mustard oil and seven and thirty vessels of the same kind clean empty. Without me and the two locked up in gaol ye number thirty-seven souls; so I will stow you away armed and accoutred each within his jar and will load two upon each mule, and upon the nineteenth mule there shall be a man in an empty jar on one side, and on the other the jar full of oil. I for my part, in guise of an oil-merchant, will drive the mules into the town, arriving at the house by night, and will ask permission of its master to tarry there until morning. After this we shall seek occasion during the dark hours to rise up and fall upon him and slay him." Furthermore the Captain spake saying, "When we have made an end of him we shall recover the gold and treasure whereof he robbed us and bring it back upon the mules."

This counsel pleased the robbers who went forthwith and purchased mules and huge leathern jars, and did as the Captain had bidden them. And after a delay of three days shortly before nightfall they arose; and over smearing all the jars with oil of mustard, each hid him inside an empty vessel. The Chief then disguised himself in trader's gear and placed the jars upon the nineteen mules; to wit, the thirty-seven vessels in each of which lay a robber armed and accoutred, and the one that was full of oil. This done, he drove the beasts before him and presently he reached Ali Baba's place at nightfall; when it chanced that the house-master was strolling after supper to and fro in front of his home.

The Captain saluted him with the salam and said, "I come from such and such a village with oil; and ofttimes have I been here a selling oil, but now to my grief I have arrived too late and I am sore troubled and perplexed as to where I shall spend the night. An thou have pity on me I pray thee grant that I tarry here in thy court yard and ease the mules by taking down the jars and giving the beasts somewhat of fodder."

Albeit Ali Baba had heard the Captain's voice when perched upon the tree and had seen him enter the cave, yet by reason of the disguise he knew him not for the leader of the thieves, and granted his request with hearty welcome and gave him full license to halt there for the night. He then pointed out an empty shed wherein to tether the mules and bade one of the slave-boys go fetch grain and water. He also gave orders to the slave-girl Morgiana saying, "A guest hath come hither and tarrieth here to night. Do thou busy thyself with all speed about his supper and make ready the guest bed for him."

Presently, when the Captain had let down all the jars and had fed and watered his mules, Ali Baba received him with all courtesy and kindness, and summoning Morgiana said in his presence, "See thou fail not in service of this our stranger nor suffer him to lack for aught. To-morrow early I would fare to the Hammam and bathe; so do thou give my slave-boy Abdullah a suit of clean white clothes which I may put on after washing; moreover make thee ready a somewhat of broth overnight that I may drink it after my return home."

Replied she, "I will have all in readiness as thou hast bidden."

So Ali Baba retired to his rest, and the Captain, having supped, repaired to the shed and saw that all the mules had their food and drink for the night. The Captain, after seeing to the mules and the jars which Ali Baba and his household held to be full of oil, finding utter privacy, whispered to his men who were in ambush, "This night at midnight when ye hear my voice, do you quickly open with your sharp knives the leathern jars from top to bottom and issue forth without delay."

Then passing through the kitchen he reached the chamber wherein a bed had been dispread for him, Morgiana showing the way with a lamp. Quoth she, "An thou need aught beside I pray thee command this thy slave who is ever ready to obey thy say!"

He made answer, "Naught else need I"; then, putting out the light, he lay him down on the bed to sleep awhile ere the time came to rouse his men and finish off the work.

Meanwhile Morgiana did as her master had bidden her: she first took out a suit of clean white clothes and made it over to Abdullah who had not yet gone to rest; then she placed the pipkin upon the hearth to boil the broth and blew the fire till it burnt briskly. After a short delay she needs must see an the broth be boiling, but by that time all the lamps had gone out and she found that the oil was spent and that nowhere could she get a light.

The slave-boy Abdullah observed that she was troubled and perplexed hereat, and quoth he to her, "Why make so much ado? In yonder shed are many jars of oil: go now and take as much soever as thou listest."

Morgiana gave thanks to him for his suggestion; and Abdullah, who was lying at his ease in the hall, went off to sleep so that he might wake betimes and serve Ali Baba in the bath.

So the handmaiden rose and with oil-can in hand walked to the shed where stood the leathern jars all ranged in rows. Now, as she drew nigh unto one of the vessels, the thief who was hidden therein hearing the tread of footsteps bethought him that it was of his Captain whose summons he awaited; so he whispered, "Is it now time for us to sally forth?"

Morgiana started back affrighted at the sound of human accents; but, inasmuch as she was bold and ready of wit, she replied, "The time is not yet come," and said to herself, "These jars are not full of oil and herein I perceive a manner of mystery. Haply the oil-merchant hatcheth some treacherous plot against my lord; so Allah, the Compassionating, the Compassionate, protect us from his snares!" Wherefore she answered in a voice made like to the Captain's, "Not yet, the time is not come." Then she went to the next jar and returned the same reply to him who was within, and so on to all the vessels one by one. Then said she in herself, "Laud to the Lord! my master took this fellow in believing him to be an oil-merchant, but lo, he hath admitted a band of robbers, who only await the signal to fall upon him and plunder the place and do him die." Then passed she on to the furthest jar and finding it brimming with oil, filled her can, and returning to the kitchen, trimmed the lamp and lit the wicks; then, bringing forth a large cauldron, she set it upon the fire, and filling it with oil from out the jar heaped wood upon the hearth and fanned it to a fierce flame the readier to boil its contents. When this was done she baled it out in potfuls and poured it seething hot into the leathern vessels one by one while the thieves unable to escape were scalded to death and every jar contained a corpse. Thus did this slave-girl by her subtle wit make a clean end of all noiselessly and unknown even to the dwellers in the house.

Now when she had satisfied herself that each and every of the men had been slain, she went back to the kitchen and shutting to the door sat brewing Ali Baba's broth. Scarce had an hour passed before the Captain woke from sleep; and, opening wide his window, saw that all was dark and silent; so he clapped his hands as a signal for his men to come forth but not a sound was heard in return. After awhile he clapped again and called aloud but got no answer; and when he cried out a third time without reply he was perplexed and went out to the shed wherein stood the jars. He thought to himself, "Perchance all are fallen asleep whenas the time for action is now at hand, so I must e'en awaken them without stay or delay." Then approaching the nearest jar he was startled by a smell of oil and seething flesh; and touching it outside he felt it reeking hot; then going to the others one by one, he found all in like condition. Hereat he knew for a surety the fate which had betided his band and, fearing for his own safety, he clomb on to the wall, and thence dropping into a garden made his escape in high dudgeon and sore disappointment.

Morgiana awaited awhile to see the Captain return from the shed but he came not; whereat she knew that he had scaled the wall and had taken to flight, for that the street-door was double locked; and the thieves being all disposed of on this wise Morgiana laid her down to sleep in perfect solace and ease of mind. When two hours of darkness yet remained, Ali Baba awoke and went to the Hammam knowing naught of the night adventure, for the gallant slave-girl had not aroused him, nor indeed had she deemed such action expedient, because had she sought an opportunity of reporting to him her plan, she might haply have lost her chance and spoiled the project. The sun was high over the horizon when Ali Baba walked back from the Baths; and he marvelled exceedingly to see the jars still standing under the shed and said, "How cometh it that he, the oil-merchant my guest, hath not carried to the market his mules and jars of oil?"

Ali Baba presently asked Morgiana what had befallen the oil-merchant his guest whom he had placed under her charge; and she answered, "Allah Almighty vouchsafe to thee six score years and ten of safety! I will tell thee in privacy of this merchant."

So Ali Baba went apart with his slave-girl, who taking him with out the house first locked the court-door; then showing him a jar she said, "Prithee look into this and see if within there be oil or aught else." Thereupon peering inside it he perceived a man at which sight he cried aloud and fain would have fled in his fright.

Quoth Morgiana, "Fear him not, this man hath no longer the force to work thee harm, he lieth dead and stone dead."

Hearing such words of comfort and reassurance Ali Baba asked "O Morgiana, what evils have we escaped and by what means hath this wretch become the quarry of Fate?"

She answered "Alhamdolillah Praise be to Almighty Allah! I will inform thee fully of the case; but hush thee, speak not aloud, lest haply the neighbours learn the secret and it end in our confusion. Look now into all the jars, one by one from first to last."

So Ali Baba examined them severally and found in each a man fully armed and accoutred and all lay scalded to death. Hereat speechless for sheer amazement he stared at the jars, but presently recovering himself he asked, "And where is he, the oil-merchant?"

Answered she, "Of him also I will inform thee. The villain was no trader but a traitorous assassin whose honied words would have ensnared thee to thy doom; and now I will tell thee what he was and what hath happened; but, meanwhile thou art fresh from the Hammam and thou shouldst first drink somewhat of this broth for thy stomach's and thy health's sake."

So Ali Baba went within and Morgiana served up the mess; after which quoth her master, "I fain would hear this wondrous story: prithee tell it to me and set my heart at ease."

Hereat the handmaid fell to relating whatso had betided in these words, "O my master, when thou badest me boil the broth and retiredst to rest, thy slave in obedience to thy command took out a suit of clean white clothes and gave it to the boy Abdullah; then kindled the fire and set on the broth. As soon as it was ready I had need to light a lamp so that I might see to skim it, but all the oil was spent, and, learning this I told my want to the slave-boy Abdullah, who advised me to draw somewhat from the jars which stood under the shed. Accordingly, I took a can and went to the first vessel when suddenly I heard a voice within whisper with all caution, 'Is it now time for us to sally forth?' I was amazed thereat and judged that the pretended merchant had laid some plot to slay thee; so I replied, 'The time is not yet come.' Then I went to the second jar and heard another voice to which I made the like answer, and so on with all of them. I now was certified that these men awaited only some signal from their Chief whom thou didst take to guest within thy walls supposing him to be a merchant in oil; and that after thou receivedst him hospitably the miscreant had brought these men to murther thee and to plunder thy good and spoil thy house. But I gave him no opportunity to win his wish. The last jar I found full of oil and taking somewhat therefrom I lit the lamp; then, putting a large cauldron upon the fire, I filled it up with oil which I brought from the jar and made a fierce blaze under it; and, when the contents were seething hot, I took out sundry cansful with intent to scald them all to death, and going to each jar in due order, I poured within them one by one boiling oil. On this wise having destroyed them utterly, I returned to the kitchen and having extinguished the lamps stood by the window watching what might happen, and how that false merchant would act next. Not long after I had taken my station, the robber captain awoke and oft-times signalled to his thieves. Then getting no reply he came downstairs and went out to the jars, and finding that all his men were slain he fled through the darkness I know not whither. So when he had clean disappeared I was assured that, the door being double locked, he had scaled the wall and dropped into the garden and made his escape. Then with my heart at rest I slept."

And Morgiana, after telling her story to her master, presently added, "This is the whole truth I have related to thee. For some days indeed have I had inkling of such matter, but withheld it from thee deeming it inexpedient to risk the chance of its meeting the neighbours' ears; now, however, there is no help but to tell thee thereof. One day as I came to the house-door I espied thereon a white chalk-mark, and on the next day a red sign beside the white. I knew not the intent wherewith the marks were made, nevertheless I set others upon the entrances of sundry neighbours, judging that some enemy had done this deed whereby to encompass my master's destruction. Therefore I made the marks on all the other doors in such perfect conformity with those I found, that it would be hard to distinguish amongst them.

"Judge now and see if these signs and all this villainy be not the work of the bandits of the forest, who marked our house that on such wise they might know it again. Of these forty thieves there yet remain two others concerning whose case I know naught; so beware of them, but chiefly of the third remaining robber, their Captain, who fled hence alive. Take good heed and be thou cautious of him, for, shouldst thou fall into his hands, he will in no wise spare thee but will surely murther thee. I will do all that lieth in me to save from hurt and harm thy life and property, nor shall thy slave be found wanting in any service to my lord."

Hearing these words Ali Baba rejoiced with exceeding joyance and said to her, "I am well pleased with thee for this thy conduct; and say me what wouldst thou have me do in thy behalf; I shall not fail to remember thy brave deed so long as breath in me remaineth."

Quoth she, "It behoveth us before all things forthright to bury these bodies in the ground, that so the secret be not known to any one." Hereupon Ali Baba took with him his slave-boy Abdullah into the garden and there under a tree they dug for the corpses of the thieves a deep pit in size proportionate to its contents, and they dragged the bodies (having carried off their weapons) to the fosse and threw them in; then, covering up the remains of the seven and thirty robbers they made the ground appear level and clean as it wont to be. They also hid the leathern jars and the gear and arms and presently Ali Baba sent the mules by ones and twos to the bazar and sold them all with the able aid of his slave-boy Abdullah.

Thus the matter was hushed up nor did it reach the ears of any; Ali Baba ceased not to be ill at ease lest haply the Captain or the surviving two robbers should wreak their vengeance on his head. He kept himself private with all caution and took heed that none learn a word of what happened and of the wealth which he had carried off from the bandits' cave.

Meanwhile the Captain of the thieves having escaped with his life, fled to the forest in hot wrath and sore irk of mind, and his senses were scattered and the colour of his visage vanished like ascending smoke. Then he thought the matter over again and again, and at last he firmly resolved that he needs must take the life of Ali Baba, else he would lose all the treasure which his enemy, by knowledge of the magical words, would take away and turn to his own use. Furthermore, he determined that he would undertake the business singlehanded; and, that after getting rid of Ali Baba, he would gather together another band of banditti and would pursue his career of brigandage, as indeed his forbears had done for many generations. So he lay down to rest that night, and rising early in the morning donned a dress of suitable appearance; then going to the city alighted at a caravanserai, thinking to himself, "Doubtless the murther of so many men hath reached the Wali's ears, and Ali Baba hath been seized and brought to justice, and his house is levelled and his good is confiscated. The townfolk must surely have heard tidings of these matters."

So he straightway asked of the keeper of the Khan, "What strange things have happened in the city during the last few days?" and the other told him all that he had seen and heard, but the Captain could not learn a whit of that which most concerned him. Hereby he understood that Ali Baba was ware and wise, and that he had not only carried away such store of treasure but he had also destroyed so many lives and withal had come off scatheless; furthermore, that he himself must needs have all his wits alert not to fall into the hands of his foe and perish.

With this resolve the Captain hired a shop in the Bazar, whither he bore whole bales of the finest stuffs and goodly merchandise from his forest treasure house; and presently he took his seat within the store and fell to doing merchant's business. By chance his place fronted the booth of the defunct Kasim where his son, Ali Baba's nephew, now traded; and the Captain, who called himself Khwajah Hasan, soon formed acquaintance and friendship with the shop keepers around about him and treated all with profuse civilities, but he was especially gracious and cordial to the son of Kasim, a handsome youth and a well-dressed, and oft-times he would sit and chat with him for a long while. A few days after it chanced that Ali Baba, as he was sometimes wont to do, came to see his nephew, whom he found sitting in his shop. The Captain saw and recognised him at sight and one morning he asked the young man, saying, "Prithee tell me, who is he that ever and anon cometh to thee at thy place of sale?" whereto the youth made answer, "He is my uncle, the brother of my father." Whereupon the Captain showed him yet greater favour and affection the better to deceive him for his own devices, and gave him presents and made him sit at meat with him and fed him with the daintiest of dishes.

Presently Ali Baba's nephew bethought him it was only right and proper that he also should invite the merchant to supper, but whereas his own house was small, and he was straitened for room and could not make a show of splendour, as did Khwajah Hasan, he took counsel with his uncle on the matter.

Ali Baba replied to his nephew: "Thou sayest well: it behoveth thee to entreat thy friend in fairest fashion even as he hath entreated thee. On the morrow, which is Friday, shut thy shop as do all merchants of repute; then, after the early meal, take Khwajah Hasan to smell the air, and as thou walkest lead him hither unawares; meanwhile I will give orders that Morgiana shall make ready for his coming the best of viands and all necesseries for a feast. Trouble not thyself on any wise, but leave the matter in my hands."

Accordingly on the next day, to wit, Friday, the nephew of Ali Baba took Khwajah Hasan to walk about the garden; and, as they were returning he led him by the street wherein his uncle dwelt. When they came to the house the youth stopped at the door and knocking said, "O my lord, this is my second home: my uncle hath heard much of thee and of thy goodness me-wards and desireth with exceeding desire to see thee; so, shouldst thou consent to enter and visit him, I shall be truly glad and thankful to thee."

Albeit Khwajah Hasan rejoiced in heart that he had thus found means whereby he might have access to his enemy's house and household, and although he hoped soon to attain his end by treachery, yet he hesitated to enter in and stood to make his excuses and walk away. But when the door was opened by the slave-porter, Ali Baba's nephew seized his companion's hand and after abundant persuasion led him in, whereat he entered with great show of cheerfulness as though much pleased and honoured. The house-master received him with all favour and worship and asked him of his welfare, and said to him "O my lord, I am obliged and thankful to thee for that thou hast strewn favour to the son of my brother and I perceive that thou regardest him with an affection even fonder than my own."

Khwajah Hasan replied with pleasant words and said, "Thy nephew vastly taketh my fancy and in him I am well pleased, for that although young in years yet he hath been endued by Allah with much of wisdom." Thus they twain conversed with friendly conversation and presently the guest rose to depart and said, "O my lord, thy slave must now farewell thee; but on some future day—Inshallah—he will again wait upon thee."

Ali Baba, however, would not let him leave and asked, "Whither wendest thou, O my friend? I would invite thee to my table and I pray thee sit at meat with us and after hie thee home in peace. Perchance the dishes are not as delicate as those whereof thou art wont to eat, still deign grant me this request I pray thee and refresh thyself with my victual."

Quoth Khwajah Hasan, "O my lord I am beholden to thee for thy gracious invitation, and with pleasure would I sit at meat with thee, but for a special reason must I needs excuse myself; suffer me therefore to depart for I may not tarry longer nor accept thy gracious offer."

Hereto the host made reply, "I pray thee, O my lord, tell me what may be the reason so urgent and weighty?"

And Khwajah Hasan answered, "The cause is this: I must not, by order of the physician, who cured me lately of my complaint, eat aught of food prepared with salt."

Quoth Ali Baba, "An this be all, deprive me not, I pray thee, of the honour thy company will confer upon me: as the meats are not yet cooked, I will forbid the kitchener to make use of any salt. Tarry here awhile and I will return anon to thee."

So saying Ali Baba went in to Morgiana and bade her not put salt into any one of the dishes; and she, while busied with her cooking, fell to marvelling greatly at such order and asked her master, "Who is he that eateth meat wherein is no salt?" He answered, "What to thee mattereth it who he may be? only do thou my bidding."

She rejoined, "'Tis well: all shall be as thou wishest"; but in mind she wondered at the man who made such strange request and desired much to look upon him. Wherefore, when all the meats were ready for serving up, she helped the slave-boy Abdullah to spread the table and set on the meal; and no sooner did she see Khwajah Hasan than she knew who he was, albeit he had disguised himself in the dress of a stranger merchant; furthermore, when she eyed him attentively she espied a dagger hidden under his robe. "So ho!" quoth she to herself, "this is the cause why the villain eateth not of salt, for that he seeketh an opportunity to slay my master whose mortal enemy he is; howbeit I will be beforehand with him and despatch him ere he find a chance to harm my lord."

Morgiana, having spread a white cloth upon the table and served up the meal, went back to the kitchen and thought out her plot against the robber Captain.

Now when Ali Baba and Khwajah Hasan had eaten their sufficiency, the slave-boy Abdullah brought Morgiana word to serve the dessert, and she cleared the table and set on fruit fresh and dried in salvers, then she placed by the side of Ali Baba a small tripod for three cups with a flagon of wine, and lastly she went off with the slave-boy Abdullah into another room, as though she would herself eat supper. Then Khwajah Hasan, that is, the Captain of the robbers, perceiving that the coast was clear, exulted mightily saying to himself, "The time hath come for me to take full vengeance; with one thrust of my dagger I will despatch this fellow, then escape across the garden and wend my ways. His nephew will not adventure to stay my hand, for an he do but move a finger or toe with that intent another stab will settle his earthly account. Still must I wait awhile until the slave-boy and the cook-maid shall have eaten and lain down to rest them in the kitchen."

Morgiana, however, watched him wistfully and divining his purpose said in her mind, "I must not allow this villain advantage over my lord, but by some means I must make void his project and at once put an end to the life of him."

Accordingly, the trusty slave-girl changed her dress with all haste and donned such clothes as dancers wear; she veiled her face with a costly kerchief; around her head she bound a fine turband, and about her middle she tied a waist cloth worked with gold and silver wherein she stuck a dagger, whose hilt was rich in filigree and jewelry. Thus disguised she said to the slave-boy Abdullah, "Take now thy tambourine that we may play and sing and dance in honour of our master's guest." So he did her bidding and the twain went into the room, the lad playing and the lass following. Then, making a low congée, they asked leave to perform and disport and play; and Ali Baba gave permission, saying, "Dance now and do your best that this our guest may be mirthful and merry."

433

Quoth Khwajah Hasan, "O my lord, thou dost indeed provide much pleasant entertainment."

Then the slave-boy Abdullah standing by began to strike the tambourine whilst Morgiana rose up and showed her perfect art and pleased them vastly with graceful steps and sportive motion; and suddenly drawing the poniard from her belt she brandished it and paced from side to side, a spectacle which pleased them most of all. At times also she stood before them, now clapping the sharp-edged dagger under her armpit and then setting it against her breast. Lastly she took the tambourine from the slave-boy Abdullah, and still holding the poniard in her right she went round for largesse as is the custom amongst merry makers. First she stood before Ali Baba who threw a gold coin into the tambourine, and his nephew likewise put in an Ashrafi; then Khwajah Hasan, seeing her about to approach him, fell to pulling out his purse, when she heartened her heart and quick as the blinding leven she plunged the dagger into his vitals, and forthwith the miscreant fell back stone dead.

Ali Baba was dismayed and cried in his wrath, "O unhappy, what is this deed thou hast done to bring about my ruin!"

But she replied, "Nay, O my lord, rather to save thee and not to cause thee harm have I slain this man: loosen his garments and see what thou wilt discover thereunder."

So Ali Baba searched the dead man's dress and found concealed therein a dagger. Then said Morgiana, "This wretch was thy deadly enemy. Consider him well: he is none other than the oil-merchant, the Captain of the band of robbers. Whenas he came hither with intent to take thy life, he would not eat thy salt; and when thou toldest me that he wished not any in the meat I suspected him and at first sight I was assured that he would surely do thee die; Almighty Allah be praised 'tis even as I thought."

Then Ali Baba lavished upon her thanks and expressions of gratitude, saying, "Lo, these two times hast thou saved me from his hand," and falling upon her neck he cried, "See thou art free, and as reward for this thy fealty I have wedded thee to my nephew." Then turning to the youth he said, "Do as I bid thee and thou shalt prosper. I would that thou marry Morgiana, who is a model of duty and loyalty: thou seest now yon Khwajah Hasan sought thy friendship only that he might find opportunity to take my life, but this maiden with her good sense and her wisdom hath slain him and saved us."

Ali Baba's nephew straightway consented to marry Morgiana. After which the three, raising the dead body bore it forth with all heed and vigilance and privily buried it in the garden, and for many years no one knew aught thereof. In due time Ali Baba married his brother's son to Morgiana with great pomp, and spread a bride-feast in most sumptuous fashion for his friends and neighbours, and made merry with them and enjoyed singing and all manner of dancing and amusements. He prospered in every undertaking and Time smiled upon him and a new source of wealth was opened to him. For fear of the thieves he had not once visited the jungle-cave wherein lay the treasure, since the day he had carried forth the corpse of his brother Kasim. But some time after, he mounted his hackney one morning and journeyed thither, with all care and caution, till finding no signs of man or horse, and reassured in his mind he ventured to draw near the door. Then alighting from his beast he tied it up to a tree, and going to the entrance pronounced the words which he had not forgotten, "Open, O Simsim!" Hereat, as was its wont, the door flew open, and entering thereby he saw the goods and hoard of gold and silver untouched and lying as he had left them. So he felt assured that not one of all the thieves remained alive, and, that save himself there was not a soul who knew the secret of the place. At once he bound in his saddle-cloth a load of Ashrafis such as his horse could bear and brought it home; and in after days he showed the hoard to his sons and sons' sons and taught them how the door could be caused to open and shut. Thus Ali Baba and his household lived all their lives in wealth and joyance in that city where erst he had been a pauper, and by the blessing of that secret treasure he rose to high degree and dignities.

435

As the morning morrowed, Scheherazade held her peace until the next day.

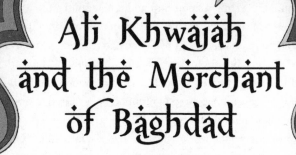

Ali Khwajah and the Merchant of Baghdad

"O dear my sister," quoth Scheherazade to Dunyazad the following evening, "be not thou downhearted; if life's span be spent, naught can avert the sharp edged sword. Yet place thy trust in all Allah Almighty and put far from the all such anxious thoughts." Whereupon she began her next tale…

Under the reign of Caliph Harun al-Rashid there dwelt in the city of Baghdad a certain merchant, Ali Khwajah hight, who had a small stock of goods wherewith he bought and sold and made a bare livelihood, abiding alone and without a family in the house of his forbears.

Now so it came to pass that each night for three nights together he saw in a vision a venerable Shaykh who bespake him thus, "Thou art beholden to make a pilgrimage to Meccah; why abidest thou sunk in heedless slumber and farest not forth as it behoveth thee?" Hearing these words he became sore startled and affrighted, so that he sold shop and goods and all that he had; and, with firm intent to visit the Holy House of Almighty Allah, he let his home on hire and joined a caravan that was journeying to Meccah the Magnified. But ere he left his natal city he placed a thousand gold pieces, which were over and above his need for the journey, within an earthen jar filled up with Asafiri or Sparrow-olives; and, having made fast the mouth thereof, he carried the jar to a merchant-friend of many years standing and said, "Belike, O my brother, thou hast heard tell that I purpose going with a caravan on pilgrimage to Meccah, the Holy City; so I have brought a jar of olives the which, I pray thee, preserve for me in trust against my return."

The merchant at once arose and handing the key of his warehouse to Ali Khwajah said, "Here, take the key and open the store and therein place the jar anywhere thou choosest, and when thou shalt come back thou wilt find it even as thou leftest it."

Hereupon Ali Khwajah did his friend's bidding and locking up the door returned the key to its master. Then loading his travelling goods upon a dromedary and mounting a second beast he fared forth with the caravan. They came at length to Meccah the Magnified, and it was the month Zu al-Hijjah wherein myriads of Moslems hie thither on pilgrimage and pray and prostrate before the Ka'abah-temple. And when he had circuited the Holy House and fulfilled all the rites and ceremonies required of palmers, he set up a shop for sale of merchandise. By chance two merchants passing along that street espied the fine stuffs and goods in Ali Khwajah's booth and approved much of them and praised their beauty and excellence. Presently quoth one to other, "This man bringeth here most rare and costly goods: now in Cairo, the capital of Egypt-land would he get full value for them, and far more than in the markets of this city."

Hearing mention of Cairo, Ali Khwajah conceived a sore longing to visit that famous capital, so he gave up his intent of return Baghdad-wards and purposed wayfaring to Egypt. Accordingly he joined a caravan and arriving thither was well-pleased with the place, both country and city; and selling his merchandise he made great gain therefrom. Then buying other goods and stuffs he purposed to make Damascus; but for one full month he tarried at Cairo and visited her sanctuaries and saintly places and after leaving her walls he solaced himself with seeing many famous cities distant several days' journey from the capital along the banks of the River Nilus.

Presently, bidding adieu to Egypt he arrived at the Sanctified House, Jerusalem, and prayed in the Temple of Banu Isra'il which the Moslems had re-edified. In due time he reached Damascus and observed that the city was well builded and much peopled, and that the fields and meads were well-watered with springs and channels and that the gardens and vergiers were laden with flowers and fruits. Amid such delights Ali Khwajah hardly thought of Baghdad; withal he ceased not to pursue his journey through

Aleppo, Mosul and Shiraz, tarrying some time at all of these towns, especially at Shiraz, till at length after seven years of wayfaring he came back to Baghdad.

For seven long years, the Baghdad merchant never once thought of Ali Khwajah or of the trust committed to his charge; till one day as his wife sat at meat with him at the evening meal, their talk by chance was of olives. Quoth she to him, "I would now fain have some that I may eat of them"; and quoth he, "As thou speakest thereof I bethink me of that Ali Khwajah who seven years ago fared on a pilgrimage to Meccah, and ere he went left in trust with me a jar of Sparrow-olives which still cumbereth the store-house. Who knoweth where he is or what hath betided him? A man who lately returned with the Hajj-caravan brought me word that Ali Khwajah had quitted Meccah the Magnified with intent to journey on to Egypt. Allah Almighty alone knoweth an he be still alive or he be now dead; however, if his olives be in good condition I will go bring some hither that we may taste them: so give me a platter and a lamp that I may fetch thee somewhat of them."

His wife, an honest woman and an upright, made answer, "Allah forbid that thou shouldst do a deed so base and break thy word and covenant. Who can tell? Thou art not assured by any of his death; perchance he may come back from Egypt safe and sound to-morrow or the day after; then wilt thou, an thou cannot deliver unharmed to him what he hath left in pledge, be ashamed of this thy broken troth and we shall be disgraced before man and dishonoured in the presence of thy friend. I will not for my part have any hand in such meanness nor will I taste the olives; furthermore, it standeth not to reason that after seven years' keeping they should be fit to eat. I do implore thee to forswear this ill purpose."

On such wise the merchant's wife protested and prayed her husband that he meddle not with Ali Khwajah's olives, and shamed him of his intent so that for the nonce he cast the matter from his mind. However, although the trader refrained that evening from taking Ali Khwajah's olives, yet he kept the design in memory until one day when, of his obstinacy and unfaith, he resolved to carry out his project; and rising up walked towards the store-room dish in hand. By chance he met his wife who said, "I am no partner with thee in this ill-action: in very truth some evil shall befal thee an thou do such deed."

He heard her but heeded her not; and, going to the store-room opened the jar and found the olives spoiled and white with mould; but presently he tilted up the jar and pouring some of its contents into the dish, suddenly

438

saw an Ashrafi fall from the vessel together with the fruit. Then, filled with greed, he turned out all that was within into another jar and wondered with exceeding wonder to find the lower half full of golden coins. Presently, putting up the moneys and the olives he closed the vessel and going back said to his wife, "Thou spakest sooth, for I have examined the jar and have found the fruit mouldy and foul of smell; wherefore I returned it to its place and left it as it was aforetime." That night the merchant could not sleep a wink for thinking of the gold and how he might lay hands thereon; and when morning morrowed he took out all the Ashrafis and buying some fresh olives in the Bazar filled up the jar with them and closed the mouth and set it in its usual place.

Now it came to pass by Allah's mercy that at the end of the month Ali Khwajah returned safe and sound to Baghdad; and he first went to his old friend, to wit, the merchant who, greeting him with feigned joy, fell on his neck, but withal was sore troubled and perplexed at what might happen. After salutations and much rejoicing on either part Ali Khwajah bespake the merchant on business and begged that he might take back his jar of Asafiri-olives which he had placed in charge of his familiar. Quoth the merchant to Ali Khwajah, "O my friend, I wot not where thou didst leave thy jar of olives; but here is the key, go down to the store-house and take all that is thine own."

So Ali Khwajah did as he was bidden and carrying the jar from the magazine took his leave and hastened home; but, when he opened the vessel and found not the gold coins, he was distracted and overwhelmed with grief and made bitter lamentation. Then he returned to the merchant and said, "O my friend, Allah, the All-present and the All-seeing, be my witness that, when I went on my pilgrimage to Meccah the Magnified, I left a thousand Ashrafis in that jar, and now I find them not. Canst thou tell me aught concerning them? An thou in thy sore need have made use of them, it mattereth not so thou wilt give them back as soon as thou art able."

The merchant, apparently pitying him, said, "O good friend, thou didst thyself with thine hand set the jar inside the store-room. I wist not that thou hadst aught in it save olives; yet as thou didst leave it, so in like manner didst thou find it and carry it away; and now thou chargest me with theft of Ashrafis. It seemeth strange and passing strange that thou shouldst make such accusation. When thou wentest thou madest no mention of any money in the jar, but saidst that it was full of olives, even as thou hast found it. Hadst thou left gold coins therein, then surely thou wouldst have recovered them."

Hereupon Ali Khwajah begged hard with much entreaty, saying, "Those thousand Ashrafis were all I owned, the money earned by years of toil: I do beseech thee have pity on my case and give them back to me."

Replied the merchant, waxing wroth with great wrath, "O my friend, a fine fellow thou art to talk of honesty and withal make such false and lying charge. Begone: hie thee hence and come not to my house again; for now I know thee as thou art, a swindler and imposter."

Hearing this dispute between Ali Khwajah and the merchant all the people of the quarter came crowding to the shop. The multitude which thronged about the merchant's shop warmly took up the matter; and thus it became well known to all, rich and poor, within the city of Baghdad how that one Ali Khwajah had hidden a thousand Ashrafis within a jar of olives and had placed it on trust with a certain merchant; moreover how, after pilgrimaging to Meccah and seven years of travel the poor man had returned, and that the rich man had gainsaid his words anent the gold and was ready to make oath that he had not received any trust of the kind.

At length, when naught else availed, Ali Khwajah was constrained to bring the matter before the Kazi, and to claim one thousand Ashrafis of his false friend. The Judge asked, "What witnesses hast thou who may speak for thee?" and the plantiff answered, "O my lord the Kazi, I feared to tell the matter to any man lest all come to know of my secret. Allah Almighty is my sole testimony. This merchant was my friend and I recked not that he would prove dishonest and unfaithful."

Quoth the Judge, "Then must I needs send for the merchant and hear what he saith on oath;" and when the defendant came they made him swear by all he deemed holy, facing Ka'abah-wards with hands uplifted, and he cried, "I swear that I know naught of any Ashrafis belonging to Ali Khwajah." Hereat the Kazi pronounced him innocent and dismissed him from court; and Ali Khwajah went home sad at heart and said to himself, "Alas, what justice is this which hath been meted out to me, that I should lose my money, and my just cause be deemed unjust! It hath been truly said, 'He loseth the lave who sueth before a knave.'"

On the next day he drew out a statement of his case; and, as the Caliph Harun al-Rashid was on his way to Friday-prayers, he fell down on the ground before him and presented to him the paper. The Commander of the Faithful read the petition and having understood the case deigned give order saying, "To-morrow bring the accuser and the accused to the audience-hall and place the petition before my presence, for I myself will enquire into this matter."

That night the Prince of True Believers, as was his wont, donned disguise to walk about the squares of Baghdad and its streets and lanes and, accompanied by Ja'afar the Barmaki and Masrur the Sworder of his vengeance, proceeded to espy what happened in the city. Immediately on issuing forth he came upon an open place in the Bazar when he heard the hubbub of children a-playing and saw at scanty distance some ten or dozen boys making sport amongst themselves in the moonlight; and he stopped awhile to watch their diversion. Then one amongst the lads, a goodly and a fair-complexioned, said to the others, "Come now and let us play the game of Kazi: I will be the Judge; let one of you be Ali Khwajah, and another the merchant with whom he placed the thousand Ashrafis in pledge before faring on his pilgrimage: so come ye before me and let each one plead his plea."

When the Caliph heard the name of Ali Khwajah he minded him of the petition which had been presented to him for justice against the merchant, and bethought him that he would wait and see how the boy would perform the part of Kazi in their game and upon what decision he would decide. So the Prince watched the mock-trial with keen interest saying to himself, "This case hath verily made such stir within the city that even the children know thereof and re-act it in their sports."

Presently, he amongst the lads who took the part of Ali Khwajah the plaintiff and his playmate who represented the merchant of Baghdad accused of theft, advanced and stood before the boy who as the Kazi sat in pomp and dignity. Quoth the Judge, "O Ali Khwajah, what is thy claim against this merchant?" and the complainant preferred his charge in a plea of full detail.

Then said the Kazi to the boy who acted merchant, "What answerest thou to this complaint and why didst thou not return the gold pieces?" The accused made reply even as the real defendant had done and denied the charge before the Judge, professing himself ready to take oath thereto.

Then said the boy-Kazi, "Ere thou swear on oath that thou hast not taken the money, I would fain see for myself the jar of olives which the plaintiff deposited with thee on trust." Then turning to the boy who represented Ali Khwajah he cried, "Go thou and instantly produce the jar that I may inspect it."

And when the vessel was brought the Kazi said to the two contentious, "See now and say me: be this the very jar which thou, the plaintiff, leftest with the defendant?" and both answered that it was and the same. Then said the self-constituted Judge, "Open now the jar and bring hither

some of the contents that I may see the state in which the Asafiri-olives actually are."

Then tasting of the fruit, "How is this? I find their flavour is fresh and their state excellent. Surely during the lapse of seven twelvemonths the olives would have become mouldy and rotten. Bring now before me two oil-merchants of the town that they may pass opinion upon them."

Then two other of the boys assumed the parts commanded and coming into court stood before the Kazi, who asked, "Are ye olive-merchants by trade?"

They answered, "We are and this hath been our calling for many generations and in buying and selling olives we earn our daily bread."

Then said the Kazi, "Tell me now, how long do olives keep fresh and well-flavoured?" and said they, "O my lord, however carefully we keep them, after the third year they change flavour and colour and become no longer fit for food, in fact they are good only to be cast away."

Thereupon quoth the boy-Kazi, "Examine me now these olives that are in this jar and say me how old are they and what is their condition and savour."

The two boys who played the parts of oil-merchants pretended to take some berries from the jar and taste them and presently they said, "O our lord the Kazi, these olives are in fair condition and full-flavoured."

Quoth the Kazi, "Ye speak falsely, for 'tis seven years since Ali Khwajah put them in the jar as he was about to go a-pilgrimaging;" and quoth they, "Say whatso thou wilt those olives are of this year's growth, and there is not an oil-merchant in all Baghdad but who will agree with us."

Moreover the accused was made to taste and smell the fruits and he could not but admit that it was even so as they had avouched. Then said the boy-Kazi to the boy-defendant, "'Tis clear thou art a rogue and a rascal, and thou hast done a deed wherefor thou richly deservest the gibbet." Hearing this the children frisked about and clapped their hands with glee and gladness, then seizing hold of him who acted as the merchant of Baghdad, they led him off as to execution.

The Commander of the Faithful, Harun al-Rashid, was greatly pleased at this acuteness of the boy who had assumed the part of judge in the play, and commanded his Wazir Ja'afar saying, "Mark well the lad who enacted the Kazi in this mock-trial and see that thou produce him on the morrow: he shall try the case in my presence substantially and in real earnest, even as we have heard him deal with it in play. Summon also the Kazi of this city that he may learn the administration of justice from this child. Moreover send word to Ali Khwajah bidding him bring with him the jar of olives, and have also in readiness two oil-merchants of the town." Thus as they walked along the Caliph gave orders to the Wazir and then returned to his palace.

So on the morrow Ja'afar the Barmaki went to that quarter of the town where the children had enacted the mock-trail and asked the schoolmaster where his scholars might be, and he answered, "They have all gone away, each to his home."

So the minister visited the houses pointed out to him and ordered the little ones to appear in his presence. Accordingly they were brought before him, when he said to them, "Who amongst you is he that yesternight acted the part of Kazi in play and passed sentence in the case of Ali Khwajah?"

The eldest of them replied, "'Twas I, O my lord the Wazir"; and then he waxed pale, not knowing why the question was put.

Cried the Minister, "Come along with me; the Commander of the Faithful hath need of thee." At this the mother of the lad was sore afraid and wept; but Ja'afar comforted her and said, "O my lady, have no fear and trouble not thyself. Thy son will soon return to thee in safety, Inshallah—God willing—and methinks the Sultan will show much favour unto him." The woman's heart was heartened on hearing these words of the Wazir and she joyfully dressed her boy in his best attire and sent him off with the Wazir, who led him by the hand to the Caliph's audience-hall and executed all the other commandments which had been issued by his liege lord.

Then the Commander of the Faithful, having taken seat upon the throne of justice, set the boy upon a seat beside him, and as soon as the contending parties appeared before him, that is Ali Khwajah and the merchant of Baghdad, he commanded them to state each man his case in presence of the child who should adjudge the suit. So the two, plaintiff and defendant recounted their contention before the boy in full detail; and when the accused stoutly denied the charge and was about to swear on oath that what he said was true, with hands uplifted and facing Ka'abah-wards, the child-Kazi prevented him, saying, "Enough! swear not on oath till thou art bidden; and first let the jar of olives be produced in Court."

Forthwith the jar was brought forward and placed before him; and the lad bade open it; then, tasting one he gave also to two oil-merchants who had been summoned, that they might do likewise and declare how old was the fruit and whether its savour was good or bad. They did his bidding and

443

said, "The flavour of these olives hath not changed and they are of this year's growth."

Then said the boy, "Methinks ye are mistaken, for seven years ago Ali Khwajah put the olives into the jar: how then could fruit of this year find their way therein?"

But they replied, "'Tis even as we say: an thou believe not our words send straightway for other oil-merchants and make enquiry of them, so shalt thou know if we speak sooth or lies."

But when the merchant of Baghdad saw that he could no longer avail to prove his innocence, he confessed everything; to wit, how he had taken out the Ashrafis and filled the jar with fresh olives.

Hearing this the boy said to the Prince of True Believers, "O gracious sovereign, last night in play we tried this cause, but thou alone has power to apply the penalty. I have adjudged the matter in thy presence and I humbly pray that thou punish this merchant according to the law of the Koran and the custom of the Apostle; and thou decree the restoring of his thousand gold pieces to Ali Khwajah, for that he hath been proved entitled to them."

The Caliph ordered the merchant of Baghdad to be taken away and be hanged, after he should have made known where he had put the thousand Ashrafis and that these should have been restored their rightful owner, Ali Khwajah. He also turned to the Kazi who had hastily adjudged the case, and bade him learn from that lad to do his duty more sedulously and conscientiously. Moreover the Prince of True Believers embraced the boy, and ordered that the Wazir give him a thousand pieces of gold from the royal treasury and conduct him safely to his home and parents. And after, when the lad grew to man's estate, the Commander of the Faithful made him one of his cup-companions and furthered his fortunes and ever entreated him with the highmost honour.

But when Queen Scheherazade had ended the story of Ali Khwajah and the merchant of Baghdad she said, "Now, O auspicious King, I would relate a more excellent history than any, shouldst thou be pleased to hear that I have to say"; and King Shahryar replied, "By Allah! what an admirable tale is this thou hast told: my ears do long to hear another as rare and commendable."

Prince Ahmad and the Fairy Peri-Banu

The following night Scheherazade began forthright to recount the next adventure. Quoth she...

In days of yore and times long gone before there was a Sultan of India who begat three sons; the eldest hight Prince Husayn, the second Prince Ali, and the youngest Prince Ahmad; moreover he had a niece, named Princess Nur al-Nihar, the daughter of his cadet brother who, dying early, left his only child under her uncle's charge. The King busied himself with abundant diligence about her instruction and took all care that she should be taught to read and write, sew and embroider, sing and deftly touch all instruments of mirth and merriment. This Princess also in beauty and loveliness and in wit and wisdom far excelled all the maidens of her own age in every land. She was brought up with the Princes her cousins in all joyance; and they ate together and played together and slept together; and the king had determined in his mind that when she reached marriageable age he would give her in wedlock to some one of the neighbouring royalties; but, when she came to years of discretion, her uncle perceived that the three Princes his sons were all three deep in love of her, and each desired in his heart to woo and to win and to wed her. Wherefore was the King sore troubled in mind and said to himself, "An I give the Lady Nur al-Nihar in wedlock to any one of her cousins, the other twain will be dissatisfied and murmur against my decision; withal my soul cannot endure to see them grieved and disappointed. And should I marry her to some stranger the three Princes my sons will be sore distressed and saddened in soul; nay, who knoweth that they may not slay themselves or go forth and betake them to some far and foreign land? The matter is a troublous and a perilous; so it behoveth me their sire to take action on such wise that if one of them espouse her, the other two be not displeased thereat."

Long time the Sultan revolved the matter in his mind; and at length he devised a device; and, sending for the three princes, addressed them saying, "O my sons, ye are in my opinion of equal merit one with other; nor can I give preference to any of you and marry him to the Princess Nur al-Nihar; nor yet am I empowered to wed her with all three. But I have thought of one plan whereby she shall be wife to one of you, and yet shall not cause aught of irk or envy to his brethren; so may your mutual love and affection remain unabated, and one shall never be jealous of the other's happiness. Brief, my device is this: Go ye and travel to distant countries, each one separating himself from the others; and do ye bring me back the thing most wondrous and marvellous of all sights ye may see upon your wayfarings; and he who shall return with the rarest of curiosities shall be husband to the Princess Nur al-Nihar. Consent ye now to this proposal; and whatso of money ye require for travel and for the purchase of objects seld-seen and singular, take ye from the royal treasury as much as ye desire."

The three Princes, who were ever submissive to their sire, consented with one voice to this proposal, and each was satisfied and confident that he would bring the King the most extraordinary of gifts and thereby win the Princess to wife. So the Sultan bade give to each what moneys he wanted without stint or account, and counselled them to make ready for the journey without stay or delay and depart their home in the Peace of Allah.

The three princely brothers forthright made them ready for journey and voyage. So they donned disguise, preferring the dress of wandering merchants; and, buying such things as they needed and taking with them each his suite they mounted steeds of purest blood and rode forth in a body from the palace. For several stages they travelled the same road until, reaching a place where it branched off in three different ways, they alighted at a Khan and ate the evening meal. Then they made compact and covenant, that whereas they had thus far travelled together they should at break of day take separate roads and each wend his own way and all seek different and distant regions, agreeing to travel for the space of one year only, after which, should they be in the land of the living, all three would rendezvous at that same caravanserai and return in company to the King their sire. Furthermore, they determined that the first who came back to the Khan should await the arrival of the next, and that two of them should tarry there in expectancy of the third. Then, all this matter duly settled, they retired to rest, and when the morning morrowed they fell on one another's necks and bade farewell; and, lastly, mounting their horses, they rode forth each in his own direction.

Now Prince Husayn, the eldest, had oft heard recount the wonders of the land Bishangarh, and for a long while had wished to visit it; so he took the road which led thither, and, joining himself to a caravan journeying that way, accompanied it by land and by water and traversed many regions, desert wilds and stony wolds, dense jungles and fertile tracts, with fields and hamlets and gardens and townships. After three months spent in wayfare at length he made Bishangarh, a region over-reigned by manifold rulers, so great was its extent and so far reaching was its power. He put up at a Khan built specially for merchants who came from the farthest lands, and from the folk who dwelt therein he heard tell that the city contained a large central market wherein men bought and sold all manner of rarities and wondrous things.

Accordingly, next day Prince Husayn repaired to the Bazar and on sighting it he stood amazed at the prospect of its length and width. It was divided into many streets, all vaulted over but lit up by skylights; and the shops on either side were substantially builded, all after one pattern and nearly of the same size, while each was fronted by an awning which kept off the glare and made a grateful shade. Within these shops were ranged and ordered various kinds of wares; there were bales of "woven air" and linens of finest tissue, plain-white or dyed or adorned with life-like patterns wherefrom beasts and trees and blooms stood out so distinctly that one might believe them to be very ferals, bosquets and gardens. There were moreover silken goods, brocaded stuffs, and finest satins from Persia and Egypt of endless profusion; in the China warehouses stood glass vessels of all kinds, and here and there were stores wherein tapestries and thousands of foot-carpets lay for sale. So Prince Husayn walked on from shop to shop and marvelled much to see such wondrous things whereof he had never even dreamt: and he came at length to the Goldsmiths' Lane and espied gems and jewels and golden and silvern vessels studded with diamonds and rubies, emeralds, pearls and other precious stones, all so lustrous and dazzling bright that the stores were lit up with their singular brilliancy. Hereat he said to himself, "If in one street only there be such wealth and jewels so rare, Allah Almighty and none save He knoweth what may be the riches in all this city."

He was not less astonished to behold the Brahmins, how their women-kind for excess of opulence bedecked themselves with the finest gems and were ornamented with the richest gear from front to foot: their very slave-boys and handmaids wore golden necklaces and bracelets and bangles studded with precious stones. Along the length of one market street were ranged hosts of flower-sellers; for all the folk, both high and low, wore wreaths and garlands: some carried nosegays in hand, other some bound fillets round their heads, while not a few had ropes and festoons surrounding and hanging from their necks. The whole place seemed one huge parterre of bloomery; even traders set bouquets in every shop and stall, and the scented air was heavy with perfume.

Strolling to and fro Prince Husayn was presently tired and would fain have sat him down somewhere to rest awhile, when one of the merchants, noting his look of weariness, with kindly courtesy prayed him be seated in his store. After saluting him with the salam the stranger sat down; and anon he saw a broker come that way, offering for sale a carpet some four yards square, and crying, "This be for sale; who giveth me its worth; to wit, thirty thousand gold pieces?"

The Prince marvelled with excessive marvel at the price, and, beckoning the dealer, examined his wares right well; then said he, "A carpet such as this is selleth for a few silverlings. What special virtue hath it that thou demand therefor the sum of thirty thousand gold coins?"

The broker, believing Husayn to be a merchant man lately arrived at Bishangarh, answered him saying, "O my lord, thinkest thou I price this carpet at too high a value? My master hath bidden me not to sell it for less than forty thousand Ashrafis." Quoth the Prince, "It surely doth possess some wondrous virtue, otherwise wouldst thou not demand so prodigious a sum;" and quoth the broker, "'Tis true, O my lord, its properties are singular and marvellous. Whoever sitteth on this carpet and willeth in thought to be taken up and set down upon other site will, in the twinkling of an eye, be borne thither, be that place nearhand or distant many a day's journey and difficult to reach." The Prince hearing these words said to himself, "Naught so wonder-rare as this rug can I carry back to the Sultan my sire to my gift, or any that afford him higher satisfaction and delight. Almighty Allah be praised, the aim of my wayfare is attained and hereby,

Inshallah! I shall win to my wish. This, if anything, will be to him a joy for ever."

Wherefore the Prince, with intent to buy the Flying Carpet, turned to the broker and said, "If indeed it have properties such as thou describest, verily the price thou askest therefor is not over-much, and I am ready to pay thee the sum required."

The other rejoined, "An thou doubt my words I pray thee put them to the test and by such proof remove thy suspicions. Sit now upon this square of tapestry, and at thy mere wish and will it shall transport us to the caravanserai wherein thou abidest: on this wise shalt thou be certified of my words being sooth, and when assured of their truth thou mayest count out to me, there and then, but not before, the value of my wares."

Accordingly, the man spread out the carpet upon the ground behind his shop and seated the Prince thereupon, he sitting by his side. Then, at the mere will and wish of Prince Husayn, the twain were at once transported as though borne by the throne of Solomon to the Khan. So the eldest of the brothers joyed with exceeding joy to think that he had won so rare a thing, whose like could nowhere be found in the lands nor amongst the Kings; and his heart and soul were gladdened for that he had come to Bishangarh and hit upon such a prodigy. Accordingly he counted out the forty thousand Ashrafis as payment for the carpet, and gave, moreover, another twenty thousand by way of sweetmeat to the broker. Furthermore, he ceased not saying to himself that the King on seeing it would forthright wed him to the Princess Nur al-Nihar; for it were clear impossible that either of his brothers, e'en though they searched the whole world over and over, could find a rarity to compare with this. He longed to take seat upon the carpet that very instant and fly to his own country, or, at least, to await his brothers at the caravanserai where they had parted under promise and covenant, pledged and concluded, to meet again at the year's end. But presently he bethought him that the delay would be long and longsome, and much he feared lest he be tempted to take some rash step; wherefore he resolved upon sojourning in the country whose King and subjects he had ardently desired to behold for many a day, and determined that he would pass the time in sight-seeing and in pleasuring over the lands adjoining. So Prince Husayn tarried in Bishangarh some months.

Now the King of that country was wont to hold a high court once every week for hearing disputes and adjudging causes which concerned foreign merchants; and thus the Prince ofttimes saw the King, but to none would he tell a word of his adventure. However, inasmuch as he was comely of countenance, graceful of gait, and courteous of accost, stout hearted and strong, wise and ware and witty, he was held by the folk in higher honour than the Sultan; not to speak of the traders his fellows; and in due time he be came a favourite at court and learned of the ruler himself all matters concerning his kingdom and his grandeur and greatness.

The Prince also visited the most famous Pagodas of that country. The first he saw was wrought in brass and orichalch of most exquisite workmanship: its inner cell measured three yards square and contained amiddlemost a golden image in size and stature like unto a man of wondrous beauty; and so cunning was the workmanship that the face seemed to fix its eyes, two immense rubies of enormous value, upon all beholders no matter where they stood. He also saw another idol-temple, not less strange and rare than this, builded in a village on a plain surface of some half acre long and broad, wherein bloomed lovely rose-trees and jasmine and herb-basil and many other sweet-scented plants, whose perfume made the air rich with fragrance. Around its court ran a wall three feet high, so that no animal might stray therein; and in the centre was a terrace well-nigh the height of a man, all made of white marble and wavy alabaster, each and every slab being dressed so deftly and joined with such nice joinery that the whole pavement albeit covering so great a space, seemed to the sight but a single stone. In the centre of the terrace stood the domed fane towering some fifty cubits high and conspicuous for many miles around: its length was thirty cubits and its breadth twenty, and the red marbles of the revetment were clean polished as a mirror, so that every image was reflected in it to the life. The dome was exquisitely carved and sumptuously ornamented without; and within were ranged in due rank and sequence rows and rows of idols. To this, the Holy of Holies, from morn till eve thousands of Brahmins, men and women, came docking for daily worship. They had sports and diversions as well as rites and ceremonies: some feasted and others danced, some sang, others played on instruments of mirth and merriment, while here and there were plays and revels and innocent merry-makings. And hither at every season flocked from distant lands hosts of pilgrims seeking to fulfil their vows and to perform their orisons; all bringing gifts of gold and silver coin and presents rare and costly which they offered to the gods in presence of the royal officers.

Prince Husayn also saw a fete once a year within the city of Bishangarh and the Ryots all, both great and small, gathered together and circumambulated the Pagodas; chiefly circuiting one which in size and grandeur surpassed all others. Great and learned Pandits versed in the

Shastras made journeys of four or five months and greeted one another
at that festival; thither too the folk from all parts of India pilgrimaged in
such crowds that Prince Husayn was astounded at the sight; and, by reason
of the multitudes that thronged around the temples, he could not see the
mode in which the gods were worshipped. On one side of the adjacent
plain which stretched far and wide, stood a new-made scaffolding of ample
size and great magnificence, nine storeys high, and the lower part supported
by forty pillars; and here one day in every week the King assembled his
Wazirs for the purpose of meting out justice to all strangers in the land.
The palace within was richly adorned and furnished with costly furniture:
without, upon the wall faces were limned homely landscapes and scenes
of foreign parts and notably all manner beasts and birds and insects even
gnats and flies, portrayed with such skill of brain and cunning of hand
that they seemed real and alive and the country-folk and villagers seeing
from afar paintings of lions and tigers and similar ravenous beasts, were
filled with awe and dismay. On the other three sides of the scaffolding were
pavilions, also of wood, built for use of the commons, illuminated and
decorated inside and outside like the first, and wroughten so cunningly that
men could turn them round, with all the people in them, and moving them
about transfer them to whatsoever quarter they willed. On such wise they
shifted these huge buildings by aid of machinery; and the folk inside could
look upon a succession of sports and games. Moreover, on each side of the
square elephants were ranged in ranks, the number amounting to well nigh
one thousand, their trunks and ears and hinder parts being painted with
cinnabar and adorned with various lively figures; their housings were of
gold brocade and their howdahs purfled with silver, carrying minstrels who
performed on various instruments, whilst buffoons delighted the crowd
with their jokes and mimes played their most diverting parts.

Of all the sports, however, which the Prince beheld, the elephant-
show amused him most and filled him with the greatest admiration. One
huge beast, which could be wheeled about where the keepers ever listed, for
that his feet rested upon a post which travelled on casters, held in his trunk
a flageolet whereon he played so sweetly well that all the people were fain to
cry Bravo! There was another but a smaller animal which stood upon one
end of a beam laid crosswise upon, and attached with hinges to, a wooden
block eight cubits high, and on the further end was placed an iron weight
as heavy as the elephant, who would press down for some time upon the
beam until the end touched the ground, and then the weight would raise
him up again. Thus the beam swung like a see saw aloft and adown; and,

as it moved, the elephant swayed to and fro and kept time with the bands of music, loudly trumpeting the while. The people moreover could wheel about this elephant from place to place as he stood balanced on the beam; and such exhibitions of learned elephants were mostly made in presence of the King.

Prince Husayn spent well nigh a year in sight-seeing amongst the fairs and festivals of Bishangarh; and, when the period of the fraternal compact drew near, he spread his carpet upon the court-ground behind the Khan wherein he lodged, and sitting thereon, together with his suite and the steeds and all he had brought with him, mentally wished that he might be transported to the caravanserai where the three brothers had agreed to meet. No sooner had he formed the thought than straightway, in the twinkling of an eye, the carpet rose high in air and sped through space and carried them to the appointed stead where, still garbed as a merchant he remained in expectation of his brothers' coming.

Hearken now, O auspicious King, to what befel Prince Ali, the second brother of Prince Husayn. On the third day after he had parted from the two others, he also joined a caravan and journeyed towards Persia; then, after a march of four months arriving at Shiraz, the capital of Iran-land, he alighted at a Khan, he and his fellow-travellers with whom he had made a manner of friendship; and, passing as a jeweller, there took up his abode with them. Next day the traders fared forth to buy wares and to sell their goods; but Prince Ali, who had brought with him naught of vendible, and only the things he needed, presently doffed his travelling dress, and in company with a comrade of the caravan entered the chief Bazar, known as the Bazistan, or cloth-market. Ali strolled about the place, which was built of brick and where all the shops had arched roofs resting on handsome columns; and he admired greatly to behold the splendid store-houses exposing for sale all manner goods of countless value. He wondered much what wealth was in the town if a single market street contained riches such as these. And as the brokers went about crying their goods for sale, he saw one of them hending in hand an ivory tube in length about a cubit, which he was offering for sale at the price of thirty thousand Ashrafis. Hearing such demand Prince Ali thought to himself, "Assuredly this fellow is a fool who asketh such a price for so paltry a thing."

Prince Ali presently asked one of the shopkeepers with whom he had made acquaintance, saying, "O my friend, is this man a maniac that he asketh a sum of thirty thousand Ashrafis for this little pipe of ivory? Surely

452

none save an idiot would give him such a price and waste upon it such a mint of money."

Said the shop man, "O my lord, this broker is wiser and warier than all the others of his calling, and by means of him I have sold goods worth thousands of sequins. Until yesterday he was in his sound senses; but I cannot say what state is his to day and whether or no he have lost his wits; but this wot I well, that if he ask thirty thousand for yon ivory tube, 'twill be worth that same or even more. Howbeit we shall see with our own eyes. Sit thee here and rest within the shop until he pass this way."

So Prince Ali abode where he was bidden and presently the broker was seen coming up the street. Then the shopman calling to him said, "O man, rare merit hath yon little pipe; for all the folk are astounded to hear thee ask so high a price therefor; nay more, this friend of mine thinketh that thou art crazy."

The broker, a man of sense, was on no wise chafed at these words but answered with gentle speech, "O my lord, I doubt not but that thou must deem me a madman to ask so high a price, and set so great a value upon an article so mean; but when I shall have made known to thee its properties and virtues, thou wilt most readily consent to take it at that valuation. Not thou alone but all men who have heard me cry my cry laugh and name me ninny."

So saying, the broker showed the Spying Tube to Prince Ali and handing it to him said, "Examine well this ivory, the properties of which I will explain to thee. Thou seest that it is furnished with a piece of glass at either end; and, shouldst thou apply one extremity thereof to thine eye, thou shalt see what thing soe'er thou listest and it shall appear close by thy side though parted from thee by many an hundred of miles."

Replied the Prince, "This passeth all conception, nor can I believe it to be veridical until I shall have tested it and I become satisfied that 'tis even as thou sayest." Hereupon the broker placed the little tube in Prince Ali's hand, and showing him the way to handle it said, "Whatso thou mayest wish to descry will be shown to thee by looking through this ivory."

Prince Ali silently wished to sight his sire, and when he placed the pipe close to his eye forthwith he saw him hale and hearty, seated on his throne and dispensing justice to the people of his dominion. Then the youth longed with great longing to look upon his lady love the Princess Nur al-Nihar; and straightway he saw her also sitting upon her bed, sound and sane, talking and laughing, whilst a host of handmaids stood around awaiting her commands. The Prince was astonished exceedingly to behold this strange and wondrous spectacle, and said to himself, "An I should wander the whole world over for ten years or more and search in its every corner and cranny, I shall never find aught so rare and precious as this tube of ivory."

Then quoth he to the broker, "The virtues of thy pipe I find are indeed those thou hast described, and right willingly I give to thee its price the thirty thousand Ashrafis." Replied the salesman, "O my lord, my master hath sworn an oath that he will not part with it for less than forty thousand gold pieces."

Hereupon the Prince, understanding that the broker was a just man and a true, weighed out to him the forty thousand sequins and became master of the Spying Tube, enraptured with the thought that assuredly it would satisfy his sire and obtain for him the hand of Princess Nur al-Nihar.

So with mind at ease Ali journeyed through Shiraz and over sundry parts of Persia; and in fine, when the year was well nigh spent he joined a caravan and, travelling back to India, arrived safe and sound at the appointed caravanserai whither Prince Husayn had foregone him. There the twain tarried awaiting the third brother's safe return.

Such, O King Shahryar, is the story of the two brothers; and now I beseech thee incline thine ear and hearken to what befel the youngest, to wit Prince Ahmad; for indeed his adventure is yet more peregrine and seld-seen of all. When he had parted from his brothers, he took the road leading to Samarkand; and, arriving there after long travel, he also like his brothers alighted at a Khan. Next day he fared forth to see the market square, which folk call the Bazistan, and he found it fairly laid out, the shops wroughten with cunning workmanship and filled with rare stuffs and precious goods and costly merchandise.

Now as he wandered to and fro he came across a broker who was hawking a Magical Apple and crying aloud, "Who will buy this fruit, the price whereof be thirty-five thousand gold pieces?"

Quoth Prince Ahmad to the man, "Prithee let me see the fruit thou holdest in hand, and explain to me what hidden virtue it possesseth that thou art asking for it so high a value."

Quoth the other, smiling and handing to him the apple, "Marvel not at this, O good my lord: in sooth I am certified that when I shall have explained its properties and thou shalt see how it advantageth all mankind, thou wilt not deem my demand exorbitant; nay, rather thou wilt gladly give a treasure house of gold so thou may possess it. Now hearken to me, O my lord, and I will tell thee what of virtue lieth in this artificial apple. If anyone be sick of a sickness however sore, nay more if he be ill nigh unto death, and perchance he smell this pome, he will forthwith recover and become well and whole of whatsoever disease he had, plague or pleurisy, fever or other malignant distemper, as though he never had been attacked; and his strength will return to him forthright, and after smelling this fruit he will be free from all ailment and malady so long as life shall remain to him."

Quoth Prince Ahmad, "How shall I be assured that what thou speakest is truth? If the matter be even as thou sayest, then verily I will give thee right gladly the sum thou demandest."

Quoth the broker, "O my lord, all men who dwell in the parts about Samarkand know full well how there once lived in this city a sage of wondrous skill who, after many years of toil and travail, wrought this apple by mixing medicines from herbs and minerals countless in number. All his good, which was great, he expended upon it, and when he had perfected it he made whole thousands of sick folk whom he directed only to smell the fruit. But, alas! his life presently came to an end and death overtook him suddenly ere he could save himself by the marvellous scent; and, as he had won no wealth and left only a bereaved wife and a large family of young children and dependents manifold, his widow had no help but provide for them a maintenance by parting with this prodigy."

While the salesman was telling his tale to the Prince a crowd of citizens gathered around them and one amongst the folk, who was well known to the broker, came forward and said, "A friend of mine lieth at home sick to the death: the doctors and surgeons all despair of his life; so I beseech thee let him smell this fruit that he may live."

Hearing these words, Prince Ahmad turned to the salesman and said, "O my friend, if this sick man of whom thou hearest can recover strength by smelling the apple, then will I straightway buy it of thee at a valuation of forty thousand Ashrafis." The man had permission to sell it for a sum of thirty-five thousand; so he was satisfied to receive five thousand by way of brokerage, and he rejoined, "'Tis well, O my lord, now mayest thou test the virtues of this apple and be persuaded in thy mind: hundreds of ailing folk have I made whole by means of it."

Accordingly the Prince accompanied the people to the sick man's house and found him lying on his bed with the breath in his nostrils; but, as soon as the dying man smelt the fruit, at once recovering strength he rose in perfect health, sane and sound. Hereupon Ahmad bought the Magical Apple of the dealer and counted out to him the forty thousand Ashrafis.

Presently, having gained the object of his travels, he resolved to join some caravan marching Indiawards and return to his father's home; but meanwhile he resolved to solace himself with the sights and marvels of Samarkand. His especial joy was to gaze upon the glorious plain highs Soghd, one of the wonders of this world: the land on all sides was a delight to the sight, emerald-green and bright, with crystal rills like the plains of Paradise; the gardens bore all manner flowers and fruits and the cities and palaces gladdened the stranger's gaze.

After some days Prince Ahmad joined a caravan of merchants wending Indiawards; and, when his long and longsome travel was ended, he at last reached the caravanserai where his two brothers, Husayn and Ali, impatiently awaited his arrival. The three rejoiced with exceeding joy to meet once more and fell on one another's necks; thanking Allah who had brought them back safe and sound, hale and hearty, after such prolonged and longsome absence. Then Prince Husayn, being the eldest, turned to them and said, "Now it behoveth us each to recount what hath betided him and announce what rare thing he hath brought back and what be the virtues thereof; and I, being the first-born, will be the foremost to tell my adventures. I bring with me from Bishangarh, a carpet, mean to look at, but such are its properties that should any sit thereon and wish in mind to visit country or city, he will at once be carried thither in ease and safety although it be distant months, nay years of journey. I have paid forty thousand gold pieces to its price; and, after seeing all the wonders of Bishangarh-land, I took seat upon my purchase and willed myself at this spot. Straightway I found myself here as I wished and have tarried in this caravanserai three months awaiting your arrival. The flying carpet is with me; so let him who listeth make trial of it."

When the senior Prince had made an end of telling his tale, Prince Ali spake next and said, "O my brother, this carpet which thou hast brought is marvel-rare and hath most wondrous gifts; nor according to thy statement hath any in all the world seen aught to compare with it." Then bringing forth the Spying Tube, he pursued, "Look ye here, I too have bought for forty thousand Ashrafis somewhat whose merits I will now show forth to you. Ye see this ivory pipe? By means of it man may descry objects hidden from his sight and distant from him many a mile. 'Tis truly a most wondrous matter and right worthy your inspection, and you two may try it an ye will. Place but an eye close to the smaller glass and form a wish in mind to see what thing soe'er your soul desireth; and, whether it be near hand or distant many hundreds of miles, this ivory will make the object look clear and close to you."

At these words Prince Husayn took the pipe from Prince Ali and, applying his eye to one end as he had been directed, then wished in his heart to behold the Princess Nur al-Nihar; and the two brothers watched him to learn what he would say. Suddenly they saw his face change colour and wither as a wilted flower, while in his agitation and distress a flood of tears gushed from his eyes; and, ere his brothers recovered from their amazement and could enquire the cause of such strangeness, he cried aloud, "Alas! and well away. We have endured toil and travail, and we have travelled so far and wide hoping to wed the Princess Nur al-Nihar. But 'tis all in vain: I saw her lying on her bed death-sick and like to breathe her last and around her stood her women all weeping and wailing in the sorest of sorrow. O my brothers, an ye would see her once again for the last time, take ye one final look through the glass ere she be no more."

Hereat Prince Ali seized the Spying Tube and peered through it and found the condition of the Princess even as his brother Husayn had described; so he presently passed it over to Prince Ahmad, who also looked and was certified that the Lady Nur al-Nihar was about to give up the ghost. So he said to his elder brothers, "We three are alike love distraught for the Princess and the dearest wish of each one is to win her. Her life is on the ebb, still I can save her and make her whole if we hasten to her without stay or delay." So saying he pulled from his pocket the Magical Apple and showed it to them crying, "This thing is not less in value than either the Flying Carpet or the Spying Tube. In Samarkand I bought it for forty thousand gold pieces and here is the best opportunity to try its virtues. The folk told me that if a sick man hold it to his nose, although on the point of death, he will wax at once well and hale again: I have myself tested it, and now ye shall see for yourselves its marvel-cure when I shall apply it to the case of Nur al-Nihar. Only, let us seek her presence ere she die."

Quoth Prince Husayn, "This were an easy matter: my carpet shall carry us in the twinkling of an eye straight to the bedside of our beloved. Do ye without hesitation sit down with me thereupon, for there is room sufficient to accommodate us three; we shall instantly be carried thither and our servants can follow us."

Accordingly, the three Princes disposed themselves upon the Flying Carpet and each willed in his mind to reach the bedside of Nur al-Nihar, when instantly they found themselves within her apartment. The handmaids and eunuchs in waiting were terrified at the sight and marvelled how these stranger men could have entered the chamber; and, as the Castratos were

fain fall upon them, brand in hand, they recognised the Princes and drew
back still in wonderment at their intrusion.

Then the brothers rose forthright from the Flying Carpet and Prince
Ahmad came forwards and put the Magical Apple to the nostrils of the
lady, who lay stretched on the couch in unconscious state; and as the scent
reached her brain the sickness left her and the cure was complete. She
opened wide her eyes and sitting erect upon her bed looked all around
and chiefly at the Princes as they stood before her; for she felt that she had
waxed hale and hearty as though she awoke after the sweetest of slumber.
Presently she arose from her couch and bade her tire-women dress her the
while they related to her the sudden coming of the three Princes, her uncle's
sons, and how Prince Ahmad had made her smell something whereby
she had recovered of her illness. And after she had made the Ablution of
Health she joyed with exceeding joy to see the Princes and returned thanks
to them, but chiefly to Prince Ahmad in that he had restored her to health
and life. The brothers also were gladdened with exceeding gladness to see
the Princess Nur al-Nihar recover so suddenly from mortal malady and,
presently taking leave of her, they fared to greet their father.

Meanwhile the Eunuchs had reported the whole matter to the
Sultan, and when the Princes came before him he rose and embraced
them tenderly and kissed them on their foreheads, filled with satisfaction
to see them again and to hear from them the welfare of the Princess, who
was dear to him as she had been his daughter. Then the three brothers
produced each one the wondrous thing he had brought from his wayfare;
and Prince Husayn first showed the Flying Carpet which in the twinkling
of an eye had transported them home from far distant exile and said, "For
outward show this carpet hath no merit, but inasmuch as it possesseth such
wondrous virtue, methinks 'tis impossible to find in all the world aught that
can compare to it for rarity."

Next, Prince Ali presented to the King his Spying Tube and said,
"The mirror of Jamshid is as vain and naught beside this pipe, by means
whereof all things from East to West and from North to South are made
clearly visible to the ken of man."

Last of all, Prince Ahmad produced the Magical Apple which
wondrously saved the dear life of Nur al-Nihar and said, "By means of
this fruit all maladies and grievous distempers are at once made whole."
Thus each presented his rarity to the Sultan, saying, "O our lord, deign
examine well these gifts we have brought and do thou pronounce which
of them all is most excellent and admirable; so, according to thy promise,

he amongst us on whom thy choice may fall shall marry the Princess Nur al-Nihar."

When the King had patiently listened to their several claims and had understood how each gift took part in restoring health to his niece, for a while he dove deep in the sea of thought and then answered, "Should I award the palm of merit to Prince Ahmad, whose Magical Apple cured the Princess, then should I deal unfairly by the other two. Albeit his rarity restored her to life and health from mortal illness, yet say me how had he known of her condition save by the virtue of Prince Ali's Spying Tube? In like manner, but for the Flying Carpet of Prince Husayn, which brought you three hither in a moment's space, the Magical Apple would have been of no avail. Wherefore 'tis my rede all three had like part and can claim equal merit in healing her; for it were impossible to have made her whole if any one thing of the three were wanting; furthermore all three objects are wondrous and marvellous without one surpassing other, nor can I, with aught of reason, assign preference or precedence to any. My promise was to marry the Lady Nur al-Nihar to him who should produce the rarest of rarities, but although strange 'tis not less true that all are alike in the one essential condition. The difficulty still remaineth and the question is yet unsolved, whilst I fain would have the matter settled ere the close of day, and without prejudice to any. So needs must I fix upon some plan whereby I may be able to adjudge one of you to be the winner, and bestow upon him the hand of Princess Nur al-Nihar, according to my plighted word; and thus absolve myself from all responsibility. Now I have resolved upon this course of action; to wit, that ye should mount each one his own steed and all of you be provided with bow and arrows; then do ye ride forth to the Maydan—the hippodrome—whither I and my Ministers of State and Grandees of the kingdom and Lords of the land will follow you. There in my presence ye shall each, turn by turn, shoot a shaft with all your might and main; and he amongst you whose arrow shall fly the farthest will be adjudged by me worthiest to win the Princess Nur al-Nihar to wife."

Accordingly the three Princes, who could not gainsay the decision of their sire nor question its wisdom and justice, backed their coursers, and each taking his bow and arrows made straight for the place appointed. The King also, when he had stored the presents in the royal treasury, arrived there with his Wazirs and the dignitaries of his realm; and as soon as all was ready, the eldest son and heir, Prince Husayn, essayed his strength and skill and shot a shaft far along the level plain. After him Prince Ali hent his bow in hand and, discharging an arrow in like direction, overshot the first; and lastly came Prince Ahmad's turn. He too aimed at the same end, but such was the decree of Destiny, that although the knights and courtiers urged on their horses to note where his shaft might strike ground, withal they saw no trace thereof and none of them knew if it had sunk into the bowels of earth or had flown up to the confines of the sky. Some, indeed, there were who with evil mind held that Prince Ahmad had not shot any bolt, and that his arrow had never left his bow. So at last the King bade no more search be made for it and declared himself in favour of Prince Ali and adjudged that he should wed the Princess Nur al-Nihar, forasmuch as his arrow had outsped that of Prince Husayn.

Accordingly, in due course the marriage rites and ceremonies were performed after the law and ritual of the land with exceeding pomp and grandeur. But Prince Husayn would not be present at the bride-feast by reason of his disappointment and jealousy, for he had loved the Lady Nur al-Nihar with a love far exceeding that of either of his brothers; and he doffed his princely dress and donning the garb of a Fakir fared forth to live a hermit's life. Prince Ahmad also burned with envy and refused to join the wedding-feast; he did not, however, like Prince Husayn, retire to a hermitage, but he spent all his days in searching for his shaft to find where it had fallen.

Now it so fortuned that one morning he went again, alone as was his wont, in quest thereof, and starting from the stead whence they had shot their shafts reached the place where the arrows of Princes Husayn and Ali had been found. Then going straight forwards he cast his glances on every side over hill and dale to his right and to his left. Prince Ahmad went searching for his shaft over hill and dale when, after covering some three parasangs, suddenly he espied it lying flat upon a rock. Hereat he marvelled greatly, wondering how the arrow had flown so far, but even more so when he went up to it and saw that it had not stuck in the ground but appeared to have rebounded and to have fallen flat upon a slab of stone. Quoth he to himself, "There must assuredly be some mystery in this matter: else how could anyone shoot a shaft to such a distance and find it fallen after so strange a fashion."

Then, threading his way amongst the pointed crags and huge boulders, he presently came to a hollow in the ground which ended in a subterraneous passage, and after pacing a few paces he espied an iron door. He pushed this open with all ease, for that it had no bolt, and entering, arrow in hand, he came upon an easy slope by which he descended. But whereas he feared to find all pitch-dark, he discovered at some distance a spacious square, a widening of the cave, which was lighted on every side with lamps and candelabra. Then advancing some fifty cubits or more his glance fell upon a vast and handsome palace, and presently there issued from within to the portico a lovely maiden lovesome and lovable, a fairy-form robed in princely robes and adorned from front to foot with the costliest of jewels. She walked with slow and stately gait, withal graceful and blandishing, whilst around her ranged her attendants like the stars about a moon of the fourteenth night. Seeing this vision of beauty, Prince Ahmad hastened to salute her with the salam and she returned it; then coming forwards greeted him graciously and said in sweetest accents, "Well come and welcome, O Prince Ahmad: I am pleased to have sight of thee. How fareth it with thy Highness and why hast thou tarried so long away from me?"

The King's son marvelled greatly to hear her name him by his name; for that he knew not who she was, as they had never seen each other aforetime—how then came she to have learnt his title and condition? Then kissing ground before her he said, "O my lady, I owe thee much of thanks and gratitude for that thou art pleased to welcome me with words of cheer in this strange place where I, alone and a stranger, durst enter with exceeding hesitation and trepidation. But it perplexeth me sorely to think how thou camest to learn the name of thy slave."

Quoth she with a smile, "O my lord, come hither and let us sit at ease within yon belvedere; and there I will give an answer to thine asking."

So they went thither, Prince Ahmad following her footsteps; and on reaching it he was filled with wonder to see its vaulted roof of exquisite workmanship and adorned with gold and lapis lazuli and paintings and ornaments, whose like was nowhere to be found in the world. The lady seeing his astonishment said to the Prince, "This mansion is nothing beside all my others which now, of my free will, I have made thine own; and when thou seest them thou shalt have just cause for wonderment." Then that sylph-like being took seat upon a raised dais and with abundant show of affection seated Prince Ahmad by her side.

Presently quoth she, "Albeit thou know me not, I know thee well, as thou shalt see with surprise when I shall tell thee all my tale. But first it behoveth me disclose to thee who I am. In Holy Writ belike thou hast read that this world is the dwelling-place not only of men, but also of a race hight the Jann in form likest to mortals. I am the only daughter of a Jinn chief of noblest strain and my name is Peri-Banu. So marvel not to hear me tell thee who thou art and who is the King thy sire and who is Nur al-Nihar, the daughter of thine uncle. I have full knowledge of all concerning thyself and thy kith and kin; how thou art one of three brothers who all and each were daft for love of Princess Nur al-Nihar and strave to win her from one another to wife. Furthermore thy sire deemed it best to send you all far and wide over foreign lands, and thou faredest to far Samarkand and broughtest back a Magical Apple made with rare art and mystery which thou boughtest for forty thousand Ashrafis; then by means whereof thou madest the Princess thy lady-love whole of a grievous malady, whilst Prince Husayn, thine elder brother, bought for the same sum of money a Flying Carpet at Bishangarh, and Prince Ali also brought home a Spying Tube from Shiraz-city. Let this suffice to show thee that naught is hidden from me of all thy case; and now do thou tell me in very truth whom dost thou admire the more, for beauty and loveliness, me or the lady Nur al-Nihar thy brother's wife? My heart longeth for thee with excessive longing and desireth that we may be married and enjoy the pleasures of life and the joyance of love. So say me, art thou also willing to wed me, or pinest thou in preference for the daughter of thine uncle? In the fulness of my affection for thee I stood by thy side unseen during the archery meeting upon the plain of trial, and when thou shottest thy shaft I knew that it would fall far short of Prince Ali's, so I hent it in hand ere it touched ground and carried it away from sight, and striking it upon the iron door caused it rebound and lie flat upon the rock where thou didst find it. And ever since that day I have been sitting in expectancy, wotting well that thou wouldst search for it until thou find it, and by such means I was certified of bringing thee hither to me." Thus spake the beautiful maiden Peri-Banu who with eyes full of love-longing looked up at Prince Ahmad; and then with modest shame bent low her brow and averted her glance.

462

When Prince Ahmad heard these words of Peri-Banu he rejoiced with joy exceeding, and said to himself, "The Princess Nur al-Nihar is not within my power to win, and Peri-Banu doth outvie her in comeliness of favour and in loveliness of form and in gracefulness of gait." In short so charmed was he and captivated that he clean forgot his love for his cousin; and, noting that the heart of his new enchantress inclined towards him, he replied, "O my lady, O fairest of the fair, naught else do I desire save that I may serve thee and do thy bidding all my life long. But I am of human and thou of non-human birth. Thy friends and family, kith and kin, will haply be displeased with thee an thou unite with me in such union."

But she made answer, "I have full sanction of my parents to marry as I list and whomsoever I may prefer. Thou sayest that thou wilt be my servant, nay, rather be thou my lord and master; for I myself and my life and all my good are very thine, and I shall ever be thy bondswoman. Consent now, I beseech thee, to accept me for thy wife: my heart doth tell me thou wilt not refuse my request."

Then Peri-Banu added, "I have told thee already that in this matter I act with fullest authority. Besides all this there is a custom and immemorial usage with us fairy-folk that, when we maidens come to marriageable age and years of understanding, each one may wed, according the dictates of her heart, the person that pleaseth her most and whom she judgeth likely to make her days happy Thus wife and husband live with each other all their lives in harmony and happiness. But if a girl be given away in marriage by the parents, according to their choice and not hers, and she be mated to a helpmate unmeet for her, because ill-shapen or ill-conditioned or unfit to win her affection, then are they twain likely to be at variance each with other for the rest of their days; and endless troubles result to them from such ill-sorted union. Nor are we bound by another law which bindeth modest virgins of the race of Adam; for we freely announce our preference to those we love, nor must we wait and pine to be wooed and won."

When Prince Ahmad heard these words of answer, he rejoiced with exceeding joy and stooping down essayed to kiss the skirt of her garment, but she prevented him, and in lieu of her hem gave him her hand. The Prince clasped it with rapture and according to the custom of that place, he kissed it and placed it to his breast and upon his eyes. Hereat quoth the Fairy, smiling a charming smile, "With my hand locked in thine plight me thy troth even as I pledge my faith to thee, that I will alway true and loyal be, nor ever prove faithless or fail of constancy."

And quoth the Prince, "O loveliest of beings, O dearling of my soul, thinkest thou that I can ever become a traitor to my own heart, I who love thee to distraction and dedicate to thee my body and my sprite; to thee who art my queen, the very empress of me? Freely I give myself to thee, do thou with me whatso thou wilt."

Hereupon Peri-Banu said to Prince Ahmad, "Thou art my husband and I am thy wife. This solemn promise made between thee and me standeth in stead of marriage-contract: no need have we of Kazi, for with us all other forms and ceremonies are superfluous and of no avail. Anon I will show thee the chamber where we shall pass the bride-night; and methinks thou wilt admire it and confess that there is none like thereto in the whole world of men."

Presently her handmaidens spread the table and served up dishes of various kinds, and the finest wines in flagons and goblets of gold dubbed with jewels. So they twain sat at meat and ate and drank their sufficiency. Then Peri-Banu took Prince Ahmad by the hand and led him to her private chamber wherein she slept; and he stood upon the threshold amazed to see its magnificence and the heaps of gems and precious stones which dazed his sight, till recovering himself he cried, "Methinks there is not in the universe a room so splendid and decked with costly furniture and gemmed articles such as this."

Quoth Peri-Banu, "An thou so admire and praise this palace what wilt thou say when sighting the mansions and castles of my sire the Jann-King? Haply too when thou shalt behold my garden thou wilt be filled with wonder and delight; but now 'tis over late to lead thee thither and night approacheth." Then she ushered Prince Ahmad into another room where the supper had been spread, and the splendour of this saloon yielded in naught to any of the others; nay, rather it was the more gorgeous and dazzling. Hundreds of wax candles set in candelabra of the finest amber and the purest crystal, ranged on all sides, rained floods of light, whilst golden flowerpots and vessels of finest workmanship and priceless worth, of lovely shapes and wondrous art, adorned the niches and the walls.

Tongue of man can never describe the magnificence of that room in which bands of virgin Peris, loveliest of forms and fairest of features, garbed in choicest garments played on sweet-toned instruments of mirth and merriment or sang lays of amorous significance to strains of heart bewitching music. Then they twain, to wit the bride and bridegroom, sat down at meat, ever and anon delaying to indulge in toyings and bashful love-play and chaste caresses. Peri-Banu with her own hands passed the choicest mouthfuls to Prince Ahmad and made him taste of each dish and dainty, telling him their names and whereof they were composed. But how shall I, O auspicious King Shahryar, avail to give thee any notion of those Jinn-made dishes or to describe with due meed of praise the delicious flavour of meats such as no mortal ever tasted or ever beheld? Then, when both had supped, they drank the choicest wines, and ate with relish sweet conserves and dry fruit and a dessert of various delicacies. At length, when they had their requirement of eating and drinking, they retired into another room which contained a raised dais of the grandest, bedecked with gold-purfled cushions and pillows wrought with seed-pearl and Achaemenian tapestries, whereupon they took seat side by side for converse and solace. Then came in a troop of Jinns and fairies who danced and sang before them with wondrous grace and art; and this pretty show pleased Peri-Banu and Prince Ahmad, who watched the sports and displays with ever-renewed delight.

At last the newly wedded couple rose and retired, weary of revelry, to another chamber, wherein they found that the slaves had dispread the genial bed, whose frame was gold studded with jewels and whose furniture was of satin and sendal flowered with the rarest embroidery. Here the guests who attended at the marriage festival and the handmaids of the palace, ranged in two lines, hailed the bride and bridegroom as they went within; and then, craving dismissal, they all departed leaving them to take their joyance in bed. On such wise the marriage-festival and nuptial merry-makings were kept up day after day, with new dishes and novel sports, novel dances and new music; and, had Prince Ahmad lived a thousand years with mortal kind, never could he have seen such revels or heard such strains or enjoyed such love-liesse.

Thus six months soon passed in the Fairy-land beside Peri-Banu, whom he loved with a love so fond that he would not lose her from his sight for a moment's space; but would feel restless and ill-at-ease whenas he ceased to look upon her. In like manner Peri-Banu was fulfilled with affection for him and strove to please her bridegroom more and more every moment by new arts of dalliance and fresh appliances of pleasure, until so absorbing waxed his passion for her that the thought of home and kindred, kith and kin, faded from his thoughts and fled his mind. But after a time his memory awoke from slumber and at times he found himself longing to look upon his father, albeit well did he wot that it were impossible to find out how the far one fared unless he went himself to visit him. So one day quoth he to Peri-Banu, "An it be thy pleasure, I pray thee give me thy command that I may leave thee for a few days to see my sire, who doubtless grieveth at my long absence and suffereth all the sorrows of separation from his son."

Peri-Banu, hearing these words was dismayed with sore dismay, for that she thought within herself that this was only an excuse whereby he might escape and leave her after enjoyment and possession had made her love pall upon the palate of his mind. So quoth she in reply, "Hast thou forgotten thy vows and thy plighted troth, that thou wishest to leave me now? Have love and longing ceased to stir thee, whilst my heart always throbbeth in raptures as it hath ever done at the very thought of thee?"

Replied the Prince, "O dearling of my soul, my queen, my empress, what be these doubts that haunt thy mind, and why such sad misgivings and sorrowful words? I know full well that the love of thee and thine affection me-wards are even as thou sayest; and did I not acknowledge this truth or

465

did I prove unthankful or fail to regard thee with a passion as warm and deep, as tender and as true as thine own, I were indeed an ingrate and a traitor of the darkest dye. Far be it from me to desire severance from thee nor hath any thought of leaving thee never to return at any time crossed my mind. But my father is now an old man well shotten in years and he is sore grieved in mind at this long separation from his youngest son. If thou wilt deign command, I would fain go visit him and with all haste return to thine arms; yet I would not do aught in this matter against thy will; and such is my fond affection for thee that I would fain be at all hours of the day and watches of the night by thy side nor leave thee for a moment of time."

Peri-Banu was somewhat comforted by this speech; and from his looks, words and acts she was certified that Prince Ahmad really loved her with fondest love and that his heart was true as steel to her as was his tongue. Whereupon she granted him leave and liberty to set forth and see his sire, whilst at the same time she gave him strict commandment not to tarry long with his kith and kin. Hearken now, O auspicious King Shahryar, to what befel the Sultan of Hindostan and how it fared with him after the marriage of Prince Ali to Princess Nur al-Nihar.

After not seeing Prince Husayn and Prince Ahmad for the space of many days the Sultan waxed exceeding sad and heavy-hearted, and one morning after Darbar, asked his Wazirs and Ministers what had betided them and where they were. Hereto the councillors made answer saying, "O our lord, and shadow of Allah upon earth, thine eldest son and fruit of thy vitals and heir apparent to thine Empire the Prince Husayn, in his disappointment and jealousy and bitter grief hath doffed his royal robes to become a hermit, a devotee, renouncing all worldly lusts and gusts. Prince Ahmad thy third son also in high dudgeon hath left the city; and of him none knoweth aught, whither he hath fled or what hath befallen him."

The King was sore distressed and bade them write without stay or delay and forthright despatch firmans and commands to all the Nabobs and Governors of the provinces, with strict injunctions to make straight search for Prince Ahmad and to send him to his sire the moment he was found. But, albeit the commandments were carried out to the letter and all the seekers used the greatest diligence none came upon any trace of him. Then, with increased sadness of heart, the Sultan ordered his Grand Wazir to go in quest of the fugitive and the Minister replied, "Upon my head be it and mine eyes! Thy servant hath already caused most careful research to be made in every quarter, but not the smallest clue hath yet come to hand: and this matter troubleth me the more for that he was dear to me as a son."

The Ministers and Grandees now understood that the King was overwhelmed with woe, tearful-eyed and heavy-hearted by reason of the loss of Prince Ahmad; whereupon bethought the Grand Wazir of a certain witch famed for the Black Art who could conjure down the stars from heaven; and who was a noted dweller in the capital. So going to the Sultan he spake highly of her skill in knowledge of the abstruse, saying "Let the King, I pray thee, send for this sorceress and enquire of her concerning his lost son."

And the King replied, "'Tis well said: let her be brought hither and haply she shall give me tidings of the Prince and how he fareth."

So they fetched the Sorceress and set her before the Sultan, who said, "O my good woman, I would have thee know that ever since the marriage of Prince Ali with the Lady Nur al-Nihar, my youngest son Prince Ahmad, who was disappointed in her love, hath disappeared from our sight and no man knoweth aught of him. Do thou forthright apply thy magical craft and tell me only this: Is he yet alive or is he dead? An he live I would learn where is he and how fareth he; moreover, I would ask, Is it written in my book of Destiny that I shall see him yet again?"

To this the Witch made reply, "O Lord of the Age and ruler of the times and tide, 'tis not possible for me at once to answer all these questions which belong to the knowledge of Hidden Things; but, if thy Highness deign grant me one day of grace, I will consult my books of gramarye and on the morrow will give thee a sufficient reply and a satisfactory."

The Sultan to this assented, saying, "An thou can give me detailed and adequate answer, and set my mind at ease after this sorrow, thou shalt have an exceeding great reward and I will honour thee with highmost honour."

Next day the Sorceress, accompanied by the Grand Wazir, craved permission to appear before the presence, and when it was granted came forward and said, "I have made ample investigation by my art and mystery and I have assured myself that Prince Ahmad is yet in the land of the living. Be not therefore uneasy in thy mind on his account; but at present, save this only, naught else can I discover regarding him, nor can I say for sure where he be or how he is to be found." At these words the Sultan took comfort, and hope sprang up within his breast that he should see his son again ere he died. Now return we to the story of Prince Ahmad. Whenas Peri-Banu understood that he was bent upon visiting his sire and she was convinced that his love her-wards remained firm and steadfast as before, she took thought and determined that it would ill become her to refuse him leave and liberty for such purpose; so she again pondered the matter in her mind and debated with herself for many an hour till at length, one day of the days, she turned to her husband and said, "Albeit my heart consenteth not to part from thee for a moment or to lose sight of thee for a single instant, still inasmuch as thou hast ofttimes made entreaty of me and hast shown thyself so solicitous to see thy sire, I will no longer baffle thy wish. But this my favour will depend upon one condition; otherwise I will never grant thy petition and give thee such permission. Swear to me the most binding of oaths that thou wilt haste thee back hither with all possible speed, and thou wilt not by long absence cause me yearning grief and anxious waiting for thy safe return to me."

Prince Ahmad, well pleased to win his wish, thanked her saying, "O my beloved, fear not for me after any fashion and rest assured I will come back to thee with all haste as soon as I shall have seen my sire; and life hath no charms for me away from thy presence. Although I must needs be severed from thee for a few days, yet will my heart ever turn to thee and to thee only."

Quoth she to her husband, Prince Ahmad, "So now, as soon as thy heart desireth, go thou and pay thy respects to thy sire; but ere thou set out I would charge thee with one charge and look that on no wise thou forget my rede and my counsel. Speak not to any a single word of this thy marriage nor of the strange sights thou hast seen and the wonders thou hast witnessed; but keep them carefully concealed from thy father and thy brethren and from thy kith and kin, one and all. This only shalt thou tell thy sire, so his mind may be set at ease that thou art buxom and happy; also that thou hast returned home for a while only with the object of seeing him and becoming assured of his welfare."

Then she gave orders to her people bidding them make ready for the journey without delay; and when all things were prepared she appointed twenty horsemen, armed cap-a-pie and fully accoutred, to accompany her husband, and gave him a horse of perfect form and proportions, swift as the blinding leven or the rushing wind; and its housings and furniture were bedeckt with precious ores and studded with jewels. Then she fell on his neck and they embraced with warmest love; and as the twain bade adieu, Prince Ahmad, to set her mind at rest, renewed his protestations and sware to her again his solemn oath. Then mounting his horse and followed by his suite (all Jinn-born cavaliers) he set forth with mighty pomp and circumstance, and riding diligently he soon reached his father's capital. Here he was received with loud acclamations, the like of which had never been known in the land.

The Ministers and Officers of State, the citizens and the Ryots all rejoiced with exceeding joy to see him once more, and the folk left their work and with blessings and low obeisances joined the cavalcade; and, crowding around him on every side, escorted him to the palace gates. When the Prince reached the threshold he dismounted and, entering the audience-hall, fell at his father's feet and kissed them in a transport of filial affection. The Sultan, well nigh distraught for delight at the unexpected sight of Prince Ahmad, rose from his throne and threw himself upon his son's neck weeping for very joy and kissed his forehead saying, "O dear my child, in despair at the loss of the Lady Nur al-Nihar thou didst suddenly fly from thy home, and, despite all research, nor trace nor sign of thee was to be found however sedulously we sought thee; and I, distracted at thy disappearance, am reduced to this condition in which thou seest me. Where hast thou been this long while, and how hast thou lived all this time?"

Replied Prince Ahmad, "'Tis true, O my lord the King, that I was downhearted and distressed to see Prince Ali gain the hand of my cousin, but that is not the whole cause of my absence. Thou mayest remember how, when we three brothers rode at thy command to yonder plain for a trial of archery, my shaft, albeit the place was large and flat, disappeared from sight and none could find where it had fallen. Now so it fortuned that one day in sore heaviness of mind I fared forth alone and unaccompanied to examine the ground thereabout and try if haply I could find my arrow. But when I reached the spot where the shafts of my brothers, Princes Husayn and Ali, had been picked up, I made search in all directions, right and left, before and behind, thinking that thereabouts mine also might come to hand; but all my trouble was in vain: I found neither shaft nor aught else. So walking onwards in obstinate research, I went a long way, and at last despairing, I would have given up the quest, for full well I knew that my bow could not have carried so far, and indeed that 'twere impossible for any marksman to have driven bolt or pile to such distance, when suddenly I espied it lying flat upon a rock some four parasangs distant from this place."

The Sultan marvelled with much marvel at his words and the Prince presently resumed, "So when I picked up the arrow, O my lord, and considered it closely I knew it for the very one I had shot, but admired in my mind how it had come to fly so far, and I doubted not but that there was a somewhat mysterious about the matter. While I thus reflected I came upon the place where I have sojourned ever since that day in perfect solace and happiness. I may not tell thee more of my tale than this; for I came only to ease thy mind on my account, and now I pray thee deign grant me thy supreme permission that I return forthright to my home of delights. From time to time I will not cease to wait upon thee and to enquire of thy welfare with all the affection of a son."

Replied the King, "O my child, the sight of thee hath gladdened mine eyes; and I am now satisfied; and not unwillingly I give thee leave to go, since thou art happy in some place so near hand; but shouldst thou at any time delay thy coming hither, say me, how shall I be able to get tidings of thy good health and welfare?"

And quoth Prince Ahmad, "O my lord the King, that which thou requirest of me is part of my secret and this must remain deep hidden in my breast: as I said before, I may not discover it to thee nor say aught that might lead to its discovery. However, be not uneasy in thy soul, for I will appear before thee full many a time and haply I may irk thee with continual coming."

"O my son," rejoined the Sultan, "I would not learn thy secret an thou would keep it from me, but there is one only thing I desire of thee, which is, that ever and anon I may be assured of thine enduring health and happiness. Thou hast my full permission to hie thee home, but forget not at least once a month to come and see me even as now thou dost, lest such forgetfulness cause me anxiety and trouble, cark and care."

So Prince Ahmad tarried with his father three days full-told, but never for a moment did the memory of the Lady Peri-Banu fade from his mind; and on the fourth day he mounted horse and returned with the same pomp and pageantry wherewith he came.

Peri-Banu joyed with exceeding joy at the sight of Prince Ahmad as he returned to his home; and it seemed to her as though they had been parted for three hundred years: such is love that moments of separation are longsome and weary as twelvemonths. The Prince offered much of excuses for his short absence and his words delighted Peri-Banu yet the more. So these twain, lover and beloved, passed the time in perfect happiness, taking their pleasure one with other. Thus a month went by and Prince Ahmad never once mentioned the name of his sire nor expressed a wish to go visit him according to his promise. Noting this change, the Lady Peri-Banu said to him one day, "Thou toldest me aforetime that once in the beginning of each month thou wouldst fare forth and travel to thy father's court and learn news of his welfare: why then neglectest thou so to do, seeing that he will be distressed and anxiously expecting thee?"

Replied Prince Ahmad, "'Tis even as thou sayest, but, awaiting thy command and thy permission, I have forborne to propose the journey to thee."

And she made answer, "Let thy faring and thy returning rest not on my giving thee liberty of leave. At the beginning of each month as it cometh round, do thou ride forth, and from this time forwards thou hast no need to ask permission of me. Stay with thy sire three days full-told and on the fourth come back to me without fail."

Accordingly, on the next day betimes in the morning Prince Ahmad took his departure and as aforetime rode forth with abundant pomp and parade and repaired to the palace of the Sultan his sire, to whom he made his obeisance. On like manner continued he to do each month with a suite of horsemen larger and more brilliant than before, whilst he himself was more splendidly mounted and equipped. And whenever the Crescent appeared in the Western sky he fondly farewelled his wife and paid his visit to the King, with whom he tarried three whole days, and on the fourth returned to dwell with Peri-Banu. But, as each and every time he went, his equipage was greater and grander than the last, at length one of the Wazirs, a favourite and cup-companion of the King, was filled with wonderment and jealousy to see Prince Ahmad appear at the palace with such opulence and magnificence. So he said in himself, "None can tell whence cometh this Prince, and by what means he hath obtained so splendid a suite."

Then of his envy and malice that Wazir fell to plying the King with deceitful words and said, "O my liege lord and mighty sovran, it ill becometh thee to be thus heedless of Prince Ahmad's proceedings. Seest thou not how day after day his retinue increaseth in numbers and puissance? What an he should plot against thee and cast thee into prison, and take from thee the reins of the realm? Right well thou wottest that inasmuch as thou didst wed Prince Ali to the Lady Nur al-Nihar thou provokedest the wrath of Prince Husayn and Prince Ahmad; so that one of them in the bitterness of his soul renounced the pomps and vanities of this world and hath become a Fakir, whilst the other, to wit; Prince Ahmad, appeareth before thy presence in such inordinate power and majesty. Doubtless they both seek their revenge; and, having gotten thee into their power, the twain will deal treacherously with thee. So I would have thee beware, and again I say beware; and seize the forelock of opportunity ere it be too late; for the wise have said:

> "'Thou canst bar a spring with a sod of clay
> But when grown 'twill bear a big host away.'"

Thus spake that malicious Wazir; and presently he resumed, "Thou knowest also that when Prince Ahmad would end his three days' visits he never asketh thy leave nor farewelleth thee nor biddeth adieu to any one of his family. Such conduct is the beginning of rebellion and proveth him to be rancorous of heart. But 'tis for thee in thy wisdom to decide."

These words sank deep in the heart of the simple-minded Sultan and grew a crop of the direst suspicions. He presently thought within himself, "Who knoweth the mind and designs of Prince Ahmad, whether they be dutiful or undutiful towards me? Haply he may be plotting vengeance; so it besitteth me to make enquiries concerning him, to discover where he dwelleth and by what means he hath attained to such puissance and opulence."

Filled with these jealous thoughts, he sent in private one day, unbeknown to the Grand Wazir who would at all times befriend Prince Ahmad, to summon the Witch; and, admitting her by a secret postern to his private chamber, asked of her saying, "Thou didst aforetime learn by thy magical art that Prince Ahmad was alive and didst bring me tidings of him. I am beholden to thee for this good office, and now I would desire of thee to make further quest into his case and ease my mind, which is sore disturbed. Albeit my son still liveth and cometh to visit me every month, yet am I clean ignorant of the place wherein he dwelleth and whence he setteth out to see me; for that he keepeth the matter close hidden from his sire. Go thou forthright and privily, without the knowledge of any, my Wazirs and Nabobs, my courtiers and my household; and make thou diligent research and with all haste bring me word whereabouts he liveth. He now sojourneth here upon his wonted visit; and, on the fourth day, without leave-taking or mention of departure to me or to any of the Ministers and Officers, he will summon his suite and mount his steed; then will he ride to some little distance hence and suddenly disappear. Do thou without stay or delay forego him on the path and lie perdue in some convenient hollow hard by the road whence thou mayest learn where he cometh; then quickly bring me tidings thereof."

Accordingly, the Sorceress departed the presence of the King; and, after walking over the four parasangs, she hid herself within a hollow of the rocks hard by the place where Prince Ahmad had found his arrow, and there awaited his arrival. Early on the morrow the Prince, as was his wont, set out upon his journey without taking leave of his sire or fare welling any of the Ministers. So when they drew nigh, the Sorceress caught sight of the Prince and of the retinue that rode before and beside him; and she saw them enter a hollow way which forked into a many of by-ways; and so steep and dangerous were the cliffs and boulders about the track that hardly could a footman safely pace that path. Seeing this the Sorceress bethought her that it must surely lead to some cavern or haply to a subterraneous passage, or to a souterrain the abode of Jinns and fairies; when suddenly the Prince and all his suite vanished from her view. So she crept out of the hiding-place wherein she had ensconced herself and wandered far and wide seeking, as dillgently as she was able, but never finding the subterraneous passage nor yet could she discern the iron door which Prince Ahmad had espied, for none of human flesh and blood had power to see this save he alone to whom it was made visible by the Fairy Peri-Banu; furthermore it was ever concealed from the prying eyes of womankind. Then said the Sorceress to herself, "This toil and moil have I undertaken to no purpose; yea, verily, I have failed to find out that wherefor I came."

So she went forthright back to the Sultan and reported to him all that had betided her, how she had lain in wait amid the cliffs and boulders and had seen the Prince and suite ride up the most perilous of paths and, having entered a hollow way, disappear in an eyetwinkling from her sight. And she ended by saying, "Albeit I strove my utmost to find out the spot wherein the Prince abideth, yet could I on no wise succeed; and I pray thy Highness may grant me time to search further into the matter and to find out this mystery which by skill and caution on my part shall not long abide concealed."

Answered the Sultan, "Be it as thou wilt: I grant thee leisure to make enquiry and after a time I shall await thy return hither."

The King largessed the Witch with a diamond of large size and of great price, saying, "Take this stone to guerdon for thy trouble and travail and in earnest of future favours; so, when thou shalt return and bring me word that thou hast searched and found out the secret, thou shalt have a Bakhshish of far greater worth and I will make thy heart rejoice with choicest joy and honour thee with highmost honour."

So the Sorceress looked forwards to the coming of the Prince, for well she knew that at the sight of each crescent he rode home to visit his sire and was bound to abide with him three days, even as the Lady Peri-Banu had permitted and had enjoined him. Now when the moon had waxed and waned, on the day before the Prince would leave home upon his monthly visit, the Witch betook her to the rocks and sat beside the place whence she imagined he would issue forth; and next morning early he and his suite, composed of many a mounted knight with his esquire a-foot, who now always accompanied him in increasing numbers, rode forth gallantly through the iron doorway and passed hard by the place where she lay in wait for him. The Sorceress crouched low upon the ground in her tattered rags; and, seeing a heap by his way, the Prince at first supposed that a slice of stone had fallen from the rocks across his path. But as he drew nigh she fell to weeping and wailing with might and main as though in sore dolour and distress, and she ceased not to crave his countenance and assistance with increase of tears and lamentations.

The Prince seeing her sore sorrow had pity on her, and reining in his horse, asked her what she had to require of him and what was the cause of her cries and lamentations. At this the cunning crone but cried the more, and the Prince was affected with compassion still livelier at seeing her tears and hearing her broken, feeble words. So when the Sorceress perceived that Prince Ahmad had ruth on her and would fain show favour to her, she heaved a heavy sigh and in woeful tones, mingled with moans and groans, addressed him in these false words, withal holding the hem of his garment and at times stopping as if convulsed with pain, "O my lord and lord of all loveliness, as I was journeying from my home in yonder city upon an errand to such a place, behold, when I came thus far upon my way, suddenly a hot fit of fever seized me and a shivering and a trembling, so that I lost all strength and fell down helpless as thou seest me; and still no power have I in hand or foot to rise from the ground and to return to my place."

Replied the Prince, "Alas, O good woman, there is no house at hand where thou mayest go and be fitly tended and tendered. Howbeit I know a stead whither, an thou wilt, I can convey thee and where by care and kindness thou shalt (Inshallah!) soon recover of thy complaint. Come then with me as best thou canst."

With loud moans and groans the Witch made answer, "So weak am I in every limb and helpless that I can by no means rise off the ground or move save with the help of some friendly hand."

The Prince then bade one of his horsemen lift up the feeble and ailing old woman and set her upon his steed; and the cavalier did his lord's bidding forthright and mounted her astraddle upon the crupper of his courser: then, Prince Ahmad rode back with her and entering by the iron door carried her to his apartment and sent for Peri-Banu. His wife hurriedly coming forth to the Prince asked him in her flurry, "Is all well and wherefore hast thou come back and what wouldst thou that thou hast sent for me?"

Prince Ahmad then told her of the old woman who was healthless and helpless, adding, "Scarce had I set out on my journey when I espied this ancient dame lying hard by the roadside, suffering and in sore distress. My heart felt pity for her to see her in such case and constrained me to bring her hither as I could not leave her to die among the rocks; and I pray thee of thy bounty take her in and give her medicines that she may soon be made whole of this her malady. An thou wilt show this favour I shall not cease to thank thee and be beholden to thee."

Peri-Banu looked at the old woman and charged a twain of her handmaidens that they carry her into a room apart and tend her with the tenderest care and the uttermost of diligence. The attendants did as she bade them and transported the Sorceress to the place she had designed. Then Peri-Banu addressed Prince Ahmad saying, "O my lord, I am pleased to see thy pitiful kindness towards this ancient dame, and I surely will look to her case even as thou hast enjoined me; but my heart misgiveth me and much I fear some evil will result from thy goodness. This woman is not so ill as she doth make believe, but practiseth deceit upon thee and I ween that some enemy or envier hath plotted a plot against me and thee. Howbeit go now in peace upon thy journey."

The Prince, who on no wise took to heart the words of his wife, presently replied to her, "O my lady, Almighty Allah forfend thee from all offence! With thee to help and guard me I fear naught of ill: I know of no foeman who would compass my destruction, for I bear no grudge against any living being, and I foresee no evil at the hands of man or Jann."

Thereupon the Prince again took leave of Peri-Banu and repaired with his attendants to the palace of his sire who, by reason of the malice of his crafty Minister, was inwardly afraid to see his son; but not the less he welcomed him with great outward show of love and affection. Meanwhile the two fairy handmaidens, to whom Peri-Banu had given charge of the Witch, bore her away to a spacious room splendidly furnished; and laid her on a bed having a mattress of satin and a brocaded coverlet. Then one of them sat by her side whilst the other with all speed fetched, in a cup of porcelain, an essence which was a sovereign draught for ague and fever. Presently they raised her up and seated her on the couch saying, "Drain thou this drink. It is the water of the Lions' Fount and whoso tasteth of the same is forthwith made whole of what disease soever he hath."

The Sorceress took the cup with great difficulty and after swallowing the contents lay back on the bed; and the handmaidens spread the quilt over her saying, "Now rest awhile and thou shalt soon feel the virtues of this medicine."

Then they left her to sleep for an hour or so; but presently the Witch, who had feigned sickness to the intent only that she might learn where Prince Ahmad abode and might inform the Sultan thereof, being assured that she had discovered all that she desired, rose up and summoning the damsels said to them, "The drinking of that draught hath restored to me all my health and strength: I now feel hale and hearty once more and my limbs are filled with new life and vigour. So at once acquaint your lady herewith, that I may kiss the hem of her robe and return my thanks for her goodness me-wards, then depart and hie me home again."

Accordingly, the two handmaidens took the Sorceress with them and showed her as they went along the several apartments, each more magnificent and kingly than the other; and at length they reached the belvedere which was the noblest saloon of all, and fitted and filled with furniture exceeding costly and curious. There sat Peri-Banu upon a throne which was adorned with diamonds and rubies, emeralds, pearls and other gems of unwonted size and water, whilst round about her stood fairies of lovely form and features, robed in the richest raiments and awaiting with folded hands her commandments. The Sorceress marvelled with extreme marvel to see the splendour of the chambers and their furniture, but chiefly when she beheld the Lady Peri-Banu seated upon the jewelled throne; nor could she speak a word for confusion and awe, but she bent down low and placed her head upon Peri-Banu's feet.

Quoth the Princess in soft speech and reassuring tones, "O good woman, it pleaseth me greatly to see thee a guest in this my palace, and I joy even more to learn that thou be wholly quit of thy sickness. So now solace thy spirits with walking all round about the place and my servants will accompany thee and show thee what there is worthy of thine inspection."

Hereat the Witch again louted low and kissed the carpet under Peri-Banu's feet, and took leave of her hostess in goodly phrase and with great show of gratitude for her favours. The handmaids then led her round the palace and displayed to her all the rooms, which dazed and dazzled her sight so that she could not find words to praise them sufficiently. Then she went her ways and the fairies escorted her past the iron doorway whereby Prince Ahmad had brought her in, and left her, bidding her God-speed and blessing her; and the foul crone with many thanks took the road to her own home. But when she had walked to some distance she was minded to see the iron door, so might she with ease know it again; so she went back, but lo and behold! the entrance had vanished and was invisible to her as to all other women. Accordingly, after searching on all sides and pacing to and fro and finding nor sign nor trace of palace or portal, she repaired in despair to the city and, creeping along a deserted path-way, entered the palace, according to her custom, by the private postern. When safely within she straightway sent word by an eunuch to the Sultan, who ordered that she be brought before him. She approached him with troubled countenance, whereat, perceiving that she had failed to carry out her purpose, he asked, "What news? Hast thou accomplished thy design or hast thou been baffled therein?"

The Sorceress, who was a mere creature of the malicious Wazir, replied, "O King of kings, this matter have I fully searched out even as thou gavest command, and I am about to tell thee all that hath betided me. The signs of sorrow and marks of melancholy thou notest upon my countenance are for other cause which narrowly concerneth thy welfare."

Then she began to recount her adventure in these terms, "Now when I had reached the rocks I sat me down feigning sickness; and, as Prince Ahmad passed that way and heard my complaining and saw my grievous condition, he had compassion on me. After some 'said and say' he took me with him by a subterranean passage and through an iron door to a magnificent palace and gave me in charge of a fairy, Peri-Banu hight, of passing beauty and loveliness, such as human eye hath never yet seen. Prince Ahmad bade her make me her guest for some few days and bring me a medicine which would complete my cure, and she to please him at once appointed handmaidens to attend upon me. So I was certified that the twain were one flesh, husband and wife. I feigned to be exceeding frail and feeble and made as though I had not strength to walk or even to stand; whereat the two damsels supported me, one on either side, and I was carried into a room where they gave me somewhat to drink and put me upon a bed to rest and sleep.

"Then thought I to myself: 'Verily I have gained the object wherefor I had feigned sickness'; and I was assured that it availed no more to practise deceit. Accordingly, after a short while I arose and said to the attendants that the draught which they had given me to drink had cut short the fever and had restored strength to my limbs and life to my frame. Then they led me to the presence of the Lady Peri-Banu, who was exceeding pleased to see me once more hale and hearty, and bade her handmaidens conduct me around the palace and show each room in its beauty and splendour; after which I craved leave to wend my ways and here am I again to work thy will."

When thus she had made known to the King all that had betided her, she resumed, "Perchance, on hearing of the might and majesty, opulence and magnificence of the Lady Peri-Banu, thou wilt be gladdened and say within thyself, ''Tis well that Prince Ahmad is wedded to this Fairy and hath gotten for himself such wealth and power'; but to the thinking of this thy slave the matter is quite other. It is not well, I dare avouch, that thy son should possess such puissance and treasures, for who knoweth but that he may by good aid of Peri-Banu bring about division and disturbance in the realm? Beware of the wiles and malice of women. The Prince is bewitched with love of her, and peradventure at her incitement he may act towards thee otherwise than right, and lay hands on thy hoards and seduce thy subjects and become master of thy kingdom; and albeit he would not of his own free will do aught to his father and his forbears save what was pious and dutiful, yet the charms of his Princess may work upon him little by little and end by making him a rebel and what more I may not say. Now mayest thou see that the matter is a weighty, so be not heedless but give it full consideration."

Then the Sorceress made ready to gang her gait when spake the King, saying, "I am beholden to thee in two things; the first, that thou tookest upon thyself much toil and travail, and on my behalf riskedst thy life to learn the truth anent my son Prince Ahmad. Secondly, I am thankful for that thou hast given me a rede so sound and such wholesome counsel."

So saying, he dismissed her with the highmost honour; but no sooner had she left the palace than he, sore distraught, summoned his second Wazir, the malicious Minister who had incited him against Prince Ahmad, and when he and his friends appeared in the presence he laid before them the whole matter and asked of them, saying, "What is your counsel, and what must I do to protect myself and my kingdom against the wiles of this Fairy?"

Replied one of his councillors, "'Tis but a trifling matter and the remedy is simple and nearhand. Command that Prince Ahmad, who is now within the city if not in the palace, be detained as one taken prisoner. Let him not be put to death, lest haply the deed may engender rebellion; but at any rate place him under arrest and if he prove violent clap him in irons."

This felon counsel pleased the malicious Minister and all his fautors and flatterers highly approved his rede. The Sultan kept silence and made no reply, but on the morrow he sent and summoned the Sorceress and debated with her whether he should or should not cast Prince Ahmad into prison.

Quoth she, "O King of kings, this counsel is clean contrary to sound sense and right reason. An thou throw Prince Ahmad into gaol, so must thou also do with all his knights and their esquires; and inasmuch as they are Jinns and Marids, who can tell their power of reprisals? Nor prison-

cells nor gates of adamant can keep them in; they will forthwith escape and report such violence to the Fairy who, wroth with extreme wrath to find her husband doomed to durance vile like a common malefactor, and that too for no default or crime but by a treacherous arrest, will assuredly deal the direst of vengeance on thy head and do us a damage we shall not be able to forfend. An thou wilt confide in me, I will advise thee how to act, whereby thou mayest win thy wish and no evil will come nigh thee or thy kingship. Thou knowest well that to Jinns and Fairies is power given of doing in one short moment deeds marvellous and wondrous, which mortals fail to effect after long years of toil and trouble. Now whenas thou goest a-hunting or on other expedition, thou requirest pavilions for thyself and many tents for thy retinue and attendants and soldiery; and in making ready and transporting such store much time and wealth are wastefully expended. I would advise, O King of kings, that thou try Prince Ahmad by the following test: do thou bid him bring to thee a Shahmiyanah so long and so broad that it will cover and lodge the whole of thy court and men-at-arms and camp-followers, likewise the beasts of burthen; and yet it must be so light that a man may hold it in the hollow of his hand and carry it whithersoever he listeth."

Then, after holding her peace for a while, she added, still addressing the Sultan, "And as soon as Prince Ahmad shall acquit himself of this commission, do thou demand of him a somewhat still greater and more wondrous wherewith I will make thee ware, and which he will find grievous of execution. On this wise shalt thou fill thy treasury with rare inventions and strange, the handicraft of Jann, nor will this cease till such time in fine when thy son shall be at his wits' end to carry out thy requirements. Then, humbled and abashed, he will never dare to enter thy capital or even thy presence; and thus shalt thou be saved from fear of harm at his hands, and thou shalt not have need to put him in gaol or, worse still, to do him dead."

Hearing these words of wisdom, the Sultan made known the Witch's device to his advisers and asked them what they deemed thereof. They held their peace and answered not a word or good or ill; while he himself highly approved it and said no more. Next day Prince Ahmad came to visit the King, who welcomed him with overflowing affection and clasping him to his bosom kissed him on eyes and forehead. Long time they sat conversing on various subjects, till at length the Sultan finding an occasion spake thus, "O dear my son, O Ahmad, for many a day have I been sad at heart and sorrowful of soul because of separation from thee, and when thou camest back I was gladdened with great gladness at sight of thee, and albeit thou didst and dost still withhold from me the knowledge of thy whereabouts,

I refrained from asking thee or seeking to find out thy secret, since it was not according to thy mind to tell me of thine abode. Now, however, I have heard say that thou art wedded to a mighty Jinniyah, of passing beauty; and the tidings please me with the highmost possible pleasure. I desire not to learn aught from thee concerning thy Fairy-wife save whatso thou wouldst entrust to me of thine own free will; but, say me, should I at any time require somewhat of thee, canst thou obtain it from her? Doth she regard thee with such favour that she will not deny thee anything thou askest of her?"

Quoth the Prince, "O my lord, what dost thou demand of me? My wife is devoted to her husband in heart and soul, so prithee let me learn what it is thou wouldst have of me and her."

Replied the Sultan, "Thou knowest that ofttimes I fare a-hunting or on some foray and fray, when I have great need of tents and pavilions and Shahmiyanahs, with herds and troops of camels and mules and other beasts of burden to carry the camp from place to place. I would, therefore, that thou bring me a tent so light that a man may carry it in the hollow of his hand, and yet so large that it may contain my court and all my host and camp and suttlers and bat-animals. An thou wouldst ask the Lady for this gift I know full well that she can give it; and hereby shalt thou save me much of trouble in providing carriage for the tentage and spare me much waste and loss of beasts and men."

The Prince replied, "O my sire the Sultan, trouble not thy thought. I will at once make known thy wish to my wife, the Lady Peri-Banu; and, albeit little I wot an fairies have the faculty of making a pavilion such as thou describest, or indeed (supposing that they have such power), an she will grant me or not grant me her aidance; and, moreover, although I cannot promise thee such present, yet whatsoever lieth in my ability to do, that will I gladly do for thy service."

Quoth the King to Prince Ahmad, "Shouldst thou perchance fail in this matter and bring me not the gift required, O my son, I will never see thy face again. A sorry husband thou, in good sooth, if thy wife refuse so mean a thing and hasten not to do all thou biddest her do; giving thee to see that thou art of small value and consequence in her eyes, and that her love for thee is a quantity well nigh to naught. But do thou, O my child, go forth and straightway ask her for the tent. An she give it thee know thou she desireth thee and thou art the dearest of all things to her; and I have been informed that she loveth thee with all her heart and soul and will by no means refuse thee aught thou requirest, were it even the balls of her eyes."

Now Prince Ahmad was ever wont to tarry three days each month with the Sultan his sire, and return to his spouse on the fourth; but this time he stayed two days only and farewelled his father on the third. As he passed into the palace Peri-Banu could not but note that he was sad at heart and downcast of face; so she asked of him, "Is all well with thee? Why hast thou come to-day and not to-morrow from the presence of the King thy father, and why carriest thou so triste a countenance?"

Whereupon, after kissing her brow and fondly embracing her, he told her the whole matter, first to last, and she made answer, "I will speedily set thy mind at rest, for I would not see thee so saddened for a moment longer. Howbeit, O my love, from this petition of the Sultan thy sire I am certified that his end draweth nigh, and he will soon depart this world to the mercy of Allah the Almighty. Some enemy hath done this deed and much of mischief hath made for thee; and the result is that thy father, all unmindful of his coming doom, doth seek diligently his own destruction."

The Prince, anxious and alarmed, thus answered his wife, "Almighty Allah be praised, the King my liege lord is in the best of health and showeth no sign of disorder or decrepitude: 'tis but this morning I left him hale and hearty, and in very sooth I never saw him in better case. Strange, indeed, that thou shouldst ken what shall betide him before I have told thee aught concerning him, and especially how he hath come to learn of our marriage and of our home."

Quoth Peri-Banu, "O my Prince, thou knowest what I said to thee whenas I saw the old dame whom thou broughtest hither as one afflicted with the ague and fever. That woman, who is a Witch of Satan's breed, hath disclosed to thy father all he sought to learn concerning this our dwelling-place. And notwithstanding that I saw full clearly she was nor sick nor sorry, but only feigning a fever, I gave her medicine to drink which cureth complaints of all kinds, and she falsely made believe that by its virtues she had recovered health and strength. So when she came to take leave of me, I sent her with two of my damsels and bid them display to her every apartment in the palace together with its furniture and decorations, that she might better know the condition of me and thee. Now all this did I on thy account only, for thou badest me show compassion to the ancient woman and I was rejoiced to see her departing safe and sound and in the best of spirits. Save her alone, no human being had ever power to know aught of this place, much less to come hither."

Prince Ahmad hearing these words thanked and praised her and said, "O sun-faced beauty, I would beg of thee to grant me a boon

whereof my father hath made request of me; to wit, a Shahmiyanah of such dimensions that it may shelter him and his many, his camp and bat-cattle and withal may be carried in the hollow of the hand. An such marvel exist I wot not, yet would I do my utmost to procure it, and carry it to him right loyally."

Quoth she, "Why trouble thyself for so small a matter? I will forthright send for it and give it thee."

Then she summoned one of her handmaids who was treasurer to her and said, "O Nur Jehan, go thou at once and bring me a pavilion of such and such a fashion." So she fared forth without delay and as quickly came back with the pavilion which, at her lady's bidding, she placed in the palm of Prince Ahmad's hand.

Prince Ahmad hent the pavilion in hand and thought to himself, "What is this Peri-Banu giveth me? Surely she doth make a mock of me."

His wife, however, reading his mind in his face fell to laughing aloud, and asked, "What is it, O my dearling Prince? Dost thou think that I am jesting and jibing at thee?"

Then she continued, addressing the treasurer Nur Jehan, "Take now yon tent from Prince Ahmad and set it upon the plain that he may see its vast size and know if it be such an one as required by the Sultan his sire."

The handmaid took the pavilion and pitched it afar from the Palace; and yet one end thereof reached thereto from the outer limit of the plain; and so immense was its size that (as Prince Ahmad perceived) there was room therein for all the King's court; and, were two armies ranged under it with their camp-followers and bat-animals, one would on no wise crowd or inconvenience the other. He then begged pardon of Peri-Banu saying, "I wot not that the Shahmiyanah was so prodigious of extent and of so marvellous a nature; wherefore I misdoubted when first I saw it."

The Treasurer presently struck the tent and returned it to the palm of his hand; then, without stay or delay, he took horse and followed by his retinue rode back to the royal presence, where after obeisance and suit and service he presented the tent. The Sultan also, at first sight of the gift, thought it a small matter, but marvelled with extreme marvel to see its size when pitched, for it would have shaded his capital and its suburbs. He was not, however, wholly satisfied, for the size of the pavilion now appeared to him superfluous; but his son assured him that it would always fit itself to its contents. He thanked the Prince for bringing him so rare a present, saying, "O my son, acquaint thy consort with my obligation to her and offer my grateful thanks for this her bounteous gift. Now indeed know I of a truth that she doth love thee with the whole of her heart and soul and all my doubts and fears are well nigh set at rest."

Then the King commanded they should pack up the tent and store it with all care in the royal treasury. Now strange it is but true, that when the Sultan received this rare present from the Prince, the fear and doubt, the envy and jealousy of his son, which the Witch and the malicious Wazir and his other ill advisers had bred in his breast, waxed greater and livelier than before; because he was now certified that in very truth the Jinniyah was gracious beyond measure to her mate and that, notwithstanding the great wealth and power of the sovereign, she could outvie him in mighty deeds for the aidance of her husband. Accordingly, he feared with excessive fear lest haply she seek opportunity to slay him in favour of the Prince whom she might enthrone in his stead. So he bade bring the Witch who had counselled him aforetime, and upon whose sleight and malice he now mainly relied. When he related to her the result of her rede, she took thought for a while; then, raising her brow said, "O King of kings, thou troublest thyself for naught: thou needest only command Prince Ahmad to bring thee of the water of the Lions' Spring. He must perforce for his honour's sake fulfil thy wish, and if he fail he will for very shame not dare to show his face again at court. No better plan than this canst thou adopt; so look to it nor loiter on thy way."

Next day at eventide, as the Sultan was seated in full Darbar surrounded by his Wazirs and Ministers, Prince Ahmad came forwards and making due obeisance took seat by his side and below him. Hereat, the King addressed him, as was his wont, with great show of favour saying, "It delighteth me mightily that thou hast brought me the tent I required of thee; for surely in my Treasury there be naught so rare and strange. Yet one other thing lack I, and couldst thou bring it me I shall rejoice with joy exceeding. I have heard tell that the Jinniyah, thy consort, maketh constant use of a water which floweth from the Lions' Spring, the drinking whereof doeth away with fevers and all other deadly diseases. I know thou art anxious that I live in health; and thou wilt gladden me by bringing somewhat of that water, so I may drink thereof when occasion shall require, and well I wot that, as thou valuest my love and affection thee wards, thou wilt not refuse to grant me my request."

Prince Ahmad on hearing this demand was struck with surprise that his sire should so soon make a second demand. So he kept silence awhile, thinking within himself, "I have managed by some means to obtain the tent from the Lady Peri-Banu, but Allah only knoweth how she will now act, and whether this fresh request will or will not rouse her wrath. Howbeit I know that she will on no wise deny me any boon I may ask of her."

So after much hesitation Prince Ahmad made reply, "O my lord the King, I have no power to do aught in this matter, which resteth only with my spouse the Princess; yet will I petition her to give the water; and, if she vouchsafe consent I will bring it straight to thee. Indeed I cannot promise thee such boon with all certainty: I would gladly do my endeavour in all and everything that can benefit thee, but to ask her for this water is a work more weighty than asking for the tent."

Next day the Prince took his departure and returned to Peri-Banu; and after loving embraces and greetings quoth he, "O my lady and light of my eyes, the Sultan my sire sendeth thee his grateful thanks for the granting of his wish; to wit, the pavilion; and now he adventureth himself once more and, certified of thy bounty and beneficence, he would pray from thy hand the boon of a little water from the Lions' Spring. Withal I would assure thee that an the giving of this water please thee not, let the matter be clean forgotten; for to do all thou willest is my one and only wish." Peri-Banu made reply, "Methinks the Sultan, thy sire, would put both me and thee to the test by requiring such boons as those suggested to him by the Sorceress."

Peri-Banu said further to Prince Ahmad, "Natheless I will grant this largesse also as the Sultan hath set his mind upon it, and no harm shall come therefrom to me or to thee, albeit 'tis a matter of great risk and danger, and it is prompted by not a little of malice and ungraciousness. But give careful heed to my words, nor neglect thou aught of them, or thy destruction is certain-sure. I now will tell thee what to do. In the hall of yonder castle which riseth on that mountain is a fountain sentinelled by four lions fierce and ravening; and they watch and ward the path that leadeth thereto, a pair standing on guard whilst the other two take their turn to rest, and thus no living thing hath power to pass by them. Yet will I make known to thee the means whereby thou mayest win thy wish without any hurt or harm befalling thee from the furious beasts."

Thus saying she drew from an ivory box a clew of thread and, by means of a needle one of those wherewith she had been plying her work, made thereof a ball. This she placed in the hands of her husband, and said, "First, be thou careful that thou keep about thee with all diligence this ball, whose use I shall presently explain to thee. Secondly, choose for thyself two horses of great speed, one for thine own riding, whilst on the other thou shalt load the carcass of a freshly slaughtered sheep cut into four quarters.

In the third place, take with thee a phial wherewith I will provide thee, and this is for carrying the water which thou, Inshallah—God willing—shalt bring back. As soon as the morn shall morrow do thou arise with the light and go forth riding thy chosen steed and leading the other alongside of thee by the reins. When thou shalt reach the iron portals which open upon the castle-court, at no great distance from the gate, do thou cast the ball of thread upon the ground before thee. Forthwith it will begin rolling onwards of its own will towards the castle door; and do thou follow it through the open entrance until such time as it stop its course. At this moment thou shalt see the four lions; and the two that wake and watch will rouse the twain that sleep and rest. All four will turn their jaws to the ground and growl and roar with hideous howlings, and make as though about to fall upon thee and tear thee limb from limb. However, fear not nor be dismayed, but ride boldly on and throw to the ground from off the led-horse the sheep's quarters, one to each lion. See that thou alight not from thy steed, but gore his ribs with thy shovel stirrup and ride with all thy might and main up to the basin which gathereth the water. Here dismount and fill the phial whilst the lions will be busied eating. Lastly, return with all speed and the beasts will not prevent thy passing by them."

Next day, at peep of morn, Prince Ahmad did according to all that Peri-Banu had bidden him and rode forth to the castle. Then, having passed through the iron portals and crossed the court and opened the door, he entered the hall, where he threw the quarters of the sheep before the lions, one to each, and speedily reached the Spring. He filled his phial with water from the basin and hurried back with all haste. But when he had ridden some little distance he turned about and saw two of the guardian lions following upon his track; however, he was on no wise daunted but drew his sabre from the sheath to prepare him for self-protection. Hereat one of the twain seeing him bare his brand for defence, retired a little way from the road and, standing at gaze, nodded his head and wagged his tail, as though to pray the Prince to put up his scymitar and to assure him that he might ride in peace and fear no peril. The other lion then sprang forwards ahead of him and kept close him, and the two never ceased to escort him until they reached the city, nay even the gate of the Palace. The second twain also brought up the rear till Prince Ahmad had entered the Palace-door; and, when they were certified of this, all four went back by the way they came. Seeing such wondrous spectacle, the towns-folk all fled in dire dismay, albeit the enchanted beasts molested no man; and presently some mounted horsemen espying their lord riding alone and unattended came up to him and helped him alight.

The Sultan was sitting in his audience-hall conversing with his Wazirs and Ministers when his son appeared before him; and Prince Ahmad, having greeted him and blessed him and, in dutiful fashion, prayed for his permanence of existence and prosperity and opulence, placed before his feet the phial full of the water from the Lions' Spring, saying, "Lo, I have brought thee the boon thou desiredst of me. This water is most rare and hard to obtain; nor is there in all thy Treasure-house aught so notable and of such value as this. If ever thou fall ill of any malady (Almighty Allah forfend this should be in thy Destiny!) then drink a draught thereof and forthwith thou shalt be made whole of whatso distemper thou hast."

When Prince Ahmad had made an end of speaking, the Sultan, with all love and affection, grace and honour, embraced him and kissed his head; then, seating him on his right said, "O my son, I am beholden to thee, beyond count and measure, for that thou hast adventured thy life and brought this water with great irk and risk from so perilous a place."

Now the Witch had erewhile informed the King concerning the Lions' Spring and of the mortal dangers which beset the site; so that he knew right well how gallant was his son's derring-do; and presently he said, "Say me, O my child, how couldst thou venture thither and escape from the lions and broughtest back the water, thyself remaining safe and sound?"

The Prince replied, "By thy favour, O my lord the Sultan, have I returned in safety from that stead mainly because I did according to the bidding of my spouse, the Lady Peri-Banu; and I have brought the water from the Lions' Spring only by carrying out her commands." Then he made known to his father all that had befallen him in going and returning; and when the Sultan noted the pre-eminent valiance and prowess of his son he only feared the more, and the malice and the rancour, envy and jealousy which filled his heart waxed tenfold greater than before. However, dissembling his true sentiments he dismissed Prince Ahmad and betaking him to his private chamber at once sent word to bid the Witch appear in the presence; and when she came, he told her of the Prince's visit and all about the bringing of the water from the Lions' Spring. She had already heard somewhat thereof by reason of the hubbub in the city at the coming of the lions; but, as soon as she had given ear to the whole account, she marvelled with mighty marvel and, after whispering in the Sultan's ear her new device, said to him in triumph, "O King of kings, this time thou shalt lay a charge on the Prince and such commandment methinks will trouble him and it shall go hard with him to execute aught thereof."

"Thou sayest well," replied the Sovran, "now indeed will I try this plan thou hast projected for me."

Wherefore, next day whenas Prince Ahmad came to the presence of his sire, the King said to him, "O dear my child, it delighteth me exceedingly to see thy virtue and valour and the filial love wherewith thou art fulfilled, good gifts chiefly shown by obtaining for me the two rarities I asked of thee. And now one other and final requirement I have of thee; and, shouldst thou avail to satisfy my desire, I shall be wellpleased in my beloved son and render thanks to him for the rest of my days."

Prince Ahmad answered, "What is the boon thou requirest? I will for my part do thy bidding as far as in me lieth." Then quoth the King in reply to the Prince, "I would fain have thee bring me a man of size and stature no more than three feet high, with beard full twenty ells in length, who beareth on his shoulder a quarter staff of steel, thirteen score pounds in weight, which he wieldeth with ease and swingeth around his head without wrinkle on brow, even as men wield cudgels of wood." On this wise the Sultan, led astray by the Doom of Destiny and heedless alike of good and evil, asked that which should bring surest destruction upon himself. Prince Ahmad also, with blind obedience out of pure affection to his parent, was ready to supply him with all he required unknowing what was prepared for him in the Secret Purpose. Accordingly he said, "O my sire the Sultan, I trow me 'twill be hard to find, all the world over, a man such as thou desirest, still I will work my best to do thy bidding."

Thereupon the Prince retired from the presence and returned, as usual, to his palace where he greeted Peri-Banu with love and gladness; but his face was troubled and his heart was heavy at the thought of the King's last behest. Perceiving his pre-occupation the Princess asked him, saying, "O dear my lord, what tidings bringest thou for me to-day?" Hereto replied he, "The Sultan at each visit requireth of me some new thing and burtheneth me with his requests; and to-day he purposeth to try me and, in the hopes of putting me to shame, he asketh somewhat which 'twere vain to hope I can find in all the world." Thereupon Prince Ahmad told her all the King had said to him.

Peri-Banu hearing these words said to the Prince, "Trouble not thyself at all in this matter. Thou didst venture at great risk to carry off for thy father water from the Lions' Spring and thou succeededst in winning thy wish. Now this task is on no wise more difficult or dangerous than was that: nay 'tis the easier for that he thou describest is none other than Shabbar, my brothergerman. Although we both have the same parents, yet it pleased

Almighty Allah to enform us in different figures and to make him unlike
his sister as being in mortal mould can be. Moreover he is valiant and
adventurous, always seeking some geste and exploit whereby to further my
interest, and right willingly doth he carry out whatso he undertaketh. He
is shaped and formed as the Sultan thy sire hath described, nor useth he
any weapons save the Nabbut or quarter staff of steel. And see now I will
send for him, but be not thou dismayed at sighting him."

Replied Prince Ahmad, "If he be in truth thine own brother
what matter how he looketh? I shall be pleased to see him as when one
welcometh a valued friend or a beloved kinsman. Wherefore should I fear
to look upon him?"

Hearing these words Peri-Banu despatched one of her attendants who
brought to her from her private treasury a chafing-dish of gold; then she
bade a fire be lit therein, and sending for a casket of noble metals studded
with gems, the gift of her kinsmen, she took therefrom some incense and
cast it upon the flames. Herewith issued a dense smoke spireing high in air
and spreading all about the palace; and a few moments after, Peri-Banu who
had ceased her conjurations cried, "Lookye my brother Shabbar cometh!
canst thou distinguish his form?"

The Prince looked up and saw a mannikin in stature dwarfish and
no more than three feet high, and with a boss on breast and a hump on
back; withal he carried himself with stately mien and majestic air. On his
right shoulder was borne his quarter staff of steel thirteen score pounds in
weight. His beard was thick and twenty cubits in length but arranged so
skilfully that it stood clear off from the ground; he wore also a twisted pair
of long mustachios curling up to his ears, and all his face was covered with
long pile. His eyes were not unlike unto pig's eyes; and his head, on which
was placed a crown-like coiffure, was enormous of bulk, contrasting with
the meanness of his stature.

Prince Ahmad sat calmly beside his wife, the Fairy, and felt no fear
as the figure approached; and presently Shabbar walked up and glanc-
ing at him asked Peri-Banu saying, "Who be this mortal who sitteth hard
by thee?"

Hereto she replied, "O my brother, this is my beloved husband, Prince
Ahmad, son of the Sultan of Hindostan. I sent thee not an invitation to
the wedding as thou wast then engaged on some great expedition; now,
however, by the grace of Almighty Allah thou hast returned triumphant
and victorious over thy foes, wherefore I have summoned thee upon a
matter which nearly concerneth me."

Hearing these words Shabbar looked graciously at Prince Ahmad, saying, "O my beloved sister, is there any service I can render to him?" and she replied, "The Sultan his sire desireth ardently to see thee, and I pray thee go forthright to him and take the Prince with thee by way of guide."

Said he, "This instant I am ready to set forth;" but said she, "Not yet, O my brother. Thou art fatigued with journeying; so defer until the morrow thy visit to the King, and this evening I will make known to thee all that concerneth Prince Ahmad." Presently the time came; so Peri-Banu informed her brother Shabbar concerning the King and his ill-counsellors; but she dwelt mainly upon the misdeeds of the old woman, the Witch; and how she had schemed to injure Prince Ahmad and despitefully prevent his going to city or court, and she had gained such influence over the Sultan that he had given up his will to hers and ceased not doing whatso she bade him.

Next day at dawn Shabbar the Jinn and Prince Ahmad set out together upon a visit to the Sultan; and when they had reached the city gates, all the folk, nobles and commons, were struck with consternation at the dwarf's hideous form; and, flying on every side in affright and running into shops and houses, barred the doors and closed the casements and hid themselves therein. So panic-stricken indeed was their flight that many feet lost shoes and sandals in running, while from the heads of others their loosened turbands fell to earth. And when they twain approached the palace through streets and squares and market-places desolate as the Desert of Samawah, all the keepers of the gates took to their heels at sight of Shabbar and fled, so there was none to hinder their entering. They walked straight on to the audience-chamber where the Sultan was holding Darbar, and they found in attendance on him a host of Ministers and Councillors, great and small, each standing in his proper rank and station. They too on seeing Shabbar speedily took flight in dire dismay and hid themselves; also the guards had deserted their posts nor cared in any way to let or stay the twain. The Sovran still sat motionless on his throne, where Shabbar went up to him with lordly mien and royal dignity and cried, "O King, thou hast expressed a wish to see me; and lo, I am here. Say now what wouldst thou have me do?"

The King made no reply to Shabbar, but held up his hands before his eyes that he might not behold that frightful figure, and turning his head would fain have fled in terror. Shabbar was filled with fury at this rudeness on the part of the Sultan, and was wroth with exceeding wrath to think that he had troubled himself to come at the bidding of such a craven, who

489

now on seeing him would fain run away. So the Jinn, without an instant's delay, raised his quarter staff of steel, and, swinging it twice in air, before Prince Ahmad could reach the throne or on any wise interfere, struck the Sultan so fiercely upon the poll that his skull was smashed and his brains were scattered over the floor.

And when Shabbar had made an end of this offender, he savagely turned upon the Grand Wazir who stood on the Sultan's right and incontinently would have slain him also, but the Prince craved pardon for his life and said, "Kill him not: he is my friend and hath at no time said one evil word against me. But such is not the case with the others, his fellows." Hearing these words the infuriated Shabbar fell upon the Ministers and ill-counsellors on either side, to wit, all who had devised evil devices against Prince Ahmad, and slew them each and every and suffered none to escape save only those who had taken flight and hidden themselves. Then, going from the hall of justice to the courtyard, the Dwarf said to the Wazir whose life the Prince had saved, "Harkye, there is a Witch who beareth enmity against my brother, the husband of my sister. See that thou produce her forthright; likewise the villain who filled his father's mind with hate and malice, envy and jealousy against him, so may I quite them in full measure for their misdeeds."

The Grand Wazir produced them all, first the Sorceress, and then the malicious minister with his rout of fautors and flatterers, and Shabbar felled them one after the other with his quarter staff of steel and killed them pitilessly, crying to the Sorceress, "This is the end of all thy machinations with the King, and this is the fruit of thy deceit and treachery; so learn not to feign thyself sick." And in the blindness of his passion he would have slain all the inhabitants of the city, but Prince Ahmad prevented him and pacified him with soft and flattering words.

Hereupon Shabbar habited his brother in the royal habit and seated him on the throne and proclaimed him Sultan of Hindostan. The people all, both high and low, rejoiced with exceeding joy to hear these tidings, for Prince Ahmad was beloved by every one; so they crowded to swear fealty and bring presents and Nazaranahs and raised shouts of acclamation crying out, "Long live King Ahmad!" When all this was done, Shabbar sent for his sister, Peri-Banu, and made her Queen under the title of Shahr-Banu; and in due time taking leave of her and of King Ahmad, the Jinni returned to his own home.

After these things King Ahmad summoned Prince Ali his brother and Nur al-Nihar and made him governor of a large city hard by the capital, and dismissed him thither in high state and splendour. Also he commissioned an official to wait upon Prince Husayn and tell him all the tidings, and sent word saying, "I will appoint thee ruler over any capital or country thy soul desireth; and, if thou consent, I will forward thee letters of appointment." But inasmuch as the Prince was wholly content and entirely happy in Darwaysh-hood, he cared naught for rule or government or aught of worldly vanities; so he sent back the official with his duty and grateful thanks, requesting that he might be left to live his life in solitude and renunciation of matters mundane.

Now when Queen Scheherazade had made an end of telling her story and yet the night was not wholly spent, King Shahryar spake saying, "This thy story, admirable and most wonderful, hath given me extreme delight; and I pray thee do thou tell us another tale till such time as the last hours of this our night be passed." She replied, "Be it as thou wilt, O auspicious King: I am thy slave to do as thou shalt bid."

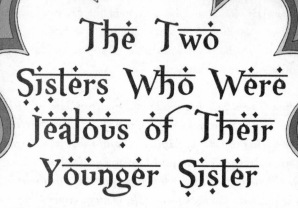

The Two Sisters Who Were Jealous of Their Younger Sister

The following evening, Scheherazade began to relate her next tale. Quoth she…

In days of yore and in times long gone before there lived a king of Persia, Khusrau Shah hight, renowned for justice and righteousness. His father, dying at a good old age, had left him sole heir to all the realm and, under his rule, the tiger and the kid drank side by side at the same Ghat; and his treasury was ever full and his troops and guards were numberless. Now it was his wont to don disguise and, attended by a trusty Wazir, to wander about the street at night-time. Whereby things seld-seen and haps peregrine became known to him, the which, should I tell thee all thereof, O auspicious King, would weary thee beyond measure. So he took seat upon the throne of his forbears and when the appointed days of mourning were ended, according to the custom of that country, he caused his exalted name, that is Khusrau Shah, be struck upon all the coins of the kingdom and entered into the formula of public prayer. And when stablished in his sovranty he went forth as aforetime on one evening accompanied by his Grand Wazir, both in merchant's habit, walking the streets and squares, the

markets and lanes, the better to note what might take place both of good
and of bad.

By chance they passed, as the night darkened, through a quarter where
dwelt people of the poorer class; and as they walked on, the Shah heard
inside a house women talking with loud voices; then going near, he peeped
in by the door-chink, and saw three fair sisters who having supped together
were seated on a divan talking one to other. The King thereupon applied
his ear to the crack and listened eagerly to what they said, and heard each
and every declaring what was the thing she most desired.

Quoth the eldest, "I would I were married to the Shah's head Baker
for then should I ever have bread to eat, the whitest and choicest in the city,
and your hearts would be fulfilled with envy and jealousy and malice at my
good luck."

Quoth the second, "I would rather wive with the Shah's chief
Kitchener and eat of dainty dishes that are placed before his Highness,
wherewith the royal bread which is common throughout the Palace cannot
compare for gust and flavour."

And quoth the third and youngest of the three, and by far the most
beautiful and lively of them all, a maiden of charming nature, full of wit
and humour; sharp-witted, wary and wise, when her turn came to tell her
wish, "O sisters, my ambition is not as ordinary as yours. I care not for
fine bread nor glutton-like do I long for dainty dishes. I look to somewhat
nobler and higher: indeed I would desire nothing less than to be married
by the King and become the mother of a beautiful Prince, a model of form
and in mind as masterful as valorous. His hair should be golden on one side
and silvern on the other: when weeping he should drop pearls in place of
tears, and when laughing his rosy lips should be fresh as the blossom new-
blown."

The Shah was amazed with exceeding amazement to hear the wishes
of the three sisters, but chiefly of the youngest and determined in himself
that he would gratify them all. Wherefore quoth he to the Grand Wazir,
"Mark well this house And on the morrow bring before me these maidens
whom we heard discoursing;" and quoth the Wazir, "O Asylum of the
Universe, I hear but to obey."

Thereupon the twain walked back to the palace and laid them down
to rest. When morning morrowed, the Minister went for the sisters and
brought them to the King, who, after greeting them and heartening their
hearts, said to them in kindly tone, "O ye maidens of weal, last night what
was it that in merry word and jest ye spake one to other? Take heed ye

tell the Shah every whit in full detail, for all must become known to us; something have we heard, but now the King would have ye recount your discourse to his royal ears."

At these words of the Shah the sisters, confused and filled with shame, durst not reply but stood before him silent with heads bent low; and despite all questioning and encouragement they could not pluck up courage. However, the youngest was of passing comeliness in form and feature and forthwith the Shah became desperately enamoured of her; and of his live began reassuring them and saying, "O ye Princesses of fair ones, be not afraid nor troubled in thought; nor let bashfulness or shyness prevent you telling the Shah what three wishes you wished, for fain would he fulfil them all."

Thereat they threw themselves at his feet and, craving his pardon for their boldness and freedom of speech, told him the whole talk, each one repeating the wish she had wished; and on that very day Khusrau Shah married the eldest sister to his chief Baker, and the second sister to his head Cook, and bade make all things ready for his own wedding with the youngest sister. So when the preparations for the royal nuptials had been made after costliest fashion, the King's marriage was celebrated with royal pomp and pageantry, and the bride received the titles of Light of the Harem and Banu of Iran-land. The other two maidens were likewise married, one to the King's Baker the other to his Cook, after a manner according to their several degrees in life and with little show of grandeur and circumstance.

Now it had been only right and reasonable that these twain having won each her own wish, should have passed their time in solace and happiness, but the decree of Destiny doomed otherwise; and, as soon as they saw the grand estate whereto their youngest sister had risen, and the magnificence of her marriage-festival, their hearts were fired with envy and jealousy and sore despite and they resolved upon giving the rein to their hatred and malignancy and to work her some foul mischief. On this wise they remained for many months consumed with rancour, day and night; and they burned with grief and anger whenever they sighted aught of her superior style and state.

One morning as the two met at the Hammam and found privacy and opportunity, quoth the eldest sister to the second, "A grievous thing it is indeed that she, our youngest sister, no lovelier than ourselves, should thus be raised to the dignity and majesty of Queendom and indeed the thought is overhard to bear."

494

Quoth the other, "O sister mine, I also am perplexed and displeased at this thing, and I know not what of merit the Shah could have seen in her that he was tempted to choose her for his consort. She ill befitteth that high estate with that face like a monkey's favour; and, save her youth, I know nothing that could commend her to his Highness that he should so exalt her above her fellows. To my mind thou and not she art fit to share the royal bed; and I nurse a grudge against the King for that he hath made this jade his Queen."

And the eldest sister rejoined, "I likewise marvel beyond all measure; and I swear that thy youth and beauty, thy well-shaped figure and lovely favour and goodliness of gifts past challenge or compare, might well have sufficed to win the King and have tempted him to wed and bed with thee and make thee his crowned Queen and Sovran Lady in lieu of taking to his arms this paltry strumpet. Indeed he hath shown no sense of what is right and just in leaving thee disappointed; and on this account only the matter troubleth me with exceeding trouble."

The two sisters took counsel each with other how they might abase their youngest sister in the Shah's sight and cause her downfall and utter ruin. Day and night they conned over the matter in their minds and spoke at great length about it when they ever met together, and pondered endless plans to injure the Queen their sister, and if possible bring about her death; but they could fix upon none. And, whilst they bore this despite and hatred towards her and diligently and deliberately sought the means of gratifying their bitter envy, hatred and malice, she on the other hand regarded them with the same favour and affection as she had done before marriage and thought only how to advantage their low estate.

Now when some months of her wedded life had passed, the fair Queen was found to be with child whereof the glad tidings filled the Shah with joy; and straightway he commanded all the people of the capital and throughout the whole Empire keep holiday with feasts and dancing and every manner jollity as became so rare and important an occasion. But as soon as the news came to the ears of the two Envious Sisters they were constrained perforce to offer their congratulations to the Queen; and, after a long visit, as the twain were about to crave dismissal they said, "Thanks be to Almighty Allah, O our sister, who hath shown us this happy day. One boon have we to ask of thee: to wit, that when the time shall come for thee to be delivered of a child, we may assist as midwives at thy confinement, and be with thee and nurse thee for the space of forty days."

The Queen in her gladness made reply, "O sisters mine, I fain would have it so; for at a time of such need I know of none on whom to rely with such dependence as upon you. During my coming trial your presence with me will be most welcome and opportune; but I can do only what thing the Shah biddeth anor can I do aught save by his leave. My advice is thus: Make known this matter to your mates who have always access to the royal presence, and let them personally apply for your attendance as midwives; I doubt not but that the Shah will give you leave to assist me and remain by my side, considering the fond relationship between us three." Then the two sisters returned home full of evil thoughts and malice, and told their wishes to their husbands who, in turn, bespake Khusrau Shah, and proffered their petition with all humility, little knowing what was hidden from them in the Secret Purpose. The King replied, "When I shall have thought the matter over in my mind, I will give you suitable orders."

So saying he privately visited the Queen and to her said, "O my lady, an it please thee, methinks 'twould be well to summon thy sisters and secure their aidance, when thou shalt be labouring of child, in lieu of any stranger: and if thou be of the same mind as myself let me at once learn and take steps to obtain their consent and concert ere thy time arriveth. They will wait on thee with more loving care than any hired nurse and thou wilt find thyself the safer in their hands."

Replied the Queen, "O my lord the Shah, I also venture to think that 'twould be well to have my sisters by my side and not mere aliens at such an hour."

Accordingly he sent word to them and from that day they dwelt within the palace to make all ready for the expected confinement; and on this wise they found means to carry out their despiteful plot which during so many days they had devised to scanty purpose. When her full tale of months had been told, the Banu was brought to bed of a man-child marvellous in beauty, whereat the fire of envy and hatred was kindled with redoubled fury in the sisters' breasts. So they again took counsel not suffered ruth nor natural affection to move their cruel hearts; and presently, with great care and secrecy, they wrapped the new-born in a bit of blanket and putting him into a basket cast him into a canal which flowed hard by the Queen's apartment. They then placed a dead puppy in the place of the prince and showed it to the other midwives and nurses, averring that the Queen had given birth to such abortion. When these untoward tidings reached the King's ear he was sore discomforted and waxed wroth with exceeding wrath.

The King, enflamed with sudden fierceness, drew his sword and would have slain his Queen had not the Grand Wazir, who happened to be in his presence at the time, restrained his rage and diverted him from his unjust design and barbarous purpose. Quoth he, "O Shadow of Allah upon earth, this mishap is ordained of the Almighty Lord whose will no man hath power to gainsay. The Queen is guiltless of offence against thee, for what is born of her is born without her choice, and she indeed hath no hand therein."

With this and other sage counsels he dissuaded his lord from carrying out his fell purpose and saved the guiltless Queen from a sudden and cruel death. Meanwhile the basket wherein lay the newly-born Prince was carried by the current into a rivulet which flowed through the royal gardens; and, as the Intendant of the pleasure grounds and pleasaunces chanced to walk along the bank, by the decree of Destiny he caught sight of the basket floating by, and he called a gardener, bidding him lay hold of it and bring it to him that he might see what was therein. The man ran along the rivulet side; and, with a long stick drawing the basket to land, showed it to the Intendant who opened it and beheld within a newborn babe, a boy of wondrous beauty wrapped in a bit of blanket; at which sight he was astounded beyond measure of surprise.

Now it chanced that the Intendant, who was one of the Emirs and who stood high in favour with the Sovran, had no children: withal he never ceased offering prayers and vows to Almighty Allah that he might have a son to keep alive his memory and continue his name. Delighted at the sight he took home the basket with the babe and giving it to his wife said, "See how Allah hath sent to us this man-child which I just now found floating upon the waters; and do thou apply thee forthright and fetch a wet-nurse to give him milk and nourish him; and bring him up with care and tenderness as though he were thine own."

So the Intendant's wife took charge of the child with great gladness and reared him with her whole heart, diligently as though born of her own womb; nor did the Intendant say aught to any, or seek to find out whose might be the child lest haply some one claim and take it from him. He was certified in his mind that the boy came from the Queen's quarter of the palace, but deemed inexpedient to make too strict enquiry concerning the matter; and he and his spouse kept the secret with all secrecy.

A year after this the Queen gave birth to a second son, when her sisters, the Satanesses full of spite, did with this babe, even as they had done by the first: they wrapped it in a cloth and set it in a basket which they

497

threw into the stream, then gave out that the Queen had brought forth a kitten. But once more, by the mercy of Allah Almighty, this boy came to the hands of that same Intendant of the gardens who carried him to his wife and placed him under her charge with strict injunctions to take care of the second foundling sedulously as she had done with the first.

The Shah, enraged to hear the evil tidings, again rose up to slay the Queen; but as before the Grand Wazir prevented him and calmed his wrath with words of wholesome rede and a second time saved the unhappy mother's life. And after another year had gone by the Banu was brought to bed and this time bore a daughter by whom the sisters did as they had done by her brothers: they set the innocent inside a basket and threw her into the stream; and the Intendant found her also and took her to his wife and bade her rear the infant together with the other two castaways. Hereupon the Envious Sisters, wild with malice, reported that the Queen had given birth to a musk-ratling; whereat King Khusrau could no longer stay his wrath and indignation. So he cried in furious rage to the Grand Wazir, "What, shall the Shah suffer this woman, who beareth naught but vermin and abortions, to share the joys of his bed? Nay more, the King can no longer allow her to live, else she will fill the palace with monstrous births: in very sooth, she is herself a monster, and it behoveth us to rid this place of such unclean creature and accursed."

So saying the Shah commanded them do her to death; but the ministers and high officers of estate who stood before the presence fell at the royal feet and besought pardon and mercy for the Queen. The Grand Wazir also said with folded hands, "O Shahihshah—O King of the kings—thy slave would fain represent that 'tis not in accordance with the course of justice or the laws of the land to take the life of a woman for no fault of her own. She cannot interfere with Destiny, nor can she prevent unnatural births such as have thrice betided her; and such mishaps have oftentimes befallen other women, whose cases call for compassion and not punishment. An the King be displeased with her then let him cease to live with her, and the loss of his gracious favour will be a penalty dire enough; and, if the Shah cannot suffer the sight of her, then let her be confined in some room apart, and let her expiate her offence by alms deed and charity until 'Izrail, the Angel of Death, separate her soul from her flesh."

Hearing these words of counsel from his aged Councillor, Khusrau Shah recognised that it had been wrong to slay the Queen, for that she could on no wise do away with aught that was determined by Fate and Destiny; and presently he said to the Grand Wazir, "Her life is spared at thine intercession, O wise man and ware; yet will the King doom her to a weird which, haply, is hardly less hard to bear than death. And now do thou forthright make ready, by the side of the Cathedral-mosque, a wooden cage with iron bars and lock the Queen therein as one would confine a ferocious wild beast. Then every Mussulman who wendeth his way to public prayers shall spit in her face ere he set foot within the fane, and if any fail to carry out this command he shall be punished in like manner. So place guards and inspectors to enforce obedience and let me hear if there be aught of gainsaying."

The Wazir durst not make reply but carried out the Shah's commandments; and this punishment inflicted upon the blameless Queen had far better befitted her Envious Sisters. The cage was made ready with all speed; and, when the forty days after purification of child-bed had come to an end, the Banu was locked therein; and, according to the King's commandment, all who came to prayer in the Great Mosque would first spit in her face. The hapless woman, well knowing that she was not worthy of this ignominy, bore her sufferings with all patience and fortitude; nor were they few who deemed her blameless and undeserving to endure these torments and tortures inflicted upon her by the Shah; and they pitied her and offered prayers and made vows for her release.

Meanwhile the Intendant of the gardens and his wife brought up the two Princes and the Princess with all love and tenderness; and, as the children grew in years, their love for these adopted ones increased in like proportion. They gave the eldest Prince the name Bahman, and to his brother Parwez, and as the maiden was of rare of beauty and passing of loveliness and graciousness, they called her Perizadah.

When the Princes became of years to receive instruction, the Intendant of the gardens appointed tutors and masters to teach them reading and writing and all the arts and sciences: the Princess also, showing like eagerness to acquire knowledge, was taught letters by the same instructors, and soon could read and write with as perfect fluency as could her brothers. Then they were placed under the most learned of the Philosophers and the Olema, who taught them the interpretation of the Koran and the sayings of the Apostle; the science of geometry as well as poetry and history, and even the abstruse sciences and the mystic doctrines of the Enlightened; and their teachers were astonished to find how soon and how far all three made progress in their studies and bid fair to outstrip even the sages however learned. Moreover, they all three were reared to horsemanship and skill in the chase, to shooting with shafts and lunging with lance and sway with

499

sabre and jerking the Jerid, with other manly and warlike sports. Besides all this the Princess Perizadah was taught to sing and play on various instruments of mirth and merriment, wherein she became the peerless pearl of her age and time. The Intendant was exceeding glad of heart to find his adopted children prove themselves such proficients in every branch of knowledge; and presently, forasmuch as his lodging was small and unfit for the growing family, he bought at a little distance from the city a piece of land sufficiently large to contain fields and meadows and copses. Here he fell to building a mansion of great magnificence; and busied himself day and night with supervising the architects and masons and other artificers. He adorned the walls inside and out with sculptural work of the finest and paintings of the choicest, and he fitted every apartment with richest furniture. In the front of his mansion he bade lay out a garden and stocked it with scented flowers and fragrant shrubs and fruit trees whose produce was as that of Paradise. There was moreover a large park girt on all sides by a high wall wherein he reared game, both fur and feather, as sport for the two Princes and their sister.

And when the mansion was finished and fit for habitation, the Intendant, who had faithfully served the Shah for many generations of men, craved leave of his lord that he might bid adieu to the city and take up his abode in his new country seat; and the King, who had always looked upon him with the eye of favour, granted to him the required boon right heartily; furthermore, to prove his high opinion of his old servant and his services, he inquired of him if he had aught to request that it might granted to him.

Replied the other, "O my liege lord, thy slave desireth naught save that he may spend the remnant of his days under the shadow of the Shah's protection, with body and soul devoted to his service, even as I served the side before the son." The Shah dismissed him with words of thanks and comfort, when he left the city and taking with him the two Princes and their sister, he carried them to his newly-built mansion. Some years before this time his wife had departed to the mercy of Allah, and he had passed only five or six months in his second home when he too suddenly felt sick and was admitted into the number of those who have found ruth. Withal he had neglected every occasion of telling his three foundlings the strange tale of their birth and how he had carried them to his home as castaways and had reared them as rearlings and had cherished them as his own children. But he had time to charge them, ere he died, that they three should never cease to live together in love and honour and affection and respect one towards other. The loss of their protector caused them to grieve with bitter grief for they all thought he was their real father; so they bewailed them and buried him as befitted; after which the two brothers and their sister dwelt together in peace and plenty.

But one day of the days the Princes, who were full of daring and of the highest mettle, rode forth a-hunting and Princess Perizadah was left alone at home when an ancient woman of the Moslems, a recluse and a devotee, came to the door and begged leave to enter within and repeat her prayers, as it was then the canonical hour and she had but time to make the Wuzu-ablution. Perizadah bade being her and saluted her with the salam and kindly welcomed her; then, when the holy woman had made an end of her orisons, the handmaids of the Princess, at her command, conducted her all through the house and grounds, and displayed to her the rooms with their furniture and fittings, and lastly the garden and orchard and game-park. She was well pleased with all she saw and said within herself, "The man who built this mansion and laid out these parterres and vergiers was verily an accomplished artist and a wight of marvellous skill."

At last the slaves led her back to the Princess who, awaiting her return, was sitting in the belvedere; and quoth she to the devotee, "Come, O good my mother, do thou sit beside me and make me happy by the company of a pious recluse whom I am fortunate enough to have entertained unawares, and suffer I listen to thy words of grace and thereby gain no small advantage in this world and the next. Thou hast chosen the right path and straight whereon to walk, and that which all men strive for and pine for."

The holy woman would fain have seated herself at the feet of the Princess, but she courteously arose and took her by the hand and constrained her to sit beside her. Quoth she, "O my lady, mine eyes never yet beheld one so well-mannered as thou art: indeed, I am unworthy to sit with thee, natheless, as thou biddest, I will e'en do thy bidding."

As they sat conversing each with other the slave-girls set before them a table whereon were placed some platters of bread and cakes with saucers full of fruits both fresh and dried, and various kinds of cates and sweetmeats. The Princess took one of the cakes and giving it to the good woman said, "O my mother, refresh thyself herewith and eat of the fruits such as thou likest. 'Tis now long since thou didst leave thy home and I trow thou hast not tasted aught of food upon the road." Replied the holy woman, "O lady of gentle birth, I am not wont to taste of dainty dishes such as these, but I can ill refuse thy provision, since Allah the Almighty deigneth send me food and support by so liberal and generous a hand as thine."

And when they twain had eaten somewhat and cheered their hearts, the Princess asked the devotee concerning the manner of her worship and of her austere life; whereto she made due answer and explained according to her knowledge. The Princess then exclaimed, "Tell me, I pray thee, what thou thinkest of this mansion and the fashion of its building and the furniture and the appurtenances; and say me is all perfect and appropriate, or is aught still lacking in mansion or garden?"

And she replied, "Since thou deignest ask my opinion, I confess to thee that both the buildings and the parterres are finished and furnished to perfection; and the belongings are in the best of taste and in the highest of ordinance. Still to my thinking there be three things here wanting, which if thou hadst the place would be most complete."

The Princess Perizadah adjured her saying, "O my aunt, I beseech thee tell me what three articles yet are lacking, that I may lose no pains nor toil to obtain them"; and as the maiden pressed her with much intreaty, the devotee was constrained to tell her.

Quoth she, "O gentle lady, the first thing is the Speaking-Bird, called Bulbul-i-hazar-dastan; he is very rare and hard to find but, whenever he poureth out his melodious notes, thousands of birds fly to him from every side and join him in his harmony. The next thing is the Singing-Tree, whose smooth and glossy leaves when shaken by the wind and rubbed against one another send forth tuneful tones which strike the ear like the notes of sweet-voices minstrels ravishing the heart of all who listen. The third thing is the Golden-Water of transparent purity, whereon should but one drop be dripped into a basin and this be placed inside the garden it presently will fill the vessel brimful and will spout upwards in gerbes playing like a fountain that jets: moreover it never ceaseth playing, and all the water as it shooteth up falleth back again inside the basin, not one gout thereof being lost."

Replied the Princess, "I doubt not but thou knowest for a certainty the very spot where these wondrous things are to be found; and I pray thee tell me now the place and means whereby I may take action to obtain them."

The holy woman thus answered the Princess, "These three rarities are not to be found, save on the boundary-line that lieth between the land of Hind and the confining countries, a score of marches along the road that leadeth Eastwards from this mansion. Let him who goeth forth in quest of them ask the first man he meeteth on the twentieth stage concerning the spot where he may find the Speaking-Bird, the Singing-Tree and the Golden-Water; and he will direct the seeker where to come upon all three."

When she had made an end of speaking the Devotee, with many blessings and prayers and vows for her well-being, farewelled the lady Perizadah and fared forth homewards. The Princess, however, ceased not to ponder her words and ever to dwell in memory upon the relation of the holy woman who, never thinking that her hostess had asked for information save by way of curiosity, nor really purposed in mind to set forth with intent of finding the rarities, ahd heedlessly told all she knew and had given a clue to the discovery. But Perizadah kept these matters deeply graven on the tablets of her heart with firm resolution to follow the directions and, by all means in her power, to gain possession of these three wonders. Withal, the more she reflected the harder appeared the enterprise, and her fear of failing only added to her unease.

Now whilst she sat perplexed with anxious thought and anon terrified with sore affright, her brothers rode back from the hunting-ground; and they marvelled much to see her sad of semblance and low-spirited, wondering the while what it was that troubles her. Presently quoth Prince Bahman, "O sister mine, why art thou so heavy of heart this day? Almighty Allah forbid thou ill in health or that aught have betided thee to cause thy displeasure or to make thee melancholy. Tell us I beseech thee what it is, that we may be sharers in thy sorrow and be alert to aid thee."

The Princess answered not a word, but after long silence raised her head and looked up at her brothers; then casting down her eyes she said in curt phrase that naught was amiss with her. Quoth Prince Bahman, "Full well I wot that there is a somewhat on my mind which thou hesitateth to tell us; and now hear me swear a strong oath that I will never leave thy side till thou shalt have told us what cause it is that troubleth thee. Haply thou art aweary of our affection and thou wouldest undo the fraternal tie which hath united us from our infancy."

When she saw her brothers so distressed and distraught, she was compelled to speak and said, "Albeit, O my dearlings, to tell you wherefore I am sad and sorrowful may cause you grief, still there is no help but I explain the matter to you twain. This mansion, which our dear father (who hath found ruth) builded for us, is perfect in every attribute nor lacketh it any condition of comfort or completion. Howbeit I have found out by chance this day that there are yet three things which, were they set within these walls, of the house and grounds, would make our place beyond compare, and in the wide world there would be naught with it to pair. These three things are the Speaking-Bird an the Singing-Tree and the Golden-Water; and ever since I heard of them my heart is filled with extreme desire to

503

place them within our domain and excessive longing to obtain them by any means within my power. It now behoveth you to help me with your best endeavour and to consider what person will aid me in getting possession of these rarities."

Replied Prince Bahman, "My life and that of my brother are at thy service to carry out thy purpose with heart and soul; and, couldst thou give me but a clue to the place where these strange things are found, I would sally forth in quest of them at day-break as soon as the morning shall morrow."

When Prince Parwez understood that his brother was about to make this journey, he spake saying, "O my brother, thou art eldest of us, so do thou stay at home while I go forth to seek for these three things and bring them to our sister. And indeed it were more fitting for me to undertake a task which may occupy me for years."

Replied Prince Bahman, "I have full confidence in thy strength and prowess, and whatso I am able to perform thou canst do as well as I can. Still it is my firm resolve to fare forth upon this adventure alone and unaided, and thou must stay and take care of our sister and our house."

So next day Prince Bahman learned from the Princess the road whereon he was to travel and the marks and signs whereby to find the place. Presently, he donned armour and arms and bidding the twain adieu, he took horse and was about to ride forth with the stoutest of hearts, whereat Princess Perizadah's eyes brimmed with tears and in faltering accents she addressed him saying, "O dear my brother, this bitter separation is heart-breaking; and sore sorrowful am I to see thee part from us. This disunion and thine absence in a distant land cause me grief and woe far exceeding that wherewith I mourned and pined for the rarities wherefor thou quittest us. If only we might have some news of thee from day to day then would I feel somewhat comforted and consoled; but not 'tis clear otherwise and regret is of none avail."

Prince Bahman made answer in these words: "O sister mine, I am fully determined in mind to attempt this derring-do; be thou not however anxious or alarmed, for Inshallah—God willing—I shall return successful and triumphant. After my departure shouldst thou at any time feel in fear for my safety, then by this token which I leave thee thou shalt know of my fate and lot, good or evil." Then, drawing from his waist-shawl a little hunting-knife like a whittle, he gave it to Princess Perizadah, saying, "Take now this blade and keep it ever by thee; and shouldst thou at any day or hour be solicitous concerning my condition, draw it from its sheath; and if the steel be clean and bright as 'tis now then know that I am alive and safe and sound; but an thou find stains of blood thereon then shalt thou know that I am slain, and naught remaineth for thee to do save to pray for me as for one dead."

With these words of solace the Prince departed on his journey, and travelled straight along the road to India, turning nor to right hand nor to left but ever keeping the same object in view. Thus a score of days was spent in journeying from the land of Iran, and upon the twentieth he reached the end of his travel. Here he suddenly sighted an ancient man of frightful aspect sitting beneath a tree hard by his thatched hut wherein he was wont to shelter himself from the rains of spring and the heats of summer and the autumnal miasmas and the wintry frosts. So shotten in years was this Shaykh that hair and beard, mustachios and whiskers were white as snow, and the growth of his upper lip was so long and so thick that it covered and concealed his mouth, while his beard swept the ground and the nails of his hands and feet had grown to resemble the claws of a wild beast. Upon his head he wore a broad-brimmed hat of woven palm-leaves like that of a Malabar fisherman, and all his remaining habit was a strip of matting girded around his waist. Now this Shaykh was a Darwaysh who for many years had fled the world and all worldly pleasures; who lived a holy life of poverty and chastity and other-worldliness whereby his semblance had become such as I, O auspicious King, have described to thee.

From early dawn that day Prince Bahman had been watchful and vigilant, ever looking on all sides to descry some one who could supply him with information touching the whereabouts of the rarities he sought; and this was the first human being he had sighted on that stage, the twentieth and last of his journey. So he rode up to him, being assured that the Shaykh must be the wight of whom the holy woman had spoken. Then Prince Bahman dismounting and making low obeisance to the Darwaysh, said, "I my father, Allah Almighty prolong thy years and grant thee all thy wishes!"

Whereto the Fakir made answer but in accents so indistinct that the Prince could not distinguish a single word he said; and presently Bahman understood that his moustache was on such wise closed and concealed his mouth that his utterance became indistinct and he only muttered when he would have spoken. He therefore haltered his horse to a tree and pulling out a pair of scissors said, "O holy man, thy lips are wholly hidden by this overlong hair; suffer me, I pray thee, clip the bristling growth which over-spreadeth thy face and which is so long and thick that thou art fearsome to behold; nay, more like to a bear than to a human being."

The Darwaysh with a nod consented, and when the Prince had clipped it and trimmed the growth, his face once more looked young and fresh as that of a man in the prime of youth. Presently quoth Bahman to him, "Would Heaven that I had a mirror wherein to show thee thy face, so wouldst thou see how youthful thou seemest, and how thy favour hath become far more like that of folk than whilom it was."

These flattering words pleased the Darwaysh who smiling said, "I thank thee much for this thy goodly service and kindly offices; and, if in return, I can do aught of favour for thee, I pray thee let me know, and I will attempt to satisfy thee in all things with my very heart and soul."

Then said the Prince, "O holy man, I have come hither from far distant lands along a toilsome road in quest of three things; to wit, a certain Speaking-Bird, a Singing-Tree and a Golden-Water; and this know I for certain that they are all to be found hard by this site."

The Prince, turning to the Darwaysh, continued, "O Devotee, albeit well I wot that the three things I seek are in this land and nearhand, yet I know not the exact spot wherein to find them. An thou have true information concerning the place and will inform me thereof, I on my part will never forget thy kindness, and I shall have the satisfaction of feeling that this long and toilsome wayfare hath not been wholly vain."

Hearing these words of the Prince, the Darwaysh changed countenance and his face waxed troubled and his colour wan; then he bent his glance downwards and sat in deepest silence. Whereat the other said, "O holy father, dost thou not understand the words wherewith I have bespoken thee? An thou art ignorant of the matter prithee let me know straightway that I may again fare onwards until such time as I find a man who can inform me thereof."

After a long pause the Darwaysh made reply, "O stranger, 'tis true I ken full well the site whereof thou are in search; but I hold thee dear in that thou hast been of service to me; and I am loath for thine own sake to tell thee where to find that stead." And the Prince rejoined, "Say me, O Fakir, why dost thou withhold this knowledge from me, and wherefore art thou not lief to let me learn it?"

Replied the other, "'Tis a hard road to travel and full of perils and dangers. Besides thyself many have come hither and have asked the path of me, and I refused to tell them, but they heeded not my warning and pressed me sore and compelled me to disclose the secret which I would have buried in my breast. Know, O my son, that all those braves have perished in their pride and not one of them hath returned to me safe and sound. Now, an thy life be dear to thee, follow my counsel and fare no further, but rather turn thee back without stay or delay and make for house and home and family."

Hereto Prince Bahman, stern in resolution, made reply, "Thou hast after kindly guise and friendly fashion advised me with the best of advice; and I, having heard all thou hast to day, do thank thee gratefully. But I reck not one jot or tittle of what dangers affront me, nor shall thy threats however fatal deter me from my purpose: moreover, if thieves or foemen haply fall upon me, I am armed at point and can and will protect myself, for I am certified that none can outvie me in strength and stowre."

To this the Fakir made reply, "The beings who will cut thy path and bar thy progress to that place are unseen of man, nor will they appear to thee on any wise: how then canst thou defend thyself against them?"

And he replied, "So be it, still I fear not and I pray thee only show me the road thither." When the Darwaysh was assured that the Prince had fully determined in mind to attempt the exploit and would by no means turn or be turned back from carrying out his purpose, he thrust his hand into a bag which lay hard by and took therefrom a ball, and said, "Alas, O my son, thou wilt not accept my counsel and I needs must let thee follow thy wilful way. Take this ball and, mounting thy horse, throw it in front of thee, and as long as it shall roll onwards do thou ride after it, but when it shall stop at the hill-foot dismount from thy horse and throw the reins upon his neck and leave him alone, for he will stay there without moving until such time as thou return. Then manfully breast the ascent, and on either side of the path, right and left, thou shalt see a scatter of huge black boulders. Here the sound of many voices in confused clamour and frightful will suddenly strike thine ears, to raise thy wrath and to fill thee with fear and hinder thy higher course uphill. Have a heed that thou be not dismayed, also beware, and again say I beware, lest thou turn thy head at any time, and cast a look backwards. An thy courage fail thee, or thou allow thyself one glance behind thee, thou shalt be transformed that very moment into a black rock; for know thou, O Prince, that all those stones which thou shalt see strewn upon thy way were men whilome and braves like thyself, who went forth with intent to gain the three things thou seekest, but frightened at those sounds lost human shape and became black boulders. However, shouldst thou reach the hill-top safe and sound, thou shalt find on the very summit a cage and perched therein the Speaking-Bird ready to answer all thy queries. So ask of him where thou mayest find the Singing-Tree and the Golden-Water, and he will tell thee all thou requirest. When thou shalt safely have seized all three thou wilt be free from further danger; yet, inasmuch as thou

507

hast not yet set out upon this journey give ear to my counsel. I beg of thee to desist from this thy purpose and return home in peace whilst thou hast yet the power."

The Prince made answer to the Darwaysh, "Until, O thou holy man, such time as I win to my purpose I will not go back; no, never; therefore adieu." So he mounted his horse and threw the ball in front of him; and it rolled forward at racing-speed and he, with gaze intent thereupon, rode after it and did not suffer it to gain upon him. When it had reached the hill whereof the Darwaysh spake, it ceased to make further way, whereupon the Prince dismounted and throwing the reins on his horse's neck left him and fared on afoot to the slope. As far as he could see, the line of his path from the hill-foot to the head was strown with a scatter of huge black boulders; withal his heart felt naught of fear. He had not taken more than some four or five paces before a hideous din and a terrible hubbub of many voices arose, even as the Darwaysh had forewarned him. Prince Bahman, however, walked on valiantly with front erect and fearless tread, but he saw no living thing and heard only the Voices sounding all around him.

Some said, "Who is yon fool man and whence hath he come? Stop him, let him not pass!" Others shouted out, "Fall on him, seize this zany and slay him!" Then the report waxed louder and louder still, likest to the roar of thunder, and many Voices yelled out, "Thief! Assassin! Murderer!" Another muttered in taunting undertones, "Let him be, fine fellow that he is! Suffer him to pass on, for he and he only shall get the cage and the Speaking-Bird."

The Prince feared naught but advanced hot foot with his wonted verve and spirit; presently, however, when the Voices kept approaching nearer and nearer to him and increased in number on every side, he was sore perplexed. His legs began to tremble, he staggered and in fine overcome by fear he clean forgot the warning of the Darwaysh and looked back, whereat he was incontinently turned to stone like the scores of knights and adventurers who had foregone him.

Meantime the Princess Perizadah ever carried the hunting-knife, which Bahman her brother had given her, sheathed as it was in her maiden zone. She had kept it there ever since he set out upon his perilous expedition, and whenever she felt disposed she would bare the blade and judge by its sheen how fared her brother. Now until that day when he was transmewed to stone she found it, as often as she looked at it, clean and bright; but on the very evening when that evil fate betided him perchance Prince Parwez said to Perizadah, "O sister mine, give me I

pray thee the hunting-knife that I may see how goeth it with our brother."
She took it from her waist-belt and handed it to him; and as soon as he
unsheathed the knife lo and behold! he saw gouts of gore begin to drop
from it. Noting this he dashed the hunting-knife down and burst out into
loud lamentations, whilst the Princess who divined what had happened
shed a flood of bitter tears and cried with sighs and sobs, "Alas, O my
brother, thou hast given thy life for me. Ah, woe is me and well-away!
why did I tell thee of the Speaking-Bird and the Singing-Tree and the
Golden-Water? Wherefore did I ask that holy woman how she liked our
home, and hear of those three things in answer to my question? Would
to Heaven she had never crossed our threshold and darkened our doors!
Ungrateful hypocrite, dost thou requite me on such wise for the favour
and the honour I was fain to show thee; and what made me ask of thee the
means whereby to win these things? If now I obtain possession of them
what will they advantage me, seeing that my brother Bahman is no more?
What should I ever do with them?"

Thus did Perizadah indulge her grief bewailing her sad fate; while
Parwez in like manner moaned for his brother Bahman with exceeding
bitter mourning. At last the Prince, who despite his sorrow was assured
that his sister still ardently desired to possess the three marvels, turned
to Perizadah and said, "It behoveth me, O my sister, to set out forthright
and to discover whether Bahman our brother met his death by doom of
Destiny, or whether some enemy have slain him; and if he hath been killed
then must I take full vengeance on his murtherer."

Perizadah besought him with much weeping and wailing not to
leave her, and said, "O joy of my heart, Allah upon thee, follow not in the
footsteps of our dear departed brother or quit me in order to attempt a
journey so rife in risks. I care naught for those things in my fear lest I lose
thee also while attempting such enterprise."

But Prince Parwez would in no wise listen to her lament and next
day took leave of her, but ere he fared she said to him, "The hunting-knife
which Bahman left with me was the means of informing us concerning
the mishap which happened to him; but, say me how I shall know what
happeneth to thee?"

Then he produced a string of pearls which numbered one hundred
and said, "As long as thou shalt see these pearls all parted one from other
and each running loose upon the string, then do thou know that I am alive;
but an thou shouldst find them fixed and adhering together then be thou
ware that I am dead."

The Princess taking the string of pearls hung it around her neck, determined to observe it hour after hour and find out how it fared with her second brother. After this Prince Parwez set out upon his travels and at the twentieth stage came to the same spot where Bahman had found the Darwaysh and saw him there in like condition. Then, after saluting him with the salam, the Prince asked, "Canst thou tell me where to find the Speaking-Bird and the Singing-Tree and the Golden-Water; and by what manner of means I may get possession of them? An thou can I pray thee inform me of this matter."

The Darwaysh strave to stay Prince Parwez from his design and shewed him all the dangers on the way. Quoth he, "Not many days ago one like unto thee in years and in features came hither and enquired of me concerning the matter you now seekest. I warned him of the perils of the place and would have weaned him from his wilful ways, but he paid no wise heed to my warnings and refused to accept my counsel. He went off with full instructions from me on how to find those things he sought; but as yet he hath not returned, and doubtless he also hath perished like the many who preceded him upon that perilous enterprise."

Then said Prince Parwez, "O holy father, I know the man of whom thou speakest, for that he was my brother; and I learned that he was dead, but have no inkling of the cause whereby he died."

Replied the Darwaysh, "O my lord, I can inform thee on this matter; he hath been transmewed into a black stone, like the others of whom I just now spake to thee. If thou wilt not accept my advice and act accordingly to my counsel thou also shalt perish by the same means as did thy brother; and I solemnly forewarn thee to desist from this endeavour."

Prince Parwez having pondered these words, presently made reply, "O Darwaysh, I thank thee again and again and am much beholden to thee that thou art fain of my welfare and thou hast given me the kindest of counsel and the friendliest of advice; nor am I worthy of such favours bestowed upon a stranger. But now remaineth naught for me to beseech that thou wilt point out the path, for I am fully purposed to fare forwards and in no wise to desist from my endeavour. I pray thee favour me with full instructions for the road even as thou favouredst my brother."

Then said the Darwaysh, "An thou wilt not lend ear to my warnings and do as I desire thee, it mattereth to me neither mickle nor little. Choose for thyself and I by doom of Destiny must perforce forward thy attempt and albeit, by reason of my great age and infirmities, I may not conduct thee to the place I will not grudge thee a guide."

Then Prince Parwez mounted his horse and the Darwaysh taking one of many balls from out his scrip placed it in the youth's hands, directing him the while what to do, as he had counselled his brother Bahman; and, after giving him much advice and many warnings he ended with saying, "O my lord, have a heed not to be perplexed and terrified by the threatening Voices, and sounds from unseen beings, which shall strike thine ear; but advance dauntless to the hill-top where thou shalt find the cage with the Speaking-Bird and the Singing-Tree and the Golden-Water."

The Fakir then bid him adieu with words of good omen and the Prince set forth. He threw the ball upon the ground before him and, as it rolled up the path, he urged his horse to keep pace with it. But when he reached the hill-foot and saw that the ball had stopped and lay still, he dismounted forthright and paused awhile ere he should begin to climb and conned well in his mind the directions, one and all, given to him by the Darwaysh. Then, with firm courage and fast resolve, he set out afoot to reach the hill-top.

But hardly had he begun to climb before he heard a voice beside him threatening him in churlish tongue and crying, "O youth of ill-omen, stand still that I may trounce thee for this thine insolence." Hearing these insulting words of the Invisible Speaker, Prince Parwez felt his blood boil over; he could not refrain his rage and in his passion he clean forgot the words of wisdom wherewith the Fakir was warned him. He seized his sword and drawing it from the scabbard, turned about to slay the man who durst insult him in such wise; but he saw no one and, in the act of looking back both he and his horse became black stones.

Meanwhile the Princess ceased not at all hours of the day and watches of the night to consult the string of pearls which Parwez had left her; she counted them overnight when she retired to rest, she slept with them around her neck during the hours of darkness, and when she awoke at the dawn of day she first of all consulted them and noted their condition. Now at the very hour when her second brother was turned to stone she found the pearls sticking one to other so close together that she might not move a single bead apart from its fellows and she knew thereby that Prince Parwez also was lost to her for ever.

The Princess Perizadah was sore grieved at so sudden a blow and said to herself, "Ah! Woe is me and well-away! How bitter will be living without the love of such brothers whose youthtide was sacrificed for me! 'Tis but right that I share their fate whate'er be my lot; else what shall I have to say on the Day of Doom and the Resurrection of the Dead and the Judgment of Mankind?"

Wherefore next morning, without further let or stay, she donned disguise of man's attire; and, warning her women and slaves that she would be absent on an errand for a term of days during which they would be in charge of the house and goods, she mounted her hackney and set out alone and unattended. Now, inasmuch as she was skilled in horsemanship and had been wont to accompany her brothers when hunting and hawking, she was better fitted than other women to bear the toils and travails of travel. So on the twentieth day she arrived safe and sound at the hermitage-hut where, seeing the same Shaykh, she took seat beside him and after salaaming to him and greeting him she asked him, "O holy father, suffer me to rest and refresh myself awhile in this site of good omen; then deign point out to me, I pray thee, the direction of the place, at no far distance herefrom, wherein are found a certain Speaking-Bird and a Singing-Tree and a Golden-Water. An thou wilt tell me I shall deem this the greatest of favour."

Replied the Darwaysh, "Thy voice revealeth to me that thou art a woman and no man, albeit attired in male's apparel. Well I wot the stead whereof thou speakest and which containeth the marvellous things thou hast named. But say me, what is thy purpose in asking me?"

The Princess made reply, "I have been told many a tale anent these rare and wondrous things, and I would fain get possession of them and bear them to my home and make them its choicest adornments."

And said the Fakir, "O my daughter, in very truth these matters are exceeding rare and admirable: right fit are they for fair ones like thyself to win and take back with thee, but thou hast little inkling of the dangers manifold and dire that encompass them. Better far were it for thee to cast away this vain thought and go back by the road thou camest."

Replied the Princess, "O holy father and far-famed anchorite, I come from a distant land whereto I will nevermore return, except after winning my wish; no, never! I pray thee tell me the nature of those dangers and what they be, that hearing thereof my heart may judge if I have or have not the strength and the spirit to meet them."

Then the Shaykh described to the Princess all the risks of the road as erst he had informed Princes Bahman and Parwez; and he ended with saying, "The dangers will display themselves as soon as thou shalt begin to climb the hill-head where is the home of the Speaking-Bird. Then, if thou be fortunate enough to seize him, he will direct thee where to find the Singing-Tree and the Golden-Water. All the time thou climbest the hill, Voices from throats unseen and accents fierce and fell shall resound in thine ears. Furthermore, thou shalt see black rocks and boulders strewn upon thy path; and these, thou must know, are the transformed bodies of men who with exceeding courage attempted the same enterprise, but filled with sudden fear and tempted to turn and to look backwards were changed into stones. Now do thou steadily bear in mind what was their case. At the first they listened to those fearful sounds and cursings with firm souls, but anon their hearts and minds misgave them, or, haply, they fumed with fury to hear the villain words addressed to them and they turned about and gazed behind them, whereat both men and horses became black boulders."

But when the Darwaysh had told her every whit, the Princess made reply, "From what thou sayest it seemeth clear to me that these Voices can do nothing but threaten and frighten by their terrible din; furthermore that there is naught to prevent a man climbing up the hill, nor is there any fear of any one attacking him; all he hath to do is on no account to look behind him."

And after a short pause she presently added, "O Fakir, albeit a woman yet I have both nerve and thews to carry me through this adventure. I shall not heed the Voices nor be enraged thereat, neither will they have any power to dismay me: moreover, I have devised a device whereby my success on this point is assured."

"And what wilt thou do?" asked he, and she answered, "I will stop mine ears with cotton so may not my mind be disturbed and reason perturbed by hearing those awesome sounds."

The Fakir marvelled with great marvel and presently exclaimed, "O my lady, methinks thou art destined to get possession of the things thou seekest. This plan hath not occurred to any hitherto and hence it is haply that one and all have failed miserably and have perished in the attempt. Take good heed to thyself, however, not run any risk other than the enterprise requireth."

She replied, "I have no cause for fear since this one and only danger is before me to prevent happy issue. My heart doth bear me witness that I shall surely gain the guerdon wherefor I have undertaken such toil and trouble. But now do thou tell me what I must do, and whither to win my wish I must wend."

The Darwaysh once more besought her to return home, but Perizadah refused to listen and remained as firm and resolute as before; so when he saw that she was fully bent upon carrying out her purpose he exclaimed, "Depart, O my daughter, in the peace of Almighty Allah and His blessing; and may He defend thy youth and beauty from all danger."

Then taking from his bag a ball he gave it her and said, "When thou art seated in saddle throw this before thee and follow it whitherso it lead

513

thee; and when it shall stop at the hill-foot then dismount and climb the slope. What will happen after I have already told thee."

The Princess, after farewelling the Fakir, straightway bestrode her steed and threw the ball in front of his hooves as she had been bidden do. It rolled along before her in the direction of the hill and she urged her hackney to keep up with it, until reaching the hill it suddenly stopped. Hereat the Princess dismounted forthwith and having carefully plugged both her ears with cotton, began to breast the slope with fearless heart and dauntless soul; and as soon as she had advanced a few steps a hubbub of voices broke out all around her, but she heard not a sound, by reason of her hearing being blunted by the cotton-wool. Then hideous cries arose with horrid din, still she heard them not; and at last they grew to a storm of shouts and shrieks and groans and moans flavoured with foul language such as shameless women use when railing one at other. She caught now and then an echo of the sounds but recked naught thereof and only laughed and said to herself, "What care I for their scoffs and jeers and fulsome taunts? Let them hoot on and bark and bay as they may: this at least shall not turn me from my purpose."

As she approached the goal the path became perilous in the extreme and the air was so filled with an infernal din and such awful sounds that even Rustam would have quailed thereat and the bold spirit of Asfandiyar have quaked with terror. The Princess, however, pressed on with uttermost speed and dauntless heart till she neared the hill-top and espied above her the cage in which the Speaking-Bird was singing with melodious tones; but, seeing the Princess draw nigh, he broke out despite his puny form in thundering tones and cried, "Return, O fool: hie thee back not dare come nearer."

Princess Perizadah heeded not his clamour a whit but bravely reached the hill-top, and running over the level piece of ground made for the cage and seized it saying, "At last I have thee and thou shalt not escape me."

She then pulled out the cotton-wool wherewith she had stopped her ears, and heard the Speaking-Bird reply in gentle accents, "O lady valiant and noble, be of good cheer for no harm or evil shall betide thee, as hath happened to those who essayed to make me their prize. Albeit I am encaged I have much secret knowledge of what happeneth in the world of men and I an content to become thy slave, and for thee to be my liege lady. Moreover I am more familiar with all that concerneth thee even than thou art thyself; and one day of the days I will do thee a service which shall deserve thy gratitude. What is now thy command? Speak that I may fulfil thy wish."

Princess Perizadah was gladdened by these words, but in the midst of her joy she grieved at the thought of how she had lost her brothers whom she loved with a love so dear, and anon she said to the Speaking-Bird, "Full many a thing I want, but first tell me of the Golden-Water, of which I have heard so much, be nigh unto this place and if so do thou show me where to find it."

The Bird directed her accordingly and the Princess took a silver flagon she had brought with her and filled it brimful from the magical fount. Then quoth she to the Bird, "The third and last prize I have come to seek is the Singing-Tree; discover to me where that also can be found."

The Bird replied, "O Princess of fair ones, behind thy back in yonder clump that lieth close at hand groweth the Tree"; so she went forthright to the copse and found the Tree she sought singing with sweetest toned voice.

But inasmuch as it was huge in girth she returned to her slave the Bird and said, "The Tree indeed I found but 'tis lofty and bulky; how then shall I pull it up?" and he made answer, "Pluck but a branchlet of the Tree and plant it in thy garden; 'twill at once take root and in shortest time be as gross and fair a growth as that in yonder copse."

So the Princess broke off a twig, and now that she had secured the three things, whereof the holy woman spake to her, she was exceeding joyful and turning to the Bird said, "I have in very deed won my wish, but one thing is yet wanting to my full satisfaction. My brothers who ventured forth with this same purpose are lying hereabouts turned into black stones; and I fain would have them brought to life again and the twain return with me in all satisfaction and assurance of success. Tell me now some plan whereby mine every desire may be fulfilled."

The Speaking-Bird replied, "O Princess, trouble not thyself, the thing is easy. Sprinkle some of the Golden-Water from the flagon upon the black stones lying round about, and by virtue thereof each and every shall come to life again, thy two brothers as well as the others."

So Princess Perizadah's heart was set at rest and taking the three prizes with her she fared forth and scattered a few drops from the silver flagon upon each black stone as she passed it when, lo and behold! they came to life as men and horses. Amongst them were her brothers who she at once knew and falling on their necks she embraced them, and asked in tones of surprise, "O my brothers, what do ye here?"

To this they answered, "We lay fast asleep."

Quoth she, "Strange indeed that ye take delight in slumber away from me and ye forget the purpose wherefor ye left me; to wit, the winning of

the Speaking-Bird and the Singing-Tree and the Golden-Water. Did ye not see this place all bestrown with dark hued rocks? Look now and say if there be aught left of them. These men and horses now standing around us were all black stones as ye yourselves also were; but, by the boon of Almighty Allah, all have come to life again and await the signal to depart. And if now ye wish to learn by what strange miracle both ye and they have recovered human shape, know ye that it hath been wrought by virtue of a water contained in this flagon which I sprinkled in the rocks with leave of the Lord of all Living. When I had gained possession of this cage and its Speaking-Bird, and also of the Singing-Tree, a wand whereof ye see in my hand, and lastly of the Golden-Water, I would not take them home with me unless ye twain could also bear me company; so I asked of this Bird the means whereby ye could be brought to life again. He made me drop some drops of the Golden-Water on the boulders and when I had done this ye two like all the others returned to life and to your proper forms."

Hearing these her words the Princes Bahman and Parwez thanked and praised their sister Perizadah; and all the other she had saved showered thanks and blessings on her hear saying with one accord, "O our lady, we are now thy slaves; nor can a lifelong service repay the debt of gratitude we owe thee for this favour thou hast shown us. Command and we are ready to obey thee with our hearts and our souls."

Quoth Perizadah, "The bringing back to life of these my brothers were my aim and purpose, and in so doing ye too have profited thereby; and I accept your acknowledgements as another pleasure. But now do ye mount each and every man his horse and ride back by the way ye came to your homes in Allah's peace."

On this wise the Princess dismissed them and made herself ready to depart; but, as she was about to bestride her steed, Prince Bahman asked permission of her that he might hold in hand the cage and ride in front of her. She answered, "Not so, O brother mine; this Bird is now my slave and I will carry him myself. An thou wilt, take thou this twig with thee, but hold the cage only till I am seated in saddle."

She then mounted her hackney and, placing the cage before her on the pommel, bade her brother Parwez take charge of the Golden-Water in the silver flagon and carry it with all ease and the Prince did her bidding without gainsaying. And when they were all ready to ride forth, including the knights and the squires whom Perizadah had brought to life by sprinkling the Water, the Princess turned to them and said, "Why delay we our departure and how is it that none offereth to lead us?" But as all hesitated she gave command, "Now let him amongst you number whose noblesse and high degree entitle him to such distinction fare before us and show us the way."

Then all with one accord replied, "O Princess of fair ones, there be none amongst us worthy of such honour, nor may any wight dare to ride before thee."

So when she saw that none amongst them claimed preeminence or right of guidance, and none desired to take precedence of the rest, she made excuse and said, "O my lords, 'tis not for me by right to lead the way, but since ye order I must needs obey." Accordingly she pushed on to the front, and after came her brothers and behind them the rest. And as they journeyed on all desired to see the holy man, and thank him for his favours and friendly rede, but when they reached the spot where he dwelt they found him dead, and they knew not if old age had taken him away, or if he perished in his prize because the Princess Perizadah had found and carried off the three things whereof he had been appointed by Destiny guard and guide.

All the company rode on, and as each one arrived at the road which led him to his natal land he took leave of the Lady Perizadah and went his way, until all were gone and the Princess and her brothers were the only left. At last they reached their journey's end safe and sound, and on entering their mansion Perizadah hung the cage inside the garden hard by the belvedere and no sooner did the Speaking-Bird begin to sing than flights of ring-doves and bulbuls and nightingales and skylarks and parrots and other songsters came flocking around him from afar and anear. Likewise she set the twig, which she had taken from the Singing-Tree, in a choice parterre also hard by the belvedere, and forthright it took root and put forth boughs and buds and grew goodly in growth, till it became a trunk as large as that from which she had plucked the twig, whilst from its leafage went forth bewitching sounds rivalling the music of the parent tree. She lastly bid them carve her a basin of pure white marble and set it in the centre of the pleasure grounds; then she poured therein the Golden-Water and forthright it filled the bowl and sot upwards like a spouting fountain some twenty feet in height; moreover the gerbes and jets fell back whence they came and not one drop was lost: whereby the working of the waters was unbroken and ever similar.

Now but few days passed ere the report of these three wonders was bruited abroad and flocked the folk daily from the city to solace themselves with the sight, and the gates stood always open wide and all who came had

entrance to the house and gardens and free leave to walk about at will and see these rarities which affected them with admiration and delight. Then also, as soon as both the Princes had recovered from the toils of travel, they began to go a-hunting as heretofore; and it chanced one day they rode forth several miles from home and were both busies in the chase, when the Shah of Iran-land came by decree of Destiny to the same place for the same purpose. The Princes, seeing a band of knights and huntsmen drawing near, were fain to ride home and to avoid such meeting; so they left the hunting-grounds and turned them homewards. But as Fate and lot would have it they hit upon the very road whereby King Khusrau Shah was coming, and so narrow was the path that they could not avoid the horsemen by wheeling round and wending another way. So they drew rein perforce and dismounting they salaamed and did obeisance to the Shah and stood between his hands with heads held low. The Sovran, seeing the horses' fine trappings and the Princes' costly garments, thought that the two youths were in the suite of his Wazirs and his Ministers of state and much wished to look upon their faces; he therefore bade them raise their heads and stand upright in the presence and they obeyed his bidding with modest mien and downcast eyes. He was charmed to behold their comeliness of favour and their graceful forms and their noble air and their courtly mien; and, after gazing at them for some time in not a little wonder and admiration, he asked them who they were and what might be their names and where they abode.

Hereto Prince Bahman made reply, "O Asylum of the Universe, we are the sons of one whose life was spent in serving the Shah, the Intendant of the royal gardens and pleasaunces. As his days grew to a close he builded him a home without the town for us to dwell in till we should grow to man's estate and become fit to do thy Highness suit and service and carry out thy royal commands." The Shah furthermore asked them, "How is it that ye go a-hunting? This is a special sport of Kings and is not meant for the general of his subjects and dependants."

Prince Bahman rejoined, "O Refuge of the World, we are yet young in years and being brought up at home we know little of courtly customs; but, as we look to bear arms in the armies of the Shah we fain would train our bodies to toil and moil."

This answer was honoured by the royal approof and the King rejoined, "The Shah would see how ye deal with noble game; so choose ye whatever quarry ye will and bring it down in the presence."

The Princes hereat remounted their horses and joined the Sovran; and when they reached the thickmost of the forest, Prince Bahman started a tiger and Prince Parwez rode after a bear; and the twain used their spears with such skill and good will that each killed his quarry and laid it at the Shah's feet. Then entering the wood again Prince Bahman slew a bear, and Prince Parwez, a tiger and did as before; but when they would have ridden off the third time the King forbade them saying, "What! would ye strip the royal preserve of all the game? This be enough and more than enough, that Shah wished only to put your valour to the proof and having seen it with his own eyes he is fully satisfied. Come now with us and stand before us as we sit at meat."

Prince Bahman made reply, "We are not worthy of the high honour and dignity wherewith thou favourest us thy humble servants. We dutifully and humbly petition thy Highness to hold us excused for this day; but if the Asylum of the Universe deign appoint some other time thy slaves will right gladly execute thy auspicious orders."

Khusrau Shah, astonished at their refusal, asked the cause thereof when Prince Bahman answered, "May I be thy sacrifice, O King of kings, we have at home an only sister; and all three are bound together with bonds of the fondest affection; so we brothers go not anywhere without consulting her nor doth she aught save according to our counsel."

The King was pleased to see such fraternal love and union and presently quoth he, "By the head of the Shah, he freely giveth you leave to go to-day: consult your sister and meet the Shadow of Allah to-morrow at this hunting-ground, and tell him what she saith and if she content to let to twain and wait upon the Shah at meat."

So the Princes farewelled and prayed for him; then rode back home; but they both forgot to tell their sister how they had fallen in with the King; and of all that passed between them they remembered not one word. Next day again they went a-hunting and on returning from the chase the Shah enquired of them, "Have ye consulted with your sister if ye may serve the King, and what saith she thereto? Have ye obtained permission from her?"

On hearing these words the Princes waxed aghast with fear; the colour of their faces changed, and each began to look into the other's eyes. Then Bahman said, "Pardon, O Refuge of the World, this our transgression. We both forgot the command and remembered not to tell our sister."

Replied the King, "It mattereth not! ask her to-day and bring me word to-morrow." But it so happened that on that day also they forgot the message yet the King was not annoyed at their shortness of memory, but taking from his pocket three little balls of gold, and tying them in a kerchief of sillk he handed them to Prince Bahman saying, "Put these balls in thy waist shawl,

so shalt thou not forget to ask thy sister; and if perchance the matter escape thy memory, when thou shalt go to bed and take off thy girdle, haply the sound of them falling to the ground will remind thee of thy promise."

Despite this strict injunction of the Shadow of Allah the Princes on that day also clean forgot the order and the promise they had made to the King. When, however, night came on, and Prince Bahman went to his bed-chamber for sleep, he loosed his girdle and down fell the golden balls and at the sound the message of the Shah flashed across his thought. So he and his brother Parwez at once hastened to Perizadah's bower, where she was about retiring to rest; and, with many excuses for troubling her at so unseasonable an hour, reported to her all that happened. She lamented their thoughtlessness which for three successive days had caused them to forget the royal behest and ended with saying, "Fortune hath favoured you, O my brothers, and brought you suddenly to the notice of the Asylum of the Universe, a chance which often hath led to the height of good. It grieveth me sore that on your over regard for our fraternal love and union ye did not take service with the King when he deigned command you. Moreover ye have far greater cause for regret and repentance than I in that ye failed to plead a sufficient excuse and that which ye offered must have sounded rude and churlish. A right dangerous thing it is to thwart Kingly wishes. In his extreme condescension the Shah commandeth you to take service with him and ye, in rebelling against his exalted orders have done foolishly and ye have caused me much trouble of mind. Howbeit I will sue counsel from my slave the Speaking-Bird and see what he may say; for when I have ever any hard and weighty question to decide I fail not to ask his advice."

Hereupon the Princess set the cage by her side and after telling her slave all that her brothers had made known to her, asked admonition of him regarding what they should do. The Speaking-Bird made answer, "It behoveth the Princes to gratify the Shah in all things he requireth of them; moreover, let them make ready a feast for the King and humbly pray them to visit this house, and thereby testify to him loyalty and devotion to his royal person."

Then said the Princess, "O Bird, my brothers are most dear to me nor would I suffer them leave my sight for one moment if it were possible; and Allah forfend that this daring on their part do injury to our love and affection."

Said the Speaking-Bird, "I have counselled thee for the best and have offered thee the right rede; nor do thou fear aught in following it, for naught save good shall come therefrom."

"But," quoth the Princess, "an the Shadow of Allah honour us by crossing the threshold of this house needs must I present myself before him with face unveiled?"

"By all means," quoth the Speaking-Bird, "this will not harm thee, nay rather 'twill be to thine advantage."

Early next day the two Princes Bahman and Parwez rode as aforetime to the hunting-ground and met Khusrau Shah, who asked them, saying, "What answer bring ye from your sister?"

Hereupon the elder brother advancing said, "O Shadow of Allah, verily we are thy slaves and whatever thou deign bid that we are ready to obey. These less than the least have referred the matter to their sister and have obtained their consent; nay more, she blamed and chided them for that they did not hurry to carry out the commands of the Refuge of the World the moment they were delivered. Therefore being sore displeased at us, she desireth us on her behalf to plead forgiveness with the Shahinshah for this offence by us offered."

Replied the King, "No crime have ye committed to call forth the royal displeasure: nay more, it delighteth the Shadow of Allah exceedingly to see the love ye twain bear towards your sister."

Hearing such words of condescension and kindliness from the Shah, the Princes held their peace and hung their heads for shame groundwards; and the King who that day was not keen, according to his custom, after the chase, whenever he saw the brothers hold aloof, called them to his presence and heartened their hearts with words of favour; and presently, when a-weary of sport, he turned the head of his steed palace-ward and deigned order the Princes to ride by his side. The Wazirs and Councillors and Courtiers one and all fumed with envy and jealousy to see two unknowns entreated with such especial favour; and as they rode at the head of the suite adown the market-street all eyes were turned upon the youths and men asked one of other, "Who be the two who ride beside the Shah? Belong they to this city, or come they from some foreign land?"

And the folk praised and blessed them saying, "Allah send our King of kings two Princes as godly and gallant as are these twain who ride beside him. If our hapless Queen who languisheth in durance had brought forth sons, by Allah's favour they would now be of the same age as these young lords."

But as soon as the cavalcade reached the palace the King alighted from his horse and led the Princes to his private chamber, a splendid retreat magnificently furnished, wherein a table had been spread with sumptuous meats and rarest cates; and having seated himself thereat he motioned them to do likewise. Hereupon the brothers making low obeisance also took their seats and ate in well-bred silence with respectful mien.

Then the Shah, desiring to warm them into talk and thereby to test their wit and wisdom, addressed them on themes galore and asked of them many questions; and, inasmuch as they had been taught well and trained in every art and science, they answered with propriety and perfect ease. The Shah struck with admiration bitterly regretted that Almighty Allah had not vouchsafed to him sons so handsome in semblance and so apt and so learned as these twain; and, for the pleasure of listening to them, he lingered at meat longer than he was wont to do. And when he rose from table and retired with them to his private apartment he still sat longwhile talking with them and at last in his admiration he exclaimed, "Never until this day have I set eyes on youths so well brought up and so comely and so capable as are these, and methinks 'twere hard to find their equals anywhere." In time quoth he, "The time waxeth late, so now let us cheer our hearts with music." And forthright the royal band of minstrels and musicians began to sing and perform upon instruments of mirth and merriment, whilst dancing-girls and boys displayed their skill, and mimes and mummers played their parts. The Princes enjoyed the spectacle with extreme joy and the last hours of the afternoon passed in royal revelry and regale.

But when the sun had set and evening came on, the youths craved dismissal from the Shah with many expressions of gratitude for the exalted favours he had deigned bestow on them; and ere they fared forth the King of kings bespake them, saying, "Come ye again on the morrow to our hunting-ground as heretofore, and thence return to the palace. By the beard of the Shah, he fain would have you always with him, and solace him with your companionship and converse."

Prince Bahman, prostrating himself before the presence, answered, "'Tis the very end and aim of all our wishes, O Shadow of Allah upon Earth, that on the morrow when thou shalt come from the chase and pass by our poor house, thou graciously deign enter and rest in it awhile, thereby conferring the highmost of honours upon ourselves and upon our sister. Albeit the place is not worthy of the Shahinshah's exalted presence, yet at times do mighty Kings condescend to visit the huts of their slaves."

The King, ever more and more enchanted with their comeliness and pleasant speech, vouchsafed a most gracious answer, saying, "The dwelling place of youths in your estate and degree will certainly be goodly and right worthy of you; and the Shah willingly consenteth for the morrow to become the guest of you twain and of your sister whom, albeit he have not yet seen, he is assured to find perfect in all gifts of body and mind. Do ye twain therefore about early dawn-tide expect the Shah at the usual trysting-place."

The Princes then craved leave to wend their ways; and going home said to their sister, "O Perizadah, the Shah hath decreed that to-morrow he will come to our house and rest here awhile after the hunt."

Said she, "An so it be, needs must we see to it that all be made ready for a royal banquet and we may not be put to shame when the Shadow of Allah shall deign shade us. There is no help but that in this matter I ask of my slave, the Speaking-Bird, what counsel he would give; and that I prepare according thereto such meats as are meet for him and are pleasing to the royal palate."

The Princes both approved of her plan and went to seek repose; whereupon Perizadah sent for the cage and setting it before her said, "O Bird, the Shah hath made a promise and hath decreed that he will deign honour this our house on the morrow, wherefore we must needs make ready for our liege lord the best of banquets and I bid thee say me what dishes should the kitcheners cook for him?"

The Speaking-Bird replied, "O my lady, thou hast the most skilful of cooks and confectioners. Do thou bid them dress for thee the choicest dainties, but above all others see thou with thine own eyes that they set before the Shah a dish of new green cucumbers stuffed with pearls."

Quoth the Princess in utter wonderment, "Never until this time heard I of such a dainty! How? Cucumbers with a filling of pearls! And what will the King, who cometh to eat bread and not to gaze on stones, say to such meat? Furthermore, I have not in my possession pearls enough to serve for even a single cucumber."

Replied the Speaking-Bird, "This were an easy matter: do thou dread naught but only act as I shall advise thee. I seek not aught save thy welfare and would on no wise counsel thee to thy disadvantage. As for the pearls thou shalt collect them on this wise: go thou to-morrow betimes to the pleasure-gardens and bid a hole be dug at the foot of the first tree in the avenue by thy right hand, and there shalt thou find of pearls as large a store as thou shalt require."

So after dawn on the next day Princess Perizadah bade a gardener-lad accompany her and fared to the site within the pleasure-gardens whereof the Speaking-Bird had told her. Here the boy dug a hole both deep and wide when suddenly his spade struck upon somewhat hard, and he removed with

523

his hands the earth and discovered to view a golden casket well nigh one foot square. Hereupon the young gardener showed it to the Princess who explained, "I brought thee with me for this very reason. Take heed and see that no harm come to it, but dig it out and bring it to me with all care."

When the lad did her bidding she opened it forthright and found it filled with pearls and unions fresh from the sea, round as rings and all of one and the same size perfectly fitted for the purpose which the Speaking-Bird had proposed. Perizadah rejoiced with extreme joy at the sight and taking up the box walked back with it to the house; and the Princes who had seen their sister faring forth betimes with the gardener-lad and had wondered why she went to the park thus early unaccording to her wonted custom, catching sight of her from the casement quickly donned their walking dresses and came to meet her. And as the two brothers walked forward they saw the Princess approaching them with somewhat unusual under her arm, which when they met, proved to be a golden casket whereof they knew naught. Quoth they, "O our sister at early light we espied thee going to the pleasure-grounds with a gardener-lad empty handed, but now thou bringest back this golden casket; so disclose to us where and how thou hast found it; and haply there may be some hoard close hidden in the parterre?"

Perizadah replied, "Sooth ye say, O my brothers: I took this lad with me and made him dig under a certain tree where we came upon this box of pearls, at the sight whereof methinks your hearts will be delighted."

The Princess straightway opened the box and her brothers sighting the pearls and unions were amazed with extreme amazement and rejoiced greatly to see them. Quoth the Princess, "Come now ye twain with me, for that I have in hand a weighty matter"; and quoth Prince Bahman, "What is there to do? I pray thee tell us without delay for never yet hast thou kept aught of thy life from us."

She made reply, "O my brothers, I have naught to hide from you, nor think ye any ill of me, for I am now about to tell you all the tale." Then she made known to them what advice the Speaking-Bird had given to her; and they, conning the matter over in their minds, marvelled much why her slave had bidden them set a dish of green cucumbers stuffed with pearls before the Shah, nor could they devise any reason for it.

Presently the Princess resumed, "The Speaking-Bird indeed is wise and ware; so methinks this counsel must be for our advantage; and at any rate it cannot be without some object and purpose. It therefore behoveth us to do even as he hath commanded." Hereupon the Princess went to her own chamber and summoning the head cook said to him, "This day the Shah, the Shadow of Allah upon Earth, will condescend here to eat the noon-meal. So do thou take heed that the meats be of choisest flavour and fittest to set before the Asylum of the World, but of all the dishes there is one thou alone must make and let not another have a hand therein. This shall be of the freshest green cucumbers with a stuffing of unions and pearls."

The head Cook listened to this order of the Princess with wonderment and said in himself, "Who ever heard of such a dish or dreamed of ordering such a one."

The Lady seeing his astonishment betrayed in his semblance without the science of thought-reading, said to him, "It seemeth from thy countenance that thou deemest me daft of wit to give thee such order. I know that no one ever tasted a dish of the kind, but what is that to thee? Do thou e'en as thou art bidden. Thou seest this box brimful on pearls; so take of them as many as thou needest for the dish, and what remaineth over leave in the box."

The Kitchener who could answer nothing in his confusion and amazement, chose as many precious stones as he required, and presently fared away to superintend the meats being cooked and made ready for the feast. Meanwhile the Princess went over the house and grounds and gave directions to the slaves about the ordinance thereof, leading especial attention to the carpets and divans, the lamps and all other furniture. Next day at break of dawn Princes Bahman and Parwez rode forth in rich attire to the appointed place where they first met the Shah, who was also punctual to his promise and vouchsafed to join them in the hunt.

Now when the sun had risen high and its rays waxed hot, the King gave up the chase, and set forth with the Princes to their house; and as they drew nigh thereto the cadet pushed forwards and sent word to the Princess that the Asylum of the World was coming in all good omen. Accordingly, she hastened to receive him and stood waiting his arrival at the inner entrance; and after, when the King rode up to the gate and dismounting within the court stepped over the threshold of the house-door, she fell down at his feet and did worship.

Hereat her brothers said, "O Asylum of the World, this is our sister of whom we spake"; and the Shah with gracious kindness and condescension raised her by the hand, and when he saw her face he marvelled much at its wondrous comeliness and loveliness.

He thought in himself, "How like she is to her brothers in favour and form, and I trow there be none of all my lieges in city or country who can

compare with them for beauty and noble bearing. This country-house also exceedeth all that I have ever seen in splendour and grandeur." The Princess then led the Shah through the house and showed him all the magnificence thereof, while he rejoiced with extreme joy at everything that met his sight.

So when King Khusrau had considered whatso was in the mansion he said to the Princess, "This home of thine is far grander than any palace owned by the Shah, who would now stroll about the pleasure-garden, never doubting but that it will be delightsome as the house."

Hereat the Princess threw wide open the door whence the grounds could be seen; and at once the King beheld before and above all other things, the fountain which cast up incessantly, in gerbes and jets, water clear as crystal withal golden of hue. Seeing such prodigy he cried, "This is indeed a glorious gusher: never before saw I one so admirable. But say me where is its source, and by what means doth it shoot up in spurts so high? Whence cometh this constant supply and in what fashion was it formed? The Shah would fain see it near hand."

"O King of kings, and Lord of the lands," quoth the Princess, "be pleased to do whatso thou desirest." Thereupon they went up to the fountain and the Shah stood gazing upon it with delight when behold, he heard a concert of sugar-sweet voices choiring with the harmony and melody of wit-ravishing music.

So he turned him around and gazed about him to discover the singers, but no one was in sight; and albeit he looketh both hard and near all was in vain, he heard the voices but he could descry no songster. At length completely baffled he exclaimed, "Whence come these most musical of sounds; and rise they from the bowels of earth or are they floating in the depths of air? They fill the heart with rapture, but strangely surprise the senses to see that no one singer is in sight."

Replied the Princess with a smile "O Lord of lords, there are no minstrels here and the strains which strike the Shah's ear come from yonder tree. Deign walk on, I pray thee, and examine it well."

So be advanced thereto, ever more and more enchanted with the music, and he gazed now at the Golden-Water and now at the Singing-Tree till lost in wonderment and amazement; then, "O Allah," said he to himself, "is all this Nature-made or magical, for in very deed the place is full of mystery?"

Presently, turning to the Princess quoth he, "O my lady, prithee whence came ye by this wondrous tree which hath been planted in the middlemost of this garden: did anyone bring it from some far distant land as a rare gift, and by what name is it known?"

Quoth Perizadah in reply, "O King of kings, this marvel hight Singing-Tree groweth not in our country. 'Twere long to recount whence and by what means I obtained it; and suffice it for the present to say that the Tree, together with the Golden-Water and the Speaking-Bird, were all found by me at one and the same time. Deign now accompany thy slave and look upon this third rarity; and when the Shah shall have rested and recovered from the toils and travails of hunting, the tale of these three strange things shall be told to the Asylum of the World in fullest detail."

Hereto the King replied, "All the Shah's fatigue hath gone for gazing upon these wonders; and now to visit the Speaking-Bird."

The Princess took the King and when she had shown to him the Speaking-Bird, they returned to the garden where he never ceased considering the fountain with extreme surprise and presently exclaimes, "How is this? No spring whence cometh all this water meeteth the Shah's eye, and no channel; nor is there any reservoir large enough to contain it."

She replied, "Thou speakest sooth, O King of kings! This jetting font hath no source; and it springeth from a small marble basin which I filled from a single flagon of the Golden-Water; and by the might of Allah Almighty it increased and waxed copious until it shot up in this huge gerbe which the Shah seeth. Furthermore it ever playeth day and night; and, marvellous to relate, the water falling back from that height into the basin minisheth not in quantity nor is aught of it spilt or wasted."

Hereat the King, filled with wonder and astonishment, bade go back to the Speaking-Bird; whereupon the Princess led him to the belvedere whence he looked out upon thousands of all manner fowls carolling in the trees and filling air with their hymns and prises of the Creator; so he asked his guide, "O my lady, whence come these countless songsters which haunt yonder tree and make the welkin resound with their melodious notes; yet they affect none other of the trees?"

Quoth Perizadah, "O King of kings, they are all attracted by the Speaking-Bird and flock hither to accompany his song; and for that his cage hangeth to the window of this belvedere they prefer only the nearest of the trees; and here he may be heard singing sweeter notes than any of the others, nay in a plaint more musical than that of any nightingale."

And as the Shah drew nigh the cage and gave ear to the Bird's singing, the Princess called to her captive saying, "Ho, my slave the Bird, dost thou not perceive the Asylum of the Universe is here that thou payest him not due homage and worship?"

Hearing these words the Speaking-Bird forthright ceased his shrilling and at the same moment all the other songsters sat in deepest silence; for they were loyal to their liege lord nor durst any one utter a note when he held his peace. The Speaking-Bird then spake in human voice saying, "O great King, may Almighty Allah by His Might and Majesty accord thee health and happiness"; so the Shah returned the salutation and the Slave of Princess Perizadah ceased not to shower blessings upon his head.

Meanwhile the tables were spread after sumptuous fashion and the choicest meats were set before the company which was seated in due order and degree, the Shah placing himself hard by the Speaking-Bird and close to the casement where the cage was hung. Then the dish of green cucumbers having been set before him, he put forth his hand to help himself, but drew it back in wonderment when he saw that the cucumbers, ranged in order upon the plate, were stuffed with pearls which appeared at either end. He asked the Princess and her brothers, "What is this dish? It cannot be meant for food; then wherefore is it placed before the Shah? Explain to me, I command you, what this thing meaneth."

They could not give an answer unknowing what reply to make, and as all held their peace the Speaking-Bird answered for them saying, "O King of the Age and the Time, dost thou deem it strange to see a dish of cucumbers stuffed with pearls? How much stranger then it is that thou wast not astonished to hear that the Queen thy Consort had, contrary to the laws of Allah's ordinance, given birth to such animals as dog and cat and musk-rat. This should have caused thee far more of wonder, for who hath ever heard of woman bearing such as these?"

Hereat the Shah made answer to the Speaking-Bird, "All that thou sayest is right indeed and I know that such things are not after the law of Almighty Allah; but I believed the reports of the midwives, the wise women who were with the Queen such time she was brought to bed, for they were not strangers but her own sisters, born of the same parents as herself. How then could I do otherwise than trust their words?"

Quoth the Speaking-Bird, "O King of kings, indeed the truth of the matter is not hidden from me. Albeit they be the sisters of thy Queen, yet seeing the royal favours and affection towards their cadette they were consumed with anger and hatred and despite by reason of their envy and jealousy. So they devised evil devices against her and their deceits at last succeeded in diverting thy thoughts from her, and in hiding her virtues from thy sight. Now are their malice and treason made manifest to thee; and, if thou require further proof, do thou summon them and question them of the case. They cannot hide it from thee and will be reduced to confess and crave thy pardon."

The Speaking-Bird also said to Khusrau Shah, "These two royal brothers so comely and stalwart and this lovely Princess, their sister, are thine own lawful children to whom the Queen thy Consort gave birth. The midwives, thy sisters-in-law, by reason of the blackness of their hearts and faces bore them away as soon as they were born: indeed every time a child was given to thee they wrapped it in a bit of blanket and putting it in a basket committed it to the stream which floweth by the palace to the intent that it might die an obscure death. But it so fortuned that the Intendant of thy royal gardens espied these baskets one and all as they floated past his grounds, and took charge of the infants he found therein. He then caused them to be nursed and reared with all care and, whilst they were growing up to man's estate, he looked to their being taught every art and science; and whilst his life endured he dealt with them and brought them up in love and tenderness as though they had been his very own. And now, O Khusrau Shah, wake from thy sleep of ignorance and heedlessness, and know that these two Princes Bahman and Parwez and the Princess Perizadah their sister are thine own issue and thy rightful heirs."

When the King heard these words and was assured of the purport being true and understood the evil doing of those Satans, his sisters-in-law, he said, "O Bird, I am indeed persuaded of thy soothfastness, for when I first saw these youths at the hunting-ground my bowels yearned with affection towards them and my heart felt constrained to love them as though they had been my own seed. Both they and their sister have drawn my affections to them as a magnet draweth iron: and the voice of blood crieth to me and compelleth me to confess the tie and to acknowledge that they are my true children, borne in the womb of my Queen, whose direful Destiny I have been the means of carrying out."

Then turning to the Princes and their sister he said with tearful eyes and broken voice, "Ye are my children and henceforth do ye regard me as your father."

At this they ran to him with rare delight and falling on his neck embraced him. Then they all sat down to meat and when they had finished eating, Khusrau Shah said to them, "O my children, I must now leave you, but Inshallah—Allah willing—I will come again to-morrow and bring with me the Queen your mother."

So saying he farewelled them fondly and mounting his horse departed to his palace; and no sooner had he seated himself upon his throne than

he summoned the Grand Wazir and commanded him saying, "Do thou send this instant and bind in heaviest bonds those vile women, the sisters of my Queen; for their ill deeds have at last come to light and they deserve to die the death of murtherers. Let the Sworder forthright make sharp his sword; for the ground thirsteth for their blood. Go see thyself that they are beheaded without stay or delay: await not other order, but instantly obey my commandment."

The Grand Wazir went forth at one and in his presence the Envious Sisters were decapitated and this underwent fit punishment for their malice and their evil doing. After this, Khusrau Shah with his retinue walked afoot to the Cathedral-mosque whereby the Queen had been imprisoned for so many years in bitter grief and tenderly embraced her. Then seeing her sad plight and her careworn countenance and wretched attire he wept and cried, "Allah Almighty forgive me this mine unjust and wrongful dealing towards thee. I have put to death thy sisters who deceitfully and despitefully raised my wrath and anger against thee, the innocent, the guiltless; and they have received due retribution for their misdeeds."

The King spake kindly and fondly to his Consort, and told her all that had betided him, and what the Speaking-Bird had made known to him, ending with these words, "Come now with me to the palace where thou shalt thee thy two sons and daughter grown up to become the loveliest of things. Hie with me and embrace them and take them to thy bosom, for they are our children, the light of our eyes. But first do thou repair to the Hammam and don thy royal robes and jewels."

Meanwhile tidings of these events were noised about the city how the King had at length shown due favour to the Queen, and had released her from bondage with his own hands and prayed forgiveness for the wrongs he had done to her; and how the Princes and the Princess had been proved to be her true-born children, and also how Khusrau Shah had punished her sisters who conspired against her; so joy and gladness prevailed both in city and kingdom, and all the folk blessed the Shah's Banu and cursed the Satanesses her sisters. And next day when the Queen had bathed in the Hammam and had donned royal dress and regal jewels, she went to meet her children together with the King who led up to her the Princes Bahman and Parwez and the Princess Perizadah and said, "See, here are thy children, fruit of thy womb and core of thy heart, thine own very sons and thy daughter: embrace them with all a mother's love and extend thy favour and affection to them even as I have done. When thou didst give them birth, thine ill-omened sisters bore them away from thee and cast them into yonder stream and said that thou hadst been delivered first of a puppy, then of a kitten and lastly of a musk-ratling. I cannot console myself for having credited their calumnies and the only recompense I can make is to place in thine embrace these three thou broughtest forth, and whom Allah Almighty hath restored to us and hath made right worthy to be called our children."

Then the Princes and Princess fell upon their mother's neck and fondly embraced her weeping tear-floods of joy. After this the Shah and the Banu sat down to meat together with their children; and when they had made an end of eating, King Khusrau Shah repaired to the garden with his Consort that he might show her the Singing-Tree and the fountain of Golden-Water, whereat the Queen was filled with wonder and delight. Next they turned to the belvedere and visited the Speaking-Bird of whom, as they sat at meat, the King had spoken to her in highest praise, and the Queen rejoiced in his sweet voice and melodious singing. And when they had seen all these things, the King mounted horse, Prince Bahman riding on his right hand and on his left Prince Parwez, while the Queen took Princess Perizadah with her inside her litter, and thus they set forth for the palace.

As the royal cavalcade passed the city walls and entered the capital with royal pomp and circumstance, the subjects who had heard the glad tidings thronged in multitudes to see their progress and volleyed shouts of acclamation; and as the lieges had grieved aforetime to see the Queen-consort imprisoned, so now they rejoiced with exceeding joy to find her free once more. But chiefly they marvelled to look upon the Speaking-Bird, for the Princess carried the cage with her, and as they rode along thousands of sweet-toned songsters came swarming round them from every quarter, and flew as an escort to the cage, filling the air with marvellous music; while flocks of others, perching upon the trees and the housetops, carolled and warbled as it were to greet their lord's cage accompanying the royal cavalcade. And when the palace was reached, the Shah and his Queen and his children sat down to a sumptuous banquet; and the city was illuminated, and everywhere dancings and merry-makings testified to the joy of the lieges; and for many days these revels and rejoicings prevailed throughout the capital and the kingdom where every man was blithe and happy and had feastings and festivities in his house.

After these festivals King Khusrau Shah made his elder son Bahman heir to his throne and kingdom and committed to his hands the affairs of state in their entirety, and the Prince administered affairs with such wisdom and success that the greatness and glory of the realm were increased twofold. The Shah also entrusted to his youngest son Parwez the charge of his army, both of horsemen and foot-soldiers; and Princess Perizadah was given by her sire in marriage to a puissant King who reigned over a mighty country; and lastly the Queen-mother forgot in perfect joy and happiness the pangs of her captivity. Destiny ever afterwards endowed them, one and all, with days the most delectable and they led the liefest of lives until at last there came to them the Destroyer of delights and the Sunderer of societies and the Depopulator of palaces and the Garnerer of graveyards and the Reaper for Resurrection-day, and they became as though they had never been. So laud be to the Lord who dieth not and who knoweth no shadow of change.

And as Scheherazade perceived the dawn of day, she ceased saying her permitted say. Quoth she "And this is all that hath come down to us of 'The Story of Two Sisters Who Were Jealous of Their Younger Sister.' But I have also heard, O King, a tale called 'Abu Kir the Dyer and Abu Sir the Barber.'"

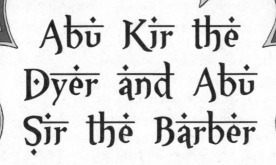

Abu Kir the Dyer and Abu Sir the Barber

*Quoth Scheherazade, "With joy and good greet,
it reached me O auspicious King, that…*

There dwelt once, in Alexandria city, two men, of whom one was a dyer, by name Abu Kir, and the other a barber Abu Sir; and they were neighbours in the market-street, where their shops stood side by side. The dyer was a swindler and a liar, an exceeding wicked wight, as if indeed his head-temples were hewn out of a boulder rock or fashioned of the threshold of a Jewish synagogue, nor was he ashamed of any shameful work he wrought amongst the folk. It was his wont, when any brought him cloth for staining, first to require of him payment under pretence of buying dyestuffs therewith.

So the customer would give him the wage in advance and wend his ways, and the dyer would spend all he received on meat and drink; after which he would sell the cloth itself as soon as ever its owner turned his back and waste its worth in eating and drinking and what not else, for he ate not but of the daintiest and most delicate viands nor drank but of the best of that which doth away the wit of man. And when the owner of the cloth came to him, he would say to him, "Return to me to-morrow before sunrise and thou shalt find thy stuff dyed."

So the customer would go away, saying to himself, "One day is near another day," and return next day at the appointed time, when the dyer would say to him, "Come to-morrow; yesterday I was not at work, for I had with me guests and was occupied with doing what their wants required till they went: but to-morrow before sunrise come and take thy cloth dyed." So he would fare forth and return on the third day, when Abu Kir would say to him, "Indeed yesterday I was excusable, for my wife was brought to bed in the night and all day I was busy with manifold matters; but to-morrow, without fail, come and take thy cloth dyed."

When the man came again at the appointed time, he would put him off with some other pretence, it mattered little what, and would swear to him; nor would he cease to promise and swear to him, as often as he came, till the customer lost patience and said, "How often wilt thou say to me, 'To-morrow?' Give me my stuff: I will not have it dyed." Whereupon the dyer would make answer, "By Allah, O my brother, I am abashed at thee; but I must tell the truth and may Allah harm all who harm folk in their goods!" The other would exclaim, "Tell me what hath happened;" and Abu Kir would reply, "As for thy stuff I dyed that same on matchless wise and hung it on the drying rope but 'twas stolen and I know not who stole it."

If the owner of the stuff were of the kindly he would say, "Allah will compensate me"; and if he were of the ill-conditioned, he would haunt him with exposure and insult, but would get nothing of him, though he complained of him to the judge. He ceased not doing thus till his report was noised abroad among the folk and each used to warn other against Abu Kir who became a byword amongst them. So they all held aloof from him and none would be entrapped by him save those who were ignorant of his character; but, for all this, he failed not daily to suffer insult and exposure from Allah's creatures.

By reason of this his trade became slack and he used to go to the shop of his neighbour the barber Abu Sir and sit there, facing the dyery and with his eyes on the door. Whenever he espied any one who knew him not standing at the dyery-door, with a piece of stuff in his hand, he would leave the barber's booth and go up to him saying, "What seekest thou, O thou?"; and the man would reply, "Take and dye me this thing." So the dyer would ask, "What colour wilt thou have it?" For, with all his knavish tricks his hand was in all manner of dyes; but he was never true to any one; wherefore poverty had gotten the better of him. Then he would take the stuff and say, "Give me my wage in advance and come to-morrow and take the stuff." So the stranger would advance him the money and wend his way; whereupon

Abu Kir would carry the cloth to the market-street and sell it and with its price buy meat and vegetables and tobacco and fruit and what not else he needed; but, whenever he saw any one who had given him stuff to dye standing at the door of his shop, he would not come forth to him or even show himself to him.

On this wise he abode years and years, till it fortuned one day that he received cloth to dye from a man of wrath and sold it and spent the proceeds. The owner came to him every day, but found him not in his shop; for, whenever he espied any one who had claim against him, he would flee from him into the shop of the barber Abu Sir. At last, that angry man finding that he was not to be seen and growing weary of such work, repaired to the Kazi and bringing one of his serjeants to the shop, nailed up the door, in presence of a number of Moslems, and sealed it, for that he saw therein naught save some broken pans of earthenware to stand him instead of his stuff; after which the serjeant took the key, saying to the neighbours, "Tell him to bring back this man's cloth then come to me and take his shop key"; and went his way, he and the man.

Then said Abu Sir to Abu Kir, "What ill business is this? Whoever bringeth thee aught thou losest it for him. What hath become of this angry man's stuff?"

Answered the dyer, "O my neighbour, 'twas stolen from me." "Prodigous!" exclaimed the barber. "Whenever any one giveth thee aught, a thief stealeth it from thee! Art thou then the meeting-place of every rogue upon town? But I doubt me thou liest: so tell me the truth." Replied Abu Kir, "O my neighbour, none hath stolen aught from me."

Asked Abu Sir, "What then dost thou with the people's property?" and the dyer answered, "Whenever any one giveth me aught to dye, I sell it and spend the price."

Quoth Abu Sir, "Is this permitted thee of Allah?" and quoth Abu Kir, "I do this only out of poverty, because business is slack with me and I am poor and have nothing." And he went on to complain to him of the dulness of his trade and his lack of means.

Abu Sir in like manner lamented the little profit of his own calling, saying, "I am a master of my craft and have not my equal in this city; but no one cometh to me to be polled, because I am a pauper; and I loathe this art and mystery, O my brother."

Abu Kir replied, "And I also loathe my own craft, by reason of its slackness; but, O my brother, what call is there for abiding in this town? Let us depart from it, I and thou, and solace ourselves in the lands of mankind, carrying in our hands our crafts which are in demand all the world over; so shall we breathe the air and rest from this grievous trouble." And he ceased not to commend travel to Abu Sir, till the barber became wishful to set out; so they agreed upon their route, at which decision Abu Kir rejoiced and improvised these lines:

> "Leave thy home for abroad an wouldst rise on high,
>   And travel whence benefits five-fold rise;
> The soothing of sorrow and winning of bread,
>   Knowledge, manners and commerce with good men and wise.
> An they say that in travel are travail and care,
>   And disunion of friends and much hardship that tries;
> Yet to generous youth death is better than life
>   In the house of contempt betwixt haters and spies."

When they agreed to travel together Abu Kir said to Abu Sir, "O my neighbour, we are become brethren and there is no difference between us, so it behoveth us to recite the Fatihah that he of us who gets work shall of his gain feed him who is out of work, and whatever is left, we will lay in a chest; and when we return to Alexandria, we will divide it fairly and equally."

"So be it," replied Abu Sir, and they repeated the Opening Chapter of the Koran on this understanding.

Then Abu Sir locked up his shop and gave the key to its owner, whilst Abu Kir left his door locked and sealed and let the key lie with the Kazi's serjeant; after which they took their baggage and embarked on the morrow in a galleon upon the salt sea. They set sail the same day and fortune attended them, for, of Abu Sir's great good luck, there was not a barber in the ship albeit it carried an hundred and twenty men, besides captain and crew. So, when they loosed the sails, the barber said to the dyer, "O my brother, this is the sea and we shall need meat and drink; we have but little provaunt with us and haply the voyage will be long upon us; wherefore methinks I will shoulder my budget and pass among the passengers, and may be some one will say to me, 'Come hither, O barber, and shave me,' and I will shave him for a scone or a silver bit or a draught of water: so shall we profit by this, I and thou too."

"There's no harm in that," replied the dyer and laid down his head and slept, whilst the barber took his gear and water-tasse and throwing over his shoulder a rag, to serve as napkin (because he was poor), passed among the passengers.

Quoth one of them, "Ho, master, come and shave me."

So he shaved him, and the man gave him a half-dirham; whereupon quoth Abu Sir, "O my brother, I have no use for this bit; hadst thou given me a scone 'twere more blessed to me in this sea, for I have a shipmate and we are short of provision."

So he gave him a loaf and a slice of cheese and filled him the tasse with sweet water. The barber carried all this to Abu Kir and said, "Eat the bread and cheese and drink the water."

Accordingly he ate and drank, whilst Abu Sir again took up his shaving gear and, tasse in hand and rag on shoulder, went round about the deck among the passengers. One man he shaved for two scones and another for a bittock of cheese, and he was in demand, because there was no other barber on board. Also he bargained with every one who said to him, "Ho, master, shave me!" for two loaves and a half dirham, and they gave him whatever he sought, so that, by sundown, he had collected thirty loaves and thirty silvers with store of cheese and olives and botargoes. And besides these he got from the passengers whatever he asked for and was soon in possession of things galore. Amongst the rest he shaved the Captain, to whom he complained of his lack of victual for the voyage, and the skipper said to him, "Thou art welcome to bring thy comrade every night and sup with me and have no care for that so long as ye sail with us."

Then he returned to the dyer, whom he found asleep; so he roused him; and when Abu Kir awoke, he saw at his head an abundance of bread and cheese and olives and botargoes and said, "Whence gottest thou all this?"

"From the bounty of Allah Almighty," replied Abu Sir. Then Abu Kir would have fallen to, but the barber said to him, "Eat not of this, O my brother; but leave it to serve us another time; for know that I shaved the Captain and complained to him of our lack of victual: whereupon quoth he, 'Welcome to thee! Bring thy comrade and sup both of ye with me every night.' And this night we sup with him for the first time."

But Abu Kir replied, "My head goeth round with sea-sickness and I cannot rise from my stead; so let me sup off these things and fare thou alone to the Captain."

Abu Sir replied, "There is no harm in that;" and sat looking at the other as he ate, and saw him hew off gobbets, as the quarryman heweth stone from the hill-quarries and gulp them down with the gulp of an elephant which hath not eaten for days, bolting another mouthful ere he had swallowed the previous one and glaring the while at that which was

before him with the glowering of a Ghul, blowing and blowing as bloweth the hungry bull over his beans and bruised straw.

Presently up came a sailor and said to the barber, "O craftsmaster, the Captain biddeth thee come to supper and bring thy comrade."

Quoth the barber to the dyer, "Wilt thou come with us?"; but quoth he, "I cannot walk."

So the barber went by himself and found the Captain sitting before a tray whereon were a score or more of dishes and all the company were awaiting him and his mate. When the Captain saw him he asked, "Where is thy friend?"; and Abu Sir answered, "O my lord, he is sea-sick."

Said the skipper, "That will do him no harm; his sickness will soon pass off; but do thou carry him his supper and come back, for we tarry for thee." Then he set apart a porringer of Kababs and putting therein some of each dish, till there was enough for ten, gave it to Abu Sir, saying, "Take this to thy chum."

He took it and carried it to the dyer, whom he found grinding away with his dog-teeth at the food which was before him, as he were a camel, and heaping mouthful on mouthful in his hurry. Quoth Abu Sir, "Did I not say to thee, 'Eat not of this'? Indeed the Captain is a kindly man. See what he hath sent thee, for that I told him thou wast sea-sick."

"Give it here," cried the dyer. So the barber gave him the platter, and he snatched it from him and fell upon his food, ravening for it and resembling a grinning dog or a raging lion or a Rukh pouncing on a pigeon or one well-nigh dead for hunger who seeing meat falls ravenously to eat. Then Abu Sir left him and going back to the Captain, supped and enjoyed himself and drank coffee with him; after which he returned to Abu Kir and found he had eaten all that was in the porringer and thrown it aside, empty. So he took it up and gave it to one of the Captain's servants, then went back to Abu Kir and slept till the morning.

On the morrow, he continued to shave, and all he got by way of meat and drink he gave to his shipmate, who ate and drank and sat still, rising not save to do what none could do for him, and every night the barber brought him a full porringer from the Captain's table. They fared thus twenty days until the galleon cast anchor in the harbour of a city; whereupon they took leave of the skipper and landing, entered the town and hired them a closet in a Khan. Abu Sir furnished it and buying a cooking pot and a platter and spoons and what else they needed, fetched meat and cooked it; but Abu Kir fell asleep the moment he entered the Caravanserai and awoke not till Abu Sir aroused him and set a tray of food before him. When he awoke, he ate and saying to Abu Sir, "Blame me not, for I am giddy," fell asleep again.

Thus he did forty days, whilst, every day, the barber took his gear and making the round of the city, wrought for that which fell to his lot, and returning, found the dyer asleep and aroused him. The moment he awoke he fell ravenously upon the food, eating as one who cannot have his fill nor be satisfied; after which he went asleep again. On this wise he passed other forty days and whenever the barber said to him, "Sit up and be comfortable and go forth and take an airing in the city, for 'tis a gay place and a pleasant and hath not its equal among the cities," he would reply, "Blame me not, for I am giddy."

Abu Sir cared not to hurt his feelings nor give him hard words; but, on the forty-first day, he himself fell sick and could not go abroad; so he engaged the porter of the Khan to serve them both, and he did the needful for them and brought them meat and drink whilst Abu Kir would do nothing but eat and sleep. The man ceased not to wait upon them on this wise for four days, at the end of which time the barber's malady redoubled on him, till he lost his senses for stress of sickness; and Abu Kir, feeling the sharp pangs of hunger, arose and sought in his comrade's clothes, where he found a thousand silver bits. He took them and, shutting the door of the closet upon Abu Sir, fared forth without telling any; and the doorkeeper was then at market and thus saw him not go out.

Presently Abu Kir betook himself to the bazar and clad himself in costly clothes, at a price of five hundred half-dirhams; then he proceeded to walk about the streets and divert himself by viewing the city which he found to be one whose like was not among cities; but he noted that all its citizens were clad in clothes of white and blue, without other colour.

Presently he came to a dyer's and seeing naught but blue in his shop, pulled out to him a kerchief and said, "O master, take this and dye it and win thy wage."

Quoth the dyer, "The cost of dyeing this will be twenty dirhams"; and quoth Abu Kir, "In our country we dye it for two."

"Then go and dye it in your own country! As for me, my price is twenty dirhams and I will not bate a little thereof."

"What colour wilt thou dye it?"

"I will dye it blue."

"But I want it dyed red."

"I know not how to dye red."

"Then dye it green."

"I know not how to dye green."

"Yellow."

"Nor yet yellow."

Thereupon Abu Kir went on to name the different tints to him, one after other, till the dyer said, "We are here in this city forty masterdyers, not one more nor one less; and when one of us dieth, we teach his son the craft. If he leave no son, we abide lacking one, and if he leave two sons, we teach one of them the craft, and if he die, we teach his brother. This our craft is strictly ordered, and we know how to dye but blue and no other tine whatsoever."

Then said Abu Kir, "Know that I too am a dyer and wot how to dye all colours; and I would have thee take me into thy service on hire, and I will teach thee everything of my art, so thou mayst glory therein over all the company of dyers."

But the dyer answered, "We never admit a stranger into our craft."

Asked Abu Kir, "And what if I open a dyery for myself?"; whereto the other answered, "We will not suffer thee to do that on any wise"; whereupon he left him and going to a second dyer, made him the like proposal; but he returned him the same answer as the first; and he ceased not to go from one to other, till he had made the round of the whole forty masters; but they would not accept him either to master or apprentice.

Then he repaired to the Shaykh of the Dyers and told him what had passed, and he said, "We admit no strangers into our craft."

Hereupon Abu Kir became exceeding wroth and going up to the King of that city, made complaint to him, saying, "O King of the age, I am a stranger and a dyer by trade"; and he told him whatso had passed between himself and the dyers of the town, adding, "I can dye various kinds of red, such as rose-colour and jujubel-colour and various kinds of green, such as grass-green and pistachio-green and olive and parrot's wing, and various kinds of black, such as coal-black and Kohl-black, and various shades of yellow, such as orange and lemon-colour," and went on to name to him the rest of the colours. Then said he, "O King of the age, all the dyers in thy city can not turn out of hand any one of these tincts, for they know not how to dye aught but blue; yet will they not admit me amongst them, either to master or apprentice."

Answered the King, "Thou sayst sooth for that matter, but I will open to thee a dyery and give thee capital and have thou no care anent them; for whoso offereth to do thee let or hindrance, I will hang him over his shop-door."

Then he sent for builders and said to them, "Go round about the city with this master-dyer, and whatsoever place pleaseth him, be it shop or Khan or what not, turn out its occupier and build him a dyery after his wish. Whatsoever he biddeth you, that do ye and oppose him not in aught."

And he clad him in a handsome suit and gave him two white slaves to serve him, and a horse with housings of brocade and a thousand dinars, saying, "Expend this upon thyself against the building be completed."

Accordingly Abu Kir donned the dress and mounting the horse, became as he were an Emir. Moreover the King assigned him a house and bade furnish it; so they furnished it for him.

On the morrow he mounted and rode through the city, whilst the architects went before him; and he looked about him till he saw a place which pleased him and said, "This stead is seemly"; whereupon they turned out the owner and carried him to the King, who gave him as the price of his holding, what contented him and more.

Then the builders fell to work, whilst Abu Kir said to them, "Build thus and thus and do this and that," till they built him a dyery that had not its like; whereupon he presented himself before the King and informed him that they had done building the dyery and that there needed but the price of the dye-stuffs and gear to set it going.

Quoth the King, "Take these four thousand dinars to thy capital and let me see the first fruits of thy dyery." So he took the money and went to the market where, finding dye-stuffs plentiful and well-nigh worthless, he bought all he needed of materials for dyeing; and the King sent him five hundred pieces of stuff, which he set himself to dye of all colours and then he spread them before the door of his dyery.

When the folk passed by the shop, they saw a wonder-sight whose like they had never in their lives seen; so they crowded about the entrance, enjoying the spectacle and questioning the dyer and saying, "O master, what are the names of these colours?" Quoth he, "This is red and that yellow and the other green" and so on, naming the rest of the colours. And they fell to bringing him longcloth and saying to him, "Dye it for us like this and that and take what hire thou seekest."

When he had made an end of dyeing the King's stuffs, he took them and went up with them to the Divan; and when the King saw them he rejoiced in them and bestowed abundant bounty on the dyer. Furthermore, all the troops brought him stuffs, saying, "Dye for us thus and thus;" and he dyed for them to their liking, and they threw him gold and silver. After this his fame spread abroad and his shop was called the Sultan's Dyery. Good

541

came in to him at every door and none of the other dyers could say a word to
him, but they used to come to him kissing his hands and excusing themselves
to him for past affronts they had offered him and saying, "Take us to thine
apprentices." But he would none of them for he had become the owner of
black slaves and handmaids and had amassed store of wealth.

On this wise fared it with Abu Kir; but as regards Abu Sir, after the
closet door had been locked on him and his money had been stolen, he
abode prostrate and unconscious for three successive days, at the end of
which the Concierge of the Khan, chancing to look at the door, observed
that it was locked and bethought himself that he had not seen and heard
aught of the two companions for some time. So he said in his mind, "Haply
they have made off, without paying rent, or perhaps they are dead, or what
is to do with them?" And he waited till sunset, when he went up to the door
and heard the barber groaning within. He saw the key in the lock; so he
opened the door and entering, found Abu Sir lying, groaning, and said to
him, "No harm to thee: where is thy friend?"

Replied Abu Sir, "By Allah, I came to my senses only this day and
called out; but none answered my call. Allah upon thee, O my brother, look
for the purse under my head and take from it five half-dirhams and buy me
somewhat nourishing, for I am sore anhungered."

The porter put out his hand and taking the purse, found it empty and
said to the barber, "The purse is empty; there is nothing in it."

Whereupon Abu Sir knew that Abu Kir had taken that which was therein
and had fled and he asked the porter, "Hast thou not seen my friend?"

Answered the doorkeeper, "I have not seen him these three days; and
indeed methought you had departed, thou and he."

The barber cried, "Not so; but he coveted my money and took it and
fled seeing me sick."

Then he fell a-weeping and a-wailing but the doorkeeper said to him,
"No harm shall befal thee, and Allah will requite him his deed."

So he went away and cooked him some broth, whereof he ladled out
a plateful and brought it to him; nor did he cease to tend him and maintain
him with his own monies for two months' space, when the barber sweated
and the Almighty made him whole of his sickness.

Then he stood up and said to the porter, "An ever the Most High
Lord enable me, I will surely requite thee of thy kindness to me; but none
requiteth save the Lord of His bounty!"

Answered the porter, "Praised be He for thy recovery! I dealt not thus
with thee but of desire for the face of Allah the Bountiful."

Then the barber went forth of the Khan and threaded the market-streets of the town, till Destiny brought him to the bazar wherein was Abu Kir's dyery, and he saw the vari-coloured stuffs dispread before the shop and a jostle of folk crowding to look upon them. So he questioned one of the townsmen and asked him, "What place is this and how cometh it that I see the folk crowding together?"; whereto the man answered, saying, "This is the Sultan's Dyery, which he set up for a foreigner Abu Kir hight; and whenever he dyeth new stuff, we all flock to him and divert ourselves by gazing upon his handiwork, for we have no dyers in our land who know how to stain with these colours; and indeed there befel him with the dyers who are in the city that which befel."

And he went on to tell him all that had passed between Abu Kir and the master-dyers and how he had complained of them to the Sultan who took him by the hand and built him that dyery and give him this and that: brief, he recounted to him all that had occurred. At this the barber rejoiced and said in himself, "Praised be Allah who hath prospered him, so that he is become a master of his craft! And the man is excusable, for of a surety he hath been diverted from thee by his work and hath forgotten thee; but thou actedst kindly by him and entreatedst him generously, what time he was out of work; so, when he seeth thee, he will rejoice in thee and entreat thee generously, even as thou entreatedst him."

According he made for the door of the dyery and saw Abu Kir seated on a high mattress spread upon a bench beside the doorway, clad in royal apparel and attended by four blackamoor slaves and four white Mamelukes all robed in the richest of raiment. Moreover, he saw the workmen, ten negro slaves, standing at work; for, when Abu Kir bought them, he taught them the craft of dyeing, and he himself sat amongst his cushions, as he were a Grand Wazir or a mighty monarch putting his hand to naught, but only saying to the men, "Do this and do that."

So the barber went up to him and stood before him, deeming he would rejoice in him when he saw him and salute him and entreat him with honour and make much of him; but, when eye fell upon eye, the dyer said to him, "O scoundrel, how many a time have I bidden thee stand not at the door of the workshop? Hast thou a mind to disgrace me with the folk, thief that thou art? Seize him."

So the blackamoors ran at him and laid hold of him; and the dyer rose up from his seat and said, "Throw him."

Accordingly they threw him down and Abu Kir took a stick and dealt him an hundred strokes on the back; after which they turned him over and

he beat him other hundred blows on his belly. Then he said to him, "O scoundrel, O villian, if ever again I see thee standing at the door of this dyery, I will forthwith send thee to the King, and he will commit thee to the Chief of Police, that he may strike thy neck. Begone, may Allah not bless thee!"

So Abu Sir departed from him, broken-hearted by reason of the beating and shame that had betided him; whilst the bystanders asked Abu Kir, "What hath this man done?"

He answered, "The fellow is a thief, who stealeth the stuffs of folk; he hath robbed me of cloth, how many a time! and I still said in myself, 'Allah forgive him!' He is a poor man; and I cared not to deal roughly with him; so I used to give my customers the worth of their goods and forbid him gently; but he would not be forbidden: and if he come again, I will send him to the King, who will put him to death and rid the people of his mischief." And the bystanders fell to abusing the barber after his back was turned.

Such was the behaviour of Abu Kir; but as regards Abu Sir, he returned to the Khan, where he sat pondering that which the dyer had done by him and he remained seated till the burning of the beating subsided, when he went out and walked about the markets of the city. Presently, he bethought him to go to the Hammam bath; so he said to one of the townsfolk, "O my brother, which is the way to the Baths?"

Quoth the man, "And what manner of thing may the Baths be?" and quoth Abu Sir, "'Tis a place where people wash themselves and do away their dirt and defilements, and it is of the best of the good things of the world."

Replied the townsman, "Get thee to the sea," but the barber rejoined, "I want the Hammam-baths."

Cried the other, "We know not what manner of this is the Hammam, for we all resort to the sea; even the King, when he would wash, betaketh himself to the sea."

When Abu Sir was assured that there was no bath in the city and that the folk knew not the Baths nor the fashion thereof, he betook himself to the King's Divan and kissing ground between his hands called down blessings on him and said, "I am a stranger and a Bath-man by trade, and I entered thy city and thought to go to the Hammam; but found not one therein. How cometh a city of this comely quality to lack a Hammam, seeing that the bath is of the highest of the delights of this world?"

Quoth the King, "What manner of thing is the Hammam?"

So Abu Sir proceeded to set forth to him the quality of the bath, saying, "Thy capital will not be a perfect city till there be a Hammam therein."

"Welcome to thee!" said the King and clad him in a dress that had not its like and gave him a horse and two blackamoor slaves, presently adding four handmaids and as many white Mamelukes: he also appointed him a furnished house and honoured him yet more abundantly than he had honoured the dyer. After this he sent builders with him saying to them, "Build him a Hammam in what place soever shall please him."

So he took them and went with them through the midst of the city, till he saw a stead that suited him. He pointed it out to the builders and they set to work, whilst he directed them, and they wrought till they builded him a Hammam that had not its like. Then he bade them paint it, and they painted it rarely, so that it was a delight to the beholders; after which Abu Sir went up to the King and told him that they had made an end of building and decorating the Hammam, adding, "There lacketh naught save the furniture." The King gave him ten thousand dinars wherewith he furnished the Bath and ranged the napkins on the ropes; and all who passed by the door stared at it and their mind confounded at its decorations.

So the people crowded to this spectacle, whose like they had never in their lives seen, and solaced themselves by staring at it and saying, "What is this thing?"

To which Abu Sir replied, "This is a Hammam"; and they marvelled thereat. Then he heated water and set the bath aworking, and he made a jetting fountain in the great basin, which ravished the wit of all who saw it of the people of the city. Furthermore, he sought of the King ten Mamelukes not yet come to manhood, and he gave him ten boys like moons; whereupon Abu Sir proceeded to shampoo them, saying, "Do in this wise with the bathers."

Then he burnt perfumes and sent out a crier to cry aloud in the city, saying, "O creatures of Allah, get ye to the Baths which be called the Sultan's Hammam!"

So the lieges came thither and Abu Sir bade the slave-boys wash their bodies. The folk went down into the tank and coming forth, seated themselves on the raised pavement, whilst the boys shampooed them, even as Abu Sir had taught them; and they continued to enter the Hammam and do their need therein gratis and go out, without paying, for the space of three days.

On the fourth day the barber invited the King, who took horse with his Grandees and rode to the Baths, where he put off his clothes and entered; then Abu Sir came in to him and rubbed his body with the bag-gloves, peeling from his skin dirt-rolls like lamp-wicks and showing them to the

King, who rejoiced therein, and clapping his hand upon his limbs heard them ring again for very smoothness and cleanliness; after which thorough washing Abu Sir mingled rose-water with the water of the tank and the King went down therein. When he came forth, his body was refreshed and he felt a lightness and liveliness such as he had never known in his life. Then the barber made him sit on the dais and the boys proceeded to shampoo him, whilst the censers fumed with the finest lign-aloes.

Then said the King, "O master is this the Hammam?"; and Abu Sir said, "Yes."

Quoth the King, "As my head liveth, my city is not become a city indeed but by this Bath," presently adding, "But what pay takest thou for each person?"

Quoth Abu Sir, "That which thou biddest will I take"; whereupon the King cried, "Take a thousand gold pieces for every one who washeth in thy Hammam."

Abu Sir, however, said, "Pardon, O King of the age! All men are not alike, but there are amongst them rich and poor, and if I take of each a thousand dinars, the Hammam will stand empty, for the poor man cannot pay this price."

Asked the King, "How then wilt thou do for the price!"; and the barber answered, "I will leave it to their generosity. Each who can afford aught shall pay that which his soul grudgeth not to give, and we will take from every man after the measure of his means. On this wise will the folk come to us and he who is wealthy shall give according to his station and he who is wealth-less shall give what he can afford. Under such condition the Hammam will still be at work and prosper exceedingly; but a thousand dinars is a Monarch's gift, and not every man can avail to this."

The Lords of the Realm confirmed Abu Sir's words, saying, "This is the truth, O King of the age! Thinkest thou that all folk are like unto thee, O glorious King?"

The King replied, "Ye say sooth; but this man is a stranger and poor and 'tis incumbent on us to deal generously with him, for that he hath made in our city this Hammam whose like we have never in our lives seen and without which our city were not adorned nor hath gotten importance; wherefore, an we favour him with increase of fee 'twill not be much."

But the Grandees said, "An thou wilt guerdon him be generous with thine own monies, and let the King's bounty be extended to the poor by means of the low price of the Hammam, so the lieges may bless thee; but, as for the thousand dinars, we are the Lords of thy Land, yet do our souls grudge to pay it; and how then should the poor be pleased to afford it?"

Quoth the King, "O my Grandees, for this time let each of you give him an hundred dinars and a Mameluke, a slave girl and a blackamoor"; and quoth they, "'Tis well; we will give it; but after to-day whoso entereth shall give him only what he can afford, without grudging."

"No harm in that," said the King; and they gave him the thousand gold pieces and three chattels. Now the number of the Nobles who were washed with the King that day was four hundred souls; so that the total of that which they gave him was forty thousand dinars, besides four hundred Mamelukes and a like number of negroes and slave-girls. Moreover the King gave him ten thousand dinars, besides ten white slaves and ten handmaidens and a like number of blackamoors; whereupon coming forward Abu Sir kissed the ground before him and said, "O auspicious Sovereign, lord of justice, what place will contain me all these women and slaves?"

Quoth the King, "O weak o'wit, I bade not my nobles deal thus with thee but that we might gather together unto thee wealth galore; for may be thou wilt bethink thee of thy country and family and repine for them and be minded to return to thy mother-land; so shalt thou take from our country muchel of money to maintain thyself withal, what while thou livest in thine own country."

And quoth Abu Sir, "O King of the age (Allah advance thee!), these white slaves and women and negroes befit only Kings and hadst thou ordered me ready money, it were more profitable to me than this army; for they must eat and drink and dress, and whatever betideth me of wealth, it will not suffice for their support."

The King laughed and said, "By Allah thou speakest sooth! They are indeed a mighty host, and thou hast not the wherewithal to maintain them; but wilt thou sell them to me for an hundred dinars a head?"

Said Abu Sir, "I sell them to thee at that price."

So the King sent to his treasurer for the coin and he brought it and gave Abu Sir the whole of the price without abatement and in full tale; after which the King restored the slaves to their owners, saying, "Let each of you who knoweth his slaves take them; for they are a gift from me to you."

So they obeyed his bidding and took each what belonged to him; whilst Abu Sir said to the King, "Allah ease thee, O King of the age, even as thou hast eased me of these Ghuls, whose bellies none may fill save Allah!" The King laughed, and said he spake sooth; then, taking the Grandees of his Realm from the Hammam returned to his palace; but the barber passed the night in counting out his gold and laying it up in bags and sealing them;

and he had with him twenty black slaves and a like number of Mamelukes and four slave girls to serve him.

Now when morning morrowed, he opened the Hammam and sent out a crier to cry, saying, "Whoso entereth the Baths and washeth shall give that which he can afford and which his generosity requireth him to give." Then he seated himself by the pay-chest and customers flocked in upon him, each putting down that which was easy to him, nor had eventide evened ere the chest was full of the good gifts of Allah the Most High.

Presently the Queen desired to go to the Hammam, and when this came to Abu Sir's knowledge, he divided the day on her account into two parts, appointing that between dawn and noon to men and that between midday and sundown to women. As soon as the Queen came, he stationed a handmaid behind the pay-chest; for he had taught four slave-girls the service of the Hammam, so that they were become expert bathwomen and tire-women. When the Queen entered, this pleased her and her breast waxed broad and she laid down a thousand dinars. Thus his report was noised abroad in the city, and all who entered the bath he entreated with honour, were they rich or poor; good came in upon him at every door and he made acquaintance with the royal guards and got him friends and intimates. The King himself used to come to him one day in every week, leaving with him a thousand dinars and the other days were for rich and poor alike; and he was wont to deal courteously with the folk and use them with the utmost respect.

It chanced that the King's sea-captain came in to him one day in the bath; so Abu Sir did off his dress and going in with him, proceeded to shampoo him and entreated him with exceeding courtesy. When he came forth, he made him sherbet and coffee; and when he would have given him somewhat, he swore that he would not accept him from aught. So the captain was under obligation to him, by reason of his exceeding kindness and courtesy and was perplexed how to requite the bath-man his generous dealing.

Thus fared it with Abu Sir: but as regards Abu Kir, hearing all the people recounting wonders of the Baths and saying, "Verily, this Hammam is the Paradise of this world! Inshallah, O such an one, thou shalt go with us to-morrow to this delightful bath," he said to himself, "Needs must I fare like the rest of the world, and see this bath that hath taken folk's wits."

So he donned his richest dress and mounting a she-mule and bidding the attendance of four white slaves and four blacks, walking before and behind him, he rode to the Hammam. When he alighted at the door, he smelt the scent of burning aloes-wood and found people going in and out and the benches full of great and small. So he entered the vestibule and saw Abu Sir, who rose to him and rejoiced in him: but the dyer said to him, "Is this the way of well-born men? I have opened me a dyery and am become master-dyer of the city and acquainted with the King and have risen to prosperity and authority: yet camest thou not to me nor askest of me nor saidst, 'Where's my comrade?' For my part I sought thee in vain and sent my slaves and servants to make search for thee in all the Khans and other places; but they knew not whither thou hadst gone, nor could any one give me tidings of thee."

Said Abu Sir, "Did I not come to thee and didst thou not make me out a thief and bastinado me and dishonour me before the world?" At this Abu Kir made a show of concern and asked, "What manner of talk is this? Was it thou whom I beat?"; and Abu Sir answered, "Yes, 'twas I."

Whereupon Abu Kir swore to him a thousand oaths that he knew him not and said, "There was a fellow like thee, who used to come every day and steal the people's stuff, and I took thee for him."

And he went on to pretend penitence, beating hand upon hand and saying, "There is no Majesty and there is no Might save in Allah, the Glorious, the Great? Indeed we have sinned against thee; but would that thou hadst discovered thyself to me and said, I am such an one! Indeed the fault is with thee, for that thou madest not thyself known unto me, more especially seeing that I was distracted for much business."

Replied Abu Sir, "Allah pardon thee, O my comrade! This was foreordained in the Secret Purpose, and reparation is with Allah. Enter and put off thy clothes and bathe at thine ease." Said the dyer, "I conjure thee, by Allah, O my brother, forgive me!"; and said Abu Sir, "Allah acquit thee of blame and forgive thee! Indeed this thing was decreed to me from all eternity."

Then asked Abu Kir, "Whence gottest thou this high degree?"; and answered Abu Sir, "He who prospered thee prospered me; for I went up to the King and described to him the fashion of the Hammam and he bade me build one."

And the dyer said, "Even as thou art beknown of the King, so also am I; and, Inshallah—God willing—I will make him love and favour thee more than ever, for my sake, he knoweth not that thou art my comrade, but I will acquaint him of this and commend thee to him."

But Abu Sir said, "There needeth no commendation; for He who moveth man's heart to love still liveth; and indeed the King and all his court affect me and have given me this and that."

And he told him the whole tale and said to him, "Put off thy clothes behind the chest and enter the Hammam, and I will go in with thee and rub thee down with the glove."

So he doffed his dress and Abu Sir, entering the bath with him, soaped him and gloved him and then dressed him and busied himself with his service till he came forth, when he brought him dinner and sherbets, whilst all the folk marvelled at the honour he did him. Then Abu Kir would have given him somewhat; but he swore that he would not accept aught from him and said to him, "Shame upon such doings! Thou art my comrade, and there is no difference between us."

Then Abu Kir observed, "By Allah, O my comrade, this is a mighty fine Hammam of thine, but there lacketh somewhat in its ordinance."

Asked Abu Sir, "And what is that?" and Abu Kir answered, "It is the depilatory, to wit, the paste compounded of yellow arsenic and quicklime which removeth the hair with comfort. Do thou prepare it and next time the King cometh, present it to him, teaching him how he shall cause the hair to fall off by such means, and he will love thee with exceeding love and honour thee."

Quoth Abu Sir, "Thou speakest sooth, and Inshallah, I will at once make it."

Then Abu Kir left him and mounted his mule and going to the King said to him, "I have a warning to give thee, O King of the age!"

"And what is thy warning?" asked the King; and Abu Kir answered, "I hear that thou hast built a Hammam."

Quoth the King, "Yes: there came to me a stranger and I builded the Baths for him, even as I builded the dyery for thee; and indeed 'tis a mighty fine Hammam and an ornament to my city"; and he went on to describe to him the virtues of the bath.

Quoth the dyer, "Hast thou entered therein?"; and quoth the King, "Yes."

Thereupon cried Abu Kir, "Alhamdolillah (praised be God) who save thee from the mischief of yonder villain and foe of the Faith, I mean the bathkeeper!"

The King enquired, "And what of him?"; and Abu Kir replied, "Know, O King of the age that, an thou enter the Hammam again, after this day, thou wilt surely perish."

"How so?" said the King; and the dyer said, "This bath-keeper is thy foe and the foe of the Faith, and he induced thee not to stablish this Bath but because he designed therein to poison thee. He hath made for thee somewhat and he will present it to thee when thou enterest the Hammam, saying, 'This is a drug which, if one apply to his parts below the waist, will remove the hair with comfort.' Now it is no drug, but a drastic dreg and a deadly poison; for the Sultan of the Christians hath promised this obscene fellow to release to him his wife and children, an he will kill thee; for they are prisoners in the hands of that Sultan. I myself was captive with him in their land, but I opened a dyery and dyed for them various colours, so that they conciliated the King's heart to me and he bade me ask a boon of him. I sought of him freedom and he set me at liberty, whereupon I made my way to this city and seeing yonder man in the Hammam, said to him, 'How didst thou effect thine escape and win free with thy wife and children?' Quoth he, 'We ceased not to be in captivity, I and my wife and children, till one day the King of the Nazarenes held a court whereat I was present, amongst a number of others; and as I stood amongst the folk, I heard them open out on the Kings and name them, one after other, till they came to the name of the King of this city, whereupon the King of the Christians cried out "Alas!" and said, "None vexeth me in the world, but the King of such a city! Whosoever will contrive me his slaughter I will give him all he shall ask." So I went up to him and said, "An I compass for thee his slaughter, wilt thou set me free, me and my wife and my children?" The King replied "Yes; and I will give thee to boot whatso thou shalt desire." So we agreed upon this and he sent me in a galleon to this city, where I presented myself to the King and he built me this Hammam. Now, therefore, I have nought to do but to slay him and return to the King of the Nazarenes, that I may redeem my children and my wife and ask a boon of him. Quoth I, 'And how wilt thou go about to kill him?'; and quoth he, 'By the simplest of all devices; for I have compounded him somewhat wherein is poison; so, when he cometh to the bath, I shall say to him, "Take this paste and anoint therewith thy parts below the waist for it will cause the hair to drop off." So he will take it and apply it to himself and the poison will work in him a day and a night, till it reacheth his heart and destroyeth him; and meanwhile I shall have made off and none will know that it was I slew him.'"

"When I heard this," added Abu Kir, "I feared for thee, my benefactor, wherefore I have told thee of what is doing."

As soon as the King heard the dyer's story, he was wroth with exceeding wrath and said to him, "Keep this secret." Then he resolved to visit the Hammam, that he might dispel doubt by supplying certainty; and when he entered, Abu Sir doffed his dress and betaking himself as of wont to the service of the King, proceeded to glove him; after which he said to him,

"O King of the age, I have made a drug which assisteth in plucking out the lower hair."

Cried the King, "Bring it to me": so the barber brought it to him and the King, finding it nauseous of smell, was assured that it was poison; wherefore he was incensed and called out to his guards, saying, "Seize him!"

Accordingly they seized him and the King donned his dress and returned to his palace, boiling with fury, whilst none knew the cause of his indignation; for, of the excess of his wrath he had acquainted no one therewith and none dared ask him. Then he repaired to the audience-chamber and causing Abu Sir to be brought before him, with his elbows pinioned, sent for his Sea-captain and said to him, "Take this villain and set him in a sack with two quintals of lime unslacked and tie its mouth over his head. Then lay him in a cock-boat and row out with him in front of my palace, where thou wilt see me sitting at the lattice. Do thou say to me, 'Shall I cast him in?' and if I answer, 'Cast him!' throw the sack into the sea, so the quick-lime may be slaked on him to the intent that he shall die drowned and burnt."

"Hearkening and obeying"; quoth the Captain and taking Abu Sir from the presence carried him to an island facing the King's palace, where he said to him, "Ho thou, I once visited thy Hammam and thou entreatedst me with honour and accomplishedst all my needs and I had great pleasure of thee: moreover, thou swarest that thou wouldst take no pay of me, and I love thee with a great love. So tell me how the case standeth between thee and the King and what abominable deed thou hast done with him that he is wroth with thee and hath commanded me that thou shouldst die this foul death."

Answered Abu Sir, "I have done nothing, nor weet I of any crime I have committed against him which meriteth this!"

Rejoined the Captain, "Verily, thou wast high in rank with the King, such as none ever won before thee, and all who are prosperous are envied. Haply some one was jealous of thy good fortune and threw out certain hints concerning thee to the King, by reason whereof he is become enraged against thee with rage so violent: but be of good cheer; no harm shall befal thee; for, even as thou entreatedst me generously, without acquaintanceship between me and thee, so now I will deliver thee. But, an if I release thee, thou must abide with me on this island till some galleon sail from our city to thy native land, when I will send thee thither therein."

Abu Sir kissed his hand and thanked him for that; after which the Captain fetched the quicklime and set it in a sack, together with a great stone, the size of a man, saying, "I put my trust in Allah!" Then he gave the barber a net, saying, "Cast this net into the sea, so haply thou mayst take somewhat of fish. For I am bound to supply the King's kitchen with fish every day; but to-day I have been distracted from fishing by this calamity which hath befallen thee, and I fear lest the cook's boys come to me in quest of fish and find none. So, an thou take aught, they will find it and thou wilt veil my face, whilst I go and play off my practice in front of the palace and feign to cast thee into the sea."

Answered Abu Sir, "I will fish the while; go thou and God help thee!" So the Captain set the sack in the boat and paddled till he came under the palace, where he saw the King seated at the lattice and said to him, "O King of the age, shall I cast him in?"

"Cast him!" cried the King, and signed to him with his hand, when lo and behold!; something flashed like leven and fell into the sea. Now that which had fallen into the water was the King's seal-ring; and the same was enchanted in such way that, when the King was wroth with any one and was minded to slay him, he had but to sign to him with his right hand, whereon was the signet-ring, and therefrom issued a flash of lightning, which smote the object, and thereupon his head fell from between his shoulders; and the troops obeyed him not, nor did he overcome the men of might save by means of the ring. So, when it dropped from his finger, he concealed the matter and kept silence, for that dared not say, "My ring is fallen into the sea," for fear of the troops, lest they rise against him and slay him.

On this wise it befel the King; but as regards Abu Sir, after the Captain had left him on the island he took the net and casting it into the sea presently drew it up full of fish; nor did he cease to throw it and pull it up full, till there was a great mound of fish before him. So he said in himself, "By Allah, his long while I have not eaten fish!"; and chose himself a large fat fish, saying, "When the Captain cometh back, I will bid him fry it for me, so I may dine on it."

Then he cut its throat with a knife he had with him; but the knife stuck in its gills and there he saw the King's signet-ring; for the fish had swallowed it and Destiny had driven it to that island, where it had fallen into the net. He took the ring and drew it on his little finger, not knowing its peculiar properties.

Presently, up came two of the cook's boys in quest of fish and seeing Abu Sir, said to him, "O man, whither is the Captain gone?"

"I know not," said he and signed to them with his right hand; when, behold, the heads of both underlings dropped off from between their

shoulders. At this Abu Sir was amazed and said, "Would I wot who slew them!" And their case was grievous to him and he was still pondering it, when the Captain suddenly returned and seeing the mound of fishes and two men lying dead and the seal-ring on Abu Sir's finger, said to him, "O my brother, move not thy hand whereon is the signet-ring; else thou wilt kill me."

Abu Sir wondered at this speech and kept his hand motionless; whereupon the Captain came up to him and said, "Who slew these two men?"

"By Allah, O my brother I wot not!"

"Thou sayst sooth; but tell me whence hadst thou that ring?"

"I found it in this fish's gills."

"True," said the Captain, "for I saw it fall flashing from the King's palace and disappear in the sea, what time he signed towards thee, saying, 'Cast him in.' So I cast the sack into the water, and it was then that the ring slipped from his finger and fell into the sea, where this fish swallowed it, and Allah drave it to thee, so that thou madest it thy prey, for this ring was thy lot; but kennest thou its property?"

Said Abu Sir, "I knew not that it had any properties peculiar to it"; and the Captain said, "Learn, then, that the King's troops obey him not save for fear of this signet-ring, because it is spelled, and when he was wroth with any one and had a mind to kill him, he would sign at him therewith and his head would drop from between his shoulders; for there issued a flash of lightning from the ring and its ray smote the object of his wrath, who died forthright."

At this, Abu Sir rejoiced with exceeding joy and said to the Captain, "Carry me back to the city"; and he said, "That will I, now that I no longer fear for thee from the King; for, wert thou to sign at him with thy hand, purposing to kill him, his head would fall down between thy hands; and if thou be minded to slay him and all his host, thou mayst slaughter them without let or hindrance."

So saying, he embarked him in the boat and bore him back to the city. Abu Sir landed and going up to the palace, entered the council-chamber, where he found the King seated facing his officers, in sore cark and care by reason of the seal-ring and daring not tell any of his folk anent its loss.

When he saw Abu Sir, he said to him, "Did we not cast thee into the sea? How hast thou contrived to come forth of it?"

Abu Sir replied, "O King of the age, whenas thou badest throw me into the sea, thy Captain carried me to an island and asked me of the cause of thy wrath against me, saying, 'What hast thou done with the King,

that he should decree thy death?' I answered, 'By Allah, I know not that
I have wrought him any wrong!' Quoth he, 'Thou wast high in rank with
the King, and haply some one envied thee and threw out certain hints
concerning thee to him, so that he is become incensed against thee. But
when I visited thee in thy Hammam, thou entreatedst me honourably, and
I will requite thee thy hospitality to me by setting thee free and sending thee
back to thine own land.' Then he set a great stone in the sack in my stead
and cast it into the sea; but, when thou signedst to him to throw me in,
thy seal-ring dropped from thy finger into the main, and a fish swallowed
it. Now I was on the island a-fishing, and this fish came up in the net with
the others; whereupon I took it, intending to broil it; but, when I opened
its belly, I found the signet-ring therein; so I took it and put it on my finger.
Presently, up came two of the servants of the kitchen, questing fish, and I
signed to them with my hand, knowing not the property of the seal-ring,
and their heads fell off. Then the Captain came back, and seeing the ring
on my finger, acquainted me with its spell; and behold, I have brought it
back to thee, for that thou dealtest kindly by me and entreatedst me with the
utmost honour, nor is that which thou hast done me of kindness lost upon
me. Here is thy ring; take it! But an I have done with thee aught deserving
of death, tell me my crime and slay me and thou shalt be absolved of sin
in shedding my blood."

So saying, he pulled the ring from his finger and gave it to the King
who, seeing Abu Sir's noble conduct, took the ring and put it on and felt life
return to him afresh. Then he rose to his feet and embracing the barber,
said to him, "O man, thou art indeed of the flower of the well-born! Blame
me not, but forgive me the wrong I have done thee. Had any but thou
gotten hold of this ring, he had never restored it to me."

Answered Abu Sir, "O King of the age, an thou wouldst have me
forgive thee, tell me what was my fault which drew down thine anger upon
me, so that thou commandedst to do me die."

Rejoined the King, "By Allah, 'tis clear to me that thou art free and
guiltless in all things of offence since thou hast done this good deed; only
the dyer denounced thee to me in such and such words"; and he told him
all that Abu Kir had said.

Abu Sir replied, "By Allah, O King of the age, I know no King of
the Nazarenes nor during my days have ever journeyed to a Christian
country, nor did it ever come into my mind to kill thee. But this dyer was my
comrade and neighbour in the city of Alexandria where life was straitened
upon us; therefore we departed thence, to seek our fortunes, by reason of

the narrowness of our means at home, after we had recited the Opening Chapter of the Koran together, pledging ourselves that he who got work should feed him who lacked work; and there befel me with him such and such things."

Then he went on to relate to the King all that had betided him with Abu Kir the dyer; how he had robbed him of his dirhams and had left him alone and sick in the Khan-closet and how the door-keeper had fed him of his own monies till Allah recovered him of his sickness, when he went forth and walked about the city with his budget, as was his wont, till he espied a dyery, about which the folk were crowding; so he looked at the door and seeing Abu Kir seated on a bench there, went in to salute him, whereupon he accused him of being a thief and beat him a grievous beating; brief, he told him his whole tale, from first to last, and added, "O King of the age, 'twas he who counselled me to make the depilatory and present it to thee, saying, 'The Hammam is perfect in all things but that it lacketh this'; and know, O King of the age, that this drug is harmless and we use it in our land where 'tis one of the requisites of the bath; but I had forgotten it: so, when the dyer visited the Hammam I entreated him with honour and he reminded me of it, and enjoined me to make it forthwith. But do thou send after the porter of such a Khan and the workmen of the dyery and question them all of that which I have told thee."

Accordingly the King sent for them and questioned them one and all and they acquainted him with the truth of the matter. Then he summoned the dyer, saying, "Bring him barefooted, bareheaded and with elbows pinioned!"

Now he was sitting in his house, rejoicing in Abu Sir's death; but ere he could be ware, the King's guards rushed in upon him and cuffed him on the nape, after which they bound him and bore him into the presence, where he saw Abu Sir seated by the King's side and the door-keeper of the Khan and workmen of the dyery standing before him. Quoth the door-keeper to him, "Is not this thy comrade whom thou robbedst of his silvers and leftest with me sick in the closet doing such and such by him?"

And the workmen said to him, "Is not this he whom thou badest us seize and beat?"

Therewith Abu Kir's baseness was made manifest to the King and he was certified that he merited torture yet sorer than the torments of Munkar and Nakir. So he said to his guards, "Take him and parade him about the city and the market-streets; then set him in a sack and cast him into the sea."

Whereupon quoth Abu Sir, "O King of the age, accept my intercession for him, for I pardon him all he hath done with me."

But quoth the King, "An thou pardon him all his offences against thee, I cannot pardon him his offences against me."

And he cried out, saying, "Take him." So they took him and paraded him about the city, after which they set him in a sack with quicklime and cast him into the sea, and he died, drowned and burnt.

Then said the King to the barber, "O Abu Sir, ask of me what thou wilt and it shall be given thee."

And he answered, saying, "I ask of thee to send me back to my own country, for I care no longer to tarry here." Then the King gifted him great store of gifts, over and above that which he had whilome bestowed on the crew of this galleon were Mamelukes; so he gave him these also, after offering to make him his Wazir whereto the barber consented not. Presently he farewelled the King and set sail in his own ship manned by his own crew; nor did he cast anchor till he reached Alexandria and made fast to the shore there. Then he landed and one of his Mamelukes, seeing a sack on the beach, said to Abu Sir, "O my lord, there is a great heavy sack on the sea-shore, with the mouth tied up and I know not what therein." So Abu Sir came up and opening the sack, found therein the remains of Abu Kir, which the sea had borne thither. He took it forth and burying it near Alexandria, built over the grave a place of visitation and endowed it with mortmain writing over the door these couplets:

> Man is known among me as his deeds attest;
> Which make noble origin manifest:
> Backbite not, lest other men bite thy back;
> Who saith aught, the same shall to him be addrest:
> Shun immodest words and indecent speech
> When thou speakest in earnest or e'en in jest.
> We bear with the dog which behaves itself
> But the lion is chained lest he prove a pest:
> And the desert carcases swim the main
> While union-pearls on the sandbank rest:
> No sparrow would hustle the sparrow-hawk,
> Were it not by folly and weakness prest:
> A-sky is written on page of air
> 'Who doth kindly of kindness shall have the best!'
> 'Ware of gathering sugar from bitter gourd:

'Twill prove to its origin like in taste.

After this Abu Sir abode awhile, till Allah took him to Himself, and they buried him hard by the tomb of his comrade Abu Kir; wherefore that place was called Abu Kir and Abu Sir; but it is now known as Abu Kir only. This, then, is that which hath reached us of their history, and glory be to Him who endureth for ever and aye and by whose will interchange the night and the day.

When Scheherazade ceased speaking Dunyazad exclaimed, "O my own sister, by Allah in very sooth this is a right pleasant tale and a delectable; never was heard the like of it, but prithee tell me now another story to while away what yet remaineth of the waking hours of this our night." She replied, "With love and gladness if the King give me leave, I will tell the tale of 'Judar and His Brethren.'"

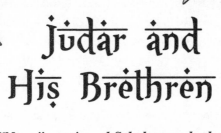

Judar and His Brethren

"Now," continued Scheherazade the next evening, "I have another tale to tell anent Judar and his two brothers...

There was once a man and a merchant named Omar and he had for issue three sons, the eldest called Sálim, the youngest Judar, and the cadet Salím. He reared them all till they came to man's estate, but the youngest he loved more than his brothers, who seeing this, waxed jealous of Judar and hated him. Now when their father, who was a man shotten in years, saw that his two eldest sons hated their brother, he feared lest after his death trouble should befall him from them. So he assembled a company of his kinsfolk, together with divers men of learning and property distributors of the Kazi's court, and bidding bring all his monies and cloth, said to them, "O folk, divide ye this money and stuff into four portions according to the law." They did so, and he gave one part to each of his sons and kept the fourth himself, saying, "This was my good and I have divided it among them in my lifetime; and this that I have kept shall be for my wife, their mother, wherewithal to provide for her subsistence whenas she shall be a widow."

A little while after this he died, and neither of the two elder brothers was content with his share, but sought more of Judar, saying, "Our father's wealth is in thy hands." So he appealed to the judges; and the Moslems who had been present at the partition came and bore witness of that which they knew, wherefore the judge forbade them from one another; but Judar and his brothers wasted much money in bribes to him. After this, the twain left him awhile; presently, however, they began again to plot against him and he appealed a second time to the magistrate, who once more decided in his favour; but all three lost much money which went to the judges. Nevertheless Sálim and Salím forbore not to seek his hurt and to carry the case from court to court, he and they losing till they had given all their good for food to the oppressors and they became poor, all three.

Then the two elder brothers went to their mother and flouted her and beat her, and seizing her money drove her away. So she betook herself to her son Judar and told him how his brothers had dealt with her and fell to cursing the twain.

Said he, "O my mother, do not curse them, for Allah will requite each of them according to his deed. But, O mother mine, see, I am become poor, and so are my brethren, for strife occasioneth loss ruin-rife, and we have striven amain, and fought, I and they, before the judges, and it hath profited us naught: nay, we have wasted all our father left us and are disgraced among the folk by reason of our testimony one against other. Shall I then contend with them anew on thine account and shall we appeal to the judges? This may not be! Rather do thou take up thine abode with me, and the scone I eat I will share with thee. Do thou pray for me and Allah will give me the means of thine alimony. Leave them to receive of the Almighty the recompense of their deed, and console thyself with the saying of the poet who said:

> "'If a fool oppress thee bear patiently;
> And from Time expect thy revenge to see:
> Shun tyranny; for if mount oppressed
> A mount, 'twould be shattered by tyranny.'"

And he soothed and comforted her till she consented and took up her dwelling with him. Then he gat him a net and went a-fishing every day in the river or the banks about Bulak and old Cairo or some other place in which there was water; and one day he would earn ten coppers, another twenty and another thirty, which he spent upon his mother and himself, and they ate well and drank well. But, as for his brothers, they plied no craft

and neither sold nor bought; misery and ruin and overwhelming calamity
entered their houses and they wasted that which they had taken from
their mother and became of the wretched naked beggars. So at times they
would come to their mother, humbling themselves before her exceedingly
and complaining to her of hunger; and she (a mother's heart being pitiful)
would give them some mouldy, sour smelling bread or, if there were any
meat cooked the day before, she would say to them, "Eat it quick and go
ere your brother come; for 'twould be grievous to him and he would harden
his heart against me, and ye would disgrace me with him." So they would
eat in haste and go.

One day among days they came in to their mother, and she set cooked
meat and bread before them. As they were eating, behold, in came their
brother Judar, at whose sight the parent was put to shame and confusion,
fearing lest he should be wroth with her; and she bowed her face earthwards
abashed before her son. But he smiled in their faces, saying, "Welcome, O
my brothers! A blessed day! How comes it that ye visit me this blessed day?"
Then he embraced them both and entreated them lovingly, saying to them,
"I thought not that ye would have left me desolate by your absence nor that
ye would have forborne to come and visit me and your mother."

Said they, "By Allah, O our brother, we longed sore for thee and
naught withheld us but abashment because of what befell between us and
thee; but indeed we have repented much. 'Twas Satan's doing, the curse of
Allah the Most High be upon him! And now we have no blessing but thyself
and our mother."

"And I have no blessing but you twain," said Judar.

And his mother exclaimed, "Allah whiten thy face, and increase thy
prosperity, for thou art the most generous of us all, O my son!"

Then he said "Welcome to you both! Abide with me; for the Lord is
bountiful and good aboundeth with me." So he made peace with them,
and they supped and righted with him; and next morning, after they had
broken their fast, Judar shouldered his net and went out, trusting in The
Opener whilst the two others also went forth and were absent till midday,
when they returned and their mother set the noon meal before them.

At nightfall Judar came home, bearing meat and greens, and they
abode on this wise a month's space, Judar catching fish and selling it and
spending their price on his mother and his brothers, and these eating and
frolicking till, one day, it chanced he went down to the river bank and
throwing his net, brought it up empty. He cast it a second time, but again
it came up empty and he said in himself, "No fish in this place!" So he

removed to another and threw the net there, but without avail. And he ceased not to remove from place to place till night fall, but caught not a single sprat and said to himself, "Wonderful! Hath the fish fled the river or what?" Then he shouldered the net and made for home, chagrined, concerned, feeling for his mother and brothers and knowing not how he should feed them that night.

Presently, he came to a baker's oven and saw the folk crowding for bread, with silver in their hands, whilst the baker took no note of them. So he stood there sighing, and the baker said to him, "Welcome to thee, O Judar! Dost thou want bread?"

But he was silent and the baker continued, "An thou have no dirhams, take thy sufficiency and thou shalt get credit."

So Judar said, "Give me ten coppers' worth of bread and take this net in pledge."

Rejoined the baker, "Nay, my poor fellow, the net is thy gate of earning thy livelihood, and if I take it from thee, I shall close up against thee the door of thy subsistence. Take thee ten Nusfs' worth of bread and take these other ten, and to-morrow bring me fish for the twenty."

"On my head and eyes be it!" quoth Judar and took the bread and money saying, "To-morrow the Lord will dispel the trouble of my case and will provide me the means of acquittance." Then he bought meat and vegetables and carried them home to his mother, who cooked them and they supped and went to bed.

Next morning he arose at daybreak and took the net, and his mother said to him, "Sit down and break thy fast."

But he said, "Do thou and my brothers break fast," and went down to the river about Bulak where he ceased not to cast once, twice, thrice; and to shift about all day, without aught falling to him, till the hour of mid-afternoon prayer, when he shouldered his net and went away sore dejected. His way led him perforce by the booth of the baker who, when he saw him counted out to him the loaves and the money, saying, "Come, take it and go; an it be not to-day, 'twill be to-morrow."

Judar would have excused himself, but the baker said to him, "Go! There needeth no excuse; an thou had netted aught, it would be with thee; so seeing thee empty-handed, I knew thou hadst gotten naught; and if to-morrow thou have no better luck, come and take bread and be not abashed, for I will give thee credit."

So Judar took the bread and money and went home. On the third day also he sallied forth and fished from tank to tank until the time of afternoon prayer, but caught nothing; so he went to the baker and took the bread and silver as usual. On this wise he did seven days running, till he became disheartened and said in himself, "To-day I go to the Lake Karun."

So he went thither and was about to cast his net, when there came up to him unawares a Maghrabi, a Moor, clad in splendid attire and riding a she-mule with a pair of gold embroidered saddle bags on her back and all her trappings also orfrayed. The Moor alighted and said to him, "Peace be upon thee, O Judar, O son of Omar!"

"And on thee likewise be peace, O my lord the pilgrim!" replied the fisherman. Quoth the Maghrabi, "O Judar, I have need of thee and, given thou obey me, thou shalt get great good and shalt be my companion and manage my affairs for me."

Quoth Judar, "O my lord, tell me what is in thy mind and I will obey thee, without demur."

Said the Moor, "Repeat the Fatihah, the Opening Chapter of the Koran."

So he recited it with him and the Moor bringing out a silken cord, said to Judar, "Pinion my elbows behind me with this cord, as fast as fast can be, and cast me into the lake; then wait a little while; and, if thou see me put forth my hands above the water, raising them high ere my body show, cast thy net over me and drag me out in haste; but if thou see me come up feet foremost, then know that I am dead; in which case do thou leave me and take the mule and saddle bags and carry them to the merchants' bazaar, where thou wilt find a Jew by name Shamayah. Give him the mule and he will give thee an hundred dinars, which do thou take and go thy ways and keep the matter secret with all secrecy."

So Judar tied his arms tightly behind his back and he kept saying, "Tie tighter." Then said he "Push me till I fall into the lake"; so he pushed him in and he sank. Judar stood waiting some time till, behold, the Moor's feet appeared above the water, whereupon he knew that he was dead. So he left him and drove the mule to the bazaar, where seated on a stool at the door of his storehouse he saw the Jew who spying the mule, cried, "In very sooth the man hath perished," adding, "and naught undid him but covetise." Then he took the mule from Judar and gave him an hundred dinars, charging him to keep the matter secret.

So Judar went and bought what bread he needed, saying to the baker, "Take this gold piece!"; and the man summed up what was due to him and said, "I still owe thee two days' bread."

"Good," said Judar, and went on to the butcher, to whom he gave a gold

piece and took meat, saying, "Keep the rest of the dinar on account."

Then he bought vegetables and going home, found his brothers importuning their mother for victual, whilst she cried, "Have patience till your brother come home, for I have naught." So he went in to them and said, "Take and eat;" and they fell on the food like cannibals. Then he gave his mother the rest of his gold saying, "If my brothers come to thee, give them wherewithal to buy food and eat in my absence."

He slept well that night and next morning he took his net and going down to Lake Karun stood there and was about to cast his net, when behold, there came up to him a second Maghribi, riding on a she-mule more handsomely accoutred than he of the day before and having with him a pair of saddle bags of which each pocket contained a casket.

"Peace be with thee, O Judar!" said the Moor: "And with thee be peace, O my lord, the pilgrim!" replied Judar. Asked the Moor, "Did there come to thee yesterday a Moor riding on a mule like this of mine?"

Hereat Judar was alarmed and answered, "I saw none," fearing lest the other say, "Whither went he?" and if he replied, "He was drowned in the lake," that haply he should charge him with having drowned him; wherefore he could not but deny.

Rejoined the Moor, "Hark ye, O unhappy! this was my brother, who is gone before me."

Judar persisted, "I know naught of him." Then the Moor enquired, "Didst thou not bind his arms behind him and throw him into the lake, and did he not say to thee, 'If my hands appear above the water first, cast thy net over me and drag me out in haste; but, if my feet show first, know that I am dead and carry the mule to the Jew Shamayah, who shall give thee an hundred dinars?'"

Quoth Judar, "Since thou knowest all this why and wherefore dost thou question me?"; and quoth the Moor, "I would have thee do with me as thou didst with my brother."

Then he gave him a silken cord, saying, "Bind my hands behind me and throw me in, and if I fare as did my brother, take the mule to the Jew and he will give thee other hundred dinars."

Said Judar, "Come on"; so he came and he bound him and pushed him into the lake, where he sank. Then Judar sat watching and after awhile, his feet appeared above the water and the fisher said, "He is dead and damned! Inshallah, may Maghribis come to me every day, and I will pinion them and push them in and they shall die; and I will content me with an hundred dinars for each dead man."

Then he took the mule to the Jew, who seeing him asked, "The other is dead?"

Answered Judar, "May thy head live!"; and the Jew said, "This is the reward of the covetous!" Then he took the mule and gave Judar an hundred dinars, with which he returned to his mother.

"O my son," said she, "whence hast thou this?" So he told her, and she said, "Go not again to Lake Karun, indeed I fear for thee from the Moors."

Said he, "O my mother, I do but cast them in by their own wish, and what am I to do? This craft bringeth me an hundred dinars a day and I return speedily; wherefore, by Allah, I will not leave going to Lake Karun, till the race of the Magharibah is cut off and not one of them is left."

So, on the morrow which was the third day, he went down to the lake and stood there, till there came up a third Moor, riding on a mule with saddle bags and still more richly accoutred than the first two, who said to him, "Peace be with thee, O Judar, O son of Omar!"

And the fisherman saying in himself, "How comes it that they all know me?" returned his salute.

Asked the Maghribi, "Have any Moors passed by here?"

"Two," answered Judar. "Whither went they?" enquired the Moor, and Judar replied, "I pinioned their hands behind them and cast them into the lake, where they were drowned, and the same fate is in store for thee."

The Moor laughed and rejoined, saying, "O unhappy! Every life hath its term appointed." Then he alighted and gave the fisherman the silken cord, saying, "Do with me, O Judar, as thou didst with them."

Said Judar, "Put thy hands behind thy back, that I may pinion thee, for I am in haste, and time flies."

So he put his hands behind him and Judar tied him up and cast him in. Then he waited awhile; presently the Moor thrust both hands forth of the water and called out to him, saying, "Ho, good fellow, cast out thy net!"

So Judar threw the net over him and drew him ashore, and lo! in each hand he held a fish as red as coral. Quoth the Moor, "Bring me the two caskets that are in the saddle bags."

So Judar brought them and opened them to him, and he laid in each casket a fish and shut them up. Then he pressed Judar to his bosom and kissed him on the right cheek and the left, saying, "Allah save thee from all stress! By the Almighty, hadst thou not cast the net over me and pulled me out, I should have kept hold of these two fishes till I sank and was drowned, for I could not get ashore of myself."

Quoth Judar, "O my lord the pilgrim, Allah upon thee, tell me the true history of the two drowned men and the truth anent these two fishes and the Jew."

The Maghribi answered, "Know, O Judar, that these drowned men were my two brothers, by name Abd al-Salam and Abd al-Ahad. My own name is Abd al-Samad, and the Jew also is our brother; his name is Abd al-Rahim and he is no Jew but a true believer of the Maliki school. Our father, whose name was Abd al-Wadud, taught us magic and the art of solving mysteries and bringing hoards to light, and we applied ourselves thereto, till we compelled the Ifrits and Marids of the Jinn to do us service. By and by, our sire died and left us much wealth, and we divided amongst us his treasures and talismans, till we came to the books, when we fell out over a volume called 'The Fables of the Ancients,' whose like is not in the world, nor can its price be paid of any, nor is its value to be evened with gold and jewels; for in it are particulars of all the hidden hoards of the earth and the solution of every secret.

"Our father was wont to make use of this book, of which we had some small matter by heart, and each of us desired to possess it, that he might acquaint himself with what was therein. Now when we fell out there was in our company an old man by name Cohen Al-Abtan, who had reared our sire and taught him divination and gramarye, and he said to us, 'Bring me the book.' So we gave it him and he continued, 'Ye are my son's sons, and it may not be that I should wrong any of you. So whoso is minded to have the volume, let him address himself to achieve the treasure of Al-Shamardal and bring me the celestial planisphere and the Kohl phial and the seal ring and the sword. For the ring hath a Marid that serveth it called Al-Ra'ad al-Kasif; and whoso hath possession thereof, neither King nor Sultan may prevail against him; and if he will, he may therewith make himself master of the earth, in all the length and breadth thereof. As for the brand, if its bearer draw it and brandish it against an army, the army will be put to the rout; and if he say the while, "Slay yonder host," there will come forth of that sword lightning and fire, that will kill the whole many. As for the planisphere, its possessor hath only to turn its face toward any country, east or west, with whose sight he hath a mind to solace himself, and therein he will see that country and its people, as they were between his hands and he sitting in his place; and if he be wroth with a city and have a mind to burn it, he hath but to face the planisphere towards the sun's disc, saying, 'Let such a city be burnt,' and that city will be consumed with fire. As for the Kohl phial, whoso pencilleth his eyes therefrom, he shall espy all the treasures of the earth.

And I make this condition with you which is that whoso faileth to hit upon the hoards shall forfeit his right; and that none save he who shall achieve the treasure and bring me the four precious things which be therein shall have any claim to take this book.'

"So we all agreed to this condition, and he continued, 'O my sons, know that the treasure of Al-Shamardal is under the commandment of the sons of the Red King, and your father told me that he had himself essayed to open the treasure, but could not; for the sons of the Red King fled from him into the land of Egypt and took refuge in a lake there, called Lake Karun, whither he pursued them, but could not prevail over them, by reason of their stealing into that lake, which was guarded by a spell.'"

"'So your father returned empty handed and unable to win to his wish; and after failing he complained to me of his ill-success, whereupon I drew him an astrological figure and found that the treasure could be achieved only by means of a young fisherman of Cairo, hight Judar bin Omar, the place of foregathering with whom was at Lake Karun, for that he should be the means of capturing the sons of the Red King and that the charm would not be dissolved, save if he should bind the hands of the treasure seeker behind him and cast him into the lake, there to do battle with the sons of the Red King. And he whose lot it was to succeed would lay hands upon them; but, if it were not destined to him he should perish and his feet appear above water. As for him who was successful, his hands would show first, whereupon it behoved that Judar should cast the net over him and draw him ashore.'"

"Now quoth my brothers Abd al-Salam and Abd al-Ahad, 'We will wend and make trial, although we perish'; and quoth I, 'And I also will go'; but my brother Abd al-Rahim (he whom thou sawest in the habit of a Jew) said, 'I have no mind to this.' Thereupon we agreed with him that he should repair to Cairo in the disguise of a Jewish merchant, so that, if one of us perished in the lake, he might take his mule and saddle bags and give the bearer an hundred dinars. The first that came to thee the sons of the Red King slew, and so did they with my second brother; but against me they could not prevail and I laid hands on them."

Cried Judar, "And where is thy catch?"

Asked the Moor, "Didst thou not see me shut them in the caskets?"

"Those were fishes," said Judar.

"Nay," answered the Maghribi, "they are Ifrits in the guise of fish. But, O Judar," continued he, "thou must know that the treasure can be opened only by thy means: so say, wilt thou do my bidding and go with me

to the city Fez and Mequinez where we will open the treasure?; and after I will give thee what thou wilt and thou shalt ever be my brother in the bond of Allah and return to thy family with a joyful heart."

Said Judar, "O my lord the pilgrim, I have on my neck a mother and two brothers, whose provider I am; and if I go with thee, who shall give them bread to eat?"

Replied the Moor, "This is an idle excuse! if it be but a matter of expenditure, I will give thee a thousand ducats for thy mother, wherewith she may provide herself till thou come back: and indeed thou shalt return before the end of four months."

So when Judar heard mention of the thousand dinars, he said, "Here with them, O Pilgrim, and I am thy man"; and the Moor, pulling out the money, gave it to him, whereupon he carried it to his mother and told her what had passed between them, saying, "Take these thousand dinars and expend of them upon thyself and my brothers, whilst I journey to Marocco with the Moor, for I shall be absent four months, and great good will betide me; so bless me, O my mother!"

Answered she, "O my son, thou desolatest me and I fear for thee."

"O my mother," rejoined he, "no harm can befall him who is in Allah's keeping, and the Maghribi is a man of worth"; and he went on to praise his condition to her.

Quoth she, "Allah incline his heart to thee! Go with him, O my son; peradventure, he will give thee somewhat." So he took leave of his mother and rejoined the Moor Abd al-Samad, who asked him, "Hast thou consulted thy mother?"

"Yes," answered Judar; "and she blessed me."

"Then mount behind me," said the Maghribi. So Judar mounted the mule's crupper and they rode on from noon till the time of mid-afternoon prayer, when the fisherman was an-hungered; but seeing no victual with the Moor, said to him, "O my lord the pilgrim, belike thou hast forgotten to bring us aught to eat by the way?"

Asked the Moor, "Art thou hungry?" and Judar answered, "Yes."

So Abd al-Samad alighted and made Judar alight and take down the saddle bage; then he said to him, "What wilt thou have, O my brother?"

"Anything."

"Allah upon thee, tell me what thou hast a mind to."

"Bread and cheese."

"O my poor fellow! bread and cheese besit thee not; wish for something good."

"Just now everything is good to me."

"Dost thou like nice browned chicken?"

"Yes!"

"Dost thou like rice and honey?"

"Yes!" And the Moor went on to ask him if he liked this dish and that dish till he had named four and twenty kinds of meats; and Judar thought to himself, "He must be daft! Where are all these dainties to come from, seeing he hath neither cook nor kitchen? But I'll say to him, 'Tis enough!" So he cried, "That will do: thou makest me long for all these meats, and I see nothing."

Quoth the Moor, "Thou art welcome, O Judar!" and, putting his hand into the saddle bags, pulled out a golden dish containing two hot browned chickens. Then he thrust his hand a second time and drew out a golden dish, full of kabobs; nor did he stint taking out dishes from saddle bags, till he had brought forth the whole of the four and twenty kinds he had named, whilst Judar looked on. Then said the Moor, "Fall to poor fellow!" and Judar said to him, "O my lord, thou carriest in yonder saddle bags kitchen and kitcheners!"

The Moor laughed and replied, "These are magical saddle bags and have a servant, who would bring us a thousand dishes an hour, if we called for them."

Quoth Judar, "By Allah, a meat thing in saddle bags!" Then they ate their fill and threw away what was left; after which the Moor replaced the empty dishes in the saddle bags and putting in his hand, drew out an ewer. They drank and making the Wuzu-ablution, prayed the mid-afternoon prayer; after which Abd al-Samad replaced the ewer and the two caskets in the saddle bags and throwing them over the mule's back, mounted and cried, "Up with thee and let us be off," presently adding, "O Judar, knowest thou how far we have come since we left Cairo?"

"Not I, by Allah," replied he, and Abd al-Samad, "We have come a whole month's journey."

Asked Judar, "And how is that?"; and the Moor answered, "Know, O Judar, that this mule under us is a Marid of the Jinn who every day performeth a year's journey; but, for thy sake, she hath gone an easier pace."

Then they set out again and fared on westwards till nightfall, when they halted and the Maghribi brought out supper from the saddle bags, and in like manner, in the morning, he took forth wherewithal to break their fast. So they rode on four days, journeying till midnight and then alighting and sleeping until morning, when they fared on again; and all that Judar had a mind to, he sought of the Moor, who brought it out of the saddle bags.

On the fifth day, they arrived at Fez and Mequinez and entered the city, where all who met the Maghribi saluted him and kissed his hands; and he continued riding through the streets, till he came to a certain door, at which he knocked, whereupon it opened and out came a girl like the moon, to whom said he, "O my daughter, O Rahmah, open us the upper chamber."

"On my head and eyes, O my papa!" replied she and went in, swaying her hips to and fro with a graceful and swimming gait like a thirsting gazelle, movements that ravished Judar's reason, and he said, "This is none other than a King's daughter."

So she opened the upper chamber, and the Moor, taking the saddle bags from the mule's back, said, "Go, and God bless thee!" when lo! the earth clove asunder and swallowing the mule, closed up again as before.

And Judar said, "O Protector! praised be Allah, who hath kept us in safety on her back!" Quoth the Maghribi, "Marvel not, O Judar. I told thee that the mule was an Ifrit; but come with us into the upper chamber."

So they went up into it, and Judar was amazed at the profusion of rich furniture and pendants of gold and silver and jewels and other rare and precious things which he saw there. As soon as they were seated, the Moor bade Rahmah bring him a certain bundle and opening it, drew out a dress worth a thousand dinars, which he gave to Judar, saying, "Don this dress, O Judar, and welcome to thee!"

So Judar put it on and became a fair ensample of the Kings of the West. Then the Maghribi laid the saddle bags before him, and, putting in his hand, pulled out dish after dish, till they had before them a tray of forty kinds of meat, when he said to Judar, "Come near, O my master! eat and excuse us for that we know not what meats thou desirest; but tell us what thou hast a mind to, and we will set it before thee without delay."

Replied Judar, "By Allah, O my lord the pilgrim, I love all kinds of meat and unlove none; so ask me not of aught, but bring all that cometh to thy thought, for save eating to do I have nought."

After this he tarried twenty days with the Moor, who clad him in new clothes every day, and all this time they ate from the saddle bags; for the Maghribi bought neither meat nor bread nor aught else, nor cooked, but brought everything out of the bags, even to various sorts of fruit. On the twenty-first day, he said, "O Judar up with thee; this is the day appointed for opening the hoard of Al-Shamardal."

So he rose and they went afoot without the city, where they found two slaves, each holding a she-mule. The Moor mounted one beast and Judar the other, and they ceased not riding till noon, when they came to a stream of running water, on whose banks Abd al-Samad alighted saying, "Dismount, O Judar!" Then he signed with his hand to the slaves and said, "To it!"

So they took the mules and going each his own way, were absent awhile, after which they returned, one bearing a tent, which he pitched, and the other carpets, which he spread in the tent and laid mattresses, pillows and cushions there around. Then one of them brought the caskets containing the two fishes; and another fetched the saddle bags; whereupon the Maghribi arose and said, "Come, O Judar!"

So Judar followed him into the tent and sat down beside him; and he brought out dishes of meat from the saddle bags and they ate the undurn meal. Then the Moor took the two caskets and conjured over them both, whereupon there came from within voices that said, "Adsumus, at thy service, O diviner of the world! Have mercy upon us!" and called aloud for aid. But he ceased not to repeat conjurations and they to call for help, till the two caskets flew in sunder, the fragments flying about, and there came forth two men, with pinioned hands saying, "Quarter, O diviner of the world! What wilt thou with us?"

Quoth he, "My will is to burn you both with fire, except ye make a covenant with me, to open to me the treasure of Al-Shamardal." Quoth they, "We promise this to thee, and we will open the treasure to thee, so thou produce to us Judar bin Omar, the fisherman, for the hoard may not be opened but by his means, nor can any enter therein save Judar."

Cried the Maghribi "Him of whom ye speak, I have brought, and he is here, listening to you and looking at you."

Thereupon they covenanted with him to open the treasure to him, and he released them. Then he brought out a hollow wand and tablets of red carnelian which he laid on the rod; and after this he took a chafing dish and setting charcoal thereon, blew one breath into it and it kindled forthwith.

Presently he brought incense and said, "O Judar, I am now about to begin the necessary conjurations and fumigations, and when I have once begun, I may not speak, or the charm will be naught; so I will teach thee first what thou must do to win thy wish."

"Teach me," quoth Judar. "Know," quoth the Moor, "that when I have recited the spell and thrown on the incense, the water will dry up from the

571

river's bed and discover to thee, a golden door, the bigness of the city gate, with two rings of metal thereon; whereupon do thou go down to the door and knock a light knock and wait awhile; then knock a second time a knock louder than the first and wait another while; after which give three knocks in rapid succession, and thou wilt hear a voice ask, 'Who knocketh at the door of the treasure, unknowing how to solve the secrets?' Do thou answer, 'I am Judar the fisherman son of Omar': and the door will open and there will come forth a figure with a brand in hand who will say to thee: 'If thou be that man, stretch forth thy neck, that I may strike off thy head.' Then do thou stretch forth thy neck and fear not; for, when he lifts his hand and smites thee with the sword, he will fall down before thee, and in a little thou wilt see him a body sans soul; and the stroke shall not hurt thee nor shall any harm befall thee; but, if thou gainsay him, he will slay thee.

"When thou hast undone his enchantment by obedience, enter and go on till thou see another door, at which do thou knock, and there will come forth to thee a horseman riding a mare with a lance on his shoulder and say to thee, 'What bringeth thee hither, where none may enter ne man ne Jinni?' And he will shake his lance at thee. Bare thy breast to him and he will smite thee and fall down forthright and thou shalt see him a body without a soul; but if thou cross him he will kill thee.

"Then go on to the third door, whence there will come forth to thee a man with a bow and arrows in his hand and take aim at thee. Bare thy breast to him and he will shoot at thee and fall down before thee, a body without a soul; but if thou oppose him, he will kill thee.

"Then go on to the fourth door and knock and it shall be opened to thee, when there will come forth to thee a lion huge of bulk which will rush upon thee, opening his mouth and showing he hath a mind to devour thee. Have no fear of him, neither flee from him: but when he cometh to thee, give him thy hand and he will bite at it and fall down straightway, nor shall aught of hurt betide thee.

"Then enter the fifth door, where thou shalt find a black slave, who will say to thee, 'Who art thou?' Say, 'I am Judar!' and he will answer, 'If thou be that man, open the sixth door.'

"Then do thou go up to the door and say, 'O Isa, tell Musa to open the door'; whereupon the door will fly open and thou wilt see two dragons, one on the left hand and another on the right, which will open their mouths and fly at thee, both at once. Do thou put forth to them both hands and they will bite each a hand and fall down dead; but an thou resist them, they will slay thee.

"Then go on to the seventh door and knock, whereupon there will come forth to thee thy mother and say, 'Welcome, O my son! Come, that I may greet thee!' But do thou reply, 'Hold off from me and doff thy dress.' And she will make answer, 'O my son, I am thy mother and I have a claim upon thee for suckling thee and for rearing thee: how then wouldst thou strip me naked?' Then do thou say, 'Except thou put off thy clothes, I will kill thee!' and look to thy right where thou wilt see a sword hanging up. Take it and draw it upon her, saying, 'Strip!' whereupon she will wheedle thee and humble herself to thee; but have thou no ruth on her nor be beguiled, and as often as she putteth off aught, say to her, 'Off with the rave'; nor do thou cease to threaten her with death, till she doff all that is upon her and fall down, whereupon the enchantment will be dissolved and the charms undone, and thou wilt be safe as to thy life.

"Then enter the hall of the treasure, where thou wilt see the gold lying in heaps; but pay no heed to aught thereof, but look to a closet at the upper end of the hall, where thou wilt see a curtain drawn. Draw back the curtain and thou wilt descry the enchanter, Al-Shamardal, lying upon a couch of gold, with something at his head round and shining like the moon, which is the celestial planisphere. He is baldrick'd with the sword; his finger is the ring and about his neck hangs a chain, to which hangs the Kohl phial. Bring me the four talismans, and beware lest thou forget aught of that which I have told thee, or thou wilt repent and there will be fear for thee."

And he repeated his directions a second and a third and a fourth time, till Judar said, "I have them by heart: but who may face all these enchantments that thou namest and endure against these mighty terrors?"

Replied the Moor, "O Judar, fear not, for they are semblances without life"; and he went on to hearten him, till he said, "I put my trust in Allah."

Then Abd al-Samad threw perfumes on the chafing dish, and addressed himself to reciting conjurations for a time when, behold, the water disappeared and uncovered the river-bed and discovered the door of the treasure, whereupon Judar went down to the door and knocked. Therewith he heard a voice saying, "Who knocketh at the door of the treasure, unknowing how to solve the secrets?"

Quoth he, "I am Judar son of Omar"; whereupon the door opened and there came forth a figure with a drawn sword, who said to him, "Stretch forth thy neck."

So he stretched forth his neck and the species smote him and fell down, lifeless. Then he went on to the second door and did the like, nor

did he cease to do thus, till he had undone the enchantments of the first six doors and came to the seventh door, whence there issued forth to him his mother, saying, "I salute thee, O my son!" He asked, "What art thou?" and she answered, "O my son, I am thy mother who bare thee nine months and suckled thee and reared thee."

Quoth he, "Put off thy clothes."

Quoth she, "Thou art my son, how wouldst thou strip me naked?"

But he said "Strip, or I will strike off thy head with this sword"; and he stretched out his hand to the brand and drew it upon her saying, "Except thou strip, I will slay thee."

Then the strife became long between them and as often as he redoubled on her his threats, she put off somewhat of her clothes and he said to her, "Doff the rest," with many menaces; while she removed each article slowly and kept saying, "O my son, thou hast disappointed my fosterage of thee," till she had nothing left but her petticoat trousers.

Then said she, "O my son, is thy heart stone? Wilt thou dishonour me by discovering my shame? Indeed, this is unlawful, O my son!"

And he answered, "Thou sayest sooth; put not off thy trousers."

At once, as he uttered these words, she cried out, "He hath made default; beat him!"

Whereupon there fell upon him blows like rain drops and the servants of the treasure flocked to him and dealt him a tunding which he forgot not in all his days; after which they thrust him forth and threw him down without the treasure and the hoard doors closed of themselves, whilst the waters of the river returned to their bed. Abd al-Samad the Maghribi took Judar up in haste and repeated conjurations over him, till he came to his senses but still dazed as with drink, when he asked him, "What hast thou done, O wretch?"

Answered Judar, "O my brother, I undid all the opposing enchantments, till I came to my mother and there befell between her and myself a long contention. But I made her doff her clothes, O my brother, till but her trousers remained upon her and she said to me, 'Do not dishonour me; for to discover one's shame is forbidden.' So I left her her trousers out of pity, and behold, she cried out and said, 'He hath made default; beat him!' Whereupon there came out upon me folk, whence I know not, and tunding me with a belabouring which was a Sister of Death, thrust me forth; nor do I know what befell me after this."

Quoth the Moor, "Did I not warn thee not to swerve from my directions? Verily, thou hast injured me and hast injured thyself: for if thou hadst made her take off her petticoat trousers, we had won to our wish; but now thou must abide with me till this day next year." Then he cried out to the two slaves, who struck the tent forthright and loaded it on the beasts; then they were absent awhile and presently returned with the two mules; and the twain mounted and rode back to the city of Fez, where Judar tarried with the Maghribi, eating well and drinking well and donning a grand dress every day, till the year was ended and the anniversary day dawned.

Then the Moor said to him, "Come with me, for this is the appointed day."

And Judar said, "'Tis well." So the Maghribi carried him without the city, where they found the two slaves with the mules, and rode on till they reached the river. Here the slaves pitched the tent and furnished it; and the Moor brought forth the tray of food and they ate the morning meal; after which Abd al-Samad brought out the wand and the tablets as before and, kindling the fire in the chafing dish, made ready the incense.

Then said he, "O Judar, I wish to renew my charge to thee." "O my lord the pilgrim," replied he, "if I have forgotten the bastinado, I have forgotten the injunctions."

Asked the Moor, "Dost thou indeed remember them?" and he answered, "Yes."

Quoth the Moor, "Keep thy wits, and think not that the woman is thy very mother; nay, she is but an enchantment in her semblance, whose purpose is to find thee defaulting. Thou camest off alive the first time; but, an thou trip this time, they will slay thee."

Quoth Judar, "If I slip this time, I deserve to be burnt of them."

Then Abd al-Samad cast the perfumes into the fire and recited the conjurations, till the river dried up; whereupon Judar descended and knocked. The door opened and he entered and undid the several enchantments, till he came to the seventh door and the semblance of his mother appeared before him, saying, "Welcome, O my son!"

But he said to her, "How am I thy son, O accursed? Strip!"

And she began to wheedle him and put off garment after garment, till only her trousers remained; and he said to her, "Strip, O accursed!" So she put off her trousers and became a body without a soul. Then he entered the hall of the treasures, where he saw gold lying in heaps, but paid no heed to it and passed on to the closet at the upper end, where he saw the enchanter Al-Shamardal lying on a couch of gold, baldrick'd with the sword, with the ring on his finger, the Kohl phial on his breast and the celestial planisphere hanging over his head.

So he loosed the sword and taking the ring, the Kohl phial and the planisphere, went forth, when behold, a band of music sounded for him and the servants of the treasure cried out, saying, "Mayest thou be assained with that thou hast gained, O Judar!"

Nor did the music leave sounding, till he came forth of the treasure to the Maghribi, who gave up his conjurations and fumigations and rose up and embraced him and saluted him. Then Judar made over to him the four hoarded talismans, and he took them and cried out to the slaves, who carried away the tent and brought the mules.

So they mounted and returned to Fez-city, where the Moor fetched the saddle bags and brought forth dish after dish of meat, till the tray was full, and said, "O my brother, O Judar, eat!" So he ate till he was satisfied, when the Moor emptied what remained of the meats and other dishes and returned the empty platters to the saddle bags.

Then quoth he, "O Judar, thou hast left home and native land on our account and thou hast accomplished our dearest desire; wherefore thou hast a right to require a reward of us. Ask, therefore, what thou wilt, it is Almighty Allah who giveth unto thee by our means. Ask thy will and be not ashamed, for thou art deserving."

"O my lord," quoth Judar, "I ask first of Allah the Most High and then of thee, that thou give me yonder saddle bags."

So the Maghribi called for them and gave them to him, saying, "Take them, for they are thy due; and, if thou hadst asked of me aught else instead, I had given it to thee. Eat from them, thou and thy family; but, my poor fellow, these will not profit thee, save by way of provaunt, and thou hast wearied thyself with us and we promised to send thee home rejoicing. So we will join to these other saddle bags, full of gold and gems, and forward thee back to thy native land, where thou shalt become a gentleman and a merchant and clothe thyself and thy family; nor shalt thou want ready money for thine expenditure. And know that the manner of using our gift is on this wise. Put thy hand therein and say, 'O servant of these saddle bags, I conjure thee by the virtue of the Mighty Names which have power over thee, bring me such a dish!' And he will bring thee whatsoever thou askest, though thou shouldst call for a thousand different dishes a day."

So saying, he filled him a second pair of saddle bags half with gold and half with gems and precious stones; and, sending for a slave and a mule, said to him, "Mount this mule, and the slave shall go before thee and show thee the way, till thou come to the door of thy house, where do thou take the two pair of saddle bags and give him the mule, that he may bring it back. But admit none into thy secret; and so we commend thee to Allah!"

"May the Almighty increase thy good!" replied Judar and, laying the two pairs of saddle bags on the mule's back, mounted and set forth. The slave went on before him and the mule followed him all that day and night, and on the morrow he entered Cairo by the Gate of Victory, where he saw his mother seated, saying, "Alms, for the love of Allah!" At this sight he well nigh lost his wits and alighting, threw himself upon her: and when she saw him she wept. Then he mounted her on the mule and walked by her stirrup, till they came to the house, where he set her down and, taking the saddle bags, left the she-mule to the slave, who led her away and returned with her to his master, for that both slave and mule were devils.

As for Judar, it was grievous to him that his mother should beg; so, when they were in the house, he asked her, "O my mother, are my brothers well?"; and she answered, "They are both well."

Quoth he, "Why dost thou beg by the wayside?"

Quoth she, "Because I am hungry, O my son," and he, "Before I went away, I gave thee an hundred dinars one day, the like the next and a thousand on the day of my departure."

"O my son, they cheated me and took the money from me, saying, 'We will buy goods with it.' Then they drove me away, and I fell to begging by the wayside, for stress of hunger."

"O my mother, no harm shall befall thee, now I am come; so have no concern, for these saddle bags are full of gold and gems, and good aboundeth with me."

"Verily, thou art blessed, O my son! Allah accept of thee and increase thee of His bounties! Go, O my son, fetch us some victual, for I slept not last night for excess of hunger, having gone to bed supperless."

"Welcome to thee, O my mother! Call for what thou wilt to eat, and I will set it before thee this moment; for I have no occasion to buy from the market, nor need I any to cook."

"O my son, I see naught with thee."

"I have with me in these saddle bags all manner of meats."

"O my son, whatever is ready will serve to stay hunger."

"True, when there is no choice, men are content with the smallest thing; but where there is plenty, they like to eat what is good: and I have abundance; so call for what thou hast a mind to."

"O my son, give me some hot bread and a slice of cheese."

"O my mother, this befitteth not thy condition."

577

"Then give me to eat of that which befitteth my case, for thou knowest it."

"O my mother," rejoined he, "what suit thine estate are browned meat and roast chicken and peppered rice and it becometh thy rank to eat of sausages and stuffed cucumbers and stuffed lamb and stuffed ribs of mutton and vermicelli with broken almonds and nuts and honey and sugar and fritters and almond cakes."

But she thought he was laughing at her and making mock of her; so she said to him, "Yauh! Yauh! what is come to thee? Dost thou dream or art thou daft?"

Asked he, "Why deemest thou that I am mad?" and she answered, "Because thou namest to me all manner rich dishes. Who can avail unto their price, and who knoweth how to dress them?"

Quoth he, "By my life! thou shalt eat of all that I have named to thee, and that at once;" and quoth she, "I see nothing;" and he, "Bring me the saddle bags."

So she fetched them and feeling them, found them empty. However, she laid them before him and he thrust in his hand and pulled out dish after dish, till he had set before her all he had named. Whereupon asked she, "O my son, the saddle bags are small and moreover they were empty; yet hast thou taken thereout all these dishes. Where then were they all?"; and he answered, "O my mother, know that these saddle bags, which the Moor gave me, are enchanted and they have a servant whom, if one desire aught, he hath but to adjure by the Names which command him, saying, 'O servant of these saddle bags, bring me such a dish!' and he will bring it."

Quoth his mother, "And may I put out my hand and ask of him?"
Quoth he, "Do so."

So she stretched out her hand and said, "O servant of the saddle bags, by the virtue of the Names which command thee, bring me stuffed ribs."

Then she thrust in her hand and found a dish containing delicate stuffed ribs of lamb. So she took it out, and called for bread and what else she had a mind to: after which Judar said to her, "O my mother, when thou hast made an end of eating, empty what is left of the food into dishes other than these, and restore the empty platters to the saddle bags carefully." So she arose and laid them up in a safe place.

"And look, O mother mine, that thou keep this secret," added he; "and whenever thou hast a mind to aught, take it forth of the saddle bags and give alms and feed my brothers, whether I be present or absent."

Then he fell to eating with her and behold, while they were thus occupied, in came his two brothers, whom a son of the quarter had apprised of his return, saying, "Your brother is come back, riding on a she-mule, with a slave before him, and wearing a dress that hath not its like."

So they said to each other, "Would to Heaven we had not evilly entreated our mother! There is no hope but that she will surely tell him how we did by her, and then, oh our disgrace with him!"

But one of the twain said, "Our mother is soft-hearted, and if she tell him, our brother is yet tenderer over us than she; and, given we excuse ourselves to him, he will accept our excuse."

So they went in to him and he rose to them and saluting them with the friendliest salutation, bade them sit down and eat. So they ate till they were satisfied, for they were weak with hunger; after which Judar said to them, "O my brothers, take what is left and distribute it to the poor and needy."

"O brother," replied they, "let us keep it to sup withal." But he answered, "When supper time cometh, ye shall have more than this."

So they took the rest of the victual and going out, gave it to every poor man who passed by them, saying, "Take and eat," till nothing was left. Then they brought back the dishes and Judar said to his mother, "Put them in the saddle bags." And when it was eventide, he entered the saloon and took forth of the saddle bags a table of forty dishes; after which he went up to the upper room and, sitting down between his brothers, said to his mother, "Bring the supper."

So she went down to the saloon and, finding there the dishes ready, laid the tray and brought up the forty dishes, one after other. Then they ate the evening meal, and when they had done, Judar said to his brothers, "Take and feed the poor and needy." So they took what was left and gave alms thereof, and presently he brought forth to them sweetmeats, whereof they ate, and what was left he bade them give to the neighbours.

On the morrow, they brake their fast after the same fashion, and thus they fared ten days, at the end of which time quoth Sálim to Salím, "How cometh it that our brother setteth before us a banquet in the morning, a banquet at noon, and a banquet at sundown, besides sweetmeats late at night, and all that is left he giveth to the poor? Verily, this is the fashion of Sultans. Yet we never see him buy aught, and he hath neither kitchener nor kitchen, nor doth he light a fire. Whence hath he this great plenty? Hast thou not a mind to discover the cause of all this?"

Quoth Salím, "By Allah, I know not: but knowest thou any who will tell us the truth of the case?"

Quoth Sálim, "None will tell us save our mother."

So they laid a plot and repairing to their mother one day, in their brother's absence, said to her, "O our mother, we are hungry."

Replied she, "Rejoice, for ye shall presently be satisfied"; and going into the saloon, sought of the servant of the saddle bags hot meats, which she took out and set before her sons.

"O our mother," cried they, "this meat is hot; yet hast thou not cooked, neither kindled a fire."

Quoth she, "It cometh from the saddle bags;" and quoth they, "What manner of thing be these saddle bags?"

She answered, "They are enchanted; and the required is produced by the charm:" she then told her sons their virtue, enjoining them to secrecy.

Said they, "The secret shall be kept, O our mother, but teach us the manner of this."

So she taught them the fashion thereof and they fell to putting their hands into the saddle bags and taking forth whatever they had a mind to. But Judar knew naught of this.

Then quoth Sálim privily to Salím, "O my brother, how long shall we abide with Judar servant-wise and eat of his alms? Shall we not contrive to get the saddle bags from him and make off with them?"

"And how shall we make shift to do this?"

"We will sell him to the galleys." "How shall we do that?"

"We two will go to the Rais, the Chief Captain of the Sea of Suez and bid him to an entertainment, with two of his company. What I say to Judar do thou confirm, and at the end of the night I will show thee what I will do."

So they agreed upon the sale of their brother and going to the Captain's quarters said to him, "O Rais, we have come to thee on an errand that will please thee."

"Good," answered he; and they continued, "We two are brethren, and we have a third brother, a lewd fellow and good-for-nothing. When our father died, he left us some money, which we shared amongst us, and he took his part of the inheritance and wasted it in frowardness and debauchery, till he was reduced to poverty, when he came upon us and cited us before the magistrates, avouching that we had taken his good and that of his father, and we disputed the matter before the judges and lost the money. Then he waited awhile and attacked us a second time, until he brought us to beggary; nor will he desist from us, and we are utterly weary of him; wherefore we would have thee buy him of us."

Quoth the Captain, "Can ye cast about with him and bring him to me here? If so, I will pack him off to sea forthright."

Quoth they "We cannot manage to bring him here; but be thou our guest this night and bring with thee two of thy men, not one more; and when he is asleep, we will aid one another to fall upon him, we five, and seize and gag him. Then shalt thou carry him forth the house, under cover of the night, and after do thou with him as thou wilt."

Rejoined the Captain, "With all my heart! Will ye sell him for forty dinars?" and they, "Yes, come after nightfall to such a street, by such a mosque, and thou shalt find one of us awaiting thee."

And he replied, "Now be off."

Then they repaired to Judar and waited awhile, after which Sálim went up to him and kissed his hand. Quoth Judar, "What ails thee, O my brother?"

And he made answer, saying, "Know that I have a friend, who hath many a time bidden me to his house in thine absence and hath ever hospitably entreated me, and I owe him a thousand kindnesses, as my brother here wotteth. I met him to-day and he invited me to his house, but I said to him, 'I cannot leave my brother Judar.' Quoth he, 'Bring him with thee'; and quoth I, 'He will not consent to that; but if ye will be my guests, thou and thy brothers' (for his brothers were sitting with him); and I invited them thinking that they would refuse. But he accepted my invitation for all of them, saying, 'Look for me at the gate of the little mosque, and I will come to thee, I and my brothers.' And now I fear they will come and am ashamed before thee. So wilt thou hearten my heart and entertain them this night, for thy good is abundant, O my brother? Or if thou consent not, give me leave to take them into the neighbours' houses."

Replied Judar, "Why shouldst thou carry them into the neighbours' houses? Is our house then so strait or have we not wherewith to give them supper? Shame on thee to consult me! Thou hast but to call for what thou needest and have rich viands and sweetmeats and to spare. Whenever thou bringest home folk in my absence, ask thy mother, and she will set before thee victual more than enough. Go and fetch them; blessings have descended upon us through such guests."

So Sálim kissed his hand and going forth, sat at the gate of the little mosque till after sundown, when the Captain and his men came up to him, and he carried them to the house. When Judar saw them he bade them welcome and seated them and made friends of them, knowing not what the future had in store for him at their hands. Then he called to his mother for

supper, and she fell to taking dishes out of the saddlebags, whilst he said, "Bring such and such meats," till she had set forty different dishes before them. They ate their sufficiency and the tray was taken away, the sailors thinking the while that this liberal entertainment came from Sálim.

When a third part of the night was past, Judar set sweetmeats before them and Sálim served them, whilst his two brothers sat with the guests, till they sought to sleep. Accordingly Judar lay down and the others with him, who waited till he was asleep, when they fell upon him together and gagging and pinioning him, before he was awake, carried him forth of the house, under cover of the night.

He was at once packed off to Suez, where they shackled him and set him to work as a galley slave; and he ceased not to serve thus in silence a whole year.

So far concerning Judar; but as for his brothers, they went in next morning to his mother and said to her, "O our mother, our brother Judar is not awake."

Said she, "Do ye wake him." Asked they, "Where lieth he?" and she answered, "With the guests."

They rejoined, "Haply he went away with them whilst we slept, O mother. It would seem that he had tasted of strangerhood and yearned to get at hidden hoards; for we heard him at talk with the Moors, and they said to him, 'We will take thee with us and open the treasure to thee.'"

She enquired, "Hath he then been in company with Moors?"; and they replied, saying, "Were they not our guests yester-night?"

And she, "Most like he hath gone with them, but Allah will direct him on the right way; for there is a blessing upon him and he will surely come back with great good." But she wept, for it was grievous to her to be parted from her son.

Then said they to her, "O accursed woman, dost thou love Judar with all this love, whilst as for us, whether we be absent or present, thou neither joyest in us nor sorrowest for us? Are we not thy sons, even as Judar is thy son?"

She said, "Ye are indeed my sons: but ye are reprobates who deserve no favour of me, for since your father's death I have never seen any good in you; whilst as for Judar, I have had abundant good of him and he hath heartened my heart and entreated me with honour; wherefore it behoveth me to weep for him, because of his kindness to me and to you."

When they heard this, they abused her and beat her; after which they sought for the saddle bags, till they found the two pairs and took the enchanted one and all the gold from one pouch and jewels from the other of the unenchanted, saying, "This was our father's good."

Said their mother, "Not so, by Allah! It belongeth to your brother Judar, who brought it from the land of the Magharibah."

Said they, "Thou liest, it was our father's property; and we will dispose of it, as we please."

Then they divided the gold and jewels between them; but a brabble arose between them concerning the enchanted saddle bags, Sálim saying, "I will have them;" and Salím, saying, "I will take them"; and they came to high words.

Then said she, "O my sons, ye have divided the gold and the jewels, but this may not be divided, nor can its value be made up in money; and if it be cut in twain, its spell will be voided; so leave it with me and I will give you to eat from it at all times and be content to take a morsel with you.

"If ye allow me aught to clothe me, 'twill be of your bounty, and each of you shall traffic with the folk for himself. Ye are my sons and I am your mother; wherefore let us abide as we are, lest your brother come back and we be disgraced." But they accepted not her words and passed the night, wrangling with each other.

Now it chanced that a Janissary of the King's guards was a guest in the house adjoining Judar's and heard them through the open window. So he looked out and listening, heard all the angry words that passed between them and saw the division of the spoil. Next morning he presented himself before the King of Egypt, whose name was Shams al-Daulah, and told him all he had heard, whereupon he sent for Judar's brothers and put them to the question, till they confessed; and he took the two pairs of saddle bags from them and clapped them in prison, appointing a sufficient daily allowance to their mother.

Now as regards Judar, he abode a whole year in service at Suez, till one day, being in a ship bound on a voyage over the sea, a wind arose against them and cast the vessel upon a rock projecting from a mountain, where she broke up and all on board were drowned and none gat ashore save Judar. As soon as he landed he fared on inland, till he reached an encampment of Badawi, who questioned him of his case, and he told them he had been a sailor.

Now there was in camp a merchant, a native of Jiddah, who took pity on him and said to him, "Wilt thou take service with me, O Egyptian, and I will clothe thee and carry thee with me to Jiddah?"

So Judar took service with him and accompanied him to Jiddah, where he showed him much favour. After awhile, his master the merchant set out on a pilgrimage to Meccah, taking Judar with him, and when they reached the city, the Cairene repaired to the Haram temple, to circumambulate the Ka'abah.

As he was making the prescribed circuits, he suddenly saw his friend Abd al-Samad the Moor doing the like; and when the Maghribi caught sight of him, he saluted him and asked him of his state; whereupon Judar wept and told him all that had befallen him. So the Moor carried him to his lodging and entreated him with honour, clothing him in a dress of which the like was not, and saying to him, "Thou hast seen the end of thine ills, O Judar." Then he drew out for him a geomantic figure, which showed what had befallen Sálim and Salím and said to Judar, "Such and such things have befallen thy brothers and they are now in the King of Egypt's prison; but thou art right welcome to abide with me and accomplish thine ordinances of pilgrimage and all shall be well."

Replied Judar, "O my lord, let me go and take leave of the merchant with whom I am and after I will come back to thee."

"Dost thou owe money?" asked the Moor, and he answered, "No."

Said Abd al-Samad, "Go thou and take leave of him and come back forth right, for bread hath claims of its own from the ingenuous."

So Judar returned to the merchant and farewelled him, saying, "I have fallen in with my brother."

"Go bring him here," said the merchant, "and we will make him an entertainment."

But Judar answered, saying, "He hath no need of that; for he is a man of wealth and hath many servants."

Then the merchant gave Judar twenty dinars, saying, "Acquit me of responsibility"; and he bade him adieu and went forth from him. Presently, he saw a poor man, so he gave him the twenty dinars and returned to the Moor, with whom he abode till they had accomplished the pilgrimage rites when Abd al-Samad gave him the seal ring, that he had taken from the treasure of Al-Shamardal, saying, "This ring will win thee thy wish, for it enchanteth and hath a servant, by name Al-Ra'ad al-Kasif; so whatever thou hast a mind to of the wants of this world, rub this ring and its servant will appear and do all thou biddest him."

Then he rubbed the ring before him, whereupon the Jinni appeared, saying, "Adsum, O my lord! Ask what thou wilt and it shall be given thee. Hast thou a mind to people a ruined city or ruin a populous one? to slay a king or to rout a host?" "O Ra'ad," said Abd al-Samad, "this is become thy lord; do thou serve him faithfully."

Then he dismissed him and said to Judar, "Rub the ring and the servant will appear and do thou command him to do whatever thou desirest, for he will not gainsay thee. Now go to thine own country and take care of the ring, for by means of it thou wilt baffle thine enemies; and be not ignorant of its puissance."

"O my lord," quoth Judar, "with thy leave, I will set out homewards."

Quoth the Maghribi, "Summon the Jinni and mount upon his back; and if thou say to him, 'Bring me to my native city this very day,' he will not disobey thy commandment." So he took leave of Moor Abd al-Samad and rubbed the ring, whereupon Al-Ra'ad presented himself, saying, "Adsum; ask and it shall be given to thee."

Said Judar, "Carry me to Cairo this day;" and he replied, "Thy will be done;" and, taking him on his back, flew with him from noon till midnight, when he set him down in the courtyard of his mother's house and disappeared. Judar went in to his mother, who rose weeping, and greeted him fondly, and told him how the King had beaten his brothers and cast them into gaol and taken the two pairs of saddle bags; which when he heard, it was no light matter to him and he said to her, "Grieve not for the past; I will show thee what I can do and bring my brothers hither forth right."

So he rubbed the ring, whereupon its servant appeared, saying, "Here am I! Ask and thou shalt have."

Quoth Judar, "I bid thee bring me my two brothers from the prison of the King."

So the Jinni sank into the earth and came not up but in the midst of the gaol where Sálim and Salím lay in piteous plight and sore sorrow for the plagues of prison, so that they wished for death, and one of them said to the other, "By Allah, O my brother, affliction is longsome upon us! How long shall we abide in this prison? Death would be relief."

As he spoke, behold, the earth clove in sunder and out came Al-Ra'ad, who took both up and plunged with them into the earth. They swooned away for excess of fear, and when they recovered, they found themselves in their mother's house and saw Judar seated by her side.

Quoth he, "I salute you, O my brothers! you have cheered me by your presence." And they bowed their heads and burst into tears. Then said he, "Weep not, for it was Satan and covetise that led you to do thus. How could you sell me? But I comfort myself with the thought of Joseph,

585

whose brothers did with him even more than ye did with me, because they cast him into the pit. Repent unto Allah and crave pardon of Him, and He will forgive you both, for He is the Most Forgiving, the Merciful. As for me, I pardon you and welcome you: no harm shall befall you." Then he comforted them and set their hearts at ease and related to them all he had suffered, till he fell in with Shaykh Abd al-Samad, and told them also of the seal ring.

They replied, "O our brother, forgive us this time; and, if we return to our old ways, do with us as thou wilt."

Quoth he, "No harm shall befall you; but tell me what the King did with you."

Quoth they, "He beat us and threatened us with death and took the two pairs of saddle bags from us."

"Will he not care?" said Judar, and rubbed the ring, whereupon Al-Ra'ad appeared.

When his brothers saw him, they were frighted and thought Judar would bid him slay them; so they fled to their mother, crying, "O our mother, we throw ourselves on thy generosity; do thou intercede for us, O our mother!"

And she said to them, "O my sons, fear nothing!"

Then said Judar to the servant, "I command thee to bring me all that is in the King's treasury of goods and such; let nothing remain and fetch the two pairs of saddle bags he took from my brothers."

"I hear and I obey," replied Al-Ra'ad; and, disappearing straightway gathered together all he found in the treasury and returned with the two pairs of saddle bags and the deposits therein and laid them before Judar, saying, "O my lord, I have left nothing in the treasury."

Judar gave the treasure to his mother bidding her keep it and laying the enchanted saddle bags before him, said to the Jinni, "I command thee to build me this night a lofty palace and overlay it with liquid gold and furnish it with magnificent furniture: and let not the day dawn, ere thou be quit of the whole work."

Replied he, "Thy bidding shall be obeyed"; and sank into the earth. Then Judar brought forth food and they ate and took their ease and lay down to sleep.

Meanwhile, Al-Ra'ad summoned his attendant Jinn and bade them build the palace. So some of them fell to hewing stones and some to building, whilst others plastered and painted and furnished; nor did the day dawn ere the ordinance of the palace was complete; whereupon Al-Ra'ad came to Judar and said to him, "O my lord, the palace is finished and in best order, an it please thee to come and look on it."

So Judar went forth with his mother and brothers and saw a palace, whose like there was not in the whole world; and it confounded all minds with the goodliness of its ordinance. Judar was delighted with it while he was passing along the highway and withal it had cost him nothing. Then he asked his mother, "Say me, wilt thou take up thine abode in this palace?" and she answered, "I will, O my son," and called down blessings upon him. Then he rubbed the ring and bade the Jinni fetch him forty handsome white handmaids and forty black damsels and as many Mamelukes and negro slaves.

"Thy will be done," answered Al-Ra'ad and betaking himself, with forty of his attendant Genii to Hind and Sind and Persia, snatched up every beautiful girl and boy they saw, till they had made up the required number. Moreover, he sent other four score, who fetched comely black girls, and forty others brought male chattels and carried them all to Judar's house, which they filled. Then he showed them to Judar, who was pleased with them and said, "Bring for each a dress of the finest."

"Ready!" replied the servant.

Then quoth he, "Bring a dress for my mother and another for myself, and also for my brothers."

So the Jinni fetched all that was needed and clad the female slaves, saying to them, "This is your mistress: kiss her hands and cross her not, but serve her, white and black."

The Mamelukes also dressed themselves and kissed Judar's hands; and he and his brothers arrayed themselves in the robes the Jinni had brought them and Judar became like unto a King and his brothers as Wazirs. Now his house was spacious; so he lodged Sálim and his slave girls in one part thereof and Salím and his slave girls in another, whilst he and his mother took up their abode in the new palace; and each in his own place was like a Sultan.

So far concerning them; but as regards the King's Treasurer, thinking to take something from the treasury, he went in and found it altogether empty, even as saith the poet:

> 'Twas as a hive of bees that greatly thrived;
> But, when the bee swarm fled, 'twas clean unhived.

So he gave a great cry and fell down in a fit. When he came to himself, he left the door open and going in to King Shams al-Daulah, said to him,

"O Commander of the Faithful, I have to inform thee that the treasury hath become empty during the night."

Quoth the King, "What hast thou done with my monies which were therein?"

Quoth he, "By Allah, I have not done aught with them nor know I what is come of them! I visited the place yesterday and saw it full; but to-day when I went in, I found it clean empty, albeit the doors were locked, the walls were unpierced and the bolts are unbroken; nor hath a thief entered it."

Asked the King, "Are the two pairs of saddle bags gone?"

"Yes," replied the Treasurer; whereupon the King's reason flew from his head, and he rose to his feet, saying, "Go thou before me." Then he followed the Treasurer to the treasury and he found nothing there, whereat he was wroth with him; and he said to them, "O soldiers! know that my treasury hath been plundered during the night, and I know not who did this deed and dared thus to outrage me, without fear of me."

Said they, "How so?"; and he replied, "Ask the Treasurer."

So they questioned him, and he answered, saying, "Yesterday I visited the treasury and it was full, but this morning when I entered it I found it empty, though the walls were unpierced and the doors unbroken."

They all marvelled at this and could make the King no answer, when in came the Janissary, who had denounced Sálim and Salím, and said to Shams al-Daulah, "O King of the age, all this night I have not slept for that which I saw."

And the King asked, "And what didst thou see?"

"Know, O King of the age," answered the Kawwas, "that all night long I have been amusing myself with watching builders at work; and, when it was day, I saw a palace ready edified, whose like is not in the world. So I asked about it and was told that Judar had come back with great wealth and Mamelukes and slaves and that he had freed his two brothers from prison, and built this palace, wherein he is as a Sultan."

Quoth the King, "Go, look in the prison."

So they went thither and not finding Sálim and Salím, returned and told the King, who said, "It is plain now who be the thief; he who took Sálim and Salím out of prison it is who hath stolen my monies."

Quoth the Wazir, "O my lord, and who is he?"; and quoth the King, "Their brother Judar, and he hath taken the two pairs of saddle bags; but, O Wazir do thou send him an Emir with fifty men to seal up his goods and lay hands on him and his brothers and bring them to me, that I may hang them."

And he was sore enraged and said, "Ho, off with the Emir at once, and fetch them, that I may put them to death."

But the Wazir said to him, "Be thou merciful, for Allah is merciful and hasteth not to punish His servants, whenas they sin against Him. Moreover, he who can build a palace in a single night, as these say, none in the world can vie with him; and verily I fear lest the Emir fall into difficulty for Judar. Have patience, therefore, whilst I devise for thee some device of getting at the truth of the case, and so shalt thou win thy wish, O King of the age."

Quoth the King, "Counsel me how I shall do, O Wazir."

And the Minister said, "Send him an Emir with an invitation; and I will make much of him for thee and make a show of love for him and ask him of his estate; after which we will see. If we find him stout of heart, we will use sleight with him, and if weak of will, then do thou seize him and do with him thy desire."

The King agreed to this and despatched one of his Emirs, Othman hight, to go and invite Judar and say to him, "The King biddeth thee to a banquet"; and the King said to him, "Return not, except with him."

Now this Othman was a fool, proud and conceited; so he went forth upon his errand, and when he came to the gate of Judar's palace, he saw before the door an eunuch seated upon a chair of gold, who at his approach rose not, but sat as if none came near, though there were with the Emir fifty footmen. Now this eunuch was none other than Al-Ra'ad al-Kasif, the servant of the ring, whom Judar had commanded to put on the guise of an eunuch and sit at the palace gate. So the Emir rode up to him and asked him, "O slave, where is thy lord?"; whereto he answered, "In the palace"; but he stirred not from his leaning posture; whereupon the Emir Othman waxed wroth and said to him, "O pestilent slave, art thou not ashamed, when I speak to thee, to answer me, sprawling at thy length, like a gallows bird?"

Replied the eunuch "Off and multiply not words."

Hardly had Othman heard this, when he was filled with rage and drawing his mace would have smitten the eunuch, knowing not that he was a devil; but Al-Ra'ad leapt upon him and taking the mace from him, dealt him four blows with it.

Now when the fifty men saw their lord beaten, it was grievous to them; so they drew their swords and ran to slay the slave; but he said, "Do ye draw on us, O dogs?" and rose at them with the mace, and everyone whom he smote, he broke his bones and drowned him in his blood. So they fell back before him and fled, whilst he followed them, beating them, till he

had driven them far from the palace gate; after which he returned and sat down on his chair at the door, caring for none.

But as for the Emir and his company, they returned, discomfited and tunded, to King Shams al-Daulah, and Othman said, "O King of the age, when I came to the palace gate, I espied an eunuch seated there in a chair of gold and he was passing proud for, when he saw me approach, he stretched himself at full length albeit he had been sitting in his chair and entreated me contumeliously, neither offered to rise to me. So I began to speak to him and he answered without stirring, whereat wrath get hold of me and I drew the mace upon him, thinking to smite him. But he snatched it from me and beat me and my men therewith and overthrew us. So we fled from before him and could not prevail against him."

At this, the King was wroth and said, "Let an hundred men go down to him."

Accordingly, the hundred men went down to attack him; but he arose and fell upon them with the mace and ceased not smiting them till he had put them to the rout; when he regained his chair; upon which they returned to the King and told him what had passed, saying, "O King of the age, he beat us and we fled for fear of him."

Then the King sent two hundred men against him, but these also he put to the rout, and Shams Al-Daulah said to his Minister, "I charge thee, O Wazir, take five hundred men and bring this eunuch in haste, and with him his master Judar and his brothers."

Replied the Wazir, "O King of the age, I need no soldiers, but will go down to him alone and unarmed."

"Go," quoth the King, "and do as thou seest suitable."

So the Wazir laid down his arms and donning a white habit, took a rosary in his hand and set out afoot alone and unattended. When he came to Judar's gate, he saw the slave sitting there; so he went up to him and seating himself by his side courteously, said to him, "Peace be with thee!"; whereto he replied, "And on thee be peace, O mortal! What wilt thou?"

When the Wazir heard him say "O mortal," he knew him to be of the Jinn and quaked for fear; then he asked him, "O my lord, tell me, is thy master Judar here?"

Answered the eunuch, "Yes, he is in the palace."

Quoth the Minister, "O my lord, go thou to him and say to him, 'King Shams Al-Daulah saluteth thee and biddeth thee honour his dwelling with thy presence and eat of a banquet he hath made for thee.'"

Quoth the eunuch, "Tarry thou here, whilst I consult him." So the Wazir stood in a respectful attitude, whilst the Marid went up to the palace and said to Judar, "Know, O my lord, that the King sent to thee an Emir and fifty men, and I beat them and drove them away. Then he sent an hundred men and I beat them also; then two hundred, and these also I put to the rout. And now he hath sent thee his Wazir unarmed, bidding thee visit him and eat of his banquet. What sayst thou?"

Said Judar, "Go, bring the Wazir hither."

So the Marid went down and said to him, "O Wazir, come speak with my lord."

"On my head be it," replied he and going in to Judar, found him seated, in greater state than the King, upon a carpet, whose like the King could not spread, and was dazed and amazed at the goodliness of the palace and its decoration and appointments, which made him seem as he were a beggar in comparison.

So he kissed the ground before Judar and called down blessings on him; and Judar said to him, "What is thy business, O Wazir?"

Replied he, "O my lord, thy friend King Shams Al-Daulah saluteth thee with the salaam and longeth to look upon thy face; wherefore he hath made thee an entertainment. So say, wilt thou heal his heart and eat of his banquet?"

Quoth Judar, "If he be indeed my friend, salute him and bid him come to me."

"On my head be it," quoth the Minister.

Then Judar bringing out the ring rubbed it and bade the Jinni fetch him a dress of the best, which he gave to the Wazir saying, "Don this dress and go tell the King what I say."

So the Wazir donned the dress, the like whereof he had never donned, and returning to the King told him what had passed and praised the palace and that which was therein, saying, "Judar biddeth thee to him."

So the King called out, "Up, ye men; mount your horses and bring me my steed, that we may go to Judar!" Then he and his suite rode off for the Cairene palace.

Meanwhile Judar summoned the Marid and said to him, "It is my will that thou bring me some of the Ifrits at thy command in the guise of guards and station them in the open square before the palace, that the King may see them and be awed by them; so shall his heart tremble and he shall know that my power and majesty be greater than his."

Thereupon Al-Ra'ad brought him two hundred Ifrits of great stature and strength, in the guise of guards, magnificently armed and equipped,

591

and when the King came and saw these tall burly fellows his heart feared them. Then he entered the palace, and found Judar sitting in such state as nor King nor Sultan could even. So he saluted him and made his obeisance to him, yet Judar rose not to him nor did him honour nor said "Be seated," but left him standing, so that fear entered into him and he could neither sit nor go away and said to himself, "If he feared me, he would not leave me thus unheeded peradventure he will do me a mischief, because of that which I did with his brothers."

Then said Judar, "O King of the age, it beseemeth not the like of thee to wrong the folk and take away their good."

Replied the King, "O my lord, deign excuse me, for greed impelled me to this and fate was thereby fulfilled; and, were there no offending, there would be no forgiving."

And he went on to excuse himself for the past and pray to him for pardon and indulgence till he recited amongst other things this poetry:

"O thou of generous seed and true nobility,
Reproach me not for that which came from me to thee
We pardon thee if thou have wrought us any wrong
And if I wrought the wrong I pray thee pardon me!"

And he ceased not to humble himself before him, till he said, "Allah pardon thee!" and bade him be seated. So he sat down and Judar invested him with garments of pardon and immunity and ordered his brothers spread the table. When they had eaten, he clad the whole of the King's company in robes of honour and gave them largesse; after which he bade the King depart.

So he went forth and thereafter came every day to visit Judar and held not his Divan save in his house: wherefore friendship and familiarity waxed great between them, and they abode thus awhile, till one day the King, being alone with his Minister, said to him, "O Wazir, I fear lest Judar slay me and take the kingdom away from me."

Replied the Wazir, "O King of the age, as for his taking the kingdom from thee, have no fear of that, for Judar's present estate is greater than that of the King, and to take the kingdom would be a lowering of his dignity; but, if thou fear that he kill thee, thou hast a daughter: give her to him to wife and thou and he will be of one condition."

Quoth the King, "O Wazir, be thou intermediary between us and him"; and quoth the Minister, "Do thou invite him to an entertainment and pass the night with him in one of thy saloons. Then bid thy daughter don her richest dress and ornaments and pass by the door of the saloon. When he seeth her, he will assuredly fall in love with her, and when we know this, I will turn to him and tell him that she is thy daughter and engage him in converse and lead him on, so that thou shalt seem to know nothing of the matter, till he ask her to thee to wife. When thou hast married him to the Princess, thou and he will be as one thing and thou wilt be safe from him; and if he die, thou wilt inherit all he hath, both great and small."

Replied the King, "Thou sayst sooth, O my Wazir," and made a banquet and invited thereto Judar who came to the Sultan's palace and they sat in the saloon in great good cheer till the end of the day.

Now the King had commanded his wife to array the maiden in her richest raiment and ornaments and carry her by the door of the saloon. She did as he told her, and when Judar saw the Princess, who had not her match for beauty and grace, he looked fixedly at her and said, "Ah!"; and his limbs were loosened; for love and longing and passion and pine were sore upon him; desire and transport get hold upon him and he turned pale.

Quoth the Wazir, "May no harm befall thee, O my lord! Why do I see thee change colour and in suffering?"

Asked Judar, "O Wazir, whose daughter is this damsel? Verily she hath enthralled me and ravished my reason."

Replied the Wazir, "She is the daughter of thy friend the King; and if she please thee, I will speak to him that he marry thee to her."

Quoth Judar, "Do so, O Wazir, and as I live, I will bestow on thee what thou wilt and will give the King whatsoever he shall ask to her dowry; and we will become friends and kinsfolk."

Quoth the Minister, "It shall go hard but thy desire be accomplished." Then he turned to the King and said in his ear, "O King of the age, thy friend Judar seeketh alliance with thee and will have me ask of thee for him the hand of thy daughter, the Princess Asiyah; so disappoint me not, but accept my intercession, and what dowry soever thou askest he will give thee."

Said the King, "The dowry I have already received, and as for the girl, she is his handmaid; I give her to him to wife and he will do me honour by accepting her." So they spent the rest of that night together and on the morrow the King held a court, to which he summoned great and small, together with the Shaykh al-Islam.

Then Judar demanded the Princess in marriage and the King said, "The dowry I have received."

Thereupon they drew up the marriage contract and Judar sent for the saddle bags containing the jewels and gave them to the King as settlement upon his daughter. The drums beat and the pipes sounded and they held high festival, whilst Judar went in unto the girl. Thenceforward he and the King were as one flesh and they abode thus for many days, till Shams al-Daulah died; whereupon the troops proclaimed Judar Sultan, and he refused; but they importuned him, till he consented and they made him King in his father-in-law's stead. Then he bade build a cathedral-mosque over the late King's tomb in the Bundukaniyah quarter and endowed it.

Now the quarter of Judar's house was called Yamaniyah; but, when he became Sultan he built therein a congregational mosque and other buildings, wherefore the quarter was named after him and was called the Judariyah quarter. Moreover, he made his brother Sálim his Wazir of the right and his brother Salím his Wazir of the left hand; and thus they abode a year and no more; for, at the end of that time, Sálim said to Salím, "O my brother, how long is this state to last? Shall we pass our whole lives in slavery to our brother Judar? We shall never enjoy luck or lordship whilst he lives," adding, "so how shall we do to kill him and take the ring and the saddle bags?"

Replied Salím, "Thou art craftier than I; do thou devise, whereby we may kill him."

"If I effect this," asked Sálim, "wilt thou agree that I be Sultan and keep the ring and that thou be my right-hand Wazir and have the saddle bags?"

Salím answered, "I consent to this"; and they agreed to slay Judar their brother for love of the world and of dominion. So they laid a snare for Judar and said to him, "O our brother, verily we have a mind to glory in thee and would fain have thee enter our houses and eat of our entertainment and solace our hearts."

Replied Judar, "So be it, in whose house shall the banquet be?"

"In mine," said Sálim "and after thou hast eaten of my victual, thou shalt be the guest of my brother."

Said Judar, "'Tis well," and went with him to his house, where he set before him poisoned food, of which when he had eaten, his flesh rotted from his bones and he died. Then Sálim came up to him and would have drawn the ring from his finger, but it resisted him; so he cut off the finger with a knife. Then he rubbed the ring and the Marid presented himself, saying, "Adsum! Ask what thou wilt."

Quoth Sálim, "Take my brother Salím and put him to death and carry forth the two bodies, the poisoned and the slaughtered, and cast them down before the troops."

So the Marid took Salím and slew him; then, carrying the two corpses forth, he cast them down before the chief officers of the army, who were sitting at table in the parlour of the house. When they saw Judar and Salím slain, they raised their hands from the food and fear gat hold of them and they said to the Marid, "Who hath dealt thus with the Sultan and the Wazir?"

Replied the Jinni, "Their brother Sálim."

And behold, Sálim came up to them and said, "O soldiers, eat and make merry, for Judar is dead and I have taken to me the seal ring, whereof the Marid before you is the servant; and I bade him slay my brother Salím lest he dispute the kingdom with me, for he was a traitor and I feared lest he should betray me. So now I am become Sultan over you; will ye accept of me? If not, I will rub the ring and bid the Marid slay you all, great and small."

They replied, "We accept thee to King and Sultan."

Then he bade bury his brothers and summoned the Divan; and some of the folk followed the funeral, whilst others forewent him in state procession to the audience hall of the palace, where he sat down on the throne and they did homage to him as King; after which he said, "It is my will to marry my brother Judar's wife."

Quoth they, "Wait till the days of widowhood are accomplished."

Quoth he, "I know not days of widowhood nor aught else. As my head liveth, I needs must go in unto her this very night."

So they drew up the marriage contract and sent to tell the Princess Asiyah, who replied, "Bid him enter."

Accordingly, he went in to her and she received him with a show of joy and welcome; but by and by she gave him poison in water and made an end of him. Then she took the ring and broke it, that none might possess it thenceforward, and tore up the saddle bags; after which she sent to the Shaykh al-Islam and other great officers of state, telling them what had passed and saying to them, "Choose you out a King to rule over you."

"And this is all that hath come down to us of the story of Judar and his brethren," said Scheherazade, as she perceived the dawn of day and ceased saying her permitted say. "But I have also heard, O King, a tale called 'The Rogueries of Dalilah the Crafty.'"

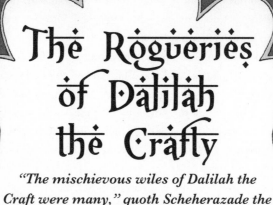

The Rogueries of Dalilah the Crafty

**"The mischievous wiles of Dalilah the
Craft were many," quoth Scheherazade the
following night...**

There lived in the time of Harun al-Rashid a man
named Ahmad al-Danaf and another Hasan
Shuman hight, the twain past-masters in fraud and
feints, who had done rare things in their day; wherefore the Caliph
invested them with caftans of honour and made them Captains
of the Watch for Baghdad (Ahmad of the right hand and Hasan
of the left hand); and appointed to each of them a stipend of a
thousand dinars a month and forty stalwart men to be at their bidding. Moreover to Calamity Ahmad was committed the watch of
the district outside the walls. So Ahmad and Hasan went forth in
company of the Emir Khalid, the Wali or Chief of Police, attended each by his forty followers on horse-back, and preceded by the
Crier, crying aloud and saying, "By command of the Caliph! None
is captain of the watch of the right hand but Ahmad al-Danaf and
none is captain of the watch of the left hand but Hasan Shuman,
and both are to be obeyed when they bid and are to be held in all
honour and worship."

Now there was in the city an old woman called Dalilah the
Wily, who had a daughter by name Zaynab the Coney-catcher.

They heard the proclamation made and Zaynab said to Dalilah, "See, O my mother, this fellow, Ahmad al-Danaf! He came hither from Cairo, a fugitive, and played the double-dealer in Baghdad, till he got into the Caliph's company and is now become captain of the right hand, whilst that mangy chap Hasan Shuman is captain of the left hand, and each hath a table spread morning and evening and a monthly wage of a thousand dinars; whereas we abide unemployed and neglected in this house, without estate and without honour, and have none to ask of us." Now Dalilah's husband had been town-captain of Baghdad with a monthly wage of one thousand dinars; but he died leaving two daughters, one married and with a son by name Ahmad al-Lakit or Ahmad the Abortion; and the other called Zaynab, a spinster. And this Dalilah was a past mistress in all manner of craft and trickery and double dealing; she could wile the very dragon out of his den and Iblis himself might have learnt deceit of her. Her father had also been governor of the carrier-pigeons to the Caliph with a solde of one thousand dinars a month. He used to rear the birds to carry letters and messages, wherefore in time of need each was dearer to the Caliph than one of his own sons. So Zaynab said to her mother, "Up and play off some feint and fraud that may haply make us notorious in Baghdad, so perchance we shall win our father's stipend for ourselves."

Replied the old trot, "As thy head liveth, O my daughter, I will play off higher-class rogueries in Baghdad than ever played Calamity Ahmad or Hasan the Pestilent."

So saying, she rose and threw over her face the Lisam-veil and donned clothes such as the poorer Sufis wear, petticoat-trousers falling over her heels, and a gown of white wool with a broad girdle. She also took a pitcher and filled it with water to the neck; after which she set three dinars in the mouth and stopped it up with a plug of palm-fibre. Then she threw round her shoulder, baldrick-wise, a rosary as big as a load of firewood, and taking in her hand a flag, made of parti-coloured rags, red and yellow and green, went out, crying, "Allah! Allah!" with tongue celebrating the praises of the Lord, whilst her heart galloped in the Devil's race-course, seeking how she might play some sharping trick upon town. She walked from street to street, till she came to an alley swept and watered and marble-paved, where she saw a vaulted gateway, with a threshold of alabaster, and a Moorish porter standing at the door, which was of sandalwood plated with brass and furnished with a ring of silver for knocker.

Now this house belonged to the Chief of the Caliph's Serjeant-ushers, a man of great wealth in fields, houses and allowances, called the Emir

Hasan Sharr al-Tarik, or Evil of the Way, and therefor called because his blow forewent his word. He was married to a fair damsel, Khatun hight, whom he loved and who had made him swear, on the night of his going in unto her, that he would take none other to wife over her nor lie abroad for a single night. And so things went on till one day, he went to the Divan and saw that each Emir had with him a son or two. Then he entered the Hammam-bath and looking at his face in the mirror, noted that the white hairs in his beard overlay its black, and he said in himself, "Will not He who took thy sire bless thee with a son?"

So he went in to his wife, in angry mood, and she said to him, "Good evening to thee"; but he replied, "Get thee out of my sight: from the day I saw thee I have seen naught of good."

"How so?" quoth she.

Quoth he, "On the night of my going in unto thee, thou madest me swear to take no other wife over thee, and this very day I have seen each Emir with a son and some with two. So I minded me of death; and also that to me hath been vouchsafed neither son nor daughter and that whoso leaveth no male hath no memory. This, then, is the reason of my anger, for thou art barren; and knowing thee is like planing a rock."

Cried she, "Allah's name upon thee. Indeed, I have worn out the mortars with beating wool and pounding drugs, and I am not to blame; the barrenness is with thee, for that thou art a snub-nosed mule and thy sperm is weak and watery and impregnateth not neither getteth children."

Said he, "When I return from my journey, I will take another wife"; and she, "My luck is with Allah!" Then he went out from her and both repented of the sharp words spoken each to other.

Now as the Emir's wife looked forth of her lattice, as she were a Bride of the Hoards for the jewellery upon her, behold, there stood Dalilah espying her and seeing her clad in costly clothes and ornaments, said to herself, "'Twould be a rare trick, O Dalilah, to entice yonder young lady from her husband's house and strip her of all her jewels and clothes and make off with the whole lot." So she took up her stand under the windows of the Emir's house, and fell to calling aloud upon Allah's name and saying, "Be present, O ye Walis, ye friends of the Lord!" Whereupon every woman in the street looked from her lattice and, seeing a matron clad, after Sufi fashion, in clothes of white wool, as she were a pavilion of light, said, "Allah bring us a blessing by the aidance of this pious old person, from whose face issueth light!"

And Khatun, the wife of the Emir Hasan, burst into tears and said to her handmaid, "Get thee down, O Makbulah, and kiss the hand of Shaykh Abu Ali, the porter, and say to him, 'Let yonder Religious enter to my lady, so haply she may get a blessing of her.'"

So she went down to the porter and kissing his hand, said to him, "My mistress telleth thee, 'Let yonder pious old woman come in to me, so may I get a blessing of her'; and belike her benediction may extend to us likewise."

The gate-keeper went up to Dalilah and kissed her hand, but she forbade him, saying, "Away from me, lest my ablution be made null and void. Thou, also, art of the attracted God-wards and kindly looked upon by Allah's Saints and under His especial guardianship. May He deliver thee from this servitude, O Abu Ali!"

Now the Emir owed three months' wage to the porter who was straitened thereby, but knew not how to recover his due from his lord; so he said to the old woman, "O my mother, give me to drink from thy pitcher, so I may win a blessing through thee."

She took the ewer from her shoulder and whirled it about in air, so that the plug flew out of its mouth and the three dinars fell to the ground. The porter saw them and picked them up, saying in his mind, "Glory to God! This old woman is one of the Saints that have hoards at their command! It hath been revealed to her of me that I am in want of money for daily expenses; so she hath conjured me these three dinars out of the air." Then said he to her, "Take, O my aunt, these three dinars which fell from thy pitcher"; and she replied, "Away with them from me! I am of the folk who occupy not themselves with the things of the world, no never! Take them and use them for thine own benefit, in lieu of those the Emir oweth thee."

Quoth he, "Thanks to Allah for succour! This is of the chapter of revelation!"

Thereupon the maid accosted her and kissing her hand, carried her up to her mistress. She found the lady as she were a treasure, whose guardian talisman had been loosed; and Khatun bade her welcome and kissed her hand. Quoth she, "O my daughter, I come not to thee save for thy weal and by Allah's will."

Then Khatun set food before her; but she said, "O my daughter, I eat naught except of the food of Paradise and I keep continual fast breaking it but five days in the year. But, O my child, I see thee chagrined and desire that thou tell me the cause of thy concern."

"O my mother," replied Khatun, "I made my husband swear, on my wedding-night, that he would wive none but me, and he saw others with

children and longed for them and said to me, 'Thou art a barren thing!' I answered, 'Thou art a mule which begetteth not'; so he left me in anger, saying, 'When I come back from my journey, I will take another wife,' for he hath villages and lands and large allowances, and if he begat children by another, they will possess the money and take the estates from me."

Said Dalilah, "O my daughter, knowest thou not of my master, the Shaykh Abu al-Hamlat, whom if any debtor visit, Allah quitteth him his debt, and if a barren woman, she conceiveth?"

Khatun replied, "O my mother, since the day of my wedding I have not gone forth the house, no, not even to pay visits of condolence or congratulation."

The old woman rejoined, "O my child, I will carry thee to him and do thou cast thy burden on him and make a vow to him: haply when thy husband shall return from his journey and lie with thee thou shalt conceive by him and bear a girl or a boy: but, be it female or male, it shall be a dervish of the Shaykh Abu al-Hamlat."

Thereupon Khatun rose and arrayed herself in her richest raiment, and donning all her jewellery said, "Keep thou an eye on the house," to her maid, who replied, "I hear and obey, O my lady."

Then she went down and the porter Abu Ali met her and asked her, "Whither away, O my lady?"

"I go to visit the Shaykh Abu al-Hamlat;" answered she; and he, "Be a year's fast incumbent on me! Verily yon Religious is of Allah's saints and full of holiness, O my lady, and she hath hidden treasure at her command, for she gave me three dinars of red gold and divined my case, without my asking her, and knew that I was in want."

Then the old woman went out with the young lady Khatun, saying to her, "Inshallah, O my daughter, when thou hast visited the Shaykh Abu al-Hamlat, there shall betide thee solace of soul and by leave of Almighty Allah thou shalt conceive, and thy husband the Emir shall love thee by the blessing of the Shaykh and shall never again let thee hear a despiteful word."

Quoth Khatun, "I will go with thee to visit him, O my mother!"

But Dalilah said to herself, "Where shall I strip her and take her clothes and jewellery, with the folk coming and going?"

Then she said to her, "O my daughter, walk thou behind me, within sight of me, for this thy mother is a woman sorely burdened; everyone who hath a burden casteth it on me and all who have pious offerings to make give them to me and kiss my hand."

So the young lady followed her at a distance, whilst her anklets tinkled and her hair-coins clinked as she went, till they reached the bazar of the merchants. Presently, they came to the shop of a young merchant, by name Sidi Hasan who was very handsome and had no hair on his face. He saw the lady approaching and fell to casting stolen glances at her, which when the old woman saw, she beckoned to her and said, "Sit down in this shop, till I return to thee."

Khatun obeyed her and sat down in the shop-front of the young merchant, who cast at her one glance of eyes that cost him a thousand sighs. Then the old woman accosted him and saluted him, saying, "Tell me, is not thy name Sidi Hasan, son of the merchant Mohsin?"

He replied, "Yes, who told thee my name?"

Quoth she, "Folk of good repute direct me to thee. Know that this young lady is my daughter and her father was a merchant who died and left her much money. She is come of marriageable age and the wise say, 'Offer thy daughter in marriage and not thy son'; and all her life she hath not come forth the house till this day. Now a divine warning and a command given in secret bid me wed her to thee; so, if thou art poor, I will give thee capital and will open for thee instead of one shop two shops."

Thereupon quoth the young merchant to himself, "I asked Allah for a bride, and He hath given me three things, to wit, coin, clothing, and coynte." Then he continued to the old trot, "O my mother, that where-to thou directest me is well; but this long while my mother saith to me, 'I wish to marry thee,' but I object replying, 'I will not marry except on the sight of my own eyes.'"

Said Dalilah, "Rise and follow my steps, and I will show her to thee, naked."

So he rose and took a thousand dinars, saying in himself, "Haply we may need to buy somewhat or pay the fees for drawing up the marriage contract."

The old woman bade him walk behind the young lady at a distance but within shot of sight and said to herself, "Where wilt thou carry the young lady and the merchant that thou mayest strip them both whilst his shop is still shut?"

Then she walked on and Khatun after her, followed by the young merchant, till she came to a dyery, kept by a master dyer, by name Hajj Mohammed, a man of ill-repute; like the colocasia seller's knife cutting male and female, and loving to eat both figs and pomegranates. He heard the tinkle of the ankle rings and, raising his head, saw the lady and the young man. Presently the old woman came up to him and, after salaming

to him and sitting down opposite him, asked him, "Art thou not Hajj Mohammed the dyer?"

He answered, "Yes, I am he: what dost thou want?"

Quoth she, "Verily, folks of fair repute have directed me to thee. Look at yonder handsome girl, my daughter, and that comely beardless youth, my son; I brought them both up and spent much money on both of them. Now, thou must know that I have a big old ruinous house which I have shored up with wood, and the builder saith to me, 'Go and live in some other place, lest belike it fall upon thee; and when this is repaired return hither.' So I went forth to seek me a lodging, and people of worth directed me to thee, and I wish to lodge my son and daughter with thee."

Quoth the dyer in his mind, "Verily, here is fresh butter upon cake come to thee." But he said to the old woman, "'Tis true I have a house and saloon and upper floor; but I cannot spare any part thereof, for I want it all for guests and for the indigo-growers my clients."

She replied, "O my son, 'twill be only for a month or two at the most, till our house be repaired, and we are strange folk. Let the guest-chamber be shared between us and thee, and by thy life, O my son, an thou desire that thy guests be ours, we will welcome them and eat with them and sleep with them." Then he gave her the keys, one big and one small and one crooked, saying to her "The big key is that of the house, the crooked one that of the saloon and the little one that of the upper floor."

So Dalilah took the keys and fared on, followed by the lady who forwent the young merchant, till she came to the lane wherein was the house. She opened the door and entered, introducing the damsel to whom said she, "O my daughter, this (pointing to the saloon) is the lodging of the Shaykh Abu al-Hamlat; but go thou into the upper floor and loose thy outer veil and wait till I come to thee." So she went up and sat down. Presently appeared the young merchant, whom Dalilah carried into the saloon, saying, "Sit down, whilst I fetch my daughter and show her to thee."

So he sat down and the old trot went up to Khatun who said to her, "I wish to visit the Shaykh, before the folk come."

Replied the beldame, "O my daughter, we fear for thee."

Asked Khatun, "Why so?" and Dalilah answered, "Because here is a son of mine, a natural who knoweth not summer from winter, but goeth ever naked. He is the Shaykh's deputy and, if he saw a girl like thee come to visit his chief, he would snatch her earrings and tear her ears and rend her silken robes. So do thou doff thy jewellery and clothes and I will keep them for thee, till thou hast made thy pious visitation."

Accordingly the damsel did off her outer dress and jewels and gave them to the old woman, who said, "I will lay them for thee on the Shaykh's curtain, that a blessing may betide thee."

Then she went out, leaving the lady in her shift and petticoat-trousers, and hid the clothes and jewels in a place on the staircase; after which she betook herself to the young merchant, whom she found impatiently awaiting the girl, and he cried, "Where is thy daughter, that I may see her?"

But she smote palm on breast and he said "What aileth thee?" Quoth she, "Would there were no such thing as the ill neighbour and the envious! They saw thee enter the house with me and asked me of thee; and I said, 'This is a bridegroom I have found for my daughter.' So they envied me on thine account and said to my girl, 'Is thy mother tired of keeping thee, that she marrieth thee to a leper?' There-upon I swore to her that she should not see thee save naked."

Quoth he, "I take refuge with Allah from the envious," and baring his fore-arm, showed her that it was like silver.

Said she, "Have no fear; thou shalt see her naked, even as she shall see thee naked"; and he said, "Let her come and look at me. Then he put off his pelisse and sables and his girdle and dagger and the rest of his raiment, except his shirt and bag-trousers, and would have laid the purse of a thousand dinars with them, but Dalilah cried, "Give them to me, that I may take care of them." So she took them and fetching the girl's clothes and jewellery shouldered the whole and locking the door upon them went her ways.

When the old woman had taken the property of the young merchant and the damsel and wended her ways, having locked the door upon them, she deposited her spoils with a druggist of her acquaintance and returned to the dyer, whom she found sitting, awaiting her. Quoth he, "Inshallah, the house pleaseth thee?"; and quoth she, "There is a blessing in it; and I go now to fetch porters to carry hither our goods and furniture. But my children would have me bring them a panade with meat; so do thou take this dinar and buy the dish and go and eat the morning meal with them."

Asked the dyer, "Who shall guard the dyery meanwhile and the people's goods that be therein?" and the old woman answered, "Thy lad!"

"So be it," rejoined he, and taking a dish and cover, went out to do her bidding.

So far concerning the dyer who will again be mentioned in the tale; but as regards the old woman, she fetched the clothes and jewels she had left with the druggist and going back to the dyery, said to the lad, "Run after

thy master, and I will not stir hence till you both return."

"To hear is to obey," answered he and went away, while she began to collect all the customers' goods.

Presently, there came up an ass-driver, a scavenger, who had been out of work for a week and who was an Hashish-eater to boot; and she called him, saying, "Hither, O donkey-boy!"

So he came to her and she asked, "Knowest thou my son the dyer?"; whereto he answered, "Yes, I know him."

Then she said, "The poor fellow is insolvent and loaded with debts, and as often as he is put in prison, I set him free. Now we wish to see him declared bankrupt and I am going to return the goods to their owners; so do thou lend me thine ass to carry the load and receive this dinar to its hire. When I am gone, take the handsaw and empty out the vats and jars and break them, so that if there come an officer from the Kazi's court, he may find nothing in the dyery."

Quoth he, "I owe the Hajj a kindness and will do something for Allah's love."

So she laid the things on the ass and, the Protector protecting her, made for her own house; so that she arrived there in safety and went in to her daughter Zaynab, who said to her, "O my mother, my heart hath been with thee! What hast thou done by way of roguery?"

Dalilah replied, "I have played off four tricks on four wights; the wife of the Serjeant-usher, a young merchant, a dyer and an ass-driver, and have brought thee all their spoil on the donkey-boy's beast."

Cried Zaynab, "O my mother, thou wilt never more be able to go about the town, for fear of the Serjeant-usher, whose wife's raiment and jewellery thou hast taken, and the merchant whom thou hast stripped naked, and the dyer whose customers' goods thou hast stolen and the owner of the ass."

Rejoined the old woman, "Pooh, my girl! I reck not of them, save the donkey-boy, who knoweth me."

Meanwhile the dyer bought the meat-panade and set out for the house, followed by his servant with the food on head. On his way thither, he passed his shop, where he found the donkey-boy breaking the vats and jars and saw that there was neither stuff nor liquor left in them and that the dyery was in ruins. So he said to him, "Hold thy hand, O ass-driver"; and the donkey-boy desisted and cried, "Praised be Allah for thy safety, O master! Verily my heart was with thee."

"Why so?"

"Thou art become bankrupt and they have filed a docket of thine insolvency." "Who told thee this?"

"Thy mother told me, and bade me break the jars and empty the vats, that the Kazi's officers might find nothing in the shop, if they should come."

"Allah confound the far One!" cried the dyer; "My mother died long ago."

And he beat his breast, exclaiming, "Alas, for the loss of my goods and those of the folk!"

The donkey-boy also wept and ejaculated, "Alas, for the loss of my ass!"; and he said to the dyer, "Give me back my beast which thy mother stole from me."

The dyer laid hold of him by the throat and fell to buffeting him, saying, "Bring me the old woman"; whilst the other buffeted him in return saying, "Give me back my beast." So they beat and cursed each other, till the folk collected around them and one of them asked, "What is the matter, O Master Mohammed?"

The ass-driver answered, "I will tell thee the tale," and related to them his story, saying, "I deemed I was doing the dyer a good turn; but, when he saw me he beat his breast and said, 'My mother is dead.' And now, I for one require my ass of him, it being he who hath put this trick on me, that he might make me lose my beast."

Then said the folk to the dyer, "O Master Mohammed, dost thou know this matron, that thou didst entrust her with the dyery and all therein?"

And he replied, "I know her not; but she took lodgings with me to-day, she and her son and daughter."

Quoth one, "In my judgment, the dyer is bound to indemnify the ass-driver."

Quoth another, "Why so?"

"Because," replied the first, "he trusted not the old Woman nor gave her his ass save only because he saw that the dyer had entrusted her with the dyery and its contents."

And a third said, "O master, since thou hast lodged her with thee, it behoveth thee to get the man back his ass."

Then they made for the house, and the tale will come round to them again. Meanwhile, the young merchant remained awaiting the old woman's coming with her daughter, but she came not nor did her daughter; whilst the young lady in like manner sat expecting her return with leave from her son, the God-attended one, the Shaykh's deputy, to go in to the holy presence. So weary of waiting, she rose to visit the Shaykh by herself and went down

into the saloon, where she found the young merchant, who said to her, "Come hither! where is thy mother, who brought me to marry thee?"

She replied, "My mother is dead, art thou the old woman's son, the ecstatic, the deputy of the Shaykh Abu al-Hamlat?"

Quoth he, "The swindling old trot is no mother of mine; she hath cheated me and taken my clothes and a thousand dinars."

Quoth Khatun, "And me also hath she swindled for she brought me to see the Shaykh Abu al-Hamlat and in lieu of so doing she hath stripped me."

Thereupon he, "I look to thee to make good my clothes and my thousand dinars;" and she, "I look to thee to make good my clothes and jewellery."

And, behold, at this moment in came the dyer and seeing them both stripped of their raiment, said to them, "Tell me where your mother is."

So the young lady related all that had befallen her and the young merchant related all that had betided him, and the Master-dyer exclaimed, "Alas, for the loss of my goods and those of the folk!"; and the ass-driver ejaculated, "Alas, for my ass! Give me, O dyer, my ass!" Then said the dyer, "This old woman is a sharper. Come forth, that I may lock the door." Quoth the young merchant, "'Twere a disgrace to thee that we should enter thy house dressed and go forth from it undressed."

So the dyer clad him and the damsel and sent her back to her house where we shall find her after the return of her husband. Then he shut the dyery and said to the young merchant, "Come, let us go and search for the old woman and hand her over to the Wali, the Chief of Police." So they and the ass-man repaired to the house of the master of police and made their complaint to him.

Quoth he, "O folk, what want ye?" and when they told him he rejoined, "How many old women are there not in the town! Go ye and seek for her and lay hands on her and bring her to me, and I will torture her for you and make her confess." So they sought for her all round the town; and an account of them will presently be given.

As for old Dalilah the Wily, she said, "I have a mind to play off another trick," to her daughter who answered, "O my mother, I fear for thee;" but the beldam cried, "I am like the bean husks which fall, proof against fire and water." So she rose, and donning a slave-girl's dress of such as serve people of condition, went out to look for some one to defraud.

Presently she came to a by-street, spread with carpets and lighted with hanging lamps, and heard a noise of singing-women and drumming of tambourines. Here she saw a handmaid bearing on her shoulder a boy, clad in trousers laced with silver and a little Aba-cloak of velvet, with a pearl embroidered Tarbush-cap on his head, and about his neck a collar of gold set with jewels. Now the house belonged to the Provost of the Merchants of Baghdad, and the boy was his son. He had a virgin daughter, to boot, who was promised in marriage, and it was her betrothal they were celebrating that day. There was with her mother a company of noble dames and singing-women, and whenever she went upstairs or down, the boy clung to her. So she called the slave-girl and said to her, "Take thy young master and play with him, till the company break up." Seeing this, Dalilah asked the handmaid, "What festivities are these in your mistress's house?" and was answered "She celebrates her daughter's betrothal this day, and she hath singing-women with her."

Quoth the old woman to herself, "O Dalilah, the thing to do is to spirit away this boy from the maid." She began crying out, "O disgrace! O ill luck!" Then pulling out a brass token, resembling a dinar, she said to the maid, who was a simpleton, "Take this ducat and go in to thy mistress and say to her, 'Umm al-Khayr rejoiceth with thee and is beholden to thee for thy favours, and on the day of assembly she and her daughters will visit thee and handsel the tiring-women with the usual gifts.'"

Said the girl, "O my mother, my young master here catcheth hold of his mamma, whenever he seeth her"; and she replied "Give him to me, whilst thou goest in and comest back." So she gave her the child and taking the token, went in; whereupon Dalilah made off with the boy to a by-lane, where she stripped him of his clothes and jewels, saying to herself, "O Dalilah, 'twould indeed be the finest of tricks, even as thou hast cheated the maid and taken the boy from her, so now to carry on the game and pawn him for a thousand dinars."

So she repaired to the jewel-bazar, where she saw a Jew goldsmith seated with a cage full of jewellery before him, and said to herself, "'Twould be a rare trick to chouse this Jew fellow and get a thousand gold pieces worth of jewellery from him and leave the boy in pledge for it."

Presently the Jew looked at them and seeing the boy with the old woman, knew him for the son of the Provost of the Merchants. Now the Israelite was a man of great wealth, but would envy his neighbour if he sold and himself did not sell; so espying Dalilah, he said to her, "What seekest thou, O my mistress?"

She asked, "Art thou Master Azariah the Jew?" having first enquired his name of others; and he answered, "Yes."

Quoth she, "This boy's sister, daughter of the Shahbandar of the Merchants, is a promised bride, and to-day they celebrate her betrothal; and she hath need of jewellery. So give me two pair of gold ankle-rings, a brace of gold bracelets, and pearl ear-drops, with a girdle, a poignard and a seal-ring."

He brought them out and she took of him a thousand dinars' worth of jewellery, saying, "I will take these ornaments on approval; and whatso pleaseth them, they will keep and I will bring thee the price and leave this boy with thee till then."

He said, "Be it as thou wilt!" So she took the jewellery and made off to her own house, where her daughter asked her how the trick had sped. She told her how she had taken and stripped the Shahbandar's boy, and Zaynab said, "Thou wilt never be able to walk abroad again in the town."

Meanwhile, the maid went in to her mistress and said to her, "O my lady, Umm al-Khayr saluteth thee and rejoiceth with thee and on assembly-day she will come, she and her daughters, and give the customary presents."

Quoth her mistress, "Where is thy young master?"

Quoth the slave-girl, "I left him with her lest he cling to thee, and she gave me this, as largesse for the singing-women."

So the lady said to the chief of the singers, "Take thy money"; and she took it and found it a brass counter; whereupon the lady cried to the maid, "Get thee down, O whore, and look to thy young master."

Accordingly, she went down and finding neither boy nor old woman, shrieked aloud and fell on her face. Their joy was changed into annoy, and behold, the Provost came in, when his wife told him all that had befallen and he went out in quest of the child, whilst the other merchants also fared forth and each sought his own road.

Presently, the Shahbandar, who had looked everywhere, espied his son seated, naked, in the Jew's shop and said to the owner, "This is my son."

"'Tis well," answered the Jew. So he took him up, without asking for his clothes, of the excess of his joy at finding him; but the Jew laid hold of him, saying, "Allah succour the Caliph against thee!"

The Provost asked, "What aileth thee, O Jew?"; and he answered, "Verily the old woman took of me a thousand dinars' worth of jewellery for thy daughter, and left this lad in pledge for the price; and I had not trusted her, but that she offered to leave the child whom I knew for thy son."

Said the Provost, "My daughter needeth no jewellery, give me the boy's clothes." Thereupon the Jew shrieked out, "Come to my aid, O

Moslems!" but at that moment up came the dyer and the ass-man and the young merchant, who were going about, seeking the old woman, and enquired the cause of their jangle.

So they told them the case and they said, "This old woman is a cheat, who hath cheated us before you."

Then they recounted to them how she had dealt with them, and the Provost said, "Since I have found my son, be his clothes his ransom! If I come upon the old woman, I will require them of her." And he carried the child home to his mother, who rejoiced in his safety.

Then the Jew said to the three others "Whither go ye?"; and they answered, "We go to look for her."

Quoth the Jew, "Take me with you," presently adding, "Is there any one of you knoweth her?"

The donkey-boy cried, "I know her;" and the Jew said, "If we all go forth together, we shall never catch her; for she will flee from us. Let each take a different road, and be our rendezvous at the shop of Hajj Mas'ud, the Moorish barber." They agreed to this and set off, each in a different direction.

Presently, Dalilah sallied forth again to play her tricks and the ass-driver met her and knew her. So he caught hold of her and said to her, "Woe to thee! Hast thou been long at this trade?"

She asked, "What aileth thee?"; and he answered, "Give me back my ass."

Quoth she, "Cover what Allah covereth, O my son! Dost thou seek thine ass and the people's things?"

Quoth he, "I want my ass; that's all"; and quoth she, "I saw that thou wast poor: so I deposited thine ass for thee with the Moorish barber. Stand off, whilst I speak him fair, that he may give thee the beast."

So she went up to the Maghrabi and kissed his hand and shed tears. He asked her what ailed her and she said, "O my son, look at my boy who standeth yonder. He was ill and exposed himself to the air, which injured his intellect. He used to buy asses and now, if he stand he saith nothing but, 'My ass!' if he sit he crieth, 'My ass!' and if he walk he crieth, 'My ass!' Now I have been told by a certain physician that his mind is disordered and that nothing will cure him but drawing two of his grinders and cauterising him twice on either temple. So do thou take this dinar and call him to thee, saying, 'Thine ass is with me.'"

Said the barber, "May I fast for a year, if I do not give him his ass in his fist!" Now he had with him two journeymen, so he said to one of them, "Go, heat the irons."

Then the old woman went her way and the barber called to the donkey-boy, saying, "Thine ass is with me, good fellow! come and take him, and as thou livest, I will give him into thy palm."

So he came to him and the barber carried him into a dark room, where he knocked him down and the journeymen bound him hand and foot. Then the Maghrabi arose and pulled out two of his grinders and fired him on either temple; after which he let him go, and he rose and said, "O Moor, why hast thou used me with this usage?"

Quoth the barber, "Thy mother told me that thou hadst taken cold whilst ill, and hadst lost thy reason, so that, whether sitting or standing or walking, thou wouldst say nothing but 'My ass!' So here is thine ass in thy fist." Said the other, "Allah requite thee for pulling out my teeth."

Then the barber told him all that the old woman had related and he exclaimed, "Allah torment her!"; and the twain left the shop and went out, disputing. When the barber returned, he found his booth empty, for, whilst he was absent, the old woman had taken all that was therein and made off with it to her daughter, whom she acquainted with all that had befallen and all she had done. The barber, seeing his place plundered, caught hold of the donkey-boy and said to him, "Bring me thy mother."

But he answered, saying, "She is not my mother; she is a sharper who hath cozened much people and stolen my ass."

And lo! at this moment up came the dyer and the Jew and the young merchant, and seeing the Moorish barber holding on to the ass-driver who was fired on both temples, they said to him, "What hath befallen thee, O donkey-boy?"

So he told them all that had betided him and the barber did the like; and the others in turn related to the Moor the tricks the old woman had played them. Then he shut up his shop and went with them to the office of the Police-master to whom they said, "We look to thee for our case and our coin."

Quoth the Wali, "And how many old women are there not in Baghdad! Say me, doth any of you know her?"

Quoth the ass-man, "I do; so give me ten of thine officers."

He gave them half a score archers and they all five went out, followed by the sergeants, and patrolled the city, till they met the old woman, when they laid hands on her and carrying her to the house of the Chief of Police, stood waiting under his office windows till he should come forth. Presently, the warders fell asleep, for excess of watching with their chief, and old Dalilah feigned to follow their example, till the ass-man and his fellows slept likewise, when she stole away from them and, going in to the Wali's Harim, kissed the hand of the mistress of the house and asked her "Where is the Chief of Police?"

The lady answered, "He is asleep; what wouldst thou with him?"

Quoth Dalilah, "My husband is a merchant of chattels and gave me five Mamelukes to sell, whilst he went on a journey. The Master of Police met me and bought them of me for a thousand dinars and two hundred for myself, saying, 'Bring them to my house.' So I have brought them."

Hearing the old woman's story she believed it and asked her, "Where are the slaves?"

Dalilah replied, "O my lady, they are asleep under the palace window"; whereupon the dame looked out and seeing the Moorish barber clad in a Mameluke habit and the young merchant as he were a drunken Mameluke and the Jew and the dyer and the ass-driver as they were shaven Mamelukes, said in herself, "Each of these white slaves is worth more than a thousand dinars."

So she opened her chest and gave the old woman the thousand ducats, saying, "Fare thee forth now and come back anon; when my husband waketh, I will get thee the other two hundred dinars from him."

Answered the old woman, "O my lady, an hundred of them are thine, under the sherbert-gugglet whereof thou drinkest, and the other hundred do thou keep for me against I come back," presently adding, "Now let me out by the private door." So she let her out, and the Protector protected her and she made her way home to her daughter, to whom she related how she had gotten a thousand gold pieces and sold her five pursuers into slavery, ending with, "O my daughter, the one who troubleth me most is the ass-driver, for he knoweth me."

Said Zaynab, "O my mother, abide quiet awhile and let what thou hast done suffice thee, for the crock shall not always escape the shock."

When the Chief of Police awoke, his wife said to him, "I give thee joy of the five slaves thou hast bought of the old woman."

Asked he, "What slaves?"

And she answered, "Why dost thou deny it to me? Allah willing, they shall become like thee people of condition."

Quoth he, "As my head liveth, I have bought no slaves! Who saith this?"

Quoth she, "The old woman, the brokeress, from whom thou boughtest them; and thou didst promise her a thousand dinars for them and two hundred for herself."

Cried he, "Didst thou give her the money?"

And she replied, "Yes; for I saw the slaves with my own eyes, and on each is a suit of clothes worth a thousand dinars; so I sent out to bid the sergeants have an eye to them."

The Wali went out and, seeing the five plaintiffs, said to the officers, "Where are the five slaves we bought for a thousand dinars of the old woman?"

Said they, "There are no slaves here; only these five men, who found the old woman, and seized her and brought her hither. We fell asleep, whilst waiting for thee, and she stole away and entered the Harim. Presently out came a maid and asked us, 'Are the five with you with whom the old woman came?'; and we answered, 'Yes.'"

Cried the Master of Police, "By Allah, this is the biggest of swindles!"; and the five men said, "We look to thee for our goods."

Quoth the Wali, "The old woman, your mistress, sold you to me for a thousand gold pieces."

Quoth they, "That were not allowed of Allah; we are free-born men and may not be sold, and we appeal from thee to the Caliph."

Rejoined the Master of Police, "None showed her the way to the house save you, and I will sell you to the galleys for two hundred dinars apiece."

Just then, behold, up came the Emir Hasan Sharr al-Tarik who, on his return from his journey, had found his wife stripped of her clothes and jewellery and heard from her all that had passed; whereupon quoth he, "The Master of Police shall answer me this" and repairing to him, said "Dost thou suffer old women to go round about the town and cozen folk of their goods? This is thy duty and I look to thee for my wife's property."

Then said he to the five men, "What is the case with you?"

So they told him their stories and he said, "Ye are wronged men," and turning to the Master of Police, asked him, "Why dost thou arrest them?"

Answered he, "None brought the old wretch to my house save these five, so that she took a thousand dinars of my money and sold them to my women." Whereupon the five cried, "O Emir Hasan, be thou our advocate in this cause."

Then said the Master of Police to the Emir, "Thy wife's goods are at my charge and I will be surety for the old woman. But which of you knoweth her?"

They cried, "We all know her: send ten apparitors with us, and we will take her."

So he gave them ten men, and the ass-driver said to them, "Follow me,

612

for I should know her with blue eyes."

Then they fared forth and lo! they meet old Dalilah coming out of a by-street: so they at once laid hands on her and brought her to the office of the Wali who asked her, "Where are the people's goods?"

But she answered, saying, "I have neither gotten them nor seen them."

Then he cried to the gaoler, "Take her with thee and clap her in gaol till the morning;" but he replied, "I will not take her nor will I imprison her lest she play a trick on me and I be answerable for her."

So the Master of Police mounted and rode out with Dalilah and the rest to the bank of the Tigris, where he bade the lamp-lighter crucify her by her hair. He drew her up by the pulley and bound her on the cross; after which the Master of Police set ten men to guard her and went home. Presently, the night fell down and sleep overcame the watchmen.

Now a certain Badawi had heard one man say to a friend, "Praise be to Allah for thy safe return! Where hast thou been all this time?"

Replied the other, "In Baghdad where I broke my fast on honey-fritters."

Quoth the Badawi to himself "Needs must I go to Baghdad and eat honey-fritters therein"; for in all his life he had never entered Baghdad nor seen fritters of the sort. So he mounted his stallion and rode on towards Baghdad, saying in his mind, "'Tis a fine thing to eat honey-fritters! On the honour of an Arab, I will break my fast with honey-fritters and naught else!" and he rode on till he came to the place where Dalilah was crucified and she heard him utter these words. So he went up to her and said to her, "What art thou?"

Quoth she, "I throw myself on thy protection, O Shaykh of the Arabs!" and quoth lie, "Allah indeed protect thee! But what is the cause of thy crucifixion?"

Said she, "I have an enemy, an oilman, who frieth fritters, and I stopped to buy some of him, when I chanced to spit and my spittle fell on the fritters. So he complained of me to the Governor who commanded to crucify me, saying, 'I adjudge that ye take ten pounds of honey-fritters and feed her therewith upon the cross. If she eat them, let her go, but if not, leave her hanging.' And my stomach will not brook sweet things."

Cried the Badawi, "By the honour of the Arabs, I departed not the camp but that I might taste of honey-fritters! I will eat them for thee."

Quoth she, "None may eat them, except he be hung up in my place."

So he fell into the trap and unbound her; whereupon she bound him in her stead, after she had stripped him of his clothes and turband and put them on; then covering herself with his burnouse and mounting his horse, she rode to her house, where Zaynab asked her, "What meaneth this plight?" and she answered, "They crucified me;" and told her all that had befallen her with the Badawi.

This is how it fared with her; but as regards the watchmen, the first who woke roused his companions and they saw that the day had broken. So one of them raised his eyes and cried, "Dalilah."

Replied the Badawi, "By Allah! I have not eaten all night. Have ye brought the honey-fritters?"

All exclaimed, "This is a man and a Badawi," and one of them asked him, "O Badawi, where is Dalilah and who loosed her?"

He answered, "'Twas I; she shall not eat the honey-fritters against her will; for her soul abhorreth them."

So they knew that the Arab was ignorant of her case, whom she had cozened, and said to one another, "Shall we flee or abide the accomplishment of that which Allah hath written for us?"

As they were talking, up came the Chief of Police, with all the folk whom the old woman had cheated, and said to the guards, "Arise, loose Dalilah."

Quoth the Badawi, "We have not eaten to-night. Hast thou brought the honey-fritters?"

Whereupon the Wali raised his eyes to the cross and seeing the Badawi hung up in the stead of the old woman, said to the watchmen, "What is this?"

"Pardon, O our lord!"

"Tell me what hath happened"

"We were weary with watching with thee on guard and said, 'Dalilah is crucified.' So we fell asleep, and when we awoke, we found the Badawi hung up in her room; and we are at thy mercy."

"O folk, Allah's pardon be upon you! She is indeed a clever cheat!"

Then they unbound the Badawi, who laid hold of the Master of Police, saying, "Allah succour the Caliph against thee! I look to none but thee for my horse and clothes!"

So the Wali questioned him and he told him what had passed between Dalilah and himself. The magistrate marvelled and asked him, "Why didst thou release her?" and the Badawi answered, "I knew not that she was a felon."

Then said the others, "O Chief of Police, we look to thee in the matter of our goods; for we delivered the old woman into thy hands and she was in thy guard; and we cite thee before the Divan of the Caliph."

Now the Emir Hasan had gone up to the Divan, when in came the Wali with the Badawi and the five others, saying, "Verily, we are wronged men!"

"Who hath wronged you?" asked the Caliph; so each came forward in turn and told his story, after which said the Master of Police, "O Commander of the Faithful, the old woman cheated me also and sold me these five men as slaves for a thousand dinars, albeit they are free-born."

Quoth the Prince of True Believers, "I take upon myself all that you have lost"; adding to the Master of Police, "I charge thee with the old woman."

But he shook his collar, saying, "O Commander of the Faithful, I will not answer for her; for, after I had hung her on the cross, she tricked this Badawi and, when he loosed her, she tied him up in her room and made off with his clothes and horse."

Quoth the Caliph, "Whom but thee shall I charge with her?"; and quoth the Wali, "Charge Ahmad al-Danaf, for he hath a thousand dinars a month and one-and-forty followers, at a monthly wage of an hundred dinars each."

So the Caliph said, "Harkye, Captain Ahmad!"

"At thy service, O Commander of the Faithful," said he; and the Caliph cried, "I charge thee to bring the old woman before us."

Replied Ahmad, "I will answer for her." Then the Caliph kept the Badawi and the five with him, whilst Ahmad and his men went down to their hall, saying to one another, "How shall we lay hands on her, seeing that there are many old women in the town?"

And quoth Ahmad to Hasan Shuman, "What counsellest thou?"

Whereupon quoth one of them, by name Ali Kitf al-Jamal, to Al-Danaf, "Of what dost thou take counsel with Hasan Shuman? Is the Pestilent one any great shakes?"

Said Hasan, "O Ali, why dost thou disparage me? By the Most Great Name, I will not company with thee at this time!" and he rose and went out in wrath.

Then said Ahmad, "O my braves, let every sergeant take ten men, each to his own quarter and search for Dalilah."

All did his bidding, Ali included, and they said, "Ere we disperse let us agree to rendezvous in the quarter Al-Kalkh." It was noised abroad in the city that Calamity Ahmad had undertaken to lay hands on Dalilah the Wily, and Zaynab said to her, "O my mother, an thou be indeed a trickstress, do thou befool Ahmad al-Danaf and his company."

Answered Dalilah, "I fear none save Hasan Shuman;" and Zaynab said, "By the life of my browlock, I will assuredly get thee the clothes of all the one-and-forty."

Then she dressed and veiled herself and going to a certain druggist, who had a saloon with two doors, salamed to him and gave him an ashrafi and said to him, "Take this gold piece as a douceur for thy saloon and let it to me till the end of the day." So he gave her the keys and she fetched carpets and so forth on the stolen ass and furnishing the place, set on each raised pavement a tray of meat and wine. Then she went out and stood at the door, with her face unveiled and behold, up came Ali Kitf al-Jamal and his men. She kissed his hand; and he fell in love with her, seeing her to be a handsome girl, and said to her, "What dost thou want?"

Quoth she, "Art thou Captain Ahmad al-Danaf?" and quoth he, "No, but I am of his company and my name is Ali Camel-shoulder."

Asked she, "Whither fare you?" and he answered, "We go about in quest of a sharkish old woman, who hath stolen folk's good, and we mean to lay hands on her. But who art thou and what is thy business?"

She replied, "My father was a taverner at Mosul and he died and left me much money. So I came hither, for fear of the Dignities, and asked the people who would protect me, to which they replied, 'None but Ahmad al-Danaf.'"

Said the men, "From this day forth, thou art under his protection"; and she replied, "Hearten me by eating a bit and drinking a sup of water."

They consented and entering, ate and drank till they were drunken, when she drugged them with Bhang and stripped them of their clothes and arms; and on likewise she did with the three other companions.

Presently, Calamity Ahmad went out to look for Dalilah, but found her not, neither set eyes on any of his followers, and went on till he came to the door where Zaynab was standing. She kissed his hand and he looked on her and fell in love with her.

Quoth she, "Art thou Captain Ahmad al-Danaf?" and quoth he, "Yes: who art thou?"

She replied, "I am a stranger from Mosul. My father was a vintner at that place and he died and left me much money wherewith I came to this city, for fear of the powers that be, and opened this tavern. The Master of Police hath imposed a tax on me, but it is my desire to put myself under thy protection and pay thee what the police would take of me, for thou hast the better right to it."

Quoth he, "Do not pay him aught: thou shalt have my protection and welcome."

Then quoth she, "Please to heal my heart and eat of my victual."

So he entered and ate and drank wine, till he could not sit upright, when she drugged him and took his clothes and arms. Then she loaded her purchase on the Badawi's horse and the donkey-boy's ass and made off with it, after she had aroused Ali Kitf al-Jamal.

Camel-shoulder awoke and found himself naked and saw Ahmad and his men drugged and stripped: so he revived them with the counter-drug and they awoke and found themselves naked. Quoth Calamity Ahmad, "O lads, what is this? We were going to catch her, and lo! this strumpet hath caught us! How Hasan Shuman will rejoice over us! But we will wait till it is dark and then go away."

Meanwhile Pestilence Hasan said to the hall-keeper, "Where are the men?" and as he asked, up they came naked; and he recited these two couplets:

"Men in their purposes are much alike,
　But in their issues difference comes to light:
Of men some wise are, others simple souls;
　As of the stars some dull, some pearly bright."

Then he looked at them and asked, "Who hath played you this trick and made you naked?" and they answered, "We went in quest of an old woman, and a pretty girl stripped us."

Quoth Hasan, "She hath done right well."

They asked, "Dost thou know her?" and he answered, "Yes, I know her and the old trot too."

Quoth they, "What shall we say to the Caliph?" and quoth he, "O Danaf, do thou shake thy collar before him, and he will say, 'Who is answerable for her'; and if he ask why thou hast not caught her; say thou, 'We know her not; but charge Hasan Shuman with her.' And if he give her into my charge, I will lay hands on her."

So they slept that night and on the morrow they went up to the Caliph's Divan and kissed ground before him. Quoth he, "Where is the old woman, O Captain Ahmad?"

But he shook his collar. The Caliph asked him why he did so, and he answered, "I know her not; but do thou charge Hasan Shuman to lay hands on her, for he knoweth her and her daughter also."

Then Hasan interceded for her with the Caliph, saying, "Indeed, she hath not played off these tricks, because she coveted the folk's stuff, but to show her cleverness and that of her daughter, to the intent that thou shouldst continue her husband's stipend to her and that of her father to her daughter. So an thou wilt spare her life I will fetch her to thee."

Cried the Caliph, "By the life of my ancestors, if she restore the people's goods, I will pardon her on thine intercession!"

And said the Pestilence, "Give me a pledge, O Prince of True Believers!" Whereupon Al-Rashid gave him the kerchief of pardon. So Hasan repaired to Dalilah's house and called to her. Her daughter Zaynab answered him and he asked her, "Where is thy mother?"

"Upstairs," she answered; and he said, "Bid her take the people's goods and come with me to the presence of the Caliph; for I have brought her the kerchief of pardon, and if she will not come with a good grace, let her blame only herself." So Dalilah came down and tying the kerchief about her neck gave him the people's goods on the donkey-boy's ass and the Badawi's horse.

Quoth he, "There remain the clothes of my Chief and his men"; and quoth she, "By the Most Great Name, 'twas not I who stripped them!"

Rejoined Hasan, "Thou sayst sooth, it was thy daughter Zaynab's doing, and this was a good turn she did thee."

Then he carried her to the Divan and laying the people's goods and stuff before the Caliph, set the old trot in his presence. As soon as he saw her, he bade throw her down on the carpet of blood, whereat she cried, "I cast myself on thy protection, O Shuman."

So he rose and kissing the Caliph's hands, said, "Pardon, O Commander of the Faithful! Indeed, thou gavest me the kerchief of pardon."

Said the Prince of True Believers, "I pardon her for thy sake: come hither, O old woman; what is thy name?"

"My name is Wily Dalilah," answered she, and the Caliph said "Thou art indeed crafty and full of guile." Whence she was dubbed Dalilah the Wily One.

Then quoth he, "Why hast thou played all these tricks on the folk and wearied our hearts?" and quoth she, "I did it not of lust for their goods, but because I had heard of the tricks which Ahmad al-Danaf and Hasan Shuman played in Baghdad and said to myself, 'I too will do the like.' And now I have returned the folk their goods."

But the ass-driver rose and said "I invoke Allah's law between me and her; for it sufficed her not to take my ass, but she must needs egg on the

Moorish barber to tear out my eye-teeth and fire me on both temples."

Thereupon the Caliph bade give him an hundred dinars and ordered the dyer the like, saying, "Go; set up thy dyery again." So they called down blessings on his head and went away.

The Badawi also took his clothes and horse and departed, saying, "'Tis henceforth unlawful and forbidden me to enter Baghdad and eat honey-fritters." And the others took their goods and went away.

Then said the Caliph, "Ask a boon of me, O Dalilah!" and she said, "Verily, my father was governor of the carrier-pigeons to thee and I know how to rear the birds; and my husband was town-captain of Baghdad. Now I wish to have the reversion of my husband and my daughter wisheth to have that of her father."

The Caliph granted both their requests and she said, "I ask of thee that I may be portress of thy Khan." Now he had built a Khan of three stories, for the merchants to lodge in, and had assigned to its service forty slaves and also forty dogs he had brought from the King of the Sulaymaniyah, when he deposed him; and there was in the Khan a cook-slave, who cooked for the chattels and fed the hounds for which he let make collars.

Said the Caliph, "O Dalilah, I will write thee a patent of guardianship of the Khan, and if aught be lost therefrom, thou shalt be answerable for it."

"'Tis well," replied she; "but do thou lodge my daughter in the pavilion over the door of the Khan, for it hath terraced roofs, and carrier-pigeons may not be reared to advantage save in an open space."

The Caliph granted her this also and she and her daughter removed to the pavilion in question, where Zaynab hung up the one-and-forty dresses of Calamity Ahmad and his company. Moreover, they delivered to Dalilah the forty pigeons which carried the royal messages, and the Caliph appointed the Wily One mistress over the forty slaves and charged them to obey her. She made the place of her sitting behind the door of the Khan, and every day she used to go up to the Caliph's Divan, lest he should need to send a message by pigeon-post and stay there till eventide whilst the forty slaves stood on guard at the Khan; and when darkness came on they loosed the forty dogs that they might keep watch over the place by night.

"Such were the doings of Dalilah the Wily One in Baghdad," quoth Scheherazade, as she perceived the dawn of day and ceased her permitted say. "And much like them were the adventures of Mercury Ali."

The Adventures of Mercury Ali of Cairo

**Quoth Scheherazade the following evening,
"Now as regards the works of Mercury Ali…**

Thre lived once at Cairo, in the days of Salah the Egyptian, who was Chief of the Cairo Police and had forty men under him, a sharper named Ali, for whom the Master of Police used to set snares and think that he had fallen therein; but, when they sought for him, they found that he had fled like zaybak, or quicksilver, wherefore they dubbed him Ali Zaybak or Mercury Ali of Cairo.

Now one day, as he sat with his men in his hall, his heart became heavy within him and his breast was straitened. The hall-keeper saw him sitting with frowning face and said to him, "What aileth thee, O my Chief? If thy breast be straitened take a turn in the streets of Cairo, for assuredly walking in her markets will do away with thy irk." So he rose up and went out and threaded the streets awhile, but only increased in cark and care.

Presently, he came to a wine-shop and said to himself, "I will go in and drink myself drunken." So he entered and seeing seven rows of people in the shop, said, "Harkye, taverner! I will not sit except by myself." Accordingly, the vintner placed him in a chamber alone and set strong pure wine before him whereof he drank till he lost his senses. Then he sallied forth again and walked till he came to the road called Red, whilst the people left the street clear before him, out of fear of him.

Presently, he turned and saw a water-carrier trudging along, with his skin and gugglet, crying out and saying, "O exchange! There is no drink but what raisins make, there is no love-delight but what of the lover we take and none sitteth in the place of honour save the sensible freke!" So he said to him, "Here, give me to drink!" The water-carrier looked at him and gave him the gugglet which he took and gazing into it, shook it up and lastly poured it out on the ground.

Asked the water-carrier, "Why dost thou not drink?"; and he answered, saying, "Give me to drink." So the man filled the cup a second time and he took it and shook it and emptied it on the ground; and thus he did a third time.

Quoth the water-carrier, "An thou wilt not drink, I will be off."

And Ali said, "Give me to drink." So he filled the cup a fourth time and gave it to him; and he drank and gave the man a dinar.

The water-carrier looked at him with disdain and said, belittling him, "Good luck to thee! Good luck to thee, my lad! Little folk are one thing and great folk another!"

Now when Mercury Ali heard this, he caught hold of the man's gaberdine and drawing on him a poignard of price, such an one as that whereof the poet speaketh in these two couplets:

> Watered steel-blade, the world perfection calls,
> Drunk with the viper poison foes appals,
> Cuts lively, burns the blood whene'er it falls;
> And picks up gems from pave of marble halls.

Cried Mercury Ali to him, "O Shaykh, speak reasonably to me! Thy water-skin is worth if dear three dirhams, and the gugglets I emptied on the ground held a pint or so of water."

Replied the water-carrier "'Tis well," and Ali rejoined, "I gave thee a golden ducat: why, then dost thou belittle me? Say me, hast thou ever seen any more valiant than I or more generous than I?" Answered the water-carrier; "I have indeed, seen one more valiant than thou and eke more generous than thou; for, never, since women bare children, was there on earth's face a brave man who was not generous."

Quoth Ali, "And who is he thou deemest braver and more generous than I?"

Quoth the other, "Thou must know that I have had a strange adventure. My father was a Shaykh of the Water-carriers who give drink in Cairo and, when he died, he left me five male camels, a he-mule, a shop and a house; but the poor man is never satisfied; or, if he be satisfied he dieth. So I said to myself, 'I will go up to Al-Hijaz'; and, taking a string of camels, bought goods on tick, till I had run in debt for five hundred ducats, all of which I lost in the pilgrimage. Then I said in my mind, 'If I return to Cairo the folk will clap me in jail for their goods.' So I fared with the pilgrims-caravan of Damascus to Aleppo and thence I went on to Baghdad, where I sought out the Shaykh of the Water-carriers of the city and finding his house I went in and repeated the opening chapter of the Koran to him.

"He questioned me of my case and I told him all that had betided me, whereupon he assigned me a shop and gave me a water-skin and gear. So I sallied forth a-morn trusting in Allah to provide, and went round about the city. I offered the gugglet to one, that he might drink; but he cried, 'I have eaten naught whereon to drink; for a niggard invited me this day and set two gugglets before me'; so I said to him, 'O son of the sordid, hast thou given me aught to eat that thou offerest me drink after it? Wherefore wend thy ways, O water-carrier, till I have eaten somewhat: then come and give me to drink.' Thereupon I accosted another and he said, 'Allah provide thee!' And so I went on till noon, without taking hansel, and I said to myself, 'Would Heaven I had never come to Baghdad!'

"Presently, I saw the folk running as fast as they could; so I followed them and behold, a long file of men riding two and two and clad in steel, with double neck-rings and felt bonnets and burnouses and swords and bucklers. I asked one of the folk whose suite this was, and he answered, 'That of Captain Ahmad al-Danaf.'

"Quoth I, 'And what is he?' and quoth the other, 'He is town-captain of Baghdad and her Divan, and to him is committed the care of the suburbs. He getteth a thousand dinars a month from the Caliph and Hasan Shuman hath the like. Moreover, each of his men draweth an hundred dinars a month; and they are now returning to their barrack from the Divan.' And lo! Calamity Ahmad saw me and cried out, 'Come give me drink.'

"So I filled the cup and gave it him, and he shook it and emptied it out, like unto thee; and thus he did a second time. Then I filled the cup a third time and he took a draught as thou diddest; after which he asked me, 'O water-carrier, whence comest thou?'

"And I answered, 'From Cairo,' and he, 'Allah keep Cairo and her citizens! What may bring thee thither?'

"So I told him my story and gave him to understand that I was a debtor fleeing from debt and distress. He cried, 'Thou art welcome to Baghdad'; then he gave me five dinars and said to his men, 'For the love of Allah be generous to him.'

"So each of them gave me a dinar and Ahmad said to me, 'O Shaykh, what while thou abidest in Baghdad thou shalt have of us the like every time thou givest us to drink.'

"Accordingly, I paid them frequent visits and good ceased not to come to me from the folk till, one day, reckoning up the profit I had made of them, I found it a thousand dinars and said to myself, 'The best thing thou canst do is to return to Egypt.'

"So I went to Ahmad's house and kissed his hand, and he said, 'What seekest thou?' Quoth I, 'I have a mind to depart'; and I repeated these two couplets:

"Sojourn of stranger, in whatever land,
  Is like castle based upon the wind:
  The breaths of breezes level all he raised.
  And so on homeward-way's the stranger's mind.

"I added, 'The caravan is about to start for Cairo and I wish to return to my people.' So he gave me a she-mule and an hundred dinars and said to me, 'I desire to send somewhat by thee, O Shaykh! Dost thou know the people of Cairo?'

"'Yes,' answered I.

"And he said, 'Take this letter and carry it to Ali Zaybak of Cairo and say to him, "Thy Captain saluteth thee and he is now with the Caliph."'

"So I took the letter and journeyed back to Cairo, where I paid my debts and plied my water-carrying trade; but I have not delivered the letter, because I know not the abode of Mercury Ali."

Quoth Ali, "O elder, be of good cheer and keep thine eyes cool and clear: I am that Ali, the first of the lads of Captain Ahmad: here with the letter!" So he gave him the missive and he opened it and read these two couplets:

"O adornment of beauties to thee write I
  On a paper that flies as the winds go by:
  Could I fly, I had flown to their arms in desire,
  But a bird with cut wings; how shall ever he fly?

"But after salutation from Captain Ahmad al-Danaf to the eldest of his sons, Mercury Ali of Cairo. Thou knowest that I tormented Salah al-Din the Cairene and befooled him till I buried him alive and reduced his lads to obey me, and amongst them Ali Kitf al-Jamal; and I am now become town-captain of Baghdad in the Divan of the Caliph who hath made me over-seer of the suburbs. An thou be still mindful of our covenant, come to me; haply thou shalt play some trick in Baghdad which may promote thee to the Caliph's service, so he may appoint thee stipends and allowances and assign thee a lodging, which is what thou wouldst see and so peace be on thee."

When Ali read this letter, he kissed it and laying it on his head, gave the water-carrier ten dinars; after which he returned to his barracks and told his comrades and said to them, "I commend you one to other." Then he changed all his clothes and, donning a travelling cloak and a tarboosh, took a case, containing a spear of bamboo-cane, four-and-twenty cubits long, made in several pieces, to fit into one another.

Quoth his lieutenant, "Wilt thou go a journey when the treasury is empty?" and quoth Ali, "When I reach Damascus I will send you what shall suffice you."

Then he set out and fared on, till he overtook a caravan about to start, whereof were the Shahbandar, or Provost of the Merchants, and forty other traders. They had all loaded their beasts, except the Provost, whose loads lay upon the ground, and Ali heard his caravan-leader, who was a Syrian, say to the muleteers, "Bear a hand, one of you!" But they reviled him and abused him. Quoth Ali in himself, "None will suit me so well to travel withal as this leader."

Now Ali was beardless and well-favoured; so he went up to and saluted the leader who welcomed him and said, "What seekest thou?"

Replied Ali, "O my uncle, I see thee alone with forty mule-loads of goods; but why hast thou not brought hands to help thee?"

Rejoined the other, "O my son, I hired two lads and clothed them and put in each one's pocket two hundred dinars; and they helped me till we came to the Dervishes' Convent, when they ran away."

Quoth Ali, "Whither are you bound?" and quoth the Syrian, "to Aleppo," when Ali said, "I will lend thee a hand."

Accordingly they loaded the beasts and the Provost mounted his she-mule and they set out he rejoicing in Ali; and presently he loved him and made much of him and on this wise they fared on till nightfall, when they dismounted and ate and drank. Then came the time of sleep and Ali lay down on his side and made as if he slept; whereupon the Syrian stretched himself near him and Ali rose from his stead and sat down at the door of the merchant's pavilion. Presently the Syrian turned over and would have taken Ali in his arms, but found him not and said to himself, "Haply he hath promised another and he hath taken him; but I have the first right and another night I will keep him."

Now Ali continued sitting at the door of the tent till nigh upon daybreak, when he returned and lay down near the Syrian, who found him by his side, when he awoke, and said to himself, "If I ask him where he hath been, he will leave me and go away."

So he dissembled with him and they went on till they came to a forest, in which was a cave, where dwelt a rending lion. Now whenever a caravan passed, they would draw lots among themselves and him on whom the lot fell they would throw to the beast. So they drew lots and the lot fell not save upon the Provost of the Merchants. And lo! the lion cut off their way awaiting his prey, wherefore the Provost was sore distressed and said to the leader, "Allah disappoint the fortunes of the far one and bring his journey to naught! I charge thee, after my death, give my loads to my children."

Quoth Ali the Clever One, "What meaneth all this?" So they told him the case and he said, "Why do ye run from the tom-cat of the desert? I warrant you I will kill him."

So the Syrian went to the Provost and told him of this and he said, "If he slay him, I will give him a thousand dinars," and said the other merchants, "We will reward him likewise one and all."

With this Ali put off his mantle and there appeared upon him a suit of steel; then he took a chopper of steel and opening it turned the screw; after which he went forth alone and standing in the road before the lion, cried out to him. The lion ran at him, but Ali of Cairo smote him between the eyes with his chopper and cut him in sunder, whilst the caravan-leader and the merchants looked on.

Then said he to the leader, "Have no fear, O nuncle!" and the Syrian answered, saying, "O my son, I am thy servant for all future time."

Then the Provost embraced him and kissed him between the eyes and gave him the thousand dinars, and each of the other merchants gave him twenty dinars. He deposited all the coin with the Provost and they slept that night till the morning, when they set out again, intending for Baghdad, and fared on till they came to the Lion's Clump and the Wady of Dogs, where lay a villain Badawi, a brigand and his tribe, who sallied forth on them.

The folk fled from the highwaymen, and the Provost said, "My monies are lost!" when, lo! up came Ali in a buff coat hung with bells, and bringing out his long lance, fitted the pieces together.

Then he seized one of the Arab's horses and mounting it cried out to the Badawi Chief, saying, "Come out to fight me with spears!" Moreover he shook his bells and the Arab's mare took fright at the noise and Ali struck the Chief's spear and broke it. Then he smote him on the neck and cut off his head. When the Badawin saw their chief fall, they ran at Ali, but he cried out, saying, "Allaho Akbar—God is Most Great!"—and, falling on them broke them and put them to flight. Then he raised the Chief's head on his spear-point and returned to the merchants, who rewarded him liberally and continued their journey, till they reached Baghdad.

Thereupon Ali took his money from the Provost and committed it to the Syrian caravan-leader, saying, "When thou returnest to Cairo, ask for my barracks and give these monies to my deputy." Then he slept that night and on the morrow he entered the city and threading the streets enquired for Calamity Ahmad's quarters; but none would direct him thereto.

So he walked on, till he came to the square Al-Nafz, where he saw children at play, and amongst them a lad called Ahmad al-Lakit, and said to himself, "O my Ali, thou shalt not get news of them but from their little ones."

Then he turned and seeing a sweetmeat-seller bought Halwa of him and called to the children; but Ahmad al-Lakit drove the rest away and coming up to him, said, "What seekest thou?"

Quoth Ali, "I had a son and he died and I saw him in a dream asking for sweetmeats: wherefore I have bought them and wish to give each child a bit."

So saying, he gave Ahmad a slice, and he looked at it and seeing a dinar sticking to it, said "Begone! I am no catamite: seek another than I."

Quoth Ali, "O my son, none but a sharp fellow taketh the hire, even as he is a sharp one who giveth it. I have sought all day for Ahmad al-Danaf's barrack, but none would direct me thereto; so this dinar is thine an thou wilt guide me thither."

Quoth the lad, "I will run before thee and do thou keep up with me, till I come to the place, when I will catch up a pebble with my foot and kick it against the door; and so shalt thou know it."

Accordingly he ran on and Ali after him, till they came to the place, when the boy caught up a pebble between his toes and kicked it against the door so as to make the place known. Ali laid hold of him and would have taken the dinar from him, but could not; so he said to him, "Go: thou deservest largesse for thou art a sharp fellow, whole of wit and stout of heart. Inshallah, if I become a captain to the Caliph, I will make thee one of my lads."

Then the boy made off and Ali Zaybak went up to the door and knocked; whereupon quoth Ahmad al-Danaf, "O doorkeeper, open the door; that is the knock of Quicksilver Ali the Cairene." So he opened the door and Ali entered and saluted with the salam Ahmad who embraced him, and the forty greeted him.

Then Calamity Ahmad gave him a suit of clothes, saying, "When the Caliph made me captain, he clothed my lads and I kept this suit for thee."

Then they seated him in the place of honour and setting on meat they ate well and drink they drank hard and made merry till the morning, when Ahmad said to Ali, "Beware thou walk not about the streets of Baghdad, but sit thee still in this barrack."

Asked Ali, "Why so? Have I come hither to be shut up? No, I came to look about me and divert myself."

Replied Ahmad, "O my son, think not that Baghdad be like Cairo. Baghdad is the seat of the Caliphate; sharpers abound therein and rogueries spring therefrom as worts spring out of earth."

So Ali abode in the barrack three days when Ahmad said to him, "I wish to present thee to the Caliph, that he may assign thee an allowance."

But he replied, "When the time cometh." So he let him go his own way. One day, as Ali sat in the barrack, his breast became straitened and his soul troubled and he said in himself, "Come, let us up and thread the ways of Baghdad and broaden my bosom."

So he went out and walked from street to street, till he came to the middle bazar, where he entered a cook-shop and dined; after which he went out to wash his hands. Presently he saw forty slaves, with felt bonnets and steel cutlasses, come walking, two by two; and last of all came Dalilah the Wily, mounted on a she-mule, with a gilded helmet which bore a ball of polished steel, and clad in a coat of mail, and such like. Now she was returning from the Divan to the Khan of which she was portress; and when she espied Ali, she looked at him fixedly and saw that he resembled Calamity Ahmad in height and breadth. Moreover, he was clad in a striped Aba-cloak and a burnous, with a steel cutlass by his side and similar gear, while valour shone from his eyes, testifying in favour of him and not in disfavour of him.

So she returned to the Khan and going in to her daughter, fetched a table of sand, and struck a geomantic figure, whereby she discovered that the stranger's name was Ali of Cairo and that his fortune overcame her fortune and that of her daughter.

Asked Zaynab, "O my mother, what hath befallen thee that thou hast recourse to the sand-table?"

Answered Dalilah, "O my daughter, I have seen this day a young man who resembleth Calamity Ahmad, and I fear lest he come to hear how thou didst strip Ahmad and his men and enter the Khan and play us a trick, in revenge for what we did with his chief and the forty; for methinks he has taken up his lodging in Al-Danaf's barrack." Zaynab rejoined, "What is this? Methinks thou hast taken his measure."

Then she donned her fine clothes and went out into the streets. When the people saw her, they all made love to her and she promised and sware and listened and coquetted and passed from market to market, till she saw Ali the Cairene coming, when she went up to him and rubbed her shoulder against him. Then she turned and said "Allah give long life to folk of discrimination!"

Quoth he, "How goodly is thy form! To whom dost thou belong?" and quoth she, "To the gallant like thee"; and he said, "Art thou wife or spinster?"

"Married," said she.

Asked Ali, "Shall it be in my lodging or thine?" and she answered, "I am a merchant's daughter and a merchant's wife and in all my life I have never been out of doors till to-day, and my only reason was that when I made ready food and thought to eat, I had no mind thereto without company. When I saw thee, love of thee entered my heart: so wilt thou deign solace my soul and eat a mouthful with me?"

Quoth he, "Whoso is invited, let him accept." Thereupon she went on and he followed her from street to street, but presently he bethought himself and said, "What wilt thou do and thou a stranger? Verily 'tis said, 'Whoso doth whoredom in his strangerhood, Allah will send him back disappointed.' But I will put her off from thee with fair words."

So he said to her, "Take this dinar and appoint me a day other than this;" and she said, "By the Mighty Name, it may not be but thou shalt go home with me as my guest this very day and I will take thee to fast friend."

So he followed her till she came to a house with a lofty porch and a wooden bolt on the door and said to him, "Open this lock."

Asked he "Where is the key?" and she answered, "'Tis lost." Quoth he, "Whoso openeth a lock without a key is a knave whom it behoveth the ruler to punish, and I know not how to open doors without keys."

With this she raised her veil and showed him her face, whereat he took one glance of eyes that cost him a thousand sighs. Then she let fall her veil on the lock and repeating over it the names of the mother of Moses, opened it without a key and entered. He followed her and saw swords and steel-weapons hanging up; and she put off her veil and sat down with him. Quoth he to himself, "Accomplish what Allah bath decreed to thee," and bent over her, to take a kiss of her cheek; but she caught the kiss upon her palm, saying, "This beseemeth not but by night." Then she brought a tray of food and wine, and they ate and drank; after which she rose and drawing water from the well, poured it from the ewer over his hands, whilst he washed them.

Now whilst they were on this wise, she cried out and beat upon her breast, saying, "My husband had a signet-ring of ruby, which was pledged to him for five hundred dinars, and I put it on; but 'twas too large for me, so I straitened it with wax, and when I let down the bucket, that ring must have dropped into the well. So turn thy face to the door, the while I doff my dress and go down into the well and fetch it."

Quoth Ali, "'Twere shame on me that thou shouldst go down there I being present; none shall do it save I." So he put off his clothes and tied the rope about himself and she let him down into the well.

Now there was much water therein and she said to him, "The rope is too short; loose thyself and drop down." So he did himself loose from the rope and dropped into the water, in which he sank fathoms deep without touching bottom; whilst she donned her mantilla and taking his clothes, returned to her mother and said, "I have stripped Ali the Egyptian and cast him into the Emir Hasan's well, whence alas for his chance of escaping!"

Presently, the Emir Hasan, the master of the house, who had been absent at the Divan, came home and, finding the door open, said to his Syce, "Why didst thou not draw the bolt?"

"O my lord," replied the groom, "indeed I locked it with my own hand."

The Emir cried, "As my head liveth, some robber hath entered my house!"

Then he went in and searched, but found none and said to the groom, "Fill the ewer, that I may make the Wuzu-ablution."

So the man lowered the bucket into the well but, when he drew it up, he found it heavy and looking down, saw something therein sitting; whereupon he let it fall into the water and cried out, saying, "O my lord, an Ifrit came up to me out of the well!"

Replied the Emir, "Go and fetch four doctors of the law, that they may read the Koran over him, till he go away."

So he fetched the doctors and the Emir said to them, "Sit round this well and exorcise me this Ifrit."

They did as he bade them; after which the groom and another servant lowered the bucket again and Ali clung to it and hid himself under it patiently till he came near the top, when he sprang out and landed among the doctors, who fell a-cuffing one another and crying out, "Ifrit! Ifrit!"

The Emir looked at Ali and seeing him a young man, said to him, "Art thou a thief?"

"No," replied Ali. "Then what dost thou in the well?" asked the Emir; and Ali answered, "I was asleep and dreamt a wet dream; so I went down to the Tigris to wash myself and dived, whereupon the current carried me under the earth and I came up in this well." Quoth the other, "Tell the truth."

So Ali told him all that had befallen him, and the Emir gave him an old gown and let him go. He returned to Calamity Ahmad's lodging and related to him all that had passed. Quoth Ahmad, "Did I not warn thee that Baghdad is full of women who play tricks upon men?"

And quoth Ali Kitf al-Jamal, "I conjure thee by the Mighty Name, tell me how it is that thou art the chief of the lads of Cairo and yet hast been stripped by a girl?" This was grievous to Ali and he repented him of not having followed Ahmad's advice.

Then the Calamity gave him another suit of clothes and Hasan Shuman said to him, "Dost thou know the young person?"

"No," replied Ali; and Hasan rejoined, "'Twas Zaynab, the daughter of Dalilah the Wily, the portress of the Caliph's Khan; and hast thou fallen into her toils, O Ali?"

Quoth he, "Yes," and quoth Hasan, "O Ali, 'twas she who took thy Chief's clothes and those of all his men."

"This is a disgrace to you all!"

"And what thinkest thou to do?"

"I purpose to marry her."

"Put away that thought far from thee, and console thy heart of her."

"O Hasan, do thou counsel me how I shall do to marry her."

"With all my heart: if thou wilt drink from my hand and march under my banner, I will bring thee to thy will of her."

"I will well."

So Hasan made Ali put off his clothes; and, taking a cauldron heated therein somewhat as it were pitch, wherewith he anointed him and he became like unto a blackamoor slave. Moreover, he smeared his lips and cheeks and pencilled his eyes with red Kohl. Then he clad him in a slave's habit and giving him a tray of kabobs and wine, said to him, "There is a black cook in the Khan who requires from the Bazar only meat; and thou art now become his like; so go thou to him civilly and accost him in friendly fashion and speak to him in the blacks' lingo, and salute him, saying, ''Tis long since we met in the beer-ken.' He will answer thee, 'I have been too busy: on my hands be forty slaves, for whom I cook dinner and supper, besides making ready a tray for Dalilah and the like for her daughter Zaynab and the dogs' food.' And do thou say to him, 'Come, let us eat kabobs and lush swipes.' Then go with him into the saloon and make him drunken and question him of his service, how many dishes and what dishes he hath to cook, and ask him of the dogs' food and the keys of the kitchen and the larder; and he will tell thee; for a man, when he is drunken, telleth all he would conceal were he sober. When thou hast done this drug him and don his clothes and sticking the two knives in thy girdle, take the vegetable-basket and go to the market and buy meat and greens, with which do thou return to the Khan and enter the kitchen and the larder and cook the food. Dish it up and put Bhang in it, so as to drug the dogs and the slaves and Dalilah and Zaynab and lastly serve up. When all are asleep, hie thee to the upper chamber and bring away every suit of clothes thou wilt find hanging there. And if thou have a mind to marry Zaynab, bring with thee also the forty carrier-pigeons."

So Ali went to the Khan and going in to the cook, saluted him and said, "'Tis long since I have met thee in the beer-ken."

The slave replied, "I have been busy cooking for the slaves and the dogs."

Then he took him and making him drunken, questioned him of his work.

Quoth the kitchener, "Every day I cook five dishes for dinner and the like for supper; and yesterday they sought of me a sixth dish, yellow rice, and a seventh, a mess of cooked pomegranate seed."

Ali asked, "And what is the order of thy service?" and the slave answered, "First I serve up Zaynab's tray, next Dalilah's; then I feed the slaves and give the dogs their sufficiency of meat, and the least that satisfies them is a pound each."

But, as fate would have it, he forgot to ask him of the keys. Then he drugged him and donned his clothes; after which he took the basket and went to the market. There he bought meat and greens; and, presently returning to the Khan, he saw Dalilah seated at the gate, watching those who went in and came out, and the forty slaves with her, armed. So he heartened his heart and entered; but Dalilah knew him and said to him, "Back, O captain of thieves! Wilt thou play a trick on me in the Khan?"

Thereupon he (dressed as a slave) turned and said to her, "What sayest thou, O portress?"

She asked, "What hast thou done with the slave, our cook? say me if thou hast killed or drugged him?"

He answered, "What cook? Is there here another slave-cook than I?"

She rejoined, "Thou liest, thou art Mercury Ali the Cairene."

And he said to her, in slaves' patois, "O portress, are the Cairenes black or white? I will slave for you no longer."

Then said the slaves to him, "What is the matter with thee, O our cousin?"

Cried Dalilah, "This is none of your uncle's children, but Ali Zaybak the Egyptian; and meseems he hath either drugged your cousin or killed him."

But they said, "Indeed this is our cousin Sa'adu'llah the cook;" and she, "Not so, 'tis Mercury Ali, and he hath dyed his skin."

Quoth the sharper, "And who is Ali? I am Sa'adu'llah."

Then she fetched unguent of proof, with which she anointed Ali's forearm and rubbed it; but the black did not come off; whereupon quoth the slaves "Let him go and dress us our dinner."

Quoth Dalilah, "If he be indeed your cousin, he knoweth what you sought of him yesternight and how many dishes he cooketh every day."

So they asked him of this and he said, "Every day I cook you five dishes for the morning and the like for the evening meal, lentils and rice and broth and stew and sherbet of roses; and yesternight ye sought of me a sixth dish and a seventh, to wit yellow rice and cooked pomegranate seed."

And the slaves said "Right!"

Then quoth Dalilah, "In with him and if he know the kitchen and the larder, he is indeed your cousin; but, if not, kill him."

Now the cook had a cat which he had brought up, and whenever he entered the kitchen it would stand at the door and spring to his back, as soon as he went in. So, when Ali entered, the cat saw him and jumped on his shoulders; but he threw it off and it ran before him to the door of the kitchen and stopped there. He guessed that this was the kitchen door; so he took the keys and seeing one with traces of feathers thereon, knew it for the kitchen key and therewith opened the door. Then he entered and setting down the greens, went out again, led by the cat, which ran before him and stopped at another door. He guessed that this was the larder and seeing one of the keys marked with grease, knew it for the key and opened the door therewith; where-upon quoth the slaves, "O Dalilah, were he a stranger, he had not known the kitchen and the larder, nor had he been able to distinguish the keys thereof from the rest; verily, he is our cousin Sa'adu'llah."

Quoth she, "He learned the places from the cat and distinguished the keys one from the other by the appearance: but this cleverness imposeth not upon me."

Then he returned to the kitchen where he cooked the dinner and, carrying Zaynab's tray up to her room, saw all the stolen clothes hanging up; after which he went down and took Dalilah her tray and gave the slaves and the dogs their rations. The like he did at sundown and drugged Dalilah's food and that of Zaynab and the slaves.

Now the doors of the Khan were opened and shut with the sun. So Ali went forth and cried out, saying, "O dwellers in the Khan, the watch is set and we have loosed the dogs; whoso stirreth out after this can blame none save himself."

But he had delayed the dogs' supper and put poison therein; consequently when he set it before them, they ate of it and died while the slaves and Dalilah and Zaynab still slept under Bhang. Then he went up and took all the clothes and the carrier-pigeons and, opening the gate made off to the barrack of the forty, where he found Hasan Shuman the Pestilence who said to him, "How hast thou fared?" Thereupon he told him what had passed and he praised him.

Then he caused him to put off his clothes and boiled a decoction of herbs wherewith he washed him, and his skin became white as it was; after which he donned his own dress and going back to the Khan, clad the cook in the habit he had taken from him and made him smell to the counter-drug; upon which the slave awoke and going forth to the greengrocer's, bought vegetables and returned to the Khan.

Such was the case with Al-Zaybak of Cairo; but as regards Dalilah the Wily, when the day broke, one of the lodgers in the Khan came out

of his chamber and, seeing the gate open and the slaves drugged and the dogs dead, he went in to her and found her lying drugged, with a scroll on her neck and at her head a sponge steeped in the counter-drug. He set the sponge to her nostrils and she awoke and asked, "Where am I?" The merchant answered, "When I came down from my chamber I saw the gate of the Khan open and the dogs dead and found the slaves and thee drugged."

So she took up the paper and read therein these words, "None did this deed save Ali the Egyptian."

Then she awoke the slaves and Zaynab by making them smell the counter-Bhang and said to them, "Did I not tell you that this was Ali of Cairo?" presently adding to the slaves, "But do ye conceal the matter."

Then she said to her daughter, "How often have I warned thee that Ali would not forego his revenge? He hath done this deed in requital of that which thou diddest with him and he had it in his power to do with thee other than this thing; but he refrained therefrom out of courtesy and a desire that there should be love and friendship between us."

So saying, she doffed her man's gear and donned woman's attire and, tying the kerchief of peace about her neck, repaired to Ahmad al-Danaf's barrack. Now when Ali entered with the clothes and the carrier-pigeons, Hasan Shuman gave the hall-keeper the price of forty pigeons and he bought them and cooked them amongst the men.

Presently there came a knock at the door and Ahmad said, "That is Dalilah's knock: rise and open to her, O hall-keeper." So he admitted her and asked her, "What bringeth thee hither, O ill-omened old woman? Verily, thou and thy brother Zurayk the fishmonger are of a piece!"; and she answered, "O captain I am in the wrong and this my neck is at thy mercy; but tell me which of you it was that played me this trick?"

Quoth Calamity Ahmad, "'Twas the first of my lads."

Rejoined Dalilah, "For the sake of Allah intercede with him to give me back the carrier-pigeons and what not, and thou wilt lay me under great obligation."

When Hasan heard this he said, "Allah requite thee, O Ali! Why didst thou cook the pigeons?" and Ali answered, "I knew not that they were carrier-pigeons."

Then said Ahmad, "O hall-keeper bring us the cooked pigeons." So he brought them and Dalilah took a piece and tasting it, said, "This is none of the carrier-pigeons' flesh, for I fed them on grains of musk and their meat is become even as musk."

Quoth Shuman, "An thou desire to have the carrier-pigeons, comply with Ali's will." Asked she "What is that?"

And Hasan answered, "He would have thee marry him to thy daughter Zaynab." She said, "I have not command over her except of affection"; and Hasan said to Ali the Cairene, "Give her the pigeons."

So he gave them to her, and she took them and rejoiced in them. Then quoth Hasan to her, "There is no help but thou return us a sufficient reply"; and Dalilah rejoined, "If it be indeed his wish to marry her, it availed nothing to play this clever trick upon us: it behoveth him rather to demand her in marriage of her mother's brother and her guardian, Captain Zurayk, him who crieth out, saying, 'Ho! a pound of fish for two farthings!' and who hangeth up in his shop a purse containing two thousand dinars."

When the forty heard this, they all rose and cried out, saying, "What manner of blather is this, O harlot? Dost thou wish to bereave us of our brother Ali of Cairo?"

Then she returned to the Khan and said to her daughter, "Ali the Egyptian seeketh thee in marriage." Whereat Zaynab rejoiced, for she loved him because of his chaste forbearance towards her, and asked her mother what had passed.

So she told her, adding, "I made it a condition that he should demand thy hand of thine uncle, so I might make him fall into destruction."

Meanwhile Ali turned to his fellows and asked them, "What manner of man is this Zurayk?" and they answered, "He was chief of the sharpers of Al-Irak land and could all but pierce mountains and lay hold upon the stars. He would steal the Kohl from the eye and, in brief, he had not his match for roguery; but he hath repented his sins and foresworn his old way of life and opened him a fishmonger's shop. And now he hath amassed two thousand dinars by the sale of fish and laid them in a purse with strings of silk, to which he hath tied bells and rings and rattles of brass, hung on a peg within the doorway. Every time he openeth his shop he suspendeth the said purse and crieth out, saying, 'Where are ye, O sharpers of Egypt, O prigs of Al-Irak, O tricksters of Ajam-land? Behold, Zurayk the fishmonger hath hung up a purse in front of his shop, and whoso pretendeth to craft and cunning, and can take it by sleight, it is his.' So the long fingered and greedy-minded come and try to take the purse, but cannot; for, whilst he frieth his fish and tendeth the fire, he layeth at his feet scone-like circles of lead; and whenever a thief thinketh to take him unawares and maketh a snatch at the purse he casteth at him a load of lead and slayeth him or doeth him a damage. So O Ali, wert thou to tackle him, thou wouldst be as

one who jostleth a funeral cortege, unknowing who is dead; for thou art no match for him, and we fear his mischief for thee. Indeed, thou hast no call to marry Zaynab, and he who leaveth a thing alone liveth without it."

Cried Ali, "This were shame, O comrades; needs must I take the purse: but bring me a young lady's habit."

So they brought him women's clothes and he clad himself therein and stained his hands with Henna, and modestly hung down his veil. Then he took a lamb and killing it, cut out the long intestine which he cleaned and tied up below; moreover he filled it with blood and bound it between his thighs; after which he donned petticoat-trousers and walking boots. He also made himself a pair of false breasts with birds' crops and filled them with thickened milk and tied round his hips and over his belly a piece of linen, which he stuffed with cotton, girding himself over all with a kerchief of silk well starched. Then he went out, whilst all who saw him exclaimed, "What a fine pair of hind cheeks!"

Presently he saw an ass-driver coming, so he gave him a dinar and mounting, rode till he came to Zurayk's shop, where he saw the purse hung up and the gold glittering through it. Now Zurayk was frying fish, and Ali said, "O ass-man, what is that smell?" Replied he, "It's the smell of Zurayk's fish."

Quoth Ali, "I am a woman with child and the smell harmeth me; go, fetch me a slice of the fish."

So the donkey-boy said to Zurayk, "What aileth thee to fry fish so early and annoy pregnant women with the smell? I have here the wife of the Emir Hasan Sharr al-Tarik, and she is with child; so give her a bit of fish, for the babe stirreth in her womb. O Protector, O my God, avert from us the mischief of this day!"

Thereupon Zurayk took a piece of fish and would have fried it, but the fire had gone out and he went in to rekindle it. Meanwhile Ali dismounted and sitting down, pressed upon the lamb's intestine till it burst and the blood ran out from between his legs. Then he cried aloud, saying, "O my back! O my side!" Whereupon the driver turned and seeing the blood running, said, "What aileth thee, O my lady?"

Replied Ali, "I have miscarried"; where-upon Zurayk looked out and seeing the blood fled affrighted into the inner shop.

Quoth the donkey-driver, "Allah torment thee, O Zurayk! The lady hath miscarried and thou art no match for her husband. Why must thou make a stench so early in the morning? I said to thee, 'Bring her a slice,' but thou wouldst not."

Thereupon, he took his ass and went his way and, as Zurayk still did not appear, Ali put out his hand to the purse; but no sooner had he touched it than the bells and rattles and rings began to jingle and the gold to chink. Quoth Zurayk, who returned at the sound, "Thy perfidy hath come to light, O gallows-bird! Wilt thou put a cheat on me and thou in a woman's habit? Now take what cometh to thee!"

And he threw a cake of lead at him, but it went agley and lighted on another; whereupon the people rose against Zurayk and said to him, "Art thou a trades-man or a swashbuckler? An thou be a tradesman, take down thy purse and spare the folk thy mischief."

He replied, "Bismillah, in the name of Allah! On my head be it."

As for Ali, he made off to the barrack and told Hasan Shuman what had happened, after which he put off his woman's gear and donning a groom's habit which was brought to him by his chief took a dish and five dirhams. Then he returned to Zurayk's shop and the fishmonger said to him, "What dost thou want, O my master?" He showed him the dirhams and Zurayk would have given him of the fish in the tray, but he said, "I will have none save hot fish."

So he set fish in the earthen pan and finding the fire dead, went in to relight it; whereupon Ali put out his hand to the purse and caught hold of the end of it. The rattles and rings and bells jingled and Zurayk said, "Thy trick hath not deceived me. I knew thee for all thou art disguised as a groom by the grip of thy hand on the dish and the dirhams."

So saying, he threw the lead at him, but he avoided it and it fell into the pan full of hot fish and broke it and overturned it, fat and all, upon the breast and shoulders of the Kazi, who was passing. The oil ran down inside his clothes to his privy parts and he cried out, "O my privities! What a sad pickle you are in! Alas, unhappy I! Who hath played me this trick?"

Answered the people, "O our lord, it was some small boy that threw a stone into the pan: but for Allah's word, it had been worse."

Then they turned and seeing the loaf of lead and that it was Zurayk who had thrown it, rose against him and said to him, "O Zurayk, this is not allowed of Allah! Take down the purse or it shall go ill for thee."

Answered he, "I will take it down, Inshallah!"

Meanwhile Ali returned to the barrack and told his comrades who cried, "Where is the purse?" all that had passed and they said, "Thou hast exhausted two-thirds of his cunning."

Then he changed his groom's dress for the garb of a merchant and going out, met a snake-charmer, with a bag of serpents and a wallet containing

his kit to whom said he, "O charmer, come and amuse my lads, and thou shalt have largesse."

So he accompanied him to the barrack, where he fed him and drugging him with Bhang, doffed his clothes and put them on. Then he took the bags and repairing to Zurayk's shop began to play the reed-pipe. Quoth Zurayk, "Allah provide thee!"

But Ali pulled out the serpents and cast them down before him; whereat the fishseller, who was afraid of snakes, fled from them into the inner shop. Thereupon Ali picked up the reptiles and, thrusting them back into the bag, stretched out his hand and caught hold of the end of the purse. The rings again rang and the bells and rattles jangled, and Zurayk cried, "Wilt thou never cease to play me tricks? Now thou feignest thyself a serpent-charmer!"

So saying, he took up a piece of lead, and hurled it at Ali; but it missed him and fell on the head of a groom, who was passing by, following his master, a trooper, and knocked him down. Quoth the soldier, "Who felled him?" and the folk said, "'Twas a stone fell from the roof."

So the soldier passed on and the people, seeing the piece of lead, went up to Zurayk and cried to him, "Take down the purse!" and he said, "Inshallah, I will take it down this very night!"

Ali ceased not to practice upon Zurayk till he had made seven different attempts but without taking the purse. Then he returned the snake-charmer his clothes and kit and gave him due benevolence; after which he went back to Zurayk's shop and heard him say, "If I leave the purse here to-night, he will dig through the shop-wall and take it; I will carry it home with me."

So he arose and shut the shop; then he took down the purse and putting it in his bosom set out home, till he came near his house, when he saw a wedding in a neighbour's lodging and said to himself, "I will hie me home and give my wife the purse and don my fine clothes and return to the marriage."

And Ali followed him. Now Zurayk had married a black girl, one of the freed women of the Wazir Ja'afar and she had borne him a son, whom he named Abdallah, and he had promised her to spend the money in the purse on the occasion of the boy's circumcision and of his marriage-procession. So he went into his house and, as he entered, his wife saw that his face was overcast and asked him, "What hath caused thy sadness?"

Quoth he, "Allah hath afflicted me this day with a rascal who made seven attempts to get the purse, but without avail"; and quoth she, "Give it to me, that I may lay it up against the boy's festival-day."

Now Ali, who had followed him, lay hidden in a closet whence he could see and hear all. So he gave her the purse and changed his clothes, saying, "Keep the purse safely, O Umm Abdallah, for I am going to the wedding."

But she said, "Take thy sleep awhile." So he lay down and fell asleep. Presently, Ali rose and going on tiptoe to the purse, took it and went to the house of the wedding and stood there, looking on at the fun.

Now meanwhile, Zurayk dreamt that he saw a bird fly away with the purse and awaking in affright, said to his wife, "Rise; look for the purse." So she looked and finding it gone, buffeted her face and said, "Alas the blackness of thy fortune, O Umm Abdallah! A sharker hath taken the purse."

Quoth Zurayk, "By Allah it can be none other than rascal Ali who hath plagued me all day! He hath followed me home and seized the purse; and there is no help but that I go and get it back." Quoth she, "Except thou bring it, I will lock on thee the door and leave thee to pass the night in the street."

So he went up to the house of the wedding, and seeing Ali looking on, said to himself, "This is he who took the purse; but he lodgeth with Ahmad al-Danaf."

So he forewent him to the barrack and, climbing up at the back, dropped down into the saloon, where he found everyone asleep. Presently there came a rap at the door and Zurayk asked, "Who is there!"

"Ali of Cairo," answered the knocker; and Zurayk said, "Hast thou brought the purse?" So Ali thought it was Hasan Shuman and replied, "I have brought it; open the door."

Quoth Zurayk, "Impossible that I open to thee till I see the purse; for thy chief and I have laid a wager about it."

Said Ali, "Put out thy hand." So he put out his hand through the hole in the side-door and Ali laid the purse in it; whereupon Zurayk took it and going forth, as he had come in, returned to the wedding. Ali stood for a long while at the door, but none opened to him; and at last he gave a thundering knock that awoke all the men and they said, "That is Ali of Cairo's peculiar rap."

So the hall-keeper opened to him and Hasan Shuman said to him, "Hast thou brought the purse?" Replied Ali, "Enough of jesting, O Shuman: didst thou not swear that thou wouldest not open to me till I showed thee the purse, and did I not give it thee through the hole in the side door? And didst thou not say to me, 'I am sworn never to open the door till thou show me the purse?'"

Quoth Hasan, "By Allah, 'twas not I who took it, but Zurayk!" Quoth Ali, "Needs must I get it again," and repaired to the house of the wedding, where he heard the buffoon say, "Bravo, O Abu Abdallah! Good luck to thee with thy son!"

Said Ali, "My luck is in the ascendant," and going to the fishmonger's lodging, climbed over the back wall of the house and found his wife asleep. So he drugged her with Bhang and clad himself in her clothes. Then he took the child in his arms and went round, searching, till he found a palm-leaf basket containing buns, which Zurayk of his niggardliness, had kept from the Greater Feast.

Presently, the fishmonger returned and knocked at the door, whereupon Ali imitated his wife's voice and asked, "Who is at the door?"

"Abu Abdallah," answered Zurayk and Ali said, "I swore that I would not open the door to thee, except thou broughtest back the purse."

Quoth the fish-monger, "I have brought it." Cried Ali, "Here with it into my hand before I open the door"; and Zurayk answered, saying, "Let down the basket and take it therein."

So sharper Ali let down the basket and the other put the purse therein, whereupon Ali took it and drugged the child. Then he aroused the woman and making off by the back way as he had entered, returned with the child and the purse and the basket of cakes to the barrack and showed them all to the forty, who praised his dexterity. There-upon he gave them cakes, which they ate, and made over the boy to Hasan Shuman, saying, "This is Zurayk's child; hide it by thee." So he hid it and fetching a lamb, gave it to the hall-keeper who cooked it whole, wrapped in a cloth, and laid it out shrouded as it were a dead body.

Meanwhile Zurayk stood awhile, waiting at the door, then gave a knock like thunder and his wife said to him, "Hast thou brought the purse?"

He replied, "Didst thou not take it up in the basket thou diddest let down but now?" and she rejoined, "I let no basket down to thee, nor have I set eyes on the purse."

Quoth he, "By Allah the sharper hath been beforehand with me and hath taken the purse again!"

Then he searched the house and found the basket of cakes gone and the child missing and cried out, saying, "Alas, my child!"

Whereupon the woman beat her breast and said, "I and thee to the Wazir, for none hath killed my son save this sharper, and all because of thee."

Cried Zurayk, "I will answer for him." So he tied the kerchief of truce about his neck and going to Ahmad al-Danaf's lodging, knocked at the door.

The hall-keeper admitted him and as he entered Hasan Shuman asked him, "What bringeth thee here?"

He answered, "Do ye intercede with Ali the Cairene to restore me my child and I will yield to him the purse of gold."

Quoth Hasan, "Allah requite thee, O Ali! Why didst thou not tell me it was his child?"

"What hath befallen him?" cried Zurayk, and Hasan replied, "We gave him raisins to eat, and he choked and died and this is he."

Quoth Zurayk "Alas, my son! What shall I say to his mother?"

Then he rose and opening the shroud, saw it was a lamb barbecued and said, "Thou makest sport of me, O Ali!"

Then they gave him the child and Calamity Ahmad said to him, "Thou didst hang up the purse, proclaiming that it should be the property of any sharper who should be able to take it, and Ali hath taken it; so 'tis the very property of our Cairene."

Zurayk answered "I make him a present of it;" but Ali said to him, "Do thou accept it on account of thy niece Zaynab."

And Zurayk replied, "I accept it."

Then quoth the forty, "We demand of thee Zaynab in marriage for Ali of Cairo"; but quoth he, "I have no control over her save of kindness."

Hasan asked, "Dost thou grant our suit?" and he answered, "Yes, I will grant her in marriage to him who can avail to her mahr or marriage-settlement."

"And what is her dowry?" enquired Hasan; and Zurayk replied, "She hath sworn that none shall mount her breast save the man who bringeth her the robe of Kamar, daughter of Azariah the Jew and her crown and girdle and pantoufle of gold."

Ali cried, "If I do not bring her the clothes this very night, I renounce my claim to her." Rejoined Zurayk, "O Ali, thou art a dead man if thou play any of thy pranks on Kamar."

"Why so?" asked Ali and the other answered, "Her father, Jew Azariah, is a skilful, wily, perfidious magician who hath the Jinn at his service. He owneth without the city a castle, whose walls are one brick of gold and one of silver and which is visible to the folk only whilst he is therein: when he goeth forth, it disappeareth. He brought his daughter this dress I speak of from an enchanted treasure, and every day he layeth it in a charger of gold and, opening the windows of the palace, crieth out, 'Where are

the sharpers of Cairo, the prigs of Al-Irak, the master-thieves of Ajam-land? Whoso prevaileth to take this dress, 'tis his.' So all the long-fingered ones essayed the adventure, but failed to take it, and he turned them by his magic into apes and asses."

But Ali said, "I will assuredly take it, and Zaynab shall be displayed therein."

So he went to the shop of the Jew and found him a man of stern and forbidding aspect, seated with scales and stone-weights and gold and silver and nests of drawers and so forth before him, and a she-mule tethered hard by.

Presently he rose and shutting his shop, laid the gold and silver in two purses, which he placed in a pair of saddle-bags and set on the she-mule's back. Then he mounted and rode till he reached the city-outskirts followed, without his knowledge, by Ali, when he took out some dust from a pocket-purse and, muttering over it, sprinkled it upon the air. No sooner had he done this than sharper Ali saw a castle which had not its like, and the Jew mounted the steps upon his beast which was a subject Jinni; after which he dismounted and taking the saddle-bags off her back, dismissed the she-mule and she vanished. Then he entered the castle and sat down.

Presently, he arose and opening the lattices, took a wand of gold, which he set up in the open window and, hanging thereto a golden charger by chains of the same metal, laid in it the dress, whilst Ali watched him from behind the door, and presently he cried out, saying, "Where are the sharpers of Cairo? Where are the prigs of Al-Irak, the master-thieves of the Ajam-land? Whoso can take this dress by his sleight, 'tis his!"

Then he pronounced certain magical words and a tray of food spread itself before him. He ate and conjured a second time, whereupon the tray disappeared; and yet a third time, when a table of wine was placed between his hands and he drank. Quoth Ali, "I know not how I am to take the dress except if he be drunken."

Then he stole up behind the Jew whinger in grip; but the other turned and conjured, saying to his hand, "Hold with the sword"; whereupon Ali's right arm was held and abode half-way in the air hending the hanger. He put out his left hand to the weapon, but it also stood fixed in the air, and so with his right foot, leaving him standing on one foot. Then the Jew dispelled the charm from him and Ali became as before.

Presently Azariah struck a table of sand and found that the thief's name was Mercury Ali of Cairo; so he turned to him and said, "Come nearer! Who art thou and what dost thou here?"

He replied, "I am Ali of Cairo, of the band of Ahmad al-Danaf. I sought the hand of Zaynab, daughter of Dalilah the Wily, and she demanded thy daughter's dress to her dowry; so do thou give it to me and become a Moslem, an thou wouldst save thy life."

Rejoined the Jew, "After thy death! Many have gone about to steal the dress, but failed to take it from me; wherefore an thou deign be advised, thou wilt begone and save thyself; for they only seek the dress of thee, that thou mayst fall into destruction; and indeed, had I not seen by geomancy that thy fortune overrideth my fortunes I had smitten thy neck."

Ali rejoiced to hear that his luck overcame that of the Jew and said to him, "There is no help for it but I must have the dress and thou must become a True Believer."

Asked the Jew, "Is this thy will and last word," and Ali answered, "Yes."

So the Jew took a cup and filling it with water, conjured over it and said to Ali, "Come forth from this shape of a man into the form of an ass." Then he sprinkled him with the water and straightway he became a donkey, with hoofs and long ears, and fell to braying after the manner of asinines.

The Jew drew round him a circle which became a wall over against him, and drank on till the morning, when he said to Ali, "I will ride thee to-day and give the she-mule a rest."

So he locked up the dress, the charger, the rod and the charms in a cupboard and conjured over Ali, who followed him. Then he set the saddle-bags on his back and mounting, fared forth of the Castle, whereupon it disappeared from sight and he rode into Baghdad, till he came to his shop, where he alighted and emptied the bags of gold and silver into the trays before him. As for Ali, he was tied up by the shop-door, where he stood in his asinine form hearing and understanding all that passed, without being able to speak. And behold, up came a young merchant with whom fortune had played the tyrant and who could find no easier way of earning his livelihood than water-carrying. So he brought his wife's bracelets to the Jew and said to him, "Give me the price of these bracelets, that I may buy me an ass."

Asked the Jew, "What wilt thou do with him?" and the other answered, "O master, I mean to fetch water from the river on his back, and earn my living thereby."

Quoth the Jew, "Take this ass of mine." So he sold him the bracelets and received the ass-shaped Ali of Cairo in part payment and carried him home.

Quoth Ali to himself, "If the Ass-man clap the pannel on thee and load thee with water-skins and go with thee half a score journeys a day he will ruin thy health and thou wilt die."

So, when the water-carrier's wife came to bring him his fodder, he butted her with his head and she fell on her back; whereupon he sprang on her and smiting her brow with his mouth, put out and displayed that which his begetter left him. She cried aloud and the neighbours came to her assistance and beat him and raised him off her breast.

When her husband the intended water-carrier came home, she said to him, "Now either divorce me or return the ass to his owner." He asked, "What hath happened?" and she answered, "This is a devil in the guise of a donkey. He sprang upon me, and had not the neighbours beaten him off my bosom he had done with me a foul thing."

So he carried the ass back to the Jew, who said to him, "Wherefore hast thou brought him back?" and he replied, "He did a foul thing with my wife."

So the Jew gave him his money again and he went away; and Azariah said to Ali, "Hast thou recourse to knavery, unlucky wretch that thou art, in order that he may return thee to me? But since it pleaseth thee to be an ass, I will make thee a spectacle and a laughing stock to great and small."

Then he mounted him and rode till he came without the city, when he brought out the ashes in powder and conjuring over it sprinkled it upon the air and immediately the Castle appeared. He entered and taking the saddle-bags off the ass's back set up the rod and hung to it the charger wherein were the clothes proclaiming aloud, "Where be the clever ones of all quarters who may avail to take this dress?"

Then he conjured as before and meat was set before him and he ate and then wine when he drank; after which he took a cup of water and muttering certain words thereover, sprinkled it on the ass Ali, saying, "Quit this form and return to thy former shape."

Ali straightway became a man once more and Azariah said to him, "O Ali, take good advice and be content with my mischief. Thou hast no call to marry Zaynab nor to take my daughter's dress, for 'tis no easy matter for thee: so leave greed and 'twill be better for thee; else will I turn thee into a bear or an ape or set on thee an Ifrit, who will cast thee behind the Mountain Kaf."

He replied, "I have engaged to take the dress and needs must I have it and thou must Islamise or I will slay thee."

Rejoined the Jew, "O Ali, thou art like a walnut; unless it be broken it cannot be eaten." Then he took a cup of water and conjuring over it, sprinkled Ali with somewhat thereof, saying, "Take thou shape of bear"; whereupon he instantly became a bear and the Jew put a collar about his neck, muzzled him and chained him to a picket of iron. Then he sat down and ate and drank, now and then throwing him a morsel of his orts and emptying the dregs of the cup over him, till the morning, when he rose and laid by the tray and the dress and conjured over the bear, which followed him to the shop. There the Jew sat down and emptied the gold and silver into the trays before Ali, after binding him by the chain; and the bear there abode seeing and comprehending but not able to speak.

Presently up came a man and a merchant, who accosted the Jew and said to him, "O Master, wilt thou sell me yonder bear? I have a wife who is my cousin and is sick; and they have prescribed for her to eat bears' flesh and anoint herself with bears' grease."

At this the Jew rejoiced and said to himself, "I will sell him to this merchant, so he may slaughter him and we be at peace from him."

And Ali also said in his mind, "By Allah, this fellow meaneth to slaughter me; but deliverance is with the Almighty."

Then said the Jew, "He is a present from me to thee."

So the merchant took him and carried him into the butcher, to whom he said, "Bring thy tools and company me."

The butcher took his knives and followed the merchant to his house, where he bound the beast and fell to sharpening his blade: but, when he went up to him to slaughter him, the bear escaped from his hands and rising into the air, disappeared from sight between heaven and earth; nor did he cease flying till he alighted at the Jew's castle.

Now the reason thereof was on this wise. When the Jew returned home, his daughter questioned him of Ali and he told her what had happened; whereupon she said, "Summon a Jinni and ask him of the youth, whether he be indeed Mercury Ali or another who seeketh to put a cheat on thee."

So Azariah called a Jinni by conjurations and questioned him of Ali; and he replied, "'Tis Ali of Cairo himself. The butcher hath pinioned him and whetted his knife to slaughter him."

Quoth the Jew, "Go, snatch him up and bring him hither, ere the butcher cut his throat."

So the Jinni flew off and, snatching Ali out of the butcher's hands, bore him to the palace and set him down before the Jew, who took a cup of water and conjuring over it, sprinkled him therewith, saying, "Return to thine own shape."

And he straightway became a man again as before. The Jew's daughter Kamar, seeing him to be a handsome young man, fell in love with him and he fell in love with her; and she said to him, "O unlucky one, why dost thou go about to take my dress, enforcing my father to deal thus with thee?"

Quoth he, "I have engaged to get it for Zaynab the Coney-catcher, that I may wed her therewith."

And she said, "Others than thou have played pranks with my father to get my dress, but could not win to it," presently adding, "So put away this thought from thee."

But he answered, "Needs must I have it, and thy father must become a Moslem, else I will slay him."

Then said the Jew, "See, O my daughter, how this unlucky fellow seeketh his own destruction," adding, "Now I will turn thee into a dog."

So he took a cup graven with characters and full of water and conjuring over it, sprinkled some of it upon Ali, saying, "Take thou form of dog." Whereupon he straightway became a dog, and the Jew and his daughter drank together till the morning, when the father laid up the dress and charger and mounted his mule. Then he conjured over the dog, which followed him, as he rode towards the town, and all dogs barked at Ali as he passed, till he came to the shop of a broker, a seller of second-hand goods, who rose and drove away the dogs, and Ali lay down before him. The Jew turned and looked for him, but finding him not, passed onwards.

Presently, the broker shut up his shop and went home, followed by the dog, which, when his daughter saw enter the house, she veiled her face and said, "O my papa, dost thou bring a strange man in to me?"

He replied, "O my daughter, this is a dog." Quoth she, "Not so, 'tis Ali the Cairene, whom the Jew Azariah hath enchanted"; and she turned to the dog and said to him, "Art not Ali of Cairo?"

And he signed to her with his head, "Yes."

Then her father asked her, "Why did the Jew enchant him?" and she answered, "Because of his daughter Kamar's dress; but I can release him."

Said the broker, "An thou canst indeed do him this good office, now is the time," and she, "If he will marry me, I will release him."

And he signed to her with his head, "Yes."

So she took a cup of water, graven with certain signs and conjuring over it, was about to sprinkle Ali therewith, when lo and behold! she heard a great cry and the cup fell from her hand. She turned and found that it was her father's handmaid, who had cried out; and she said to her, "O my mistress, is't thus thou keepest the covenant between me and thee? None taught thee this art save I, and thou didst agree with me that thou wouldst do naught without consulting me and that whoso married thee should marry me also, and that one night should be mine and one night thine."

And the broker's daughter said, "'Tis well."

When the broker heard the maid's words, he asked his daughter, "Who taught the maid?" and she answered, "O my papa, enquire of herself."

So he put the question and she replied, "Know, O my lord, that, when I was with Azariah the Jew, I used to spy upon him and listen to him, when he performed his gramarye; and when he went forth to his shop in Baghdad, I opened his books and read in them, till I became skilled in the Cabbala-science. One day, he was warm with wine and would have me lie with him, but I objected, saying, 'I may not grant thee this except thou become a Moslem.' He refused and I said to him, 'Now for the Sultan's market.' So he sold me to thee and I taught my young mistress, making it a condition with her that she should do naught without my counsel, and that whoso might wed her should wed me also, one night for me and one night for her."

Then she took a cup of water and conjuring over it, sprinkled the dog therewith; saying, "Return thou to form of man." And he straightway was restored to his former shape; whereupon the broker saluted him with the salam and asked him the reason of his enchantment.

So Ali told him all that had befallen him; and he answered by telling him all that had passed, when the broker said to him, "Will not my daughter and the handmaid suffice thee?" but he answered, "Needs must I have Zaynab also."

Now suddenly there came a rap at the door and the maid said, "Who is at the door?"

The knocker replied, "Kamar, daughter of Azariah the Jew; say me, is Ali of Cairo with you?"

Replied the broker's daughter, "O thou daughter of a dog! If he be with us, what wilt thou with him? Go down, O maid, and open to her."

So the maid let her in, and when she looked upon Ali and he upon her, he said, "What bringeth thee hither O dog's daughter?"

Quoth she, "I testify that there is no god but the God and I testify that Mohammed is the Apostle of God." And, having thus Islamised, she asked him, "Do men in the Faith of Al-Islam give marriage portions to women or do women dower men?"

Quoth he, "Men endow women."

"Then," said she, "I come and dower myself for thee, bringing thee, as my marriage-portion, my dress together with the rod and charger and chains and the head of my father, the enemy of thee and the foeman of Allah." And she threw down the Jew's head before him.

Now the cause of her slaying her sire was as follows. On the night of his turning Ali into a dog, she saw, in a dream, a speaker who said to her, "Become a Moslemah." She did so; and as soon as she awoke next morning she expounded Al-Islam to her father who refused to embrace the Faith; so she drugged him with Bhang and killed him.

As for Ali, he took the gear and said to the broker, "Meet me to-morrow at the Caliph's Divan, that I may take thy daughter and the handmaid to wife." Then he set out rejoicing, to return to the barrack of the forty. On his way he met a sweetmeat-seller, who was beating hand upon hand and saying, "There is no Majesty and there is no Might save in Allah, the Glorious, the Great! Folk's labour hath waxed sinful and man is active only in fraud!"

Then said he to Ali, "I conjure thee, by Allah, taste of this confection!"

So Ali took a piece and ate it and fell down senseless, for there was Bhang therein; whereupon the sweetmeat-seller seized the dress and the charger and the rest of the gear and thrusting them into the box where he kept his sweetmeats hoisted it up and made off. Presently he met a Kazi, who called to him, saying, "Come hither, O sweetmeat-seller!"

So he went up to him and setting down his sack laid the tray of sweetmeats upon it and asked, "What dost thou want?"

"Halwa and dragees," answered the Kazi and, taking some in his hand, said, "Both of these are adulterated."

Then he brought out sweetmeats from his breast-pocket and gave them to the sweetmeat-seller, saying, "Look at this fashion; how excellent it is! Eat of it and make the like of it." So he ate and fell down senseless, for the sweetmeats were drugged with Bhang, whereupon the Kazi bundled him into the sack and made off with him, charger and chest and all, to the barrack of the forty.

Now the Judge in question was Hasan Shuman and the reason of this was as follows. When Ali had been gone some days in quest of the dress and they heard no news of him, Calamity Ahmad said to his men, "O lads, go and seek for your brother Ali of Cairo."

So they sallied forth in quest of him and among the rest Hasan Shuman the Pestilence, disguised in a Kazi's gear. He came upon the sweetmeat-seller and, knowing him for Ahmad al-Lakit suspected him of having played some trick upon Ali; so he drugged him and did as we have seen.

Meanwhile, the other forty fared about the streets and highways making search in different directions, and amongst them Ali Kitf al-Jamal, who espying a crowd, made towards the people and found the Cairene Ali lying drugged and senseless in their midst.

So he revived him and he came to himself and seeing the folk flocking around him asked, "Where am I?"

Answered Ali Camel-shoulder and his comrades, "We found thee lying here drugged but know not who drugged thee."

Quoth Ali, "'Twas a certain sweetmeat-seller who drugged me and took the gear from me; but where is he gone?"

Quoth his comrades, "We have seen nothing of him; but come, rise and go home with us."

So they returned to the barrack, where they found Ahmad al-Danaf, who greeted Ali and enquired if he had brought the dress.

He replied, "I was coming hither with it and other matters, including the Jew's head, when a sweetmeat-seller met me and drugged me with Bhang and took them from me."

Then he told him the whole tale ending with, "If I come across that man of goodies again, I will requite him."

Presently Hasan Shuman came out of a closet and said to him, "Hast thou gotten the gear, O Ali?"

So he told him what had befallen him and added, "If I know whither the rascal is gone and where to find the knave, I would pay him out. Knowest thou whither he went?"

Answered Hasan, "I know where he is," and opening the door of the closet, showed him the sweetmeat-seller within, drugged and senseless. Then he aroused him and he opened his eyes and finding himself in presence of Mercury Ali and Calamity Ahmad and the forty, started up and said, "Where am I and who hath laid hands on me?"

Replied Shuman, "'Twas I laid hands on thee;" and Ali cried, "O perfidious wretch, wilt thou play thy pranks on me?"

And he would have slain him: but Hasan said to him, "Hold thy hand for this fellow is become thy kinsman."

"How my kinsman?" quoth Ali; and quoth Hasan, "This is Ahmad al-Lakit son of Zaynab's sister."

Then said Ali to the prisoner, "Why didst thou thus, O Lakit?" and he replied, "My grandmother, Dalilah the Wily, bade me do it; only because

Zurayk the fishmonger fore-gathered with the old woman and said, 'Mercury Ali of Cairo is a sharper and a past master in knavery, and he will certainly slay the Jew and bring hither the dress.' So she sent for me and said to me, 'O Ahmad, dost thou know Ali of Cairo?' Answered I, 'Indeed I do and 'twas I directed him to Ahmad al-Danaf's lodging when he first came to Baghdad.' Quoth she, 'Go and set thy nets for him, and if he have brought back the gear, put a cheat on him and take it from him.' So I went round about the highways of the city, till I met a sweetmeat-seller and buying his clothes and stock-in-trade and gear for ten dinars, did what was done."

Thereupon quoth Ali, "Go back to thy grandmother and Zurayk, and tell them that I have brought the gear and the Jew's head and tell them to meet me to-morrow at the Caliph's Divan, there to receive Zaynab's dowry."

And Calamity Ahmad rejoiced in this and said, "We have not wasted our pains in rearing thee, O Ali!"

Next morning Ali took the dress, the charger, the rod and the chains of gold, together with the head of Azariah the Jew mounted on a pike, and went up, accompanied by Ahmad al-Danaf and the forty, to the Divan, where they kissed ground before the Caliph, who turned and seeing a youth of the most valiant aspect, enquired of Calamity Ahmad concerning him and he replied, "O Commander of the Faithful, this is Mercury Ali the Egyptian captain of the brave boys of Cairo, and he is the first of my lads."

And the Caliph loved him for the valour that shone from between his eyes, testifying for him and not against him. Then Ali rose; and, casting the Jew's head down before him, said, "May thine every enemy be like this one, O Prince of True Believers!"

Quoth Al-Rashid, "Whose head is this?" and quoth Ali, "'Tis the head of Azariah the Jew."

"Who slew him?" asked the Caliph. So Ali related to him all that had passed, from first to last, and the Caliph said, "I had not thought thou wouldst kill him, for that he was a sorcerer."

Ali replied, "O Commander of the Faithful, my Lord made me prevail to his slaughter."

Then the Caliph sent the Chief of Police to the Jew's palace, where he found him lying headless; so he laid the body on a bier, and carried it to Al-Rashid, who commanded to burn it. Whereat, behold, up came Kamar and kissing the ground before the Caliph, informed him that she was the daughter of Jew Azariah and that she had become a Moslemah.

Then she renewed her profession of Faith before the Commander of the Faithful and said to him "Be thou my intercessor with sharper Ali that he take me to wife."

She also appointed him her guardian to consent to her marriage with the Cairene, to whom he gave the Jew's palace and all its contents, saying, "Ask a boon of me." Quoth Ali, "I beg of thee to let me stand on thy carpet and eat of thy table;" and quoth the Caliph, "O Ali, hast thou any lads?"

He replied, "I have forty lads; but they are in Cairo."

Rejoined the Caliph, "Send to Cairo and fetch them hither," presently adding, "But, O Ali, hast thou a barrack for them?"

"No," answered Ali; and Hasan Shuman said, "I make him a present of my barrack with all that is therein, O Commander of the Faithful."

However, the Caliph retorted, saying, "Thy lodging is thine own, O Hasan"; and he bade his treasurer give the court architect ten thousand dinars, that he might build Ali a hall with four daises and forty sleeping-closets for his lads.

Then said he, "O Ali, hast thou any further wish, that we may command its fulfilment?" and said Ali, "O King of the age, be thou my intercessor with Dalilah the Wily that she give me her daughter Zaynab to wife and take the dress and gear of Azariah's girl in lieu of dower."

Dalilah accepted the Caliph's intercession and accepted the charger and dress and what not, and they drew up the marriage contracts between Ali and Zaynab and Kamar, the Jew's daughter and the broker's daughter and the handmaid. Moreover, the Caliph assigned him a solde with a table morning and evening, and stipends and allowances for fodder; all of the most liberal. Then Ali the Cairene fell to making ready for the wedding festivities and, after thirty days, he sent a letter to his comrades in Cairo, wherein he gave them to know of the favours and honours which the Caliph had bestowed upon him and said, "I have married four maidens and needs must ye come to the wedding."

So, after a reasonable time the forty lads arrived and they held high festival; he homed them in his barrack and entreated them with the utmost regard and presented them to the Caliph, who bestowed on them robes of honour and largesse. Then the tiring-women displayed Zaynab before Ali in the dress of the Jew's daughter, and he went in unto her and found her a pearl unthridden and a filly by all save himself unridden. Then he went in unto the three other maidens and found them accomplished in beauty and loveliness. After this it befel that Ali of Cairo was one night on guard by the Caliph who said to him, "I wish thee O Ali, to tell me all that hath befallen

thee from first to last with Dalilah the Wily and Zaynab the Coney-catcher and Zurayk the Fishmonger."

So Ali related to him all his adventures and the Commander of the Faithful bade record them and lay them up in the royal muniment-rooms. So they wrote down all that had befallen him and kept it in store with other histories for the people of Mohammed the Best of Men. And Ali and his wives and comrades abode in all solace of life, and its joyance, till there came to them the Destroyer of Delights and Sunderer of Societies; and Allah (be He extolled and exalted!) is All-knowing!

The Tale of Scheherazade Concluded

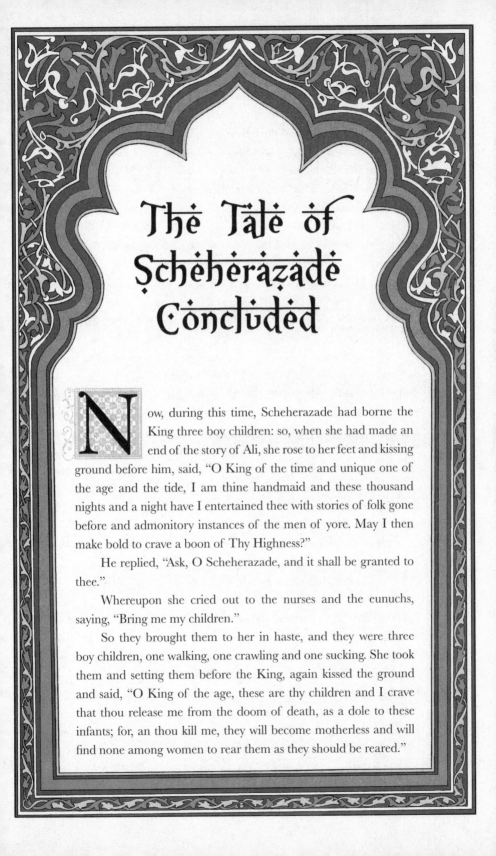

Now, during this time, Scheherazade had borne the King three boy children: so, when she had made an end of the story of Ali, she rose to her feet and kissing ground before him, said, "O King of the time and unique one of the age and the tide, I am thine handmaid and these thousand nights and a night have I entertained thee with stories of folk gone before and admonitory instances of the men of yore. May I then make bold to crave a boon of Thy Highness?"

He replied, "Ask, O Scheherazade, and it shall be granted to thee."

Whereupon she cried out to the nurses and the eunuchs, saying, "Bring me my children."

So they brought them to her in haste, and they were three boy children, one walking, one crawling and one sucking. She took them and setting them before the King, again kissed the ground and said, "O King of the age, these are thy children and I crave that thou release me from the doom of death, as a dole to these infants; for, an thou kill me, they will become motherless and will find none among women to rear them as they should be reared."

When the King heard this, he wept and straining the boys to his bosom, said, "By Allah, O Scheherazade, I pardoned thee before the coming of these children, for that I found thee chaste, pure, ingenuous and pious! Allah bless thee and thy father and thy mother and thy root and thy branch! I take the Almighty to witness against me that I exempt thee from aught that can harm thee."

So she kissed his hands and feet and rejoiced with exceeding joy, saying, "The Lord make thy life long and increase thee in dignity and majesty!" presently adding, "Thou marvelledst at that which befel thee on the part of women; yet there betided the Kings of the Chosroes before thee greater mishaps and more grievous than that which hath befallen thee, and indeed I have set forth unto thee that which happened to Caliphs and Kings and others with their women, but the relation is longsome and hearkening groweth tedious, and in this is all sufficient warning for the man of wits and admonishment for the wise."

Then she ceased to speak, and when King Shahryar heard her speech and profited by that which she said, he summoned up his reasoning powers and cleansed his heart and caused his understanding revert and turned to Allah Almighty and said to himself, "Since there befel the Kings of the Chosroes more than that which hath befallen me, never, whilst I live, shall I cease to blame myself for the past. As for this Scheherazade, her like is not found in the lands; so praise be to Him who appointed her a means for delivering His creatures from oppression and slaughter!" Then he arose from his seance and kissed her head, whereat she rejoiced, she and her sister Dunyazad, with exceeding joy.

When the morning morrowed, the King went forth and sitting down on the throne of the Kingship, summoned the Lords of his land; whereupon the Chamberlains and Nabobs and Captains of the host went in to him and kissed ground before him. He distinguished the Wazir, Scheherazade's sire, with special favour and bestowed on him a costly and splendid robe of honour and entreated him with the utmost kindness, and said to him, "Allah protect thee for that thou gavest me to wife thy noble daughter, who hath been the means of my repentance from slaying the daughters of folk. Indeed I have found her pure and pious, chaste and ingenuous, and Allah hath vouchsafed me by her three boy children; wherefore praised be He for his passing favour." Then he bestowed robes of honour upon his Wazirs, and Emirs and Chief Officers and he set forth to them briefly that which had betided him with Scheherazade and how he had turned from his former ways and repented him of what he had done and purposed to take the Wazir's daughter, Scheherazade, to wife and let draw up the marriage-contract with her.

When those who were present heard this, they kissed the ground before him and blessed him and his betrothed Scheherazade, and the Wazir thanked her. Then Shahryar made an end of his sitting in all weal, whereupon the folk dispersed to their dwelling-places and the news was bruited abroad that the King purposed to marry the Wazir's daughter, Scheherazade. Then he proceeded to make ready the wedding gear, and presently he sent after his brother, King Shah Zaman, who came, and King Shahryar went forth to meet him with the troops. Furthermore, they decorated the city after the goodliest fashion and diffused scents from censers and burnt aloes-wood and other perfumes in all the markets and thoroughfares and rubbed themselves with saffron, what while the drums beat and the flutes and pipes sounded and mimes and mountebanks played and plied their arts and the King lavished on them gifts and largesse; and in very deed it was a notable day.

When they came to the palace, King Shahryar commanded to spread the tables with beasts roasted whole and sweetmeats and all manner of vi-ands and bade the crier cry to the folk that they should come up to the Divan and eat and drink and that this should be a means of reconciliation between him and them. So, high and low, great and small came up unto him and they abode on that wise, eating and drinking, seven days with their nights.

Then the King shut himself up with his brother and related to him that which had betided him with the Wazir's daughter, Scheherazade, during the past three years and told him what he had heard from her of proverbs and parables, chronicles and pleasantries, quips and jests, stories and anecdotes, dialogues and histories and elegies and other verses; whereat King Shah Zaman marvelled with the uttermost marvel and said, "Fain would I take her younger sister to wife, so we may be two brothers-german to two sisters-german, and they on likewise be sisters to us; for that the calamity which befel me was the cause of our discovering that which befel thee and all this time of three years past I have taken no delight in woman, save that I lie each night with a damsel of my kingdom, and every morning I do her to death; but now I desire to marry thy wife's sister Dunyazad."

When King Shahryar heard his brother's words, he rejoiced with joy exceeding and arising forthright, went in to his wife Scheherazade and acquainted her with that which his brother purposed, namely that he sought her sister Dunyazad in wedlock; whereupon she answered, "O King of the age, we seek of him one condition, to wit, that he take up his abode with

us, for that I cannot brook to be parted from my sister an hour, because we were brought up together and may not endure separation each from other. If he accept this pact, she is his handmaid."

King Shahryar returned to his brother and acquainted him with that which Scheherazade had said; and he replied, "Indeed, this is what was in my mind, for that I desire nevermore to be parted from thee one hour. As for the kingdom, Allah the Most High shall send to it whomso He chooseth, for that I have no longer a desire for the kingship."

When King Shahryar heard his brother's words, he rejoiced exceedingly and said, "Verily, this is what I wished, O my brother. So Alhamdolillah—Praised be Allah—who hath brought about union between us." Then he sent after the Kazis and Olema, Captains and Notables, and they married the two brothers to the two sisters. The contracts were written out and the two Kings bestowed robes of honour of silk and satin on those who were present, whilst the city was decorated and the rejoicings were renewed. The King commanded each Emir and Wazir and Chamberlain and Nabob to decorate his palace and the folk of the city were gladdened by the presage of happiness and contentment. King Shahryar also bade slaughter sheep and set up kitchens and made bride-feasts and fed all comers, high and low; and he gave alms to the poor and needy and extended his bounty to great and small. Then the eunuchs went forth, that they might perfume the Hammam for the brides; so they scented it with rosewater and willow-flower-water and pods of musk and fumigated it with Kakili eagle-wood and ambergris.

Then Scheherazade entered, she and her sister Dunyazad, and they cleansed their heads and clipped their hair. When they came forth of the Hammam-bath, they donned raiment and ornaments; such as men were wont prepare for the Kings of the Chosroes; and among Scheherazade's apparel was a dress purfled with red gold and wrought with counterfeit presentments of birds and beasts. And the two sisters encircled their necks with necklaces of jewels of price, in the like whereof Iskander rejoiced not, for therein were great jewels such as amazed the wit and dazzled the eye; and the imagination was bewildered at their charms, for indeed each of them was brighter than the sun and the moon. Before them they lighted brilliant flambeaux of wax in candelabra of gold, but their faces outshone the flambeaux, for that they had eyes sharper than unsheathed swords and the lashes of their eyelids bewitched all hearts. Their cheeks were rosy red and their necks and shapes gracefully swayed and their eyes wantoned like the gazelle's; and the slave-girls came to meet them with instruments of music.

Then the two Kings entered the Hammam-bath, and when they came forth, they sat down on a couch set with pearls and gems, whereupon the two sisters came up to them and stood between their hands, as they were moons, bending and leaning from side to side in their beauty and loveliness. Presently they brought forward Scheherazade and displayed her, for the first dress, in a red suit; whereupon King Shahryar rose to look upon her and the wits of all present, men and women, were bewitched for that she was even as saith of her one of her describers:

> A sun on wand in knoll of sand she showed,
> Clad in her cramoisy-hued chemisette:
> Of her lips' honey-dew she gave me drink
> And with her rosy cheeks quencht fire she set.

Then they attired Dunyazad in a dress of blue brocade and she became as she were the full moon when it shineth forth. So they displayed her in this, for the first dress, before King Shah Zaman, who rejoiced in her and well-nigh swooned away for love-longing and amorous desire; yea, he was distraught with passion for her, whenas he saw her, because she was as saith of her one of her describers in these couplets:

> She comes apparelled in an azure vest
> Ultramarine as skies are deckt and dight:
> I view'd th' unparallel'd sight, which showed my eyes
> A Summer-moon upon a Winter-night.

Then they returned to Scheherazade and displayed her in the second dress, a suit of surpassing goodliness, and veiled her face with her hair like a chin-veil. Moreover, they let down her side-locks and she was even as saith of her one of her describers in these couplets:

> O hail to him whose locks his cheeks o'ershade,
> Who slew my life by cruel hard despight:
> Said I, "Hast veiled the Morn in Night?" He said,
> "Nay I but veil Moon in hue of Night."

Then they displayed Dunyazad in a second and a third and a fourth dress and she paced forward like the rising sun, and swayed to and fro in the insolence of beauty; and she was even as saith the poet of her in these couplets:

The sun of beauty she to all appears
And, lovely coy she mocks all loveliness:
And when he fronts her favour and her smile
A-morn, the sun of day in clouds must dress.

Then they displayed Scheherazade in the third dress and the fourth and the fifth and she became as she were a Ban-branch snell or a thirsting gazelle, lovely of face and perfect in attributes of grace, even as saith of her one in these couplets:

She comes like fullest moon on happy night.
Taper of waist with shape of magic might:
She hath an eye whose glances quell mankind,
And ruby on her cheeks reflects his light:
Enveils her hips the blackness of her hair;
Beware of curls that bite with viper-bite!
Her sides are silken-soft, that while the heart
Mere rock behind that surface 'scapes our sight:
From the fringed curtains of her eyne she shoots
Shafts that at furthest range on mark alight.

Then they returned to Dunyazad and displayed her in the fifth dress and in the sixth, which was green, when she surpassed with her loveliness the fair of the four quarters of the world and outvied, with the brightness of her countenance, the full moon at rising tide; for she was even as saith of her the poet in these couplets:

A damsel 'twas the tirer's art had decked with snare and sleight,
And robed with rays as though the sun from her had borrowed
    light:
She came before us wondrous clad in chemisette of green,
As veiled by his leafy screen Pomegranate hides from sight:
And when he said, "How callest thou the fashion of thy dress?"
She answered us in pleasant way with double meaning dight,
"We call this garment creve-coeur; and rightly is it hight,
For many a heart wi' this we brake and harried many a sprite."

Then they displayed Scheherazade in the sixth and seventh dresses and clad her in youth's clothing, whereupon she came forward swaying from side to side and coquettishly moving and indeed she ravished wits and hearts and ensorcelled all eyes with her glances. She shook her sides and swayed her haunches, then put her hair on sword-hilt and went up to King Shahryar, who embraced her as hospitable host embraceth guest, and threatened her in her ear with the taking of the sword; and she was even as saith of her the poet in these words:

> Were not the Murk of gender male,
> Than feminines surpassing fair,
> Tirewomen they had grudged the bride,
> Who made her beard and whiskers wear!

Thus also they did with her sister Dunyazad, and when they had made an end of the display the King bestowed robes of honour on all who were present and sent the brides to their own apartments. Then Scheherazade went in to King Shahryar and Dunyazad to King Shah Zaman and each of them solaced himself with the company of his beloved consort and the hearts of the folk were comforted. When morning morrowed, the Wazir came in to the two Kings and kissed ground before them; wherefore they thanked him and were large of bounty to him.

Presently they went forth and sat down upon couches of Kingship, whilst all the Wazirs and Emirs and Grandees and Lords of the land presented themselves and kissed ground. King Shahryar ordered them dresses of honour and largesse and they prayed for the permanence and prosperity of the King and his brother. Then the two Sovrans appointed their sire-in-law the Wazir to be Viceroy in Samarcand and assigned him five of the Chief Emirs to accompany him, charging them attend him and do him service. The Minister kissed the ground and prayed that they might be vouchsafed length of life: then he went in to his daughters, whilst the Eunuchs and Ushers walked before him, and saluted them and farewelled them. They kissed his hands and gave him joy of the Kingship and bestowed on him immense treasures; after which he took leave of them and setting out, fared days and nights, till he came near Samarcand, where the townspeople met him at a distance of three marches and rejoiced in him with exceeding joy.

So he entered the city and they decorated the houses and it was a notable day. He sat down on the throne of his kingship and the Wazirs did him homage and the Grandees and Emirs of Samarcand and all prayed that he might be vouchsafed justice and victory and length of continuance. So he bestowed on them robes of honour and entreated them with distinction and they made him Sultan over them. As soon as his father-in-law had departed for Samarcand, King Shahryar summoned the Grandees of his realm and made them a stupendous banquet of all manner of delicious meats and exquisite sweetmeats. He also bestowed on them robes of honour and guerdoned them and divided the kingdoms between himself and his brother in their presence, whereat the folk rejoiced.

Then the two Kings abode, each ruling a day in turn, and they were ever in harmony each with other while on similar wise their wives continued in the love of Allah Almighty and in thanksgiving to Him; and the peoples and the provinces were at peace and the preachers prayed for them from the pulpits, and their report was bruited abroad and the travellers bore tidings of them to all lands. In due time King Shahryar summoned chroniclers and copyists and bade them write all that had betided him with his wife, first and last; so they wrote this and named it *The Arabian Nights and A Night*. The book came to thirty volumes and these the King laid up in his treasury. And the two brothers abode with their wives in all pleasance and solace of life and its delights, for that indeed Allah the Most High had changed their annoy into joy; and on this wise they continued till there took them the Destroyer of delights and the Severer of societies, the Desolator of dwelling-places and Garnerer of grave-yards, and they were translated to the ruth of Almighty Allah; their houses fell waste and their palaces lay in ruins and the Kings inherited their riches.

Then there reigned after them a wise ruler, who was just, keen-witted and accomplished and loved tales and legends, especially those which chronicle the doings of Sovrans and Sultans, and he found in the treasury these marvellous stories and wondrous histories, contained in the thirty volumes aforesaid. So he read in them a first book and a second and a third and so on to the last of them, and each book astounded and delighted him more than that which preceded it, till he came to the end of them. Then he admired whatso he had read therein of description and discourse and rare traits and anecdotes and moral instances and reminiscences and bade the folk copy them and dispread them over all lands and climes; wherefore their report was bruited abroad and the people named them *The Marvels and Wonders of the Arabian Nights*.

This is all that hath come down to us of the origin of this book, and Allah is All-knowing. So Glory be to Him whom the shifts of Time waste not away, nor doth aught of chance or change affect His sway: whom one case diverteth not from other case and Who is sole in the attributes of perfect grace. And prayer and peace be upon the Lord's Pontiff and Chosen One among His creatures, our lord MOHAMMED the Prince of mankind through whom we supplicate Him for a goodly and a godly

FINIS.

ABOUT THE TRANSLATOR

Richard Francis Burton was born in England in 1821 and spent much of his childhood in France and Italy. In 1842, he accepted a commission with the Bombay Army and, under the auspices of the East India Company, worked as a surveyor and intelligence officer in India until 1850. Fluent in numerous eastern languages, he disguised himself as an Afghani in 1853 to travel through Medina, Mecca, and other sacred cities forbidden to non-Muslims. He also undertook expeditions to Ethiopia and Somaliland, and the books he wrote about his travels—including *Personal Narrative of a Pilgrimage to El-Medinah and Mecca* (1855–1856) and *First Footsteps in East Africa* (1856)—were considered groundbreaking introductions to Islamic culture for western readers. In *The Lake Regions of Central Africa* (1860), Burton chronicled his two-year search with explorer John Speke to find the source of the Nile, during which they discovered Lake Tanganyika. Burton began translating the collection of eastern folk tales known as *A Thousand and One Nights* (or *The Arabian Nights*) in the 1850s. It was published in sixteen volumes beginning in 1884 and supplemented with additional stories in 1886, the same year Burton received a knighthood. Long regarded a seminal work of world literature, Burton's translation has never been out of print. Burton wrote many other travelogues and cultural studies before his death in 1890.